The Cavern of Deep Harmony

By
Jo Carolyn Anzalone

Xulon Press

Xulon Press
2301 Lucien Way #415
Maitland, FL 32751
407.339.4217
www.xulonpress.com

Printed in the United States of America.

ISBN-13: 9781545613146

This book is dedicated to my husband, Rev. Carl Anzalone. It is in loving him, in being loved by him, that I know first-hand what it means to love completely, sacrificially, and without end or edges.

Introduction

This story is the result of a life-long interest in the world of the blind, especially what the concept of that world is like for someone born blind, someone who has never seen it. Though I myself do not know that world from inside it, I've sought out those who do and spent hours in conversation with them, asking questions, struggling to understand. I do not even know exactly why I've always wanted to understand, only that I have. My only personal experience of blindness came when I was a sophomore in college, had an accident involving my eyes, and was in the infirmary for a long time with both eyes bandaged. That, of course, is nothing at all like what the born blind person knows or even the person who has been sighted and then lost it. While I was inside my own small experience, I explored it as best I could, what it was like to eat without seeing your plate, what it was like to pour something into a glass you could not see. My college was in the South and while I was bandaged, we had our only snow of the winter. I asked everyone who came to visit me to describe what that was like and discovered how difficult it seems to be for so many to do that effectively.

I visited the Seeing Eye in Morristown, New Jersey, and it was there I saw guide dogs in action and discovered they know who is sighted and who is not. If one walks down an aisle with dogs lying in it, they get up and move for the blind but not for the sighted. I grew up with German shepherds, my mother often having three at a time, and one of them is who I base my guide dog in this story on, a one hundred and twenty pound fellow with golden fur and a black saddle. When I was in the 8th grade, my history teacher's husband was blind and he'd often come to school with his dog, telling us stories of how they worked together, how a dog had given its life for him, how another kept him from stepping into an empty elevator shaft.

Through the years I've read everything I could find about the blind life, written both by the born blind and those who lost their sight and to them I owe an extraordinary debt, especially for such concepts as gazing, the meaning of rain, and Psalm 139. I was surprised to discover how many of them were college professors and when I came to write this story, I made my main character a professor of literature at a university in Pittsburgh, where I live. My sighted son was for a number of years a professor of literature so that choice came naturally.

This is also the story of a great love between a man and a woman and an exploration of what it is like for him to invite a sighted woman to share his world, what it is like for her to know she will never be seen by him, her desire to understand what the world is like for him. His entire life he has been comfortable in his world, the only world he has ever known, then something happens and abruptly he's presented with it suddenly being vital to him to understand what seeing...is...and he must grapple with that, with the utter impossibility of that, with how his comfort and his confidence are impacted by it.

Chapter 1

Blind eyes closed, Marshall stood on the porch of the bed and breakfast, smelling the scents that came toward him off the lake. Though it was still morning, someone was already waterskiing. He heard the motor of the small boat then a yell followed by a splash as the skier lost his balance. With his toe, he found the edge of the porch, stepped down onto the top step and sat, leaning his left shoulder against the railing post. The bed and breakfast faced east so the morning sun was on his face, warm despite the late October chill in the air. He wasn't wearing his dark glasses, didn't see any need for them, not at the moment.

A large furry body came and sat beside him, pressing close to his right side. Smiling, he slid his arm around the back of the big German shepherd. "Seems like a fine morning, Wadsworth," he said, turning to rub his cheek in the soft fur of the dog's neck. He'd planned on writing more this morning, but the thought of sitting at his desk in the second-floor room he was renting was not nearly so inviting as the sound of crisp leaves rustling in the wind. "You up for a walk, boy?"

Yes, that was a much better idea. Not only would it blow any cobwebs out of his mind, the male protagonist in his book was currently walking through a large forest. It would be legitimate research, it would. He'd left Wadsworth's harness lying on a wicker chair just to the right of the main entrance of the house, so rose, followed closely by the dog, and picked it up, fastening it easily with long years of practice. They had been a team for three years now and had gotten to the point where each seemed to understand exactly what the other was thinking. Wadsworth was a big shepherd, nearly one hundred and twenty pounds, and a bright golden color with a perfect black saddle. Not that Marshall knew about the saddle. What he knew was how broad and deep Wadsworth's chest was, how sleek his fur felt under stroking hands.

It had been an adjustment at first, getting used to Wadsworth after so many years with Mellow, the female yellow lab he'd had since his undergrad days at Northwestern University. She'd gone to Boston with him during the time it took to get his PhD in American literature at Harvard, had been with him as he'd begun teaching at Duquesne University in Pittsburgh. Then had come the day when she'd bumped him hard so he fell to the side, taking the impact herself of the motorcycle that had come roaring out of the small alleyway. For two months he'd tried life without a guide dog, something in him not ready to bond with a new animal. But he found his life circumscribed without a dog, without the greater freedom one gave him, and soon was back at the Seeing Eye in New Jersey being introduced to the young shepherd named Wadsworth after Henry Wadsworth Longfellow, a poet whose work he loved. He'd knelt on one knee beside the dog, feeling unsure as memories of Mellow flooded him. Then a large and very wet tongue suddenly licked up the full side of his short, neatly-trimmed beard and with no further thought his arms had gone around the furry neck. They had been inseparable ever since.

Harold Malone, the innkeeper, came out the door just as Marshall finished attaching the harness. "Headin' out somewhere, are you?"

"Thought Wadsworth and I might take a bit of a walk this morning, Harold. There are woods not far behind the house, aren't there?"

"Yep. Pretty big section of them, actually. You feel ok about going in them alone?"

Marshall smiled. "Not alone, Harold. Wadsworth's going with me."

Harold was not familiar in dealing with a blind person and to him the idea of going into woods you could not see was beyond comprehension. "Well, I wouldn't go too far into 'em," Harold suggested. "There's a wide, fairly flat path starts just behind the parking area. If you stay on that and don't go too far, you should be ok."

"Thanks," Marshall replied genially, used to the over-concern of the sighted. Marshall, though, didn't know the meaning of the word 'hesitation'. He'd been born blind so that was simply the way the world was. He saw no need for fear in venturing forth and had, indeed, created untold gray hairs on his mother's head with all his boyhood adventures. Now at thirty-six, he was a mature, confident man, widely-traveled and completely comfortable in his world.

Harold stood on the porch watching the closely-linked man and dog going down the main walk, make a sharp turn to the right and head toward the parking area. Wadsworth walked just to Marshall's left and slightly in front. Harold still couldn't get used to the sight of the quick, sure stride of the blind man. "But why the heck he wants to go walk in the woods...." he muttered to himself. After all, he couldn't see the brightly-colored autumn leaves or the billowing white clouds in the blue sky above them. What was the purpose in it? He shook his head and went back inside to see if Martha, his wife, needed anything from the store. He and Martha had run this bed and breakfast, the Morning Glory Inn, for twenty-five years now and Marshall was the first blind guest they'd ever had.

The path, as Harold had said, was indeed wide and its dirt felt firm and solid enough under Marshall's feet. The warm sun on his back disappeared as he and Wadsworth entered the forest itself, though he still felt it now and again as they passed through areas where the trees thinned a bit. The air was almost heady with the powerful scent of rich soil and fallen leaves. From time to time a puddle lay on part of the path, but Wadsworth led him carefully around those, not breaking stride. There had been a heavy downpour for much of the night and the leaves had that particular wet smell that thick layers of them lying on a forest floor can have.

Utterly trained, Wadsworth merely eyed the scolding squirrels they passed and even the quiet peering of half-seen deer that paused in their foraging to watch with wide, alert eyes the man and dog. Marshall felt relaxed, enjoying himself immensely, letting the forest scents wash over and around him, listening to the sound of his own footfalls, Wadsworth's breathing, the brushing of leaves against each other. The woods were full of birds. He'd learned to recognize them all and paused, smiling, lifting his head up as several Canada geese streamed past overhead, honking to one another. Autumn had its own particular sounds. He was especially pleased when the fallen leaves were dry and crisp and crunched as he walked through them. Not today, though. The forest was just beginning to dry a bit in the morning sun.

He began to put himself in Morgan Kent's shoes as he walked. In his novel, Morgan was walking through a Virginia forest, but there were many similarities. As was so often the case with him, he soon lost himself in line after line of descriptive phrases that he would later write down. He was thinking so deeply that he failed to notice Wadsworth was guiding him more carefully, that there were more roots, more rocks in a severely narrowing path.

The dog led him around a large rock half-blocking the path then not only stopped completely but turned himself broadside across Marshall's path. "What's up, boy?" he asked, jarred out of his reverie, the dog's side pressed against his knees.

What he could not see was that during the night's downpour, a usually small stream had been deflected from its path by a fallen tree and come tumbling down the slope, washing away the path completely just before the trail made a sharp turn at the edge of a deep gully. He pulled Wadsworth slightly to his left and felt ahead carefully with his right foot. The ground was saturated with water and as he let his weight come forward a bit, the edge crumbled into the gully. Even as he felt himself falling, Marshall remembered to let go of Wadsworth's harness so he wouldn't pull him down, too. He fell in a collapsing mess of mud and loose stones, wet leaves and shale, crying out once as his left shoulder impacted a large branch. He sort of bounced off that, his right hip coming down against the side of the gully, then he literally turned head over heels and ended up flat on his back atop the mud and rocks at the bottom.

He lay there, his whole body vibrating from the shock of it. Mud and grit were in his eyes and, worse, his mouth. His right arm seemed trapped under something heavy, so he lifted his left hand to wipe the mud away from his face. The movement brought a sharp pain slicing through his shoulder and he dropped the hand, sinking his teeth into his lower lip to stifle a moan. But it was his mouth that was his most immediate concern. As he'd landed, a flow of mud splashed over him and into his mouth. His teeth and tongue were coated with it and bits of it kept trying to slide down toward his throat. Using his tongue, he tried to push some of it out, managing somewhat but not enough so that he could call out. He stopped then and just listened. Wadsworth was barking frantically some distance above him. From the sound, he figured he must have fallen at least twenty-five feet. The sound moved back and forth and he could tell that the dog was trying to find a way down to him.

"Wa...," he tried, but choked.

More mud and loose rock slid down the side of the gully, half-burying him, and a continuous stream of cold, muddy water flowed under and around him. He pulled hard on his right arm, suddenly afraid his face would be covered if more soil should slide, but he was completely immobile. The sound of Wadsworth's barking seemed to fill his world as he lay there trying to breathe. Silently he willed, *Get help, boy. Go get some help!*

CHAPTER 2

Martha, the older woman who'd checked her into the B&B, had been very pleasant, very welcoming, but still Eden found herself lying atop the covers on the canopy bed, staring out the window toward the lake, wondering just why she'd come. Her suitcase remained unpacked on the stand at the foot of the bed, her jacket tossed crookedly on the window seat. She'd kicked off her shoes, sending them flying helter skelter across the room. It was a beautiful day. Why couldn't the rains have continued? At least they matched her mood better than all this disgusting sunlight.

Having risen at the crack of dawn, she'd driven the three hours northeast from Pittsburgh just so she could get out of the city as quickly as possible. Her cousin Connie, used to Eden's flights from unpleasant situations, had recently stumbled across the website for the Morning Glory Inn and suggested it to Eden.

"Morning Glory Inn?" Eden had frowned. "Is it entirely covered by twining vines?"

"No, see," Connie had replied, calling her cousin over to the computer. "It looks really pretty."

"Hmmm?" Eden mumbled, peering over Connie's shoulder. "I don't know that I want... pretty."

"Sure you do!" Connie chirped. "Look. It's got a big porch, a swing, even a lake."

"Not particularly fond of lakes. You know that."

"Well, it's too cold for swimming already anyway. You can just sit on the porch and look at the darn thing."

"Do I have to?"

"What? Look at the lake? Nah, you can ignore the lake. Just rest, eat some nice breakfasts, read a few books."

"Sounds exciting."

"You want excitement? You can just stay here. I'll figure out something."

Eden didn't know what she wanted. "I'm so stupid," she muttered.

"Ok, I'll agree with that," Connie laughed, "but why in particular?"

"Oh, I don't even know, Connie! I just feel stupid today. I feel, done, over, lost. I don't know. I just feel...off."

Connie studied her cousin. Deep auburn hair that brushed her shoulders, eyes almost a clear green, perfectly oval face with a small, straight nose above a mouth that used to smile all the time. "You don't look very 'over' to me, kid."

"That's part of the problem, don't you see? I was thirty-four last month. I feel like I've already lived my life and now I just look back on it, remember it, and that's all."

Connie smiled fondly at her younger cousin. Tomorrow it would be four years since Miles had been killed. Miles, the quintessential Irish cop with the laughing eyes and lilting tenor voice. Miles, shot down on what looked like a routine drunk driver stop. Friendly, jovial, open Miles, everybody's buddy, everybody's friend.

"I think you need to get out of the city for a little while, Eden. Just relax, take some time to think. Maybe you'll come up with something new you want to do. Are you tired of the paper? Is that it?"

"No, it's not the paper, Connie. It's me. It's what's left of me. I don't think there's enough left, not really, to make a go of anything. The job on the newspaper, that's not so bad, you know. It's about the only thing that's not so bad, though."

"Yeah, if you didn't have that you'd probably stay in your apartment alone every evening, wouldn't you?"

"Probably would," Eden agreed. "Especially after Collier." Collier was an architect she'd dated for six months last year. "Pompous ass."

Connie laughed. "That's true! He was definitely that. At least you didn't marry the guy."

Eden rolled her eyes and looked back at the picture of the Morning Glory Inn on the website. It was a large, pale yellow Victorian house with lots of dormers and bay windows, sharp gables limned in white gingerbread, a big porch all the way across the front that faced the lake. Already a bit late in the fall, but there would still be a lot of leaves yet on the trees. Maybe a few twining vines wouldn't be so bad.

"I really would like to just sort of be alone tomorrow," she sighed.

Connie tapped the computer screen. "Go for it, Eden. You said you've got vacation time from the paper. Call Marti and tell him you're going to be out of the office for a while. He'll understand. He knows about...."

Yes, Marti knew about Miles. You couldn't know Eden and not know about Miles. It was as though half of her, probably more than half, lay buried in Queen of Heaven. "But it's prime fall movie season," Eden protested, not taking her eyes off the house. "So many reviews to write. I can't...."

"Barbara can do them, you know she can. She'd love to. Come on, kid, give yourself a break." She jerked her head toward the computer. "It's callin' your name. Eeeeeee-den. Eeeeeee-den. Eeeeeee-den. Come to me!"

Eden laughed. It WAS a lovely place. Maybe a few days away from the city would perk her up? If she stayed here, memories of Miles would be everywhere. Last year she'd rather wallowed in them, in fact, going to all the places he used to take her, sitting in her car outside the house he'd grown up in, then going to the cemetery and standing there until the sun set. She'd gotten all too professional at wallowing in the last four years. But this inn, there was nothing that connected it to Miles. Did she want that? Did she really want to be so away from everything that still shouted out his name to her?

"You need to go, Eden," Connie said seriously, interrupting her thoughts. "Really you do."

So here she was, lying on the bed and not at all sure she'd done the right thing. Getting up, she padded in her stocking feet to the window seat, tossed her jacket on the back of a rocking chair and sat down, propping her elbows on the white window sill and her chin on her elbows. The morning sun glinted off the lake and she could still see reds and yellows in the maples and sweet gums where the woods came down to the shore off to the left. She remembered when she was little how she would gather the leaves and press them in the big old atlas her father had. It had been a while since she'd walked in the woods. The largest area of trees she usually saw any more was when she visited Miles' grave.

Darn! There, she'd done it! She'd brought him fresh again into her day. There was no way she could not, though, not really. Four years ago this morning. She remembered brushing her hair while he sang *Four Green Fields* in the shower. How odd, somehow, that he had shaved, had tied his shoelaces, had eaten the bagel and cream cheese, had kissed her good-bye. Like always. Simple things, things he did every single day. Only that day was the last time. And you didn't even know it. You didn't know it so you didn't treasure what he did as he did it. And then he was gone. Poof! Gone. No more *Four Green Fields*, no more shoelaces, no more bagels, and no more kisses good-bye. She smacked her forehead against the windowpane just a little too hard.

Keeping her face there against the glass, she stared at the lake for a long while. Then a large V of Canada geese flew over the water, heading south. "Going somewhere," she murmured, "not like me." Inhaling deeply, she leaned back away from the window and turned her head, her eye falling on the jacket she'd tossed. Hmm? Seemed about the right weight for going outside. Maybe she'd just check out the gardens around the house for a bit, let the sun shine on her face. She unpacked, hanging her clothes in the large wardrobe, and changed into a pair of soft gray slacks and a peach-colored pull-over sweater. Slipping on her tennis shoes, she picked up the jacket and headed down the staircase.

Once out the door, she paused on the top step. Did she want to go down by the lake or just walk in the gardens? As she stood there, an orange maple leaf blew by, landed on the walk at the bottom of the steps and did a series of three cartwheels before settling flat. Ah, yes, leaves. Maybe she'd gather some leaves and press them in a book, do something she'd done back in happy days. She felt downright cheerful at the thought of gathering leaves, so turned the corner and headed toward the parking area and the path she saw that led toward the woods behind the inn.

Now she was glad the rains had stopped and the sun was drying the leaves. Wet leaves didn't press nearly so well as dry ones. Just at the edge of the woods grew a yellow maple with several sweeping branches hanging low. She stepped off the path and walked under the tree, liking the way the sunlight played on the leaves, making some of them almost transparent. Choosing three or four of the larger, unblemished ones, she pulled them off the branch and carried them with her as she went back to the path. She remembered so clearly being about nine and gathering leaves with her father.

"Ah, Dad," she smiled, the leaves making her feel connected to him.

She found red maple leaves, multicolored sweet gum leaves, bright orange sassafras, yellow oak leaves with brown markings. "Way too many," she thought aloud. '"I'll have to sort them when I get back to the inn." The sun went behind a cloud just then and she shivered in the suddenly chill air. "Maybe I should go back. This is way more than I need anyway."

She'd just turned on the path when something large broke through the underbrush off to one side. She froze, knowing bears lived in these forests.

Chapter 3

It had been warm when Marshall had headed out and he'd only worn tan slacks and a cream shirt with its sleeves rolled halfway up his forearms. As he lay there with the muddy water flowing under and around him, he began to shiver, though. It was almost November and the water had a definite chill to it. The bottom of the gully was also in complete shadow, which made everything even colder.

His eyes hurt. Grit had gotten underneath his lids and a thin coating of mud was drying atop them. Well, nothing he could do about that. He tried and tried to get the mud out of his mouth, but a layer of grit still coated his tongue and teeth and occasional larger bits constantly threatened to slide toward his throat.

Idiot! he thought, berating himself. He knew better than to let his weight come forward onto an exploring foot like that, especially after Wadsworth had blocked him as he had. The sound of Wadsworth's barking had stopped a moment ago. He must've gone back down the trail. Surely someone would see the dog and his tell-tale harness and figure something was amiss? Long minutes passed, though, and the struggle to keep from choking was steadily getting more difficult. He had to sit up! Pulling again on his right arm, he was still not able to budge it. Something pinned it just above the wrist. His fingers felt slightly numb. That worried him.

His left arm was free, but even lying still the pain flared in his shoulder. He had to try, though, and attempted to turn his body toward the right side. Sharp pain made him gasp and he lay back, choking from the mud he'd sucked further down his throat. He gagged, coughed hard, and managed to move it up toward his tongue. Air was becoming terribly precious and getting it past the mud steadily harder. He was able to push a bit more of it with his tongue and it dribbled over his lips, clotting in his beard.

The running water, also thick with mud, had risen and now covered his ears, blotting out all sound. He began to have somewhat of a floating sensation, knew it was probably lack of oxygen, that he wasn't actually floating but as he began to drift away on the tide of it, he stopped feeling the rocks that protruded against his back. Floating felt much more comfortable and he was losing the will to resist it.

He remembered the pool in his friend Dave's back yard and how when he was a boy he would stand at the deep end, his toes curled over the concrete edge. He remembered letting himself go, letting himself just...fall. In that brief moment as the air rushed around him, he experienced a little surge of delight. For him, he was falling into nothingness, toward something he could only trust was there. Then he'd hit the water, sink beneath it, feeling it around him and the emptiness was gone. Down he would go, not trying to rise, lying on the bottom as long as he could, feeling his breath bubbling roundly out of him. Then up he'd float, rising with his bubbles, spreading his arms and lying there on the surface, rocked by the little waves. Floating was one of his favorite things, lying there between the waters and the sky. Despite the chill that seemed now to be sinking into his flesh, he found himself there again, floating in the pool, suspended between earth and heaven. He smiled and the movement of the smile let mud flow around his tongue and toward his throat, but there was nothing left to stop it and so he began to sink again to the bottom of the pool.

Eden screamed, backing up along the path, dropping her leaves. Too far. It was too far back to the inn and she could never outrun a bear. Her heart pounded and when some low leaves parted and she got a fleeting glimpse of black fur, she screamed again, tripped and fell hard on her rear. Her eyes were closed. She couldn't look! It was right there, was right on her! She flung up her arms in a feeble effort to protect her face.

Trembling, she sat there as it circled around her. She should have rolled onto her belly. From what she read, that's what one did during a bear attack, rolled onto your belly and folded your arms over the back of your neck. Too late, its wet nose was poking at her. She felt it jam into her arms twice. Then it barked, loud, and right in her ear. Her whole body jerked. It had to bark again and yet again before it penetrated into her mind that it was a bark and not a growl.

Slowly she lowered her arms enough to peer at the thing. It was a dog, a huge dog but, nonetheless, a dog. It kept circling her, almost bouncing on its paws, barking and now and then poking at her with its nose.

"Go away!" she shouted at it. It wasn't a bear, thank goodness, but it was still plenty big enough to do a lot of damage if it wanted. She saw that it was a German shepherd. Oh, lordy! She'd heard tales of German shepherds gone bad. That same hard, cold fear she'd felt about the bear came back, lodging in her gut. "Go away!" she half-screamed, half-sobbed at it.

Wadsworth, trained to be aware of human needs and circumstances, stopped, and stood quietly, staring at the strange person sitting on the path. He whuffed deep in his throat, took two steps backwards, then came up to her and whuffed again, this time taking the bottom of her jacket in his mouth and pulling.

"Let GO!" she shouted, scrabbling to her knees. Wadsworth held onto the jacket, though. She smacked him across his face. "Let go, I said!"

He let go and backed off a few paces, regarding her. Whuffing again, he backed up, came toward her, looked down the trail then back at her and whuffed again. She managed to get all the way to her feet. He didn't seem like he really intended to harm her somehow. He repeated what he'd just done as she watched. "What's up?" she finally asked. "Did little Timmy fall in the well?" She'd seen Lassie. After all, who hasn't seen Lassie? "You doing your impression of a collie?"

Wadsworth came right up to her but didn't touch her, just looked up at her face, whuffed, and began to back up. Her gaze centered in on the strange contraption fastened around the dog's body. What the heck was that? "You somc sort of working dog?" she wondered aloud. It looked almost like it could be used to pull a little cart. She glanced down the trail. Surely no child would take a wagon down there? It was becoming narrow where they were, with roots and rocks breaking up what had been a fairly smooth surface earlier. She began to feel curious. "Something down that way, boy? Is that what you're trying to tell me?"

She took one step down the trail. Wadsworth whuffed and backed up more. She'd seen too many movies in her time. After all, that's what she did. She reviewed movies for the paper. This was way too much like stepping onto a sound stage. This just could not be what she'd begun to think it was. No way. But the dog kept backing up, keeping its eyes on her. She took another step and it backed up more. This was just too strange! What if there were a child further on, its cart crashed somehow? She couldn't just go blithely back to the inn without checking. Miles would definitely have checked. Darn! Couldn't she leave that behind for more than an instant? But it was true. Miles would have followed the dog. She sighed, looking at her leaves scattered, some of them already blowing away. Tomorrow, she would just gather more tomorrow.

"All right, dog," she said firmly. "I'll bite." Then she laughed at what she'd said. "At least you didn't bite, eh?" She walked toward it. "Lead the way."

Wadsworth turned and dashed down the trail, pausing when he got too far ahead of the human, making sure she could see him, see where he was going. She wasn't nearly as fast as he'd have liked, but she'd have to do.

Eden panted, trying to keep up with the dog. He seemed in some dreadful hurry but she got a stitch in her side and stopped, leaning against a tree to catch her breath. The dog halted about thirty feet further up the trail, giving her one short, sharp bark. "I'm coming! I'm coming!" she grumped.

The path had become little more than a deer track with large rocks more concentrated nearby and huge roots of trees jutting up across it. She had to pick her way carefully in order not to twist an ankle. Surely no kid would bring a cart this far? The dog disappeared around a sharp bend and she could hear him barking at something. Some sort of gully washer had rampaged through this area in the night, obliterating the path altogether and she came up to the dog right at the edge of a steep drop-off. The edge of the big gully had obviously collapsed and the dog was staring down into the shadowy bottom, dancing back and forth in agitation. She followed the line of his gaze and gasped. Someone was there! Squinting, she tried to make out details, but there was so much mud, so many rocks and broken branches she could only tell that it was a person, nothing more. Again her heart began to pound. How would she ever get down there?

Wadsworth was determined. He went about twenty feet further along the top of the gully, finally finding a place where he could pick his way down by clambering over a large fallen tree and through some jumbled rocks. She had followed him and watched as he started down. A rock rolled from under his paws and he yelped, scrambling atop a larger one nearby. Down there? She was going to have to follow the dog down *there*? Blowing out a long breath, she hauled herself up and over the tree. The dog was almost at the bottom and she hurried as fast as she could, trying to remember where he'd stepped and the rocks had remained in place.

When she got to the bottom, miraculously, she thought, still in one piece except for a long scrape down her left forearm, the dog was already beside the person. At least she thought it was a person. One couldn't really tell yet. A small, muddy stream was pouring down the side of the gully and she had to walk in it, white tennis shoes or no white tennis shoes. She was beyond caring. The mud squished up to her ankles, hiding small rocks and branches under its goo. Several times she nearly fell but at last she came up beside the dog. He was frantically licking the face of the person, and, yes, now she could see for sure it was a person, and from the looks of it, a full-grown man. Not much of him remained above the mud, though. She leaned forward, looking down at him. He appeared to be dead, yet the dog still licked his face.

"Mister!" she called loudly. "Can you hear me?"

The man neither responded nor moved. Then she saw his mouth was partially open and a lot of mud had gotten inside. She fell to her knees in the mud, feeling for a pulse as Miles had taught her. Yes, weak, thready, but still there. Just barely there. Pulling out a scarf from her jacket pocket, she began to wipe at his mouth. She needed fresh water. She just seemed to be smearing the stuff around! The way it was, it had to be clogging his throat. She got behind his head, trying to lift his shoulders but discovered his right arm was firmly pinned by a branch. So she moved to his left side, pushing hard, and managed to roll him half-way to his right. She tried to lift his head again but now her hands were slippery with mud, so she sat down just above his head, slid her arms under him, and shoved him as hard as she could over her right thigh. His head was now hanging down and forward and she pounded on his back with her right fist while using her left fingers to almost claw the mud from his mouth.

Finally he began to cough, long, gut-wracking coughs that seemed to go on and on. She pounded his back some more until she was too tired to continue and leaned back against a rock behind her. Whoever he was, he lay twisted to the side over her thigh, gasping in air while the dog licked his face.

"Good dog," she sighed, then closed her eyes a minute, gathering strength to move again.

Chapter 4

He had been settling through the waters to the bottom of the pool and as he floated downward, the need to breathe became somehow irrelevant. Then, without warning, a shark was in the pool, had grabbed him between rows of razored teeth and was shaking him. Breathing suddenly became a desperate requirement and his throat, his lungs, his diaphragm spasmed with wrenching coughs so that air might find its way where it needed to go. Coughing was everything there was. Nothing more, nothing else existed. He had no sense of place or time, only that the air must flow. And when it could, he gasped it in and the gasping was all there was. Being itself was centered in his lungs and all awareness was only there, involved only with that.

As they gradually became satisfied, as their need was met, he lay there over her leg utterly spent. In the coming of the quiet, pain, too, found entrance. His body was twisted to the right and his left shoulder sent shards of broken pain across his back. Violent coughing had only made things worse. He clamped his teeth on a moan, but the edges of it escaped despite his efforts. Vaguely he was aware Wadsworth was furiously licking his face, as though his tongue could remove the layers of mud. He couldn't, at the moment, remember where he was or why he was stuck in this position that wrenched him to his core and then kept going. His hearing seemed gone and he didn't know why, didn't remember about the mud. Touching his teeth together produced a horrid gritting feeling and though his eyes stung, they seemed glued shut. He had to move, had to untwist his body, had to relieve the grating pull on his shoulder, but he couldn't. He opened his mouth but nothing more than a mangled groan could form.

"You say something?" Eden leaned forward, touching the back of his head. She tugged on him, pulling his shoulder so that he came off her leg, his head lolling back against her stomach. Unknown to her, the procedure sent a lightning bolt searing through his back and he passed completely out. She looked down at his quiet face, so caked with mud she had no idea how old he might be, what he might look like. The dog was still trying to lick at his face, but she made him stop.

"Don't think that's doing any real good, boy," she said. "All you're doing is getting mud on your tongue." Suddenly the tag on his collar caught her eye and she reached out and turned it so she could read it. 'Wadsworth' it said and beneath that was an address in Mount Lebanon, a suburb south of Pittsburgh.

"Wadsworth?" His ears pricked up at the sound of his name. "What the heck kinda name is that for a dog?" Still she was somehow glad for knowing it. "Looks like we're in this together, you and me, boy." She tilted her head, looking around. "And what we're in is a pretty darn steep-sided, wet gully." She patted the dog's neck. "So you're a local boy, eh, and from a spiffy neighborhood, too." She smiled at him. "What's a nice dog like you doin' in a place like this?" Then she looked down at the head in her lap. *And who are you,* she wondered, *and how in heaven did you get yourself in a pickle like this?*

But the matter confronting her was what was she going to do about it? His right arm was still trapped by the branch and was completely submerged under the mud. That had to be addressed. But if she laid him back so she could reach the branch, his head would sink back into the mud, which was even deeper now as the flow around them continued. It was getting colder. Why was it getting colder? She looked up at the patch of sky she could see through the canopy of trees. It was solid gray. Where had the sunshine gone? She was wet, sitting in deep mud, and the light jacket just wasn't doing much to make that better. And him? He was completely sopping and had no jacket at all. The seriousness of the situation washed over her. She had to think of something and think of it fast. But what?

She tried scooching forward so his head rested higher on her torso and she was closer to the pinning branch, but it remained out of her reach. She could just brush it with her fingertips. There was nothing to rest his head on, nothing but herself. Or the dog. She eyed him. Was he trained enough that he would do what she needed? Only one way to find out.

"Wadsworth," she said, "you obviously care about this guy so you've gotta do what I tell you. Ok?" She slid to her left, holding the man's head in her hands. "Here, Wadsworth," she motioned, getting the dog to come close so that as she kept sliding there was room for him. "Down. Lie down, boy." Despite the mud, the big dog crouched down. She slid entirely free and gently settled the man's head on the dog's back. The harness thing worked as sort of a cradle, holding his head in place. "Now don't you move, Waddy. You stay right where you are."

She stood up and squished her way around them to the branch. It wasn't that it was huge, just that it had two sections, a smaller limb growing out of the larger, and as it had fallen into the gully with him, the corner made by the two parts had come down on his arm, pinning it like a clamp. The smaller branch had buried its tip deep into the ground. That she discovered with fingers probing through the mud. The larger portion lay over his wrist, its broken end wedged between two big rocks. She positioned herself on the far side of the branch, reached down through the mud and gripped the wood. Tugging as hard as she could, she finally was able to wiggle the smaller piece loose and pulled it back and away from his arm.

"Did it!" she crowed to the watching dog.

The man moaned again and turned his head, making it slide off Wadsworth's back. "Oh, no!" she cried, slogging toward them, putting a hand out just in time to stop it from hitting the mud. She knelt there beside the dog, her hand supporting the man's head. The world seemed made entirely of mud. The man was coated completely and only the dog's back, neck and head were not solid with it, though even they had large splashes. She herself was not much better. She wondered what Connie would say if she could see her now, see what she looked like, what she was doing. "She'd probably just be glad I wasn't mooning in the graveyard," she said wryly.

The man seemed to be coming around. His features, well, what she could see of them, tightened in pain and his mouth squared over clenched teeth. Oh, gads, he was hurt. Of course he was hurt. You didn't fall headlong into a gully like this and not be hurt, did you? Somehow she'd just been thinking of him as trapped, that he'd be ok if she just got him loose. He made a small series of grunting sounds as if he were trying to get control of some pain. She felt suddenly awkward and didn't know what to say to him.

"H...hello," she ventured, but he didn't respond. "Can you open your eyes?" No, of course he couldn't. They were caked with mud. Opening them was probably the last thing he'd want to do. "Look," she said, "I need to get you out of here."

She studied the gully in the direction opposite from the way they'd entered it. It looked like it tapered upwards and they just might be able to make their way to the top. That is, if he could walk. It suddenly dawned on her his legs could be broken. He turned his head again and she knew he was awake, so she got behind him and pushed until he was in a sitting position.

He'd come back to himself with almost a start and felt his head sliding to one side. Then something, someone, seemed to stop it, hold it. He swore he could feel fingers. Whose fingers? Why would someone need to hold his head? He lay there, breathing through the pain in his shoulder, trying to figure out where he was. So much depended on his sense of hearing, but for some reason the world had gone entirely quiet. That, in itself, was disorienting. He was cold, terribly cold, and his shoulder hurt like blue blazes.

None of this made any sense. *Think, Marshall,* he silently ordered himself. What had he been doing? Pittsburgh? Was he in Pittsburgh? No, that didn't seem right. He'd gone somewhere, hadn't he? His book. That was it. He was working on his book. It was his Sabbatical and he'd gone...where?...to write. The inn. He was staying at the inn by the lake. With Wadsworth. Of course, with Wadsworth. Then what? What day was it? He couldn't seem to remember what day it was.

Then someone was pushing on him, making him sit up. Oh, God, that hurt! Why couldn't he hear? He needed to hear! He couldn't even smell anything. He didn't know when he'd ever felt quite so closed in. It was as though he'd been shoved into some small corner of the world where everything was taken away so that there was nothing left, nothing to let him know where he was. *No,* he said to a quiet panic that threatened to rise inside him. *No, I will not permit that.*

It was then he felt a hand slide around his right fingers. Ah, so someone was in this small corner with him. He wanted to speak, to let them know he was aware of their presence, but a small rasping croak was all the sound he could make. His throat felt raw and swollen, his teeth and tongue gritted unpleasantly, and he was very, very thirsty. But he curled his fingers around the hand, finding it very small compared to his.

Somehow he was on his feet. He felt Wadsworth press against his left leg and the small hand moved, supporting his elbow. He should move his feet. Wherever he was, he should move his feet, take a step. There was some need not to stay where he was. Nothing seemed very clear to him, but he knew that much. He needed to move his feet. But they seemed swallowed, encased in something and it took great effort just to lift one enough to set it forward. But he did. It was like walking into a wall and yet keeping on going. It was all very unreal. Existence had been reduced to touch. That was all that was left, but that was filled with pain. Nevertheless, he put one foot in front of the other, endlessly. He stumbled often for there were...things...in his way.

He did not discern them as rocks or branches, only as things that must be gotten past though he could not remember why he must get past them, only that he must. Sometimes the arm went around his waist and he leaned toward the supporting warmth of the being who walked with him, if what he was doing could be called walking. It was a going forward, a going propelled by nothing more than sheer, dogged willpower.

Some while later he felt the land flatten out and the going forward seemed easier, except his feet were heavy with some weight not his own, except despite the shivering cold his shoulder was on fire, except that if he did not get fresh water down his throat the universe would end.

Never would she forget that journey up and out of the gully. The man seemed barely conscious and leaned heavily on her as they made their way through areas of rocks jumbled with weeds and vines, slippery with wet leaves, blocked by branches. How he kept going she'd never know. She didn't even know how she'd kept going. Just ahead she saw with relief the area where she'd first met Wadsworth. Now the path would be flatter, wider. The trees were not so thick here and she glanced up at the sky. The clouds were a heavy, leaden gray. No, it wouldn't. It simply would not rain on them.

"We've got to hurry," she said, knowing he wouldn't really hear her. "Please, we've got to hurry."

His full weight suddenly sagged against her, almost making her knees buckle. Bracing herself, she let him slide to the ground as gently as she could. Oh, Lord, he'd passed out again. She sat down, leaning against a tree, and pulled his head into her lap again, waiting. A raindrop hit her cheek and as she tilted her head up, a light spattering fell across her face. She blew out a long breath, tired to the bone, and looked at his face. "I don't suppose you'd wake up now and we could jog to the inn?"

The mud on his face had dried to a pasty, light color and she watched the raindrops begin to hit it, making a scattered pattern of dark spots. He was cold. She knew he had to be cold, and now it was going to rain on him. She couldn't get him any further. She just couldn't. Wadsworth sat, pressing close to them. What if? She reached into the inner, breast pocket of her jacket and pulled out a small notepad and pen she always kept with her in case some sudden thought for a review should strike her when she was out. She scribbled, *Need help. Am on forest trail. Man hurt. Come ASAP*. Folding it, she slipped it under a tight part of Wadsworth's harness.

"Go!" she ordered, pointing down the trail. "GO!"

Wadsworth looked at her a moment, then whined and touched his nose to the man's face. "GO!" she repeated. He hesitated a moment more, not wanting to leave, but seeming to understand what she wanted. He took several steps down the trail, stopped and looked back, whined again, then turned and loped off, disappearing around a curve. "Good dog," she whispered after him, her voice almost breaking.

The rain started in earnest and she leaned forward over the man, trying to shelter his face. But a wind had begun to blow and the rain came in at a sharp angle. After a few minutes she became fascinated watching the water wet the dried mud on him. Soon sections of it began to wash away and she started to see areas of his skin, realized that he had a short, dark beard and neatly-trimmed moustache. Using her fingers, she helped smooth away still more of the mud. He was younger than she'd thought. For some reason she'd begun to think of him as an older man, perhaps in his fifties, though still well-muscled. But he didn't look much older than she did now that she could see his features. He was, in fact, startlingly handsome. They both lived in Pittsburgh and she wondered if she'd ever seen him in passing. Probably not. He lived in Mount Lebanon and she in Crafton, very different sorts of neighborhoods.

A very sodden dog scratched repeatedly at the door of the Morning Glory Inn. Martha opened it to investigate and saw the shepherd standing there. "Oh, no, you don't, mister! You're not coming into my house all wet like that." She took a few steps back down the hall and peered into the parlor where her husband sat at his desk, doing paperwork. "Harold, did you see Marshall come in? His dog's at the door. Soaking wet, he is, too, and I don't want him inside."

Harold looked up from the e-mail guest registration. "Can't say as I did, Martha. Saw him this morning before I left for the store. Said he was goin' for a walk. Had his dog with him. You say the dog's on the porch?" He got up and followed her to the door. Sure enough Wadsworth stood there, wet, splashed with mud, and when he saw

Harold, he started barking.

"What's up with you, dog?" Harold said, stepping out on the porch carefully so the animal wouldn't be able to come inside. "Where's your master?"

Wadsworth turned in a tight circle then looked at Harold and whined. "I swear I think something's up with this dog," he said over his shoulder to Martha, who stood watching through the screen door. "What is it, boy? What's got you all riled up?" Then he saw the bit of damp white paper sticking out from under a section of the harness. "Hold on there. Let me have a look-see at what this is."

He pulled out the folded paper, which was damp enough that it tore completely in half. Holding it together, Harold was still able to read what was written. "Good Lord, Martha, somebody's gone and got hurt. Note here's askin' for help on the forest trail."

He stepped back in the house, grabbing a raincoat off a hook. "You call Mike down at the station. Tell him what the note says." He handed the paper to her, stuffing one arm in the raincoat as he talked. "I'm going to take the dog and see what's up." With that he went back out the door and set off at a trot after Wadsworth, who was heading into the woods.

Chapter 5

Would the dog go to the inn, or at least to some other place? She wasn't used to dogs that did what one wanted them to. Connie had some sort of little, fluffy thing that only seemed to bark constantly and was always under your feet. Her younger brother had had a mutt, some stray he'd found in an alley. But Spike was only interested in eating and that was when he wasn't more interested in sleeping. So far Wadsworth continually amazed her. She hoped to God he'd keep doing that. But what if he got somewhere and nobody noticed the little paper? What if it slid loose and was even now lying in some puddle?

She shivered, chilled through, much of her hair plastered in wet strands across her face. The rain ran down her back, funneled by her jacket collar because she was leaning forward over the man. Most of the mud was washed off his face now, but some watery portions of it had pooled over his closed lids. With her fingers she gently tried to brush it away. Then she curved both of her arms around his head and leaned way forward so that her body was only a couple of inches from his face.

He'd awakened as the first cold raindrops spattered his cheeks and gradually became aware he was lying on his back again, his head resting on something fairly soft. He didn't move, though. At even the thought of moving again his body said, *No*. So he simply lay quietly, feeling the rain pelting down on him. He was cold completely through, and though the rain increased that, there was also something good in the way he felt it washing away much of the mud, especially the mud caking his face. He remembered the fall now, remembered lying there, trapped, with mud rising around him. He understood now why he couldn't hear. But the rain was running in rivulets down the sides of his face, into his ears, and gradually some sense of sound began to return.

He was also aware of fingers wiping his face. He had no idea to whom they might belong, but it involved too much effort to try and puzzle it out. Whosever they were, they were helping rid him of the mud and all he felt was a quiet sense of gratitude. They stopped for a while and then returned to his eyes. He could feel them gently passing over his lids. His eyes still hurt, though, and he knew he had mud under his lids as well. He tried to open them, thinking maybe the rain might wash there, too, but couldn't seem to manage even that. Then the rain almost completely stopped hitting his face and he smelled, what was that, roses? Yes, a definite scent of roses was just above him, faded considerably but still there. He almost laughed, knowing that was ridiculously impossible in the midst of this late-Autumn rain. It had to be a trick of his mind.

He remembered as a boy talking with his grandmother about heaven. He thought it must smell like roses, like the roses his mother had over the archway that framed the entrance walk to their house. But she, and she knew about such things, said, no, heaven smelled like lilies, not roses. But he was too cold now even to think and felt himself drifting again.

Harold pounded through the puddles as fast as he could go, trying not to lose sight of the big dog, praying all the while he himself didn't have a heart attack. There, just ahead, where the wide path began to peter out, he could see two people as the dog ran up to them. For just a moment he paused, leaning forward, his hands resting on his thighs as he breathed heavily. Then he started forward again, realized he'd never seen the woman before, but that it was Marshall lying on the ground.

As he dropped to his knees beside the two figures, the woman, who had been leaning forward, jerked up, startled by his presence. "Harold Malone," he introduced himself, "from the inn by the trailhead."

"Oh, Mr. Malone!" she cried, tears of relief sparking in her eyes. "Thank God!"

"What's happened to Mr. Sinclair here?"

"You know him?"

"Sure do. He's staying at my inn. Been there a good month already."

"He's hurt. I don't know exactly where, but his dog led me to him. He had fallen in a deep gully back further in the woods."

Harold shook his head, sighing. "I told the man to keep to the flat part of the trail."

Eden let the remark pass, only a vague second given to why Mr. Malone would say that. "He walked this far with me," she explained, "but then he collapsed again. I sent the dog...."

"Yeah, found the note. Good idea, young lady. My wife's called the rescue unit. They should be here before much longer. But why are you out here?"

"Eden," she said, "Eden McLaughlin. I checked into the inn just this morning. Martha said you were at the store."

"You a woods-walker sort, too, eh?"

She smiled slightly. "Was hoping to gather some leaves. Then Wadsworth kidnapped me." She turned to pat the wet dog. "He's one smart boy."

"That kind usually are. Have to be, I guess."

"German shepherds?" she asked, not getting his meaning. But before he could say more, three men came running down the trail. Wadsworth stood, moving to place himself between Marshall and the men, but Eden said, "It's ok, Waddy. They're here to help him."

He eyed them carefully as they came near then moved back to the far side, sitting close, putting one forepaw on Marshall's left arm where it lay in the wet leaves.

"What we got here, Harold?" one of the men asked.

"Fell into the big gully," Harold said. "Don't know exactly how he's hurt. Lady says he walked this far."

Mike looked from the man to the dog still wearing the harness. "Good Lord, Harold, why in heaven's name would he be near the gully?"

Eden, almost paralyzed herself with cold and fatigue, couldn't understand the references they kept making. "The path had been washed out," she added, "and the edge crumbled."

"That's got to be twenty-five, thirty feet down," Mike whistled, kneeling in Harold's place as the innkeeper moved aside. Another man helped Eden to her feet, wrapping a waterproof blanket around her, leaving Marshall flat on the ground. "You said he walked here?"

"Yes, but it was very hard for him. Oh, and he was almost buried in mud back in the gully. I'm pretty sure his eyes are full of it. He came all this way with them closed. Don't know how he did it."

Mike gave her an odd look and turned to his examination of the man. "Who is he?" he asked Harold.

"Sinclair, Dr. Marshall Sinclair. From Pittsburgh."

"Doctor?"

"One of those PhD sorts, not a doctor doctor. Teaches Lit at Duquesne."

Eden looked at the man lying so quietly on the leaves. Somehow she hadn't...expected. She puffed her cheeks out, shaking her head. That made it all the more strange, finding him at the bottom of a gully like that. One just did not stumble upon literature professors in gullies every day.

Marshall was vaguely aware that things were being done to him. He felt the prick as the IV needle was inserted, felt hands probing him here and there, knew he was being lifted onto something. The scent of roses was gone. Then whatever he was lying on was picked up and began moving. Men were talking but he was too tired to listen. He wanted the roses back.

The next thing he knew he was in some sort of moving vehicle and someone was tucking a heating blanket around him, saying something about low core temperature. He wondered who they were talking about. He'd missed completely the scene where Harold had offered to drive Wadsworth the fifteen miles to the little community hospital that served the area, missed that Wadsworth was having none of it, had broken free and jumped into the back of the EMT vehicle. Eden was sitting in a small jumpseat, still shivering. Mike wanted her taken to the hospital, too. The dog would make it crowded, but he grinned wryly. "Let him be," he ordered the man who was trying to grab the harness. "He's earned the right to stay with his guy."

Marshall drifted in and out, aware from time to time of things going on around him. He felt his wet clothes being peeled off, knew he was being washed and then warm blankets placed closely around him. But he'd found a nice fuzzy place in his mind and laid his consciousness down in it, curling it tightly until it disappeared.

"How is he?" Eden asked the nurse. She was standing in the doorway of the room and was clean herself, dressed in baggy green scrubs, a woolen blanket around her shoulders.

"He'll be asleep for a while now," the nurse replied, finishing her adjusting of his IV drip. "Pain meds, you know."

No one would really tell her much and when she saw Mike turning a corner at the far end of the corridor, she ran after him. "Look," she said, when he, too, hesitated, "I'm the one who found him and he's got nobody here but me. Please, Mike."

He looked at her a moment. Her hair was dry now but had been brushed straight and simple to her shoulders. She had dark smudges of fatigue and stress around her eyes, but she was still very pretty, and was looking at him earnestly with those emerald eyes of hers. "His left shoulder was completely dislocated," he said softly, "and it seems he's pulled a lot of tendons and muscles in that area. Has a bit of a concussion and his right wrist is lacerated where you said that branch had pinned him. Main thing is his core temp got so low. If he'd spent the rest of the day down there, he'd probably be dead by now, that is if he didn't drown in the mud first." He put his hand on her arm. "So you really did save his life, you and that dog of his."

"Wadsworth! Where's Wadsworth?" She'd forgotten about him.

Mike smiled. "One of my men hosed him down, got him all clean, found some food for him. From what I hear tell he's lying behind the nurses' station watching every person who comes and goes."

"They let him in the hospital?"

"Dogs like that, they get to go most everywhere. Betsy, the head nurse, has a thing for dogs, it seems. She's the one who decided he could stay. Not sure Doc Peterson knows it, though. Probably why Betsy's got him sort of tucked away there. Speaking of which, where're you spending the night?"

"Nice couch in the lounge. I just sort of wanted to be here."

"Let me see if I can arrange a room for you. I'll talk to Betsy. Hospital's kinda quiet tonight. Sometimes they do things like that. Loyal dogs, heroic women, they deserve a break."

She smiled. "I'm not very heroic, Mike."

"Hey, in my book you are. Took guts, you know, going down into that gully, getting him out. Not sure how a little thing like you managed it, anyway."

"I had to," she said simply. "It had to be done and I was the only one there."

He grinned. "That's what I mean."

"About that room? I think I'm going to fall over any second."

"Back in a jiff," he said, then pointed to a small bench in the hall. "Sit!"

Obediently, she settled in the vinyl seat, pulling the blanket around her tightly. Her left arm throbbed a bit where the long scrape had been bandaged. Closing her eyes, her mind was filled with the image of Marshall's face as the rain began to wash the mud away.

Mike returned in about five minutes. "I've got...," he began, but saw she'd fallen asleep. A big man in his mid-40's, with silvering hair and a moustache to match, Mike gently scooped her up and carried her down the hall.

Chapter 6

Despite her tiredness, Eden woke up repeatedly during the night. Her dreams were wildly erratic combinations of things. Marshall had fallen down a crevice in a glacier and several polar bears were sitting on him. Miles was with her and dropped a rope ladder down into the crevice, explaining to her how she had to carry Wadsworth down the ladder on her shoulders and be careful not to sing or the bears would throw leaves at her. That was one of the more sensible dreams. When she woke with a start, she peered at the clock on the wall of the room Mike had arranged for her. Three AM. Sliding her feet into the hospital slippers, she padded quietly down the corridor. A young nurse at the station had her back turned and she flitted past unseen, pausing with her hand on Marshall's door.

She knew she shouldn't stay out in the hallway too long, so she pushed the door open. The room was dimly lit and she saw there were two beds, but Marshall was the only occupant of the room. Well, other than Wadsworth, who blinked sleepily at her from under the bed. "You here, too, eh?" she whispered, crouching to rub his ears. His tail thumped against the metal under-structure of the bed and she stood quickly, putting her finger to her lips. "Shhh!"

Marshall lay on his back, an IV drip in his left arm. She noted his right wrist was bandaged. Bruises she'd not seen earlier had appeared now on his forearms. There was a fairly large one on his left cheekbone and she expected the rest of him bore similar marks. He still had a heating blanket tucked around him and the room itself felt quite warm. Mike had told her that his eyes had been irrigated repeatedly. "You're going to be all right," she whispered more to herself than to him. The concept of drowning in cold mud sent a fresh shiver down her spine.

She sat in a chair between the two beds and just watched him sleep. Wadsworth crept out from under the bed, sat right in front of her knees and rested his head in her lap. She stroked his neck. "You were wonderful, Waddy," she told him softly. "He's going to be so proud of you when he finds out what you did."

Thinking back over the last three anniversaries of Miles' death, she had to admit this one was the most different. It had almost become the day this man sleeping in the bed two feet away had died. She wasn't sure why, couldn't form it into words, but the fact of that, that this man had almost died on the same day as Miles, would have died if she hadn't gone down into the gully, made her feel bonded to him somehow. Something was, in some odd way, a bit redeemed. She hadn't been there when Miles died, and there had been nothing she could do to save him. But today, today she had made a difference. Something newly strong had taken root inside her and she felt almost a sense of gratitude to this man for nearly dying so that she could prevent it.

"I'm still tired," she explained to the dog. "Don't mind me. My mind's all warped sideways right now."

Back in her own bed, she thought about it some more. There had been an early snow the day Miles was killed and he died right there beside his squad car, snowflakes falling on his face. She'd always imagined the scene, him lying there, his curly hair golden against the snow, fresh flakes settling on his ruddy face with its scattering of freckles. Now the scene switched back and forth from her imagined memories of Miles to the ones she'd just seen with her eyes, Marshall's face coated in mud and the raindrops starting to spatter darkly on it, the mud beginning to run down his cheeks. It all braided together in her tired brain, the days, the dyings, the faces.

In the morning there was a light tap on her door and Martha came in with a small case. Last night she'd told Harold what she'd need and Martha had packed it for her. She'd also packed for Marshall, only there she had to use her own judgment as to what to bring. Eden would be going back to the inn with Martha this morning, but the doctor wanted to keep Marshall at least through the day.

"They might let him out this evening. Said they'd wait and see how he was doing," Martha explained. She stepped out to the station to talk with the nurses while Eden dressed in the fawn-colored wool slacks and thick chocolate brown sweater she'd requested. Martha knew all the nurses and they were busily telling her what Mike had said about how Eden had gone down into the gully to rescue the professor. They smiled at her as she came up to the desk and one of the nurses handed her a bag with the clothing Eden had worn yesterday. "Here, I'll take that," Martha said firmly. "Let me see what I can do with them."

Eden looked down the corridor toward Marshall's room, undecided if she should stop by or not. Martha saw the look and said, "Doc just went in."

Well, that settled that. She'd be able to speak with Marshall this evening at the inn. She felt almost shy about the prospect, though. Good Lord, she'd had the man's head in her lap twice, had had her arm around his middle, had held his hand. He'd even toppled over almost on top of her. It wasn't like she'd never been near the guy before. But the thing was, she figured he probably didn't remember any of that. She rubbed the fingertips of her right hand on her palm, thinking of when she'd brushed mud from his face. *Silly goose,* she berated herself. But, without thinking, her fingertips moved, touching her own cheek as she followed Martha to the main entrance.

Mike came to the hospital about an hour later, bringing Wadsworth's harness with him. It, too, had gotten coated in mud yesterday and he'd spent some while cleaning it. He walked up to the nurses' station. "Hey, Betsy, ok if I drop this off in Sinclair's room? He may need it if he goes home today."

Wadsworth, who had slunk way back under the bed when Doctor Peterson had been there earlier, watched with guarded eyes as the door opened and another man came in. He remembered this one, though, and his tail thumped.

"So that's where you are!" Mike laughed softly. "It's ok, boy, you can come out. I brought your gear."

"His harness?" a slightly raw voice came from the bed.

"Yeah. It was all muddy. I sorta cleaned it a bit."

Marshall was sitting propped up on his pillow, his left arm in a sling. He extended his right hand in the direction the man's voice had come from. "Marshall Sinclair," he said.

"Mike, Mike Johnson. I'm one of the EMT's brought you in yesterday."

"Good," Marshall replied. "I was hoping to get a chance to thank you. I can't tell you how much I appreciate your getting me out of that gully."

"Out of...? You've got that one wrong. You were more'n halfway back to the inn before we got to you."

"But...I couldn't...."

"You don't remember the little gal?"

"Little gal?"

"Yeah, stayin' at the inn. Wadsworth here went and got her. Took her right to you."

"A...girl?"

Mike laughed. "Ok, a woman then. From what I hear tell she was out looking at the leaves and, as she says, Wadsworth kidnapped her."

"But...."

"I know what you mean. Don't see how she did it myself, but she got you loose and out of that big ditch all by herself. Saved your life."

"How...?" Marshall began but Mike's beeper went off.

"Gotta go," he said. "You got a great dog there," he added as he went out the door.

Marshall lay quietly after Mike left, trying to get his mind to go over yesterday step by step. He remembered walking down the wide path, the scents, the sounds that were triggering lines for his book. Then Wadsworth had stopped, had tried to block him, but he'd taken one more step, trying to feel with his foot what lay ahead. It was when his weight shifted forward that the edge had crumbled. He'd fallen. His shoulder had crashed into something and he'd turned in the air. There was mud everywhere and he couldn't seem to move very well. He shifted his right arm. Yes, it'd been pinned. He remembered trying to pull his hand free. And pain, searing through his shoulder and back. That would be the left shoulder. Then what? Everything seemed to converge into the mud and the pain, get all fuzzy and somehow lost. What had happened then?

More pain. He was choking. And someone was pushing on him, moving him. Could that have been this girl, woman, the EMT mentioned? Nothing was fitting together. He'd gotten out of the gully, was way down the trail before the EMTs got to him? That had to be a fair distance. He didn't remember any of it. Had it rained? He did seem to recollect rain hitting his face. He lay back, trying to recall what he could about the rain. Cold. That was the main thing. He remembered cold so deep even his liver felt cold. And fingers. What? Fingers? Yes, fingers on his face, touching, moving. What were they doing?

There had been some scent, some out-of-place scent. He couldn't remember what it was, only that it didn't fit there in the cold rain. He shivered again there in his warm bed, just thinking about the cold.

He slept much of the day and nurses came in and out, checking his temperature, adjusting things. About four, Peterson came back, said that he could go to the inn but that he needed to keep his left arm in a sling for awhile, would probably need some therapy to get it back in working order. Told him to rest a lot, not push it, and definitely not to go on any long walks in the woods. A male nurse came in and helped him dress. He grinned a little when he figured out what clothes Martha had chosen for him.

Harold drove out and picked him up. Wadsworth sat happily in the back seat, glad to be away from all the scents in the hospital. They rode in silence for a bit then Marshall asked, "The woman who found me, she's staying at the inn?"

"Yep, checked in that morning after you'd already set out."

"Will she still be there? I mean now, is she still staying there?"

"Yep. Came up from Pittsburgh, just like you."

He raised his eyebrows, finding that interesting. "Can you...?"

"Eden," Harold supplied. "Eden McLaughlin. Widow. Works on one of the Pittsburgh papers. Can't remember which one."

Marshall chewed silently on that bit of information for a moment. Here he'd been thinking of her as a girl but she was probably an older woman. All the more amazing that she could get him out of the gully. "I'd like to thank her," he said finally.

Eden was sitting on a couch in the living room when she heard the door of Harold's car slam. She knew he'd gone to pick Marshall up. Setting aside the book she was reading, she watched the front door, suddenly nervous. What would he think when he saw her sitting there? Would he remember her at all? Because of the mud, he'd never really looked at her and the last time she'd seen him, he'd been asleep. She blew out a long breath, feeling silly. Then Harold entered, holding the door for Marshall, who was walking behind him. Marshall came into the room dressed almost in the classic uniform of a lit professor, brown slacks, a tweed jacket with suede elbow patches. He had on a pair of very dark sunglasses and his left arm was in a sling, but it was the way he was holding Wadsworth's harness as he walked. It was all so unmistakable. She bit her lower lip, amazed at her own denseness.

Of course! Wadsworth was a Seeing Eye dog.

Chapter 7

Eden simply sat there and stared at Marshall as Martha bustled in, making a fuss over him. How could she have possibly been so blasted oblivious? "Dumb as a dodo," she muttered under her breath. She'd gotten so distracted trying to follow Wadsworth that she'd just completely stopped thinking about what the harness could be for. Then when she saw Marshall almost entombed in the mud, all her concentration had been on getting him free, getting him out, getting him help. By the time the EMTs arrived, she was so exhausted her brain was fried. But...still.

She watched him greet Martha, and felt like sinking beneath the cushions of the couch, but his voice captured her, held her up. It was very deep, though he was speaking softly. It was the first time she'd heard it and it just...fit.

She saw Wadsworth looking at her, his tail wagging slightly, but he was in harness and remained steady at Marshall's side. Marshall was explaining to Martha and Harold that it was really awkward for both him and Wadsworth right now because a guide dog was trained always to walk on his person's left, but with his left arm in a sling, he couldn't hold the harness, so they were having to make do with the right side. "It's amazing what a difference it makes," he said.

Martha looked over at Eden and then back to Marshall. "She's here, you know."

"She?"

"Eden. The one who got you out of the gully."

"I'd like very much to meet her, Martha, tell her how grateful I am."

Martha signaled for Eden to come join them. Eden bit her lower lip. On his feet, dressed as he was, he was a whole different ballgame from the mud-coated man of yesterday. "Come on," Martha urged, so she got to her feet and walked across the room to stand beside the older woman.

"Marshall, this is Eden McLaughlin."

Dropping the harness, he extended a large hand in her direction, waiting for her to take it. She'd held it before, there in the gully, but she stared at it a few seconds before lifting her own. "Hello," she said.

"Mrs. McLaughlin," he replied, his lips curving in a smile. "There are no words adequate to tell you...."

"Eden," she interrupted. "Please, call me Eden."

"Eden," he repeated. "Thank you. I mean that with my whole heart."

She had no idea what to say. He was several inches taller than she was, seemed taller somehow today than yesterday as he stood in front of her. Some sense of what...presence? ...radiated from him. Yesterday it had been coated in mud and pain. Today the intensity of it took her somewhat aback. Miles had been nothing like this. If one were to make a statue of Miles, one would mold it from wet red clay. There was a roundedness to Miles. Not that he was at all plump, but his face was round, his eyes were round and blue, his laugh, even his voice was round. Marshall had been chiseled from granite or marble. He wasn't round, not at all.

She'd left her hand in his and was studying his face now that she knew he was not staring back at her. What was it she was feeling as she looked at him? She had no experience of blindness other than a sort of vague horror of the thought of it. He was so handsome, so vital. How could he be blind? It seemed somehow like a terrible waste. She found herself wondering how long he'd been blind, how it had happened to him. It had to have been utterly traumatic, changing everything, limiting everything. She felt a great sense of disappointment for his sake rising in her.

"I'm sorry," she said, the words slipping out before she thought.

"Sorry? What are you sorry for, Eden?"

Good Lord! Had she said that out loud? "For...for not being able to get you out more quickly. It, um, seemed to take me a long time."

He smiled again. "I wasn't doing a very good job of getting myself out, I fear. So however long it took you is quite all right by me."

"Your arm was really stuck under that branch and the mud kept rising. It was...."

"It sounds perfectly dreadful," Martha said. "I'm just amazed you were able to do what you did, Eden." She clucked her tongue a couple of times for emphasis. "But now I've got a nice supper all fixed." She laughed. "I know it's a bed and breakfast, but today we're doing supper, too. It'll just be the two of you, I'm afraid. Mr. and Mrs. Simpson and their daughter checked out before lunch and we don't have any other guests coming in until the weekend."

She led the way to the dining room. The oval mahogany table was set for two. "Aren't you and Harold eating?" Eden asked.

"Oh, we'll be eating in the kitchen. We always like to let our guests dine on their own. Come on, have a seat. This way, Marshall." She pulled out a chair with its back to the fireplace. "Got a nice fire going to keep you warm."

Marshall sat down and Wadsworth settled on the floor just at his side. Eden took the chair on the opposite side of the table facing him. "Thank you, Martha," Marshall said, sliding his chair in. "The fire feels really good."

He heard Eden slide her own chair in. She was sitting quietly, not saying anything. He'd not expected somehow to be dining alone this evening with his rescuer. "I'm glad," he said, "to have this chance to thank you again. I'd like to hear more about Wadsworth, what he did to get you there."

She smiled, then remembered he couldn't see her smile. This was hard, his blindness, and she didn't know quite what to do around him now that she was aware of it. No wonder he didn't really need to open his muddy eyes yesterday. Then it dawned on her that his ears had been clogged with mud, too. How had that been for him, that world with no sight and no sound? She remembered reading a book about Helen Keller when she'd been a girl, had even done a report on it, but somehow it had never been real to her. Well, it was real enough to him, now wasn't it?

"Wadsworth is amazing," she finally answered. "I'm not used to dogs that, um, do things."

He chuckled. "Yes, Wadsworth does a lot of things." He leaned a bit, patting the dog's neck. "Don't you, boy?"

"Have you had him long?"

"Three years now. We're together just about all the time."

Three years. Well, then he'd been blind for at least that long. "I heard you teach. Does he go to school with you?" For the life of her, she couldn't quite imagine how he taught a college class of sighted students.

"He does. He's a great hit with the kids, in fact. They love to hear stories about the things he's done. Which leads me back to what he did yesterday. Just what did he do?"

She almost snorted at the memory of their meeting. "I thought he was a bear."

"A bear?" He chuckled again.

"I was fairly far into the woods, where the path starts to narrow, had my hands full of leaves when he came crashing out of the underbrush. Scared me to death until I realized he was a dog. Then he was most insistent I follow him. Tugged on my jacket even. He just wouldn't give up."

Marshall's lips curved into a fond smile.

"You really love him, don't you?" she observed.

"There's a saying about guide dogs that goes 'My eyes have a wet nose.' That's him, but he's a whole lot more than that, too. Yes, I love him very much." As if in response, Wadsworth's tail thumped the floor happily.

"What happened next?" he asked.

"Well, we got to the edge of the gully where it had crumbled and he found a way down. I just sort of followed him. You were almost entirely covered in the mud. Waddy kept licking you. Got his tongue all muddy."

"Waddy?"

"Um, well, I just sort of started calling him that. I saw his tag so I knew his name. We kinda became friends trying to get you out of there."

His smile broadened, showing even white teeth. "I rather like that. Waddy. He's named after Henry Wadsworth Longfellow."

"Ah, the daffodil guy." Darn, she didn't like the really black dark glasses. She wanted to be sitting across from him, knowing he was looking at her. It wasn't right, not at all, that he couldn't.

Marshall controlled his smile. "Not quite the daffodil guy. You're thinking of Wordsworth, not Wadsworth. Longfellow was the Hiawatha guy. But I'm very interested in Wordsworth, too. In fact, next spring I'm hoping to go to the Lake District, Wadsworth and I, in time for the daffodils. It's something I've always wanted to do, walk there beside the lakes in spring."

He was serious. He was actually serious. What could he possibly get out of being in the midst of acres of daffodils he couldn't see? "That sounds nice," she said lamely.

However, he'd caught the nuance in her voice. "It doesn't make sense to you?"

"What?" Good Lord, how did he know what she was thinking?

"That I would want to walk there," he added.

"No, I didn't mean, well, it's just...I don't understand. How would you know the daffodils were there?" She couldn't believe she'd actually asked the man that!

"Because I know a single daffodil. I've held one in my hands and touched all its parts." The fingers of his right hand moved gracefully as he spoke. "When you get on intimate terms with one flower and then trail your hand over a row of them, it becomes easy to take that and multiply it. And then you add the breeze that blows there in the early spring and the soft sounds the flowers and leaves make rubbing against one another, the lapping of the water at the edges of the lake. You add the birds you know who live in the area, probably the bleating of some spring lambs, the rustle of the branches with their leaves just coming out. Spring has its own wonderful scent, the plowed earth, the water itself, the flowers.

And then you put in the knowledge that you're there, right there in the place where the poet walked, the place that inspired his words and it just comes together."

She paused, her fork halfway to her lips, looking at him, realizing he knew more about daffodils than she'd ever taken the time to find out. She knew they were yellow mostly and had little trumpet-thingies, but she'd never run her fingers over one, never gotten to know a single daffodil, how had he put it, intimately.

She cleared her throat. "You...you teach literature, right?"

"I do. I think I've loved words all my life. But you must, too. You work for a newspaper, don't you?"

"Yes, I write for the entertainment section. Museum openings, concerts, that sort of thing. Movie reviews, too."

"Ah, I like movies."

"You do?"

"I usually go the DVD route. I had a colleague at Duquesne who'd watch them with me. He was wonderful at describing what happened between the moments of dialogue. He took a position in Florida this fall, though. It's hard to find someone really good at that."

Gads, he liked movies. That was a new thought for her. She studied him a moment more, mentally trying to remove his glasses so she could see his whole face as she had there in the rain and when he was sleeping in the hospital.

There he was sitting across the table from her, carrying on a conversation with her, yet he couldn't seem to get a handle on just who she was. There was something a bit guarded about her. From her voice and manner, she didn't seem as old as he'd thought. Harold had said she was widowed. Perhaps that was why she was guarded? She obviously was unfamiliar with things relating to blindness, but he was used to that, finding it to be the case more often than not. So it was her fingers he remembered touching his face, his eyes? Somehow he was having a hard time relating that to the person he was dining with. In his memory, the touch had been soft, almost intimate, but the woman across from him maintained a certain stiffness that didn't fit. But then, just because she had saved his life didn't necessarily mean she had to feel comfortable around him.

"Are you here for long?" he tried.

"I'm not sure yet. Just sort of playing it by ear. And you?"

"I'm rather a long-termer. At least I was. I'm on Sabbatical and writing a book. But with my left arm all laid up for a while, I'm not sure just how much writing I'll be doing."

"That does make it awkward, doesn't it."

"Very," he nodded.

"Perhaps I could help?"

His eyebrows went up. "You mean...?"

"I could type, or whatever it is you use, what you dictate. I'm not really working on anything of my own right now."

"I have a special keyboard attachment for the computer. Works better for me than the old brailler, and my secretary ...," he paused, leaning forward. "You'd actually do that?"

"My pleasure. Could be interesting. Might even inspire me to attempt something of my own. I've always kinda wanted to do something more than just the newspaper."

"First you save me and then you save my book. You're an amazing woman, Mrs. McLaughlin."

"Eden."

"Right, Eden. As in 'garden of.'"

"Hardly!" she laughed. "More of a weed patch."

"Somehow I doubt that."

And though she wasn't so sure herself that she was wrong, she was rather pleased that he doubted it.

Chapter 8

Martha brought out an apple pie for dessert. She was a short, plumpish woman, with a cap of white curls framing her open, pleasant face. As she set the warm pie on the table, Marshall grinned and said, "Good Lord, Martha. My nose thinks it's died and gone to heaven."

Indeed the smell filling the room was marvelous: apples, cinnamon, brown sugar. Eden watched as Martha cut a huge slice, plopped it on a plate and set it in front of Marshall. Her pleasure in being able to serve him was clearly writ on her features. Eden wished Marshall could see how happy his little remark had made their hostess. His not being able to see Martha or the pie took her mind back to the daffodils with a sudden start. She went over what he'd said, not that he remembered what daffodils looked like and could transpose that into the Lake Country, but that he'd run his fingers over one. She stared openly at him as he lifted a forkful of pie to his lips. Had he never seen a daffodil, ever? Was that what he meant? Did he know their form completely but not that they were yellow? Did he not know about yellow? The thought absolutely appalled her. How could she find out without being rude and asking him directly?

She ate a bite of pie, so preoccupied she didn't even taste it. "Was Wadsworth your first guide dog?" she asked offhandedly.

"My third," he replied, wiping his lips. "I had a golden retriever during my teens, but he was retired, lived with my mother after that. A guide dog usually serves for around seven years, but I had Mellow for longer than that. She was my second, a yellow lab. Went off to college with me. A really wonderful animal."

"Then you got Wadsworth?"

"You have to go back to the Seeing Eye and train with a new dog each time you get one. They need to make sure you work as a team before they send you out in the world. But, yes, Wadsworth is my third dog."

"Um, how young can you get one?"

He smiled, laying down his fork. "Small children aren't able to handle one. It's rather a workout walking with a guide dog. So when I was little, I used a cane or my brother or

I just...went. My mother had a hard time with that, I'm afraid. She didn't appreciate my love for climbing trees."

"You've been blind since you were a child?" There, she'd asked it.

"Always," he said.

"Always?"

"Came into the world this way," he grinned, "but they decided to keep me anyway."

"I didn't...."

"It's fine, Eden. I don't mind at all your asking."

Her mind was racing. So he'd really never seen a daffodil. Never. She'd couldn't begin to imagine it. He returned to eating his pie, somehow realizing that she was thinking. She was actually running through a lot of emotions. When she got past being appalled, she found that she was angry that this should be so for him. She took a bite of pie and almost choked on it, coughing and then taking a long drink of coffee.

"Are you all right?" he asked.

"Went down wrong pipe," she gasped.

"I did that with mud yesterday," he offered pleasantly.

"So you did." She was glad he'd brought that up again. "How did it happen that Wadsworth let you go over the gully's edge anyway?"

"It wasn't his fault, not at all. Mine entirely. He stopped and even tried to block me with his body." He patted the dog again, accompanied by more tail thumping. "But I thought if I explored carefully with my foot, I could determine where to walk. Made the mistake, though, of letting my weight come forward before I was sure. Blasted careless of me. And the edge just crumbled away. Took me down with it. I should have known better. I did know better. So it was stupidity and not blindness that nearly did me in."

"Did you send him for help, then?"

"I couldn't. Too much mud in my mouth. He decided that all on his own."

"He's very smart."

"Evidently smarter than I am," Marshall chuckled.

There was a pause that lasted a couple of minutes as they finished their pie. "Have you been to the Morning Glory before?" he asked, wondering where it might lead.

"First time. My cousin found it on the internet, thought it would do me good to get away right now."

"And has it?"

"What?"

"Done you good? I imagine you didn't expect to spend your first day covered in mud."

She thought about that a minute. Actually yesterday had been easier for her than she'd imagined. He'd distracted her so from herself that she hadn't moped around thinking about Miles. "No, I didn't expect that. But it was ok. You helped."

"Glad to be of service, though I don't see how I could have been of any help to you. It was entirely the other way round."

"Not really. Not...." Did she really want to explain? "It was an anniversary of sorts."

"Wedding?"

"No, not a wedding."

"I'm sorry. I don't mean to pry, Eden."

She looked down at her plate and then remembered he wouldn't be staring at her anyway. Suddenly she realized she wanted him to understand. "Miles, my husband, he was killed four years ago yesterday."

Marshall pressed his lips together, not having expected that. He said, "I'm so sorry, Eden," then thought how insufficient that was.

"He was a cop. Irish. Liked to sing. Guess I didn't think I'd lose him that soon."

"How long were you married?"

"Two years. Now he's been gone twice as long as that." She couldn't believe, really, that she was sitting there with a stranger telling him about her feelings. But she looked at her hands in her lap and they held the memory of touching his eyelids. Did that make him more than a stranger? She didn't know. Curling her fingers tightly into her palm, she pressed her thumb over them like a clamp, studying them. Did she owe it to Miles not to think about that, not to remember it? She squeezed her own eyes shut.

Martha bustled back into the room to take away the pie dishes and found her sitting there like that, head down, eyes shut. Marshall was simply sitting quietly across from her, looking slightly grim. She put her hand on Eden's shoulder, startling her. "Are you ok, Eden, dear?"

"A bit of a headache. I think I'll go up to my room now, if that's all right."

"You go right along. You had quite the day yesterday." She stood watching as Eden bade Marshall a quick good-night and then headed for the stairs. When she heard Eden's door close, she said to Marshall. "Looked a bit peaked. Probably just needs to rest a bit."

Marshall sat there a moment more, then got up and went into the parlor, Wadsworth in attendance. Harold came in, half a mug of coffee in his hand, cleared his throat loudly as he'd decided to do so Marshall would know he was in the room. Marshall had been there a month and Harold was still not used to his blindness but he liked the man, liked to talk with him when he got the chance. "You feeling better this evening?"

"A lot, thanks. After they got my arm back in its socket, a great deal of that pain simply stopped." He ran his palm down his right leg. "Still have a lot of aches and bruises, though. Must have really tumbled against things as I went down." His right hip, in fact, ached rather profoundly.

"Good twenty-five, maybe thirty feet down to the bottom of that thing. Surprised you didn't break your neck." Harold had a definite tendency toward bluntness of speech.

"How do you think she did it, Harold? Eden. How do you think she got me out of there? I barely remember anything about it."

"Don't know as I could've done it myself so I can't imagine how a slender little thing like her did it. She's got guts, that one. Then after she got you up and out, she walked you halfway back down the trail. You collapsed on her right where it widens out and she got the idea of writing a note and putting it under your dog's harness. That's what got me out there. Pouring rain, it was, too. Absolute buckets."

"I have some memory of the rain. I imagine if I'd have still been in the gully when that started, I'd probably have drowned."

"'Spect so," he agreed. "She looked like a drowned pup herself when I found you, sitting there with your head in her lap, leaning over, trying to keep the rain off you."

Marshall licked his lips, trying to place the woman he'd just had dinner with in that totally different situation. Martha came in, still wiping her hands on a dish towel. "Anything I can get you men?"

Marshall got to his feet. "Thanks, but no, Martha. I believe I'm going to retire for the night myself." He smiled. "That was outstanding pie, by the way."

When he was settled in his bed, Wadsworth sprawled on the rug beside it, he lay there trying to ignore his hip and shoulder, trying to center his mind on what Eden had done. He wished he could recall things more clearly. Everything had become this big mush of mud and pain and wet and cold, and fingers touching his face, and the scent of something he strained to remember but just couldn't quite manage. He dropped his right arm off the side of the bed and Wadsworth lifted his head to lick it. He left it there, the dog's warm tongue somehow a needed connection in that moment. Sometimes, he mused, it was the lightest touch that kept us from floating away.

Chapter 9

Eden woke with the morning sun on her face. She'd fallen into bed and forgotten to close the curtains. Stretching, she lay there, letting her eyes run absently along the ruffle of the canopy. Why had she practically fled the scene last night at dinner? She was usually much more collected than that. It was Marshall. She knew it was. He disturbed her in ways she had no name for. She found his person almost magnetically attractive yet at the same time felt awkward and unsure because of his blindness. It was the push-pull of the whole thing that was keeping her off-balance. Not since reading Helen Keller's biography for that 5th grade report had she thought about what it meant to be blind, and she hadn't really thought about it all that much back then. Florence Nightingale had been taken by Marsha and Queen Elizabeth the First by Joyce. It was either Helen Keller or Betsy Ross. That was about her level of interest in it. Her hand had been reaching for the shelf when Pam snatched away Betsy so she read about water pumps instead of flags. It didn't really matter. It was a report and had to be gotten out of the way. Helen was an alien being who lived in an alien world. She got a B+, put the book back on the shelf, and went out to roller skate. Except for a movie or two where a character was blind, loss of sight had not crossed her path again, not until yesterday. And Marshall, he'd not lost it. He'd never had it. He must live in a world almost as alien as Helen Keller's. Yet he'd sat there eating his apple pie, drinking his coffee, having conversation with her in a way that seemed entirely normal. She just could not get the two separate concepts to mesh.

She closed her eyes, trying to put herself into his world. It was impossible. Even with her lids down, she knew the wallpaper was pale pink, knew what the clouds looked like out the window, knew the canopy was white with scattered pink cabbage roses, that there was a discolored place on the hardwood floor where an old leak had stained it. If he were lying there, he would not know those things. How could life possibly be if you didn't know these things?

She knew she'd become suddenly fascinated with it all, fascinated because it simply was his world. They'd sat together at table, yet his perception of it had to be entirely different than hers. The thought that he was so near, doing the same things she was, and yet so totally in his own sphere of awarenesses gripped her imagination. She hadn't been so caught up in anything in years, in four years, to be exact.

And Miles, would he mind? She'd carried him with her invisibly for so long, she felt like she was doing him some disservice to be so interested in something that he'd never had any part of, something that didn't involve him in any way. She'd settled into a familiar pattern of taking him with her, wherever she went, whatever she thought. It was how, in the beginning, she'd been able to get through still being alive when he was not, but it had become habit over time, had become a padding between herself and the stream of life.

Almost absent-mindedly she dressed in Navy blue slacks and a cowl-necked lighter blue sweater then went downstairs. A large coffee urn sat on a sideboard and she poured herself a mug, turning when Harold entered the room.

"Mornin'," he said with a dip of his head, heading toward his desk in the adjoining room. Harold was a tall, weathered man, who walked with just a slight stoop of his lean body as though the years were beginning to weigh on him a bit.

She followed him part-way. "Have...have you seen Marshall this morning?" she asked.

"On the dock last I saw."

Martha came in with a platter of hot blueberry muffins. "He was up early, Eden. Said he'd slept too much yesterday. Here, why don't you take him one of these muffins?" She popped two muffins into a large napkin and handed them to Eden, her face entirely innocent.

Eden took the napkin and her mug and wandered toward the front door. Yes, there he was down at the edge of the lake where the old wooden dock jutted about twenty feet over the water. Martha came up behind her, lifting Eden's coat off the rack and settling it over her shoulders, then without a word turned, and humming softly went toward the kitchen.

She went out on the porch, standing at the top of the stairs, looking at Marshall. His back was to her and he was outlined by the morning sun. His legs were apart and Wadsworth sat, leaning slightly against his right calf. He was wearing a rust-colored leather jacket and even from the back she could tell that though his right arm was in the sleeve, it was just draped over his left shoulder.

The night had, indeed, been rather difficult. It had taken him a while to fall asleep despite a lingering sense of exhaustion, and then if he turned to the left, his shoulder woke him or if he turned to the right, his hip did. He'd risen before dawn and sat for a long time on the front porch even though it was quite chilly. When Martha found him there, she brought out a plaid afghan and put it over his legs then returned with a steaming cup of coffee. Martha had raised five children, all of whom now lived in distant states, but the mothering instinct still waxed strong in her breast. She had decided Marshall needed mothering and busily attended to it. He allowed it with good grace, as his own mother had been quite like that.

As he sat there his thoughts wandered from day before yesterday to Eden and on to his book. If she were truly willing, perhaps he might actually get something accomplished on that while his shoulder healed. He leaned forward, resting his right elbow on his knee, his mind going over the chapter he was working on. Later, he went back inside, got another cup of coffee and headed down to the dock, a rather awkward maneuver because his right hand needed to hold the harness, so he'd tucked the mug in his left and tried valiantly not to slosh as it was pressed close to his abdomen.

Once at the end of the dock, he dropped the harness and transferred the mug to his right hand. The sun was on his face, though not really very warm, and he stood there quietly, listening to the little lapping sound the lake water made against the pilings of the dock. There weren't any boats out yet today, but a flight of Canada geese had settled on the lake to his right and were honking at one another. A fish surfaced and splashed, making him recall days when his Dad and brother, Jeffrey, had gone fishing with him.

He heard footsteps on the wooden dock behind him and judging by their lightness, thought it was a woman, most likely Eden. He smiled slightly to himself, rather glad for her company. "Good morning," he said pleasantly as she came up on his left side, standing about two feet away.

"Hello, Marshall," she replied. "Sorry I left the table so abruptly last night."

He turned his head toward her, his dark glasses in place. "It's all right. You had every reason to be tired."

His face was positively golden in the morning light, and the sun reflected in his glasses. Again she was struck by his presence, by some gravitas of bearing, some innate dignity. She was silent a moment, trying to imagine him a boy climbing trees.

"What are you thinking?" he asked, surprising her.

After a little pause, "I was trying to picture you climbing a tree," she admitted.

"Now?" he grinned.

"When you were a boy. You said you liked to do that."

He turned his face back into the sun. "We had this big crabapple in the front yard. It had twisty branches low to the ground and I found it extremely easy to get fairly high up in it. I had a favorite seat up there." He smiled. "It's a good memory."

"Was that the only tree?"

"There were others, a maple down the street, a younger oak not far into the woods. The crabapple was my favorite, though."

She studied his profile, nice straight nose, good chin. He seemed aware of her study and though he didn't turn his head, asked, "Is there something, Eden?"

"It's just that...that...I've never met anyone before in quite so, um, dramatic circumstances. And here we are now, standing in this peaceful morning. It makes me wonder if it was all real, the gully, I mean."

"Quite real," he said, moving his sling slightly, causing a bit of a grimace to pass quickly over his face. "But it is nice here now, isn't it?"

She shivered. "Bit chilly, though."

"You're cold. Would you like to go back up to the house, Eden? I imagine Martha's got a huge breakfast ready by now."

"Oh! I forgot! She sent you a pre-breakfast muffin." Eden unwrapped the two rather cooled muffins and started to hand one to him, but he had the coffee mug in his one good hand. "Here," she said quickly, "let me take your cup." Awkwardly, she tried juggling her own mug of coffee and the two muffins while taking his cup from him, succeeding in dropping both muffins on the dock. She expected Wadsworth to lunge for them, but he sat where he was, simply watching them roll past the toes of Marshall's shoes.

"He didn't grab them," she commented, astonished. Any other dog she'd ever met would have gobbled them right down. "They're right there in front of him and he's just looking at them."

"He's trained to do that, Eden. A guide dog can't be distracted by food." He bent to his right, patting Wadsworth. "Good boy," he affirmed.

Eden stooped and picked them up. The geese had come up onto the bank not far away and she tossed the muffins toward them. "Waddy, you are one heckuva dog." His tail thumped in acknowledgement as he regarded her with large brown eyes. "Yes, let's do go in now. My fingers are getting frozen. There's a heavy frost this morning, you know." Or did he know? Being with him brought up questions she'd never dealt with before. Constantly.

After the muffins had fallen, she'd tucked the napkin in her coat pocket and was holding both mugs by their handles in her left hand. Marshall took up the harness in his right hand and turned toward the inn. "Wadsworth, forward," he said quietly and the dog set off at a brisk pace.

She had to hurry to keep up. "Do guide dogs always walk that fast?"

"As a rule, yes," he replied. "Takes a while to get used to it."

They came to the end of the dock and headed up the brick walkway to the house. Wadsworth stopped at the bottom step so Marshall would know where they were. He mounted them confidently, seeming to know just how many steps there were. She had no idea and found herself counting them as she went up. Details. Details she'd never paid any attention to before.

Marshall had been right. Martha had, indeed, made a huge breakfast. She hovered around Marshall a bit at the table, making sure he was aware of everything she'd cooked. Eden watched him, noting the fond grace with which he handled the motherly woman. She found something in herself settling contentedly down on the cushioned dining room chair. He was like a fireplace, giving off some deep peace and warmth and comfort, that made one want to pull one's chair close and just...be. How strange. How could he be like that? He had been utterly helpless when she'd first come across him, yet here he was radiating this sense of, what was it, what did she feel around him? Safety? No, that couldn't be it. For Pete's sake, the man was blind. Yet there he sat like some sturdy bluff between her and...what? That was the question. Between her and what? What was in the wind she suddenly felt his presence could block from her? And why was she even thinking things like this? It made no sense. Was she not the one who had saved him, right there at the brink of death, had she not saved him? Did that not make her the sheltering bluff? Why wouldn't her mind be still and let her just eat breakfast?

Too late she realized he had asked her something. "Sorry. I guess I was thinking."

"You know about my tree climbing. I was just wondering what similar things young Eden might have done."

With a mental broom, she swept all her straying thoughts into a pile in the corner. "Um, well, let's see. I wasn't much of a tree climber myself, I'm afraid. Liked to roller skate a lot, though. Had the skinned knees to prove it."

"Ah," he said, leaning back in his chair. "Roller skating is a lot of fun."

"You skated?"

"In rinks a few times, yes. My older brother Jeffrey was determined I had to do everything he did. I guess I was pretty much determined that way myself."

"How?" she asked without thinking how that might sound.

"The skating? Jeffrey held my hand and off we went." He tipped his head down, smiling at recollections. "Where my mother was over-protective, Jeff was entirely the opposite. No sitting at home for me while he went off with his friends. No, they all pitched in and took me everywhere." He chuckled. "They even had me driving a car in the cemetery one night. My mother never knew about that one."

"He sounds marvelous. How much older is he?"

His chin tipped up toward the ceiling. "Three years. He was three years older, almost three and a half."

She caught the 'was.' "Is...is...?"

"Afghanistan. About two years ago. Marine corps."

She sighed. So he knew about great loss, too. "Oh, Marshall." She couldn't think of what to say.

"He was still three when I was born. Always seemed to have this uncanny understanding that I couldn't see. When he was four and I was one, he figured out this way to teach me to walk. Got a cardboard box and held onto one edge while I held onto the other, then he'd walk backwards. Led me all around the house and yard like that. He was always coming up with something similar, something to help me go fearlessly into his sighted world."

"He seems to have done a good job."

"So much of what I've become as a man is due to him. He was simply the best, the very best." He inhaled deeply. "But the rest of my life I owe to you, Eden. I wouldn't be having it if it weren't for you."

His right hand lay on the table top just to the side of his plate. More than anything in the world at that moment she wanted to rest hers atop it. But she didn't, of course. She just looked at it and wanted to.

Chapter 10

Immediately following breakfast, Eden went up to her room and called Connie. "You're not coming back already?" were the first words out of Connie's mouth when she heard Eden's voice on the phone.

"No, no. In fact, I'm calling to say I've decided to extend my stay. I've got a lot of vacation time piled up at the paper. You know how I've not used any in ages. So I'm going to call there next and tell them I'm taking it now, all of it."

"All of it? Eden, that's quite a lot. What in heaven's name have you found up there that's so interesting?"

"I'll tell you more about that later, Con. Right now I just know it's something I need to do, want to do. Just wanted to let you know, ok?"

"Sure. I'm just a bit puzzled. Hadda twist your arm to get you up there and now you don't want to come back. Sounds a bit strange, I hope you know."

Eden laughed. "I know. But everything's all right. Really it is."

When Eden finished her second phone call and walked down the hall toward the stairs, she heard piano music. Curious, she came into the parlor and found Marshall seated at Martha's old upright, the fingers of his right hand picking out notes. "It sounds like raindrops," she commented.

"Close," he grinned. "It's called *The Wisdom of Snow*. Has a definite 'falling' quality to it, doesn't it?" He played a bit more. "There are no words, just the music. Sounds better with the left hand, too."

"Marshall Sinclair, is there anything you can't do?" she chuckled.

He turned on the bench. "I'm actually not all that good at portrait painting," he answered, trying to look serious.

"But he sings quite nicely," Martha added, coming into the room. "We've had our own little songfest going here in the evenings. Here, Darlin', move over."

Marshall slid to the side and Martha took a seat on the piano bench and started playing *Stout-hearted Men*.

Marshall groaned dramatically. "Martha! Nelson Eddy?"

"Come on, mister," she said determinedly, "you can do it."

And so he did, a deep, full-bodied baritone filling the room as Martha played, a rather satisfied smile lurking around the corners of her mouth. Eden stood there listening, absolutely transfixed. Miles had sung, but his voice was an Irish tenor. Marshall's was so different, rich and full and strong. She sat in an easy chair to one side of the room and when they'd finished, urged them to continue. Martha began *You'll Never Walk Alone* and Marshall briefly touched his hand to his face, rubbing lightly across his lips, then began singing. When he sang the words, "hold your head up high and don't be afraid of the dark," Eden's eyes stung with quick tears, watching him. He was simply grand. And he was not at all afraid of the dark.

And then she realized that this was the first time she'd cried for anybody since Miles and she was crying because Marshall was so beautiful and he was unafraid in his dark but she didn't understand his dark and how he could be so unafraid. There was no way, ever, even if she lost her sight tomorrow that she could really grasp his darkness yet she found herself desperately wanting to. He was right there, just a few feet away, and yet somehow so separate from where she was. It was like they were each encased in their own distinct bubbles. As she got the mental image of that, though, she also remembered how when two bubbles came into contact, they often merged. Could that happen? Could she get beyond the walls of his bubble, of hers, and find some space that they shared? She didn't know why it mattered, but it did. She had held his life in her hands, quite literally, not knowing about the bubbles. Now he was himself again, now she knew, but what she wanted was the way it had been when she had wiped his face, his eyes, and he had not dwelt in some different land she could never visit.

Martha looked over, saw the tears in Eden's eyes, but said nothing. She merely turned to Marshall and asked, "Need some hot apple cider after that?"

"Sounds good. You, too, Eden?"

"Most definitely," she said brightly, wiping quickly at her eyes. "Thank you both. I really enjoyed that."

He stood up from the piano bench and walked straight to the chair near hers, taking a seat. Wadsworth was napping under the window. "You know where the chair is so easily." She was becoming less hesitant about saying what she was thinking. He seemed not to mind her questions.

"I've been here a month. After a little while, you learn the locations of things. So long as they're not moved," he added. "Martha watches over me like the proverbial hawk. If a guest so much as moves a footstool, she's right there putting it back in place."

He sighed then and leaned his right temple against the curve of the wing-backed chair. "You look tired," she said.

"I am," he admitted. "I think not sleeping much last night is catching up with me."

"Why don't you rest a little then? I have some more phone calls to make in my room. I'll see, uh, I'll come back later and maybe we can talk about your book some."

"It's ok, Eden, to use the word 'see'. I use it all the time myself."

After she left, Marshall closed his eyes. Wadsworth got up, moved over to one side of the chair and flopped back down again. Half-asleep, Marshall reached up, took off his glasses, and let his hand fall with them onto his lap.

Half an hour later Eden returned to the parlor. Wadsworth lifted his head to see who was coming, saw it was her and laid it back down again. Walking quietly, she crossed the room and sat down on the footstool in front of Marshall. His eyes were closed but the darn black glasses were off and she could see his whole face for the first time since the hospital. Then he was still a stranger, but now she was getting some grasp of who he was. With his glasses off, the bruise along his cheekbone showed clearly. The bruise, his face in such repose, eyes closed brought clearly back to her their time in the rain and she felt connected again to him as that person and somehow was able to begin reconciling the two Marshalls who had seemed so different to her. Harold was outside raking leaves, Martha was bustling about in her kitchen, and no one else was in the house, so she got to her knees right beside his legs and just watched him for a long time.

Always she had thought she knew herself, understood what made herself tick, knew her own motivations. But right now she wasn't so sure anymore. She had just met this man yet was so extraordinarily drawn to him. She'd not even felt this...this...what was it? This sense of...of...going toward. Yes, that was it. Not even when she'd met Miles. Miles was laughter and ballgames in the midst of large crowds of his buddies. Always there'd been buddies. She liked them, got along with them fine, enjoyed being part of a larger group. Most of them were cops like Miles and very close with one another. Wherever they went, there were always several others along, watching each other's back. Except for that night in the snow when he'd been alone. They hung around for a time in the days after the funeral, knowing he'd want them to make sure she was all right. After a while, they began to drift away and her main companion was her cousin, Connie. There'd been no more evenings in Irish pubs with beer and back slapping and ballads. She hadn't really wanted it, not after Miles was gone. It was because of Miles that she'd ever been a part of it in the first place.

She hadn't wanted to date, not for a long time after Miles. Then last year she'd ventured into a relationship with Collier, the architect. He was eight years older, had lived alone all his adult life, and had a splendid condo in the Trimont tower overlooking the city. Everything there was perfectly arranged, absolutely clean, and totally uncomfortable. Just like him. It was how he was, how he needed things to be, and how she was not. It wasn't that she was a slob, not at all, but that comfort was important to her. She liked to go into a room and live in it. His rooms were works of art with invisible *Do Not Touch* signs posted everywhere. It would never have worked.

Now here she was kneeling beside the sleeping Marshall and he seemed to her like some beckoning roadway that she wanted to travel. Something lay just around the bend of him, something she felt this rising desire to find and, strangely, she felt that if she found whatever it was, it would somehow explain her to herself and something that was lacking would be filled. Not that she put all this into words in thought clear and reasoning as she watched him sleep. She just knew it without consciousness of the knowing.

Three men. Miles and his world of police blue and golden hair and the foam of beer on laughing lips. Collier, all in minimalist black and white, with clean, straight lines and a horror of lace. And Marshall, whom she'd found in autumn, in a place of crisply-colored leaves and wild geese and the lappings of lake water. Marshall, tweed and suede and rust-toned leather, warm cider and apple pie, plaid afghans and books. Fireplaces and quiet grace and walking without fear in places all unseen.

Martha poked her head in the room to make sure he was all right and paused, riveted by the expression on the young widow's face as she knelt beside his chair. She had saved him and now, though sound asleep, he'd begun something quite akin to saving her. The older woman smiled and then hurried to shush Harold who was coming a bit too noisily in the front door.

Chapter 11

Without even realizing she had done it, Eden had laid her palm on his right leg as she watched him sleep. Harold's coming in the front door had roused Marshall enough so that he gradually became aware of her hand. He didn't move his head at all nor open his eyes, he simply slid his own hand down a bit and covered hers with it. She started slightly, but remained where she was, kept her hand where it was. And so they stayed that way for several quiet moments.

As he woke to awareness of her hand, he was, in that state of just awakening, back in the rain on the path and her hands were on his cheeks. Of everything that happened to him after he fell, that was the one most real moment. Now here her hand was again, only he came to know that he was dry and not in so very much pain as then. He didn't know, really, why she was there, why her hand was on his leg, but he liked the sense of it there. In the rain and mud, her hands had been his brief connection with relief. That he had not died, not drowned in the mud, was not going to die that day...because of her hands.

They were small, slender hands and he wanted to cover the one on his leg, to surround it with himself and shelter it as it had sheltered him, to offer to it warmth in some small return. When he'd moved it there, there was a rightness to it that surprised him. When one is not looking at all for rightness and yet it comes, it requires a certain degree of attention. He had not thought to leave it there, just a brief, acknowledging, covering touch and then a moving on, but he did not wish to move on and so he simply let it remain. Hers lay quietly compliant beneath his much larger one, indicating in no way that he should lift his away.

He could hear her breathing. She made the slightest sound deep in her throat and it was then he did lift his hand and touch her cheek. She remained perfectly still and his fingers moved on, walking softly down her cheekbone as his thumb pad followed the line of her jaw. Two fingers traced her lips then, barely touching, lightly found the form of her nose. He began to wonder if this might be too much and made to move his hand away, but her fingers took his wrist and moved it back, guiding it to her eyes. She wanted him to touch her eyes as she had touched his. Silently he accepted her invitation, finding her lids closed. He traced the arch of her brow then let his fingers follow down her temple to her cheek again. It was then he curled them back and rested his hand again in his lap. "Thank you," he whispered, honored.

She didn't want to open her eyes. The whole thing had been somehow magical and even when his hand was gone, she felt it still. By the time she did open them, he was settling his dark glasses back into place. "Why," she asked softly, "why the glasses?"

He tipped his head to one side and gave her a small smile. "Not for me. It's not for me."

"Why then?"

"Because...," he hesitated, "because the light is not there and it bothers some people." He was thinking of Beatrice. He'd asked her to marry him just before he'd gotten his doctorate. She, a native Bostonian, was getting an advanced degree in music theory. They'd been more or less together for nearly two years but she didn't like his eyes, had told him they were definitely not the windows of his soul because their shutters were closed and gave her the creeps. He'd met other people like that from time to time. A few kids when he was young and too free and active to bother with dark glasses. Some pretty cruel teasing, a few black eyes produced by Jeffrey's fists on bully's faces, but Beatrice had come to it gradually, after he'd let himself become committed to her. In the end, it was probably why they'd parted company. It had come down to her saying, "Good grief, Marshall, at least keep them closed!"

"Eyes that do not see," he continued, "have a different appearance to them, so I am told, especially ones that have never seen. I just, well, it's just better this way, with the glasses."

She saw she'd touched some sort of nerve with him and let it rest, but for one final question. "Ok, then, what color are they?"

"Jeffrey always said they were green, though Mom insisted on some days they were blue."

She smiled, liking the thought of him with green eyes. "Mine are green, too."

"And your hair?"

"Sort of a really deep auburn, almost a chestnut maybe."

"Ah, a lovely color," he said, which made her wonder how he knew, and so she asked.

"Colors are an 'iffy' thing for people like me," he admitted, "but Jeffrey used to work with me on it, finding things that were not only a color, but said something about the essence of the color, like freshly-mown grass, for instance. He'd mow our yard then come get me and stand me in the middle of it and say, 'Smell hard, Marshy. That's green.'" He smiled at the memory. "He found something for all the colors, their scent, their sound, their feel. We'd lie under the maple tree on a June day, listening the breeze blowing the leaves against each other. I even wrote a short story once called 'Green Is the Whisper of Leaves.'"

"So what is auburn then?"

"When you're standing on a hilltop and the sun is low in the sky and hot on your face and you wait there a while as it disappears a moment behind a cloud. Then suddenly it's there again, just briefly before it sets, and there's this flow of warmth on your face after the chill. Not hot like before, but spreading over it soft and comfortable and somehow deeper and richer than just the regular heat. That's auburn."

She knew that never again in her life could she ever brush her hair and not hear his deep voice saying those words. Profoundly touched, she had to blink away more tears. "I like you, Dr. Marshall Sinclair. I like you a lot."

He touched her cheek again, encountering a single tear as it tracked downward. Saying nothing, he wiped it away with his thumb pad, then curved his hand around to touch her hair. "Thank you," he murmured, meaning it in many ways.

"Oh, God," she moaned, pressing her palms to her face.

Quickly, he moved his hand from her hair, afraid he'd offered offense. "Eden? I... I'm...."

"No!" she said, almost fiercely. "Don't say you're sorry. Please. Don't say that. It's just... I...I'm...."

She was flooded with emotions, so many they collided and jammed together and almost hurt. She knew she was embarrassing herself now, but she scrambled to her feet, finding one leg had gone entirely asleep while she knelt, lurched, tripped over Wadsworth, who never moved out of the way of sighted people, and fell hard against the side table, almost knocking the lamp off and ending up back on her knees again.

Marshall was instantly beside her, his right hand gripping her shoulder. "Eden?" He could feel her trembling under his hand.

Why wouldn't the parlor floor open up when she needed it to? She hid her face against his shirtfront.

"Eden, what is it?"

"Me," she said, her voice muffled. "It's just...me."

He sat all the way down, pulling her to him as best he could with one arm. "Tell me." He ran his hand down the back of her hair. "Please?"

She could hear his heart beating. That was all she could think of at the moment, that she could hear his heart beating.

As she rested quietly against him, it was then he knew. Very faint, as though she hadn't applied any fresh this morning, but still definitely there. "Roses," he whispered almost in awe. It was the scent out of place in the cold rain. It was her. She had to have been bending very closely over him, sheltering him with her body. Scent, touch, both so vital to him, such connections for him, and she had offered him both not even knowing what it meant to him. So terribly cold, in so much pain that he almost floated free of the world, the touch of her fingers on his face, the slight drift of roses bade him stay. The top of her head was right under his chin and he rested his lips on her hair. Not a kiss, just a resting of lips, just a beginning.

Chapter 12

She sat there against him feeling like an ember that had fallen loose some while back, had rolled alone out onto the hearth and was losing its glow. Then someone had come and scooted her back and she was pressed against the log that she was a part of once more. She didn't even know the man, had only just met him, yet there she was, content because she was home. Never in her life had she had such a sense of that, such an awareness of 'homing.'

How it could be she did not know. Right now she did not care. His heartbeat had become the center of not less than everything. She was a little afraid that if she held this homing in her hands, examined it carefully, that it might slide between her fingers and simply plop on the carpet. Perhaps it was only because of their strange meeting, maybe it was only that which made her feel bonded to him? It certainly was not at all normal for her to feel this way, act this way on such short acquaintance. But she didn't care about that, not right now. She hadn't really understood the degree to which she'd sat alone on the hearth, not until she was pressed against him, not until she knew about home.

But what must he be thinking of her? And the possibilities of that jarred her, shredding away her comfort and shrouding it with a sense of embarrassed self that was unable just to be. So her mind left the fireplace and began bumping about the room, looking for something to say, anything at all, in that way minds have when self is suddenly thrust out into the footlights of the stage and feels it must speak. She licked her lips as she performed a last, inner ripping loose from what her heart wanted, yielding to the jarring urgings of her less attuned mind.

"Marshy?"

He laughed, little puffs of his breath ruffling the top of her hair. And she felt him pulling back, felt his presence lift from off her hair as though an anointing oil had been sucked back into its vessel. And there was the loss of it. But she plastered a semi-smile on her face only because she needed it there to mask the loss that was not, after all, really hers to lose. He could not possibly know what the moment meant to her so she tried to recover as though the moment had not been, or, if it had, had not been what she imagined of it. His arm came down from around her and he rested his palm flat on the floor, bracing himself.

"Yes, Marshy. Jeffrey was the only one who ever called me that, and only when I was very little."

"I like it. It sounds very affectionate." She combed her fingers through her hair, trying to restore some lost order, realizing as she did so that she must've hit her ribcage as she fell against the table. There'd most likely be a big bruise before long. No matter. It was nothing compared with what had happened to him.

Wadsworth, unsure about what was going on, hovered near and began to lick Marshall's face, then Eden's. She spluttered as a large, wet tongue swiped across her nose. Marshall laughed again. "He's licking you? He never licks anybody but me. He must think you're special."

"It's a compliment?"

"A big one," he chuckled, reaching up to pull on Wadsworth's collar to make him stop.

Suddenly his smile faded and his face grew serious. "What happened, Eden? I need you to talk to me."

"Oh, Lord, no," she breathed, not really meaning to have said it aloud.

He put his hand on her arm as though he knew exactly where it was. "Yes, Eden." His deep voice was very soft, yet very compelling. "Come, sit on the couch with me." He moved to get his feet under him, unable to stop a slight gasp of pain. Recovering quickly, he even helped her to her feet, maintaining a light hold on her arm as they walked across the room to the couch. He was aware of the tenseness in her body, something that had been totally absent just a moment before when she leaned against his chest.

She sat about a foot to his right, playing with her fingers in her lap. Wadsworth settled in front of them, almost across their feet. "Who are you, Eden?" he asked softly.

"Who am I?"

"Yes, tell me who Eden is."

No one had ever asked that before. She wasn't even sure she'd asked it of herself. Briefly she placed a palm across her eyes, then let it drop back into her lap. He was waiting, quietly, patiently.

She blew out a long breath. "When I was a kid I wanted to be a photojournalist for National Geographic. My Dad had all the issues going back to 1929. His whole den was shelves of yellow." Then she wondered if he knew about that, but let it pass. "And I always liked to write poems, little stories, pretend news articles. Majored in journalism at Carlow. I guess I always kind of found my sense of identity in what I wrote, in the pictures I took. And I always loved movies. When the National Geographic thing didn't turn out to be a reality, I sort of found a place for myself writing about the movies I saw. Other people's stories. Other people's pictures. But I got paid, get paid, for what I have to say about them. I like it, but it's not quite... enough. Not anymore." She paused, absently running the fingers of her right hand around and around the palm of her left. "Nothing's really been enough, not for a long time."

"Since when, Eden?"

"Since Miles. I guess since then. I think I'd sort of settled into a certain kind of life with him and then it was just suddenly gone. Over. Completely, utterly over. And then...."

"Then?"

"Not much. Not much at all. I dream from time to time, always improbable things. Tibet. The Andes. The Li River. Places I'd love to see, write about. But what I do is go see *Seven Years In Tibet* or *The Painted Veil* and there I am in what other people wrote and other people saw. Other people's stories. And I wonder if my story ended in the snow that night."

"The snow?"

"Yes, Miles was killed in the snow. Shot in the neck by a man whose car he'd pulled over."

Marshall's hand came out, cupping over both of hers in her lap. "It was a terrible thing, a big thing, Eden, but not the end of your story. Not at all. Maybe the end of a chapter, yes, but here you are and your story is still being written."

"It's just so often it doesn't feel like that. It's more like I'm just repeating the same page most days. Except for two days ago. That was definitely a new page."

He smiled. "I shall have to fall into gullies more often then."

She looked at him, at his genuine smile. "I'm so glad I was there."

"Possibly not as glad as I am."

"You have no idea," she added, looking back at her lap and sighing. "I'm not very good at being unhappy. I always enjoyed life, enjoyed being me growing up, then I sort of just got swept along into Miles' life. There was kind of an odd balance to it, probably because of his job. It was like dancing right at the edge of a cliff. You enjoyed yourself and you laughed and joked, but the cliff was always nearby and you never really forgot it, not even when you were laughing the hardest. Maybe you even remembered it more then and so you laughed harder. Then he fell off and nobody was there to pick him up. That double-sided laughter all just stopped and you discovered you'd forgotten how to just laugh, that kind of laugh where there was no cliff, so you didn't laugh much after that. I think I've been trying to find my way back to that, that cliffless laughter. But it's hard."

His fingers squeezed a bit on hers. "Who am I?" she murmured and then for the first time put something into words. "I think I'm a writer who's not found her story."

"Sometimes," he said, his voice really, really soft, "our story finds us."

Chapter 13

She leaned her head against the high back of the couch, closing her eyes. She hadn't talked so much about what she was thinking for a long, long time. His hand was still cupped over both of hers and she slid one out, putting it atop his, rather sandwiching it gently. He left it there.

How strange the last few days had been. For a month he'd quietly been here at the inn, mostly keeping to himself, working on his book, enjoying casual chats with other guests over breakfasts. In the evenings Martha almost always played the piano a while and when she discovered he could sing, had made them into sort of a regular duo. From time to time another guest would join in, singing or playing a duet with Martha. It was all very genial but not something that really grabbed hold of some deep part of your being. Then the very morning Eden had checked in, he'd almost died. That, in itself, was odd enough to catch one's attention, but the fact that it was she who had clambered down into the gully and gotten him out added vast new dimension to it. If she had not come to the inn, if she had not decided to gather leaves, then he would be dead. It was no more nor less complicated than that. That was the bottom line of the whole thing.

But, then, layers were added to it, the effect of her hands, the scent of roses, on him when he'd been barely conscious. The sense of her presence as she stood beside him on the dock. What she'd done just now, holding herself so quietly against his chest. He liked her presence. There was no getting around it. He simply liked it when she was near. He was getting used to the sound of her voice now, could tell it was her just by her footsteps. And his hand at this very moment? He was content completely to let it rest there between hers. She must be thinking quietly. He could hear the even sound of her breathing and had no need to break her meditation.

He let his own mind drift back over the things he'd come to know about her. Auburn and green. He liked the combination. And she loved to write, even yearned to write. That he knew. That he understood perfectly. Absently, she began to run the fingertips of her top hand over his knuckles, tracing down his fingers. Something stirred within him, down in his very core.

On her part, she wasn't even really aware what she was doing. It just felt so natural to move her hand on his that the thought they'd just met was not even present. Then Wadsworth shifted and gave a long doggy sigh. She opened her eyes and looked down at her lap.

"Oh, I'm sorry," she whispered, moving her right hand to lie on the couch beside her.

He didn't say anything, merely began doing the same thing with his fingers to her single hand remaining under his. He had a way of saying things were all right without actually saying them. She watched, fascinated, as his sensitive fingers explored her hand, moving around, between each finger so lightly, yet somehow so thoroughly. Then he guided her hand to turn so her palm was up and he continued, tracing down its lines, sliding over the ball of her thumb. It was such a simple thing and yet the most marvelous that had ever happened to her body. It was her hand, only her hand, yet she felt as though she had been touched by him, been known by him everywhere. She'd never experienced anything even close to it before and everything that was female in her responded to it. How could he do that with nothing more than her hand? It was one of those moments after which you know you are utterly changed, that nothing will ever be the same, ever again. She knew completely that no one could ever touch her again in quite this way, that nothing could ever be so good.

Then he stopped, his palm lying crossways over hers, and cupped his fingertips around the edges of her hand, leaving it there. A tremble of response went through her, head to toe, and he squeezed his fingers just slightly tighter, completely aware of what he'd said to her in his silent touching.

She waited. What would he say? What could he possibly say in words? The corners of his mouth curved slightly and he opened his lips, speaking very softly, very seriously and clearly.

"Much have I travell'd in the realms of gold,

And many goodly states and kingdoms seen,

Round many western islands have I been,

Which bards in fealty to Apollo hold,

Oft of one wide expanse had I been told,

That deep-brow'd Homer ruled as his demesne,

Yet did I never breathe its pure serene,

Till I heard Chapman speak out loud and bold,

Then I felt like some watcher of the skies,

When a new planet swims into his ken,

Or like stout Cortez when with eagle eyes,

He star'd at the Pacific-and all his men,

Looked at each other with a wild surmise,

Silent, upon a peak in Darien."

"John Keats' *On First Looking Into Chapman's Homer*, he explained. "Cortez is standing on a mountain in Panama and has just seen the Pacific Ocean for the first time. It's my favorite piece, this old sonnet, about a sudden discovery of something that was already there."

He lifted her hand then, and placed one soft, warm kiss on the back of it, repeating, "Silent, upon a peak in Darien."

CHAPTER 14

He left her speechless. Literally. She simply could not force a sound up her throat. Her vocal cords seemed to have ceased functioning. She could blink, though, so she did that over and over. She had been in one place and now she was in another. How long ago had it been that she sat on the footstool watching him sleep? Now his lips were hovering just above her hand and the sound of his deep voice, the words he'd spoken sparked up and down her nervous system sending signals in a language she'd forgotten she could speak, if she had even ever known.

She looked at his tipped-down face and he was infinitely dear. How? When? She knew, though, that it had all started when the raindrops had begun spattering the dried mud on his face. She just hadn't known she knew. His face. She reached out now, touching the soft, short beard at the side of his cheek. His breath caught, stopped for a moment, then he let it out, long and sighingly slow, turned his face into her hand and kissed her palm.

She was almost dizzy. Her soul had plunged into some unthinkable depth and was swimming forward through waters thick with things she had no names for, only that her arms were out before her and he was there, had grasped her hands and when he did, the waters became something she could breathe. And so she did, drawing in great breaths of it while his fingers laced with hers. None of this came as words, or image, or even thought but only as awareness, as knowing.

"How?" she finally managed.

"Shhh!" He touched her mouth with a single fingertip then moved it back to rest on his own as though he were lost in some wildwood of thought. Then he smiled that slight, little smile again and leaned forward, softly surrounding her upper lip with his mouth, sliding down to her lower, then taking them both at once. He did not go further than that. It was enough. For now it was enough, and when he pulled his head back, his hand lingered on her cheek.

"Marshall."

"Hmmm?"

"I just wanted to say your name, to hear the sound of it...now."

"Eden." He cocked his head slightly to one side. "God planted a garden eastward in Eden."

"How?" she asked again.

"I don't know. Some things just are."

"I think I'm lost."

"Or found."

"Can someone be both lost and found at the same moment?" she asked.

"Perhaps. Are you?" His hand was still on her cheek.

"I think so. Except I can't really think."

"That's all right."

"It is?"

"Yes." And he kissed her again. Just soft and light and warm, and his tongue traced across her lower lip.

"Marshall?"

"Hmmm?"

"Will you not ever stop doing that?"

His lips curved back into a smile and he leaned toward her again, kissing each of her eyes then down her cheek to her lips. This time he kissed her more thoroughly and she parted her lips, welcoming him. The kiss was long and much more intimate.

He kept his face near hers and she leaned her forehead against his. "I didn't expect you," she breathed.

"I was waiting," he said simply.

"In a gully."

"That, too."

"Were you...waiting?"

"I'm not sure I knew I was, but I was."

She leaned back a bit. "But I, I wasn't looking. I think I'd stopped."

"Finding has its own timing."

"You...you were just...there," she said, still amazed by the fact.

"Barely."

"Do you know, do you really know, how close you came to not...not...."

"Some," he said, "but I'm not sure it matters, not now."

"I didn't know it was you. I didn't know you...were you." Good heavens! She hadn't. She really hadn't known the stranger so covered in mud was...him. The thought of it now, of him, *this* him, like that was appalling. She cupped his face with both her hands. "How could I not know?"

"Lots of mud?" he offered.

"That's not what I mean."

"I know," he smiled.

"Kiss me."

He did.

Chapter 15

Eden drove the two of them for lunch to a small tavern known locally for its great salads and sandwiches. They sat on the same side of a booth, their hips and legs touching then drove to a small park where she found a secluded glen. The early afternoon had warmed considerably under a bright sun and she spread a wool blanket on the grass. Wadsworth flopped just off its edge and, off duty, watched the squirrels and one waddly groundhog, a bit sluggish this late in the year.

"He's got his back turned," Eden whispered gratefully to Marshall as he settled down beside her, the leather of his jacket making slight creaking sounds.

"Wadsworth?" Who, of course, turned his head at the sound of his name.

"Yeah, him," Eden laughed. "I'm not used to an audience, canine or not."

"He's very discreet."

"I suspect so, but...still." The dog turned his attention back to the groundhog, whom he currently found much more interesting than the two humans sitting on the blanket.

"Tell me," he said.

"Tell you what?"

"Describe where we are." He truly wanted to see how she'd go about it. Jeffrey had been really good at it, giving him a sense of space and environment, but no one else had ever bothered quite so intently as his brother had.

She took his right hand, pulling it into her lap. "Well, I know you know green and where we're sitting is still rather green since our first real frost was this morning. So we're this little island on my brown blanket in the middle of a sea of green about, oh, fifty feet across and slanting to your left down toward a line of trees. A lot of the leaves are down already, but there's one big oak with a bunch of really crisp-looking pale brown leaves still holding tight. I think the oaks do that, hold onto their old leaves because they're about the last of the trees to trust the spring and put out new ones. Oaks are big, strong trees and stand out from the others by their shape and size and some aura of magic they have about them."

He listened to every word, loving the sound of her voice, what she said, the way she said it. She was trying really hard to make it real for him. "There's a lot of underbrush there so it looks like it would be hard to walk and the woods go back a long way, so that they just sort of disappear into shadows of shadows and you can't tell where it all ends. About ten feet to your left is a single big rock sticking up through the grass, about five feet across and maybe two feet high. It's kind of flat on the top and makes you want to go over and stand on it just because you can. There's one tall clump of grass tucked in right next to the side, too close for the mower to reach. It's got several big tufts of seed heads on it curving against the rock. Behind us, the meadow slopes up to a bit of a ridge and right in the middle of that is the dirt path we followed to get here. There's a single evergreen that looks a lot like a huge Christmas tree just to the left of where the path begins at the edge of the meadow and just to the left of it are three stumps, fairly large ones, where trees have been cut down and the grass hasn't grown yet in the dirt area that used to be under their branches. Wadsworth is watching a fat grayish-brown ground hog at the edge of the meadow straight in front of us. It's poking around near a half-rotted log and a cluster of saplings."

He squeezed her hand appreciatively. "Thank you." Tipping his head back, he let the sun shine on his face, glinting off his glasses. "All my life I've tried to imagine what seeing is. But I can't, not really. It must be something to be able to gather all that information like you did. It has to be truly amazing. I think sometimes of trying to describe music, voices, any sound at all to someone who's never heard. There's just no way to convey it. You have to hear to understand sound. Yes, you can lay your hands on the piano top and feel the vibration, the resonance of it, but you don't really know what hearing is. It's like that with me and sight."

"Does it bother you?"

"Not in the least. If I can't even imagine it, I can't really miss it. I know it must be wonderful," he paused and reached out, brushing his hand over the grass, "but green for me is touch and scent and even taste. There's a definite presence to green that makes it different from, say, brown, but what green is to you is a language I can never speak."

She was filled with a thousand things to say and nothing to say all at once. He seemed to realize that and lay carefully back on the blanket so his right shoulder came down first, taking the weight of his body. She lay beside him on his right, facing him. He nuzzled his nose into her cheek and she sighed contentedly, cuddling close to him, her head resting on his upper arm. He kissed the tip of her nose. She felt as though she were in some dream but such a thing was way too trite to say and, besides, his lips had found hers again and she had much more important things to do with her mouth than form words.

She found, lying there, his lips warm on hers, that neither sight nor sightlessness mattered. Her eyes were closed and everything was a matter of nerve endings and mutuality of touch and wanting. Right here, right now, in this moment, in this way, they were in the same world and their experience of it was the same. She was almost overcome by the intense closeness of it, the lack of separation of it and wondered vaguely if it were possible to live forever on a blanket held in his embrace.

They lay there a long time, kissing quietly, exploring in that way one does when 'other' has been so newly found. His hand curved up behind her head, his fingers playing with long strands of her hair. He lay half-tipped onto his right side, but after a while his left shoulder began to complain from the strain the position caused and he had to lie back. She was concerned because she saw the crease form between his brows. "Are you all right?"

"Mmm hmm," he murmured, his eyes closed behind his glasses. "Just need to rest the shoulder a bit."

His right arm was still around her and she nestled into him enough that she could hear his heart beating without putting weight on his chest. She let her lids shut again, entering into a place once more where sound and touch were the guideposts of being. His fingers still played with her hair, sending the gentlest tingling sensations down into her scalp. Her head moved a bit, carried by the rhythm of his breathing, but it was the sound of his heart that her consciousness began to orbit.

After a few minutes she felt his hand drop away to the blanket and she looked up at his face. His lips were slightly parted and she could tell he'd fallen asleep. As she settled her cheek back against him, she whispered, "I love you, Marshall Sinclair," and in that dichotomy of feeling that had been hers the last couple of days, was both amazed and not the least bit surprised.

Chapter 16

She must have dozed because some change in the 'feel' of things caused her to open her eyes with a start. What was it? She was aware Marshall's arm was still under her head. It was his heartbeat. That was it. No longer the steady, slow rhythm of rest, it was beating fast, really fast. Fully awake, she now saw that he had a deep crease on his forehead and his tongue flicked out just a bit, touching his lower lip. He must be dreaming, she decided, but whatever it was was obviously disturbing. Then it hit her. He was lying on his back, his right arm pinned beneath her head, his left bound in the sling. In his sleep, it must have triggered the memory of the gully. It flooded over her, how unimaginably awful it must have been for him to be so entirely, immovably trapped and to be choking on mud, all in a black and soundless world.

She sat so his arm would be free, and leaned close, whispering, "Marshall, you're not in the gully. You're here, in the meadow, with me."

He jerked awake. "Jeff?"

"No, it's me, Eden."

Wadsworth, who seemed to think a good face licking would fix just about anything, began busily setting about the task. "Mmpft!" Marshall spluttered, pushing at the dog with his right hand. When Wadsworth backed off, he reached out toward her with the hand and she took it in both hers and pressed it to her cheek. "Eden," he said, letting out a long breath.

"I think you were back in the gully."

He nodded. It was taking a moment for his heart to slow to normal. He could still taste the mud on his tongue, feel its slow slide down the back of his throat.

"Want to talk about it?"

Still breathing deeply in and out, in his mind he heard again the sound of Jeffrey's voice. "Never tuck anything away, Marshy. Never hide anything from yourself, not even for a minute. You've got to bring what's gotten to you out in the open and deal with it, especially you."

With Jeff around, he'd never even had the chance to sit on a fear and let it fester, so he'd grown up very honest and open with his feelings. "Yes," he said, blowing out a last, heavy breath, "I was there." He shook his head, not liking it that the dream had been so vivid. It meant he was still dealing with what had happened. A sudden ache of missing

Jeffrey blew through him. He must've let it show slightly on his face, as her grip on his hand tightened, and he smiled at her. That was another reaction Jeff had taught him. A smile is a natural response to seeing someone else smile. As soon as young Jeffrey had realized that fact, he'd say, "I'm smiling at you, Marshy. Smile back. Listen for the sound of a smile in my voice, in my touch, and smile back at me." He'd done that so often that it had become natural for Marshall, who didn't have to think about it anymore. It was just there in his responses, part of who he was.

"Jeffrey always got me to talk about things," he explained. "I'd fall out of a tree, or get brushed by a truck, or lose my balance on the top of a wall, things like that, and he'd be there, making sure I didn't carry away any fear from it."

"Good Lord," she gasped softly.

"What?"

"The things he got you to do."

Marshall chuckled. "Well, truth be told, a lot of them were my own idea. But this last thing was different." He tipped his chin up a bit. "I think it was the almost total sensory deprivation of it."

"The mud had blocked your hearing?"

He nodded. "I couldn't move. Even scent was gone because of the mud. I was just... there...in some place I'd never quite experienced before and all that existed was pain and this deep, penetrating coldness. Nothing but that. And then I couldn't breathe." He turned his face toward her again. "I think that must be when you came."

"I almost went to the gardens," she said, her voice very low, "or down toward the lake. I...I can't imagine what...."

"But you didn't," he replied. "You went for the leaves."

"There was this single maple leaf that changed my mind," she remembered. "It just rolled across the sidewalk and I suddenly knew it was toward the leaves I needed to go."

"I think there's a poem there somewhere," he smiled. It was how his mind worked. "One of those little moments of life we don't really know are important as they happen, yet they turn out to have been beginnings."

She smiled, looking at his face, then wondered if she'd ever get past the wanting of him to be able to see her smile. Maybe because it all was so new for her, maybe, given time, the wanting would fade? But there she was, presuming there would be time. They were just now taking their first tentative steps toward one another and she was, well, projecting. It was a thing she'd not done in years.

"So you're alive because of a maple leaf, are you?" she said, shoving her thoughts back into some semblance of order.

"It's as basic as that, yes," he agreed. "And in the end, you were there."

"But it wasn't the end."

His lips curved. "No, it wasn't the end." He knew he'd started to let go, knew he'd begun to drift away, and in that very moment she'd come, bringing with her all her beginnings.

"I came here, you know, because...," she was silent for a long moment, "because of endings. I think I've walked around for a long time with an ending in my arms, not knowing what to do with it, how to put it down. It's just always there, between me and everything, like some big, foggy cloud I can feel but can't grab."

He lifted his hand, holding it flat in the air until she understood that he wanted her to put her palm against his. He said nothing, just waited silently, his flesh warm against hers. She stared at it, awareness of what he meant coming to her slowly.

"No cloud," she murmured barely audibly. Between his hand and hers there was no cloud. Then he curved his fingers, lacing them through hers.

Chapter 17

Wadsworth was getting restless. He wasn't in harness so wasn't "working", which left him free to want to run. Standing, he stepped onto the blanket and poked his nose against Marshall's neck as if to say, "Ok, enough of this sitting about."

Marshall chuckled and turned, ruffling the fur of his neck. "He wants some playtime. He hasn't really had any the last couple of days." Adjusting the position of his sling, he apologized to the dog. "I can't roll around with you today, boy," he said regretfully.

"What do you usually do to play with him?" Eden asked.

"Oh, we chase around and he trips me and I fall down and then he jumps on me and we tumble about a bit."

Eden's eyes widened. "Not with that shoulder!"

"Right, not with this shoulder." He ruffled Wadsworth's fur some more. "You heard that, I hope?" He turned his head toward Eden. "Would there be a pinecone or something lying near the blanket?"

"There's a couple just here," she replied, leaning out to pick up two fat cones not far away.

He took one of them in his right hand, turning it over with his fingers to make sure it wasn't sharp. Wadsworth keenly watched his every movement, his muscles gathering in anticipation. Marshall pulled back his right arm and threw the cone as hard as he could. Instantly Wadsworth was off after it, covering the ground in great leaping strides.

"Uhh!" Marshall moaned, clenching his teeth. The pitch had pulled the sprained muscles and tendons of his left shoulder. He clutched his right hand around his shoulder. "That was stupid," he gritted.

Wadsworth was quickly back, dropping the cone onto Marshall's lap, but Eden grabbed it up and tossed it, maybe a third of the distance Marshall had. "He's too fast!" she gasped. "And, you, you'd better lie back a bit and rest that shoulder. I'll do what I can to entertain Waddy."

"Deal," Marshall sighed, lowering himself gingerly back onto the blanket just as Wadsworth returned again, this time stepping with his front paws onto Marshall's stomach.

"Off, beast!" Eden laughed, actually concerned as she pushed on Wadsworth's broad chest. "I thought your job was to serve and protect, not mutilate your master."

"He's not in harness," Marshall said again. "When he's not, he's just my big ol' dog."

Wadsworth, agreeing, happily licked Marshall's chin, picked up the dropped cone, and set it high on his chest from where it promptly rolled off.

"I've got it," Eden announced, tossing it again. She did that over and over for nearly half an hour while Marshall lay perfectly still, trying to calm his shoulder. "You said, what was her name, Mellow? wasn't a shepherd."

"Yellow lab. Most guide dogs nowadays are some sort of lab or retriever. They don't use shepherds very much anymore."

"Why not?"

"Too protective. Some of them can get a bit aggressive about it."

"But Wadsworth...?"

"He comes from a long line of guide dogs. His father and grandfather both sired lots of good ones with such a proven reputation, that they keep using them. I think they mostly match them with grown men, though. They're very careful about the matches they make, and Wadsworth is a big shepherd, 120 pounds of dog, so it takes a bigger, stronger blind person to handle him." He winced. "Which, however, is not me at the moment."

"Would you tell me more about when you were a boy, what it was like for you then?"

"You really want to know?"

"Mmm hmm," she said, lying beside him, hoping Wadsworth would get the message she was tired of throwing the cone. The dog tried a few more times to get her to toss it, but finally settled beside Marshall, his chin resting across his master's thigh.

"All my first memories revolve around Jeffrey. I guess that's inevitable."

"You say he knew you were blind, even when he was very little?"

"Somehow he did. The other kids his age didn't really seem to understand, but Jeffrey was different. I was really premature, very small for a while, and my mother told me how he would hover around, watching over me even when he was just three himself. By the time I was two or so, I'd caught up with my growth and he wouldn't let me stay in the playpen where my mother thought I'd be safe. I didn't want to stay in the playpen, either, so between the two of us my mother seldom had a peaceful moment."

"What sorts of things would he do, other than teaching you to walk with the box, I mean?"

"He wanted me to know what things were so he was always putting something in my hands for me to feel or taste or use. It's very hard when you're discovering the world small bit by small bit to understand what a whole, large thing is like so he'd take me to the driveway and have me feel all the different parts of my father's car, then sit me down and put a toy car in my hands and we'd go over the same parts kind of back and forth with the real car so I'd grasp somewhat what a full-sized car is like."

"I'd never thought of that," she murmured.

"Even with something as simple as a chair," he continued. "I learned a chair by feeling its rungs and its legs and its seat and its back, but on my own a whole chair wouldn't be real for me. So he'd bring home a chair he'd borrowed from some little girl's dollhouse and let me feel it. He did that with as many small versions of big things as he could get hold of. I still have no real idea how right I am in how I perceive certain things. There's no way to communicate that to a sighted person. And, then, well, there are things there just are no small versions of, like the sky."

"And rainbows," she said softly to herself.

He held out his right hand to her again and she slid hers into it. His fingers curved around hers then glided slowly over the surface of her palm. "This is how I see," he whispered. His fingers continued moving over her hand. "This is how I gaze at your hand. It's smooth, warm and I can hold it in my own hand and as I keep holding it that's as close as I come to what gazing is for you. Jeffrey wanted to be sure I didn't find lack in myself, that my perceptions mattered, were another way of seeing. He wanted my blindness to be something much less important than who I am as a person."

Entranced, she watched his fingers moving over her hand. He'd done something similar back at the B&B, and the pure delight of it was instantly there again. His touch made her feel 'known' in a new way, a deeper, more thorough way. His thumb pad moved around her wrist, lightly turning her hand, sliding up the back of it, along the ridges of her knuckles. She trembled slightly.

He lifted his head toward her face as though asking a question. "I like it when you gaze," she said almost inaudibly.

Setting her hand gently down, his fingers moved to her neck, sliding from her jaw line down around under her ear then across to the hollow where his thumb made light circles as his forefinger explored up the length of her collar bone. She closed her eyes, tipping her head back, baring her throat to him. He slid his whole palm up the length of her neck, fingers spreading out, meeting at the tip of her chin, then spreading again, curving up to her lips, one fingertip lightly passing over the warm, wet softness inside her lower lip.

A sudden breeze kicked up, blowing the edge of the blanket over her leg. Wadsworth lifted his head, looking around, then shifted his position and settled back alongside Marshall, his large tail swishing into his master's face. Marshall made a sound half-sigh, half-chuckle and moved his hand from Eden's face.

"It's getting cloudy," he said. "Probably rain by suppertime."

She looked up at the gray clouds moving in from the west, low stratus ones blowing toward them over the distant treetops. He was right. For someone who could only guess at what the sky was, he was pretty good. They got to their feet and, together, folded the blanket. She held his arm and, harness-free, Wadsworth bounced along nearby as they headed up the smooth slope to where she'd parked the car.

Chapter 18

Back at the inn, they'd each gone to their separate rooms for a while, both having phone calls to make to Pittsburgh. Marshall's cell phone had been swallowed up by the mud and he was making do with the inn's phone extension in his room. He called Alice, his secretary, and asked her to procure him a new phone with the special features his old one had had. She said she'd get it in the mail to him tomorrow.

He sat in an armchair for a while, chin resting on his right hand, and just thought about things. If it hadn't been for the need to keep his left arm and shoulder stationary and for Wadsworth's interruption, he might very well have....

"You wanted to," he murmured to himself. He was still somewhat surprised at that. He was usually quite cautious, possibly overly-so, in developing any relationships with women, especially since Beatrice, who'd found him interesting, different, even exciting at first but in the long haul she really wanted a sighted partner. It took someone special, he guessed, to commit to a blind man. Eden was a totally different sort of woman from Beatrice, but he just didn't know, not yet, not for sure, how she'd feel over time. He did know that he hoped she wanted to find out. It was the first time in a long while he'd hoped that. In the short time he'd known her, he felt connected in some strange way, and that she had capacities for understanding, a deeper level of patience.

"What do you think, Wadsworth?" He dropped his hand to the dog's neck and Wadsworth thumped his thick tail two or three times. "She tosses a good pinecone, don't you agree?"

He was thirty-six and getting used now to living alone, possibly too used to it. Though he'd dated a number of women, Beatrice was the only one he'd actually thought he might marry and that was steadily getting further and further in the past. It was easy just doing what he needed or wanted to do every day, just him and Wadsworth. But he lifted his fingers, touching his lips, remembering the feel of Eden and smiled to himself.

Raindrops began a slow patter against the window and he listened quietly for a while then suddenly wanted to share it with her, share the meaning of rain with her. "Come on, boy," he said, striding toward the door, not bothering with harness or leash.

He walked briskly down the hall, his fingertips trailing lightly along the wall, then stopped outside her door. She was playing music so he paused, his hand on her door and just listened. It was the soundtrack of *The King and I* and the song that had just begun was *I Have Dreamed.* He knocked softly and she opened the door.

He stood there, his hand on the door frame, Wadsworth at his side. He hesitated a moment then sang rather softly, "I have dreamed that your arms are lovely; I have dreamed what a joy you'll be. I have dreamed every word you've whispered when you're close, close to me." He chuckled and swept into a grand bow.

Eden had just been thinking of going down the hall to ask Marshall if he'd like to go to the parlor with her when the light knock came on her door. Opening it, she saw him standing there, looking slightly awkward for the briefest moment. Then he sang the first four lines of the song she was playing and bowed. She was utterly silent, totally blown away, and completely at a loss for words. She saw the smile on his face begin to fade and realized he was taking her silence for disapproval. Quickly she reached out and took his hand. "Thank you, I loved it."

"I guess it was pretty silly of me. I was just about to knock when I heard the music from your room and I...I...."

"I'm so glad you did. I'm a sucker for show tunes. I think I know all the words by heart. I just can't sing them well like you do."

She could tell he still felt a little embarrassed and decided the only way to deal with him was total, upfront honesty. "Marshall, I didn't say anything for a minute because, well, because you took me by surprise. I'm not used to opening my door and finding a handsome man singing to me. But I liked it, I liked it so much, in fact, I had no words that were quite good enough to say how much."

"It's the first time I've ever done something like that," he admitted. "I thought of you listening to the song and when you opened the door it just...."

"I'm glad it just," she smiled."It was a lovely gift on what's turning out to be a rainy afternoon, I'm afraid."

"Ah, that's why I came," he said. "I wanted to share the rain with you."

"Share the rain?" She had no idea what he meant.

"Yes, the rain is wonderful. I wanted to share with you just how wonderful." He stepped back. "Will you come with me to the porch?"

When they had their coats on and the afghan Martha had insisted they take out with them all tucked around their laps and legs on the porch swing, Marshall said, "Just close your eyes a moment and listen, Eden, listen with everything that's in you."

He was holding her hand in his as they sat, his chin tipped slightly in that way he had when listening intently, an expression of serene pleasure on his face. She closed her eyes as he'd asked, at first mostly aware of him breathing next to her. It was, for her, his presence and not the rain that was important, but she knew he wanted her to understand something that mattered to him, and since that was important, she turned her focus outward toward the steady rain falling. She heard it gurgling through the downspout and spattering on the concrete walk, but wasn't sure just what it was he wanted her to notice about it so she opened her eyes, watching him.

Moving his hand, he reached it straight out in front of him, then to the side where he ran his fingers down the chain from which the porch swing hung, then further out, touching briefly the railing and the top of a yew just beyond. "This," he said, "is how I am aware of the world and when the rain stops, my world shrinks back to what I can touch. But the rain," he took her hand again, "drapes itself almost like a blanket over everything, and things that were incomplete for me, that I was only aware of from time to time, are now there fully, and I am centered in and connected to the world around me. I know the bush is just beyond the railing because I've touched it and remember it, but it gives me no sign of its presence until I touch it again." He began rubbing his thumb pad over her knuckles as he spoke, his voice low, intense with his yearning that she understand his meaning. "But when it's raining it's all very different and my surroundings speak to me," he continued, "and I understand where the house is in relation to the lawn and the lawn to the lake as though some impediment has been lifted and the world is now revealed to me. It's a gracious thing for me, the sounds of the rain, and an experience of profound beauty. Jeffrey used to try to describe to me what it was like for him to open the curtains and look out at the view beyond with the morning light falling on the trees and the rooftops. Rain for me is much like that, as though I can open my own curtains and see my own view. I don't have to wait until I touch it, don't have to feel removed from it, but all of it is there for me."

He turned his face to her just as though he were looking earnestly at her. "Listen, Eden, really listen and you'll hear what the rain is saying, hear how it's creating this world for me. Listen to the almost thudding, heavy sound as it hits the roof shingles over the porch, then the rather happy gurgle of the downspouts. The spout on the left of the porch is blocked at the end and the water pattern of sound is different as it forces its way through. Do you hear how different it sounds, the tones it makes, describing my surroundings for me? In the rain I know there is lawn on either side of the sidewalk, that the land slopes away down toward the lake. It spatters on the wooden dock. Can you hear the difference of the rainsounds on the grass from those on the dock? Then there's the distinct sound of water on water as it splashes into the lake, the little cascading sound of it running down the steps close by and the almost blanketed sound it makes on the evergreen bushes. It makes a crisp sort of sharp sound on the dry leaves of the trees in the distance. There are layers of sound, Eden, the light drip dripping of it off the railing and the distinct sound it makes on the metal of the cars in the parking lot. For me it's as though I can touch all of it at once and the world becomes full and complete in the rain. Without the rainsounds, all the sounds I hear are disconnected but the rain gives them dimension, a sense of place and joins them all together."

She sighed, a somewhat ragged sigh because she was so filled with emotion looking at him, listening to him. "Do you have any idea how beautiful you are?" It was what she was thinking and the thought formed itself into words before she could stop them, so she just continued. "You have the most beautiful mind I've ever met."

He smiled slightly and kissed her knuckles. "It's the rain that's beautiful."

"It is, yes," she agreed, "but it's you who make it so. You took me, you know, you took me into it, into your world, and I think I understand, just a bit."

She closed her eyes again, trying to listen to the rain with new awareness. He'd said he wanted to share the rain with her. She was filled with a quiet sense of the preciousness of what he offered. There was always such a depth to what he said, something so opposite to the casual talk most men tried with her. It was what she wanted, what she needed. She could no longer deal with casual.

"Thank heavens for the maple leaf," she almost whispered, more to herself than to him.

"The one that blew across the sidewalk at the bottom of the steps?"

"Yes, that one. I wish I'd saved it."

"It served its purpose."

"It did, that it did," she smiled. "And didn't you say there was a poem somewhere in that leaf?"

He chuckled. "I did, indeed."

"So, where is it?"
"Now?"
"Right now."
He blew out a laughing breath. "Well, a poem on the spot like this generally tends to come out free verse."
"Free is fine," she joined his laugh.
"Give me a second." He tipped his chin again. She loved his up-tipped profile.
"Ok, here goes. Free verse, mind." He pursed his lips a moment then began:

"It came,
 its fragile thinness
  blown on Autumn's wind
Across
the chilled concrete
  of her morning's path.
Unknown,
its mission served
  as herald of the way,
Messenger
sent to guide
  a choice yet unmade,
A vastness
of decision
  with life and future
Hanging there
in the veined
  delicateness...
A wheeling
mapled portent
  skipping past."

He sat back a bit. "A bit feeble, but very free, eh?"
"You did that just now, just off the top of your head?"
"Was it ok?"
"'A wheeling mapled portent'? I'd say, yeah, it's ok."
He laughed. "Maybe a bit much, eh?"
"Not at all. I like it. Say it again so I can remember it."
"Again? Eden, it just blew through my brain like the maple leaf. I don't think it's still there."
"Well, try. I need it."
"You need it?"
"I definitely need it."

Between the two of them they recalled most of it. "I've got to write it down before it's gone again," she said, rising. "Come on inside with me so I can find some paper."

Hanging their coats on the rack near the door, they made their way into the parlor where Martha was mending a seam on a handmade pillow. "You two look chilled," she announced, laying aside her needlework and standing. "Hot chocolate or hot cider?"

"Chocolate for me," Eden replied, rubbing her hands briskly together near the fire.

"For me, too. Thanks, Martha," Marshall added.

"Oh, is there paper in the desk?" Eden asked before Martha had fully crossed the room. "I need to write something down before I forget."

"Top drawer, left," Martha smiled. "I'll be back in just a minute."

Eden pulled out the desk chair and sat down, getting a blank sheet of note paper. "You may have to help me again."

"All right," Marshall agreed, walking carefully around where he knew the coffee table would be and taking a seat on the couch. He had no way of knowing Martha had set her needlework there and sat down atop it. "Aaah!" He stood quickly, barking his shins on the table.

Wadsworth, who had just been circling, ready to settle down under the window, was instantly at his side, poking a wet nose into his palm. Marshall turned, feeling the couch, finding the pillow, a spool of thread, and a very sharp needle.

Eden had been looking at the paper, not at him, and so had not been aware of where he was trying to sit. "One of life's little hazards," he said ruefully, moving the pillow off to the side. "I've actually inadvertently sat on someone's lap, more than once." He sat carefully at the far end of the couch, wiping his hand over the seat first. "Not since I've had dogs, though," he continued after he was settled. "A dog will always lead you to an unoccupied seat, even in a crowded restaurant. But on my own, it's a different story. As you see," he smiled.

Quickly she scribbled the words to his poem. The lines were short and she found that after the second repetition, she'd got them firmly in mind. Rising, she came and sat on the coffee table in front of him. "Marshall?" She rested her hands on his knees.

"Yes, Eden?"

"Would you do something for me?"

"What is it you want, Eden?"

"I want you to take off your dark glasses."

She saw his jaw square and a muscle on one side begin to twitch. "Why?"

"I saw you in the rain. When you were talking about the rain, I really saw you. But I want to see you here, inside, too."

He sucked in a long breath, sitting there silently, tense. "I'd rather not," he finally said.

"I know," she replied, "but I need you to trust me enough to let me see you."

He licked his lips, his mind filled with Beatrice. "They don't look back at you, Eden, my eyes. They don't look back."

"I know that." Her hand curved around his where it rested on his thigh. "But it would mean a lot to me to see your whole face."

"You saw it there in the woods," he countered.

"All muddy, yes," she smiled, "but your eyes were closed."

"I had mud in...."

"Please," she interrupted. "I'm not going to run away. I promise."

"You can't know that," he barely whispered.

"I can," she said. "I do know that."

Very, very slowly he raised his hand and took off his glasses, letting his hand fall with them beside him onto the couch. His eyes were closed, long lashes fanned across his cheeks, traces of the big bruise still there on one cheekbone. "Please," she asked again.

He sighed, then pressed his lips together, letting his lids open bit by bit. He kept his face directly towards her, expressionless as he could manage, and waited. He really did not want to do this, not yet, not after Beatrice.

They were green, green like the sea on a summer day with reflections of the sky mixing in, a few freckles of amber here and there. They were beautiful eyes and it broke something in her heart that he could not see her, but she loved them, loved them because they were his. Her own eyes sparked with tears that he had done this for her and she felt this really odd combination of gratitude, yearning, wonder, and even a bit of anger that he'd been made to feel that they were somehow ugly. Leaning her weight on her hands on his knees, she shifted her body forward until her face was close to his. Then she kissed them, one by one, she kissed his eyes

Chapter 19

At dinner, he'd not worn his dark glasses, and sat across the small table from her, the candle between them flickering on the planes of his face. She was fascinated, watching the play of shadow and light over his strong features. This time, when his right hand lay beside his plate, she reached and placed hers atop it, thinking how much things had changed since their first dinner when she'd wanted to, but hadn't felt she had the right.

Their table was in a corner, very private. The restaurant was small, had interior walls of rough stone, a beamed ceiling, and wide plank flooring. As she held her hand over his, she described it to him. "It's almost completely lit by candlelight," she smiled. "I like it."

The waiter came and she pulled her hand back as he set their water glasses down. "If you reach your right hand out just a bit, the wall is right there," she said. "It looks like fieldstone, very rough, kind of a dark gray."

He ran his fingertips over the first stone they encountered. "I've always been fond of stone walls. The exterior of my house is rough stone."

"Tell me about your home, Marshall. I'm fairly familiar with Mount Lebanon. I know most of the older homes there are built of either stone or brick."

"It's the house I grew up in," he began, "so I know every inch of it quite well."

"Did your parents move to a smaller place then?"

"No." His voice was soft, low.

"No?" she repeated the word even more softly. "Then...?"

"I'm the only one left."

She sat back in her chair, looking at him, remembering all the things he'd told her about his family. She'd formed such a mental image of the four of them, everybody loving everybody else, the other three taking time, being careful to make sure young Marshall grew up confident and secure despite his blindness. How could they be gone, all of them? She knew about Jeffrey in Afghanistan, but his parents, too?

"About six months after we got the news Jeff had been killed, Dad took Mom to France. They'd been talking about it for a couple of years and...," he paused, licked his lower lip thoughtfully, then continued, "...and Dad thought it would do her good. She'd always wanted to see the lavender fields of Provence in bloom. Jeff's death was really hard for her. He'd always been so larger than life, so strong, everybody always turned to him. He just had a way of...of making things better."

He paused again, absently using his fingers to make little folds in his cloth napkin. "Tour bus went off a mountain road."

"Oh, Marshall," she breathed. "I...I...."

"Couldn't sell the place, you know. But I don't really spend all that much time there. Have a room at the University that's handier for me when I'm teaching. Works out better."

He lifted his chin a bit and she thought for a moment he was looking at her across the table, but it was only the way the candlelight was reflected in his eyes. Her own stung sharply as emotions surged through her. "I want...."

"What, Eden? What do you want?"

"It sounds silly."

"Not to me it won't."

"I want to surround you. I want somehow for me to be able to wrap myself around you and draw you inside of me so there's nothing between us. I've never felt like that before, like I can't stand it another second if we're not occupying the same space. I...," then she saw his face was working, his jaw muscle was moving, his lips were pressed together, and he was closing his eyes tightly. Oh, no! Had she said the wrong thing, had she said too much? Color drained from her face as she watched his, watched him trying to...to...what?

"Eden," he said, seeming to have some difficulty forming the word. "Eden...." Suddenly he stood, the big dog at his side instantly at attention. "Wadsworth, door!" he ordered, his voice low but firm as he found his grip on the harness.

Eden felt sick, almost dizzy, thought she might actually faint on the spot. He was going to...leave?

But he took only one step, which brought him closer to her, and said, "Outside. Come outside." Then he and Wadsworth were making their way between the tables toward the distant doorway.

She watched him, rooted to the spot for a long moment, having no idea what was happening, feeling somehow shaken to her core. Her mouth was extremely dry and she took a long drink from her water goblet, her hand trembling so much she let large dribbles run down her chin. Dazedly she blotted them with her napkin, still not quite able to get to her feet. She folded the napkin into a neat rectangle, put it back in its place and set her unused fork on it, centering it carefully atop the napkin. Then she looked at the door again. He must already be outside. A couple of other diners were openly staring at her.

Slowly she stood, bracing herself a moment with a tight grip on the back of her chair before following where Marshall had gone. Her feet felt heavier than they had in the deep mud of the gully. It would be cold outside, so she lifted her coat off the rack near the entrance, noticing his leather jacket was still hanging there. Both coats draped over her arm, she pushed the door open and stepped out onto the small entrance porch. The sharp night air washed over her, but she made no move to put on her coat.

He was a bit off to the left, had dropped Wadsworth's harness, and was pacing back and forth near a row of clipped yews. She'd said too much. It was too soon. What had she been thinking? He was talking about his parents' bus going off a mountain and she'd replied that she wanted him inside her? Her white face flooded with sudden red. Good Lord! It sounded, didn't it, like she'd made some sexual remark as a response to the death of his parents! She was horrified.

Grimly, she walked up to him. "Marshall," she began, "I didn't...."

But she didn't get to finish her explanation. He pulled her to him with his good arm and unerringly his lips found hers and he kissed her until her breath was gone. Both coats slipped unheeded to the grass. Her legs went so rubbery that had his arm not been so firmly around her, she might have joined the coats on the ground. He kissed her again and again and again, then with his lips still lightly brushing hers he murmured, "I couldn't do that in there, and I had to do that."

When he realized she could barely stand, he helped her to a nearby bench, sitting beside her, still holding her. Her brain was spinning wildly, jerked from one intense emotion to another. She kept her eyes closed, clutching at his shirt, not at all sure she might not yet topple over. He didn't seem aware of the confusion, the panic that had enveloped her in the restaurant. Her heart was still racing madly, her stomach was in knots. He'd wanted to kiss her? She thought he was angry, was leaving, and he wanted to kiss her?

"Eden," he said, his voice soft, tender. "Eden, I love you, darling."

It was the first time he'd said that to her. She threw up in his lap.

Both of them sat there, rather stunned. Weakly, she pulled a tissue from her pocket, wiped her mouth, then looked at his face. His lips were parted, as though he wanted to say something but couldn't quite speak. Finally he clamped his tongue between his lips. By this time her emotions were beyond her control. He hadn't been angry with her, he'd wanted to kiss her, and now he was sitting there with his tongue like that and her lunch all over his pants and she was so relieved that she began to giggle, then hiccup, then cry and giggle more at the same time.

"Eden?" Now he was confused, really, really confused. He had professed his love and she'd...vomited? Now she was laughing? He'd pulled his tongue in and now his teeth were tightly clamped. Wadsworth was sniffing interestedly at his lap and he pushed him away. "Sit, damn it!" He had no idea how to feel, what he was supposed to feel. "Eden?" he tried again.

She couldn't stop hiccupping and tears still ran down her cheeks as a silly giggle escaped her lips from time to time no matter how hard she tried to stop them. Then she shivered violently. Her skin had gone all clammy just before she'd thrown up and now the cold air was becoming too much. She shivered again, hiccupping loudly.

"Your coat," he said, "where's your coat?"

"G...ground. Be...behind bench."

He reached back, felt around, located it and pulled it up around her shoulders. "Talk to me," he gritted. "What's going on?"

She was silent a moment, just breathing deeply, trying to gather the pieces of herself together. Ah, better! She closed her eyes, breathing in through her nose and out through her mouth, feeling her heartbeats steadying, slowing. The scent from his lap wasn't exactly helping to calm her stomach, though. Finally able to form words, she said, "I thought you were disgusted with me."

"Now?"

"Not now, well, maybe now, too, but in the restaurant you got up so suddenly and just...left. I...I thought I'd offended you."

"Offended me?" What was she talking about?

"About the wanting you inside me stuff. Your face went all strange and I thought...."

His lips curved slightly. "You had moved me more than I could say, darling. And I desperately needed to kiss you, so I...."

"So you wanted to go outside," she whispered, "but I didn't know why. I thought...I thought...oh, Marshall, you scared me to death. I...I...."

"Is that why you're upset? You thought I was angry?"

"Umm hmm," she hiccupped. "You just left so fast. I couldn't think, couldn't imagine. It just seemed like I'd said everything wrong."

"Oh, Eden," he smiled, sliding his arm around her shoulders. "You said everything right. Don't you know that?"

She hiccupped.

"Come here," he said softly, pulling her against him. "I understood what you meant. It was the most beautiful thing anyone has ever said to me." He kissed her very, very gently, neither of them caring that her skirt was now in contact with his lap. "I'm so sorry I scared you, darling. I had something entirely different in mind."

She hiccupped. "Kiss me again."

Chapter 20

There was a gas station just a bit down the road from the restaurant and they went there, both into the side door to the men's room, locking the door behind them.

Eden soaked paper towels in water and tried to sponge them off a bit, laughing and hiccupping all the while. Wadsworth barked and Marshall couldn't help but laugh as well.

A loud pounding sounded on the door and a male voice bellowed, "What in hell's going ON in there?"

The door swung inward, revealing a blind man, a large guide dog, and a hiccupping woman. "Um, nothing," Eden giggled. "Absolutely not a thing." Then she grabbed Marshall's hand and the three of them walked rapidly toward where she'd parked her car by the restaurant.

They were both fairly wet and she spread clumps of paper towels across the front seat before they got in.

"We never had dinner," Marshall commented as she started the engine. His stomach growled.

Eden scanned down the street. There was a fast food place two blocks further with a drive-in window. "Want a burger?" she asked, smiling at his profile in the dim light.

"Anything," he grinned. "At this point, anything."

So, they sat there in the car and ate burgers, fries, and chocolate shakes, and Eden laughed and chewed and forgot how scared she'd been not long before. There was something so companionable, so rather 'familiar' about eating burgers in a car at night. And in the near darkness, as she talked with him, it didn't really even seem like he couldn't look back at her.

Martha was busy in her kitchen when they arrived at the inn, so they just hurried up the stairs. In the hallway outside his room, he kissed her again, then said, "I'd better wash off." The odor from his pants was still rather rank despite her sponging attempts.

She wanted to say, "Need help?"...but didn't. She wasn't sure why. Maybe she wanted him to suggest it?

He was thinking of it, but somehow with his shoulder the way it was, he, well, he wanted to be whole, be mobile completely when he first made love to her. Now, any use of his left arm would be impossibly painful, and he wanted more than that for her sake. Perhaps that was foolish of him? He thought it probably was somehow, but he'd settled his mind into it. It wouldn't be all that long. He was a patient man. He just hoped she was a patient woman.

So he cupped her cheek with his palm, kissed her gently. "I'll see you downstairs in about half an hour."

She stood there a moment in the hall after his door closed, then sighed. How plain the invitation in her eyes had been. But then, he couldn't see that, now could he? She knew he loved her, loved to touch her, yet he didn't go further than that. Was it her? Could it be his shoulder? Was that it? She just wasn't sure. All she knew was that she ached with longing for him every moment she wasn't with him. Was it not the same for him? She rested her hand lightly on his closed door, then went to her own room, unzipping her skirt and letting it slide to the floor. A bubble bath. Yes, if she must bathe alone, a bubble bath.

She went to the small bathroom and ran warm water in the claw-foot porcelain tub, pouring in more of the bubble crystals than she usually would. Disrobing, she snuggled down into the tub, leaning her neck against the back curve, letting her eyes close. After a few minutes, she drifted into a light doze.

Marshall washed very carefully. It was a more complicated process with his shoulder so useless, and as careful as he was, the bit of movement it required, had him clenching his teeth. No, bathing with Eden right now was not right. He wanted to be able to devote his attention to her, not have her have to nurse him through pain. But he wished that were not the case. He wished they were together and his wet hand tingled with the thought of stroking down her sudsy back.

Dressed again, he picked out a CD he'd brought, using his Braille labeling system, and carried it with him down to the parlor. Martha was there, arranging some dried seed heads in a small vase on the side table. "You two have a nice dinner?" she asked fondly.

"Very nice," he replied, then held out the CD. "All right if I put this on?"

"Fine by me," she smiled. "I like your taste in music. You go right ahead, Marshall dear. I've got cookies in the oven I need to tend to."

Eden woke with a start. She hadn't meant to nap. What time was it? He'd said he'd be waiting for her in the parlor. She finished her bath, dressed quickly and hurried down the stairs. The scent of warm cookies filled the air as she crossed to the parlor. Ah, there he was. He was alone, sitting on the couch, leaning back, his eyes closed, listening to music. She didn't recognize it as Puccini's *O Mio Babbino Caro*, she just knew she'd heard it before and that it was lovely.

She'd paused at the doorway and stayed there now, just watching him. He had such a quiet, beautiful look on his face, and his right hand was moving. The sight riveted her. His hand was moving to the music, not exactly like a conductor's would, but somehow...more. She had no words for it. It moved not with the music but in the music, with an utterly graceful flow of motion. It seemed to her he was touching the notes as they filled the air.

The music changed to a different piece, also one she knew she'd heard before but could put no name to. It had a definite waltz beat to it, one two three, one two three, and with her hand on the doorframe, she closed her eyes. There he was, dressed in an Austrian cavalryman's uniform from the early 1800's, form-fitting white pants tucked into tall black boots, his jacket hung with golden epaulets and roping. He held out his hand to her, looking her in the eye, inviting her to dance. She offered her fingers and he swept her out onto a ballroom floor, her long, full gown billowing as they moved.

Opening her eyes, she watched him again. Suddenly she felt like a voyeur. It wasn't right, watching him so intently when he wasn't aware of her presence. But that was part of being blind, wasn't it? That must happen all the time. You didn't know someone was there until they made some noise, until they decided to let you know. Her throat constricted. It wasn't right, it just wasn't right, that someone like him was closed into a dark box.

She realized again with a great piercing that he lived in a differently-perceived world from hers. Even the music. The music was, for her, a visual thing. Listening to it had led her into the ballroom scenario, a place of color and brightness, a place made alive visually. But not for him. He sat there, listening to the same sounds, but it was all different for him. She couldn't grasp what it was like for him and he wouldn't be able at all to understand what it was like for her. Tears wet her cheeks and she reached a hand out toward him, though he was completely across the room.

Martha found her standing there like that. "Eden, sweetheart," she whispered. "What's the matter?"

"I can't touch him, Martha. I simply can't touch him."

"Well, not if you stay in this doorway, dear heart."

"That's not what I mean," she sighed heavily. "He's somewhere I can't go. I can't be where he is while he's listening to the music. I'm locked off from it, Martha. Completely."

"Does that mean you can't love him?"

Eden smiled wryly. "There's no way I cannot love him, Martha. But I can't go where he is."

"Not if you stay in the doorway," Martha repeated. "There's trying and then there's watching from the door."

"Trying?"

"Yes, trying. Even if you can't make it all the way, there's still trying, and trying can be a wonderful thing. Trying is a way of saying 'I love you'. Much better than watching and feeling shut out. Much better." She headed back to the kitchen.

"Trying," Eden said to herself. He'd made the rain as real for her as he could, hadn't he? Maybe he could take her with him into his experience of music?"

She walked into the room, saying his name as she came. He stood, smiling, extending his hand much in the same way she'd imagined in her ballroom fantasy. She gulped. It was her own desire that he could see, her own wish that he know color and light the way she did, that made her feel this sense of anger and frustration and sadness for his sake. But he never felt that for himself. He'd said plainly that he couldn't yearn for things he couldn't even imagine. He was fine and happy as he was. She was the one who suffered for him. Could she stop that? Could she get to some place where she was as content with his blindness as he was? She knew she needed to.

"Eden," he said happily, "I was hoping you'd come while *Va' Pensiero* was still on. It's one of my favorites."

She took his hand. "Is that the one that's just ending?"

"It is," he grinned, moving to the table beside the couch where the CD player was. "Let me play it again from the beginning."

She sat beside him on the couch. "It sounds like it would be lovely to dance to," she ventured.

"It's wonderful," he agreed, "but I generally need a large and very empty place to dance. For the safety of others," he added with a chuckle. "Once my mother took me to a gym when it was closed. She brought a tape player and put on music and for the first time I got to lead a woman wherever I wanted without fear of ramming into other couples." His face lit up at the memory.

"Your mother was a wonderful woman," she said quietly.

"She was," he nodded. "But this is what I do in places like we're in now." He took her hand and put it crossways atop his own. "Listen," he urged, "really listen."

She closed her eyes and he began to move his hand. She had no idea how he managed, but he took her whole soul with him into the music. Forgetting about the ballroom, she let go of preconceptions and found herself in some far reach of space where her spirit lay atop his and the two of them flowed as one through utter limitlessness. And for the first time she understood that he was not in a box but in this place without boundaries and she was there with him. There was nothing visual about it, nor any need for it. It was all feeling and awareness and movement and riding on the sound of music. She had never felt so together with another person.

The music ended and still she was there with him, her eyes closed. "I don't want to take my hand off yours," she breathed.

He lifted her hand to his cheek, rubbing it gently back and forth. "You don't have to." The next piece began and he took her with him into it. His presence, his understanding, his grasp of the music radiated somehow into her and she knew they were dancing, that he had taken her, dancing, into the music in some profound, inexpressible way.

When the CD ended, he let his hand settle into her lap, her hand still resting atop his. She just sat there silently, needing to let the waves of the music slide slowly away as though a series of thin veils floated gently, one by one, down to her feet. Opening her eyes, she looked at his hand. "Marshall Sinclair," she whispered, "I think I love you almost more than I can bear."

Chapter 21

Martha peeked in the door to see if they wanted some fresh cookies, but when she saw them cuddled so close on the couch, merely smiled and went back to the kitchen.

"I think I've heard that last piece," Eden was saying, her temple resting against his, "but doesn't it usually have voices behind it?"

"You're right," he said, "almost always a choral backup, sometimes quite a large group of singers. This CD of mine just has the orchestral parts. Sometimes I like it that way. Leaves me freer somehow to go where I want with the music."

He leaned over and started *Va' Pensiero* from the beginning, this time with his head resting against hers, his hand quiet with hers in her lap, but sang the words just above a whisper in Italian, his lips not far from her ear.

She sat there wondering if anyone had ever actually just upped and died from sheer happiness. And it was there again, that almost desperate need to be closer than merely side by side. They said sometimes folks were blessed enough to find their other half and the image she'd always gotten of that was of two pieces, like maybe an apple cut in half or something, anyway, two pieces that matched closing together. But that wasn't what she was feeling. She didn't want one smooth side of her pressed against one smooth side of him. That wasn't it at all. What she yearned for was for all of her to be contained by all of him and all of him to be contained by all of her. You couldn't really get a mental image of that, now could you?

His breath as he sang was on her hair and the sensation of it went down each individual strand to her scalp with a delightful tingle. He doesn't have to do more than this and he leaves me panting, she thought. What would it be like to...? Something deep in her core trembled then went all soft and squishy. She didn't think she'd ever felt so completely female in her life.

The music was over, his lips were still against her hair, his hand in her lap. She lifted his hand to her throat just above her collar bone and pressed it slightly, then let hers drop away. He kept his hand there, still, for a moment then his thumb pad began a soft stroking up her neck, moving on, back and forth along her jaw line.

There was something about the way she offered him her neck that moved him deeply. Her neck was slender, delicate, and his hands were large. It was as though she were saying silently to him that she trusted him with the most vulnerable part of herself. He could feel her pulse beating rapidly under his fingers, the slight vibration in her flesh as he moved his hand. No one had ever offered themselves to him quite so completely and everything male in him responded to it. His thumb found her lower lip, explored across it, inside it, then in one smooth motion he locked his own mouth over it, nearly consumed with hunger for her.

He forgot himself, forgot his shoulder, and turned to take her in both arms, a wrenching movement that sent electric pain shooting across and through and around the upper left side of his body. He gasped with the blinding suddenness of it, stiffening, which only made it intensify.

She realized instantly what he had done and her eyes flew open, finding him with jaw squared against the pain and a small trickle of blood seeping from where he'd bitten his lower lip. "Oh, Marshall!" she cried, stricken by the expression on his face. "I'm sorry. I'm so sorry."

He tipped his head down, blowing out short, quick breaths before he was able to speak. "No," he gasped. "No. Not your fault. I simply forgot." He raised his head, still panting, managing a smile. "Just a second. I'll be ok."

There was a pitcher of water on a side table and she went hurriedly to it, dipping a handful of tissues she'd grabbed, then came back and dabbed at his lip. "This is why no bath, isn't it?" she asked, deciding she might as well speak her mind with him.

"No bath? Oh, you mean together?" He grinned just enough to make his lip bleed more. So, she'd thought about that, too, had she now? "Yes," he chuckled ruefully, "I'm afraid it is."

"I just needed to be sure it wasn't because you didn't want to."

"Good Lord, darling, I want to so badly I can barely stand it." Another bolt of pain shot through his shoulder and he winced.

"I'm going to get you some aspirin," she announced. "Don't go away."

"I'll be here," he panted, his eyes squeezed tightly shut.

He sat quietly while she was gone, trying to relax his muscles as that seemed to help, and taking long, slow breaths. He was concentrating so much on that, he didn't hear her return. She'd started the CD again and *Un Bel Di* filled the room. Dutifully, he swallowed the two extra-strength aspirin she presented him with, then settled his right side against her as she sat beside him again. Still taking deliberate, long breaths, he felt himself relaxing into her presence, into the music, and the pain began to drift slowly away on the tide of his rising peace.

Martha came in with a tray of cookies and hot tea. "Is he asleep?" she whispered.

"I don't know," Eden whispered back. "He's been quiet for a long while now."

"I'm awake," he said, not moving his head or opening his eyes. "Just comfortable, that's all." Then his nose wiggled just a bit. "I smell MarthaCookies, I do believe." He straightened then, running his right hand through his hair.

"Cookies 4 o'clock, teacup at 10," Martha laughed fondly, letting him know where his things were on the coffee table.

"Martha Malone, will you marry me?" he smiled.

"Already taken," she giggled.

"Drat!" he replied dramatically. But both women saw his hand move, locate Eden's, and fold it into his. Martha looked at the two of them, a deep motherly tenderness shining in her eyes.

Marshall heard Martha's footsteps leaving the room. He sniffed the air again. "Ah, good, peanut butter."

"You like peanut butter cookies, do you?"

"We had this big production thing going with them when I was a kid," he explained. "Mom would make the dough and roll it into little balls. We all sat in a row at this big kitchen table, you see. I was in the middle and my job was to take a glass that had a damp cloth secured over its bottom with a rubber band. Each time a peanut butter ball would come in front of me, I'd take the glass and squish the ball sorta flat then move it on over to Jeff, who'd take a fork and press its tines across it in the traditional peanut butter cookie pattern. Rather like an assembly line of some sort." He picked up one of the cookies, turning it over in his fingers, his thumb tracing over the impression made by Martha's fork. "Just like this," he said happily and popped it into his mouth.

"I don't think I've ever squished a peanut butter dough ball with a glass," Eden said softly.

He turned his face to her. "The kitchen table is still there." He let his words, with all their implications, simply rest there, quietly solid.

Chapter 22

Marshall and Eden were standing close together just outside her door. He kissed her, a long, tender kiss, then stepped back, intending to go to his own room.

"Marshall," she said, her voice halting his movement. "Are we going somewhere?"

He knew what she meant. "I want to."

"Will you come in for a moment?"

"That's the problem, darling. I want to do that, too."

He heard her opening her door. "Please."

Licking his lip thoughtfully, he said, "Eden...."

"Please."

He blew out a breath and followed her into her bedroom. As he didn't know the arrangement of her furniture and Wadsworth was not in harness, she led him to her bed.

"Sit with me? Talk to me?" she asked.

His right hand rested on his lap and she lifted it in hers, liking some physical point of contact between them since he couldn't see her. He smiled slightly, very aware of his own breathing, of the faster rhythm of his heart. "Eden," he tried again, "please don't ever think I don't want you, darling. I literally ache with the wanting of you. I just want...," he blew out another long breath, "I just...want...everything, absolutely everything, especially me, to be...right."

"I know," she said, her voice very low, "but I can hardly bear lying in this bed now without you beside me."

An odd little sound escaped his throat. "I don't think I could bear lying beside you and not...."

"Just a little," she urged. "I just need to feel the length of you alongside me, just a little."

"Oh, Eden," he said, shaking his head.

"Just a little," she repeated, sliding off the bed and slipping his shoes off. "I'll be gentle."

A half-strangled laugh burst out of him. "Isn't that supposed to be my line?"

"It doesn't matter whose line it is, my darling. I think I'm going to die on the spot if you don't lie beside me...just a little."

He pushed himself back and around on the bed so his right side would be next to her. He couldn't do this properly, not like he wanted, not with his top left half trussed like a turkey for roasting. He was accustomed to a grace and flow of movement, but not now. Now he felt inept, clumsy. He simply could not let her first experience of him be awkward. So as he lay back, he said, "Just lie with me a while, darling. Just be close and...."

"It's all right," she smiled, still sitting, looking down at him, entirely filled with her longing for him. "I do understand." She lay carefully beside him on his right side, sliding her arm across his chest. "Just let me listen to your heart beating." She rested her cheek atop him and closed her eyes. Ah, there it was and it had become to her the most beloved sound in the world.

Her hand slipped inside the front of his shirt, her fingers lightly playing with the hair on his chest. His whole body reacted and he began to breathe through his mouth in a desperate effort to make himself relax. He couldn't do it. His body had a mind of its own and it wanted hers. If he had been whole, he would have rolled up on his right elbow and his left hand would have done, would have touched, would have found.... But he couldn't and it was killing him that he couldn't. His right arm was under her shoulders and as she leaned up on him a little more, he used his arm to lift her closer to his face where he could find her mouth. One small, still-functioning corner of his brain kept reminding him not to attempt curving his left side up, the memory of what had happened not long before on the parlor couch still fresh in his nerve endings. So he let his mouth show her mouth what he would do if he could with the rest of him. His hand was fisted in the back of her hair, pressing her rather desperately to him.

Then he became fully aware that the reins he was keeping on himself, the reins that in their reasonableness told him certain movements would result in exquisite pain, those reins were slipping from his fingers. He pulled his mouth away from hers, sucking in gasping breaths of air. Not like this. He wanted to love her freely, completely, not with teeth gritted against agony.

She lifted her face, looking down at him, seeing his struggle plainly writ on his features. "You were right, weren't you?" she whispered.

He nodded, not quite able to speak, his eyes squeezed tightly shut.

"I'm sorry," she murmured, rolling onto her back, his arm still under her.

He let out one more long, fairly ragged breath. "Don't be sorry for wanting to love me," he said. His hand curved up, its fingers combing through her hair. "I think there's just too much wanting from both of us to be able to lie together like this."

"I just want, need, to be close to you," she sighed.

"I know," he said. "I really know." He scooped her back against him. "Maybe if we lie very still," he almost chuckled.

She nestled her head against him, not putting her hand on his chest. "Let's try," she said. "Like this, let's just try, for a while."

His breathing and pulse had begun to calm. He lay flat on his back, the only movement he allowed being his fingers in her hair. After a long, long while, even that stopped and they both slept. Wadsworth woke up somewhere in the wee hours, changed his position, flopped down again with rather much of a thud. Not used to dog sounds in the night, Eden roused, realized the lights were still on and Marshall still lay beside her. She moved her head just enough to watch his face as he slept. "I love you, you beautiful, wonderful man," she whispered. "I love you so much I almost scare myself."

As she settled back, she knew that was because of Miles in the snow. She'd read somewhere that when you love, you offer hostages to fate. She'd loved Miles as completely as she knew how at that stage of her life, and fate had taken him brutally away. Now, lying there, listening to the steady beat of Marshall's heart, she was truly somewhat frightened that she'd not only let herself love again, but let herself love more.

Thank God, she comforted herself, that he was a college professor and not a cop. Thank God for that much. And he'd already fallen off his cliff and she'd been there, been in time to save him. Not like Miles, whose blood had poured out of his neck, soaking the snow in its redness until he was white and cold and gone. For the next half hour she listened to the beating of Marshall's heart then finally slept, warm against his side.

In the morning she woke again, smiled because he was there, and asked softly, "You awake?"

"Umm hmm," he murmured.

"I can't tell. Your eyes are shut."

He smiled, opening them. "It's not instinct for blind people to open their eyes. Sometimes we forget and just keep them closed."

"I love your eyes," she said. "You have really long lashes, you know."

He laughed. "Not once in my life have I ever thought about my eyelashes."

"Well, I like them! So there! And when your eyes are closed, they fan out across your cheeks and make me want to kiss them."

"Kissable eyelashes?" He chuckled again, closing his lids. "I'm waiting."

Now she laughed and leaned over him, kissing each eye in turn.

Wadsworth got up, coming to Marshall's side of the bed and whuffing softly. "He probably needs to go out," Marshall said. Since they'd both slept in their clothes, all they had to do was slip on their shoes, go quietly down the stairs, grab their coats and step out on the porch. Marshall hadn't bothered with a leash and let Wadsworth run free in the large area between the inn and the lake.

"It snowed last night," Eden remarked. "I'd say about three inches or so." She tipped her face up toward his. "Is snow at all like rain for you?"

"Not in the least, I'm afraid. Almost the exact opposite."

"How do you mean? Doesn't it fall out of the clouds just like rain?"

"It muffles, Eden, and takes away all my points of reference. When I walk, I'm aware of textures under my feet, the differences between roads or paths or lawns. Snow blankets that. It's not so bad if Wadsworth's in harness with me, but when I'm on my own I can't tell where I am or where I need to go. When I was a boy, I'd go anyway, blundering my way through the drifts, falling over things I would have known were there except for their presence being wiped out for me by the snow. How do I tell where the curb is if the snow is deep? How do I know where the road begins? It takes away any certainty I have of where I am going."

He stopped, smiled. "But I don't want you to think it's all grim. I still make a fairly decent snowman."

She was silent, thinking. There was so much she'd never thought of, so much she didn't realize about what his world was like. She ran her hand along the top of the railing, scooping off some of the snow into her palm. "It's really light and fluffy today. I don't think it'd pack well at all or I'd make you prove that, mister."

Wadsworth barked happily as he dashed about. "He's having a good time," Marshall said. "It's good for him to run like this without his harness."

"He does look happy," she agreed. "He seems to have uncovered a pine cone and is tossing it up in the air."

"That you know that...." he said softly. "I can't even imagine how you know that." He shook his head wonderingly. "I know he's happy and he's playing in the snow, yes, but how you know about the pine cone, it's just unimaginable. What is it that eyes do that lets you gather such detailed information at such a distance?"

She bit her lip. There was simply no way to describe seeing to someone who'd never seen.

"You know," he continued, "there was this two-year study dealing with the near-death experiences of born-blind people, and what's interesting is that 80% of them had some sort of visual perception during it. They had a hard time describing it because born-blind people don't have the early developmental process of making sense of perceived objects."

"I've heard of born-blind people sometimes getting their sight through some sort of surgery or something and then being all confused because nothing makes sense to them," she added.

"Umm hmm," he nodded. "From what I understand, that's the way it is. So these people who saw during NDE's were hard-pressed to explain, but from what they were able to do, the doctors were astounded."

"It's quite a thought," she murmured. "Dying to see."

"What is says to me, Eden, is that sight is an integrated part of the essence of our spirit and it's only the physical body that may be blind, but never the spirit. So when the spirit is free, even for a moment, from the physical, it sees. It's actually rather simple in concept."

"Did you see anything, Marshall, there in the mud?"

"Nothing. I think I didn't get that far, close, but not quite that far. I sort of recall something like, well, coming loose, almost a beginning of a drifting away. But then you beat on my back and cleared my airway and stopped me dead in my tracks, so to speak."

"Live in your tracks," she amended. "I definitely need you live in your tracks."

He bent, kissing her cheekbone. "That makes two of us."

Chapter 23

"It's November now, you know," Eden mentioned as they went back upstairs to change before breakfast.

"And I've not written a further word on my book," Marshall sighed.

"You've been busy," she said with a soft chuckle.

"Very," he agreed. She had walked a bit down the hall toward her room and he extended his arm in her general direction. She returned quickly, taking his hand.

"What?" she asked.

"Just this," he smiled, tracing his hand up her arm, then higher, where he slipped it around behind her neck, pulling her gently close enough to kiss her lips.

When they parted again, she went to her door but, rather than going in, simply stood there a moment in the hallway watching him. He had his right hand on the frame of his doorway, but was also standing silently, not going in. Wadsworth stood next to him, waiting for the door to open. Marshall's face was toward her and she wondered what he was thinking. Then his hand moved, his palm wiping slowly back and forth two or three times across his mouth and chin. His hand dropped and he held it levelly in front of himself, flexing his fingers, then quietly turned and he and his dog went into his room. She stayed a moment longer, looking at his door, then touched her own fingertips lightly to her mouth before leaving the hall.

Eden was already seated at the breakfast table when he came down the stairs, Wadsworth in harness. New guests had arrived at the inn and she noticed too late that they had left luggage in the entrance hall Marshall had to cross.

"Mar...," she started to call in warning, but Wadsworth smoothly and neatly led Marshall around the bags, into the breakfast room and up to an empty chair.

She shook her head. Wadsworth must do that constantly. No big deal. She decided not to comment on it but instead said, "He's in harness?"

"I was hoping we could go into town for a while this morning, if you'd like. We haven't done that, you know. You and me, just strolling down the street, maybe looking for an antique shop or something. Would you like that?"

"I would," she smiled, aware how much she liked to smile at him even though he didn't see. "But weren't you thinking about the book?"

"I was," he admitted, taking his seat, "but there's this afternoon. I thought this morning it would be nice just to walk with you."

She smiled again and he smiled back. "I can't get over how you do that," she said.

"What?"

"Smile back at me. I know you said Jeffrey worked on that with you, but it still delights me every time."

"Jeff thought it was really important. He said that when people talked to a blind person, they still smiled even though they knew it wouldn't be seen. It's just a natural thing for a sighted person to do that without even thinking about it. But for me, I'm aware every time I smile."

He unfolded the large cloth napkin, placing it in his lap. "Smiling, you see, is, well, it's responsive. You see someone smiling at you so you smile back. Jeff said it was easy to do that when you could see. But for me I have to listen for it in a voice then hope that I'm right and smile back." He shrugged, "I might not even be smiling in quite the right direction, though. Then if I'm the one who smiles first, I don't know if the other person has actually seen it or answered with their own smile." He smiled then, a bit wryly. "But I like to smile, and I've gotten so that I can tell fairly well from vocal inflections if I'm being smiled at." He shrugged slightly.

"I'm glad you like to smile," she said softly, laying her hand atop his on the table.

Just then the new arrivals came in, followed by Martha, who introduced them as Walter and Melissa Capstan from Buffalo. Marshall had stood up at the beginning of the introductions and then held his hand out across the table. Walter's eyes went from the hand to the guide dog lying near Marshall's chair and he nodded toward Wadsworth so his wife would notice, then took Marshall's hand. "Nice to meet you," he said, his voice genuinely friendly. "Fine-looking dog you've got there."

"This is Wadsworth," Marshall grinned, "guide dog extraordinaire."

Walter and Melissa took their seats, explained how they were just there for the weekend then would be traveling on to Philadelphia to see their daughter's new baby. The four of them had an amiable breakfast, then Marshall and Eden left in her car for the drive into town. They'd just turned onto the road when Marshall said, "Bellefonte."

"Hmmm?"

"Bellefonte. Have you been there?"

"Um, I don't think so. Where is it?"

"About ten miles from State College. Shouldn't take too long to get there from here."

"What's at Bellefonte?"

"Us, for lunch."

She laughed. "We just had breakfast and you've got lunch planned?"

"There's a tavern there I'd like to take you to, Eden. When Jeffrey was at Penn State, we used to drive up to Bellefonte and eat there. It's special."

"I'd like that," she said, "but won't it take more out of your day?"

"You're my day," he replied. "You're what matters the most."

"But your book...."

"It'll wait. But you're here and I'm here and this is something I'd really like to share with you."

So they by-passed the little nearby village and continued on to Bellefonte. The road wound through huge tracts of forest land that had really started looking wintry now that the first snow had fallen. Her eyes flicked from time to time to her right, glancing at his profile. For a couple of seconds on a straight stretch of road, she closed her eyes, trying to get in touch with what it was like for him to be sitting there, not seeing the thick growth of trees on either side of their passage.

"Marshall?"

"Umm hmm."

"What's it like, riding like this in a car? What's it like for you?"

His lips curved in a smile. He loved that she wanted to understand. Not everybody did. "Whatever's out there, and I'm presuming it's a whole lot of trees, isn't making a sound as the car passes through it. Jeff tried to describe it to me, how the hills and the houses moved past, how the scene was constantly changing, but that's not real for me. For me, my whole sense of movement comes from the relationship of my body to the car. The engine makes the floorboards vibrate under my feet and when you go around a curve, I tip a little. If you speed up, I'm pressed back into my seat and if you suddenly slow down, I go forward. What's outside the windows doesn't change for me so I have no relationship with that, only with the car itself, its sounds, its feel."

She licked her lips, trying hard...again...not to mourn his blindness. That would not be what he wanted. But it was hard, sometimes it was really hard not to. It was all so new for her, this world of his, new and very different.

"Tell me more about Bellefonte," she ventured. "Why do you like the place?"

"Beautiful fountain. That's what the name means, you know, beautiful fountain. There actually was one there, but now it's covered. What I want you to see, besides the tavern, of course, are the houses. Very Victorian. It's a little gem of a town. Only about 7,000 people, but really special in how it looks. Lots of the big old homes have been turned into bed and breakfasts. My mother really loved them. We'd drive up here and walk the hilly streets, and she'd describe all the houses to me."

She moved her right hand to rest on his leg. "Thank you," she murmured.

"For...?"

"For wanting to share it with me."

He found that, yes, it was very important for him to share things with her, happy things, places that had some meaning for him. This deep sense of contentment had been steadily growing in him since, well, since her. She was the first person he'd ever wanted to come to Bellefonte with since they'd stopped their little side trip to it after Jeff's graduation from college.

As they entered the small town, Marshall directed her to look for the octagonal cupola of the Centre County Courthouse. She parked on a side street and stood looking a moment at the building. There was a weather vane atop the cupola, but it was turning and she couldn't make out what it was. "It doesn't look at all like a rooster," she commented as Marshall and Wadsworth came around to join her.

"What? The weathervane?" He chuckled. "It's a trout."

"A trout?"

"Umm hmm. Fly fishing is big around here."

He knew how many blocks they needed to go before turning a corner, where to walk to find the best of the old homes. "I know this is a bit awkward," he said, as they paused at a corner. "Wadsworth in harness, I mean. It may be good that we go a little slower since I'm having to use my right hand on the harness and neither of us are used to it. Generally we rather zoom up the street. Not very good for companionship, I'm afraid."

He was actually holding Wadsworth back somewhat so Eden could maintain a comfortable pace on his left side. "It also takes considerable concentration from both of us to do what we have to do, and talking with someone is generally distracting from that. But I figure since you're with me, your eyes will make up for any lack in my concentration. And you can read the street signs if I forget how many blocks we've come. Right now I'm looking for Linden Street."

"Half a block ahead," she announced.

"Thought so," he grinned.

"Right or left?" she asked.

"We need to go both ways, so you pick."

She turned left for no particular reason and after a bit he said, "We should be by the Garret Bed and Breakfast right about now, I think."

"Is that the white building with the Norman roof?"

"That'd be it." They stood on the sidewalk so she could see the three-story home, white for the two lower floors, with the third floor windows set in the curved-down, black roof. It had a porch all round, lots of trees, and just a comfortable, charming air about it. She commented on several other homes as they turned and headed east again, stopping outside the Reynold's Mansion. It was a really huge stone home set back away from the street on a rise. It had a roundish tower on its right, a central square tower, a large gable on its left and was at least half covered in brilliant red-leafed vining.

"Maybe too big," Eden said, "but I bet it has great rooms."

"It does. I've been in there with my mother. It has marvelous ceilings, carved wood, really nice, but, as you say, big, very big.

Further down on another street they paused in front of a very different sort of B&B. This one had lots of steps going up to its stone porch, was painted yellow with narrow blue trimmings, a perfectly round tower on its left side and an oddly cut-off right corner up which rose a huge brick chimney that seemed to disappear behind some sort of high dormer thing before reappearing and dividing into three parts. It had a glorious amount of gables and angles and sat there, bright and colorful despite a few wandering snowflakes.

"Wow!" she said.

"That's The Queen," he explained. "Nothing else quite like it. I've always wanted to stay there someday, find out what it's like inside."

"I like B&B's," Eden commented.

"Good," he chuckled. "Maybe someday?"

"Maybe someday. Yes."

They stopped by an antique store where she watched him run his hand over several pieces. "You like antiques?"

"Umm hmm," he said, his brow knit as his fingers traced the deep carving on an old sideboard. "Especially pieces like this with texture to them."

She closed her eyes, letting her fingers follow after his. Yes, she could understand why that would appeal to him.

"You hungry yet?" he suddenly asked.

She hadn't thought about it, so interested she had been in all they'd looked at, but now she stopped and did think about it, found she was. "I do believe I am," she said, her voice a bit surprised.

He laughed. "Time for the Mill then."

"The Mill?"

"The Gamble Mill Tavern. It's where I want to take you for lunch. It's an old mill, built in 1786 on the bank of Spring Creek. They turned it into a restaurant in 1986, exactly 200 years later. Let's go back to the car and I'll tell you where to look for it."

She found it easily, parked, and just sat looking through the windshield at the place for a moment. It was red brick with a center tower in the angle made by two wings that had to be at least six stories tall. A series of very Dutch-like steps made of brick flanked the top of the tower. The entrance was a series of red doors in a large brick arch, to the right of which climbed a huge expanse of vines.

"What a marvelous old place," she said.

"It's even better inside," Marshall added.

He was right. She found herself walking across a shiny hardwood floor toward a small wooden table with four ladder-back chairs. The big room had huge square beams everywhere that came down to the floor, dividing the room into sections. Each of the beams had long, slender bare branches bound around it and curving up and into the branches were woven tiny amber lights. The entire room had a golden glow to it that delighted her eyes.

"You like it?" he asked.

"It's...it's...glorious!" she sighed happily.

She saw him let go of the harness briefly, reaching out to run his hand down some of the branches, his fingers barely touching some of the lights. "Still the same," he commented gratefully. "This is what I wanted you to see."

She looked at him, his face eager and happy that she was seeing all this beauty he was not, but obviously not minding it for himself in the least. Her eyes sparked with sudden tears, which she blinked rapidly away. His mother or Jeffrey must have described the room in detail for him.

Still.

At their table, the amber glow reflected on his face. He seldom wore his dark glasses any more, at least not when he was with her, and the glow made his skin very warm and rich in color. How was this possible, she mused. How had she come to love this man so much so soon?

"You're thinking...what?" he asked softly, aware of her silence.

"You want to know?"

"I do."

"I'm thinking how infinitely dear you are to me, Marshall Sinclair, and I'm wondering how I managed to exist until I came to the Morning Glory Inn."

He smiled a close-lipped, warm smile. "Sometimes our story finds us when we're not even looking."

He'd said that to her before. "Are you , will you be, my story?" she whispered.

"I'm planning on it."

Then their waiter came.

After lunch, they drove to the Plaza Center Antique Co-op, which was, for the most part, more like a huge garage sale. They walked through it for a while, laughing over some of the odd items, pausing to check out some of the more interesting. Then she saw something on the top shelf of a cluttered area that caught her eye. "Oh, look!" she cried, without thinking.

"What is it?"

"It's an old wooden dollhouse," she said, going up to it. "It's got gingerbread on top and a bay window. I could fix it up, add more gingerbread."

He'd already found the salesperson and was asking her how much. He had it paid for before she even realized what he was doing.

"Oh, Marshall...."

"Souvenir of Bellefonte and its Victorian houses," he smiled. "Can't think of a more perfect one."

She looked at him as he stuffed his wallet back in his pocket. He was standing there surrounded by mostly junk and was to her the most wonderful thing in the world. "I can't think of a more perfect one, either," she agreed, not at all thinking about the dollhouse.

Chapter 24

The wooden dollhouse had ridden home, sharing the back seat with Wadsworth, who seemed to find the smell of it interesting and kept moving his nose over the roof and walls. Harold had carried it up to Eden's room and set it on the bureau.

"Went to Bellefonte, did you?" he remarked.

"Marshall used to go there a lot when his older brother was at Penn State," Eden explained. "It sure has a lot of bed and breakfasts."

"Folks've kinda discovered it now. Almost can't get a room in peak fall season these days. But, yeah, the B&B's there are something special all right."

"Not as special as this one," Eden said softly. "This is the most special one of all."

"'Cause of him, I 'spect."

"He might have something to do with it," she admitted, turning the dollhouse so she could study the rooms. The interior had never really been finished and in her mind she was already planning on adding wallpaper and furnishings. She'd named the house Bellefonte Manor in honor of where it had been purchased. The fact that Marshall had bought it for her only added to her delight in the little house.

Marshall tapped lightly on her doorframe. The door was still wide open and Harold left as Marshall and Wadsworth entered. Wadsworth was not in harness and went over to flop down near the window seat.

"I love the house, Marshall."

"May I?" he asked, coming up beside her, reaching his hand out to trace the contours of the structure. "Ah, it is a fine little building, isn't it? You know, there's a program, especially in the UK, where they have models about this size of cathedrals and such so that blind people can feel them and get a better concept of what the building is like. A blind college professor came up with the idea."

"I think that's simply wonderful." She took his hand and moved it down to where the bay window was. "Don't you think this needs more trim or something here?"

"It is a bit plain. I think you should just drip the thing in gingerbread."

She laughed. "I may do that. I just may do that."

Giving him a bit more time to explore the house, she then asked, "What about your book?"

"Would you really like to work a bit on that with me?"

"I'd love to."

"Ok, then. I have what we need in my room."

The two of them, accompanied by Wadsworth, went down the hall and into his room. "How do you go about this?" She was truly curious.

"Usually I just type it into my computer myself. I have a lot of special software installed that does fancy stuff just for blind people and a LaserJet printer that can print out in ink or in Braille. Back in the city I have a Sounding Board speech synthesizer that lets me just talk to the computer, but it's not here. I didn't think I'd need it. I guess I could send for it."

"Well," she interrupted, "I am here, so I can type it in for you until your shoulder heals."

"You really don't mind?"

"Mind? I'm really interested in what you might be writing."

"You know what I need, too?"

"What's that?"

"Someone to keep me straight. There are times when I'm writing a sighted character and I'm just, well, off. I need someone who sees to let me know if I'm doing right by my sighted characters."

"Have you written a novel before?"

"Not a novel, no. I've written probably a literal ton of poetry, a few short stories, but most of it has been exposition on the literary works of others, essays, commentaries, that sort of thing. This is my first."

"Tell me about it. What's it about?"

"It's set in Colonial Williamsburg not long before the Revolutionary War begins. My protagonist is a young man named Morgan Kent, recently arrived from England."

"Have you been to Williamsburg?"

"Last summer Wadsworth and I spent about two weeks there. I think we walked over every square inch of the place."

"What was your favorite thing about it?"

"The bell, the one in Bruton Parrish Church. It's the same one that was there at the time my book is set. I'd be walking down the Duke of Gloucester Street and it would peal out and every single time it just got to me. It was the exact sound George Washington, Thomas Jefferson, all of them back then heard. I'd stand very still and just let the sound of it soak through me. The same sound. It was marvelous."

"I'd love to know more of what Williamsburg was like for you. What else was special for you?"

"The walls. The tops of the brick walls are all shaped into a continuous curve. I'd run my hand along them." He smiled, remembering. "Some of them were quite long. Then there are the picket fences. Everywhere. Picket fences. And the gates to them have small cannonball counterweights to make them close automatically." He paused again, casting his mind back. "And brick walkways. They feel so different under your feet. Duke of Gloucester Street is gritty with sand and some of that gets up on the sidewalk, too. Then there's the sound of horses, the jingle of harnesses, the clop of their feet, the squeak of carriage wheels. I rode in one. Had to get the feeling of it, you know. Took me a little bit to talk the guy into letting Wadsworth come along, but he finally relented.

"And the scents! Herb gardens in every yard, magnolia trees all in lemony bloom, and boxwood. They say Williamsburg is the scent of boxwood and they're right. Neat hedges of it all over the place and when the sun is hot, the scent of it gets stronger and stronger. This spring I want to plant some of it around my house. I grew to love the smell of it. Of course there's the definite scent of road apples left by the horses. You can't have a constant stream of horse-drawn carriages and not get road apples. Sometimes Wadsworth wasn't always all that careful about leading me around them, either. I don't think road apples were part of his training. But especially the Duke of Gloucester Street had quite a lot of them. It got so that when he would put his head down to sniff at something, I knew I'd better start watching my step, so to speak.

"Sometimes," he continued, "I'd pause by a picket fence with a garden just beyond. The air would be filled with the sound of bees in the lavender. And birds. There were lots of birds. And voices. People come there from all over the world and I'd count how many different languages I'd hear in a day. Once I was sitting on the steps of the old Courthouse where the Declaration of Independence was read to the people of the town, and the fife and drum corps came marching by. It was just so easy to imagine myself back in time. I found it really helped with my feel for the book, you know."

She was silent, picturing him exploring Williamsburg by sound and scent and feel. How he went about that was steadily becoming more real for her, though she knew she'd never grasp it completely. He couldn't stand on the lawn and look down the length of the Palace

Green and see the palace itself. He had to go up to it, touch the brick walls, the wrought iron gate, get someone else to describe the high crown atop the gate he'd walk beneath. He'd have no real idea what the palace, as a building, looked like. Why did that make that dull ache for him rise in her chest? It wasn't pity. She knew that. There was nothing about Marshall that made you think of pitying him. It was more of a yearning.

She suddenly realized he was aware of her silence. When her eyes focused on him again, he had the slightest wry smile on his lips. "It's all right, Eden. Really it is. I'd like you to know that."

"I...I'm trying so hard, Marshall, to understand what it's like for you. I want to know. I just...."

"Me, too," he said softly. "This thing you do with your eyes, this other way of sensing and knowing, I wish I had some idea what it is, but I'm truly fine with what I have. I don't bemoan sight as a loss. For me it's not a loss." He leaned back in his chair. " I've had a couple of friends who once had sight and then went blind. For them the loss was enormous and adjusting to the fact of it took much time, much emotion. I've never had to go through that."

She sighed a bit raggedly. "I've never thought so much about the blind life as I have in the past few days. I feel ignorant, like there's so much I need to understand, a lot of ideas I need to get rid of, too."

"It's that way with most sighted people, probably. The general assumption is that blindness is some profound mistake that makes ordinary life impossible. In past history, with a few exceptions, that's probably been all too true. I was blessed with a family that in no way was going to let blindness mean my life was reduced. It always amazes me how ingrained the social attitudes toward blindness still are. If someone is blind, if their eyes are affected, the view is their mind must also be. Helplessness, that's the image, as though the whole body were affected, the blind beggar holding out his cup."

She was quiet, letting him talk.

"My whole life, not from my family, of course, but from other people, this view of blindness has rather beat against me. In Sparta, you know, they used to put blind babies in small earthenware tubs and set them out on the hillsides to die. If you were blind, you weren't worth being given a chance at life." He stopped. "I'm sorry. My mind suddenly flooded with too many memories, too many things I've read."

"Don't be sorry, not for a minute. I need to hear all these things if I'm to know what it's like for you."

"It's one of the reasons I became a lit professor."

"This? How?"

"It turns out the primary source those who can see have for information about those who can't is fiction. So it became important to me to understand just what the image of blind people is in fiction. There's quite a history to it."

"Like what?"

He smiled. "There's no balance to it. It's either one extreme or the other, absolute tragedy, maybe punishment for sin, or a gift bestowed that grants one purification and possibly miraculous powers. There's hardly ever any middle ground. Oedipus Rex puts out his own eyes and we are informed 'Thou art better off dead than living blind.' Then there's Milton. He went blind, you know, yet produced his best works after that. You'd think he'd have some sympathy for it but in *Samson Agonistes* he wrote, 'Blind among enemies, O worse than chains, dungeon, or beggary, or decrepit age! Inferior to the vilest now become of man or worm; the vilest here excel me. They creep, yet see; I, dark in light exposed to daily fraud, contempt, abuse, and wrong. Within doors or without, still as a fool, in power of others, never in my own; scarce half I seem to live, dead more than half, a moving grave.'" He turned his head away a moment, repeating in a whisper, "A moving grave."

"That's just terrible!" Eden said. "Terrible!"

"But widely-read, Eden. It's Milton."

"Are they all helpless and sad like that? What about what you said, the other extreme?"

He sighed. "It's just as bad in its way as the other. In those it's a blessing in disguise where the person has been deprived of sight so they will be inwardly illuminated. These characters are unbelievably noble and sweet. How often have you read something where the old wise man, the prophet, was blind. It doesn't help the blind at all that such things are written, are read, are believed. If one is evil and blind, it is the fault of the blindness. If one is totally virtuous, pure, gifted...and blind, it also due to the blindness, not the person. There is neither responsibility or credit."

He rubbed his hand across his chin. " Victor Hugo created a character named Dea to whom he gives an extra sense as compensation for her blindness. She had this ecstatic strain of perfect music in her perfect, pure soul. According to Hugo, 'blindness is a cavern to which reaches the deep harmony of the Eternal.' But what it's really saying is that in the very blindness itself, there's some magic present so whatever we might accomplish comes from it alone and has nothing to do with our own ability."

He sighed. "I've rambled on way too long, I fear. Comes from years of lecturing at university about literature. Sometimes it just wants to spill out of me."

"You know so many passages," she marveled.

"Part of the job," he smiled, "at least for me. I was," he smiled more widely, "gifted with a good memory."

She pulled her chair closer to his. "I kinda like the phrase 'the cavern of deep harmony.' Sounds like the title of a book or a poem. You should write one."

Chapter 25

For the next several weeks they spent hours every day working on his book. Often they paused and laughed with one another as they worked out some detail of phrase or sentence to make it ring true. They'd break for coffee or to take Wadsworth out for a romp. As Marshall's arm healed, Eden began driving him into the small hospital for physical therapy.

She'd had to call Connie, of course, to give some better explanation of why she was staying so long at the inn.

"A literature professor at Duquesne?"

"Umm hmm," Eden had smiled into the phone.

"You go all the way up there and meet somebody from here?"

"Looks that way."

"You sound happy."

"I am happy, Connie. Possibly the happiest I've ever been."

"More than with Miles?"

"This is very different from being with Miles, Con. It's hard to compare, really hard. But, yes, more than with Miles."

"Are you ever coming back?"

"Oh, yes. I just don't know when. Well, I do know sort of when. When Marshall comes back, I'll come back then."

"Sounds like you've got it bad, Eden."

"Not bad, Con. What I've got is good, all good. Wait till you meet him. You'll see what I mean."

"What about the blindness, though? Isn't that kind of hard to deal with?"

"Not like you might think, Con. He's so much more than that. You'll see."

They had talked for an hour.

"I'm going to have to credit you as co-author, you know," he said, leaning over, resting his chin atop her head as she sat at his desk proofreading the page they'd just finished. It was late in the evening of what had been a cold day in mid-December. That morning he'd finally said good-bye to his sling for good. The shoulder had been a long time in healing and the freedom of having the use of both hands back was wonderful.

Being blind, it had been especially difficult as he'd explained to Eden. A blind person with only one hand is much the same as a blindfolded sighted person. He told her he could carry a full cup of tea fine in one hand, but if you gave him a book to carry in the other, he would simply bumble into everything. "I need one hand free," he'd said, "because I see with that hand. With my left arm in the sling, every time I'd pick up anything, there I was, blindfolded." She'd never thought how it was for a blind person to carry something large with both hands. There was no free hand to see with.

His hands were on her shoulders and moved lightly, touching either side of her neck. Her skin tingled at the presence of his fingers and she had to stop typing, just sitting still in the desk chair as his left hand moved to the front of her throat. Every day since he'd first traced along her fingers there in the parlor she'd wondered what it would be like...if....

His hand slid delicately over her collarbone and continued down. She gasped and closed her eyes. *Oh, Lord...oh, Lord* was all her mind seemed capable of thinking. His lips found her earlobe and even the ability to think that much was gone.

"Eden," he whispered into her ear.

"Yes," she said, though he'd not verbally asked a question.

He offered her his hand, leading her to his bed. He wanted to scoop her up in his arms, but the doctor had said he shouldn't lift much for the next two or three weeks at least. But he was free now, free to lie beside her, with her, as he'd been aching to do. As fervently as he wanted her, his motions were very slow as he unbuttoned her blouse, moving his lips down each newly-bared part of her flesh. He took his time, exploring her as though she were some jeweled crown and his fingers must touch, must know every gem, every curve of gold, every fold of velvet. He loved her reverently but so thoroughly she wasn't sure toward the end if she were going to survive it.

The responses her body had made to his, the sensations that coursed through her, electrifying, almost exploding her entire nervous system, left her nearly limp. And when they finally lay together, legs entwined, his arms wrapped around her, she knew she'd never felt so a part of another human being, so absolutely overlapped in her being with his. Some ancient longing in her was utterly satisfied.

From then on her room was merely where she kept her clothes. She slept every night in his bed. Three days later she realized how foolish it was to keep paying for two rooms, and her clothes joined his, Bellefonte Manor appeared atop his dresser.

"That's what I mean," he said. "Would Morgan concentrate quite so much on the sound of distant gunfire or is that something I would do?"

She was at his desk, as usual, and had been typing his words for about an hour. Marshall seemed restless this evening and paced back and forth across the middle of the room behind her.

"I don't think he would," Eden commented. "I think he'd be paying more attention to the tracks he sees in the dust."

Marshall sneezed loudly, then cleared his throat.

"You ok?" she asked.

"Feeling a bit clogged," he admitted. "I think a cold's trying to settle in for a visit."

"Let's take an orange juice break," she suggested.

"I don't know," he replied rather wearily.

"Oatmeal cookies," she tempted. "Martha was baking again this afternoon."

"Oh, all right," he chuckled, actually quite ready to stop thinking about Morgan Kent for a while.

It was a Wednesday and, again, they were the only guests at the inn. Midweek was always slow as far as other visitors showing up, and now that it was full winter, there wouldn't be many on the weekends, either.

Martha was glad to see them coming down the stairs. "Would you...?" she began.

"We most definitely would," Eden laughed, "but can Marshall here have orange juice instead of coffee? He seems to be getting a cold."

By bedtime he was coughing a lot and worried about Eden sleeping with him. "You have very sexy germs," she protested. "They don't scare me."

On Thursday they didn't work on the book. His cough was worse and it was just too hard to dictate passages. She bundled him into a wool blanket and settled him near the fireplace, reading aloud to him from a book of Browning verse she found on a bookshelf. Martha bustled in and out with bowls of chicken soup and cups of hot tea.

"I should get a cold more often," he commented agreeably, then sneezed three times in a row.

After lunch, when Martha suggested a bit of a nap might do him some good, he found the thought of it appealing. He felt tired even though he hadn't really done much of anything all morning.

Harold shrugged on a heavy coat and went outside to bring in more firewood. Snow had fallen again in the night and a thin layer of ice had formed pretty far out into the lake. Martha was in the kitchen planning dinner. She wouldn't have Marshall going out to some restaurant when he was sick, not when she could feed him perfectly well right where he was. She smiled as she opened her smudged old recipe book. The younger couple had become rather dear to her.

Eden was sitting on the couch writing a letter when the front door opened and Harold came back inside, his arms empty of logs, and two men in ski masks walking closely behind him. Martha came out of the kitchen, wiping her hands on a towel as she so often did, and stopped, puzzled by the strange expression on her husband's face. "We have unexpected guests?" she asked, looking past him to what she could see of the men, then tensing at the sight of the masks.

"From Rockview," Harold said, his voice low, cautious.

Martha stiffened more. Rockview was the all-male state prison five miles out from Bellefonte.

"That's enough, old man," the larger of the two growled, giving Harold a shove between his shoulder blades that sent him staggering toward the dining room. "You, too," the man added, jerking his head to indicate Martha should follow her husband into the room.

The shorter, slimmer man had discovered Eden in the parlor. Wide-eyed and slightly trembling, she was dragged by her arm to the dining room.

"Anybody else here?"

"No," Eden and Martha said in unison. "It's off-season," Martha added. The two women exchanged a brief glance.

"You got a safe?" the big man asked. "We need cash, food."

"I could pack you something to eat," Martha offered.

"Never you mind that. You just sit yourself down in that there chair."

For the first time she noticed the smaller man was carrying a large roll of duct tape he'd gotten from the shed. Harold was standing perfectly straight, absolutely still, a knife pressed a bit too firmly into the middle of his back as the larger man's eyes flicked about the room, sizing everything up. While he kept the knife against Harold, the other man used the wide silver tape to strap both women firmly in their chairs. He seemed to know what he was doing and rather than merely taping their hands and feet together, taped each ankle individually to a chair leg and each wrist to the curving wood of the chair arms.

Eden closed her eyes. *Marshall,* she willed, *you stay asleep, you hear me. Don't you wake up and come downstairs. Don't you do that!* Let them take whatever they thought they needed and get the heck out of there before he came downstairs.

"Ok, mister," the man with the knife said. "Where's the cash?"

Harold blew out a long breath and led the man to his desk, indicating a locked drawer.

"Open it."

Harold unlocked it and stepped back. "Not much," he said. "Don't keep all that much around the house."

The man had grabbed a small metal box from the drawer and was quickly flipping through the bills, a scowl building as he did so. "There's got to be more!"

"Afraid not. Off-season like my wife said. Rest of it's in the bank in town. Not safe to keep it lying about, you know."

"Asshole!" the man snarled, striking Harold across the face. He forced Harold back to the dining room where he, too, was taped to a chair. "Might as well see what's in the kitchen. You go. I'll stay here with them. Get stuff that don't need cooking."

They could hear clatter coming from the kitchen as the man opened drawers and cabinets, stuffing items into a pillowcase he'd gotten out of Martha's laundry basket. He'd just come out of the kitchen munching on an oatmeal cookie when a door opened and closed upstairs and Marshall appeared at the top of the steps, calling down, "Eden, darling. I can't find the cough medicine. Did you move the bottle?"

The larger man's eyes narrowed. "You said no one else was here!" he hissed, then put his finger to his lips, motioning his comrade to come quietly on into the dining room as he himself stepped behind a door, knife poised.

Eden was frantic. Marshall had started down the steps. "He's blind," she said, trying to keep her voice low. "Just leave him alone. He's blind, for heaven's sake!"

The men watched Marshall descend the stairs, his hand gliding along the banister. He didn't look very blind to them.

"Eden?" Marshall called again. "Where've you got to, darling?"

"Answer him!" the man in the dining room whispered.

"I...I'm in here," she said, her voice rather unsteady.

"You all right?" Marshall asked, beginning to cross the entryway toward the dining room door, his fingers lightly touching the wall as he moved. He'd left Wadsworth in his room, having only intended to find out where the cough medicine was. Something sharp was suddenly pressed up under his jawbone and he stopped, completely startled.

"Don't move, mister!" an unfamiliar voice rasped into his ear.

This was surreal. Did he really have a knife at his throat? What in God's name was going on? He was aware the man was shifting position, moving more toward his front. Where was Eden?

The man was intently studying Marshall's face. After a long moment he snorted and let out a harsh laugh. "By jiminy we do have ourselves a genuine blind feller here," he called to the other man. He lowered his knife, moving again until the knife was in Marshall's back. "Dining room," he ordered. "You know how to find that?"

Marshall nodded and started forward. His hands were at his sides now and as he moved he forgot about the umbrella stand, almost falling over it. Both men laughed. Marshall pressed his lips together in a tight line.

"You got enough food?" the man with Marshall asked the other.

"Should do. Be better, though, if we had more cash."

"You got a wallet, mister?" The big man patted Marshall's pockets but Marshall had just dressed after his nap and had gone to find the cough medicine before he'd put his wallet or new cell phone in his pants.

"Shit! He ain't got nothing on him."

"Well, get him over to this here chair and let me tape him up anyways. We shouldn't hang around here too long, you know."

"I want to take the woman with us," the man near Marshall said suddenly. "Might need her if the cops get too close. Might come in handy."

"I didn't think we was going to do that. Just get us into more trouble, won't it?"

"You think we can get into more trouble than we're in?"

Eden's heart had nearly stopped. Two escaped convicts were going to take her with them. Horrid thoughts began to run through her mind.

Marshall, still standing with the knife in his back, spoke up. "Wouldn't it make more sense to take me?"

"Marshall, no!" Eden cried.

He ignored her. "Think about it. I won't be able to see where you're going, where you stop. I'll never see your faces, won't be able to pick you out of a line up some day. It would be a lot smarter, if you need a hostage, to take me along."

"He's got a point," the smaller man said. "My cousin was blind and he couldn't do shit."

Marshall was almost holding his breath, waiting for their decision. He couldn't have them taking Eden. Nothing was more important at the moment than that they not take Eden with them. He was also trying not to cough loudly, keeping his mouth closed tightly, attempting to keep the sound more contained.

Bart, the man with the knife, wasn't so sure. The blind guy was large, well-built. He might be trouble. Calvin, the other man, spoke up again. "He can't see. He ain't going to know where we are, where we been. Makes sense, don't it?"

Bart fixed his eyes on Eden. "Keys?"

"Keys?" she repeated blankly.

"Yeah, keys. Car keys."

"My purse. On the coffee table in the room where I was."

Calvin ran in and returned shortly, a set of keys dangling from his finger, several bills and a credit card in his hand. "You ready now?" he asked.

"I guess so." Bart eyed Marshall. "Looks like you've done gone and got yourself what you wanted, mister." He grabbed Marshall by the collar and spun him around. "See if you can find the door, blind man."

They left the dining room, Eden's eyes straining after Marshall. This couldn't be happening! This simply could not be happening. The last she heard was Bart ordering Marshall out onto the porch and Calvin saying, "At least let him get his coat." Then the door slammed and they were gone. She listened to the silence then heard the sound of her car engine starting. She closed her eyes, feeling like she was going to be sick to her stomach. The sound of the car disappeared and everything was quiet again except for the ticking of the mantel clock and the beating of her own heart. Then there was something else. It was Wadsworth, scratching at the inside of Marshall's bedroom door.

Chapter 26

Marshall shivered as he was hustled by Bart toward Eden's car. Bart had hold of the back side of the collar of the solid burgundy flannel shirt Marshall was wearing, pushing him rapidly along the snow-covered walkway. He heard the double-tone sound as Bart used the remote on Eden's key chain to unlock the doors, then found himself being shoved into the back seat. As Bart went around to the driver's side, Calvin got in beside Marshall.

"Here, mister," Calvin said, pushing Marshall's rust-colored leather jacket into his lap.

Bart paused, half in the car, frowning at Calvin. "What'd you do that for?" he growled.

"I went down for grand theft. I ain't no murderer," Calvin said, glaring back.

Marshall got awkwardly into his jacket, a belted one that went just below his hips. He found his long, cream-colored muffler stuffed in the right arm, where he liked to keep it so he wouldn't accidentally end up with the wrong one, and tucked it around his neck. Bart started the engine and as they went down the long driveway, Marshall slid on his leather gloves and whispered a soft, "Thanks," to the man on his right.

At the end of the drive, Bart turned left. Marshall carefully noted that. "Do you...?" he began, but Bart hissed, "Shut up!" cutting him off. He leaned back into his seat. There was nothing to do for the moment but wait and see what the two men had in mind. He was trying to estimate how far they'd travel, keep track of turns. Except for the sound of the engine and the vibration of the car, the only other noise was from the tires on the wet snow of the road and the breathing of the men. His own coughing kept interrupting his listening concentration.

After one more protracted coughing session, Calvin leaned forward toward Bart. "Shit, man, this guy's sick."

"Just a cold, that's all," Marshall said, trying to clear his throat.

"We shoulda taken the damn woman like I told you!" Bart snapped.

"Too late now," Calvin replied, sitting back in his seat.

Thank God! Marshall sighed silently. The mere concept of Eden with these two was unthinkable.

"You know the cops'll be looking for this car before long?" Calvin said.

"I'm not stupid. We're going to have to ditch it pretty soon, find us another one before....."

Woods were on both sides of the two-lane road and a doe had darted suddenly out from the right. Bart braked but the small car swerved on the snow, lost traction, and slid backwards into a culvert. Unbuckled, Marshall flew forward, his chin impacting the front headrest. Stunned for a second, he couldn't seem to move until the taste of blood in his mouth snapped him out of it. Exploring then with his tongue, he found his lower teeth had opened a gash inside his lip.

The next thing he knew was that he was being dragged out of the tilted car, a string of profanities filling the air. "I'd say you ditched the car pretty damn good," Calvin remarked, resulting only in a fresh spew of profane words from Bart.

"Ain't gonna be too hard for the cops to find it here," Calvin continued, surveying the firmly trapped vehicle. They hadn't gotten more than four miles from the inn. "Now what?"

"You know this area better'n me. Where can we get another car?" Bart asked.

"Well, ain't very many places in these parts." He turned his head, looking around. "Best bet might be the used car lot over on the highway. I could hotwire us one of them."

"Where's that?"

Calvin pointed toward the woods on their right. "Straight through there'd probably be quickest. 'Bout five mile I'd guess."

"Shit, man!"

"You want to just walk down this road, then, wait for the cops to come along and offer us a lift?" Calvin pointed out.

Bart looked at the woods. They were part of one of the large state forests that covered so much of the land in this area of Pennsylvania. But the snow on the ground would make it too easy to tell which way they'd gone. About fifty feet further along, a creek crossed under the road. The water was flowing fast enough in it that ice had only formed in the small pools made by the many rocks and along the banks. His eyes shifted to Calvin's feet. "You got them rubber boots from that old man's shed on. I got me an idea. Just a sec."

He popped open the trunk of Eden's car, rummaging around, coming up with a short length of thin rope. With a grim smile he approached Marshall and began tying his hands together in front of him. "I can't walk like that," Marshall said quietly.

"You can't walk with your hands tied?"

"Right. I need to be able to use at least one hand to feel where I'm going."

Bart stepped back, staring at Marshall's unseeing eyes for a moment, then retied it so that Marshall had about a foot of rope between his wrists. "That'll have to do you, mister." With that, he grabbed the center section of rope and tugged Marshall along down the road toward the small bridge.

"What you thinking?" Calvin asked.

"Too easy to track," Bart replied, not stopping until they were at the edge of the bridge. "You got them boots. You make a bit of a fuss with them in the snow that way." He pointed left. "Make it big enough so they'll think we all went that way. Then kinda deliberate-like, just step into the stream and head back this way. Maybe the cops'll think we all just got in the stream down there to cover our tracks. That's the more likely way we'd go anyway. Town's back that way, ain't it? We'd probably go that way to get another car."

"So what're you doing, then?"

"Mr. Blind Man and I'll just step into the stream on this side. You cover our tracks to the edge then head off the other way. He and I'll just go upstream a bit and wait for you 'bout a half mile into the woods."

Calvin nodded. "Makes sense," he agreed.

"You got a watch, Blind Man?" Bart groped for Marshall's left wrist. "Ah!" he was pleased. It had a black leather band with a buckle. No need to untie the guy's hands to get it off him. He passed the watch to Calvin. "Just before you step in the stream, drop this on the bank. They'll think he did it as a signal we took him that way."

Calvin looked at the watch. "What the heck kinda watch is this, anyway?"

"Braille," Marshall said, sighing.

"Yeah, stupid, You think Blind Man here needs a regular person watch?"

Calvin put the watch in his pocket and Bart yanked on the rope so Marshall had to step into the stream. He gasped with the shock of it as the icy waters swirled around his ankles. It wasn't deep, but it completely covered his feet. He heard Calvin stomping around back on the bank, covering their footprints, going back and forth like they'd been trying to decide which way to go then he headed off under the bridge away from Bart and Marshall.

Bart forged relentlessly ahead, just slightly turned so that his right arm could reach back and hold onto the rope. Time after time that hold kept Marshall from falling but it wasn't because he cared if Marshall fell or not, only that he didn't want the delay or the bother of it.

The streambed was strewn with smooth rocks of all sizes, the ones below water wet and slippery, the ones above it glazed with ice and even more slippery. Marshall had never had such a hard time keeping to his feet. He tried to feel ahead with a foot before putting it down, but Bart didn't allow him much chance to do that successfully. He was so concentrated on it, though, that he had no sense of the passage of either distance or time. All that existed was trying to get past the next rock, and then the next, and he coughed so much that finally Bart whirled on him and spat, "Dammit! Can't you shut that up!"

He couldn't. He tried to keep his mouth shut, but couldn't seem to get enough air through his nose alone. "Miserable, worthless...," Bart mumbled as he walked.

The thought passed briefly through Marshall's brain that his captor was obviously of the Spartan school of thought concerning the blind population. He slipped and Bart wasn't fast enough, so Marshall went down hard on one knee, bruising it deeply and getting the lower half of his right pants leg wet. "Idiot!" Bart yanked him to his feet.

So laborious was each passing second that it seemed to Marshall like hours had passed when Bart finally dragged him out of the stream in a place where there were rocky ledges. "Sit!" Bart ordered. They'd wait here for Calvin.

Marshall let his legs fold under him and sat, his breath coming in short, shallow gasps. His knees were bent and he leaned forward, cradling his head in his hands, his whole body shivering. He was still like that when, about twenty minutes later, Calvin showed up, having been able to make faster time because he was alone.

"You drop the watch?" Bart greeted him.

"Yeah, right on a big, flat rock. They'll be sure to see it if it don't get covered with snow." He tipped his head up. The snow had stopped right before the car had slid into the ditch. "Maybe it won't snow no more for a while."

"Maybe. Maybe not," Bart grumped. "But we got to get going. You take him along with you for a while. Arm's tired of hauling the worthless load of shit." He searched around and found a large, broken pine branch. "Go on. Start walking. I'm going to brush these tracks off them ledges."

Calvin squatted beside Marshall. "Can you stand up, mister?"

Marshall lifted his head. "Sure." But he was so stiff with cold that Calvin had to help him to his feet. After they'd gone several yards, Calvin looked back at the man stumbling along behind him. No way was this guy going to make it 4 1/2 miles through these woods. No way.

Bart came along a bit further back, brushing away their tracks until he felt they'd gotten far enough away from the stream. He dropped the pine branch and came up beside Calvin. "Ain't no fun hauling him along, is it?"

"Ain't much fun for him being hauled, I 'spect," Calvin replied.

After two more miles, Marshall was putting one foot in front of the other in what had become a complete mental fog for him. He tripped over a branch buried in the snow and fell flat, taking Calvin down backwards.

Bart scowled as Calvin sat up. He surveyed Marshall, still lying in the snow. "This guy ain't any good at all in the hostage department."

"Well, we got him," Calvin pointed out. "Guess we're stuck with him."

"Maybe not," Bart replied, his eyes scanning around them, fastening on a thick piece of wood about two feet long. He picked it up and walked back toward Marshall.

"Wait a minute!" Calvin cried. "What're you going to do with that?"

"What you think, stupid? I'm going to eliminate the hostage situation."

Marshall had sat groggily up, shaking his head a bit, and Bart was behind him, the wood poised like a baseball bat.

Calvin got quickly to his feet. "Don't do that!"

"Why not?" Bart spat into the snow.

"For Pete's sake, man. He's shit blind. He ain't going nowhere, ain't finding his way out of this forest. Just leave him be. It'll be just as good as whacking him in the head."

Bart looked at Marshall, who was shivering and coughing. "Well," he said, reluctantly dropping the wood, "I ain't going to leave him just sitting there free and easy like that." He walked about ten feet to an old dead evergreen, reaching up to judge the height of several of its jagged branches. "This'll do," he muttered to himself then walked back to Marshall, grabbing the rope and yanking him to his feet.

Marshall swayed, almost falling again, but Bart had a firm grip on the rope and dragged him to the pine. "Come here!" he ordered Calvin. "You hold him up a minute."

With Calvin's arms around his middle so he wouldn't topple over, Marshall's arms were jerked roughly up and Bart slid the rope over the branch. Both men stepped back, Bart with a pleased smile on his face. Marshall's hands were nearly straight up in the air, the rope connecting his wrists now pulled tightly over the branch, keeping him in a standing position.

"Come on," Bart said, heading out.

Calvin looked back over his shoulder. "It's murder," he breathed softly.

"Ain't neither," Bart laughed. "If he dies, he dies. Ain't my doing."

Marshall was so foggy he hadn't even realized what was going on. All he knew was that he was being hauled to his feet again but, then, instead of more endless slogging through the forest, he felt his arms pulled upwards and somehow being held there. It took him a good ten minutes before his head was clear enough for him to even think about what had happened. He stood perfectly still, then, straining to listen. There was no sound from either of the two men. He was puzzled. Had they simply gone? No, they wouldn't do that, would they? Didn't they need him as hostage? He listened more. Still no sound other than the wind clacking frozen branches together over his head.

His left shoulder was aching. The position was straining muscles and tendons too freshly healed. The rope must be over something, something that was holding him up. He tried to reach a bit higher with his fingertips, but the branch was just beyond his grasp. He moved forward a bit, hoping the rope would slide, but it wouldn't. He couldn't see it, but several short, sharp smaller branches off the main one had the rope firmly lodged between them. He could go neither forward nor backward. He tried bending his knees, hanging his weight on the branch. Nothing but a sift of snow onto his face from the vibrations he'd caused. "Eden," he whispered, then coughed so hard and so long he thought his rib cage would crack.

There must be a way! There had to be some way! He was not going to die today, hung up from a tree like some carcass of a deer. Perhaps if he...? He jumped slightly then bent his knees and was rewarded with a small sound like old wood was beginning to splinter. He jumped again, higher this time, letting the branch take the force of his downward plunge. This time it broke about two feet behind him, falling with him as he came down on his knees. It was right above him and as he landed, the branch struck him a glancing blow on his left temple. He stayed on his knees one second, then two, then quiet as the snow, crumpled sideways, the rope still curved over the broken branch.

Chapter 27

Mike Johnson's EMT shift was over and he was driving home in his pick-up, humming along to a Martina McBride song, patting the steering wheel with his left hand in time to the beat. "Whoa, baby!" he said aloud, coming around a curve and seeing a small car canted at an angle in the culvert alongside the road. He pulled over and got out, walking quickly up to the car to see if anyone were still inside. It was empty and he stepped back, studying it. Looked like the one Eden McLaughlin drove. He'd seen it often enough in the lot of the hospital when she'd bring Marshall in for his therapy and also near the inn. He had a habit of stopping by the inn at least a couple of times a week. Not that he'd ever admit to a weakness for Martha's cookies or anything. And now that Eden and Marshall seemed to have taken up long-term residence there, he'd have coffee and a cookie with them before heading home. Wadsworth had gotten quite used to him and when the three of them would go out for a bit of dogcercize, Mike would throw a tennis ball for Wadsworth to fetch.

He tried the driver's door as it was on the up-side of the tilt. It wasn't locked. He reached across to the glove compartment, pulling out a black vinyl folder that held the registration and insurance information. He frowned. It was Eden's car. What the heck was it doing in the ditch with nobody about and the door unlocked?

The sun was just about to set so he got a big flashlight out of his truck, finding tracks that led to the small bridge he'd just driven over. Three sets. One probably Marshall's, but who would the others belong to? He squatted, studying the footprints more carefully. All of them were too big to be Eden's. A deep frown line creasing his forehead, he went back to the car, shining his light over the front seat. Nothing. He opened the passenger door, pausing when his beam crossed the back of the driver's headrest. Damn if that wasn't blood.

Pulling out his phone, he dialed Eden's cell. No answer. He tried the main number at the inn. Also no answer, though he let it ring and ring. Maybe Harold's cell? Nothing there, either. Now that was really strange. Either Harold or Martha was almost always at the inn just in case unexpected guests stopped by.

He dialed another number. "Pete? Mike Johnson here." Peter was the county sheriff. "Listen, I'm here by Eden McLaughlin's abandoned car. I don't think she was driving it and I can't reach her or anybody at the inn. You had any word on anything connected with this?"

"Nothing, Mike," Peter replied. "I've been busy all day myself. Two inmates broke out of Rockview last night. Word was they might've been seen heading this way."

"Pete," Mike said, "I think you'd better come take a look at this car. It's in the ditch four miles toward town from the inn. I'm going to the inn now." He hung up and dashed for his truck, cutting off Peter's admonition for him to wait until a squad car got there. As he drove, he reached into his glove compartment and pulled out a revolver.

For the better part of the afternoon, Eden, Martha, and Harold had struggled to get free. Duct tape turned out to be a much more efficient way to bind someone than rope ever had, and the way Calvin had gone about it, there was nothing for anybody's fingers to reach to loosen, even had there been knots. Harold had succeeded only in making his chair fall over sideways, narrowly avoiding hitting his head on a table leg.

Eden and Martha had talked quietly at times, but mostly sat in silence, terrified for Marshall. Eden had heard the smaller man's remark about the coat as they went out the front door, but she had no way of knowing if they'd let Marshall have it or not. The coat rack by the door was completely out of her sight. Was it still hanging there?

Along toward dark Eden's cell phone rang. It was in her purse on the coffee table in the parlor. Then the phone on Harold's desk began to ring. It rang for a long time before stopping, the sound being almost immediately taken up by the cell in Harold's back pocket. Somebody was trying desperately to get hold of them.

Not very many minutes later they heard the sound of boots running up the walk way, a pause outside the door, no knock, and then the long creak as the old door swung slowly on its hinges. Almost dazedly Eden thought how carefully she listened to sounds these days.

"In here!" Harold shouted, hoping it wasn't the convicts returning.

At the sound of Harold's voice, Mike hurried to the dining room. "Good Lord!" he breathed at the scene before him. "Are you three unharmed?" He knelt beside Harold, quickly taking his pulse and then righting the chair. At first his fingers fumbled with the wide tape, not able to find the ends, then he gave up and pulled out a pocket knife and just sliced carefully through the tape where it touched the chairs.

"We're ok," Harold nodded, "but they took Marshall."

"In Eden's car?" Mike asked.

He looked at Eden, who stood, rubbing her wrists, her eyes sparking with tears. "They were going to take me," she said, not really looking at anyone, "but he talked them into taking him instead."

Mike was quickly on the phone to Pete again, who was half-way to Eden's car. "It's them, Pete. Took Marshall Sinclair hostage when they left the inn. Yeah, everybody here's ok, a bit shook up, but ok. There're tracks by the car, Pete, three males, heading to the creek. Yeah, ok, I'll do that. Thanks, Pete."

Eden clutched his arm. "What are you saying, Mike? Tracks by my car? Aren't they still in my car?"

Mike shook his head. "Didn't get very far, I'm afraid, Eden. Saw it in a ditch about four miles from here. Nobody anywhere around." He decided not to mention the blood on the head rest.

"You said you saw tracks going to the stream?" Harold asked.

"Three sets, yes."

"Probably going to high tail it up the creek bed," Harold surmised. "Make it hard to follow."

"They're on foot?" Eden asked blankly. "Marshall's on foot?"

"Looks like, Eden," Mike said.

She looked at him, her chin trembling. "He's sick, Mike. Don't you see? He can't be out there on foot. He just can't!" Then she remembered his coat and ran toward the front door, followed by a concerned Mike. "Thank heavens it's gone!" she sobbed gratefully. "It's gone!"

"What's gone, Eden?"

"His leather jacket. They let him have it after all." Suddenly her knees didn't want to support her all that well and, holding her elbows, he led her to the couch. "Martha," he asked, "you up for making some hot tea or something?"

"Sure fire," she said briskly, heading for her kitchen, wading purposefully through the mess Calvin had made and putting on a kettle to boil.

Mike sat beside Eden. "You say Marshall's sick? What kind of sick?"

"It started as a bad cold, Mike, but by today he had a terrible cough."

Mike pressed his lips together. Not good.

Mike's cell rang. It was Pete, calling from the location of Eden's car. "I think you should talk with Harold," Mike said. "He can tell you what happened here at the inn."

Harold sat at the dining room table, his forehead leaning heavily on one hand as he described the two men. The ski masks made identification more difficult, but with what he said about their height and weight and manner, there was no doubt as to who they were. Calvin Hobbs, in for three counts of grand theft auto and Bart Sommersby, repeat offender drug dealer, small-time thief, now in for manslaughter.

Eden listened to Harold's voice from the other room. "Do you think they'd hurt him?"

"Now why would they go and hurt him?" Mike said kindly. "He's their ticket out of a tough situation." He had absolutely no confidence in what he was telling her, however.

She sat quietly twisting her fingers together, remembering what Marshall had said about snow back at the beginning of November when he'd stood beside her on the porch as Wadsworth played. *It's not so bad if Wadsworth's in harness with me, but when I'm on my own, I can't tell where I am or where I need to go. Any certainty I have of where I'm going disappears.*

Yes, that's what he'd said. What if the men decided just to abandon him somewhere? He'd be alone, like that, not knowing where he needed to go. A tear tracked down her cheek. If only he had Wadsworth with him.

"Wadsworth!" she blurted out. "He's upstairs, shut in Marshall's room."

She ran for the stairs, the sound of his scratching getting louder. "Oh, Waddy!" she cried, opening the door and falling to her knees beside the big dog. "They took him, Waddy, they've got him." She spoke to him as though he'd understand her words.

Mike had followed her, standing at the top of the stairs, his hand still on the rail, watching her. Wadsworth paused in the bedroom doorway just long enough to permit a brief hug from Eden, then barreled past Mike and down the steps. He padded quickly through the entryway, his nose to the floor, circled around the dining room then went to the front door and began his scratching again.

Harold opened the door and Wadsworth ran to the parking lot, stopping beside where Eden usually parked her car. He lifted his head, sniffing the air, then looked back at the inn where Eden, Mike, and Harold were all watching him from the porch.

"Dog might be of some use," Harold suggested. "Sure wants to find his man."

Mike got on his phone again. "Pete, I've got Sinclair's guide dog here at the inn. Be ok if I bring him down to the creek? He might pick up on some sort of scent that could help."

Marshall stirred in the snow, roused by his own coughing and his need to gasp for air. He had to sit up! He couldn't get his breath lying down like that. Pushing with both arms, he managed a sitting position, then wiped at his temple with one hand, coming away with blood on his glove. He knew there was blood because he touched his finger to his tongue. What he didn't know was if it were day or night. Not that that really mattered to his perception of anything, but it might be good to know how long he'd lain there, how long since they'd left the inn. There was, however, absolutely no way for him to tell.

His head was pounding, had been a good while even before the branch had fallen on him. The rope between his hands was still around the branch and he spent a while figuring out how to work it over the smaller parts that had it pinned. When that was done he pulled his hands as far apart as he could get them. Hadn't been too bad when one of the men had been pulling him along, but on his own he couldn't get anywhere with them bound a foot apart. The larger branch, now lying beside him, had some ragged parts to it where old growth had broken off years ago. He ran his hand along the branch, feeling for the biggest of these then set about rubbing the rope back and forth across it. He had to stop and cough every little bit so it took him some while, but finally the fibers of the rope parted and his arms were free to move. He didn't bother working at the knots on either wrist and so each had a small section of rope dangling from it.

He had almost no feeling in his legs or feet and knew he had to get up, get moving, get some circulation back into them. Using the branch as a prop, he hoisted himself to his feet, wiggling his toes and stomping before he had some returning sensation. That made them hurt like blue blazes. The air temperature had been hovering all day right under freezing and while he'd lain there, had risen a handful of degrees so that the snow was starting to melt a bit. There was a steady dripping of icy water from the limbs above him. He tipped his face, letting some of it drip into his mouth. Despite the cold, his face seemed strangely hot.

Leaning on the branch, he tried to think what he should do. Thinking seemed to take a great deal of effort, but he remembered what Bart had said about his plans to cover their tracks and lead any searchers in the wrong direction. "They aren't coming for you, old boy," he said to himself grimly. "They'll think you're headed to town." He breathed quietly, appreciating a moment without coughing. It was up to him. He knew that. It was up to him to get himself out of this mess. "If it can be gotten out of," he added aloud.

He had no idea which way they'd come from, which way he should go. The stream. If he could only find the stream and follow along, it should lead him back to the road. But where? He took a few tentative steps, his right knee protesting from where he'd fallen on the rocks in the stream. There was a definite slope to where he was. Streams were always at the bottoms of slopes, weren't they? If he went downhill, chances were he'd find the stream sooner or later.

Strong shivering took him and his teeth began to clack together. He couldn't stop them from doing it. He remembered that a lot of body heat escapes through the head and his head had been bare all this while. Leaning the branch against his hip, he used both hands to pull his muffler up and out of his jacket, then wrapped it over his head, tying it in front of his mouth to keep his lips warmer and then tucking its long ends back down in the front of his jacket so they spread across his chest. His chest had begun to hurt when he breathed, like the muscles wanted to pull away from his ribs.

Holding the broken branch like a cane in front of him, and with his left arm stretched out, fingers wide, he started down the slope. He'd gone about fifteen feet before he stumbled over a half-buried rock and fell, rolling maybe ten more feet down the slope before he managed to stop. His tree branch cane was lost somewhere along the way. He got to his knees just as a long coughing spell took him and all he could do was lean forward, his palms pressed on his thighs, coughing and gasping. He knew he should keep going, but he was just so overwhelmingly tired.

His forehead brushed against a low, rather fluffy branch of some sort of evergreen. He stretched out more, feeling beneath it. There was almost no snow under there. Layer after layer of the fat branches hung down, practically brushing the ground and there was a thick padding of years of fallen needles and old leaves. He slid into it on his belly, almost burrowing into the musty-smelling mound, wriggling into it, rolling onto his side, using his hands to scoop it up and over himself as he curled tightly, his knees pulled up, his hands under his armpits. And he slept.

Chapter 28

Eden pulled on her coat. "You're not going without me, Mike Johnson!"

He looked at the set of her shoulders, the raised chin. "All right, Eden, but at least change those shoes for some boots, will you?"

As she sat on a bench to do that, Mike snapped the leash on Wadsworth. The dog had been pacing back and forth at the doorway ever since they'd called him back to the house, making low whining noises in his throat. Mike knew that the bond between a blind person and their guide dog was the absolute peak of thousands of years of human-canine relationship. Marshall had explained to him once that as he and Wadsworth made their way together through the world, Wadsworth completely saw them as a unit. The decisions he made about where to walk were not made based on what was best for him or even what was best for Marshall, but on what was best for *them*. For Wadsworth, now, his other half was missing.

"Ready," Eden announced, tucking her pants' cuffs into the high tops of her boots.

"Hat?" Mike said simply.

She grabbed a knitted cap off the rack. "Hat."

As Mike opened the door, Wadsworth lunged forward with such force that Mike's arm was nearly jerked out of its socket. "Holy cow!" he exclaimed, running to keep up with the usually self-controlled dog. "I've never seen him act like this."

"He's never lost Marshall before," she said quietly.

"What about the gully?"

"He knew right where Marshall was. This is different. Now Wadsworth's hurting."

The winter darkness had settled in completely by the time they headed out in Mike's truck. As they drove down the road, Eden kept her eyes on the blackness of the forest surrounding them. He was out there somewhere. He was either alone or with two dangerous men. She didn't know which was worse. She closed her eyes, remembering him leaning over her chair, his chin on her head, his hands doing marvelous things to her neck. He had to be all right. The world would simply spin off its axis without Marshall to keep it steady.

They arrived where her car still sat at a crazy angle in the ditch. At least seven squad cars, their lights flashing were parked around it. The night shift EMTs were there, too, as well as several men Mike knew from town. He got out of his truck, taking Wadsworth's leash from Eden.

"K-9?" asked a state patrolman Mike didn't recognize.

"Guide dog. Belongs to the man they've taken hostage."

"The hostage is...blind?" the trooper asked, raising his eyebrows. "You hear that, Malloy?"

Another trooper looked over at them. The two of them had just arrived and not been completely filled in yet. The second trooper looked at the dark woods and the snow. "Good Lord!" he said softly.

Mike saw Pete ahead down closer to the stream and led Wadsworth that way, closely followed by Eden. "Pete!" Mike called out. "Got his dog here."

"Good," Pete replied, rubbing his gloved hands briskly together. "Bring him on down and let's see what he picks up."

One hand manning the leash and the other under Eden's right elbow, Mike made his way down to the bank just to the right of where the stream flowed under the bridge. "Tracks lead off that way," Pete said, nodding toward the bridge. "I've got crews working both sides of the creek in that direction. Ma'am," he said, touching his hat brim as Eden approached.

"We've got to find him soon," she said earnestly. "It's not just that he's blind," her eyes brimmed briefly, "but he's very sick."

Pete looked at Mike. "Why in the name of all that's holy would they take a sick blind man as hostage? What on earth were they thinking?"

"It was me," Eden said, her voice low.

"What was that, Ma'am?"

"They planned on taking me, you see," she continued, biting her lip, "but he made them think it would be better to take him."

Pete met Mike's eyes again as Mike shrugged slightly and said, "He loves her."

Pete smiled gently at Eden. "We'll find him, Ma'am. Don't you worry about that. The creek that way runs right past town. I've got officers all over the place there in case they try to steal another vehicle. We'll get them before the night's out."

Wadsworth, however, was not the least interested in the downstream portion of the creek. Marshall's scent came down to the bank and simply stopped. It didn't go either way. But some deep instinct of connection made him pull upstream.

"Now, that is strange," Pete said, watching the dog. "The only tracks go that way, yet the dog says 'no'. What do you make of that, Mike?"

"I think we need to look both directions," Mike stated. "Wadsworth always seems to know where his man has gone."

"All right," Pete sighed. "I'll send a crew upstream, too, then. But it's too dark now to see much of anything. I'll have them do a sweep tonight and if they don't find anything, we'll have to wait till morning, I'm afraid. Nothing to do about it."

"But," Eden protested, "you can't just leave him out here all night. You can't."

"Ma'am, I assure you we're doing our level best and we'll continue to do it, but there's not even a moon tonight and there's only so much can be done in present conditions."

There was a large rock nearby and Eden went dejectedly to it and sat down, holding her mittens to her cold cheeks. Distant flashlights flickered up and down the small stream, accompanied by men's voices. She watched it almost dreamily, thinking how they reminded her of fireflies on a hot July night, neighborhood children chasing after them. Only this was different, cold and deadly and different. Sometime later someone offered her a cup of hot coffee from a thermos. She drank without tasting it. Mike had taken Wadsworth a way upstream, hoping for some eventual sign of a scent. They came back half an hour later, cold and wet, but with Wadsworth still staring off into the upstream forest.

"He's up there somewhere," she said to Mike. "I know it because Wadsworth knows it. He's not downstream. They're just wasting their time." She put a mitten over her eyes. "They're just wasting their time, Mike," she repeated.

"We'll come back at first light, Eden. Everybody will. It'll be easier then, ok?"

"What about him, Mike? What about him all night long? Is that going to be easier for him?"

He knew it wouldn't, but except for a few die-hard searchers who kept looking downstream, everybody else packed up for the night. Pete came up to them. "We'll have patrols out all night," he explained, "especially near the town where they're likely to look for another car. And five of my best men will keep looking all night despite conditions. We'll find him. We'll find them all."

Mike drove her back to the inn. He spent the night in a spare guest room so he could take her to the stream again as soon as the sun was up. She lay miserably in the bed she shared with Marshall, clutching his pillow, hardly closing her eyes all night. Wadsworth, who had a special place he usually slept between Marshall's side of the bed and the chest of drawers, lay with his side pressed against the door, his head cocked, listening.

Marshall was hot and began to push at the needles and leaves that covered him. He reached his right hand out, feeling for Wadsworth. "Ah, there you are, boy!" he said affectionately, then chuckled. "No, no! Now you stop that!" Wadsworth just would lick his face whenever he got a chance. "You want to go out, don't you?" He sat up, his lips curving in a smile. "Give me just a minute, boy, I seem to be a bit tired this morning."

His head was brushing against the low-hanging branches of the evergreen and he batted at them, trying to make them stay away, but they kept getting right back in his face. "Darn curtains!" he grumped. "Wadsworth, 'mind me to get new curtains. I don't think I like these anymore."

He swayed, bracing his hands on the ground on either side. "I'm supposed to go somewhere, Wadsworth," he said, then began to shake with violent coughing. When it was over, he leaned forward, his hands pressed to his body. "Think I broke my chest, Waddy." Despite the pain, he smiled again. Waddy. That's what she called him. Waddy. He liked that. Who was that who called him Waddy? He couldn't come up with her name just then. Oh, well. He liked her whoever she was even if he couldn't remember her name. Putting an arm around Wadsworth's neck, he asked seriously, "Do you 'member where I'm supposed to go?" He didn't know why, but he had this driving urge to go somewhere. Was he late for class? Was that it? He tried to think what he was lecturing on today. "Can't," he said, "can't think what that was."

Crawling out of his little bower, he managed to stand only by clutching at clumps of the evergreen beside him. "Don't feel so good, Wadsworth," he said. "Don't feel so good at all."

He felt for the dog. "No harness? Where'd you go and leave your harness?" He really needed the harness to hold onto, especially since he couldn't remember where he was supposed to go. Maybe Wadsworth remembered and just wasn't telling? That was probably it.

He was really thirsty. "You got a canteen on you, boy?" His legs just suddenly folded and he sat down hard in the slushy snow. Becoming aware his right hand lay palm-up in some sort of little puddle, he lifted a bit of the icy water to his lips. "Good," he sighed, then scooped up more and more handfuls of the snowmelt, finally wiping his wet glove across his face. "Better." His hands found Wadsworth again. "We gotta get going, boy. Someplace I have to be."

He staggered to his feet. Which way? He tried going uphill a few steps but it took too much effort so he turned around and began going the other way. "Come on, boy," he called and walked straight into a tree. He stood there, surprised, feeling the large, rough trunk with both hands. "It's a tree," he announced to Wadsworth. "What's a tree doing here?" He pushed himself away from it, feeling clammy and cold and hot all at once. "I like trees," he said conversationally to the dog. "Do you remember *Evangeline*? Lots of trees in *Evangeline*."

He smiled to himself. He might not remember where he needed to go, but he remembered *Evangeline*, so as he stumbled down the long slope, falling, getting up again, tripping on roots, getting tangled in large bushes, none of it seemed to bother him. He quoted *Evangeline* as he went. Wadsworth had written it, which was pretty darn good for a dog.

This is the forest primeval. The murmuring pines and the hemlocks.
You listening, boy? S'important.
Bearded with moss, and in garments green, indistinct in the twilight,
Stand like Druids of eld, with voices sad and prophetic...

His voice droned on and on in between fits of coughing and times when he fell and had a hard time getting back up. Once, when he'd fallen on his knees, he lifted his head and said quietly, "Downhill. That's where I've got to go...downhill." He still couldn't remember exactly why that was important, but somehow it was. "This is the forest primeval," he whispered again. There was something about that word 'forest'. Maybe the hill he had to go down was there? If he just kept walking, maybe he'd find it?

"Come *on*, boy!" he called again. Wadsworth kept wandering off. He didn't like it. He wanted Wadsworth beside him, where he was supposed to be. He paused, holding onto a slender tree for support. "Wadsworth!" he called as loudly as he could manage. But the dog didn't come. Suddenly he felt terribly, terribly alone. "Wadsworth," he breathed, then his chest hurt so bad he just slid down the tree and sat on the ground. "I miss you," he said, but it wasn't the dog. It was something else...somebody else...someone he yearned for with his whole being.

Every part of him ached and throbbed and all he could manage any more were rapid, shallow breaths, but even those hurt to take. He'd long ago pushed his muffler off his head, but now he untied it completely, letting it drop beside him. "So hot," he mumbled. "Too hot." Yet his feet were almost numb with cold. Very slowly he simply folded forward, then as he slumped to one side, murmured, "Eden, where are you?"

Chapter 29

After an indeterminate time, Marshall jerked awake. "Who's there?" he called. He'd heard a voice. He knew he had.

"It's me, Marshy."

"Jeff?"

"Who else, you dolt!" the voice came affectionately and very close.

"Oh, Jeff! I'm so glad you came!"

"What the heck you doing out here alone, Marshy?"

"Out here?"

"Yeah. You know Mom doesn't like you to go to the park by yourself."

"I'm in the park?"

"What's the matter with you, Marshy? Where do you think you are?"

"I...I'm not...sure, Jeff." Marshall's hands reached out, feeling the ground around him. "I don't think I know."

"You see! That's what worries Mom. She's always concerned that you'll get someplace and not know where it is."

"I think I've done that this time, Jeff. Tell Mom I'm sorry, ok? But I...."

He faded out again.

Eden had slept briefly just before dawn. Wadsworth's whining at the door woke her. Mike was tapping very softly.

"You up, Eden? We can leave as soon as you're ready."

"Just a minute!" she called out, sliding on her slippers and dashing to the bathroom.

She moaned, looking at herself in the mirror as she clutched both sides of the sink. "You look like crap." What did that matter, though?

Quickly she ran a brush through her tangles, didn't bother with any make up, and pulled on her clothes and boots.

Wadsworth onleash, she hurried downstairs. Mike was standing by the bay window on the front of the house, looking toward the lake, sipping from a cup of coffee. Turning at the sound of her steps, he said, "Get a bite first."

"But...."

"I insist."

"Damn you, Mike Johnson," she muttered, only half-serious.

He grinned. "It's my job to make sure folks stay healthy. Off to the kitchen with you, woman! I'm sure Martha's got something you can cram in fast." He knew it was no use to even suggest a sit-down meal. He himself was chomping at the bit to get back to the stream. The day-shift EMTs from his station were already there with their rig and he was eager to join them.

Eden gobbled a blueberry muffin, her eyes misting as she recalled the ones she'd tried to bring Marshall on the dock. Two long sips of hot tea and she was done. "Here!" she announced, striding back to the living room. "Ready to go!"

Mike had tried to feed Wadsworth, but the dog wasn't interested. He lapped up some water, but that was it. "Won't eat," he said to Eden.

"I know how he feels." The blueberry muffin had stuck in her throat and it was only by great effort she was able to get most of it down. Would he have had anything to eat? She knew the smaller guy had taken food from Martha's kitchen. Would they share with him? Was he even still with them?

The number of cars and rescue vehicles near the bridge was almost twice as large as it had been the night before. Eden, however, had a hard lump of dread lodged somewhere just behind her breastbone. Marshall had spent the entire night outside. Had the convicts built a fire that he could warm himself by?

Her eyes passed over the EMT vehicle. Today there was an ambulance as well. Tomorrow would the coroner be present? Pete had said they'd find him before the night was out. Well, it was out and where was Marshall?

A different police van was parked near the bridge and a handler was unloading a bloodhound. Mike smiled eagerly at the sight of it. "That's good, Eden, very good. They'll find them now for sure!"

All Eden had to say was, "Why didn't they use it last night, then?"

"We don't have one as part of the department here. This one is probably brought in from the prison system."

Some vague alarm went off in Eden's head. She wasn't able to put a finger on just why. Curiously, she watched the handler take the dog down to the stream's edge then present it with an article of clothing. The dog headed immediately under the bridge, downstream. Her eyes turned to Wadsworth, who was staring intently at the upstream forest. Silently she walked up to Pete, touching him on his arm to attract his attention.

"Oh, good morning, Ma'am. We hope to have some good news for you before too long."

"Who is the hound trailing?" she asked.

"Ma'am?"

"Of the three men, whose scent is he trailing?"

"Oh, well, that would be Calvin Hobbs, Ma'am. That was one of his prison shirts."

"Not Marshall?"

"Well, Ma'am, it probably doesn't make much difference, now does it? They're all together so if we find one, we find them all."

"How do you know they're all together?"

"Well, we don't, not for sure, but that's still the most likely way of it. They took your Dr. Sinclair hostage for a reason and it doesn't seem it would make sense for them not to keep him with them."

She walked back up to Mike, who had Wadsworth on leash. "The hound's tracking one of the convicts. But look at Wadsworth, Mike, just look at Wadsworth."

Wadsworth was practically vibrating as he stared at the forest. "He's up there, Mike. That's where he is, not downstream toward town. Wadsworth knows."

"Ok," he said, "let me talk to some of the guys. I'll be right back."

"Look, Mike," Pete said after Mike had explained, "as I told the young lady, it wouldn't make any sense for Sinclair to be up that way. The bloodhound knows what he's doing. This is what he's trained for and he's the best and he says Calvin Hobbs went downstream toward town. I think it's more important to send my men where they're most likely to find them, not off on some mystical chase in entirely the wrong direction."

"Is it ok by you if I take the guide dog and go upstream myself? That all right?"

"You got your revolver on the off-chance you're right?"

Mike nodded but Pete still hesitated. "Barry!" he called to a young officer. "I want you to go along with Mike here, ok. Just to cover all the bases." He leveled a look at Mike. "Don't think you'll find anything, but I don't feel right sending you off alone. You keep in touch with me, you hear?"

Mike nodded again and ran back up to Eden. "I'm going upstream myself. Pete's sending one man with me. You got your cell on? I'll let you know if we find anything." He took a long look at her face, then amended that to, "When we find something."

"No, you won't."

"What?"

"You won't have to let me know. I'm coming with you."

"Eden, this is pretty rough country. You shouldn't...."

"Marshall's there. He's blind. Do you think it's rougher for me than for him?"

"I'd rather you...."

"Do you think at this point I give a damn what anybody had rather!" she snapped. "If you won't let me come with you, I'll just go by myself. I mean that. You know I do."

Marshall had awakened again and briefly lucid, remembered where he was. He pulled himself to his feet feeling like twenty pound sandbags were draped over him in abundance. He couldn't straighten his shoulders. It hurt his chest too much when he tried, so he moved in a rather hunched-forward position. "Got to find the stream," he said. "Got to find the stream."

What he didn't realize, even though he was going downhill, was that he was headed diagonally away from the stream Bart and Calvin had brought him up. He managed to locate another fallen branch and used it as a cane to feel ahead of himself. It took so much effort, though, just to hold the blasted thing that he had to stop and rest every few minutes. Every breath came now as a wheeze and his headache was growing worse. When his branch encountered a large log, he sat down, wondering how he would ever manage to stand up again.

A spell of shaking chills took him then and sitting there became too much. He slid off, finding a long snowless patch along the side of the big log. Lying down, he pressed his back to the log and scooped some handfuls of needles and forest debris somewhat over himself before even that became too much effort. Time passed, the chills came and went and came again, then he just drifted away for a while.

"Marshy!"

"Wha...what?" He lifted his head.

"What are you doing, Marshy?"

"Try...trying to stop sh...shaking, Jeff. That's what I'm tr...trying to do."

"Well, why are you shaking like that? You fall in the pond? Mom'll skin you good!"

"Did I f...fall in the pond?"

"Yeah, Marshy, did you?"

"I don't kn...know, Jeff. I don't know wh...why I'm shaking."

"You know you scare her silly when you do things like fall in the pond."

"I...I know, Jeff. I just don't remember if I fell in the p...pond or n...not."

"Don't you think it's time you got up and came home, Marshy? You'll be late for dinner."

"Y...yeah. I sh...should get up," he agreed. He struggled up beside the log. "J...Jeff?"

"What, Marshy?"

"Wh...which way is h...home?"

"Downhill, Marshy. Home is downhill."

"Oh...right," he said vaguely. "H...home. Down h...hill."

He forgot his branch and started walking the length of the long log, trailing his left hand along it as he went. Arriving at the end of the log he found a huge tangle of roots in a massive dirt ball that had been pulled up when the tree fell. "Dirt ball," he said aloud, then finding the concept somehow very funny, chuckled and said, "Dirt ball," again. Then he stepped forward and toppled down the side of the crater left where the roots and dirt ball had once been. The sides were smooth after several years of weathering and covered with mosses and small bits of now bare vegetation. He didn't really hurt himself but just tumbled like a rag doll to the bottom, about five feet down.

Lying there on his back, he wheezed for breath then managed to call weakly, "J...Jeff?"

But Jeff did not reply.

Marshall floated in and out for a minute then finally decided Jeff must have gone home for dinner. That also meant he had to get out of whatever it was he'd fallen into by himself. Vaguely he remembered falling into something else some other time, but it was too long ago to be clear in his mind. He pushed himself to a sitting position, his gloves squishing down into soggy moss. Rolling over onto all fours, he crawled to the wall of the hole, reaching his hand up to look for something to hold onto. It came away with a big clump of moss and a bit of soil. No good. He managed to get to his feet and found his head was just above the top edge of this whateveritwas, so he dug his toes into the moss, jamming them hard until they held, and basically clawed his way up and over the lip, sprawling exhaustedly on the ground. He would be late for dinner. He knew he would.

"I'm sorry, M...Mom," he said. "I tried."

Mike and Wadsworth led the way, followed by Eden, with Barry bringing up the rear. They were picking their way upstream along the bank of the creek. The water level was higher today because of added snowmelt trickling steadily into it. The banks had no clear place for walking but were more a jumble of roots and rocks with now and then sheer dropoffs of several feet that entailed small detours. Wadsworth, though, seemed intent on forging ahead and Eden was gratified to be doing something herself at last.

The going was very slow and Wadsworth seemed impatient at being held back. Mike knew, though, that if he let the dog go, that's what he would do...go. He wouldn't wait for them but would disappear from sight in his single-minded desire to get wherever Marshall was.

Part of Eden wanted that, wanted to let him go so he'd find Marshall. She wanted Marshall to have him with him but, then, the rest of them wouldn't be able to follow, so what good would that do?

Downstream, the bloodhound had trailed Calvin to the point where he'd waded out into the deepest part of the stream in Harold's nearly knee-high rubber boots. The dog stopped, then went out into the cold water himself. One of the officers following behind the team called back to tell Pete what was up. "They probably walked in the stream, trying to throw us off. Give the dog a chance to find where they came out."

Everyone there expected the dog to continue downstream and several eyebrows went up when it turned and headed back for the bridge.

"He doesn't want to keep on toward town," the officer said, calling again. "Looks like we're headed your way."

Pete rubbed a hand across his chin and turned, looking upstream where Mike and Barry had long since disappeared from view.

"Damn!"

Chapter 30

Pete stood quietly, watching Roscoe, the bloodhound, begin to work his way along the banks upstream. Moments before, one of his men had handed him a plastic bag with a man's watch in it. With a Braille readout, there was no doubt it was Marshall's, but Roscoe had indicated clearly after many attempts to track where Calvin might have left the stream, that he'd lost all interest in the downstream area. What that said to Pete was that the convicts had gone downstream, yes, but then circled back. The watch was a clear plant.

Then his phone rang and it was Mike, his voice excited. "Pete, the guide dog really seems to be on to something. We're in an area 'bout half a mile upstream where a bunch of rocky ledges come out from the right bank. Looks to me like someone tried to cover tracks some while ago. Snowmelt makes it harder to tell now, but sure looks that way to me. Dog's all excited. Wants to go up the hill."

"Mike, we'll be coming down your way immediately. You and Barry wait right there. Don't go after them, you hear me. Wait for us!"

Mike relayed this information to Eden and Barry. Evidently Pete had not seen Eden going with them. He knew Pete would be really upset that she was along.

"Wait here?" Eden said, her eyes not moving from Wadsworth, who was straining at the leash so hard Mike could barely hold him. Then her gaze moved up the long, wooded slope. Marshall had gone that way. He was up there somewhere. "Not on your life, Mike. Not on his life."

Barry spoke up. "Ma'am, I'm sorry but we've got to do what Pete said. He's in charge here."

Eden looked at Barry, her eyes flashing. "He's not here." She started up the hill, her boots squishing in the soft, muddy soil beneath the half-melted snow.

Barry ran up, taking her forearm in his hand. "Sorry, Ma'am. I know you're upset, but I can't let you go up there."

Tears sparked on her lashes. "Officer, you can't begin to imagine just how upset I am." With that, she took him by surprise, yanked her arm free of his loose grip and pushed him hard in the center of his chest so that he fell on his rear. Then she took off running up the slope.

No way was Wadsworth going to let Eden go up the slope without him. He scrambled forward, pulling Mike to his knees. Mike, a big man and very strong, had the loop of the leash around his wrist, not just in his hand, so he managed to keep hold of the dog. "You ok, Barry?" he puffed as he scrabbled to his feet, not easy with Wadsworth still pulling so hard.

"Yeah, I'm fine, Mike." He looked with a bit of chagrin at Eden's back getting further away by the second.

"I have to go after her, Barry. You know that. What are you going to do?"

Barry got to his feet, brushing snow off his pants. "The rest of them should be along pretty quick. I'll wait here and make sure everybody goes in the right direction."

Mike smiled slightly. "Not going to be too hard to do." Eden was slipping as she ran, her hands coming down to brace herself, leaving tracks a mile wide.

"Good thing," Barry commented, "that Roscoe won't lose Calvin's scent no matter how she messes it up."

Mike adjusted the position of his revolver. He'd served for years as sort of a back-up deputy in this county of widely-scattered population. Barry observed the motion. "Damn it! I can't let you go up there without me, Mike, no matter what Pete ordered."

With Wadsworth rather heaving Mike along, the two men started up the slope after the determined woman.

Marshall lay quietly, his mind clear again for a bit. Had Wadsworth been with him and left again? He'd swear Wadsworth had been there for a while. Thinking of Wadsworth brought Henry Wadsworth Longfellow to mind again and as he lay there he quoted aloud, poetic phrases broken by coughing:

O what a glory doth this world put on
For him who, with a fervent heart, goes forth
Under the bright and glorious sky, and looks
On duties well performed, and days well spent!
For him the wind, aye, and the yellow leaves,
Shall have a voice, and give him eloquent teachings.
He shall so hear the solemn hymn that Death
Has lifted up for all, that he shall go
To his long resting-place without a tear. *

He'd begun to hear it. Not that he wanted to, but that his body was simply giving out on him and, so, that solemn 'hymn of Death' had been weaving its way through his inner ear for some time now. He knew what it was. He'd heard its beginning notes there in the muddy gully. Eden. She had found him then. There was to be no finding of him now. He knew that, too.

His fingers moved, feeling snow under them. There was something really not right about that. What was it? It took him long minutes to think what it was. It was Eden. Miles had died in the snow. That was how they'd told her they'd found his body, lying still and cold in the snow. That would be how they'd find him some day, if they ever found him. He'd be lying still and cold in the snow and someone would go to her and tell her. Eden. Hearing that...twice.

He lay there, the tactile memory of her hair sliding through his fingers, the smooth skin of her neck, very clear to him. He could hear her voice, hear it when it was full of laughter, hear it when it was full of wanting to know, hear it when it changed timbre in times of passion. Eden.

No. He could not let her hear that news twice. He forced himself to sit up, waiting while a spinning sensation slowly stopped. No. He could not be found dead in the snow. He would not.

Getting his legs painfully under him, he waited again until a spasm of coughing passed before he could pull himself to his feet. Finally standing, holding himself upright with a desperate grip on a young pine, he listened. There was...something. Was it the sound of water moving over stones? It was a bit distant still, but it sounded to him like it might be. The steady drip of moisture from the canopy above made it almost like a light rain now. He turned to face the direction the water sounds were coming from, both arms stretched out, lurching from tree support to tree support. As the burbling of the stream grew nearer, Longfellow still close to the surface of his dimming brain, he said more lines from various poetry aloud. Somehow, the sound of his own voice made him seem less totally alone.

In the green valley, where the silver brook,
From its full laver, pours the white cascade;
And, babbling low amid the tangled woods,
Slips down through moss-grown stones with endless laughter.

He coughed violently, skipped a couple of lines, then went on...

...And here, amid
The silent majesty of these deep woods,
Its presence shall uplift thy thoughts from earth,
As to the sunshine and the pure, bright air
Their tops the green trees lift. **

He stopped. The stream was right in front of him. He listened carefully. The waters were flowing to his right. That was odd. When he'd walked up the stream with the two men, had left it and he'd stood a moment on the bank, the stream had been flowing to his left. He sagged. A different stream. It had to be a different stream. Damn, damn, damn!

He needed to think, but it was so hard. Thoughts came and went, skittering and scattering like a bag of dropped marbles. "Think, Marshall!" he ordered himself sternly.

Ok, it was a different stream. Deal with it. It was at the bottom of the ridge he'd been taken up. He hadn't gone up any other ridge. He hadn't been able to. So this stream had to be somewhere at the base of that ridge, only further over to the side. That meant it probably flowed toward the same general area as the other, didn't it? If he followed it downstream, he'd be going away from the ridge and toward the road, right? If he could find the road, a car would come along sooner or later. He could wait there at the road. That was all he had to do. Find the road and wait there. He could do that.

Exploring near where he stood, he located another branch he could use as a guide cane. He could barely keep on his feet, but he willed himself forward. One more step, he kept telling himself. This step and then one more. On and on and on until he lost track of why he was doing it, only that he must do it.

The going along this particular stream was actually easier than the one they'd come up. Here the water found its way through a flatter valley bottom where, in the summer, tall grasses grew right down to its edge. Now the grass was brown and wet and bent nearly flat under the weight of melting snow. There were much fewer rocks and the trees were widely spaced and easy to locate with his branch. He found, after half an hour of this, that he could let go of thinking almost entirely and just slog along, using his branch as an extension of his arm to avoid rocks and trees. In his mind, he'd locked onto keeping the small stream to his left and just going ahead. Everything else in his brain curled into a ball and switched itself off.

Completely oblivious, he walked along the stream right under the bridge that took the two-lane road over it, never knowing the road was there.

*First Longfellow quote is from *Autumn*
**Second quote is from *The Spirit of Poetry*

Chapter 31

Roscoe was still trailing Calvin, but now that they had a definitive point of departure from the stream already, his handler, followed by a number of armed officers, hurried upstream to the area of the rock ledges. No one was there and Barry and Mike had left a large section of disturbed muddy snow.

"Woman's with 'em," the handler announced.

Pete didn't have to be told who it was. Sinclair's lady friend. Damn, but this was no place for her. Two convicts on the loose and her trailing after. He had no idea she'd gone off ahead of Mike and Barry.

Roscoe, trained to differentiate scents, had no problem picking Calvin's out of the mish mash closer to the stream. Tracks didn't matter to him. It wasn't tracks he followed, it was scent, and Calvin's scent was strong in his nose, having been emitted from his entire body, wafting into the air much like cigarette smoke, were it visible, and settling against trees, rocks, leaving pockets of 'pool scent' on the ground. He started up the long slope, locked onto a track picture.

Barry and Mike had caught up with Eden. She was tired and gasping in lungfuls of air when they came up beside her. "S...sorry," she said, eyeing Barry. "I hope I didn't hurt you."

"That was accosting an officer, you know."

She hadn't thought of it quite like that at the time. She hadn't thought of anything but getting to Marshall. "You going to arrest me?"

He grinned. "Not this time." He knew he'd probably have done the same thing in her shoes.

Now Mike and Wadsworth took the lead, and Barry came along beside Eden, helping her over rough places. They were almost to the spot where Calvin and Bart had separated from Marshall when they heard the sounds of the other officers coming up the ridge not far away. Eden was breathing hard and Mike suggested they wait just a minute to give the trackers a chance to catch up. She had a stitch in her side and didn't have much choice right then.

Pete rounded a section of low underbrush. "I told you to wait," he glowered at Barry, "and what in God's name did you think you were doing in letting a woman come along?"

"I didn't come along!" Eden snapped. "I went and they came, too. It's not their doing."

"You shouldn't be here," Pete said firmly.

"If anybody should be here, it's me," she replied, then indicated Wadsworth, "and him."

Wadsworth was still straining to go further. "Look," Eden said, "none of that matters. All that counts as that we keep going, not standing around here debating who or what." With that, she turned her back on him and started up the ridge again.

"All right!" Pete called after her exasperatedly. "Just let Roscoe take the lead, will you?"

She paused, not turning to look back, waiting silently until Roscoe and his handler and several officers passed her. Wadsworth wasn't at all interested in Roscoe. He was on his own mission and it had nothing to do with Calvin. He pulled Mike slightly to the right of the others and forged his own way forward.

Before long, they came to a small clearing where it was obvious the three men had stopped. Pete wouldn't let anybody into the area until Roscoe had gone in first and gotten a track lock on where Calvin had left it. Sure enough, two sets of tracks led off toward the back side of the ridge. When Pete was sure he knew where the convicts had gone, he let the others onto the scene. There were a lot of footprints going back and forth and it was evident something had happened here.

Wadsworth was bathed in Marshall's scent. He went here and there about the clearing wherever Marshall had been. Tracks led to a big old pine snag. Mike looked up. A dead branch had broken off recently. Directly below where it had been the snow was packed as though a body had fallen there. He looked up at the broken end of the branch still on the tree, then closed his eyes.

Eden saw his face. "What are you thinking, Mike?"

"You won't like it."

"Tell me."

"It's nothing I know for sure, but it's what looks to me that might have gone down."

Both Barry and Pete came closer, looking at the branch and the snow below it. Pete whistled. "If that doesn't beat all!"

"How could they do that?" Barry asked, shaking his head.

Eden, not used at all to crime scenes, had no idea what they were referring to.

Mike licked his lips. "Eden...."

"Mike!" she cried.

"Ok. To me," he paused, "from what I see here, it looks like...it looks possible...that," he licked his lips again. "It looks like what they did was decide not to take Marshall any further with them."

Her eyes widened. "So what did they do with him?"

"Ma'am," Pete broke in, "it's likely they had his hands tied and decided to hook him over the branch that's...," he pointed toward the jagged broken end on the tree, "that's been broken off here."

Eden's knees felt weak and Barry grabbed her elbow. "You mean, you're saying that they went off and left him tied to a tree?"

"Basically that, yes," Pete continued, rubbing his hand across his chin.

"His hands up over a branch, up high like that?" she murmured, looking up.

"'Fraid so, Ma'am."

She looked around. "But...but where is he now?"

Wadsworth was done with the area under the tree and was now straining in a different direction. "I think the dog is trying to tell us," Mike said.

"Look, Mike," Pete sighed. "I've got two convicts on the loose here and a hound who wants to trail 'em. I'll send Barry and two more of my men with you to find the professor, but the rest of us will have to go after the other two. I need to find them before they hurt anybody else. Looks to me like the guide dog will be all you need to find the guy anyway. And now we know nobody who's armed or anything is with him, so it'll be safe going that way. I'll alert the rescue team where we are, which way you're going, so they can cut across and meet you, all right?"

Wadsworth only went a short way before he came to the place where Marshall had fallen and then dragged himself under the low branches of the thick evergreen to sleep.

"Smart," Mike said, nodding his head. "Good place for him to go. Wish he'd stayed there, though."

"He probably figured nobody was coming up this way to look for him," Eden commented grimly, "and he was almost right."

They continued on down the slope. "Look at the tracks he left!" Barry said with another soft whistle. He'd never seen anything like them. They zigzagged down the slope with very plain indications of where Marshall had fallen again and yet again.

A tear tracked coldly down Eden's cheek. What had he been through? What was he going through now? How many times could he fall and still manage to get up again? And was he doing it with his hands tied? She remembered what he'd said about how he needed his hands.

When they came to the huge fallen tree, Wadsworth sniffed along where Marshall had lain, his back against the trunk, then went straight to the gaping hole beyond its root ball and looked down.

"Not there!" Eden sighed, her heart breaking. "He didn't...."

But when she, too, stood at its edge, there was the impression in the soft, snowy moss where a man had lain, its outlines marred when he'd gotten to his knees. All of them looked across to the far side, where large sections of moss had been ripped loose in his effort to get out of the pit. She closed her eyes again. The sight of his struggle to climb the far wall tore too much at her heart.

A tiny spring, not more than six inches across, flowed into the stream from the right. It came down over a flat rock upon which grew a hairy, stringy sort of moss, its delicate little tendrils weaving in soft patterns as the thin layer of clear water washed continuously over it. Marshall's right foot came squarely down atop it and the silky strands proved slipperier than ice, sending him crashing forward. He fell onto the tall bent grasses, the impact of it jarring him out of his stupor and into some semblance of consciousness.

A patch of crystallizing snow lay under his cheek and he extended his tongue, licking moisture from it. Where was he? He couldn't seem to tune into where he was or why he might be there. He found he couldn't breathe while lying on his chest but wasn't sure he could manage actually rolling onto his back. A few moments of gasping and not getting any air, though, gave him the impetus to try and he pushed with arms and legs, getting himself up onto his left side. He lay there listening to the sound of water burbling past rather close behind him. Had a pipe broken? He couldn't remember the name of the plumber his father had always used. O'Donnell? Was that it? O'Connell? Something like that. He'd have to look it up, but not right now.

He rolled, finally, onto his back, a movement which resulted in the back of his right hand coming down in the edge of the stream. Darn bathwater was way too cold. He pulled the hand up, letting it rest across his chest, but the weight of it seemed to hurt his ribs.

What had he been doing? Oh, yes, he'd been lecturing on Longfellow. Poor Longfellow. He'd loved sweet Mary Potter so much he'd followed her home from church, so struck by her beauty he couldn't bring himself to speak to her. But he'd married her, by God, he had and settled her into a house surrounded by elm trees. He took her to Europe with him. She died, young, in Rotterdam. Poor Longfellow. So he taught at Harvard for seven years, going about in his flowered vest and yellow gloves, his hair flowing behind him. Then he married Frances, Frances who gave him two sons and three daughters. For them he wrote *The Children's Hour.*

"Grave Alice and laughing Allegra and Edith with the golden hair," Marshall murmured aloud. But Frances, trying to save locks of her children's hair, attempted to seal the packages with wax and matches and the hair burst into flames. Frances was gone. So he translated Dante into English and went to Europe again. Poor Longfellow. He lost both his loves. Like Eden. Eden lost both her loves in the snow. Poor Eden.

The thought jarred him as much as the fall had. That was what he'd been doing, trying to keep Eden from becoming Poor Eden. Oh, God, yes! That was it!

He sat up, having to hold his rib cage so the bones didn't spurt out and fall in his lap. The stream. Surely he would come to the road before much longer? Hadn't he been stumbling alongside it for several days now? How far could the bridge be?

Getting to his knees, he felt around for his branch, finding it lying halfway into the stream. His legs hurt. He'd fallen so many times there was no place on them that was not bruised and aching, but it was his chest that hurt more than all the rest of him. He could only manage short, shallow little breaths but each of them impaled his chest wall on some celestial hook. After several minutes, he paused, a loneliness so vast washing over him he'd never known its like.

"No, Marshall," he gasped aloud. "Don't go there. You don't have to go there."

The sing-song rhythm of *The Song of Hiawatha* came to him. There was something comforting in the steady consistency of the meter of the thing, as though one were following a long string through a tunnel, rolling it up in your hands as you went.

Lonely in the sky was Wabunn
Though the birds sang gaily to him,
Though the wild flowers of the meadow
Filled the air with odors for him,
Though the forests and the rivers
Sang and shouted at his coming,
Still his heart was sad within him,
For he was alone in heaven.

He didn't know his cheeks were wet with his own tears as he spoke the verse. Eden. He wanted Eden and his heart now ached with the wanting more than his chest ached with the breathing.

Eden.

Downward through the evening twilight,
In the days that are forgotten,
In the unremembered ages,
From the full moon fell Nokomis....

Those four lines had always been his favorite Longfellow ever since he was a boy and had first memorized them. Back then he'd fallen in love with the sound of them, now he was in love with the meaning of them.

Eden.

He knew he'd loved her through all the unremembered ages since before the creation of the world.

Eden.

Feeling himself starting to crumple, he gripped the branch with both hands, determined to keep on his feet. His right hand was curved over the top end of the branch and he leaned forward, resting his chin on it. In the quiet of the moment he became aware of a new sound, one he'd heard before. It was the lapping of the lake against the rocks along its shores. He knew it was. He straightened. How had he gotten to the lake? The road lay between him and the lake and he'd never crossed the road, had not intended to cross the road, had planned he would stop there and wait.

Head lifted, he listened. A distant motorboat went by. It was definitely the lake. The inn was just back from the lake, but which way? When they'd left the inn in Eden's car, Bart had turned left out of the drive. That should mean the inn lay somewhere, that way. He turned, extending his branch, moving it from side to side, checking his path. He'd have to cross the stream. He'd definitely have to do that. Perhaps better here than where it flowed into the lake. Might be deeper there. Have to get his feet soaked again, but there was no help for that.

Ok, it seemed he could get down into it right where he was. No big rocks. He jabbed the branch down, testing the bed of the stream. Didn't seem deep. Maybe not more than four or five inches. Repeatedly jabbing the branch down, he made it across. The further bank was low, the bent grasses continuing on that side.

Following down the opposite bank, he got to where he was only a few yards from the lake. His diagonal path down the ridge had, all by accident, put him out not more than five hundred or so feet from Harold's dock. He didn't know that, though, had no way of knowing that, but he had found the lake and, by God, the inn was somewhere on the lakeshore.

Mike paused at the thinning edge of the forest where the grassy field began to lead down to the smaller creek. Marshall's trail led clearly toward the creek, not straight at all, still zigzagging wildly, yet toward the creek. Excitedly he got his phone out, calling his EMT crew. "Butch," he said, "Mike here. Look, buddy, we're just coming out of the state forest by Miller's Run. Looks like Marshall has made it to the creek all by himself. Don't know how he did it. But if he did what I think he did, he'd have followed it down to the road. You guys get down to the bridge over the run and see what you find there."

He turned to Eden. "This is good, Eden. This is really good. Looks like he made it to the bridge, that first one that's closer to the inn."

Her chin trembled with a combination of exhaustion and relief. "He might be there?" she asked hopefully.

"Or somebody might've picked him up. Maybe that."

They were following the creek when Mike's phone signaled. "Butch? Marshall there? No? What? Under the bridge? Look, Butch, I can see you guys now." He waved. "Be right there."

"He's not by the bridge?"

"No, Eden. He's not. Butch is going down to the stream to check for tracks. See what's up." Marshall's path along the stream was easy to see. How had he missed the bridge? Where had he gone?

When they got to the bridge, Butch and two other men were down beside the creek. "He walked under the blamed thing, Mike. Just walked right under it."

Standing there, Mike could understand how that had happened. The bridge was small, but high, with plenty of room for a man who couldn't see to pass easily under it and not know it was there.

"Damn!" he said. Wadsworth led him under the bridge and Marshall's tracks continued down the stream. "Heading toward the lake," he murmured. "Probably doesn't know it, but he's heading toward the lake."

"Is that good?" Eden asked.

"Probably, yeah. He gets to the lake, he'll have to turn left or right. Let's hope he turned left. Inn's not far down that way."

"The inn? This puts us close to the inn?" Even sighted, she'd lost all sense of direction in the forest.

He was at the end of things. That he knew. He'd come to the end of himself. It was taking as much effort to hang onto consciousness as it was to keep plodding along. And he was simply on fire. With trembling fingers he unbuttoned his jacket. It was too hot. He'd taken a wrong turn somewhere, had passed through Purgatory, and was now entering hell itself. The flames of it licked up his body, lingering with their embered fingers on his cheeks, his forehead.

Vaguely, he knew that if he fell again, he wouldn't get up. There was no more getting up left in him. His little gasps of breathing were getting shallower and shallower. He dropped the branch, no strength left to hold it longer, just plodding, one foot, another foot. On and endlessly on.

The top of his head had exploded a while back. He knew that because he could feel the wet dripping of his brains down past his ears, curving under his chin. It wasn't sweat. It had to be his brain. He felt a definite trickle down his spine. Yes. Soon it would reach his feet and he would step on it and then he'd be gone. Maybe that wouldn't be so bad. Maybe everything would stop hurting.

Eden.

He couldn't die in the snow because of Eden.

He cupped both sides of his cheeks with his palms. Maybe he could just push a little of his leaking mind back...up? Maybe he could put one foot in front of the other a while more? His right shin impacted the hard edge of something and he fell forward, lying half on-half off whatever it was.

It was Harold's dock. But he didn't know that.

Chapter 32

Even though they'd walked the better part of the day, now they ran. Mike had Wadsworth's leash in his right hand and Eden's hand in his left. She ran with her mouth open, gasping for breaths in the cold air, but she ran as fast as she could. When they got to where Marshall had crossed the creek, Wadsworth splashed across it with hardly a break in his stride. Eden almost fell, but Mike kept her on her feet. When the trail turned left near the lake and they knew he'd gone in the right direction, Eden panted, "Let him go, Mike. Let Wadsworth go now."

They paused only long enough for Mike to unhook the leash from the dog's collar and Wadsworth was off like the proverbial shot, his large body moving in a long stride that sent him along the shoreline much faster than the humans could keep pace.

He ran along the scentline of his other half, actually beyond scenting, running now only on heart and instinct. He knew. Nothing else existed for him now but this knowing. He rounded a curve in the shoreline, heading like an arrow for the dock.

Still running, Mike called his crew. "Get to Harold's," he panted. "Our man's there." He also called Harold, alerting him. He didn't know if Marshall had made it to the door or what. But he'd definitely made it.

When she got around the curve, Eden saw Marshall. Stumbling, she started to fall, quickly steadied by Mike. "Oh, God!" she gasped. "It's him!"

Both Harold and Martha had shrugged on coats and as they were coming out on the porch, saw Eden, Mike and the others running along the shore from the right. The EMT vehicle, lights flashing, raced down the drive and whipped to a stop at the near end of the parking area.

But Wadsworth was already there, had circled around Marshall twice, nudging him with his nose and, getting no response, settled near his head, his long muzzle resting across Marshall's temple.

Marshall had fallen forward when his shin struck the plank edge of the dock. He lay from the waist up on the wet boards, his arms curved around his head, his left cheek down, so that his face was turned away from the house. His legs rested on the ground, about three feet in from the shoreline where the dock was built low to the land. He had been right. It was his last fall. There was no more getting up.

Mike was the first to reach him, having to physically push Wadsworth to the side so he could tend to Marshall. His fingers flew to take a quick pulse. Still alive, but racing on overdrive. He touched his cheek. Burning hot. He was just gently turning Marshall on his back when Eden ran up.

"Is...is...?"

"He's alive, Eden, but he's sick." His eyes met hers gravely. "And I mean really sick."

Butch dashed up with a med kit. They turned Marshall so his legs were on the dock and Mike listened to his chest, his own lips set grimly. "Think it's pneumonia?" Butch asked softly.

Mike nodded. "Get the stretcher up here!"

Eden was on her knees on the other side of Marshall, her hands hovering over him as though if she touched him, he might break or dissolve or otherwise disappear before her eyes. His lips were parted, his breaths coming in painfully short little gasps. He tried to swallow, seemed to work at the effort of it for ages without an intake of breath, then finally managed, gulping at the air like some landed trout, but not really getting any. Mike clapped an oxygen mask on him and before Eden knew what was happening, Marshall was on the stretcher and two men were hurrying with him to the open back doors of the emergency vehicle, Mike running beside it, holding equipment. They hustled him into the vehicle, one of the men starting an IV while Mike got on the radio to the hospital.

It was all a blur to Eden, who heard words like "cyanotic", "possible involvement of both lungs," "extreme respiratory distress." Wadsworth stood with his front paws on the rear bumper, whining. Both he and Eden had ridden in the vehicle on the day she'd met Marshall, but now Mike leaned out the back. "Sorry, Eden. Got the whole crew this time. I'm really sorry, but you and Wadsworth will have to find...."

"I'll take them," Harold announced firmly. "You go ahead, Mike. We'll be right behind you."

Martha looked at Eden. The young woman seemed ready to fall over herself. Dark smudges lay under both eyes; she was wet and dirty and looked on the point of exhaustion.

Martha put her arms around her, leading her to their car as the rescue vehicle's sirens and lights came on and it began to speed down the drive.

Harold drove and Martha sat in the back seat because she didn't want to take her arms from around Eden. Wadsworth perched, tense, panting, to Eden's left.

"I...I...didn't get to touch him, Martha," Eden whispered, her voice breaking. "After all this time, I didn't get to touch him." Tears began to track rapidly down both cheeks.

"You will, dear heart," Martha soothed. "Really soon. You will."

"I don't think he knew I was there," Eden continued in her cracking little whisper. "I don't think he knew anybody was there." She wiped at her cheeks. "Did you see his face, Martha? Did you see his face?"

"Hush, sweet one. It'll be all right now. You'll see. It'll be all right."

Eden tipped her chin up. "He did it, you know. He did it all by himself. All that way. By himself."

"How in blazes he do that?" Harold wondered aloud. "Didn't think it was possible. All that way. And sick, too."

Eden's hand went to her neck. She'd found Marshall's muffler in the forest and even though it was damp, splattered with mud, and spotted with bits of pine debris, she'd wrapped it around her neck. Now she twisted its long ends around and around her hands. Right at the moment, it was all she had of him. Then Wadsworth whined, his nose pressed to the window, and she knew she had more than a muffler.

When she got to the hospital, Marshall had already been whisked away to some deep inner part of the emergency department. She had to wait. On a dark green vinyl seat with a long crack in it, she waited, twisting the muffler in her hands, Wadsworth half under the chair, his forequarters between her boots, whining softly now and then.

She closed her eyes, her mind going over the long trail Marshall had made, seeing again all the mashed snow where he'd fallen, the little place under the low pine where he'd nested, the pit at the end of the fallen tree. How had he managed? How had he kept going for so long?

Martha had her own worries for Marshall, her own rather profound motherly concern for him, but she tried to set it aside and offer only comfort to Eden, not wanting her to know she could use some herself. She went to the cafeteria, trying to pick out simple things for Eden, and sat beside her, offering her nothing whole but her heart. The food she placed in Eden's fingers little bits at a time, watching as the young woman sometimes lifted them to her mouth rather unaware.

After several weeks, or was it years, Mike came into the waiting room, squatting by Eden, one hand on her knee, the other stroking Wadsworth neck. "They're still working on him," he said, his voice gentle, quiet. "I'll let you know when you can see him, ok?"

He stood and Harold followed him toward a coffee machine. "How bad off is he?"

Mike looked back across the room at Eden, shaking his head. "Bad, Harold, real bad."

"Any danger the young fellow might not...?"

Mike shut his eyes and nodded.

"Lord," Harold sighed, "and her already a widow 'n all." He looked at Eden. "You going to give it to her straight?"

Mike sighed. "I don't know. Guess that's up to what the doc decides to tell her."

"Who's tending him?"

"Hersholtz."

"Good man. He'll do right by him."

"Problem is, Harold, when Marshall was already sick and should've been warm in bed, he was out there in the icy water, climbing hills, falling over and over. I lost count of how many times I could tell he'd fallen. Just so damn many times. And this thing got a really deep grip on him while he was out there. Temp's a bit over 104. He had to be fighting for breath for hours."

"You've got to remember, Mike, she followed every step he took. She knows where he went, saw the places with her own eyes. She's got to have a pretty good idea what he went through."

Mike looked back at Eden again. "You should've seen her, Harold. Pushed Barry down flat when he tried to stop her going up Cooper's Ridge. Didn't take any guff off Pete, either. Just spoke her mind and did what she needed to do. Then she stayed right with Wadsworth and me no matter how rough the going got but, you know, Harold, every minute that I was up there on that ridge and then making my way down to Miller's Run, hard as it was to get through there, I kept thinking, good Lord, what if I was doing this with my eyes closed? Once in a while I'd even shut them, just trying to get the feel of it, but I knew where I was. He wouldn't know that, wouldn't know what lay in front of him or either side, which way was easier. I can't even imagine what that was like for him." He shook his head slowly. "Just can't imagine."

"They confirm pneumonia yet?"

"'Fraid so, Harold. Both lungs. Settled in real good, like I said."

Harold sighed, looking across the waiting room where his wife sat tending to Eden. "Martha's gone and let herself get all attached to that feller, almost like he was one of her sons. Be hard for her, too, if he doesn't pull through."

More time passed. Eden dozed briefly on Martha's shoulder. Mike took Wadsworth outside for a bit. It seemed like everyone in the small, rural hospital remembered Marshall and Wadsworth from their previous time there just over a month and a half ago. Everyone who saw Wadsworth wanted to stop and pet him or talk to Mike. Wadsworth, though, wasn't having any of it. He was on edge, making a lot of little noises, constantly on alert and watching. Not once in all that time that he sat under Eden's chair did his head go down on his paws. He'd found Marshall only to have him taken away moments later and now there was no scent of him in this waiting room. It was not where he wanted to be. Running in the track of Marshall's scent in the forest had been better than this.

A man in scrubs, with glasses and a fringe of white hair circling his head, walked into the waiting area. He came straight to Eden. She and her little group were the only ones there this evening. He introduced himself as Doctor Hersholtz. He was going to let her see Marshall briefly but not Wadsworth, not yet anyway. Marshall was in the ICU right now. It was no place for dogs, he said firmly. Mike had to hold on tightly to Wadsworth's collar as Eden walked away with the doctor. She could hear his feet scrabbling on the tile floor behind her and her heart broke for him.

As they walked, Hersholtz talked with Eden about Marshall. He had severe streptococcus pneumonia in both lungs, had been cyanotic when he arrived at the hospital because his lungs weren't able to oxygenate his blood well enough. He told her Marshall was on oxygen therapy and intravenous antibiotics and that she would see an oxygen mask as well as various tubes and wires that were monitoring his heart and other vital functions.

Ok, she thought. He'll have IVs in his arms and one of those clear things they gave you oxygen through. That would be all right. He'd had that back at the end of October. She walked into his room, finding the bed cranked up a bit to ease his breathing. The oxygen mask was there and an IV was hooked up to his left arm. His hospital gown had been put on so it opened to the front and there were several wires attached to his chest, which she figured must go to the heart monitor. What she wasn't quite prepared for was the tube that disappeared inside him between two of his ribs. She couldn't say exactly why, but it was the sight of that tube in that place that rather got to her. His eyes were closed and once in a while his head turned restlessly back and forth on the white pillowcase.

"The tube, there...," she indicated his ribs. "Why is that there?"

"He's dealing with a pleural effusion, I'm afraid.'

Why did he have to add the 'I'm afraid', she wondered silently, waiting for him to explain.

"Fluid has accumulated between his pleura, that's the thin, transparent membrane covering his lungs, and the membrane that lines the inner surface of his chest wall. When the pleurae around the lungs become infected, it's called pleurisy."

She'd heard of that, but never really understood just what it was. "What does the tube do?"

"Well, Marshall's fluid has become infected as well. That's empyema, and we have to drain it because antibiotics don't penetrate well into the pleural cavity."

"What does all that mean?"

"It means he's very, very sick. We're hoping to prevent sepsis or the need to intubate him."

"You mean he might need to be put on a respirator?"

"We're hoping it doesn't come to that.

"But it might?"

"It might, yes," he nodded.

Marshall mumbled something.

"Is he conscious?"

"Not really," Hersholtz said. "Man's had one hell of a time. We're trying to get his fever down but he's got an excess build-up of carbon dioxide in his blood. I imagine he's had a heck of a headache due to that, and that build-up, in itself, causes disorientation that leads into a semi-conscious state. That'd be bad enough even if he'd spent the last twenty-four hours in bed, but he didn't. Man went to his physical limit and then kept going, wet and freezing cold, to boot. Had some light frostbite on his feet, but we're tending to that and it should be ok. But as my grandfather would say, 'He's plumb give out.' I truly have no idea how he didn't die on that ridge."

He looked with an assessing eye at Marshall. "His total exhaustion combined with all this makes it harder for him to fight, you see. He fought so long just to get off the ridge, he hasn't got much left in him to fight this sickness that's trying to take him down."

"It's not going to take him down, Doctor," Eden said. "I'm not going to let it."

"That's why you're here, Ms. McLaughlin. I want you to talk to him, let him know he's got someone he needs to fight for." He turned to go. "Don't mind if he doesn't seem to hear you. You talk to the man anyway."

When Hersholtz had gone, she pulled a chair as close to the side of the bed as she could get, gently enfolding his right hand between both of her own. His right ring finger was in a splint. Her eyes roamed over what she could see of him above the bedding. He was clean now, but the washing also served to reveal the deep bruises forming almost all over him. She'd thought his experience in the gully had bruised him, but that was nothing compared with now. At one time or another as he'd struggled down the long ridge, almost every part of his body must have impacted rock or tree or stump. She couldn't see his legs, but she'd seen the marks in the snow where he'd fallen to his knees over and over.

She kissed the back of his hand and leaned closer, her mouth close to his ear. "I'm here," she whispered. "It's Eden, Marshall. I'm right here beside you, my love. You made it. You showed everybody and you made it back, all the way back to the inn, Marshall, all the way to the inn. Now you've got to make it back from this hospital room. You hear me? There's this bed in our room upstairs in the inn and I need you beside me in it. I need you beside me," she choked a bit, "in my life, Marshall Sinclair. You hear that? I love you. Please, Marshall. Please don't leave me." Tears again tracked down her cheeks.

His head turned a couple of times, his lips moving slightly. It seemed like he was trying to say something but she couldn't make it out.

"What, Marshall? What are you saying?"

He mumbled something unintelligible, then very faintly she heard, "Snow. Can't die... in snow. Can't tell Eden...died in snow. Can't." His head turned more. "No. Not in snow. Can't. Not Miles. Can't."

She sat back in her chair, her lips parted. She understood what he meant and more tears came.

Leaning forward again, she said firmly, "Yes, Marshall, that's right. You can't die in the snow like Miles. You can't. You've got to fight. You hear me? You've got to fight to come back to me."

"Fight," he mumbled then faded too much for further words.

She sat beside him for as long as they'd let her, stroking his hand and arm, talking to him. When they made her leave, she was surprised to find Martha and Harold still in the waiting room.

"Wanted to drive you home for a change of clothes, maybe a hot bath," Harold smiled.

Suddenly the both of them seemed unutterably dear to her and she let them guide her to Harold's car. Mike had been walking Wadsworth and came, putting the dog in the back seat. He stood silently under a streetlight, watching Harold's car as it turned out of the lot.

Eden held out her hands and Wadsworth could smell Marshall on them. It was as close as he'd be able to get for a while.

Hersholtz had told her to get some sleep, that she'd have a long vigil ahead of her and she was too done in herself right now. He promised the hospital would call if anything changed in the night. As they drove back to the inn, Eden explained what the doctor had said about Marshall's condition. Harold just pressed his lips tightly together as he drove home in the winter night.

Eden bathed and, wearing a thick flannel nightgown, the one Marshall liked the feel of the soft material, she got in bed. Wadsworth lay against the door as he had the night before, but she called him over and dropped Marshall's muffler down where he could sleep beside it, but he picked the muffler up in his mouth and carried it to the spot by the door, setting it down and finally lowering his head to let his muzzle rest atop it.

Chapter 33

The tired voice went on.

"He's at it again," the night nurse said, standing in the doorway of Marshall's room. "I have no idea what it is, but he's been doing it off and on a good part of the night."

Maria was just starting her shift, taking over from Betty, who was going home. Quietly, she walked into the small ICU unit where Marshall lay, his head moving on the pillow. The low voice continued. Maria smiled, checking his IV drip.

Pete and his men had tracked Calvin and Bart out of the forest near the highway the afternoon of the previous day. Within two hours the escapees were surrounded in the back lot of the used car dealer's and apprehended. Mike arrived at the inn the following morning to drive Eden to the hospital, sharing the good news. He took Wadsworth outside for a bit and the dog presumed he was going with them, but today Wadsworth had to stay with Martha and Harold in the inn.

"I feel so bad for him," Eden said as they drove away.

"I'll come back and walk him at lunch," Mike commented. "At least let him get out a bit. I don't think either Harold or Martha could manage him, not the way he is right now wanting to get to Marshall." He looked sideways at Eden. "How're you holding up?" She still had dark smudges around her eyes.

"I'm ok. I just need for him to be all right, you know. He didn't know I was with him when I was in his room yesterday. I called the hospital this morning and they said he was still about the same."

"You being with him, Eden, that's got to make a difference. He'll pull through for you." He glanced at her again as he drove.

Hersholtz decided Marshall needed every bit of anything that might help him, so he was letting Eden stay longer today. She entered his room while Maria was still there, marking something in his chart.

"How is he?" Eden asked.

Marshall's lips were moving as the odd-sounding syllables flowed out, his head still doing that restless turning back and forth.

"He is by the sea," Maria smiled.

"By the sea?"

"He sits on the same rock every day for seven years, gazing out to sea, weeping for his home and his beloved."

Eden was lost. "Who? What are you talking about?"

"Odysseus," Maria replied, looking fondly at the man in the bed. "Book five of the *Odyssey*."

"Ulysses? Homer?"

"Yes, he's been quoting it ever since I came on duty."

"Greek? He's speaking Greek?"

Maria nodded.

"And you understand?"

Maria pointed to her name tag: Maria Papadopolous.

Eden came closer to the bed, listening carefully. It was so good to hear his voice, always, but this had some sort of flow and rhythm to it that was very different, and was lovely to her ears, especially when spoken in his deep voice despite the soft level of it at the moment and muffled by the oxygen mask. But he didn't know she was there. She could tell he was unaware of her presence.

"Is...is it all right if I stay?"

"I'm finished for now. Dr. Hersholtz should be by on morning rounds before long. He can answer any questions you have."

Eden stood beside the bed a while, simply looking down at Marshall. Wherever he had gone in his mind, he was by the sea somewhere, yearning for his beloved. Her eyes misted over as he spoke the ancient words and for a moment she covered her face with both hands. Mike, in the hallway, watched her, hating all the anxiety she had been through, was still going through. Then he grinned slightly, remembering her facing down both Barry and Pete yesterday. She had guts. He watched her a moment more then left to start his EMT shift.

She finally sat where she had the evening before, taking his hand again. She needed not only to be close, but to hold whatever part of him she could. He was here. He was alive and he was here. Her eyes kept straying to the chest tube. It didn't seem right it should be there, going into him like that. She didn't like that they had cut between his ribs to get it where it was. It was good for him. That was what mattered. But she didn't like it, still, didn't like that his chest...his...had it there, so out-of-place, an ugly thing protruding there from his beautiful chest.

Hersholtz and Maria came back and she was asked to step outside for a while, told she'd be called when she could return. She wandered back to the waiting area. Mike was there by the coffee machine, having returned to the hospital already from a near-by run where a small boy had gotten his hand caught in a grate.

"How's it going?" he asked, getting her a cup.

"I just wish he knew I was there, Mike."

"They get that fever down, oxygenate his blood some more, he'll come 'round. You'll see. He'll be fine."

She smiled at him. "I don't know what I'd have done the last couple of days without you, Mike. You got me through. Still are."

He smiled back, his graying moustache curving up with his lips. "You're special folks, the both of you," he said softly. "I've gone and got really fond of you. Both of you," he added quickly. *None of that*, he admonished himself. *She's his, heart and soul.* Besides, he truly liked Marshall. He'd always thought the man had courage to spare and now here he'd gone and proved it in spades. Still, there were times alone in his bed that he found himself wishing he'd been the one who'd fallen in the gully. Both he and Marshall had met Eden on the same day. He'd just been a few minutes too late. Even as he ran up the path in the rain toward them, he'd already been able to see just from the way she was bending over Marshall, sheltering his face with her body, her fingers wiping gently at the mud. Just from that he'd known he was too late.

Mike lived in a small log home he'd built himself, set back from the lake about three miles on past the Morning Glory Inn. He lived there alone, his ex-wife having taken their two young daughters and moved to Erie, where she was from. That was eight years ago now. His girls were getting into their early teens and he didn't get to see them nearly as often as he'd like. He hadn't really known how much he missed being close to a woman, not until he saw Eden there on the path, her chestnut hair dark with rain. Then that evening in the hospital when he'd carried her, sleeping, down the hallway to the room he'd arranged for her, her cheek warm against his shoulder, something in him he'd tried to keep a lid on all these years, that something began to yearn again.

He'd been a witness to her falling ever more in love with Marshall. It hadn't taken long at all. And he understood it completely. Marshall was an extraordinary man. At first, he'd been simply fascinated to learn more about what things were like for Marshall, but he came to feel a warm friendship for him...and Wadsworth. Marshall himself couldn't see how Wadsworth always had his eyes on him. Mike had always liked dogs, almost always had one, until last summer when Mazie, his yellow lab had died from old age. Watching Wadsworth with Marshall, playing with Wadsworth himself, made him miss Mazie. He'd get himself a new dog soon. Be a lot easier than getting a new woman.

Then Marshall, both blind and sick, had gone and offered himself as hostage in place of Eden. He would have done the same thing but, then, he was neither blind nor sick. There would be no comparison between what he'd risk and what Marshall had been willing to risk. That was how much the man loved Eden. You had to respect that. You had to stand back and simply admire something like that. All you could do was help her get him back.

Now he was in there, still fighting for his life. Mike, always very honest with himself, ran a quick check on his heart. Yes, thank God, yes. There was not one thing in him that wanted Eden at the cost of Marshall's life. Marshall had to live.

"Any man makes it down Coopers Ridge under the conditions he did, that man's not going to give up, Eden. He'll be back with you at the inn before you know it."

"I....," Eden began, grateful for Mike's unflagging support, but a young nurse came and told her she could go back to Marshall's room.

Mike watched her hurrying down the corridor then turned to go back to work.

Dr. Hersholtz, making a final entry on Marshall's chart, looked up as she came in, noting all the as-yet-unasked questions in her anxious glance. "Draining's going well," he said, indicating the chest tube. I'm hopeful we won't have to do a decortication."

Seeing her blank look in response, he explained, "Marshall's in second stage empyema thoracis. In third stage restrictive fibrous material forms, encasing the lung. Then he'd need decortication, which is, basically, going in and cutting and peeling it off the lung. Then the lung can expand again."

A horrid mental image of a scalpel scraping the outsides of Marshall's lungs filled her brain. Her hand gripped the metal back of a chair.

"But after examining him just now, like I said, I'm hopeful that won't have to be done."

At the white expression on her face, he changed his approach. "The antibiotics seem to be starting to have some effect now, Ms. McLaughlin. Fever's down just a bit, should be dropping more soon. That's an excellent sign, excellent. It's when the antibiotics don't work that we're in trouble, you know."

She tried to smile but her lips didn't seem to want to slide over her teeth very well. She was having a hard time shaking free of that image with the scalpel and the lungs. His lungs. "The...tube," she stammered, "how long?"

"Until the pleural cavity stops draining," he said.

She'd begun to hate the sound of all the technical medical terminology that had swirled about her head for a while now. Sitting, she took his quiet hand again, just wanting the warm contact of his skin against hers. Hersholtz left to continue his rounds, Maria adjusted the IV, then left, too.

His head lay still on the pillow, the Greek syllables no longer forming on his lips. "Where are you now?" she whispered. "Have you left the rock by the sea?"

Her other hand moved, resting ever so lightly on his oxygen mask above his mouth. His head turned, then, just the slightest bit.

"Eden," he murmured almost inaudibly.

"I'm here," she replied, leaning close. "I'm here, my darling."

Chapter 34

Marshall licked his lips, trying to speak. "Eden," he managed again.

"Right here, darling. Right here. I love you. I love you."

He knew she was there! She almost moaned with the relief of it.

"So tired..."

"I know, darling, I know. You went so far."

"Can't...."

"It's all right, darling. It's all right. You're right here in the hospital now. Everything's all right."

"Don't know...."

"What don't you know, sweetheart? Everything's all right. You're ok. You're going to be just fine."

"Way...don't know...way."

"What? What way, sweetheart?"

"Don't know," he repeated. "Too cold."

"Cold? Are you cold, darling? Do you need more blankets?"

"Poor Longfellow."

She sat back a bit. Poor Longfellow? What did he mean, Poor Longfellow?

"Ages...," he mumbled. "Unremembered ages."

Her lips parted and she stared at him, something thick and solid settling through the center of her joy. He didn't know she was there.

He made a sound like a long, sad sigh. "...days that are forgotten...in the unremembered ages."

Her tears over-brimmed. He wasn't back yet. Maybe he'd left that rock by the sea, but he hadn't come home to her in the hospital. Not yet. Feeling like the edges of her soul were wearing off, becoming thin and brittle, she laid her cheek down on the edge of his bed and closed her eyes.

Maria came back, finding Eden asleep like that. She knew Hersholtz would have wakened her, made her leave, but Maria went quietly about, performing the checks on Marshall she needed to do, then left.

Eden slept nearly half an hour, waking with a start, not having meant to drift off like that. Her back was stiff, so she stood, stretching her muscles. Marshall was lying peacefully now. Perhaps he'd got to a place beyond remembered pain. She had no way of knowing. Her tummy growled and she decided to go out to the waiting room where she'd seen a vending machine. Maybe some chips and a Coke would see her through till supper.

Trying to stuff several quarters into the machine, she let one slip and it rolled away on its edge. A male foot settled atop it, stopping its flight. "That supposed to be lunch?" Mike said, eyeing the small bag of chips in her hand.

She smiled wryly and shrugged. "Didn't want to take time for the cafeteria."

"Any change?"

"Hersholtz says the antibiotics seem to be starting to work, but I haven't seen any real change in him so far. When he's not speaking Greek, he's still lost in the woods." She looked at Mike more carefully. "What're you up to?"

"I'm off to the inn to walk Wadsworth. Anything there you need me to bring back?"

She hadn't thought of that. Anything he could bring back? Hmmmm? Nothing for her. Was there anything for Marshall? That triggered an idea. "Yes, Mike, there is something I'd like you to bring."

"You name it."

"In the parlor, there's that small CD player. You know the one I mean?"

He nodded.

"Will you bring me that and the CD, should be in that stack near the player, the one with the word 'Tuscany' on the cover? I have an idea I'd like to try."

"Sure thing," he smiled. "Anything else?"

"Can't think of anything right now, Mike. I know Wadsworth will be glad to see you, get out for a bit. Thanks so much for doing that."

He turned when he'd gotten about five steps away. "Oh, Eden, I talked with Pete about your car. They had it towed into town. Had a broken strut and needed two new tires. I've arranged for it to be taken to Herb's garage. He's a cousin of mine and said he'd fix it up for you. Needs one fender hammered out a bit, too, but he's good at that. Said he'd have it for you by tomorrow afternoon. Herb doesn't want to charge you for the repair. Said he didn't feel right about it seeing as how it was the convicts ran it into the ditch and all. Everybody's kind've gotten all involved in the story of the blind professor left in the forest. Story's been all over the news, you know. I bet even Pittsburgh's got it."

Pittsburgh? She hadn't thought about Pittsburgh knowing it, but with her connection to one of the largest newspapers, of course they'd splash it all over. And Marshall being a professor at Duquesne. Connie. Connie would have heard, might even have called Eden's parents in Florida. She didn't have her cell phone with her at the hospital.

"Mike!" she called after his back. "Ask Martha to give you my cell! I think it's on my dresser."

He gave her a thumbs up and disappeared out the door.

She should call Marti at the paper, too. There were lots of people she should call, but that wasn't foremost on her mind. Mike had handed her the runaway quarter so she went and sat on a chair in the corner, quickly gobbling her chips and taking long sips from the Coke can she'd finally managed to get. Marshall could wake up and she needed to be there when he did.

Stopping in the doorway of his room, she saw that he lay exactly as he had when she left. "Come back, Marshall," she whispered. "Come back to me soon." Sighing, she went in, sitting again in the chair beside his bed. Perhaps if she just talked to him?

"You should've seen Waddy, darling. He wanted to get to you so bad. Nothing was going to stop that dog. Nothing. He...." She talked steadily for nearly forty-five minutes with no response from him. Her eyes glared up at the IV bag. *Damn you!* she thought. *Why aren't you working faster?* She rubbed her fingertips as hard as she could back and forth across her forehead, trying to stave off a headache.

Mike paused in the doorway, watching her, seeing the tension in the way she held her shoulders. Taking a breath, he said, "Hey, there. I've got the stuff."

She didn't reply and he came into the room, squatting beside her chair. "Eden?"

"He's just lying there, Mike. Why is he just lying there?"

"He's exhausted, dar...Eden," he said softly, setting the shopping bag he had with him aside. "On top of the pneumonia and everything else, he's got to be totally exhausted."

"I know," she said wearily, "I know that's right. It's just I need...." A single tear began to run down her left cheek.

"Now, now," he whispered, wiping it away with his thumb. "You're practically as exhausted as he is." He reached into the bag. "Look, Martha sent you a thermos of her chicken soup."

He began to unscrew the cap of the blue container. "You can't keep on like this with just potato chips, you know." He poured some into the big plastic cap. "Here, you drink this. Come on," he urged when she hesitated.

"Mother hen!" she snorted.

"Cluck cluck," he laughed softly.

She sipped the hot soup gratefully. "It's good," she murmured, licking her lip.

"It's Martha's," he stated. "Has to be good."

"How was Waddy?"

"Restless. I had to keep him onleash. Couldn't let him run loose. He'd have taken off down the road for the hospital."

"He would," she nodded. "He's got to see Marshall pretty soon, Mike."

"I know. But Marshall will have to be in his own room, out of the ICU before I can even think of talking people into that."

"You will, though?"

"You can count on me," he smiled, getting to his feet. "Always."

"You brought the CD?"

He reached into the bag, lifting out a CD with a picture of a Tuscan villa and a sweeping green hill leading down to some red poppies. "This the right one?"

She took it from him. "Oh, yes! This is it!"

He plugged the small CD player in for her, setting it on the little table near her chair, then placed her cell phone beside it. "I've got to get back to work now, Eden. I'll come by again at the end of my shift so I'll be here to drive you home whenever you want."

"Thanks, Mike," she said, but her eyes were already scanning down the playlist on the back of the CD. There it was, track 12. Mike left and she popped the CD into the player, scanning forward until she got where she wanted, then pressed 'play', keeping the sound moderate because of where they were.

Eyes locked on his face, she waited as the melody of *Vá Pensiero* drifted out of the small player. There was nothing until about halfway through when he made a couple of low sounds.

"That's it," she urged. "You remember singing this to me in the parlor?"

She would never forget it, the sound of his whispering voice, his breath on her hair. The piece ended and she hit 12 again so it would replay. He made some more little sounds. She played it again. "You're not on some rock at the shore," she said, "and you're not up on the ridge in the forest. You're here, Marshall, here...with me." She sighed, resting her forehead on the edge of the bed, the memory of him singing so very clear.

She felt something. Not sure at first what it might be, she stayed as she was, waiting. There it was again. Her hair was being ever so lightly touched. His fingers were moving in her hair. She wanted to lift her head, to look at him, but didn't want to disturb what he was doing. So she waited, feeling his fingers drifting over her hair. Finally she had to look, so tipped her head up just enough to see him. His eyes were still closed, but his lips were curved into a slight smile.

"Marshall?"

"Auburn," he said, maintaining the smile, "like the last of the rays of the setting sun."

Chapter 35

"Oh!" she cried softly. "It's you!"

"Who else would it be?" he asked, puzzled.

"I thought maybe it was still Odysseus, or maybe Longfellow."

He turned his head more toward her, remembering to open his eyes. "You've lost me, darling."

"I almost did," she nodded. "I really almost did."

"Not like that," he smiled. "Now, you've lost me now. What are you talking about?"

"You. You kinda...went away, somewhere in the Aegean or by the shining big sea waters. I don't know."

He still had no idea what she meant. "Eden...I....."

"It's ok. It's all ok. You're back. And you're not speaking Greek."

"Greek?"

"Yep. According to the staff you entertained them with the *Odyssey* most of the night."

"I did?"

"You did, indeed. I came in on the tail end of it myself."

He blew out a breath, fogging the oxygen mask. "I don't remember."

"Doesn't matter. All I care about is that you're back." She picked up his hand. "How are you feeling?"

"You know that old saw about 'Did you get the number of the truck?'? I think I got run over by a whole convoy." He closed his eyes, trying to ease his legs into a better position, clamping his teeth as he did so. Somehow, the movement made him aware of his chest and his left hand reached up, feeling along the tube.

"What the heck is that?"

"Chest tube, draining your pleural cavity."

"My pleural cavity needs...draining?"

"Mmm hmm," she said. "Double pneumonia wasn't quite enough for you, my love. You went on into pleurisy and empyema."

"I'm not sure I want to know what that last word means," he replied with a wry smile, then coughed, which hurt terribly.

Maria came in then, saw her patient was awake and greeted him in classical Greek. He cocked one eyebrow in surprise and returned the greeting. "She's the one who told us what you were talking about this morning," Eden explained. "This is Maria Papadopoulos."

Maria took his temperature. "Fever's down. 102.5." She checked his drainage tube, read all the monitors, adjusted the IV, and made notes on his chart. "Doing good, Dr. Sinclair. Keep it up and I suspect you'll have your own room by morning."

"I'm not in a regular room?" he asked Eden as Maria left.

"ICU," she explained. "You were in really bad shape when you finally got to the inn."

"I got all the way to the inn?" He seemed to have endless questions.

"Well, to the dock. That's where we found you, half on-half off the dock. Wadsworth had gotten to you first, was lying there with his head atop your head."

"Where is he, Eden? Where's Wadsworth now?"

"At the inn. Won't let him in ICU. Mike went by at lunch, took him out for a bit, but all he wants is to get to you."

"He needs...." But his eyelids had begun to droop. "Oh, Eden," he murmured, "so hard to stay awake." He made some little sighing sounds. "Hurts. Hurts...everywhere. So tired. So...." His head tipped to the side on the pillow.

She sat there a long time after that, just holding his hand. He slept the rest of the afternoon. Maria stopped by, commenting that it was the best thing for him.

Mike had just shaved and trimmed his moustache and now stood staring at himself in the mirror over his bathroom sink. He never shaved twice in one day. He frowned at his reflection. "What do you think you're doing, Mike Johnson?" He'd shaved again because he was going to pick Eden up at the hospital. "You're acting like you're courting the woman," he admonished himself, "and you're not. You know that's impossible." Eden was spoken for. Hard as that was sometimes to swallow, he knew the fact of it. No way was he going to try and woo Eden away from Marshall. "Couldn't even if you tried." He knew that, too. Good Lord, the man spoke Greek, for Pete's sake, when he was out of his head. Greek! And he was a good man, really good. Mike liked him a lot, but all that just somehow made it harder.

Eden was, what, thirty-four? Mike had turned forty-three in mid-November. He looked at himself critically. Light brown hair with a lot of graying to it. Men in his family grayed early. He had almost startlingly light blue eyes beneath full brows and lean, straight cheeks leading down to a strong, squarish chin. After work, he'd showered, dressing in a blue and cream checked shirt and slim jeans. His wide leather belt had a large buckle with an engraved deer on it. He kinda liked big buckles. Had never been sure just why, but he did. He was tall, almost 6' 4", and the heels of his boots made him even taller. All his life he'd worked hard, first on his father's farm, then a stint in the Army, and now he worked for both the sheriff's department and as a paramedic. On his downtime, he hunted and fished and hiked...and helped rid Martha of any excess supply of cookies.

He'd met LeeAnn when he was in the Army. Things had been ok at first, but when he got out and came back home, she didn't like the rural life and started not liking him so much, either. They'd had a small house in town, but after she left and took the girls, he'd built this log cabin for himself. From scratch, too, not some kit. There was nothing quite like running your hand down a smooth log you'd peeled yourself.

Wiping his face dry, he grabbed his keys, put on the old brown leather flight jacket his uncle had worn years ago, and went out the door, stopping by the inn to tend to Wadsworth. He really liked Wadsworth, too. Another man's dog. Another man's woman. He sighed, turning off his lights in the hospital lot. "You need a life of your own," he told himself.

He'd called, so she was waiting for him just inside the glass doors, the reflection of a large 'Exit' sign, lying in a red glow on her chestnut hair. "Hi, there," he greeted casually, "sounds like the news is good."

"It is, Mike. He woke up and talked to me earlier this afternoon. In English," she added with a bit of a laugh.

It was easy to see her spirits were up now that Marshall was clearly going to pull through. "I'm real glad to hear that." He opened the door of his truck for her. "Bit of a high step there. Watch yourself." Closing her door, he walked around to the driver's side, getting in. He looked sideways at her as he started the engine. "You had anything to eat since that thermos of soup?"

"Not a bite," she replied. "I guess I'll have to see what Martha's got left over in the kitchen."

"We could stop by Annie's," he suggested.

"What's Annie's?"

"Little cafe just around the corner. Nothing fancy, but the food's great. You want to do that?"

"Sounds fine by me," she nodded. "That way I can just fall into bed when I get to the inn."

As Mike drove the four blocks, he kept mentally kicking himself. *What do you think you're DOING? Taking her out to eat like you had some right. How big of a fool do you intend to make yourself, anyway?*

He opened the cafe door for her, a series of little attached bells tinkling to announce their arrival. The window of the door had a valance of red and white checked cloth and the eight tables that made up the entire dining area each had a matching cloth with a small votive candle burning in the center.

"Hi, Annie," he said, taking Eden's coat and hanging it on a wall rack, then putting his flight jacket beside it. "Like you to meet Eden, Eden McLaughlin, from Pittsburgh."

"Glad to meet you, hon," Annie replied with a big smile. "Heard how you and Mike here traipsed all over the forest looking for that poor Dr. Sinclair."

Eden smiled back at the pleasant, stout woman. "Yes, we did. But it was a lot easier for us than it was for him."

"I bet," Annie said, shaking her head so that the brown bun at the nape of her neck woggled from side to side. Eden couldn't help wondering how it didn't just come completely loose.

Mike led Eden to a table near a large front window that looked out toward the lake. A low red and white valance didn't block the view and Eden found her eyes pulled to the lake. The moon had sailed out from between the clouds and silver light lay like a veil of blessing, somehow come loose from the heavens, settling down upon the calm waters. "It's so peaceful tonight," she murmured, "so easy to relax at last and just...be."

"You've got to be really tired, I imagine."

"I am. I don't know when I've done such a continuous stretch of exercise as we did in the forest...and the worry. That was worse."

"He's going to be all right, though. That's what matters."

"Yes," she sighed, "that's all that matters."

She picked up the menu. "I think I just want something simple and maybe kind of country." She decided on hot turkey slices and gravy over thick white bread. "I eat much of that and I'll have to roll myself out through the door!" she laughed. "But I'm going to anyway."

"Won't hurt you," he commented. "Your...," he stopped. He was going to say that her body was just lovely. "You're not the least fat."

"Not yet," she chuckled, "but check again after I eat that."

It was good, hot and tasty and good. As she sipped her tea, she looked at Mike across the table. "You're such a good friend to me, Mike, to both of us. I just want to be sure you know how much we appreciate that."

He smiled, setting his napkin carefully down. "Thanks, Eden. You two are pretty easy to be friends with."

She yawned widely, covering her mouth with her hand. "Sorry. I guess I'm more tired than I thought."

He stood. "Well, let me get you back to the inn, then, so you can get a good rest." He paid the bill and fetched her coat. "I'll come by and take you to the hospital in the morning. Your car should be ready by my lunch break so I'll get it for you and drop it by the hospital lot then you won't need me to drive you home tomorrow evening."

She looked up at him. Up was the right word. He was nearly a foot taller than she was. "You've done so much for me, Mike, and you always make me feel like it's ok, that you don't mind. I can't thank you enough for that." She stretched up on tiptoe and kissed him lightly on his left cheek. "We're so lucky to have you as our friend."

His cheek was still tingling as he drove down the dark road to his cabin after dropping her off. Damn, damn, damn!

Chapter 36

3 AM: hospital

Marshall awoke in the middle of the night, lying there, taking a moment to make sense of where he was and why. His body didn't take long to remind him. Ah, yes, he'd been flogged for an hour with a cat 'o nine tails with pieces of metal tied into each end of the whips, then dragged by a Jeep over a gravel road for some miles before being delivered to the native populace who'd cooked him for dinner. Or something like that. At least his body felt like that. Then there was that marathon he'd run twice, the route lined with angry Apaches determined to stop him with their hatchets and clubs. He mustn't forget about that.

Actually, he found he'd forgotten about a great deal of it, the doing of it, not the repercussions. He lay there aching and stinging and throbbing from head to toe, but he hadn't died strung up to a tree. He hadn't done that. He hadn't lain down in the snow and died, either. One of the clearest things he remembered was that sheer determined will not to do that. The details were a bit fuzzy, especially those after he'd made that little nest under the evergreen. He figured that's when his fever had taken over, during that time there. He remembered everything about the long walk up the icy streambed to wait for Calvin, and he remembered the slog up the steep slope to the place where they'd hooked him over the limb.

After he'd come out from under the evergreen, that's where he began to lose the clearness. Most of it had become this nightmarish mishmash of tree branches striking his face, of rocks that loomed up out of nowhere to trip him, of cold that penetrated to his bones and wouldn't stop.

Eden said he'd made it to Harold's dock. He had absolutely no memory of being anywhere even close to the dock. There was a vague bit about a stream that went on forever. All he could imagine was that primal instinct had taken over and gotten him there.

He lifted his right hand, examining it with his left. One finger broken. Not bad for all the falling he'd done on his hands, all the wild clutching at branches. He tried to lift up enough to reach his legs, but the moment his head left the pillow, shock waves of pain shot through him, sending his pulse up enough to set off an alarm on his monitor.

A night nurse was there in two seconds. "I...I'm...all right," he gasped. "I just tried to sit up."

"Well, Dr. Sinclair, I guess you found out just what a good idea that wasn't, now didn't you?"

"Maria?"

"Nope, Marcy. You just lie still like you're supposed to for now. Won't be all that long before someone will be around beating on you."

"Be...beating on me?" Not all nurses had great bedside manners just because they were nurses.

"Yep. You'll be pounded a bit. Helps you cough. Got to get all that yukky stuff up out of your lungs."

"Oh, God," he moaned. There wasn't a square inch on him that wasn't bruised or scraped. Where could they pound?

She checked his chest tube. He'd moved his left hand so it was lying across it. She picked up his hand, plopping it onto the bed. "You touch that tube, you get your hand tied to the bed frame. You don't touch the tube. You got me?"

"I got you," he said weakly. Would they really do that or was that just her way of getting him to leave it alone? He wouldn't put it past her to tie him completely to the bed and start methodically hammering in three inch nails. Maybe she'd done some of that already. He sort of felt like maybe she had.

He lay there thinking about what Marcy had said. Were they actually going to... pound...him? He thought probably they might. Well, he'd been left hung on a tree and made it to the dock. Maybe he could get out of the hospital and make it to the dock again? He seriously considered his options. If Marcy turned out to be the one who was going to do the pounding, he knew he'd have to try. He wouldn't survive a Marcy-pounding. No one would, not even people who hadn't had a ton of coal dropped on them and then set afire.

His fingers crept up over his hip, continuing on upwards, finally running lightly down several inches of the tube. It was his tube, dammit, and he'd touch it if he wanted. Then he grinned, feeling like a little boy. Problem was, being blind, he didn't know if Marcy were standing in the doorway with her sawed-off shotgun. She might be. He waited for the impact of pellets.

3 AM: Morning Glory Inn

Eden woke, not knowing why exactly. She'd been having a dream where she was lying on her back in a field of daffodils with Marshall, propped on his elbow, leaning over her, tickling her chin with a single flower stalk. She didn't like waking up and losing the dream. Getting out of bed, she padded to the window, sitting on the built-in seat and pushing the curtains open. Wadsworth joined her, laying his head on her thigh. She rubbed her finger up and down between his large, serious eyes. "Soon, sweet boy, soon. I promise."

Turning, she leaned her elbows on the windowsill. The view of the lake was better from here. At the cafe there had been the lights of other businesses and homes, several street lights, some passing traffic. Here there was just the lake, the lake and the moon, which had moved a great distance but still silvered the surface. She liked the quiet of it. Up on the ridge, even though the only sounds had been the ones she and Mike and Wadsworth made as they struggled along, there had been this drumbeat in her ears. *Find him!* it had beaten, over and over. *Hurry, hurry, hurry!*

Her thoughts moved to the dock, to the landward end where they'd found him lying. All that way. All the way to the dock. It seemed impossible that he had managed that. How? How had he done it? But even in his delirium he'd told her. He'd done it for her. He'd done it because he wouldn't die in the snow. She shook her head just a bit. How had she found someone who would love her that well, love her that much?

3 AM: Johnson cabin

He hadn't slept, not a wink. He was still amazed, even angry, at himself. He'd asked her out to eat, bumbling idiot of a man that he was. Thank goodness she was totally unaware. She'd kept using the words "we" and "our", as in "our friend." He sighed, tossing back his blankets and sitting on the side of his small bed. It wasn't much more than a cot, a one-person bed for a man who always slept alone, who would always sleep alone. Resting his elbows on his knees, he held his head in his hands, his fingers lacing through his hair. He was the "good friend." Of course he was. Why was he trying to steal little moments, taking her to the cafe just so he could be in her presence, look at her for a few minutes longer?

Barefoot, he went to the cabin door, the chill night air immediately making him shiver. Still he stood there, looking at the lake. His rowboat was tied up to the bit of a pier. Yeah. He couldn't sleep. Slipping on his boots without socks, he grabbed the old flight jacket, not putting it on till he was half way to the pier. He undid the rope, stepped into the boat, standing there a moment as it rocked a bit under his weight, then he sat and began to row. He rowed out into the moonlight where there was nothing but the night and the moon and the dark water. Pulling in the oars, he let the small boat drift, and leaned back against the side, his face tipped up to the soft light.

Chapter 37

Marshall woke in the morning feeling fingers on his wrist. Someone was taking his pulse. "Marcy?" he asked warily, his pulse speeding up just a bit.

"No, Maria," came the reply.

"Thank God," he murmured.

"She give you a hard time in the night, Dr. Sinclair?"

"Three inch nails. All over."

"Ah, yes, that would be our Marcy."

"She said people would be coming to pound me. Is that true?"

Maria chuckled at his phrasing. "Not for you. Not yet anyway. Drainage, um, pounding therapy is, um, contraindicated by pleural effusions and empyema. So you're safe."

"You mean they can't beat on me because my chest leaks?"

"Something like that."

He relaxed a bit. "Any chance Marcy's not working the night shift tonight?"

"She's on, but I think you'll be in a private room in plenty of time, so you'll miss out on her company, I'm afraid."

"Poor me," he sighed.

"Poor me, you mean," she came back. "I'll miss your Greek."

"Did I really do that? Much?"

"A lot. You have quite a memory."

"It's compensation from the gods."

"Compensation?"

"Yep. They felt guilty."

"Ah!" she said, actually understanding what he meant. "What else can you do? Besides the *Odyssey*, I mean."

"I can do *The Midnight Ride of Paul Revere*."

"In Greek?"

"I'd have to think about that."

"Well, if you come up with it, please let me know."

"So how'm I doing?"

"Fever's down more. 101.8. The miracle of modern medicine."

"Look, Maria," he said, suddenly serious, "I can feel my body from the inside but I can't see it. Would you tell me what's going on with my hide?"

"You are black and blue over about, oh, 60 to 75% of yourself. You know black and blue?"

He nodded. "In my own fashion, yes."

"Some of the bruises are just light and superficial, but others are really deep into the muscle, especially on your legs. Your right knee is swollen and a rather glorious purple. You have a lot of scratches, none terribly deep, on your face, neck, and wrists. I think the leather jacket you had on probably prevented a lot more of those to your body. The jacket itself, by the way, is a total loss. The only thing you might be able to wear again is the flannel shirt. The pants were fairly well shredded and the shoes, well, just forget the shoes."

"Anything else?"

"You have a slight concussion where it looks like something fell on your head and then scraped a bit down your temple and cheek." She'd heard the stories about the possibilities of how the convicts had left him but didn't want to comment on it in case he had no memory of it.

"That would be the tree branch," he sighed, touching his face with his hand.

"There are a lot of reporters, Dr. Sinclair. I don't know if you're aware of that or not, but there are a lot of people who want to hear your story from you." A frown passed over his face. "But they can't get to you while you're in here. I just think you should know what's facing you when you get out, though."

He sighed. "Blind guy left in woods by rabid convicts, eh?"

"Afraid so. You're big news."

It truly hadn't occurred to him. He wished it hadn't to anybody else, either.

"A lot of people from Duquesne have been calling the hospital, too. Dean, President of the University, Chairman of the Literature Department. Folks like that. Not all just the media."

He didn't want to talk to anybody, though, nobody at all...except Eden.

Eden sat on the side of her bed, phone in hand. "Yes, Mom. Everything's going pretty good now. Yes, he's doing better now. No, I didn't hurt myself. Well, I'm still not sure. Whenever he comes back to Pittsburgh. Just like I told Connie. I'll let you know. Ummm hmmm. Yes. Sure, sure, Mom."

She lay back on the bed, her feet still dangling to the floor, the phone pressed to her chest. It was always a bit awkward talking with her mother. She'd never been able to pinpoint precisely why, maybe just that her mom was so entirely different than she was. Now that her parents had left Pittsburgh and retired to St. Petersburg, Florida, she didn't see them so often and most of the keeping up was done by phone. It was on the phone that the conversational awkwardness seemed to be at its height. Her Mom's sister, Edith, who was Connie's mother, still lived in Pittsburgh and Eden had always found her the one she could talk to. In fact, she'd spoken with both Edith and Connie before calling her parents this morning.

A light tapping sounded on her door. "Eden, honey," Martha said, "Mike's here. He's walking Wadsworth but seems to be in more of a hurry this morning. Are you about ready?"

"Be right there," she called, grabbing her purse.

Mike was already in his truck with the engine running as she hurried out the door. "My, you *are* in a rush today, aren't you? You late for something?"

"Not really," he said, getting the truck in gear rather than looking at her.

He drove down the road, his eyes fixed out the windshield. She studied his profile. Something was different. "You ok, Mike?" she asked softly.

"Just fine," he replied, neatly avoiding a bag of some sort that had blown onto the road.

He didn't say more than those four words all the way to the hospital. When he pulled into a parking space, he didn't cut the engine. "You're not coming in?" she asked.

"Not this morning."

She'd had her hand on the handle ready to open the door, but paused. "Did I do something, Mike? Have I presumed too much on your friendship, expected you to do more than I should have?"

He still didn't turn his eyes toward her. "Nope," he said. "Not possible for you to do that."

"Then what is it?"

"Just got a batch of stuff on my mind today. That's all."

"Anything I can help you with?"

He pressed his lips tightly together briefly, then one corner curved into a suggestion of a wry smile. "Don't think so, Eden."

His manner worried her. She realized she missed his sparkly blue eyes and the calm, efficient way he handled everything. "Mike?"

"I'll get your car here by lunch," he said. "Park it over there near that tree so you'll know where to look. Be good for you to have your own wheels back again." His eyes finally flickered sideways, but only very, very briefly. "Best be getting on, now."

She sighed and got out of the truck, watching as he drove around the corner.

When he knew he was out of sight, he pulled over, folded his forearms on the steering wheel and rested his face on them. He couldn't do it anymore, couldn't be close to her like that and not want her. The scent of her still filled the cab of his truck. It was why he'd made sure Herb would do a hurry-up job on her car, why he was paying for it himself just to get it back to her. Herb was not a charitable sort of guy. It just sounded good that he'd want to do that for her because of the general feeling in the small town over what had happened. No way Herb'd do that for nothing, though. After this morning, he wouldn't have to pick her up again, wouldn't have to have her scent in his cab like this, have her sitting so close he could reach out and touch her when he had no right to be touching her, when all in the world he wanted to do was touch her. Be better if he just stayed away. Better for everybody.

Marshall was dozing when she came in, but woke at the sound of her steps. She leaned over the bed, lightly kissing his lips, her cheek inadvertently brushing the cannula that replaced his oxygen mask. "Sleeping Beauty," she whispered fondly.

"Hardly," he said. "I asked Maria to describe me a bit ago. Evidently I'm rather colorful."

"Positively psychedelic," she said, "but you're beautiful to me."

"It's so good to hear your voice," he sighed, reaching for her hand. "Sometimes I start to feel cut off from reality in here."

She pulled the chair close again so he could comfortably hold her hand. "I saw Maria on my way in. She said your fever's down more. Any news about the darn chest tube?"

"I'm not supposed to touch it," he whispered conspiratorially. "Night nurse threatened beheading if I did." The fingers of his left hand, however, were slightly curled over it even as he spoke.

"And I can see how well you paid attention to her." It was Dr. Hersholtz.

Marshall's hand fell guiltily to his side.

"Here, let me have a look at it." In a moment he straightened and said, "Drainage rate has slowed considerably overnight. Might even get it out before evening. We'll just have to wait and see how the day goes." He looked at the entries that had been made on the chart. "Good, good. Fever's down." He lifted Marshall's left wrist, taking his pulse, then listened to his chest sounds. "Ok," he announced, "I'm going to arrange a private room for you this morning. The orderlies will be by for you in, oh, about an hour, I'd say."

He stopped in the doorway, looking back at Eden. "And he needs as much rest as he can get, young lady. You keep that in mind, all right?"

Hersholtz had only been gone a moment when Marshall coughed several times, having to hold his left hand across his chest as he did and a wad of tissues to his mouth. "Sorry," he said, "lung-stuff still coming up."

She saw how it hurt him to cough and he explained how it wasn't just the pleurisy and all, but the combination of all the bruises and pulled muscles that made it so hard. "And then they turn me," he said. "Not good for me just to lie in one position all the time. But they have to do it for me. Can't even roll on my side or anything right now by myself." He grimaced, remembering how much even a simple turning hurt.

"Marshall?" she said, her voice low. "Is it all right, darling, if I ask you about the tree? The one at the top of the ridge where they left you."

"It's ok, Eden," he smiled. "I can talk about anything I remember. It's really ok."

"Did....did they...?"

"Yes, they did. I heard a couple of the orderlies out in the hall talking about what the police think happened. They actually have it fairly right."

"How...was...that? To be left there like that? When I got up there, I couldn't imagine anyone would do something like that."

"You were there? All the way up there?" He hadn't realized that somehow.

"I went everywhere you did. Mike, Wadsworth, and me. We trailed your whole route. Well, not down into the big hole left by the fallen tree, but everything else."

"You...you saw the fallen tree? You went that whole way?"

"I had to. You'd gone that way. I had to."

"Oh, Eden, I didn't know."

"I couldn't just stay there by the bridge and let everybody else try to find you. Besides, they started off looking in the wrong direction. But Waddy knew. He knew all along which way you'd gone. So Mike and I and some officer named Barry, we went the other way, the right way." She paused, remembering. "But tell me about the tree on the ridge."

"Not all that much to tell. I was on my knees in the snow. I had this sense that the bigger one of the convicts wanted to get rid of me. I was coughing and slowing them down and he didn't like it. I don't know what he was doing, but the other one said something that made him stop." He closed his eyes, trying to take a deep breath, but it hurt his chest too much. Then he held up both hands about a foot apart. "They'd tied me," he explained, "with about this much leeway between my wrists, and suddenly the big one just pulled me up and yanked the rope over a branch and I could hear them leaving."

She put her hand up to her mouth and kept it there as he continued. "Couldn't get the rope to move forward or back, so I just jumped a couple of times and the branch broke. Fell right on me," he said, his fingers going to the side of his face. "But it worked. Then I just kept going downhill from there, trying to find the stream again." He coughed some more and felt really tired afterwards, so she suggested he nap a bit until the orderlies came and she'd go get some coffee.

As she stood by a glass section of the wall, sipping the hot liquid, she noticed an EMT vehicle backing up to the emergency entrance a bit off to her left. Mike got out, striding quickly around to where his men were unloading a gurney with an elderly man who was having symptoms of a heart attack. His gaze passed briefly over where she was standing, but if he saw her there, he gave no sign of it and soon disappeared into that section of the hospital.

She sighed. "What happened, Mike? Where did my friend go?"

Chapter 38

When Eden got back to where Marshall was, two orderlies had just arrived and announced it was time for Marshall's move to a private room. "I'm here," she said over the clatter the orderlies were making as they positioned the gurney beside Marshall's bed in preparation to shift him over onto it.

"I'm not sick enough anymore for the ICU," Marshall said in her general direction. "They're kicking me out."

"Can you slide toward the edge, Dr. Sinclair?" one of the orderlies asked.

Marshall tried, but every muscle he'd use to push himself with protested most firmly. He still tried a bit, but the two orderlies moved close and each one got a good grip and did most of the lifting and scooting for him. They had him halfway between the two beds when a man in green scrubs darted in the doorway. "Dr. Sinclair," he said in a rather hurried voice, "can I have a statement about just how it was the two convicts left you up there atop Coopers Ridge? I'd like to...."

"Who *are* you?" Eden said loudly. She looked closely at the man. "Press! You're from the press, aren't you?"

The man just tried to push closer to Marshall. The orderly with his hands on Marshall's upper body, shifted a bit to block the reporter from getting access to the patient. "Security!" he called loudly, leaning more to look out the doorway. The reporter bumped the orderly's shoulder, which combined with his forward lean, over-balanced him and he lurched wildly, trying to keep to his feet, somehow sending the gurney out of position. His grip on Marshall slipped and the top half of Marshall's body twisted and dropped toward the space that had opened up between the two beds.

Eden shrieked, the reporter collided with the IV stand, almost knocking it over before finally managing to clutch it and keep it upright, though the bag itself still continued to swing. The second orderly made a grab for Marshall's hips as the other one scrabbled after his shoulders, both catching him in a rather awkward fashion and hefting him up and onto the gurney. Marshall came down flat on his back, completely and utterly jarred. His face went white and he lay there making deep sounds in his throat that came out half gasp-half moan through his clenched teeth. He thought for sure he was going to pass out.

Maria, who had hurried to the scene in time to witness the final hefting of Marshall, called immediately for Hersholtz. "Stand back!" she ordered the reporter and the orderlies as her fingers moved quickly to check the chest tube. By some miracle, it was still where it belonged.

Hersholtz had been checking a near-by patient and was there almost immediately. "Somebody throw that man out of the hospital!" he said brusquely, pushing past the reporter to turn his attention to Marshall. Marshall had stopped moaning and was now almost gagging for breath. "Suction!" Hersholtz snapped, but Maria was already handing him what he'd need.

After a few moment's intense concentration, Marshall was breathing again and moaning in pain again as well. "What happened?" Eden asked, her pulse still racing.

"The percussion of landing so hard on his back loosened large amounts of secretions from his lungs," Hersholtz explained, his eyes still on Marshall. "They moved up into his airways. Was more than he could handle all at once." He leaned toward Maria, whispering some directions, and she moved to inject something into his IV.

"Is he still able to be moved to his private room?" Eden asked.

Hersholtz nodded. "I'm just going to have the nurses keep really close tabs on him for a while, however."

During the awkward move, the sheet had slipped off Marshall's legs and Eden got a clear look at his swollen, purple right knee, as well as the many scrapes and bruises covering his legs fairly solidly. She closed her eyes briefly, seeing again in her mind all the signs of his falls as they had trailed him.

Maria covered his legs. Hersholtz was gone. "You two wait out in the hall just a minute," she directed the orderlies. "Give Dr. Sinclair a respite here to gather himself together."

He had his teeth clenched again now that the suctioning was over. He was beginning to feel like a grasshopper pinned to a 10th grade biology table with some teenage boy ready to dissect him. He knew the kid had already ripped off his legs and knocked them on the floor. The drop there between the beds had twisted his whole frame just enough to set every muscle and tendon screaming, and then the heavy impact atop the gurney had exploded his chest. He couldn't speak. He'd have to unclench his teeth and somehow stop those little desperate sounds his throat insisted on making even though his mind tried to shut them up. But Maria had put something in his IV drip that seemed to be soothing things a bit and he was vaguely aware the tension he'd maintained in his body was loosening. He'd had his eyes scrinched tightly shut, but now his lids settled into just being closed and his jaw relaxed enough that even his lips parted slightly as he drifted away to someplace warm and soft.

"Is...is he all right?" Eden asked anxiously.

"He'll probably sleep a while now." She called the orderlies back. "It will be easier on him if they continue the move now. Will you take the CD player with you? He can have it in his room." She smiled warmly at Eden. "Might be good if you just stepped out a while until they get him all settled."

Eden took the player with her back out to the waiting area. Mike was with a buddy of his by the coffee machine. Out of the corner of his eye, he saw her come into the room. He turned to go but noticed the slump to her shoulders. Then she sat down, the CD player sliding heedlessly the last couple of inches from her fingers to the floor.

Idiot! he said to himself, walking toward her. He hadn't been going to say anything, just leave a message with someone that her car was now in the lot. "Something the matter?" he asked, stopping about five feet out in front of her.

"They dropped him."

"Marshall? They dropped Marshall?"

"Sort of. A reporter got in disguised as some kind of hospital personnel. Came into ICU just as the orderlies were moving Marshall onto a gurney. Everything went haywire, Mike, everything. IV almost toppled over and the orderlies kind of let Marshall start to fall between the gurney and the bed. Really hurt him when they grabbed him. Then he couldn't breathe and Hersholtz did some kind of suction thing and, anyway, now he's sort of out of it and they're moving him to a private room." She'd been rubbing one palm across the other as she talked, but now she looked up at him, just waiting.

"So that's what that ruckus outside the entrance was," he said, shaking his head. "Somebody was being hustled off pretty fast." He sized Eden up. She looked rather shaken, still upset. He wanted to squat in front of her, put his hand on her knee, or sit beside her and put his arm around her shoulders. "Car's in the lot now," is all he said, however, still standing where he had been.

"Thanks, Mike," she said. "I appreciate it." She sighed. "I guess I should go to the inn and take care of Wadsworth, huh? Did you have a chance to make any arrangements for him to be allowed into the hospital?"

He hadn't. Not that he hadn't had a chance, but that he had put up such a barrier this morning that he'd actually forgotten about the dog. He didn't want to be that involved with this whole thing anymore. He scratched at his cheek. "No, Eden, I haven't had a chance to do that."

"Would you? It'd mean so much to Marshall. You know just as well as I do how much he's been through, and now they've gone and caused him more pain, useless, senseless pain. If Waddy could be there when he wakes up that would be so wonderful. Could you do that, Mike?"

There he was...trapped, trapped by a pair of luminous green eyes and by the right thing to do. He'd always been a sucker for the right thing to do, not to mention green eyes, her green eyes. Why couldn't he just blurt out that he was too busy? Or the truth? That he didn't want to because it hurt his heart too much to have to be close to her?

"Sure," he said, trying to manage a little smile. "I'll go talk to Hersholtz and if he says yes, I'll go on out to the inn, walk Wadsworth and bring him back."

She smiled up at him, a wide, clear smile that sliced right into his heart. *Please*, he prayed, *please, please don't let her say the "F" word.* He just did not want her to call him "friend" right here, right now.

"I don't know what I'd do without you," she said. She'd said that before. He didn't know what he was going to do without her, without her when she went back to Pittsburgh, went back to Pittsburgh with Marshall.

"I'd better catch Hersholtz while he's still around in ICU," he replied. "Hang in there, Eden. Everything's going to be ok. Marshall's going to be ok." Then he turned and walked quickly away, never having gotten closer than those five feet.

This time she did go to the cafeteria for lunch, plopping some sort of ham sandwich and a small dish of fruit salad on her tray. She sat alone at a table near a square pillar painted an unpleasant shade of sickly green. It was hard to choke the food down. She decided to pull off the thick crust to make it easier, but ended up pulling off large portions of the sandwich in the process.

Absently she stabbed at squishy slices of bananas mixed in with grapes and bites of pineapple. What if they'd completely dropped him all the way to the floor? His chest tube would have been yanked out right along with his IV. She could tell he was hurting so badly after that, even as much as they did drop him.

She returned her tray and found a chair that faced a bank of large windows, just sitting and staring out at the winter landscape beyond. The sky was completely gray and a few stray flakes blew past sideways in the wind. She shivered looking at it despite being in the warm cafeteria. All she wanted was to be back in the inn, one of Harold's fires crackling, the scent of Martha's cookies wafting from the kitchen, Marshall singing softly into her hair. Interesting. That was what came to her now when she thought of 'home'. When they decided to move to Florida, her parents had sold the old brick house where she'd grown up.

That had been home once, but now that was gone. Her apartment, even though it had her things, had never really become for her what something with the profoundly meaningful name of 'home' should be. But the inn, that was different. It wasn't hers and she only had a few things there, mostly clothes, but the people in it and even the look and the smells and the sounds of it, that did. And that was what she wanted. To be there...with Marshall.

She sighed longingly, heavily, and looked at the sickly green paint again. Institutional green. She was here because Marshall was here, and he was here because he wouldn't let those men take her with them into the woods. "Marshall," she murmured aloud, "I love you."

Chapter 39

Eden sat there looking out the windows longer than she had intended. Time had gotten lost somewhere in the depth of her thinking. Suddenly she looked at her watch and scrambled to her feet, heading off at a fast trot toward the elevator that would take her up to the third floor where Marshall's private room was located. She paused just outside the door, one of those wide hospital doors they can wheel a bed through. It had 303 on a small central plaque and for some reason she noticed the natural design in the grain of the wood right under that formed what looked strikingly like a large eye. Not sure just why she paused outside like she was doing, she considered that maybe it was the mere fact the door was closed. Did that mean he wasn't awake yet?

A blonde nurse passing down the long hallway with a small tray of meds said, "You can go on in, Miss McLaughlin. Dr. Hersholtz has arranged extended visiting hours for you."

"Thank you," she murmured in reply. Did everyone in the hospital know who she was? She turned, following the slim nurse with her eyes until the woman disappeared in a different doorway. Just then Mike came around the far corner from the elevators, Wadsworth onleash. The dog hurled himself forward at her sight and scent and Mike let him go.

Wadsworth barreled down the corridor straight at her as she smiled and backed up against the wall for support in case he decided to go for a full-out greeting with all 120 pounds of himself. But, excited as he was, he didn't jump up on her, just pressed close, wiggling his entire body, looking for bare skin to lick.

She squatted, letting him kiss her cheeks and neck for a moment, her arms going around him. "Oh, Waddy! They let you in." Her eyes lifted over the dog's big head to Mike, who had stopped part-way down the hall. "Thank you, Mike! This is just wonderful!"

She got the leash in her hands as she stood. Mike made no move to come forward. "Aren't you coming in to say hi to Marshall?"

"Got to get back to work," he shrugged. "Shift's not over yet. Maybe later."

As she watched him walk away, she wished she knew what had changed. Something had. That easy openness between them was gone. But Wadsworth seemed to sense Marshall beyond the closed door and her attention was pulled, literally, back to him.

"So you think your guy is in there, do you?" Giving him a last quick pat on his neck, she opened the door, bracing back to keep him from dashing in and leaping on Marshall. Just what he needed was 120 pounds on his chest right about now.

The room was larger, much more like an actual room than the little space in ICU had been with only space for one small chair beside the bed. 303 actually had a wallpaper border around the tops of the walls, was painted a warm beige and had a painting of an English cottage garden to the right of the mounted TV set. The head of Marshall's bed had been cranked up a bit, but he lay there, his eyes shut, looking as though he were still asleep. That was good because he needed rest and he wasn't hurting when he was asleep, but she had a huge dog on a leash, a dog who desperately needed some contact with the man who'd become his life. She paused, trying to decide what to do, both arms straining to keep Wadsworth in check. Wadsworth was whining, pulling hard. Gradually, she let him inch across the room toward the bed. Perhaps this was an idea whose time had not come?

But Wadsworth, well aware that after a tortuous crossing of the desert he had at last arrived at the gates of Mecca, was not going to be put off. One short, utterly piercingly sharp bark sounded in the room. Marshall's head turned a bit.

"Oh, Waddy!" Eden sighed. This was all her fault.

Only half-awake, Marshall seemed to realize, though, who was now in the room with him. One corner of his mouth quirked up slightly and as he moved his right hand to the very edge of the bed, he murmured sleepily, "My family."

Eden stared at him. Had he said what she thought he had?

Wadsworth made it to the hand and for the moment it was enough. He licked and licked and licked it, his tongue going carefully between each of Marshall's fingers as though it were terribly important not to miss a single spot. Marshall lay quietly, letting him. Purell could come later. He had no memory of Wadsworth's arrival on the dock, of how the dog had lain beside him, his muzzle on Marshall's head. For Marshall, this was the first time he'd been with Wadsworth since the moment he'd closed the bedroom door, leaving him there just to pop out and ask Eden where she'd moved his cough medicine. Both corners of his mouth curved up as the dog continued his industrious licking.

"Hi there, boy," he murmured, still not moving. He knew somehow that if he moved, moved absolutely anything but his hand, his whole body would shatter into little sharp shards. At the sound of Marshall's voice, Wadsworth's tail wagged furiously and his hand licking took on even greater fervor.

"Eden?"

"I'm here, darling." She moved close to the other side of the bed, her hand hovering, afraid to let it rest on him anywhere. Wadsworth had looked like he could be trusted at this point not to jump up on the bed. She'd watched the dog's face. Despite the evident joy of reunion, there was a certain gravity to it as though he knew by some instinct that Marshall was hurt and care needed to be taken. It was, after all, his life's work to be aware of Marshall, to anticipate his needs.

Eden leaned carefully over the bed, kissing him lightly and with no pressure on his lips. "I miss your lips," she said softly.

"I miss all the parts of you," he whispered back.

"They're all here, darling, just waiting for all of you to come back to all of them, but they're yours." Her fingers gently pushed back a bit of hair from his forehead. "Always."

"Christmas," he said.

"What?"

"Soon. Christmas."

"Oh, yes, darling. About a week now, I think. I've kind of lost track of which day today is."

He just breathed for a few moments, as though merely being awake took some effort. "Need Martha."

"You need Martha?"

"Yes. Here. Need Martha here." He blew out a long breath, almost visibly gathering himself. "Would you ask her to come see me when she can? I really need to talk to her."

"Of course, darling. I'll speak with her about that when I go back to the inn this evening."

"Good," he said, almost drifting off to sleep but catching himself.

Wadsworth had finally come to the conclusion that Marshall's hand was sufficiently cleansed and now sat quietly by the bed, his big head resting atop the damp palm. He was joined again with the other half of the two-in-one unit that framed his existence. His eyes closed and he relaxed for the first time in days, letting out a long doggy sigh of contentment mingled with relief.

Marshall wiggled one of his fingers under Wadsworth's chin. "I know, boy. I know." Then Marshall sighed himself. "I love you," he murmured.

"Wadsworth?"

"You...and Wadsworth. I've got my eyes on one side and my heart on the other. Don't know what more I could ask."

"You could ask not to be so hurt, so sick."

"It's worth it."

"But...."

"No but's. You're worth it. I couldn't, no way could I let...."

"I know."

A little shudder went through him again at the thought of those men dragging Eden off into the woods, especially Bart.

She bent near his ear. "Thank you," she whispered, "with all my heart." She kissed his temple. "You make me feel so protected, so cherished."

"It's hard," he said, his voice low, serious. "Being blind, you know, it's hard to make a woman feel protected."

"Oh, darling! You risked everything, let all this happen to you. How much more protected can a woman get?"

"I...I...just want...so much...for you. I want...."

"You, Marshall. You, who you are, as you are, that's what I want."

"I just want it to be enough," he said wearily.

"Enough? Do you have any idea, any at all, of how much more than enough you are?"

And so he quietly told her about Beatrice, about how he hadn't been enough at all, not for her, not after her initial fascination with his blindness had worn off.

"So it's left you concerned I might do the same thing, decide I'm tired of being around you?"

He pressed his lips together, not answering.

"Listen to me, Marshall Sinclair. Not only are you marvelously handsome, which is, actually, neither here nor there in the long run of things, but you are the most wonderful, amazing, intelligent, gifted, all-round glorious human being I've ever met, and you've got the whole thing backwards anyway. I'm the one, you know, I'm the one, me, who's just utterly amazed that you want me. I'm still not sure just how that happened to be, but it does seem to be and the fact of it makes me the happiest, most blessed woman on the face of the planet. This Beatrice person was a fool. There's no other word for it. A total fool of a woman who didn't recognize treasure when she had it." She inhaled deeply. "But I'm glad she didn't because maybe if she hadn't been such a fool, you wouldn't have come up to the inn and I'd....oh, Marshall, I can't even think of not ever meeting you, knowing you, hearing your voice, being with you. What I'm trying to say is that you've gone and got yourself stuck with me. You'd better know that right now. You are stuck with me for good."

His closed lips curved into a smile and for the first time that afternoon he opened his eyes, letting her see the bit of moisture sparkling there. "I love you, Eden McLaughlin."

"Back at'cha," she replied, brushing at a stray tear of her own, kissing his ear, his cheek, his nose, and then his chin.

Chapter 40

Eden stayed all afternoon. Wadsworth spent the time either contentedly resting his head on Marshall's hand or lying slightly under the bed. Marshall himself dozed off and on. During one of his little naps, she went out to the nurses' station to ask a question and found the CD player sitting on the countertop. She'd completely forgotten about it, realizing only now that she must've left it on the floor in the waiting room.

"How'd it get here?" she asked.

"One of the EMT guys," the nurse explained. "Said he found it near where you'd been sitting and recognized it as the one you had. Brought it up a while ago and left it here at the station. Said to make sure you got it."

Mike. Of course, Mike. But he hadn't brought it into the room. She sighed, picked it up and carried it to 303. Marshall was awake and talking to Wadsworth. "Don't let me interrupt," she chuckled.

"Oh, it's just guy talk. You know, rifles and wrenches and beer. That sort of thing."

"Sure!" she laughed. "There are guys and then there are guys. You're more of a suede elbow patch sorta guy. So's Waddy. If he had a jacket, I'm positive it would have a suede patch on it somewhere or other."

An odd look passed briefly across his features. Miles had been a rifles and beer guy. Suede patches weren't quite the same thing. She saw it on his face, saw what he was thinking. For a man who was so self-confident and assured in just about everything, he had a real weak spot where it came to what women might think of him. She frowned. What had Beatrice done to him anyway? There had to be a lot more to it than what he'd told her so far. She touched his cheek lightly. "I happen to adore suede, especially in patches on tweed jackets."

"Do you always know the right thing to say?" he asked softly.

"No," she said, "I don't. not by far, but what I say to you, Marshall, is what I truly feel, what I'm really thinking. I need you to know that if I say it to you, I mean it. I won't ever play games with you, won't ever say something just because it sounds right. Ok? I do love suede patches on jackets. There's such a cultured Englishness about it that just appeals to me. A suede patch announces class and intelligence and articulateness. Oh, I suppose anybody could put one on, of course, but generally speaking, that's the connotation that comes with suede patches and I like that." She leaned close again, blowing in his ear. "And, besides that, my darling one, they sneak up on my literary side and really," she blew again, "turn me on."

He laughed a little and had to press his hand to his chest. "I've got a different tweed jacket with not only suede elbow patches, but another large patch on one shoulder."

"OooOOooo...," she said, "you'd better change the subject or I'll jump your bones right where you lie!"

He laughed more, held his chest more.

"I've got the wandering CD player," she announced. "Well, scratch that. It didn't so much wander as I left the darn thing sitting on the waiting room floor. Lucky someone didn't just walk off with it. Anyway, Mike must've seen it and dropped it by the nurses' station." She found a plug for it and set it on his bedside table. "The only CD we've got here is your Tuscany one, though. I'll bring more tomorrow."

So she put it on to play and sat close to his bed, smoothing back his hair as they listened. After a while the pure orchestral version of *Time To Say Good-bye* came on. She rested the back of her hand against his cheek as it played. "I was so worried," she whispered. "I had such a horror of it's being time to say good-bye to you up there on that ridge and I couldn't do that." Her breath came out in a dry sob of an exhale. He leaned his cheek more against her fingers. "You've become so infinitely precious to me."

The music began to build and she closed her eyes, just listening. "I like this. This is beautiful, just the music. You usually hear it with a voice, like Sarah Brightman, singing the lyrics."

"Or Andrea Bocelli," he added.

"You like Bocelli?"

"A great deal, and he interests me because beside that great voice of his, he gets up on stage and sings to huge crowds he can't see."

"Was he born blind like you?"

"He had congenital glaucoma that steadily got worse, but he could see a little as a small boy. Then he had a soccer accident when he was twelve and lost what little bit of sight he had." He listened to more of the music, then added, "He sings this piece really well."

"I bet you could, too."

"Not like him," he chuckled, "and at the moment I don't think I have breath to do justice to *Yankee Doodle Dandy*, though I might give a try to *Row, Row, Row Your Boat*." But on the second 'row' he began to cough. "So much for that," he gasped out between hacks.

She sat next to him a long while as they listened together to the whole CD, her hands stroking his hair. It was about the extent of the physical contact she could have with him, but limited as it was, it was also wonderful. She would never forget that sight of the little hollow under the evergreen where he had lain, but which was cold and empty by the time she got there. Yes, touching his hair was lovely compared with that.

"You know, sweetheart," she mused, "you came up to the inn hoping for a peaceful place to write and you've nearly died twice."

"I think I'm done. At least I hope I'm done with that particular form of activity." He sighed contentedly. "Mmmm, that feels good, the way you're touching my hair."

"I'm glad something feels good." His bruises were beginning to change color now, the purple deepening, yellows appearing. The one she was studying made a perfect crescent around his right eye, from above his eyebrow and down around across his cheekbone. His breathing was evening out, slowing a bit, and she knew he was drifting off again. When she could tell he was asleep, she hooked Wadsworth's leash on his collar and led him to the door, intending to take him outside for a brief walk. He didn't want to leave the room. He'd found, at last, what he'd been looking for and he wanted to stay.

"Look here, Waddy," she said, crouching in front of where he'd stubbornly sat, "I understand this whole 'being with' thing, really I do, but a dog's just gotta, um, 'go' from time to time. He's asleep. He won't even know we're gone, ok. I promise I'll bring you right back."

Wadsworth stood up.

"I am so glad you speak English as well as you do," she chuckled. "It must come from living with a lit professor."

He allowed her to lead him out the door. She paused by the nurses' desk to explain what she was doing so someone could let Marshall know in case he awoke while they were still gone. "Will it be ok if Wadsworth spends the night in 303?"

"I'm afraid not," the nurse replied firmly. "No one would be there who could take him out if he needed to go. The nurses are too busy and it's not right to ask such a thing of them anyway."

"Well, I guess he'll just have to come back to the inn with me, then."

"Probably best," the nurse nodded. "We don't usually allow animals in the hospital in the first place. Besides, Dr. Sinclair doesn't really even need a guide dog at the moment, you know."

Eden sighed and continued on toward the elevator. The head nurse on this floor didn't have the same appreciation of the relationship between Marshall and Wadsworth that Betsy did during his initial hospital stay.

As the doors opened on the main floor, she suddenly remembered she'd need a coat. She'd had a coat when she arrived that morning. She knew she did. Where the heck had she put it? As the main waiting area seemed the most likely, she wandered in that direction, finding it hanging on the rack there.

She stayed outside longer than she'd intended, letting Wadsworth sniff around at all the places that attracted his doggish interest. The brisk air felt rather good after the warm closeness of the hospital room. When she reentered, she kept her coat on all the way to Marshall's room so she'd know where the blasted thing was the next time she'd need it. As she approached the door, a different nurse from the ones she'd seen before was just leaving.

"How's he doing?" she asked.

"Just got him all settled again," the nurse replied. "Dr. Hersholtz removed the chest tube."

Eden's face brightened. "That's a good sign then, isn't it?"

Nodding, the nurse explained that the drainage had completely stopped. So it was with a glad smile on her face that Eden opened the door. Marshall was up on his side a bit, a series of pillows propping his back to keep him there. He seemed just slightly paler than when she'd left him, probably due to the process of having the tube removed.

"You ok?" she asked, unclipping the leash.

Wadsworth had to do a bit more hand-licking since he'd been gone for a while and Marshall's hand had obviously gotten filthy in the interim.

"Tubeless," he sighed, "which is definitely an improvement."

"What did Hersholtz say?"

"He said now they'd be getting me up and out of bed before I turned into cement, or something along those lines anyway."

"Out of bed where?"

"Just around the room at first, I think, then on expeditions down the hall."

"That's good, right?"

"Well, considering the only time I don't hurt terribly much is when I'm lying perfectly still, I'm not so sure it's a good thing."

"You don't want to become cement, now do you? I mean, just think, what could I possibly do to, um, with, a block of cement in bed?"

"You may have a point there," he half-grinned. "Motivation, that's what I need."

She leaned over him, kissing his earlobe. "Lots more where that came from," she chuckled, "but I ain't kissin' no statues, mister. You got that?"

"I got you, Babe," he whispered.

"Oh, don't tell me you know who Sonny and Cher are...were."

"I know lots of good stuff," His grin widened, "despite my suede patches."

"You never cease to amaze me, Dr. Sinclair."

"Good."

They talked for a while then a male nurse came in. "Time for you to walk, Dr. Sinclair."

"How far?"

"Let's try for the bathroom. That sound good to you?"

"It'll do."

Eden went to sit in a far corner as the nurse pulled back Marshall's covers. "Legs over to the side and veeeery slowly we'll get you sitting up, ok?"

Marshall had his lips pressed in a tight, white line. The nurse helped him lift his torso up and Marshall just sat there on the side of the bed for a while, swaying slightly. "Not... sure... about this," he muttered.

"We'll just take it nice 'n easy," the nurse said. "And I'll be right here with you if you start to fall."

Marshall coughed a bit from the change in position, then let his body slide off the edge of the bed so his feet, on which the nurse had quietly slid hospital slippers, were resting on the floor. "Don't you worry about the IV. It's on wheels and I've got it. You just think about putting one foot in front of the other."

Marshall rested a palm on the top of the bed. Hadn't he done just that for hour after endless hour, put one foot in front of the other?

The nurse stood there, waiting, because Marshall didn't move.

"The bathroom?" he urged.

Marshall sighed. "Where is it? I don't know which way to head."

"Ooo, sorry, Dr. Sinclair. I forgot for a minute. At an angle to your right. I'll move along right beside you. You just come along with me."

Marshall took one step and was unable to stifle a sharp moan. Eden turned her head for a moment, looking out the window. Watching Marshall like this was nearly unbearable. He hobbled painfully, awkwardly the eight or so steps to the bathroom door. The nurse went in with him and when they came out, the expended effort of being out of bed had been almost too much for Marshall. He was quite white and his teeth were clamped down tightly on his lower lip. Halfway back to the bed, the nurse had to put his arm around Marshall or he would have crumpled on the spot.

"Ok, Dr. Sinclair, that's real good, real good for your first try. You'll see. You'll get stronger each time."

Marshall didn't reply. He just sank gratefully back to a seated position on the edge of the bed and let the nurse lift his legs and get him settled. As he pulled the covers back up, the nurse looked over at Eden. "Don't you go trying to help him do this on your own," he directed. "Doc here's a big man and you're just not going to be able to catch him if he starts to fall. You buzz the station if he needs to get up."

She nodded, rubbing at the back of her neck, realizing how tense she'd been just watching Marshall. He'd walked just fine out of the inn that last time. All this was the result of what those men had put him through. Getting up from her seat near the window after the nurse left, she sat close to his bed, touching his hair again since he'd said he liked that.

"Got to rest," he murmured.

"I know, darling. You rest." She sat there quietly, just stroking his hair, until his head tipped slightly on the pillow, and still she stroked it.

Chapter 41

Very, very lightly Martha tapped on the door to 303. She hadn't seen him since he'd collapsed halfway onto their dock, looking far more dead than alive. Briefly, she closed her eyes, not at all sure of what to expect when she entered the room.

Eden had returned after dinner to the inn, bringing a most reluctant Wadsworth along with her. Marshall wanted her to come to the hospital. That was the message that Eden had brought. She'd planned to go the following day anyway now that he was in a private room, but thought that since he'd asked for her, she'd just go on ahead for the later evening visiting hours.

"Marshall, you awake?" she asked, opening the wide door just enough to poke her head in.

"Martha. Come on in."

He was propped up with pillows in the bed, an IV still attached to his arm. He was pale, which only made his bruises stand out all the more. And such bruises! Every bit of him that she could see had a bruise or a scrape or both on it. She bit her lip, looking at him, her maternal heart aching at the sight.

He sniffed. "You've brought me peanut butter cookies!"

"I have," she chuckled, setting a small basket down on the table close to him, "and pajamas, real pajamas. Eden said you needed them."

"Ah, thanks," he murmured gratefully. "This gown thing is not my idea of good bedwear."

"You're feeling better?"

"Chest's coming along pretty well, Martha. It's the rest of me that hurts like crazy."

"No wonder," she said, shaking her head at his appearance. "I'm so proud of you," she added after a moment's silence.

"Me?"

"When that convict said he wanted to take Eden with him, my heart almost stopped right then. Back, oh, maybe twenty years or so, we had another escaped convict take a young woman from her home about five miles around the other side of the lake. Took them four days to find her body, and she'd been, well, you know. So when he said that about Eden, the thought of it was nearly more than I could handle." She paused again, reached out her hand to rest it softly on his left arm. "Then you were there and you convinced him to take you in her place. I can't tell you, Marshall, there just aren't words for how you made me feel. I was worried sick for you, too, what with your cough and...eyes... and all, but I was so darn proud of you at the same time. You stepped up, protecting her right along with the bravest of brave men. It meant so much just seeing you do that, son."

"I couldn't let them take her, Martha," he whispered.

"I know, and you didn't, but after we knew they'd taken you on foot up Cooper's Ridge, well, that was almost impossible to imagine. Then Pete called to say they'd left you up there and you were trying to get back all on your own." She shook her head again. "I don't think I stopped praying for a single minute after that."

He smiled. "Thank you, Martha. I needed every bit of that, every single bit."

"You said you wanted to talk to me about something?"

"Umm hmm," he grinned, and proceeded to tell her what was on his mind.

When he was done, she sat back in the chair, a big smile on her face. "You just leave that to me."

"I can't tell you how much I...."

"No need," she interrupted."This is something I'll love doing."

"You're sure? It could be difficult."

"I'm sure." She stood. "You go on and get some more rest. I'll let you know how it's going."

After she left, Ray, a short, rather wide male nurse entered the room. "Dr. Sinclair, you ready for a stroll down the hall?"

"Do I have to?" he sighed.

"'Fraid so."

"Not until I've got my regular pajamas on, ok?"

"Ok by me, Doc. You need some help?"

He did. Just moving his body enough to get his arms in sleeves and his legs in pants wore him out, leaving him so weak and tired that by the time Ray got him on his feet beside the bed, he could barely stand. "Can we just stay in the room?" he asked and Ray, looking at his face, agreed.

Eden, in their room upstairs at the inn, had been texting back and forth with her cousin Connie. Connie had seen a picture of Marshall in the Pittsburgh newspaper and had a lot to say to Eden about it. He had his dark glasses on in the shot and a serious expression on his face but, "He's gorgeous," Connie commented succinctly.

"Better than that," Eden sent back. "He's gorgeous inside, too."

After a few more exchanges, Eden wrote, "I need help with Christmas."

"You staying up there, I presume?"

"Yup. But I need help."

"Ok, lay it on me, cuz."

So Eden did.

"In winter? You expect me to find those in WINTER?" Connie typed.

"I do. I know you. I know you can."

"Ah, the burthen of someone else's confidence in you."

"That's not all," Eden wrote.

"More? You want more than that?"

"I do." And she explained in some detail what she wanted.

"Well, ok, I can do that without much trouble."

"You are useful as well as decorative," Eden commented.

"It's my function, my fate."

"Thank you! It means a lot to me."

"I know."

And so the evening went. She took Wadsworth outside just before bed. Bundled in a thick coat, she walked down to the dock, trying to picture Marshall there as he'd been that morning at the end of October with the sunlight bright on his face, not as he'd been more recently, but it was the second memory that haunted her, that kept thrusting itself to the forefront of her mind. How close she'd come to losing him.

She hadn't seen Miles lying there, dying in the snow, but she had seen Marshall. Only he hadn't died. But it was all too closely similar and she was shaken to her core by it, by how easily such things could come into her life, did come into her life. How did you ever settle into trust, trust that everything would be all right, that those you allowed yourself to love wouldn't be lying dead in the snow some day? There was no way, was there? You just had to love anyway; you had to risk it all and love anyway. She'd let herself think that because of the way she'd first found Marshall there in the gully engulfed in mud, the way she'd been able to get him out, keep death away from him, that death would always stay away, at least until he was very old or something.

But it didn't work like that. Death had leapt out at her again, a mere month and a half later, had waved its arms at her and made faces, daring her to try and stop it. And she had tried, had tried until she'd worn herself to the bone with the trying, but he had saved himself...this time...and death had gone into hiding once again. But it was still there, lurking. She knew that for certain. It made her want to run to Marshall, wrap him in herself and never let loose. People couldn't live like that, though. She knew that, too. It wasn't right, it wasn't living, to let the sprawled, unconscious form at the landward end of the dock keep away the man who'd stood so strikingly in the morning light at the end by the lake. To have the one, you had to accept the risk of the other.

Sighing, she turned to look back at the inn. Martha kept those electric candle things in all the windows and this time of year, especially, they created such a warm, homey glow for the place. She wished Marshall were inside, waiting for her. "Soon," she said, both to herself and Wadsworth. "Well have him back, you and I, soon." What had he said? His eyes on one side and his heart on the other? She liked that. How was he doing right at this moment, with his heart and his eyes here on the dock together?

Marshall was back in bed, trying to recover from the short walk he'd taken with Ray around his room. He'd never felt so weak, so drained of energy in his life, and he didn't like it. After the fall into the gully his strength had come back rather readily, but he hadn't had pneumonia then, either, had he? It was the one-two punch that left him feeling like this. As still as he tried to lie, the recent movements he'd had to do to get changed into his pajamas then walk about the room had geared his muscles and tendons up into full protest mode. Even perfectly quiet, sharp stabs of pain flitted here and there through him, railroad spikes driven rustily through his flesh. With concentrated effort he tried to relax the tense muscles in his forehead, knowing it would only lead to a headache.

A nurse came in to adjust his pillows, check his IV, and give him something to help him sleep. Lying back, he let his mind wander to the sounds and smells of Martha's dining room, the fire crackling warmly at his back, the apple pie Martha set at his place, the knowing that Eden was right there, too. After about half an hour he drifted off to sleep.

Eden saw Martha's car pull into the inn's lot and she and Wadsworth walked over to greet her. "He like the cookies?" Eden asked.

"I think he liked the pajamas even better," Martha chuckled.

"You two have a nice talk?" Eden probed, trying not to be too obvious in her curiosity.

"Yes, yes, we did," Martha smiled, not in the least forthcoming.

Eden sighed. "Well, I'm glad. I know he was pleased to see you, um, have you come by."

"He saw me," Martha said quietly, "in that way he has of seeing."

"You're right," Eden replied, shaking her head. "I think I'm too tired to put things correctly."

"You and Wadsworth come on back inside," Martha suggested, "have some hot cider with Harold and me."

"Sounds good," Eden agreed. "I wish...."

"Me, too," Martha whispered. "And he will."

"Oh, Martha. I just...."

"He 'just's' too, Eden. I know that for a fact." She smiled, hooked her arm through Eden's and together they went down the walk to the inn.

Chapter 42

Marshall spent the next four days in room 303. Eden brought Wadsworth with her whenever she came to visit, which was several hours every day. Though Wadsworth never really liked having to leave Marshall's room in the evening, he became rather reconciled to it since Eden always brought him back to Marshall the next morning. Whenever they were at the inn, he stayed close to her as she was his link to his other half. The two of them were developing a nice relationship of their own, founded on their mutual love for the same person.

Martha spent a lot more time on the phone than usual and also went into town more often. Christmas was coming and no one thought anything of Martha's activities. She hummed frequently and baked whenever she could. Harold kept the fireplaces going, and had even begun taking Wadsworth out for walks when Eden was busy. Eden was on her laptop and cell phone a lot, going back and forth with Connie.

Harold's brother, Stuart, had a huge old farmhouse about four miles further around the lake, a big barn of a place with more bedrooms than could be kept track of. Most of Harold and Martha's kids and their families stayed at Stuart's when they came home for Christmas because the inn was, well, an inn and needed to be available for guests. Christmas for the Malone's was rather a moveable feast in the truest sense as bounteous meals were served at both Stuart's and Harold's, with the family going back and forth between. Stuart's wife, Joan, loved cooking nearly as much as Martha did, and between them, with the help of grown daughters, bellies were always full.

This year, because there was room, Martha's daughter, Elizabeth was going to be staying at the inn for the holidays, her husband, Dale, and her six year old son, Luke, with her. Martha's four sons were all staying at Stuart's. Three of them were married and had their families along. Together with Stuart's three kids and their families, the Malones were quite a crowd.

Martha loved Christmas. It was the only time the widely-scattered family gathered these days all at the same time. She liked to decorate the inn early and thoroughly. Wreaths hung at every window and Harold had outlined all the trim of the house and several small trees in white lights, lots of white lights. In the parlor a nine-foot fir graced a corner, decorated with Eden's assistance, in a thick layer of Victorian ornaments, a large angel with a deep rose-colored velvet gown on its top branch. The banisters on the stairs and along the front porch were hung with draped evergreen garlands. Christmas treasures, fragile and antique, were set on the mantels and tabletops among still more boughs of evergreen. Yet, except for the addition of the large tree in the parlor corner, Martha made sure that every piece of furniture remained where it had been. Marshall would be coming home before Christmas. She smiled at the thought, checking her supply of peanut butter for cookies.

Three days before Christmas, he was released from the hospital. About ten that morning, Eden arrived on the third floor with Wadsworth. As she started down the hallway from the elevators, she thought of her first time here when Mike had come along to show her the way. She hadn't seen him since. She'd tried to call the cabin two or three times, but either he wasn't home or wasn't answering.

Dr. Hersholtz was making rounds and when he saw her, motioned her aside into a small alcove where there were two chairs. "I wanted to speak with you about Marshall before you left today," he said, indicating she should have a seat.

"It's all right for him to be leaving the hospital, isn't it?"

Hersholtz took the other chair, actually giving Wadsworth a small pat. "He should do fine. I mainly want you to be sure he doesn't try to overdo anything for a while. It's easy to get caught up in the holidays, I know, but he's got to get sufficient rest and plenty of sleep. That's not always easy to do at the inn this time of year so he needs someone who's watching out for him in the midst of activity. I think, truly, it would be a good idea if he spent a lot of time in his bedroom. He may think he's up for more than he's really able to handle, but his body is still just recovering from major insult both internally and externally. That little stroll he had in the forest was, for him, just as though he'd been attacked and beaten to a pulp, and he's had two concussions within a month and a half of each other, both in the same general area of the head." He paused, shaking his own head. "That sort of thing is cumulative and we don't want a third."

"I understand, Doctor," she replied. "I'll make sure he doesn't push himself."

"It takes a good while to get strength and energy back after a severe bout of pneumonia. That in itself requires a lot of rest. I thought about keeping him here until after Christmas but he was adamant on wanting to go back to the inn. You call me if you think anything's not right, ok?"

She promised, then rose to go on her way to 303. Wadsworth was doing his trembly thing, seeming to be aware something different was up. When she opened the door, Marshall was dressed in the slacks and shirt she'd brought the evening before, and sitting in the chair by the window. He looked better somehow just by being in his regular clothes and some tension that had been growing in her after listening to Hersholtz began to relax.

"You ready to blow this popsicle stand, mister?" she asked in as throaty a voice as she could manage.

"And here all along I thought it was a gin joint."

"That was in Morocco, I believe."

"Will we always have Paris?" he asked Bogartishly.

She kissed him lightly. "We will if you take me there."

He smiled widely. "Left bank or right?"

"Probably the left I should think. Isn't that where the authors are supposed to hang out?"

"Left it is, then, and I...."

But he was interrupted by the arrival of Ray, pushing an empty wheelchair. He parked the chair close to Marshall and waited while Wadsworth inspected it. "I almost brought his harness," Eden said, "but then I remembered they never let you walk out of hospitals on your own two feet."

"Nope," Ray joined in, "we don't go in for that foot stuff around here. It's wheels all the way."

Ray guided Marshall into the chair and Eden, watching carefully, saw a quickly-suppressed glimmer of pain flash across his features. The nurse adjusted the footrests and with Eden holding the leash and Marshall's small tote bag, they left 303 behind. Harold had pulled his car close to the hospital entrance, and with Ray's hand on his elbow, Marshall walked the three or four steps to its open rear door. Wadsworth jumped in beside him, immediately laying his head on Marshall's lap, letting out a loud sigh of content. It was the first time he'd been able to get that close in way too long.

Eden, holding onto the door, looked in at them affectionately. "You got him this time, Waddy," she grinned, "but just you wait." She closed the door and slid into the front passenger seat.

The Morning Glory Inn faced the lake and guests usually followed the walk around to the front door. The plan for today, though, was that Marshall would come in the back way as it was closer. Though Harold parked his car in the space nearest the back of the house, it was still a good forty paces to the house, then eight steps up to the door itself. It had snowed again in the night and this morning Harold had carefully shoveled the walk and the steps. Eden went around, opening the rear door for Marshall. "It's pretty far," she sighed.

"I'll be fine," he said, straightening himself slowly beside the car. Just that movement of standing erect strained him in several places, but he pressed his lips together and curved them into a determined smile. He walked slowly, his left arm draped around Eden's shoulders as both a guide and a bit of support. When they reached the bottom of the stairs, he paused, gripping the railing tightly. "Give me just a sec," he breathed. He hadn't had to climb stairs yet in his recovery.

Eden and Harold exchanged concerned glances. "I'll be right behind you, son," Harold said, laying his hand on Marshall's shoulder.

Marshall had to go up the stairs by putting both feet on each step. His right knee just wasn't ready to bear his full weight in a normal ascent. He hadn't really realized the effort this simple task would involve for him. About two steps from the top, he stopped completely and swayed slightly, feeling like he was going to fall.

"MARTHA!" Harold yelled.

The steps led into the kitchen and when Martha heard Harold, she quickly opened the door, letting out a flow of warm air redolent with raisins and cinnamon and brown sugar that impacted Marshall almost physically. He gathered himself together, managed a bit of a crooked smile and said, "Hullo, Martha. I'm back."

"I see that, Marshall," she clucked, her brow knit as she observed his face "and you look like you're at the end of your rope in the doing of it."

He nodded. "Think I need to sit down."

Harold, at this point, actually had his hands on Marshall's back, supporting him, and was basically all that was keeping him from toppling backwards down the steps. Martha reached out, taking his left hand, tugging just enough to get him to go forward and somehow, all in a clump, the three of them managed to get him through the big kitchen and around the corner to the parlor and down onto the couch. All the color had drained from his face and his breaths were coming in short little gasps. His head seemed too heavy for his neck and he let it rest against the high back of the couch. "Made it," he sighed.

"You sure di...," Martha began, but his head had turned to the side. "Marshall?"

"He go to sleep already or did he pass out?" Harold asked, peering at him.

"I can't tell," Martha replied, her brow knitting even more deeply. "Here, help me get him turned." As Harold lifted Marshall's legs, Eden and Martha gently settled him on the couch so he was lying down. Eden tucked a pillow under his head and Martha spread a quilt over him. Marshall lay quietly for the next hour while Harold brought more wood for the fire and the two women looked at the long flight of steps up to the second floor and then at each other.

"If he needs to," Martha said, "he can just spend the night right where he is."

Eden pulled a footstool up close to the couch, smoothing his hair back in that way he liked. He might not be aware she was doing it, but she was and it made her feel somehow comforted to do it. "I still can't get my mind around everything he went through, Martha, what it must've been like for him up there."

"He loves you, Eden. That's what got him through."

"Oh, Martha," she whispered, her cheeks suddenly wet, "I love this man so much it hurts."

His lips moved. "Love you, too," he murmured, his hand groping to find hers. "Always."

"Are you all right?"

"Fine. Just...tired. That's all. Just tired." He drifted off again, still holding her hand.

Chapter 43

He rose up gradually through the different layers of sleep, letting his consciousness hover comfortably just slightly below full waking. Where was he? He couldn't remember for a moment, but he seemed to be lying in some bower of scent. His mind, wanting to know, woke, but still he lay unmoving, exploring the wonders that reached him. Evergreen was very strong, rather dominating the other scents. There had to be cinnamon sticks not far away, used in a decoration of some sort. He was at the inn, thank God, he was at the inn.

Still not moving, he sorted out all the other delicacies that filled the air about him. Martha was baking, many things. There was fresh, hot bread, almost the best smell in the world. She was making something else with raisins and brown sugar. He'd smelled that when she'd opened the door earlier and it was still strong in the house. Tomatoes? She was making some kind of sauce. Garlic, onions, cheese, celery, oregano, basil. How glad he was to be away from the medicinal, antiseptic hospital smells he'd experienced for the last week.

What else? A bowl of fruit must be on the coffee table. Oranges, apples, pears, and grapes. He could smell them all. Still he sorted through the scents: slightly wet dog, logs stacked by the fireplace, the ones burning, releasing their wonderful woodsy scent. After the forest, he was almost surprised how much he still enjoyed that particular scent. Ah, there it was. The best scent of all, delicate, somewhat elusive to locate among all the louder ones. She was in the room with her roses. His lips curved into a quiet smile.

Eden had been in a rocking chair nearby, reading, had looked up just as he smiled. Closing her book, she came and sat on the coffee table, not aware of how, for him, she was bringing the roses of herself closer. "You're awake."

"Umm hmm," he said drowsily, inhaling a deep breath, "and I need terribly to be kissed."

"I think I can manage that." She leaned close, gently laying her lips on his.

"I like that," he sighed. "I like that a lot." Then his tummy rumbled.

Eden laughed. "Martha's been holding lunch. I can bring you a tray."

"I'm tired of trays," he said. "I'd really like to try for the table." He moved his legs to the side, pushing with his arms to sit up, trying not to let it show that it hurt. Finally upright, he blew out another breath. "There's just so much of this invalid stuff a fellow can take."

"Just wait there a sec while I go let Martha know you're awake." She walked quickly to the kitchen. "Marshall's up now, and hungry."

"Shall I fix a tray for him?"

"He says he wants to eat at the table." She shrugged. "Can't blame him. He's had every meal in bed for a week."

Martha went around the corner, finding Harold. "Will you walk with Marshall to the table, dear? I just don't quite trust him all on his own." Not after that near-collapse of his on the steps.

When Eden and Harold got back to the parlor, Marshall was standing, his left hand holding onto the back of the couch. "Smells really good," he said at the sound of their steps. "I've missed Martha's cooking."

Eden slid her right arm through his left. "No protests, mister. I'm escorting you into dine."

Harold followed close behind, and though Marshall walked slowly and rather awkwardly, he managed the route to the dining room table rather well. Martha served spaghetti with the homemade bread. It all tasted so good to him he ate a lot more than he usually would have, as Martha watched, grinning widely in pleasure. There was, for her, nothing quite so good as feeding a hungry man and, sizing Marshall up, she could tell he'd lost weight. Well, Christmas was an excellent time to put a little meat back on his bones. She'd see to that.

"You want me to help you up the stairs?" Harold asked at the end of the meal.

"If it's ok, I'd like to spend some more time downstairs. I've been shut away so long I feel kin to the man in the iron mask."

Eden holding his arm again, the two of them went back to the parlor, Harold watching carefully from a bit further away this time. "Looks like he's getting his sea legs back, Martha."

Eden guided him toward the couch, but he indicated he'd rather sit at the piano for a while. The splint on his right ring finger made it a bit difficult, but he managed to play *It's Beginning to Look a Lot Like Christmas* with only a few misses. When he finished, he let his fingertips run soundlessly back and forth over the keys for a moment, enjoying the familiar feel, the fact that he could use his left arm again. "My mother taught me," he said quietly, memories flooding through him. "She had a really good soprano. Used to sing in the church choir. In the evening sometimes she'd play and my Dad would come in. They'd sing together." His hands ran over the keys again. "It's one of my best memories. Kind of old-fashioned, I guess, more like folks used to do before there was TV. I think they tried really hard to find things I could be a part of, you know, other than everybody sitting around staring at a box I couldn't see." He played the beginning of *Danny Boy*. "They were like that."

She came up behind him, resting her hands lightly on his shoulders. "You miss them." It was a statement, not a question.

He nodded, his fingers moving into *Aura Lee*. "It's been different since they've been gone, especially Christmas."

Martha, attracted by his playing, stood in the doorway, a small kitchen pot still in her hand.

"What did you do last Christmas?" Eden asked.

"Met a couple of colleagues of mine at a pub Christmas Eve. Then Wadsworth and I walked a lot. Mount Lebanon, as you know, is one of the few suburbs that has sidewalks. Guess we did several miles of them that night. I know all the streets there really well, then, of course, Wadsworth knows them even better. Started to snow about eleven. Sat on a bench in a small park and just sort of let it snow on me. Was really quiet. In the morning I gave Wadsworth his presents. He's generally a cheap date," he grinned.

Eden, aware of Martha, turned and looked at her as Marshall talked. Martha just shook her head silently.

"What about you, darling?"

"Presents? Oh, there'd been a little party at the university. My secretary had a mug and some special coffees for me." His hand came up, resting atop hers on his left shoulder. "It's ok. I don't require much."

She kissed his hair. "I love you," she whispered.

"That's my present this year," he smiled. "I get loved by you."

"You do," she said, wanting to crush him in her arms, but holding back, knowing it would hurt him so she kissed his neck and around up, kissing his ear, then his temple, leaving her lips there. She loved him so much that, in that moment, she wasn't sure her being could contain it and thought she might well split open right there on the spot like some milkweed pod and all the soft whiteness of her love would spill out, floating around him, enveloping him.

Martha turned and left then, brushing at her cheeks with the back of her free hand. Sat alone and let it snow on him? On Christmas Eve? Not this year!

He played a few more Christmas songs, leaning back against her body as she stood behind him, liking the physical connection with her. When he stopped, he put his hand on hers again where it still lay on his shoulder. "Shall we try the stairs, you think?" he asked.

"You don't have to. Martha said you could just stay on the couch tonight."

"Nope. Don't want to be away from you another night. Had enough of that."

"All right, then, but let me get Harold. I'd like him behind you."

"I'll be fine."

"Seems like you said that on the way to the back door, if I remember right."

So Harold came and the three of them went slowly up the steps to the second floor. He paused once, catching his breath half way up, but made it to the top, where he gripped the railing post and breathed some more. "Long way," he said, trying to make light of how much the climb drained him.

"Very long," she agreed, waiting for him to recover enough to continue down the hall to their room. Wadsworth was already at the door, wagging his tail, patient for someone to let him inside. He was happy again. Things were as they should be.

Harold followed along to the door, then went back downstairs. Martha had stood at the bottom of the staircase, intently watching Marshall's progress. Again she thought of the last time he'd come down it, the two convicts waiting silently for him. But he was back now. Safe and back.

He went directly to the big four-poster bed, sitting on the edge of it. "Will you lie beside me a while?"

"Is that all right?"

"It's more than all right, my darling. I need it desperately."

He lay slowly back, not able fully to suppress a brief wince again. Eden slipped off his shoes, then hers, and crawled up beside him, not at all sure how to go about lying next to him without hurting him. But he lifted his left arm, and she tucked herself carefully along his side. His eyes were closed and his breathing was a bit labored, but he had a small, contented smile on his face as his arm curved around her. He let out a long sigh. "Home," he whispered. It was the inn, not his own house, but she was there beside him and nothing more was required than that to make it home.

Chapter 44

Marshall had spent most of the afternoon in bed, just cuddling with Eden, talking softly. Martha showed up at the door with a big tray at suppertime, bearing enough food for both of them. They ate slowly, enjoying the simplicity of being together, music playing softly in the background. He took his evening meds, finally changed into his pajamas, and they lay together again, nuzzling as much as he was able. He fell asleep about nine and Eden sat in the chair for a while, texting Connie, making sure of last minute details.

Morning broke on a day that was warm for north central Pennsylvania in late December. Martha was glad because it was the day Elizabeth and her family were arriving for the holidays. It was always easier to think of them on the road when it wasn't snowing.

Marshall and Eden came down for breakfast. He still had to take the steps one at a time, but he was determined to be out and about. In fact, since it was so warm, in the upper 50's at least, he decided to venture forth on a walk down to the dock. Martha rolled her eyes and shook her head for Eden's benefit. Since his leather jacket had not really survived his trek out of the forest, he was wearing the navy blue one he'd worn home from the hospital. Though it was thick cloth, it was similar in form to his leather one, as he liked the longer, belted jackets. Martha insisted he wear a sweater under it, not taking no for an answer, absolutely firm in her motherly way that he not get chilled. He was not a hat sort of person, but she reached up and popped one of Harold's hunting caps on his head. He indulged her with a slight grin.

Wadsworth loose, but staying nearby of his own choice, Marshall went down the walk with Eden's arm through his. "It's foggy," he said, lifting his chin.

It was, indeed, the soggy ground and the thin patches of snow sending up moisture into the warm air. Despite the splint, he held his right hand out, spreading his fingers, turning the hand slowly, feeling the fog.

They walked down to the end of the dock and stood silently a while, arm in arm. No boats were out and the Canada geese had finished their migration. The lake was quiet but for the rhythmic lap lapping of itself against the pilings of the dock and some rocks along the shoreline. Eden closed her eyes, trying to enter his world. In the darkness, the stillness was even more profound, and the tiniest break in it came clearly to her ears. The mist became tangible, touching her cheeks with its foggy veils. She listened to his breathing at her side, really listened. It sounded different somehow than it had when she had lain beside him on the bed.

Opening her eyes, she looked up at him. His lips were parted and he seemed to be working harder at what he was doing. "Marshall? Are you all right?"

"Fine, darling. I think it's a bit further out here than I remembered. I'd sit but there's no place around here for that."

He was right. All the outdoor furniture had been stored away for the winter. She sized up the distance back to the house, frowning. "Can you make it to the inn?"

"Sure. No problem. Think I'd better take it fairly slow, though." He hated the sudden weakness that had washed over him, had wanted to prolong his time there at the end of the dock with Eden, but he needed a chair, he really needed a chair.

They walked slowly, pausing now and then, but he made it ok to the inn and up the steps to the porch. Eden opened the door and walked with him to the parlor, where he settled on the couch. "Would hot tea be good?" she asked, and he nodded.

She'd heard a car arrive while they'd been on the way back up the walk, the sound of voices greeting happily behind the house. Elizabeth must be here. In the kitchen she found Martha and Elizabeth talking while Dale investigated what Martha had been cooking. Six-year-old Luke slipped unnoticed into the main part of the house.

Luke, a serious little boy with straight dark brown hair and large brown eyes framed in rather owlish glasses, went into the parlor to look at his grandmother's Christmas tree.

Eden had left Marshall sitting on the couch, but he had decided he really rather lie down, so slipped off his shoes and was full-length on the couch, his eyes closed and was taking long breaths in through his nose and letting them out his mouth with a soft, little 'aaaah' sort of sound. Luke forgot about the tree and came, standing just the other side of the coffee table, his kneecaps pressed against it.

"You dying, Mister?"

"Wha...?" Marshall was startled. He thought he was alone in the room.

"You dying?" the boy repeated.

The voice was very young, probably belonging to Martha's grandson. Marshall sucked in one last, long breath. "Not today."

"I heard Granny talking to my Mom. She said you almost died twice since you been staying here."

"Well, that is true."

"So I thought maybe you was dying again. You sure look like you're dying."

"That bad, eh?"

"Never saw anybody dying before."

Marshall chuckled. "Well, you're not seeing one now, either." He swung his legs off the couch, still letting the high back of it support his head as his weariness yet hung heavily on him. He forgot to open his eyes.

"You the man whose eyes are broken?"

"Interesting way of putting it. Well, I've never thought of it quite in that way but, yes, I'd be that fellow, most likely."

"My eyes are a little broken," Luke said softly.

"A little?"

Luke came around the coffee table and sat down on it. He took off his thick glasses and held them out so they touched Marshall's left hand. "I have to wear these."

Marshall ran his fingers around the glasses, careful not to smudge the lenses. "These seem to be big, important glasses."

Luke smiled. "I never thought of them like that."

Eden had started back into the parlor just as Luke began to talk to Marshall. Martha and Elizabeth were right behind her. All three women stopped, taken by the rather strange conversation.

"The only glasses I have are very dark glasses."

"How come? Where are your regular ones?"

"Regular ones can't help me, Luke. It is Luke, right? Not like yours can help you."

Luke had put his back on, settling them carefully, peering through them at the man who was sitting on the couch. "I never met anybody whose eyes were worse than mine." He stared at Marshall, fascinated. "If I close my eyes, can you see me then?"

"Doesn't work that way, Luke. My eyes never see, no matter what you do with yours." He'd remembered and opened his eyes a few moments ago.

"How long have they been broken?"

"Always."

"Always?"

"Umm hmm."

"Even when you were little like me?"

"Even then, yes."

Luke had to think about this. This was a new concept for him. "Don't you miss seeing?"

"Luke, I don't even know what seeing is."

Now this was really strange and new. "How can you not know that? Everybody knows what seeing is."

"Not if you've never seen anything. Then you don't." He had become aware of the presence of the women in the doorway behind him, but didn't acknowledge it, not yet. He didn't want to interrupt Luke's train of thought.

"So you're what they call 'blind'?"

"I am."

"What is blind? Can you tell me what it is?"

"No, I can't, Luke," Marshall said frankly. "I know it's the absence of seeing, but since I don't know what seeing is, how can I know what the absence of it is?"

Eden shook her head. She understood something for the first time.

"You don't miss it?"

"No, Luke, I don't miss it. I have what I have. It's enough. Really it is."

"What about him?" He pointed at Wadsworth, who was sitting near the window, watching proceedings with a cocked head.

"Him? You mean the dog?"

"Yeah, that's what I'm pointing at."

"But I can't see that, Luke, remember?"

"It's hard to remember that."

"That's Wadsworth. He's my eyes."

"You have kinda greenish eyes and his are brown. How can his eyes be your eyes?"

"His eyes aren't, um, 'broken' so he sees with his own eyes and then he lets me know where to walk so I don't run into things."

When Eden had first gone into the kitchen and been introduced to Elizabeth and Dale, she'd asked Martha about the tea, explaining how weak Marshall had suddenly felt down on the dock. Martha already had some water boiling, and quickly made tea, putting a thick slice of homemade pound cake on a small plate as well. Elizabeth and Martha talked almost daily, so Elizabeth was well aware of Marshall and most of the circumstances surrounding his stay at the inn.

"Luke," his mother said firmly, stepping into the room, "it might be a good idea to let Dr. Sinclair get a little rest right now, all right?"

"Are you really a doctor?"

"A teacher-kind of doctor, not a giving-shots kind."

"Luke." Elizabeth was a younger, female version of Harold, tall and very lean, but with her mother's friendly eyes.

"Ok, Mom." Luke got up from the coffee table and went to look at the tree.

"I'm sorry, Dr. Sinclair," Elizabeth said, coming closer as Eden set the tray for Marshall on the coffee table.

"Marshall, please. And don't be concerned about Luke. I enjoyed our little chat." He sniffed. "Pound cake?"

"Two o'clock. Tea's hot, more to your left, about nine," Eden said softly.

"Luke, are you still here?"

"By the tree."

"Tell me what it's like."

Luke turned back to the tree, studying it seriously. "It's tall, almost up to the ceiling. Has Granny's angel on it, up on top. Lots of ornaments. Can hardly see the green. Lots of sparkly things." He looked at Marshall appraisingly. "You know sparkly?"

"Like when you get handed a glass of Coke or something and it's just been poured and you hold it close to your face and the little bubbly-things tickle your nose?"

Luke smiled really big. "Yeah, like that." He looked at his mother. "Marshall knows sparkly." He turned his eyes back to the man on the couch. "Marshall can't see the tree, but he knows sparkly, and it's enough."

Marshall smiled. He liked young Luke, a lot.

"Come on, Luke," Elizabeth said. "Let's get settled in, then we'll drive over to Stuart's. I bet your uncles will be arriving there shortly."

When it was just the two of them, Eden sat beside Marshall on the couch, drinking her own cup of tea. "You feeling better now?"

"Tea and pound cake, much better than medicine."

They went up to their room and he rested a while, falling deeply asleep for a half hour, which he'd not meant to do. He woke to the scent of evergreen and thought for a minute he was in the parlor. "Eden?"

"I'm here, darling. I have something for you, for us."

He sat up. "Evergreens?"

"A tree. Just a little one about a yard tall, but it's a Christmas tree, our Christmas tree."

He walked toward the scent of roses and pine and she took his outstretched hand, guiding it to the little tree on a small table. He ran his hands over it. "It's not decorated, just has lights."

"That's because we're going to do it, you and I."

He smiled. "I haven't put an ornament on a tree since...."

"Well, you are now." She put a golden glass ball in his hand. "It's colored like the sun," she said, so he'd know.

He turned it, finding the hanger, and feeling carefully with both hands, hung it on a branch mid-way down. "Ok?"

"Perfect," she said. "Now here's a green one, like freshly-mown grass."

"You remember."

"It was important."

"Is there a red one?" he asked.

"Yes, with two green stripes."

"You hang that one. This should be a joint effort. Our first Christmas tree."

But as she reached out, his hands found hers, cupping above them, following along so that they hung the red one with two green stripes together.

Chapter 45

"Eden?" Martha said from the doorway to the parlor, where Eden was sitting on the couch beside Marshall. It was early afternoon on Christmas Eve and the two of them had been in deep conversation for a while.

"What is it, Martha?"

"I wanted you to meet our Christmas guests, a mother and her grown daughter."

Eden rose, turning to face the door. Her mouth literally dropped open. "Connie!"

Connie came into the room, a big, satisfied smile on her face. "You think Mom and I are doing without you for Christmas this year, you got another think coming, kid."

Her mother, Edith, was right behind her. Eden hurried around the couch, hugging both women at once, then stepped back, looking at her cousin. "You didn't tell me! How could you not tell me?"

"This, that look on your face. I didn't want to miss the look," Connie laughed. Peering past Eden, she whispered, "Is that...him?"

Marshall stood, turning, smiling because he had been able to hear the joy in Eden's voice.

"Oh, heavens!" Connie said in Eden's ear. "Better than the picture in the paper."

Marshall acted like he hadn't heard. "Cousin Connie, I presume?"

Connie walked around the couch. He heard her steps and held out his hand, one corner of his mouth up in a bit of a grin. She put her hand in his and he laid his other atop it. "You've made Christmas even better for Eden with your surprise."

Connie, never having heard his voice, was fascinated by its deep, rich tone. She looked from Marshall back to where Eden was standing, her arm around Edith's waist, and made a thumbs up gesture with her free hand. Eden grinned and dipped her head in an acknowledging nod. "And I cannot tell you how glad I am finally to meet you," Connie replied. "Not that Eden has really ever mentioned you to me, of course." She laughed lightly.

Eden came around, bringing Edith with her. "Marshall, I've got Connie's mom, Edith, here with me. She's my aunt but has always been more another mother for me."

"Edith," Marshall said, as Connie withdrew her hand and he moved his in the other woman's direction.

Edith, a just slightly plump woman in her sixties, with gray-streaked faded red hair that had once looked very much like Eden's, had to clear her throat before she could speak. For some years now she'd been worried about Eden, afraid she would spend the rest of her life alone. As she'd entered the parlor and stood by her niece, carefully observing the light in Eden's eyes as she looked at Marshall, the truth of what Eden had been telling her on the phone finally hit her. She cast a quick glance to her side at Eden, then took Marshall's proffered hand. Several dozen quick little thoughts were running through her mind all at once, things she might say...*I see how much Eden loves you...I'm so glad you didn't die and leave her alone again...I can tell you've been terribly sick but you seem to be on the mend...do you love her as much as she loves you?...it's wonderful you live in Pittsburgh so she won't be moving away from us, not like her mother did....*

"Merry Christmas, Marshall," she said.

"Merry Christmas, Edith," he returned. Both of his parents had been only children, so he'd never had aunts or uncles or cousins. "And to you, too, Connie. There's nothing quite like having family for the holidays."

Connie, who was taller, thinner than Eden, and with short, curly red hair so dark it was almost a burnished brown, stood, still facing Marshall, a rather sloppy grin on her face, her eyes sparkling.

Eden pulled her back a few steps as Marshall and Edith spoke. "You've got the stuff?" she whispered.

"Sheesh, Cuz," Connie giggled, "you make me sound like a crack dealer. Of course I've got the stuff. Seemed better to bring it myself than wire it. Besides, you know I had to see him for myself."

"Good?"

"All good, better than good. Good is not nearly good enough," Connie whispered. She and Eden had grown up very much like sisters. Connie was Edith's only child and was two years older than her cousin. Her house was just two blocks from Eden's when they were kids and they'd spent the better part of their days going back and forth between the two homes. The two months Eden had been at the inn had been the longest they'd ever gone without seeing one another. Connie had been married for seven years in her twenties, a marriage that had ended in a rather bitter divorce. She had no children and lived now in an apartment a short drive from Eden's.

Martha looked in the door, smiling. All three women were in a semi-circle in front of Marshall. Her smile widened. Three women. He would have three of them now to be good to him. She'd rather enjoyed being in on Connie's little secret, handling the room reservation and not saying a word. Little secrets and Christmas, they went hand in hand. Then she returned to her kitchen. Her own family would be coming over for dinner this evening, all of them, all around the dining room table with Marshall and his ladies. Harold was even now adding the extra leaves to the table, making it big enough for everyone.

She'd invited Mike, too. He'd had Christmas Eve dinner with them for many years now. This year, though, she'd had to really work on him to get him to say he'd come. He'd never been reluctant before. An observant woman, she knew why, but she also knew he'd be alone if he didn't come so she played up his close friendship with Ryan, her eldest son. Ryan was the only one of her children who'd not married. His job as a travel agent had taken him to several cities, but right now he lived in Cleveland. She smiled again, thinking of him, of how he was so determined to see every bit of the world he could. At forty-one, he'd managed to see a huge part of it.

Elizabeth was in the kitchen along with Stuart's wife, Joan, two of Joan's daughters and three of Martha's daughters-in-law. Good thing it was a huge kitchen, Martha thought as she entered, what with so many cooks 'n all.

After Harold got the leaves in the dining room table, he set up three card tables over to the side for the kids. He was just finishing this when Luke came in, studied what his grandfather was doing, then announced, "I'm not eating at the little peoples' tables this year."

"And why would that be?" Harold asked, looking fondly across the room at his serious little grandson.

"Because I want to sit next to Marshall."

"You do, now do you?"

"I do."

"Well, you go clear that with your grandmother and I'll make sure and fit in a chair for you, too."

As Marshall and the three women sat together in the parlor, Eden noticed his hand go to his breast pocket and that he had his dark glasses folded and tucked there. He was thinking about his eyes. He was meeting new people, a lot of new people today and wasn't used to not wearing his dark glasses. *Beatrice*, she thought again, hating that he should feel the slightest discomfort, especially with Edith and Connie, with whom it was totally unnecessary. Then Martha and Harold's whole family would be coming over shortly. He must be thinking of them, too. She watched as his fingers ran across the top fold of the glasses, linger a moment, then drop back to his lap.

"Right, Eden?" Connie said.

"I...I'm sorry, Con. I didn't hear what you said."

"I asked if you thought a rural Christmas like this was kind of nicer than back in the city."

She didn't really care where she was spending Christmas. All Eden needed was that Marshall be there. "Uh, yes, yes, I do think it's nicer," she mumbled, getting a rather sharp look in return from Connie, who could easily see Eden's mind was elsewhere.

"Your parents, Eden," Marshall asked, "did they not come to Pittsburgh for the holidays?"

Eden realized she hadn't mentioned them to him, mentioned where they'd be. "No, they went to, where was it this year, Con, Aruba?"

Connie nodded. "Aunt Cerise likes warm for Christmas."

"That's my mother," Eden explained. "After she left the Pennsylvania snows behind, she hasn't been all that much for returning. She and my father like to travel," she shrugged, "so for the last several years, they've found some place more exotic to be for Christmas than Pittsburgh."

Unseen by Marshall, Edith reached out and cupped her hand over Eden's right arm. He did the same thing with her left. Edith and Connie both watched his movement and shared a pleased smile.

They talked for a good while, Connie and Edith getting acquainted with Wadsworth as well, then Eden noticed that Marshall was beginning to look really tired. "Why don't you two get settled in your rooms and Marshall can rest for a little bit before dinner?"

He didn't protest. It was still an effort for him to go up the stairs, and he still had to put both feet on each step. Watching him made his condition more real for the newly-arrived women.

At the top of the stairs, Eden said, "I'll be there in just a minute, ok?"

In their room, Marshall lay on the bed, his forearm across his upper face. "Are you up for a big family dinner, darling?" she asked, concerned.

He didn't move his arm. "Just need to rest a minute. I'll be fine."

"You know you'd say you were fine if you were lying beside the tracks and a train had just severed your legs."

She saw his lips curve slightly. "I probably would."

"You sleep. I'll go visit with Connie and Aunt Edith. Their room is two doors down on the right if you need me."

He didn't answer and she could see his mouth had relaxed, so she went quietly out of their room, tapping on her family's door.

When Connie opened it, Eden said, "He's sleeping already."

"I don't think I really realized until just now how hurt he'd been, Eden."

"You should have seen him a week ago, Con. He looked like he'd arm wrestled a cement mixer. Most of the bruises are pretty faded by now, but the pneumonia has left him really weak, and his right knee makes it hard for him to walk." She sat down on the edge of one of the two beds, looking at her hands in her lap. "Nobody knows how he made it out of there. He was so sick, you have no idea how sick, and he kept falling over and over and over. The whole thing was a nightmare."

"But he did make it out, Eden," Edith said softly. "That's all that matters."

Eden nodded. "It is all that matters. It really is."

"I can tell," Edith said.

Eden turned large green eyes on her aunt. "I know I've only known him a couple of months, but he means more to me already than anything, anything, ever has."

Edith was aware of an intensity in Eden she'd never seen before. "I like him very much, darling," she said. "He seems to be everything you've said he was."

"I'm glad you came." Eden blinked back tears. "I'm so glad you came, both of you."

Edith had been widowed for fifteen years now. These two young women meant the world to her. "Christmas wouldn't be the same without you, darling, and now to have not only the three of us together, but to have him, too. We both just really wanted to meet him after all you've said, and he's a lovely man, he really is."

They talked a while longer then Eden suddenly remembered and asked, "They're not still in the car, are they?"

"Oh, they'll be fine, worry wart," Connie laughed.

"Let's go get them. Now. Please? I'd just feel better if I knew they were safe in your room."

After the younger women had made a trip out to Connie's car, and talked some more, Eden slipped quietly back into the room she shared with Marshall. He lay on his back, his arm now at his side rather than across his face, and seemed to be still sleeping. She knelt on the floor beside the bed, just appreciating his aliveness. "Thank You, God," she whispered.

"For what?"

"You're awake!"

"You're thanking God I'm awake?"

"I'm thanking Him that you're alive."

He turned his head toward her. "I'm thankful you're alive, too."

"It's not the same thing. I haven't almost kicked the bucket twice in two months."

"And you better not, either."

She laughed. "I promise."

"But, Eden, it is the same thing, you know. That you are alive is the most important thing there is to me." He moved his hand to the side of the bed, reaching out, finding her head, sliding his palm around her cheek. She turned her face into it, kissing his hand.

"Merry Christmas Eve," he said softly, and she got up, sliding onto the bed beside him, her arm over his chest, her face tucked against his neck. He put his hand atop her arm, sighing deeply.

"What are you thinking?" she asked.

"I'm thinking you are the best Christmas present I've ever had." He moved his head enough to kiss her temple then sighed contentedly again.

Chapter 46

"Suede patches."

"What?"

"Please. Suede patches for Christmas Eve dinner."

Marshall smiled. "You really want me to?"

"I really do."

"I could wear the one with the shoulder suede, too."

"Ooo, yes! Wear that!"

"You want me to look...literary?"

"Yep. You don't have a pipe, do you?"

He shook his head. "Wadsworth won't pass as a hunting hound, either, I'm afraid."

As she slipped on an emerald green silk blouse and a long black skirt with almost a cummerbund effect at the waist, he ran his hand down the line of his jackets till he felt the suede shoulder patch. "Cravat or tie?" he asked.

"You have a cravat?"

"I think there's one here somewhere, but that might be a bit much, don't you think?"

She pondered it seriously, not at all sure it would be too much. "It *is* Christmas Eve."

"In Pennsylvania, not Devonshire."

"Still...."

"I will if you'd like."

"Let me see the jacket first."

He held it out on its hanger, a deeply burnished rust-colored tweed with matching solid rust suede patches. "I like it," she approved.

Opening a drawer, he fished for the cravat. It was a dark rust-color, too. "Oh, my," she said. "Will you humor me and try it on?"

He took the clothes into the bathroom. "Not for modesty," he grinned, "but so you'll get the full effect and not piece by piece."

She brushed her hair, put on a two-strand gold chain and matching dangly earrings. She got such pleasure out of looking at him, it was hard for her not to wish he could see her. It was definitely perplexing. How did a sighted person share such things as their own enjoyment of something as simple as the way somebody looked in a special outfit? How did you get past wanting your beloved to see you?

Then the bathroom door opened and he came back into the bedroom, looking for all the world as if he'd just stepped out of a movie. He was that handsome. He was always handsome to her, but the clothes simply accentuated it. Soft rust-colored slacks and a silk handkerchief in his breast pocket completed the total coordination of what he wore. He had the cravat on, a small gold stickpin in the center. She didn't say a word and a worried expression crossed his face. "Not right?"

Coming to him, she touched his cheek. "So right it's taken my breath away."

"Tell me about you. What color?" His fingers found the collar of her blouse.

"Emerald green," she supplied, "like the scent of the Christmas tree."

"I like that."

His fingers moved down the front of her blouse, trailing over each covered button, finding her cummerbund where his hand spread out, sliding around her waist, then down her hip, delicately touching the draping folds of her skirt. She inhaled a short, sharp breath. Perhaps his way of seeing her wasn't so bad after all. "Don't stop looking," she whispered, and his hand moved up, curving over the silky mound of her breast. He left it there, letting his hand rise and fall with her breathing. "This isn't very conducive to going down to dinner," she murmured.

"I know," he agreed, his lips finding her neck.

"You two ready in there?" Connie's voice came through their door.

"Are you ready?" Marshall whispered in her ear.

"I am *so* ready," she moaned, her fingertips curving into the tweed of his sleeve. Then she sighed hugely. "Coming, Con!" she called out.

Marshall slipped his arm around her waist and they went to the door. "You know you...," Connie began, but her voice trailed off as she looked at them. Eden's eyes met hers, an understanding gaze passing between them.

Edith, standing slightly to one side, smiled broadly. "Good evening, Marshall. I'm so pleased to be sharing Christmas Eve dinner with you."

"Thank you, Edith. I'm looking forward to it."

As they entered the dining room, Eden made sure to steer him around the newly-set-up card tables and the larger space the main table now occupied with all its leaves inserted. Harold had a nice fire going with evergreens, pinecones, and bayberry candles along the mantel. So many aromas flowed out of the kitchen it was hard to identify them individually. They mixed and mingled in a delightful potpourri of dinner smells.

Harold introduced them to Stuart and his wife, Joan, and their grown children. Three of Elizabeth's brothers were there with their wives, their children vying for places at the card tables, which had their own tablecloths and small centerpieces. Martha directed Marshall to a seat, with Eden on his right, then Edith and Connie past her.

A small voice sounded just to Marshall's left. "Hello again."

"Luke?"

"Yep, it's me."

"He asked to sit by you," Martha volunteered softly. "Is that all right?"

"It's wonderful, Martha."

"See, I told you he wouldn't mind," Luke crowed. "I told them your eyes were broken and mine were a little broken so we needed to stick together."

"You are very right," Marshall nodded. "I'm glad you thought of that tonight."

"How do you eat with broken eyes?"

"Well, Luke, it's the only way I know to eat, but I understand it's supposed to be easier to know where your food and your glasses are with that thing called 'seeing'. When I make my meal myself, I know where I've put things, but times like now I don't know where things are until my hands find them or someone tells me."

"Can I tell?"

"Sure, if you like. Do you know how to tell time?"

"I just learned, but what's that got to do with finding food?"

"If my plate is a pretend clock face, and someone tells me my peas are at three and my potatoes are at seven, then I know where to find them."

"Oh! I like that! But you don't have any food on your plate yet. Uncle Ryan's not here. Your water's about, um, two, I guess. Does that help?"

"It helps a lot, Luke."

Just then there was a stir and two men in their early forties entered the dining room. "I stopped by the cabin and hauled Mike out," Ryan said, his dynamic presence rather charging the room. Both Connie and Edith had heard about all the help Mike had been, and turned to look at the newcomers. Eden looked, too, glad that Mike had come. She hadn't seen him since the day Marshall left ICU.

Ryan was running one hand through his slightly wavy light brown hair. "Hat hair," he chuckled. He had an Australian bush hat, one side of the brim curved way up, that he wore almost everywhere and had just hung it on the rack by the front door. He was tall, lean, with something almost cowboyish about him. Perhaps it was the rather weathered look to his face, as though he spent a lot of time outdoors. Even in winter he was tan, which just served to emphasize the light blue-grayness of his eyes.

"You always have hat hair," Elizabeth laughed. He reached out, mussing her hair just a bit.

"Now we match."

"Fiend!" she chortled.

"C'mon, Michael," Ryan urged. Mike was hanging back a bit by the doorway, his eyes wary, trying not to linger on Eden. Two women he didn't know were just to her right, so he let his gaze settle on them.

"Mike," Martha said, "take the seat by Connie. She's Eden's cousin from Pittsburgh. Connie, this is Mike. Ryan, that leaves one chair over here, son." She indicated a chair across the table from Edith.

"I'm glad you came, Mike," Eden said. He dipped his head and smiled with his lips closed as he took his seat. He'd seen her crossing the parking lot of the hospital with Wadsworth a couple of times, but had never made her aware of his presence. She looked marvelous this evening, that shiny deep green setting off her dark red hair.

Pulling his eyes away from her, he focused on Connie. "So you're the one who found the inn for Eden?"

"Pretty easy for me," she smiled. "Comes right along with my job."

"Your job?"

"Travel agent. So I have access to information about all the nicest places to stay."

Ryan's ears perked up. "You're an agent?"

"For quite a few years now."

"Ryan's a travel agent, too, Connie," Martha explained.

"Where?"

"Cleveland."

"Cleveland?"

"I know, I know. It's just temporary. I have a good friend who's starting an agency there. Kinda helping him get it up and running." He looked across the table at her, his eyes sparkling and full of life. "Ever been to Fiji?"

"Myself?" she asked and he nodded. "Well, I must admit I plan lots of trips for other people, but haven't really taken all that many myself."

"Would you like to go to Fiji?"

"You askin' me?" she chuckled.

Ryan cocked his head. "Might not be such a bad idea."

From then on for the rest of the dinner, the two of them went back and forth, totally absorbed in travel talk, places seen, places yet unseen, the art of planning a long trip for someone. Connie barely glanced at Mike, who once in a while quietly stole a brief look past Connie and Edith to see what Eden was doing. Martha sighed. So much for the best laid plans of mice and innkeepers.

Luke delighted in the clock concept of Marshall's plate, keeping him fully informed throughout the meal. Eden was enjoying Marshall's pleasure in the attempts of the serious little boy to guide him while he ate. Her head was more often than not turned to her left so she could observe the interaction between the two of them. Martha, at the end of the table, tried to make conversation with Mike.

"You thought of getting a new dog?" she asked, knowing how much he'd loved old Mazie.

"I do think of it from time to time, Martha," he admitted, "but I'm gone so much right now, it would be hard to manage a puppy."

"Company could be nice, though," she added.

Involuntarily, his eyes darted quickly to his left, then back to Martha. "Could be," he whispered.

Marshall ate quietly for the most part, surrounded by a sea of detached voices, a great deal of them new to him. Once in a while, he felt Eden rest her left hand on his thigh and he'd put down his fork, letting his own hand lie atop hers. There was a general warmth in the room, that sort of warmth that comes when a large family is reunited and everyone is catching up on all the news, happy to be together, laughing at all the familiar things families share through the long years. He liked the hubbub of it, though it was rather new for him, his own family having been just him, his brother, and his parents. Many conversations were going at once and it was a bit hard to sort them out, but he was aware of Connie's animated chatting with Ryan. After a while, he leaned forward, turning his head to the right. He hadn't heard Mike's voice for some time now during the meal. "Mike," he said, to attract his attention. It was hard because he never knew if someone were looking at him or otherwise engaged.

"Merry Christmas, Marshall," Mike responded.

"I haven't gotten to speak with you since, well, since....and I wanted to let you know how grateful I am that you stayed with Eden there in the woods and how you watched over Wadsworth for me. I've been hoping you'd come by the inn so I could tell you how much I appreciate your friendship and your kindness."

"She was one determined little lady," Mike replied. "Was going to go up that ridge by herself if nobody'd go with her. Did you hear how she pushed Barry?"

"Eden pushed somebody?"

"Yeah, one of the deputies. He tried to stop her from going up the slope from the place where you'd come out of the stream. She pushed him flat and headed off." He smiled to himself, remembering.

"You did that?" Marshall asked her.

"Do it again, too," she chuckled. "No way the law's comin' between me and my man. No way!"

Mike managed to keep a pleasant smile on his face. Even though he knew Marshall couldn't see it, others were watching, Eden was watching. "Like a Sherman tank," he added, "there was no stopping her."

"I wish I'd known," Marshall said softly, rubbing his thumb up and down the handle of his fork. "At the time, I wish I'd known. After what they did there at the stream by the bridge, making tracks the wrong way, I thought everybody would be looking downstream. I thought no one would come where I was."

Eden curved her hand over his on his fork. "Wadsworth knew, and I believed him. Love is stronger than evidence."

Marshall leaned close to her. "I love you so much," he murmured.

Mike carefully, intently, lifted a heaping fork full of mashed potatoes to his lips.

Chapter 47

Dinner lasted a long time, with almost as much talking and laughing as there was eating. Martha and the other women had outdone themselves with the cooking, though, and Marshall listened to the clink of forks, the settings down of glasses, the scrape of knives cutting meat. *It's a true Christmas feast*, he thought, *in the finest sense of the word.* It was interesting, good, to be in the midst of it, be a part of it.

When it got well into its second hour, though, he began to tire. He wished his energy level would get back up. From time to time because it made no actual difference to him at all, he let his lids close. After he'd sat that way for a long moment, he remembered and opened them. It was difficult for blind people always to stay aware of the fact that they could be seen. He lived with what he called his 'illusion of privacy.' He knew it was an illusion because he'd learned that though he couldn't see what someone else was doing, they could see him. It took effort, though, to stay aware of it. It was a matter of courtesy for him to turn his face in the direction of someone speaking to him, and over time he'd gotten very used to doing so.

"Do broken eyes hurt, Marshall?" Luke asked.

"Not usually, Luke. Why do you ask?"

"You were closing them and I was wondering if they hurt."

"I'm just tired. I've been rather sick of late."

"I heard about that and how the bad guys left you in the forest. They were really, really bad to do that."

"But everything's all right now and it's almost Christmas. Isn't that wonderful?"

Luke nodded, forgetting Marshall couldn't see that. "What do you want for Christmas, Marshall?"

"I already have it."

"You opened your present already?"

Marshall smiled. "It's the lady beside me. She's my present."

"A people present?"

"The very best kind."

"But don't you want something in a box?"

He leaned toward Luke, whispering confidentially. "I don't think she'd much like to be in a box, and she's all I want anyway."

Eden, hearing them, smiled but she, too, noticed how he was closing his eyes. She'd also noticed how he was keeping his back very straight, not giving in to it. There was nothing she could really do at the moment, though, to help him. The dinner plates had just been removed and the table was groaning under a massive array of desserts. Coffee, tea, hot chocolate and heated cider were on the side table, their aromas mingling with the centered scents of chocolate, cinnamon, whipped cream, cherries, raisins and more.

Marshall ate a slice of chocolate pecan pie, moving his fork slowly. He was already full but from the sounds around him, everyone was busily working on diminishing the desserts. He sighed, wanting to close his eyes again, but settling for some long, quiet blinks. Eden had moved her left leg to the side so that her knee touched his. He liked that, liked being in contact with her in that quiet, gentle way. He managed to separate out from the rest, her scent of roses and concentrated on that.

Ryan and Connie were still talking. He could hear a change in the tone of her voice when she spoke to him, something rich and excited added to it. He wondered if Eden were aware of it. Of course she would be. She and Connie were like sisters. The thought of that brought Jeffrey clearly to his mind. Christmas and Jeff. Year after year of special times. He missed his brother. The sudden missing rose right up through the middle of him, splattering itself with needle pricks on the back of his eyeballs and he blinked more, this time rapidly to hold the moisture in check.

Eden missed almost nothing any more when it came to Marshall. She leaned close. "What is it, darling?"

"Just thinking of Jeff. All this family here. I miss him."

"I wish I could've known him." She really meant it. He'd been such a marvelous big brother to Marshall. Everything she'd heard about him made her regret that she'd never have the chance for that.

"He would have loved you," Marshall said. There it came again, the needle pricks. Jeff would never know Eden. He blinked again. "Sorry," he whispered, "I don't...I seem...I mean when I'm so tired, it's harder to...."

"Do you want to go upstairs?"

"I do actually, but I don't think it's a very gracious thing to do just yet. I'll be fine."

"Train tracks," she whispered back.

"What?"

"Severed legs?"

"Oh!" he grinned a bit. "Yes, the train and the legs. Well, I will be fine. Just wrap a tourniquet around my neck or something."

Dessert went on for a long while, too. Ryan caught Mike's eye and nodded toward Marshall. Mike leaned enough to see Marshall's face. He was sitting there, a bite of pie on his fork half lifted to his mouth, but had let his eyes close again and was just holding the fork there as though not really aware of it. Mike whispered a few words to Martha and after an appraising glance at Marshall, she stood up. "Why don't we move on to the parlor," she suggested in a tone that made it not a suggestion at all. "Eden, you and Marshall go on in first, ok, and get settled."

Wadsworth, who'd been almost completely under the table during the course of the meal, came out, shook himself and waited just behind Marshall's chair. With a soft sigh, Marshall stood up, sliding his hand under Eden's elbow to let her guide him through the newly-unfamiliar territory of the rearranged dining room. He settled gratefully on the big couch, his head feeling rather heavy for his neck again, and was content to let it rest against the high, soft back. That, though, made it even harder for him to keep his eyes open. But he did, determined to be a part of the Christmas Eve gathering. Elizabeth brought him some more cider, setting it on the coffee table for him. Everyone was aware he'd only gotten out of the hospital a couple of days ago. Joan set a plate of sugar cookies near his cup.

While the leftovers were being put away and the dishes done, Ryan came in and sat in a chair near the couch. "Ryan here," he said, to announce his presence and identity. Mike went over to the fireplace, engaging himself in an intent study of the mantel decorations, which let him have his back to the room. "Sorry we didn't get to talk much at dinner," Ryan continued. "That's quite an amazing story you've got there. Glad to see you're doing pretty good after all that."

"Just my version of a peaceful stay at a country inn," Marshall smiled, his hand resting on Eden's knee, hers atop his.

"I don't think he's quite got the hang of peaceful inn-staying," she added.

Ryan chuckled. "I could arrange a New Zealand bungee jumping getaway for him."

"Shhh!" Eden said, mock seriously. "He'd probably do it."

Connie wandered into the room, a dish of homemade marzipan fruits in her hand. She held it out to Ryan. "Peach?" she asked.

He picked up one of the molded bits, not taking his eyes off her. "Indeed," he said.

"Who's going bungee jumping?"

"Ryan was suggesting it for Marshall," Eden explained.

"But only if Wadsworth does it with me," Marshall added. "I wouldn't want to get lost on my way down."

"Tish tosh!" Martha said, coming into the parlor and heading straight for the piano. "Enough of this bungee talk. It's time for some carols."

Luke had followed his grandmother, perching on the piano bench beside her. "Play Grandpa's carol," he urged.

"Your grandfather has his own Christmas carol, Luke?" Connie asked, sitting on the arm of Ryan's chair as all the seats were now taken.

"Yep. 'Hark the Harold Angels Sing.' Play it, Granny."

"You got it." And she launched right in to it. Soon everyone was singing along. This was what Marshall had done nearly every Christmas Eve of his life, his mother playing the piano, his Dad, Jeff, and him singing along with her. He must be tired. His eyes were stinging again.

They went through all the old familiar hymns, and all the *Silver Bells*, *White Christmas*, and even the *Rudolph* songs. He found it an exercise in bittersweetness, the memories of his family flooding through him bringing both the pleasure of the fact they had been and the pain of the harder fact that they were gone. But there was Eden at his side, Eden who in such a short time had become so important to him. The room was warm and he began to swim in the surrounding stream of the music, floating on the scent of her roses. He didn't even realize he was falling asleep as the voices around him moved into *I'll Be Home For Christmas*.

Luke, watching from the piano bench, whispered to Martha, "He didn't die, did he?"

Martha turned to look. "No, Luke. He didn't die. He has too much to live for." She gave him a little squeeze. "You like him, don't you?"

He nodded, adjusting his thick glasses. "He knows things."

"What kind of things, Luke?"

"Eye things. That it's not so bad to have broken eyes."

She pulled him to her, wrapping her arms around him. He was only six and his eyes were steadily getting worse. He was one of the reasons she felt such a pull toward Marshall. Together, they sat on the bench looking toward the couch. Marshall had sagged a bit toward Eden and she had rearranged herself so that his head rested against hers. She had his right hand in her hands and was gently tracing her fingers over it. "You see that, Luke?" Martha asked. "You see how she loves him? Love is the best thing in the world, my darling, and much more important than if your eyes are broken or not."

Mike had turned, a pinecone from the mantel in his hand, and was looking at them, too. *You're right, Martha,* he thought. *You are so right.*

Chapter 48

Mike left the fireplace and came, squatting in front of Marshall, lifting his free hand to take his pulse. "I expect Hersholtz warned him Christmas at the inn might be a bit too much for him?"

"He warned me, actually," Eden said. "I noticed he was beginning to flag during dinner. He probably should have gone straight to bed after that but he was determined not to miss...well, let's just say this evening is a lot different than what he did last Christmas Eve." Her eyes met Martha's across the room.

"Marshall?" Eden said softly, her lips close to his head.

"Mmmm?" he murmured, not moving.

"I think it's time to go upstairs, ok?"

"Mmmmm," he sighed, still not moving.

"Ryan," Martha said, "why don't you and Mike help him up the stairs? I don't think he'd make it right now."

"S'ok," Marshall breathed. "I'm fine."

Eden just rolled her eyes, moving so Mike could get on that side of Marshall. As Marshall straightened and then attempted to rise, Mike slipped one of his arms around his shoulder, while Ryan took the other side. "For Pete's sake," Marshall protested, though rather mildly, "I'm not...."

"We know, Marshall," Ryan smiled, "we're just here to be outriggers on your canoe. Keep you upright in the water."

"Where's water?" He was still groggy from the deep sleep he'd been in.

"No water," Ryan added, "just a long staircase."

"Oh, yes," Marshall remembered. "Steps."

"Uh huh, steps," Mike supplied. "Lots of steps."

"Ok, then," Marshall agreed, not really sure at all if he could make it up the flight on his own.

Wadsworth didn't particularly like Marshall being rather hauled off like that and kept blocking the way. Eden finally snapped his leash on and took him outside. She was the only one he'd permit to do so. Marshall sagged more and more as they went up the stairs. "Damn!" he said under his breath.

"What?" Ryan asked.

"Didn't want to mess up Christmas Eve."

"You haven't messed up a thing, Marshall," Ryan said. "Everybody else is doing just fine. I expect they'll be singing again any second now. You just tend to what you need for now, ok?"

"Eden?"

"She had to take Wadsworth out, Marshall," Mike explained. "I think he thought we were taking you away from him again."

They got him into the room and set him on the side of the bed. He hadn't opened his eyes the entire time. Ryan studied him a moment. "Duds are too fine for sleepin' in," he said. "You want a bit of help with the p j's?"

Marshall nodded. "Second drawer."

Mike went to get them, unable not to notice how Eden's things were mingled atop the dresser with Marshall's. It all made a quiet, but comprehensive, statement about their togetherness.

Ryan had gotten off Marshall's jacket and cravat and was unbuttoning his shirt. He whistled slightly at the sight of the chest beneath. Though they were mostly yellow now with just traces of purple, Marshall's chest was still covered in large bruises. Ryan had noticed the remnants of his facial bruising, but hadn't any idea of the extent of them.

Mike, the pajamas in his hand, paused and looked, too. Ryan turned his eyes up to his friend. "He looks beaten," he whispered.

"Rest of him is like that, too," Mike replied.

Marshall was starting to sag tiredly toward the pillows, so they got his pajama top on quickly and eased him down. They'd just finished with the pajamas and Ryan was pulling the covers up when Eden and Wadsworth came in the door. "Oh, you've got him all settled."

"He didn't look like he'd last until you got back," Mike explained.

Wadsworth went to the bed, finding Marshall's hand and licking it. Marshall was sleeping again and didn't acknowledge it, but the dog seemed satisfied just to find him there in the bed where he belonged.

Ryan went out the door but Mike paused, his hand on the knob. "Look, Eden, I know it's Christmas and all, but he can't do everything he thinks he can. Hersholtz probably wanted to keep him in the hospital till after the holidays. He needs rest right now, more'n he's getting. He's got a lot to heal from, a whole lot, and you may have to tie him down a bit, ok, to see that he doesn't get himself in trouble."

She nodded, thinking about the huge Christmas dinner at Stuart and Joan's tomorrow afternoon. How much did he want to go to that?

"Thanks," she said, "thank you both."

In the hallway, Mike blew out a breath. "Think you can run me home now, Ryan? I'm about Christmas Eved out."

"Sure. Let me tell Con, er, the gang that I'll be right back."

Mike didn't say anything for the first half mile as Ryan drove him to the cabin. Without turning his gaze from the windshield, Ryan asked, "Must be pretty hard, huh, being in love with a woman who's in love with such a nice guy?"

"You noticed?"

"Like a bulletin board, Mike. You've got it tacked up there in plain view."

"Oh, damn! I didn't think...."

"I don't think everybody's noticed. Mom has. Probably Elizabeth." He paused. "Eden hasn't."

"You're sure?"

"Pretty sure, Mike. I started looking for it and it wasn't there."

Mike sighed. "Good."

"You don't want her to know, do you?"

"Nope. Better that way. Better for everybody."

"Better for you?"

"Maybe not better, but a damn sight easier."

"Doesn't look all that easy, Mike."

Mike smiled grimly. "It's not. She's the best thing I've seen in, well, in ever."

"What do you know about her cousin?"

"Connie? Eden's said she's been divorced a long time. No kids. Don't really know much except that Eden regards her as a sister." He looked sideways at his friend. "You've been a bit of a bulletin board yourself, you know."

Ryan grinned. "I know. But it's ok. I don't mind if she notices me looking at her. Especially when she looks back."

Eden stood in the bedroom, the sound of the family singing again coming faintly to her ears through the thick oak door. She looked at the bed then at the door. It was Christmas Eve. Where did she want to be; what did she want to be doing? There was no decision involved. Slipping into a pale yellow silk nightgown, she got under the covers, cuddling up against Marshall, who, even in his sleep, curved his arm around her. "Merry

Christmas, my darling one," she whispered, leaning her cheek against him so she could hear his heart beating, could feel the lift and fall of his chest. That was all it took, all she needed, just the being close to him.

On his way back to the inn, Ryan passed the farm of Mr. Smythe. When he was a teenager, Ryan had worked for Smythe in the summers, taking care of his horses, helping with the chores. Snow was falling in huge, individual flakes as Ryan turned up the drive to the Smythe farmhouse and knocked on the door. He spoke for a while with the older man, who was very glad to see him, then walked out to the large barn with a big smile on his face.

Half an hour later he pulled up behind the inn. Martha heard him coming, glanced at Connie, and smiled to herself. Ryan came in the door with a swoosh of cold wind and a stomp of snowy feet. Staying on the entrance mat, he called into the parlor, "Connie! You got a warm coat?"

Connie, who admittedly had been wondering why it was taking him so long just to drive the short round trip to Mike's, smiled at the sound of her name and went toward the entrance. "I live in Pittsburgh, Malone, of course I've got a warm coat."

"Want to get it on?"

"Do I?"

"Yep. You do."

She grinned more widely and got her coat off the rack. "Hat and mittens, too," he added.

"Polar expedition?"

"Something like that."

She reached into her pocket. "No mittens. Gloves do?"

He took the gloves from her, and the simple act of his sliding one of them on her hand was somehow utterly intimate. Then he slipped his arm through hers and led her out the door and around the house. She stopped, her lips parting slightly at what she saw. It was Christmas Eve and it was absolutely perfect.

A sleigh was there, and not just any sleigh, but a red one, with one black horse harnessed to the front. It was night and it was snowing giant, almost fuzzy flakes, and he'd come to get her in a one-horse open sleigh. He handed her up to the seat then went around, getting in himself, pulling up the large green wool blanket Smythe had given him. As they headed down the drive, Bess' nostrils blowing steam in the night air, Connie tipped her head back, watching the tracery of black branches passing above them, letting the flakes settle on her eyelashes.

"I come back to the inn nearly every Christmas," Ryan said, his voice low, near her ear, "but I've never come close to finding something like you under Mom's tree."

"I almost didn't come," she sighed, "but I missed Eden. We always have Christmas together."

They drove and talked a long time and she told him about Eden and how Miles had died, about the ending of her own marriage. He told her about growing up near the lake and how he'd thought he'd be a fireman someday but had gone to college and majored in social studies instead. Then, when the only job he could get was as a teacher, he'd decided to see the world and gotten into the travel business as a means to that end.

Two hours later, just before they got to the turning to the Smythe farm, he pulled Bess to a stop. They were on a low rise overlooking the lake, which lay silver and soft as the snow sifted down over it. Connie's coat had a hood and he turned to her, sliding it back so the white flakes landed on her deep red hair. He cocked his head, just watching as the flakes melted against the warmth of her, then his hand slid behind her head and his lips found hers. "Merry Christmas," he whispered and kissed her again.

Mike lit the fire he'd laid earlier and sat on his couch a long while, his gaze lost in the crackling flames. "Best face it," he said, "there's not going to be anybody up here for you, not anybody like Eden." Sighing, he went to the 'fridge and poured himself a large glass of eggnog. On the way back to the couch, he opened a cabinet and added a big slug of rum to it.

"Here's to you, Michael Johnson." He lifted his glass in a toast to the fireplace. An old log, left over from the day before, broke and crumbled under the newer wood just at that moment. "Embers and ashes. Very appropriate."

He sat down with a flop on the couch again, some of the eggnog spilling over onto his jeans. Idly he watched the thick liquid just sit there on the denim, only beginning to absorb into the material after a long while. Perhaps he'd been up here in this place long enough? Perhaps there was somewhere else he should be? He couldn't think where, though.

The grandmother clock on the rough-hewn mantel struck midnight. He lifted his glass again, downing it in one long drink. "Merry Christmas," he said to himself then threw the coated glass into the fireplace.

Chapter 49

He was in bed. He didn't remember how he'd gotten there. Hadn't they been singing Christmas songs in the parlor? He lay quietly, trying to sort things out. Wadsworth, aware of Marshall's waking, nuzzled at his hand and got his ears scratched in response. His left hand explored to the side across the bed. Eden wasn't there. Hadn't she come to bed yet? He'd lost all track of time.

Sliding his feet into his slippers, he went to the window, resting his palm against the glass. Cold and moist. He listened. The world seemed padded. Snow. But the inside of the inn was quiet, too. Where was Eden? Where was anybody?

Going to the bathroom then the closet, he located his robe, ran his hands through his hair and went out the door, trailing his fingers along the wall till he came to the head of the stairs. He listened again. Ah, someone was in the kitchen. The distant clink of a pot, the burble of the coffee machine. It smelled suspiciously like breakfast. How could it be time for breakfast, though?

Slowly, Wadsworth at his side, he made his way down the stairs. "Martha?" he called.

"It's me," Eden replied, coming to the kitchen door. "You have great timing. The eggs are just now done."

So, it was breakfast. "Did I sleep all night?"

"You got a wonderful rest. Hardly moved."

"Where is everybody? Since it's Christmas morning, I thought there would be a lot of noise."

"Stuart's. That's what the Malone's do on Christmas morning. All of the ones at the inn truck over to Harold's brother's house for Christmas Day."

"And Connie?"

"Today I think if you find Ryan, you'll find Connie."

"And Edith is over there, too?"

"Yep. Just you and me, Babe, and, well, Waddy, of course." She let Wadsworth out the kitchen door. "Now it's just you and me and no one will come and save you when you holler for help."

"And why would I holler for help?"

She came close, pressing against him, holding a warm cinnamon bun under his nose. When he tipped his head forward, she pulled the bun away and kissed him. He chuckled and she kissed his throat.

"All alone?" he asked.

"Umm hmm."

"Absolutely no one within saving distance?"

"No one at all."

He pushed a wave back from her ear and with his lips against it, whispered faintly, "Help." Then he kissed her mouth, full and long and deep and with his lips still touching hers said, "Merry Christmas."

They ate breakfast together in the kitchen, a wet Wadsworth lying near the stove. "I like eating in the kitchen," he said. "Much better than a dining room. You're right here, right in the center of the source of things."

Suddenly he realized he was eating for the first time a meal she'd entirely cooked for him. There was something just so right about being together like they were. Being at the inn was wonderful and he'd grown really attached to both Martha and Harold, but this, this was right, him and Eden.

"Is it all right with everybody that we didn't go to Stuart's?" he asked.

"Did you want to go? I can still drive us over later."

"They'll be gone all day?"

"I think so. Most of it, anyway."

"And it's ok, though, with them if we stay here?"

"Martha thought it would be best for you. A bit of quiet, you know, but it's up to you."

He smiled, finding her hand. "You and me. I like that."

So they lingered over the rest of breakfast and while she cleaned up, he sat there at the table enjoying the sounds she made. Wadsworth had eaten, too, had been outside a second time, and followed them into the parlor. Harold had laid a fire for them and put plenty of extra wood in the bin, enough to get them through the day. She got the fire going and came to sit beside him on the couch.

His hand curved around her hip. "Silk," he murmured as the material slipped away under his fingers. He played with it a while, letting it slide and flow as he moved his hand. Finding her hip bone, he explored inward, laying his palm across the flat of her belly, feeling her rapid suck of breath in response. He was still not fully recovered physically, but it was Christmas morning, he'd had hours of sleep, they were alone and she was draped in silk. He'd told Luke she was his Christmas present. It was time for unwrapping.

He took his time, enjoying every second, every touch, making sure she did, too. The silk cooperated beautifully, sliding down, moving where he guided it over her curves, along the lines of her body. His lips followed where the silk slid away and, there on the couch where his fingers had first traced the outlines of her hand, he now sought and found the outlines, the shape of all of her.

Then they lay together, faces still so close they breathed the air together. And that was right, too.

He hadn't known how the day would go, had hoped somehow there would be a moment when he and she would be alone together in the parlor. The whole day was a joyous surprise. She lay atop him on the couch, the soft curves of her fitted against the hardness of his own body. He wondered vaguely if what he was about to do had ever been done before in quite this way. It was not what he'd planned, but with her there, now, it was so right. Making love, for him, was such a tactile thing. He could only be aware of the way her breast sloped up towards her collar bone by touching it. And now his body was touching all of her body and he felt entirely joined with her, felt he was 'seeing' all of her at once and not just part by part. So he reached up over his head, feeling for the covered candy dish Martha kept there. Carefully, he set the lid to one side. Ah, it was there.

Eden had her face buried in his neck and wasn't aware of what he was doing. But when he said her name so softly, so seriously, she looked up.

"Eden," he began, "when I was a boy, I learned much of what love means because so much of it was so freely given to me, and I came, early, to know the flow of it, and how the giving of it opens some vast source where there is always, ever, only more to give. I have loved, have loved my mother and my father, have loved my brother. I have known the love of close friendship and the love of things beautiful to the soul, but I have never loved a woman as I love you. I think I've longed for it but never walked the path that would lead me to it, not until I followed the one through the woods to a crumbling gully. My heart has been entirely surprised by finding you, has been amazed that you found me."

She was hardly breathing, listening to him.

"When someone, someone who has surprised you by their being, by their sudden presence in your life, flows into your life like liquid into some oddly-shaped container and fills it up, fills in all the caverns and even all the little spaces you didn't know were there, when someone simply...fits...I don't think measurements of time really matter. Sometimes we simply know the rightness of a thing and have no need for the passing of years to affirm what we knew from the beginning, and it's in my hope that I fill you as you fill me, Eden, my darling, that I ask if you will marry me."

His right arm had been dangling off the couch while he spoke and now he lifted it, a small white velvet box in his cupped hand. The way they were lying, he couldn't use his left hand to open it, so he simply set the little container on his chest near her face, waiting quietly.

Her eyes focused on the box then moved to his face. His eyes were open and he was looking at her so directly she felt somehow he was seeing her. But, then, he *was* seeing her. She swallowed hard, blinking back tears. With 'broken' eyes, he saw her better than anyone ever had. "I love you," she managed, raggedly. Her arms slid around him. "I get... you...for Christmas?"

"If you want me."

"If I, oh, Marshall, I cannot begin to put in words how much I want you!"

"Is that a...?"

"Yes! It's such a yes as the world has never seen!"

He smiled. "See if you like it."

She cracked open the hinged lid and there in a slot framed by white satin sat a ring, its central diamond surrounded by smaller ones set in such a way that it looked like a star. He touched it with a fingertip. "I was four before someone thought to tell me about stars. It was just a simple thing, something everybody takes for granted, nothing anybody would go out of their way to think of telling somebody else about. Of course there are stars. The night sky is full of them. But I'll always remember that moment when I first learned they existed. There was something so amazing about it to me. I know I'll never see what the night sky actually looks like, but I have this concept of it that's just wonderful to me."

He smiled. "And you, you're like that. Finding out you exist was like my finding out the stars did, and that's why I wanted your ring to be shaped like this, so when you look at it or touch it, you'll always know how amazing, how wonderful you are to me."

She was crying now, her tears dropping on his chest. He wiped them away with his thumb, murmuring little endearments. "It's just overflow," she sniffed. "There isn't room inside me for all the joy you've made and it's leaking out."

"Merry Christmas, my love," he murmured.

She lay there a while longer, just wanting to be as near him as possible. Then finally she sat up. He did, too, and taking the ring from the box, slipped it on her finger. They sat there, thigh to thigh, hip to hip, and her ring was the only article of clothing or adornment either wore. There was something delightfully primal about it and both were aware of that. He took her hand between his and said softly, "God planted a garden eastward in Eden."

Chapter 50

Marshall slipped on his satin pajama bottoms, satin in a deep, burnished gold that Eden loved. Rather than putting on her gown, Eden lay back on the pillows, watching him. It dawned on her that she was reposed on the couch very much like Rose had been in *Titanic* when she'd asked Jack to sketch her. She smiled, always having liked that scene, especially the intense look in Jack's eyes as they moved between her and his sketching paper. She looked up at Marshall. He couldn't do that, couldn't look at her in her repose as Jack had at Rose.

"What are you thinking?" he asked softly.

"How do you always know?"

He grinned. "It's that 'cavern of deep harmony'. It leaks out at the oddest moments."

She smiled up at him. "I did say I'd always tell you what I was thinking."

"You did."

"Ok, I was thinking about the movie, *Titanic*."

"I went with my friend to see that, the one who described well."

"There was a scene where Rose lies on the couch in her stateroom and Jack sketches her. I'm lying rather like she was and I was just thinking...."

"That you wish I could see you."

"How...?"

"It's a natural thing, Eden, for you to wish that."

"It's all right. I was just...."

"Shhh," he breathed, getting down on his left knee, his right still not ready for bearing pressure.

"What...?"

"Let me gaze at you."

Her arms were curled loosely around her head and he reached until he found her hands with his. He drew his hands slowly, inch by inch, down her arms, lingering where her shoulders began, his lips joining his fingertips as he wandered through her hair, up to her brow, then beginning down again, his mouth finding her eyes, her mouth, down the line of her jaw and throat. There he began to murmur to her softly in French, a hundred small kisses marking his route from collar bone to breast. His voice was low, very deep, his words cushioned somehow by his kisses. As his hands moved lower, he switched to Italian. When his lips found hers again at last, there were no words that needed to be said by either her or him, and so they kissed until he lifted his head, moving it to nest his cheek between her breasts.

She lay quietly, looking at his face, listening to the crackle of the fireplace, utterly content. She hadn't given him his present yet. That could wait. This moment was too precious to disturb. After a while, a bit of tree sap burst with a loud pop and he jerked slightly, jarred from some intense place of reverie.

Touching his temple with her fingertips, she whispered, "Merry Christmas, my love."

He straightened enough to find her left hand, tracing his thumb pad around the setting on her ring. "Look for a star," he quoted, "and you will find it. It is not far. It never will be far."

Lifting her hand, he kissed the ring. "I've always imagined what a star must look like, but now there's one here, right within my reach." He kissed it again. "And it's more beautiful than I'd ever dreamed."

When she had her gown on again, she led him to the main living room. "In here," she said, hoping she'd done the right thing.

"Flowers?"

"Come on to the sideboard." She lifted his hands. "Now feel."

His fingers moved lightly, gracefully over the blossoms, and a smile began to spread delightedly across his face. "Daffodils! You've brought me," his hands moved, finding pot after pot of them, "a host, a cloud of daffodils."

"There's more," she said, guiding his hand down inside the tall stems of a particular pot, where his fingers encountered an envelope. "These are only a down payment."

He looked puzzled. "Tickets," she explained. "Two tickets for England and a reservation at a B&B near Dove Cottage."

His mouth changed shape into an 'O'. "Early April," she added. "Your birthday handily comes when the daffodils are in bloom. I...I...wasn't sure," she stammered, "if... if...but then...the ring ...and I...."

"It's perfect!" he said. "I always thought it would be just Wadsworth and me and the lakes and the daffs, but now there's you. Will you marry me before, maybe here, and the Lake Country can be our honeymoon?"

She went into his arms. "I can't think of anything better," she sighed, then reached to pick one of the largest daffodils. "Come upstairs...now."

In their room, he sat on the bed and she let the petals of the flower move over his chest. He gasped and she smiled, "Let me gaze at you," and pushed him back on the bed. When she was done, some while later, it was doubtful either he or she would ever think of daffodils in quite the same way again.

Chapter 51

She had been sleeping beside him for well over an hour, and when she woke, she lay quietly, listening to him breathe and to the snow-muffled sounds from the world around the inn. It was Christmas Day. She lifted her left hand, looking at her ring, not at all used yet to having it there. It was Christmas Day and he'd asked her to marry him. She grinned at the memory of how he'd asked.

Propping herself up a bit on her right elbow, she turned to see him better. He was still deeply asleep, lying on his back, his left arm at his side, his right hand resting on his upper chest, the crushed daffodil still under it. He'd gripped it, there at the end, his fingers closing convulsively over the delicate yellow petals. Her gaze moved on to his side, the mark from where the chest tube had been inserted still pink and fresh. The sight of it brought clearly to her the fact of how recently he'd been in the hospital. It was good he was resting. It was enough just lying there with him enfolded in the greatest sense of oneness she'd ever known. She thought of C. S. Lewis' book, *Surprised By Joy*. Lewis had settled into a life of intellectual routine when Joy had come to England and, completely unexpectedly, he had fallen in love. She'd always liked the double meaning of the title and now she knew, she knew personally, what it was to be surprised by joy. Marshall had simply, utterly become her joy. There, completely covered in mud, her joy had been waiting for her. Who would ever have thought?

After a while her tummy began to protest that it was hungry and she slipped carefully out of bed, putting on her gown and robe again. Taking Wadsworth with her, she went downstairs, let the dog outside then went into the kitchen, prowling through the leftovers from last night to make a lunch for them. Letting Wadsworth back in, she went upstairs and found him in the shower. "Lunch when you're done!" she called through the steam.

Bundled in thick terry robes, they sat at the kitchen table. The house was toasty and warm and she had made orange spice hot tea to go with lunch. Being there, just them, was utterly comfortable, completely companionable. "I've known you all my life," she said, "I just didn't know I knew."

"I think it's like that with the halves of a whole," he nodded. "Sometimes I've had this sense of space beside me, rather odd, as though someone were there and yet not there. But, then, for the last several years, I chalked it up to my imagination. It was...."

"I know."

He nodded again. "Yes."

"When I was a little girl," she continued, "I thought sometimes I knew what it was to be really happy on Christmas Day. A child has its world, you know, what it's familiar with, what it expects, what it knows, and it's easy for a kid to find happiness in that, to think that's all there is and it's pretty good." She curved her hand over his on the table. "But this, this *is* happiness. I've never known anything quite like it."

He put his other hand over hers. "Will they come?"

"Who?"

"Your parents. If we get married here on New Year's Eve, will they come?" He was becoming more and more aware that something was rather amiss between Eden and them.

"You want to get married on New Year's Eve?"

"Would that work, you think?"

"Connie and Edith will still be here."

"I was hoping they would, but what about your parents?"

"Leave Aruba? When it's winter in Pennsylvania? I seriously doubt it."

"Not even for your wedding?"

She knew her mother wouldn't find it all that important. After all, it was merely a second wedding, not worth the trouble. That was not something she wanted to say aloud. "I'll call," she whispered. "Tomorrow. They're probably busy today."

"I love you."

It was completely the right thing to say at just that moment.

They were in the parlor after lunch, still in their robes, when the phone rang. It was Connie, calling from Stuart's. "How's Marshall today?" she asked.

"He's quite, um, good," Eden replied, smiling at Marshall, who was scratching behind Wadsworth's ears.

"How good?"

"Why?"

"Well, we were wondering if you two would like to come over here for a bit this evening. You could join us for Christmas dinner if he's up to it."

"You up for going to Stuart's for dinner?" she asked him.

"Do I have to put clothes on?"

She laughed. "Yes, I'm afraid you do have to get dressed."

"Hey, I heard that!" Connie chuckled. "You mean you two aren't dressed yet?"

"We've been, um, occupied."

"Well, can you unoccupy yourselves long enough for dinner?"

"That's asking a lot, I hope you know," Eden replied, stifling a giggle.

"You are a wanton woman," Connie laughed again.

"You have no idea."

"Look," Connie continued, "Ryan has this plan where he and I would come to get you two in the sleigh he took me for a ride in. Have you ever ridden in an actual one horse open sleigh and on Christmas at that?"

"Don't believe I have. But...."

"No but's. Just bundle Marshall up really good, ok. He'll be fine. We've got blankets and everything. It'll be fun."

Marshall was nodding at her. "I feel much better today. The sleigh ride sounds really nice."

"Ok," Eden said into the phone, "but the horses better have bells."

"They do. Ryan does the complete package. We'll be there in a couple of hours. That should give you time to, um, get dressed."

For the next hour they cuddled on the couch, sometimes talking, sometimes just holding. "Does it have a fireplace?" she asked.

"Does what?"

"The house in Mount Lebanon."

"One of those double ones. Opens to the living room on one side and the dining room on the other. Jeffrey said you could see through from room to room." He nuzzled his lips into her hair. When he went back there, back to the house he'd grown up in, he would be bringing her as his wife. He hadn't spent much time there, not since his parents' deaths. It was much bigger than he needed just for himself and he'd started just staying in a room on campus. But today he sat there thinking of the house, of her in the house, and how he wanted her to come to know the place, to be comfortable there.

"My wife," he whispered into her hair.

Chapter 52

There was the unmistakable scent of horse as he approached the sleigh, his hand under Eden's elbow. Then Bess snorted and stamped a foot, sending her bells into a wild and merry fit of jingles.

"Wonderful," he said, reaching out, resting his palm on the warm neck of the horse.

Eden smiled, her anticipation of the sleigh ride heightened by Marshall's evident pleasure. It had become like that now. Her greatest joy came from watching him be pleased about something. It didn't really matter what. If he was pleased, happy, smiling at something, her own heart filled with a rush of warmly quiet satisfaction. It was what she'd come to want more than anything, that he be happy and that she be privileged to know.

"This is Bess," Ryan introduced.

"Hello, Bess," Marshall said, letting his hand run down her neck. "So you're the one horse of this one-horse, open sleigh, are you?" Bess shook her head a bit and her bells rang again. Marshall laughed. "You can't get more Christmassy than that!"

The sleigh only had the one seat, but it was fairly wide and all four of them managed to fit into it. When the blankets had been sufficiently tucked, Ryan flipped the reins, spoke to Bess, and they headed down the drive. Wadsworth had been invited to ride but he preferred to run alongside. It felt good to stretch his legs and he stayed close enough so that he could lift his head from time to time and see Marshall. He was uneasy anymore if he lost sight of him. Their separations had disturbed the secure balance he'd always felt that Marshall would be near.

Snow was still falling, the large flakes settling on their cheeks and noses as the sleigh turned down the smaller side lane that roughly paralleled the main road that circled the lake. This lane went through the thicker parts of the woods that grew close here to the water and the lake was nearly always visible just off to their right through the trees. The late afternoon light was pale gray but brightened by all the white that lay on the land, that coated the tops of every branch and twig, every fence post and outcropping of rock.

Marshall held Eden's left hand under the thick wool blanket. For the other three, the ride was mostly a visual experience, but he sat there happily immersed in the motion of the sleigh, the sound its runners made as they shusshed through the snow, the clop of Bess' hooves, and the creak of her harness leather, her breath, and the bells.

The wind had entirely dropped and the snow fell straight down. Opening his mouth, he let the flakes settle and melt on his tongue. As they touched the bare skin of his face, each light and delicate, they made him think of Eden's lashes when her face was near to his. Her hand rested on his right thigh, his fingers curled around hers. He gave them a light squeeze, delighting in her companionable closeness during this shared moment. Even through her glove he could feel the shape of her engagement ring and moved his thumb pad over it several times.

She smiled, aware of what he was doing, and leaned more closely against his side, resting her cheek on his shoulder. She felt utterly alive. He did that. He took every moment and imbued it with the life of his presence, transforming the ordinary into the special and the special into the sublime.

Connie, to Eden's right, stole a quick glance at her cousin. Seeing Eden so content, so completely happy, it was something she'd not been sure she'd witness with Eden again. In fact, she didn't know when she'd ever seen Eden so totally wrapped in happiness as at this moment. She, too, smiled and slipped her right arm through Ryan's left. She was feeling rather happy herself the last couple of days. Maybe it was catching?

Ryan pulled the sleigh to a stop in front of Stuart's house, a home so large it nearly dwarfed the inn. The main part of it had been built as a lodge back in the late 1800's and someone had put on a decent-sized addition in the 1920's. The first story was clad in fieldstone, while the second and third stories were clapboard. Eden was describing it to Marshall as they walked together up the curving walk to the big porch that ran across the front of the house and then down one side. Stuart, a building contractor, had bought the place some thirty years ago after it had lain empty for more than two decades. Fixing it up had been his pet project and he'd made a lovely home for his family out of it.

Harold and Martha heard the bells and came out on the porch, waiting to greet them. As they went up the steps, Luke ran out the door. "You came!" he cried as he caught sight of Marshall. "I knew you'd come!"

"Couldn't have Christmas Day pass and not see my Luke," Marshall smiled, crouching a bit as the small boy came right up to him.

"You can't see me," Luke corrected.

"I see you the way I see things," Marshall said, cupping Luke's chin in his palm, "and who's to say it's not a fine way to go about it."

"It is a fine way," Eden added, then when Connie caught her eye, she blushed slightly.

Marshall suppressed a little grin and then moved his hand down to Luke's chest. "I see you with my hands, young Luke, but I also see you with my heart, and when you've been seen by a heart, you've been really, really seen."

"I like that," Luke nodded. "I think I want to learn to see with my heart."

"I think you do that already," Marshall said, patting Luke's chest lightly. "You are a very good seer."

"Even if my eyes are not so good?"

"Eyes have almost nothing to do with heart-sight, Luke. I'd like you always to remember that, ok? Always."

Luke suddenly threw his arms around Marshall's neck. "Can you be my Christmas present, too," he asked softly, "not just Eden's?"

"I'd like that," Marshall smiled, sliding his own arms around the small back. "I'd like that a lot."

Martha looked at them, her eyes wide and unblinking, taking a mental snapshot of a scene she wanted always to remember. Marshall stood, lifting Luke in his arms. "You want to do the clock-plate for me at dinner again?"

"Oh, yes!" Luke said, his face lighting up even more. "That was great yesterday."

"You were a big help. I knew where everything was."

With Luke balanced in the crook of his right arm, Marshall held out his left hand for Eden to take. He heard the sound of someone opening the door, but before he moved forward, he paused a moment, closed his eyes, and murmured very quietly, "God bless us every one."

Stepping over the threshold, he was wrapped in the scents of Christmas dinner. If it were possible, there were even more different delightful smells than from Christmas Eve. As he walked down the hallway, Luke on his arm, Eden's hand in his, the Malones and Connie and Edith all grouping around, it was, however, the sense of family, of home, that truly wrapped him and he paused again, blinking rapidly. He was...full. That was the word for it. He'd always felt full most of his life and had tried to take the sense of it with him even after his family was gone. It wasn't until here and now that he completely realized how much of that had drained from him over the last couple of years, what an effort it had been to hold close the remaining threads of it. But there, just inside the huge dining room, he knew he was full to his brim, so full that it spilled over and a tear tracked down his right cheek.

Luke saw it and touched it with a fingertip. "It's Christmas, Marshy," he said in his small voice. "Don't be sad."

Marshy. Luke had called him Marshy. Another tear followed the track of the first. "Merry Christmas, Luke," he whispered. "I'm not sad. That was a Christmas happy tear."

"You sure?"

"Umm hmm," he nodded. "I haven't been this happy in a long time."

He felt Eden squeeze his left hand. "I love you," she said softly.

"I know."

Luke had put his whole palm on Marshall's wet cheek. "Broken eyes can't see but they can cry?"

"Yes, Luke, broken eyes can cry."

"Does that mean they're not broken all the way, then? If they can cry, then that part of them still works, right?"

"That part still works, yes."

"Then heart-sight can make broken eyes cry sometimes?"

"Very often."

"Good," Luke pronounced. "I wouldn't want to have eyes so broken they couldn't cry."

"I wouldn't want that, either."

"You don't think I have to worry about that, then, Marshy?"

"I don't think you have to worry about that at all."

A chair scraped out. "Here's your chair, Marshall," Stuart said. "And, Luke, you can sit here right next to him if you like."

Marshall felt better during this dinner, not so tired. Each day he was stronger than the day before, making slow but steady progress back to his regular self. Luke was on his right tonight and Eden on his left. Connie and Ryan were side by side directly across the table, Mike seated beside Ryan. As much as he tried to keep his eyes averted, Mike couldn't help noticing the extra glow shining from Eden's face. The reason became evident after Stuart said grace when Eden held out her hand toward Connie and announced that she and Marshall had become engaged that morning. Connie whooped with delight and Ryan cast a covert glance to his side. Mike's face was expressionless except for the muscle twitching in his jaw. Ryan knew him so well, though, that he was aware of the effort it was taking for Mike not to show what he was feeling.

Mike wasn't surprised, not really. He had figured this was where it was headed with Marshall and Eden, he just hadn't known when. Swallowing hard, he made his lips curve into a smile, joining in with the congratulations that were sounding from all around the table.

"Oh, I'd love to see that," Martha said wistfully.

"You will, Martha, if what I'd like to suggest works for you," Marshall replied. "We were thinking New Year's Eve at the inn."

"At the inn? Really?" Martha gasped.

"Would that be all right?" Eden asked.

"All right? All right? My goodness! I'd love it!"

"I know it's not much notice but...."

"Who needs notice?" Martha cut her off. "We can pull it off." She looked around the huge table. "Right?"

Everyone agreed and most of Christmas dinner's conversation was given over to making plans. Marshall asked Martha if she'd play the piano for the ceremony, which pleased her immensely. "Who'll be giving you away, though, Eden?" she wondered. "Will your father be there?"

"They're out of the country right now," Eden explained, "but I have someone in mind. She looked across the table. "Mike, you've been there for me ever since the day I first got here. And when I needed to get to Marshall, you were by my side, with me every step of the way, taking me to him. Will you take me to him on my wedding day?"

Oh, God, had she really asked him to walk her down the aisle and put her hand in that of someone else? Had she really just asked *that* of him? He couldn't speak for a moment. His vocal cords had gone on strike. He was aware of Ryan's gaze fixed on him from the side. Some little part of his brain that wasn't currently paralyzed was grateful that Ryan was there, that Ryan knew. He opened his mouth a little, knowing he needed to say something, knowing everyone was waiting for him to reply to her.

"Please?" she added. "There isn't anyone in the world I'd rather have by my side for that than you, Mike."

She had him shoved out in the spotlight, didn't she? There was no room to wiggle out of it, nothing to say about why he couldn't possibly do that, about what it would cost him to do that. He was trapped in the telescopic sight of her rifled question. Swallowing again, he licked his lips, hoping his voice had decided to return. He felt Ryan grip his arm just below the elbow, hidden from view by the table. "S...sure," he got out, his voice cracking a bit on the single syllable. After he'd said it and been flooded with the smiles of the others at the table, he thought to himself that someday he'd surprise them all and simply not do the right thing. Evidently today was not that day.

"Oh, thank you, Mike!" Eden responded. "It means so much to me."

Mike dipped his head in a nod, his voice having wandered off somewhere again, his throat thick and uncooperative.

"That leaves me needing a best man," Marshall spoke up. He'd actually thought of asking Mike to fill that role, but Eden was right. It made sense for Mike to be the one to walk her down the aisle. He'd always thought Jeff would fill the role of best man some day. Now who would he ask? Then he heard Luke set his fork down on his plate. "Luke," he said seriously, "would you consider standing up with me as my best man?"

"Me? You want me?"

"I do. Will you do that for me?"

Luke looked over at his mother. "Is that ok?" he asked hopefully.

She nodded yes. "She says ok, Marshy. I can do it!"

Marshall smiled. Jeff, who had called him Marshy and who would have been his best man, was gone. But here was Luke, who also called him Marshy, and who felt this kindred relationship with him. Luke was perfect for the job. He felt utterly satisfied by the thought of it.

"Um, Marshy, what is a best man?"

"The best man stands beside the groom at the wedding, Luke. He's someone who means a lot to the groom, that's me, and is so important that he has the wedding rings in his pocket."

"Wow!"

"Does that sound ok? Would you like to do that?"

"Am I important enough for it?"

Marshall turned more toward the boy. "Luke, listen to me. I'm the one who decides who's important enough to me to be the best man and I choose you. That means, yes, you are definitely important enough to do that."

He heard a series of sniffs. "Are you ok, Luke?"

"My eyes aren't so broken, either, that they can't cry."

Chapter 53

"Cranberries are at 11 o'clock," Luke informed Marshall, then leaned close, asking, "What does a best man wear?"

Marshall turned toward Eden. "Are we talking tuxes here?"

"Not that formal, I think," she replied. "What I like you in best, actually, is what you wore to dinner yesterday."

"Married in suede?"

She pressed her mouth to his ear so no one could hear. "It's the next best thing after a single daffodil."

He choked a little on his cranberry sauce and she patted his back. "Sorry," she giggled. "But that's the truth."

"What's the truth?" Connie asked, one eyebrow dramatically cocked.

Eden made a slight face at her cousin then ignored her. "Do you feel all right about wearing the tweed jacket?"

Marshall nodded, still clearing his throat from the sauce. "Do I wear tweed, too?" Luke piped in. "What's tweed?"

"It's the kind of jacket I wore yesterday evening, Luke," Marshall explained.

"I don't think I have anything like that," the boy said sadly.

"But I did when I was a boy," Ryan interjected. "Remember that suit you made me wear, um, I had when I was about Luke's age, Mom? Isn't the box with those things still in the attic at the inn somewhere?"

Martha smiled. "I'd almost forgotten about that outfit. Yes, that was a chocolate and cream tweed. I'll look for it tomorrow."

"Is it ok to be a chocolate best man?" Luke wondered aloud.

"Yep," Marshall smiled. "I'm going to be a butterscotch groom."

"What about you, Eden?" Connie asked. "Do you have any idea of what you'd like to wear?"

"I saw a shop in Bellefonte," she answered. "It had some lovely vintage dresses in it. I bet I could find something there."

"I know the one you mean," Marshall said, putting his hand on her arm. "My mother bought several dresses there. I like the idea of your marrying me in one of their gowns."

"Sounds like a female shopping day is in order this coming week," Edith smiled. She'd always rather hoped she'd be along when Eden picked out her wedding dress.

"And you, Mike," Martha asked, "what about that nice brown suit you have? A rust-colored tie would make that fit in just fine."

"I like that, Mike," Eden said, directing a large smile at him across the table.

Mike dipped his head again. "Ok," he replied. "Fine by me."

She studied his face. He'd been so withdrawn lately. Was it really fine with him that she'd asked this of him? He saw the serious, appraising look in her eyes and managed a reassuring smile.

"Who all do you want to invite?" Harold asked. "You got folks you want to come up from Pittsburgh?"

"I don't want it to get too big, I think," Eden replied thoughtfully. "I don't want the inn all stuffed with people, you know." She looked around the dining room. "Everyone here, that's who I want to be there. You, Marshall?"

"There's a couple of people from the hospital I'd like to invite, ones who were really special while I was recovering. Just two or three. We can have some sort of dinner back in Pittsburgh later for the ones who live there." He lowered his voice. "But are you going to call your parents?"

"Tomorrow." She looked across at Edith and Connie. Connie rolled her eyes slightly.

One of Stuart's daughter's had taken music lessons for years and there was a baby grand in a corner of the enormous living room. After dinner, everyone gathered there and sang again. Martha changed places with her niece and started the first few notes of *Do You Hear What I Hear?* "Come on, Marshall," she urged. "Will you do this one for us?"

Eden walked with him up next to the piano and he rested his right palm on its top edge. Luke and Wadsworth both pressed close to his legs. His voice rang out, true and mellow, though a little softer than usual as his lungs weren't fully back to normal, and when he got to the *do you see what I see?* part, he put his left hand lightly atop Luke's hair but his face turned toward Eden as he sang *a star, a star, way up in the night, with a tail as big as a kite....* She looked down at the ring he'd given her that morning. Had it just been that morning? Hadn't she worn it forever? Hadn't she been heading toward him all her life? Lifting her eyes, she watched him standing there with the boy and the dog, his chin slightly tipped up as he sang. As she looked at him she felt as though she were standing at the rail of some weather-worn ship, gazing at the purple-blue ridge of the shore, with months of endless seas and storms behind her. "Land," she whispered to herself, knowing her soul had dropped anchor and was putting out in little boats for the harbor of him.

"Do you want to ride home in the car with us?" Harold offered as the evening wound down. "Bit cold for the sleigh."

"I'll be fine," Marshall smiled in his usual litany of reply, "and the sleigh is a marvelous way to travel on Christmas Day."

Harold shook his head. He just didn't understand how this stuff worked for Marshall, why he'd even care if he were in a car or in a sleigh if he couldn't see. But it was obvious the man got some sort of pleasure out of things like that. Blindness was an entire mystery to Harold. The docs had said Luke would, in all probability, end up in that same dark place as Marshall. He wanted to believe it wasn't so bad and watching Marshall still enjoy things was, admittedly, a bit of a comfort. But, oh, how he wished Luke didn't have to go there.

Martha saw that Marshall looked a bit tired by now and spoke quietly to Ryan. "Don't gallivant all over the countryside with them tonight, ok, son. He needs to get home and rest. You and Connie want to go for a longer ride, you do that after you drop them off."

Ryan, who was getting Bess back in harness, smiled at his mother. "What makes you think Connie and I want to go for a longer ride?"

"Well, you do, don't you?"

"You've got me," he grinned. He only had another week here before going back to Cleveland and wanted every moment he could get with Connie.

Martha stepped back, watching fondly as the two couples rode off. She stood there until they disappeared around the curve that led into the woods by the lake. The jingling of the bells grew fainter and she finally turned, going back inside to help with the last of the cleaning up. She noticed Mike was stacking firewood in the corner of the living room for Stuart and went up to him. "I just want to be sure you know, Mike, dear, how very important you are to all of us, how much you matter to us."

He paused, three logs still in his arms. "Thanks, Martha," he said quietly, then turned to lay the logs carefully on the stack.

Martha sighed and walked toward the kitchen. Luke was asleep on the couch, waiting for his parents to gather him up and drive back to the inn. He always tugged at her heart strings and she stood a moment, just looking at him with great tenderness, remembering how Marshall had spoken to him this evening.

Eden cuddled against Marshall's right side in the sleigh. The snow had stopped and silver-edged mounds of clouds moved across the sky rather quickly, diminishing in size so that the spaces between them grew steadily wider. "The stars are coming out," she breathed contentedly. It was nearly midnight and yet the world was bright all around them. She thought of the old lines...*the moon on the breast of the new-fallen snow gave the luster of mid-day to objects below.* It was like that. You didn't need lights provided by mankind. Nature, all by itself, had lit the night and reflected it on the snow so that the shadows of trees were etched as clearly on the white ground as if a spotlight were shining on them. She was trying to find words to describe it properly for Marshall, but how did you explain what a shadow was?

Connie and Ryan were cuddled, too, and whispering together as he guided the sleigh. She said something that made him laugh and he let the sleigh get too close to the edge of the road. The right-hand runner hit a large rock completely buried under the snow and rode up over it, causing the sleigh to tip sharply and suddenly. With its load of four adults, the sleigh was more easily over balanced and continued to angle up and over so the people in it were thrown out to the left on the lane.

Marshall felt the sleigh heave up, heard Ryan's shouted expletive, knew Eden was falling. There was only one thing completely filling his mind in that split second. She must not be allowed to impact the road. He grabbed for her, his right arm locking firmly about her waist, pulling her so that her body was atop his. He curved his left arm up, putting his hand behind her head as the two of them arced in what seemed like slow motion out of the sleigh. He came down flat on his back with a thud that reverberated completely through him. A split second later, she landed fully atop him and the inner explosion of the first thud rising up met the second blasting down.

Connie came down near Eden, her right ankle twisting painfully under her. Ryan landed on hands and knees in a snowdrift, shaken to his core. Eden lay atop Marshall, trying to gather her scattered senses. His arm was still protectively around her. Finally she gasped and sat up, rolling to the side off him and onto her knees. Connie was moaning and clutching her ankle as Ryan crawled the short distance to her. The sleigh had righted itself and come to a stop just down the road, Bess unhurt and still in harness.

Eden's eyes took in that fact and the thought flitted through her mind that she was glad the horse was ok. Wadsworth, who had been running just behind the sleigh, was poking his nose at Marshall's left ear. Eden turned to thank Marshall for padding her fall. He lay on his back, his arms now that she had sat up, fallen out away from his sides.

"Marshall? Darling?" She scrambled as close as she could get to him. She'd seen him unconscious, semi-conscious, and sleeping. Something was different now. His lids were only half-closed and his jaw was quite slack. She crouched, staring at him in the bright moonlight, her hands on his chest.

"Marshall?" Something long and icy made its way through her being, stabbing, ripping, shredding as it moved inexorably. *No,* she said to herself. *No. This can't be. This cannot be.*

And she took the hands of her soul and tried to yank the icy thing out, but it only settled in more deeply, more utterly coldly.

Shaking, her hands moved to his neck, feeling for his pulse. Nothing. Frantic, she pulled off her gloves, feeling again where Miles had showed her. There was no answering rhythm of blood being pumped. There was nothing. Sitting back on her heels, she stared at his face. He wasn't there. Oh, God...he'd gone. He was lying on his back, on his back in the snow, and he'd left her. The realization of it mowed her down like a scythe and a piercing, primal scream ripped out of her throat before she crumpled to the side in the snow.

Chapter 54

Ryan had reached Connie just as Eden screamed and crumpled. Both he and Connie were absolutely shocked.

"Eden!" Connie called frantically, scrabbling forward despite the pain in her ankle.

Ryan looked from Eden to Marshall, his heart sinking. "Oh, God, no!" he moaned, practically flinging himself in Marshall's direction.

Connie was patting Eden's unresponsive face when she thought she heard Ryan say something impossible about Marshall.

"What?" she croaked. "What did you say?"

"He's dead, Con. His heart's not beating."

Connie looked down at Eden. Not twice. Eden couldn't handle this twice. "*DO SOMETHING!*" she shrieked at Ryan.

Ryan was kneeling beside Marshall, his mind racing. Do what? Desperately he raised his right arm high and brought his fist down as hard as he could on Marshall's chest. It was all he could think to do.

The double impact of his body on the road and then Eden landing atop him, both with such force and coming from opposite directions, had thrown Marshall's heart into severe arrhythmia and after a few wild, irregular beats, it had simply stopped. He felt a sudden jerking loose of himself from himself, a sense of detachment from even the fact of that, and then an awareness of rising. With no idea of what was happening or where he was, he knew only that he was moving, though making no effort to move. Everything was very quiet and he flowed into the quiet, letting it take him. There seemed to be no real choice in the matter. Something had happened, had changed, but it was too much trouble somehow to try and think what it might be.

Then in his upward float, he became aware of movement other than his own. There were things around him that were also in motion. He didn't know how he knew without touching them or hearing them, but there were things around him that were not part of him and he knew they were there. They were large boughs of evergreens, draped with snow, blown by a light wind, only he did not recognize them as that. They had form, somehow they had form, but the form was not known to him for what it was. He passed by them, through them, not knowing what they were, quietly amazed that he knew they were there. Everything was very strange, utterly different. He looked up and his usual space was punctured by something, somethings, even more unutterably beyond all imagining. Many, many little punctures dotted his space. He'd never been aware of such things and had no names, no labels for pure unrecognizability. He was, though, strangely undisturbed by it all.

Then that stopped. Everything stopped, the rising, the quiet, the awareness of the other things, and he felt himself being yanked down much more rapidly than he'd been going up. He slammed back into himself with a huge gasping, grating moan.

Ryan, on his knees, fell back over on his rear, his eyes wide, his mouth dropping open. Connie gave another little shriek then began to laugh and cry at the same time. Marshall clamped both hands to his chest, making a series of loud gasping sounds. Ryan scrambled back onto his knees, trying to push Marshall's hands away. "Did I break something? Did I break something?" he muttered over and over, feeling Marshall's ribcage.

"You...you hit me?" Marshall moaned.

"As hard as I could," Ryan nodded.

"W...why?"

"Your heart stopped, Marsh. I had to do something, anything."

"St...stopped?"

"Yup. Not beating at all. Guess the fall outta the sleigh did it somehow."

"Sleigh?" Then Marshall remembered. "Eden?! Where's Eden?" He tried to sit up, gasped again with the pain of it, and sat up anyway. "Where? Eden?! "

"She's here, Marshall," Connie said. "She fainted. You were dead in the snow. It was too much." She brushed some strands of hair back from Eden's face.

Clenching his teeth, Marshall managed to get up on his knees and crawl toward the nearby sound of Connie's voice. "Where?" he asked again, feeling around with one hand.

Connie took his hand, guiding it to Eden's head.

"Ooh," he moaned, his fingertips finding Eden's closed eyes. "Eden? It's all right, darling. Wake up. Please wake up now." He sat back, pulling her into his arms, rocking slightly with her.

Ryan was on his cell phone. "Mike?" he said. "I wrecked the sleigh. About a mile your side of the inn. Marshall's heart stopped but he's ok now, I guess. Eden collapsed when she saw what happened to him. No, she hasn't roused yet. No, she doesn't seem to be hurt. Connie's got a bad ankle, though. Can you get out here with some help? Yeah. We're on the little road by the lake, not far from where the old snag fell into the water. Yeah. Right there. Ok. Soon as you can. Right. Thanks, pal."

Luke awakened to the sound of loud, excited adults, catching something about Marshall having died. He grabbed at Martha's skirt as she passed by the couch. "Did he this time, Granny? Did he really?" Tears were dripping down his little face.

"Seems he did, Luke," Martha explained. "I don't know just how, but Ryan saved him. Looks like he's going to be ok, so don't you worry. You didn't lose him. You got that? You didn't lose him." She closed her eyes briefly. *None of us lost him, thank God.*

Luke was aware most of the adults were shrugging on coats, getting ready to pile into various cars. "I've got to see him, Granny. I've *got* to!"

She knew he meant it and as she felt the same way, helped him on with his coat, slid her arms quickly into her own coat sleeves, and took him out the front door with her. "We're coming, too," she announced. Harold took one look at the set of her face and quietly opened a car door.

Ryan stood up, waving as several sets of headlights came rushing down the small road. Mike hopped out of his truck, pounding through the snow to where Marshall still sat, rocking Eden.

"She won't wake up," Marshall said as Mike knelt in front of them, announcing his presence as his hands reached out to take Eden's pulse.

"What happened to her?" Mike asked.

Connie spoke up. "She was kneeling beside Marshall, Mike. His heart had stopped and she just let out this cry and toppled over."

"You ok?" Mike looked with quick appraisal at Marshall.

"Feel like an elephant stepped on me," he replied, "but I think I'm all right."

Eden, draped, enveloped in a horror beyond imagining, had curled her consciousness into a tight little ball as deeply within herself as she could go. Vaguely aware of being moved, being touched, she nonetheless refused to let it uncurl. She simply could not face the fact of Marshall's death, would not face it. Perhaps, then, it would not be so. She hugged oblivion with tightly-clasping fingers.

Mike lifted one of her lids, shining a small light into her eye. "She didn't hit her head, did she?"

"I don't think so, Mike. I had my hand there."

Mike paused, looking at Marshall. So, he'd put himself at risk again to protect her. This time it had killed him. He looked back at Eden. And what had it done to her? "I think it'd be best if we got all of you into the hospital, ok? Everybody needs some checking out from what I can see."

Sliding his arms under Eden, he continued, "Let me carry her, Marshall. We'll just put her in Harold's car and you guys can ride in that." He stood, Eden in his arms, turning to Ryan. "Can you drive my truck? Take Connie to the hospital. We'll meet you there."

Ryan put a hand on Mike's arm. "Be careful, Mike. She's not yours to tend. Don't forget that."

Mike set his jaw and carried Eden to the car.

Luke ran up to the still-sitting Marshall. "Marshy! Marshy!" he called, flinging his arms around Marshall's neck. "Did you die this time, really die?"

"I think so," he said, trying not to grimace at the pain even Luke's little hug caused his torso. "I haven't had time really to think about it. It all happened very fast. I guess it did. I don't know."

Stuart and Harold helped him stand. Just straightening his body hurt. "I think I've gone and made some brand new bruises," he commented wryly.

Martha was there now in front of him, wanting to hug him with all her might but not doing so because she knew it would only hurt him. Tears were tracking down both her cheeks. "Oh, Marshall," she whispered. "I'm so glad you didn't leave us."

Marshall got in the back seat of Harold's car and Mike reluctantly let Eden's head and shoulders slide over onto his lap. Knowing that Marshall couldn't see him, he kept Eden's hands between his own. He didn't like how long she was staying unconscious. She'd told him, though, about Miles and he knew what it must have meant to her to see Marshall like that in the snow.

Marshall's lips were pressed tightly together as he dealt with the pain in his chest where Ryan had hit him and the pain across his back from where he'd landed on the road. His greatest pain, though, was that he'd let Eden down. After he'd spent so many hours on Cooper's Ridge vowing he would not do that to her, would not die in the snow, he'd gone and done that very thing. He knew he had a lot to think about concerning that, but it could wait. All that mattered right now was that Eden wake up. He stroked her cheek and spoke softly to her all the way to the hospital, but she didn't stir at all.

Stuart had alerted the hospital and Dr. Hersholtz was waiting for them in the ER. "You got a yoyo string on you, Marshall?" he asked as he caught sight of him walking in, bent a bit forward.

"Seems like, doesn't it? But don't worry about me right now, doctor. It's Eden I'm concerned about."

Connie had been seated in a wheelchair and was about to be taken off for x-rays. Ryan kissed her hand as a nurse wheeled her away then he began to explain what he had witnessed of the accident and what he'd done to try and get Marshall's heart started again. Hersholtz was examining Eden as he listened. "Doesn't appear she's injured at all," he announced. "Seems to be severe psychological trauma, though. The unconsciousness is how she's dealing with it. She needs to realize you're not dead, Marshall, but she's not ready to let anything in, not even good news. She's afraid such things don't exist."

"What can I do?"

"Just let her rest a bit while I check you out, ok? You're the one who died tonight."

"I'm fine," he protested, keeping his hand on Eden's shoulder.

"I know," Hersholtz said patiently, "but you're still going to have a couple of x-rays just to prove it to me."

"I don't want to leave her."

"It'll just take a minute. You'll stay with her, won't you, Mike?"

"Don't leave her, Mike," Marshall said urgently. "I don't want her to be alone."

"She won't be," he replied quietly, avoiding Ryan's piercing look.

Connie was wheeled back, her foot raised and packed in ice packs. "Sprain," she said. "Not broken."

Ryan knelt beside her chair, taking her hand in his. "I'm so sorry, Con. I just didn't see the rock."

"Not your fault," she smiled. "I made you laugh, remember."

When Marshall came back, Eden was still lying quietly. "No change," Mike said, laying her hand back beside her as Marshall came close.

"Oh, Eden," Marshall whispered. "Please be all right, darling."

"Well, Marshall," Hersholtz said, coming up with x-rays in his hands. "Doesn't look like you've got any broken bones, though I have no idea why you don't. You're going to have a rather big batch of deep bruising again, though, mostly across your shoulders and in the center of your chest." Then from what Ryan, Connie, and Marshall himself had told him, he explained what had most likely caused Marshall's heart to stop. "So that blow from Ryan did the trick," he ended. "And I'll tell you again. You do need to rest. Your body needs to take it easy for a good while yet. I can tell just by looking at you that you've been overdoing."

Edith was hovering by Connie's chair. "Oh, Mom," Connie was saying, "I don't think I've ever been so scared in my life. Marshall was lying there so still and then Eden just folded over. I think her heart just literally broke in half."

"I know, darling, I know. It was Miles all over again, only worse."

"I've never seen anyone more in love, Mom, than she is with Marshall. Losing him was...."

"She'll be all right, Connie. He'll see to that."

All through the wee hours of the night Marshall sat beside her bed, holding her hand, talking to her. Mike hovered in the doorway, not able to leave until Eden woke up and he could see she was really ok.

About 5 in the morning, Marshall lay his head on the bed and went to sleep, utterly exhausted. It was then Mike remembered what Eden had asked of him when it was

Marshall lying in the ICU. Quietly, he left the hospital, found his truck and drove to the inn. Harold was asleep on the couch, but Martha had been in the kitchen, baking, unable to sleep, and let him in. Within moments he had what he wanted and was on his way back to the hospital.

Marshall stirred when Mike laid his hand on his shoulder and then explained why he'd brought the CD player and the Tuscany music. "She thought it would work for you," he said, "maybe it'll work for her, too?"

"It's worth a try, Mike," Marshall said tiredly, rubbing a hand hard across his face.

Mike plugged the player in and Marshall, who knew the CD intimately, brought up the twelfth track. As the music started, he leaned close to her pillow, his fingers stroking her hair and sang the words to *Vá Pensiero* to her in Italian. Mike stepped just out into the hall. There was something so personal about how Marshall was doing it that he felt like an intruder even to watch.

During the pauses in lyrics, Marshall said things like, "Come on, darling. I'm here. I'm really here. You can wake up now." Then he'd continue with the music.

From a great distance, the music penetrated into her balled self. It was so...him. It carried for her all the essence of him. Her being peeped out of isolation like a little child showing a single eyeball from under a blanket. She was frightened, scared to death. She could come out and his singing could be a dream, nothing more. She'd seen his face, touched the lifelessness of his body. It was not a world she cared to inhabit. She would not inhabit it.

He started the song over, his urgings stronger, firmer. "Mmmmm," she murmured, turning her head slightly.

"That's it!" he affirmed. "Come on, darling! Wake up! Wake up for me."

He sang some more, pausing between words to rain kisses on her face and neck.

How real his presence felt to her. It couldn't be, though. Like Miles, the snow had taken him.

He nuzzled his nose into the hollow of her neck. "Eden, please."

"Mar...Marshall?"

"Yes, darling. I'm here. It's our song. Remember our song?"

"Marshall?"

He kissed all over her face. She blinked her eyes open. He was there! He was there! Huge gasping sobs took her, doubling her up, wrenching through her gut. He put his arms around her, holding on as she rocked back and forth, gulping and sobbing, her fingers digging into his shoulders.

Mike gave a quick peek in the door. She would be all right now. Marshall would be there for her. He hadn't heard Ryan come up behind him, didn't know he was there until a firm hand gripped his upper arm. He turned, meeting Ryan's eyes. "That's where she belongs. I know that. I've just got to get used to it." He smiled wanly at his friend. "How's Connie doing?"

"Pretty bad sprain, but she'll be ok. I should go let her and Edith know Eden's awake."

"Give them a moment more, ok?" Mike said, looking briefly back toward the door. "They've earned it."

Marshall sat on the side of the bed so he could hold Eden better in his arms. She couldn't seem to stop the gut-wrenching sobs. They went on and on and on until she was so worn out she couldn't physically manage them anymore and then she just clung to him, her whole body shaking, as he smoothed her hair and whispered in her ear. Finally, she quieted and went to sleep in his arms. He laid her back and then stretched out beside her, and arms circled close about her, fell into a deep slumber himself.

Hersholtz had come by when a nurse told him Eden was crying. He stood now in the doorway a moment, smiling at the sleeping couple.

"Merry Christmas," he whispered, "after all."

Chapter 55

About 8 AM Harold and Martha showed up at the hospital to take Marshall and Eden back to the inn. When Dr. Hersholtz saw them, he took them aside into a small, unoccupied lounge. "Martha," he said, holding out a tiny envelope in his hand, "Marshall was up all night long talking to Eden, singing to her, until he got her to come 'round. He's entirely worn out from yesterday. I understand he got engaged and attended the big Malone Christmas dinner at Stuart's. Dying on the way home didn't help much, and then he's gotten almost no sleep."

He put the little pouch in Martha's hand. "This is what I want you to do. When you get him home to the inn, make sure he's all settled in his room then put this in a glass of orange juice and take it to him. Tell him I said he needed a lot of vitamin C right now. Make sure he drinks it all, ok? In about five minutes he'll be sound asleep, stay that way most of the day. Man's just not resting proper. Needs some help. You can let Eden know if you want. Probably wise. Don't want her to worry about him."

Martha turned the envelope over in her hand. "Be sure he's the only one drinks that juice. I've got this measured for his size. Real strong stuff."

Harold made a little clucking sound. "You asking Martha to slip him a Mickey, eh, Doc?"

"Basically," Hersholtz nodded. "I've seen how the man is. He'll tend to other folks all day and not rest himself. Looks like I was right to consider not releasing him from here till after Christmas. Didn't know he'd go and get himself killed, though."

Harold shook his head. "Still can't believe that happened last night. Everything was so happy 'n all then Ryan calls and starts talking about how Marshall's dead in the snow and Eden's passed out."

"I imagine that rather put an end to the festivities."

"Never had 'em end quite so abrupt, Doc. Thank goodness it turned out OK. Eden's cousin Connie's back at the inn. Ryan moved his stuff into a back bedroom just a bit ago. Says he needs to be there to carry her up and down the stairs." He cast a sideways look at his wife.

"It is a good reason for him taking a room there, Harold," Martha chuckled. "Not that he has anything else on his mind."

"Feels real responsible for the sleigh tipping, though," Harold added. "Thought he'd killed Marshall."

"No use him going and loading himself up with blame," Hersholtz said. "What's done is done. Now we've just got to get everybody all fixed up again." He patted the packet in Martha's hand. "Resting good's part of that."

"I'll take care of it," Martha nodded. "Make sure it's nice and quiet for him, too."

"Don't think you'll have to worry about that," Hersholtz smiled. "I'd say this will leave him dead to the world, but that hardly seems appropriate right about now."

An aide had brought Marshall and Eden breakfast and they were just finishing when Hersholtz opened the door and ushered Martha and Harold inside. The doctor did a quick check over of Eden, suggested she take it easy for a couple of days, then turned to Marshall. "And you," he said sternly, "I don't suppose telling you to rest a lot is going to do any good."

"I'll try," Marshall said sincerely, "but I'm getting married in a few days."

"A few days?"

"At the inn, New Year's Eve. I'd like it if you could come, Dr. Hersholtz."

Hersholtz said he'd see what he could do about that, thanked Marshall for the invitation, which, admittedly, surprised him a bit, did a last admonition about getting rest, then left.

"Where's Wadsworth?" Marshall asked.

"Ryan's got him at the inn," Martha supplied. "Took him for a bit of a walk early this morning. He's, as you say, fine."

"Ok if before we leave I make a couple of quick stops here in the hospital?"

"Sure," Harold said. "Where you need to go?"

"ICU. I'd like to go there first."

The three others walked with him down the corridor, turning into the ICU. "Is Maria here?"

"Hello, Marshall," came a familiar voice. "I just came on duty. I'd say it's good to see you again, but I hear last night was rather rough on you."

"I'm fi...," he began, but caught himself. "Everything's all right," he amended. "But there's something I'd like to ask you." He slipped his arm through Eden's. "We're getting married at the inn New Year's Eve. I'd be honored if you could be there."

Maria's eyes opened a bit wider. "Why, yes, Marshall, but the honor is mine." She added something in Greek which made him smile.

On the way down the corridor, they encountered Betsy, who'd let Wadsworth spend that first night in the hospital after Marshall's incident at the gully. He invited her, too, and though she was delighted, was going to be in West Virginia at her daughter's that day.

Eden kept her hand laced through his and he was very aware that she was gripping it more tightly than usual. In the back seat of Harold's car, he wrapped his arms around her, holding her close on the drive to the inn. She seemed to be holding herself together by some force of will.

Connie was sitting on the couch in the parlor, Ryan just handing her a cup of tea, as they came in. She studied her cousin carefully, noting a deep gravity that appeared to have fastened onto her features. She sighed. Here it was, a time when Eden should be bubbling with happiness and yet any bubbles seemed submerged under the weight of last night. Marshall looked tired, had dark smudges under his eyes, and held himself slightly bent forward.

"Eden," Connie said warmly, holding out both arms.

Eden came toward Connie, bringing Marshall with her, not about to let go of his hand. "How's the ankle?" she asked, extending only her free hand.

"Better. Ryan's pampering me shamefully."

"You folks can visit later," Martha said. "Doc Hersholtz insisted Marshall go right on up to bed." She touched Marshall's arm. "He said you were up most of the night and had to rest today to make up for it. So up you go, ok? Get in your pajamas and get settled and I'll be up in a sec with some orange juice. Doctor's orders. Lots of vitamin C."

She made eye and hand signals to Eden, indicating she wanted to speak with her privately. Very reluctantly, Eden let go of Marshall's hand and followed Martha into the kitchen. "I don't want to be gone long," she protested.

"I understand," Martha said gently and explained about the orange juice. "Hersholtz said it was imperative he rest really well today."

"Thanks, Martha, for telling me about the juice. I'll make sure he drinks it and I'll stay with him."

Wadsworth followed the two of them up the stairs, relieved again now that Marshall was back. Marshall sat on the side of the bed, grimacing as he moved to take off his shirt. Eden quickly helped him and he'd just gotten into his pajamas when Martha tapped lightly on the door.

"Got the orange juice," she said softly. "Have to keep the doc happy." She handed the glass to Marshall and both she and Eden watched as he drank it. There was no problem getting him to drink the whole thing.

"Very good," he said, handing the glass back. Then, "Bess, she's ok? She didn't get hurt last night?" He hadn't really been aware of what had become of the horse.

"She didn't get injured at all, Marshall," Martha answered. "Sleigh seemed to settle back on its runners and didn't pull her down. Stuart took her back to the Smythe's. You just rest now, son. We'll have a nice quiet dinner later."

"I don't think I'll sleep that long," Marshall chuckled. "Just give me a half hour or so and I'll come downstairs."

Martha and Eden exchanged glances. "All right, Marshall," Martha said. "You do what you think best."

She left and Eden quickly slipped into a nightgown. Marshall was settling back onto his pillow and she slid in beside him. "Rest, darling. I'll be right here. I'm not going anywhere."

"Good," he murmured. "I need you in my arms." He yawned. "And you need rest, too."

"What I need is your arms," she whispered, pressing into his side. "Thank you."

"Hmmm?"

"You protected me...again. But it costs too much, darling. It costs more than I can bear."

"Can't have you getting hurt," he slurred, unable to fend off the comfortable softness that was enveloping his brain. "Can't let them take you."

"I know," she sighed. "Oh, how I know."

"Eden."

"Yes."

"Love you." Then his head tipped to the side on the pillow and his right arm slipped from his chest, lying out from his side on the bed.

She looked at him. He was lying much as he had in the snow last night, only this time his eyes were fully closed and his lips only barely parted. But it was still too much and tears began to roll freely down her cheeks. "Oh, God, Marshall," she moaned, feeling the jagged, rusty wound that still oozed in her core. She touched his face then pressed her lips to his unresponsive ones. They were warm, soft. If... if.... Then they would be stiff and cold. A huge sob wrenched its way through her, followed by short, gasping ones that made breathing hard.

With shaking fingers, she unbuttoned the shirt of his pajamas, spreading the sides apart so his chest was bare. In its center, a round bruise was forming, a bruise the size of the side of a man's fist. She kissed it then her fingers fluttered over his chest, finally stopping so she could rest both palms there, rest them there and let them ride the gentle up and down swells of his breathing. Her tears fell on her own hands, dripping across them, rolling down to his chest.

Closing her eyes, she leaned over him, laying her cheek on his chest. There it was. His heartbeat. Regular. Strong. Most importantly, there. It was there. But she'd been shaken beyond endurance. Would she ever be able to relax into its being there, ever again? Would anything ever be so simple again? She listened to it, enveloped in the rhythm of its beating. It was the one necessary sound so that she might exist.

Her arms circled around his body, holding on, holding close. Those moments last night when she'd thought he'd gone, when he had gone, would not leave her alone. It had been so fast, all of it. She was falling and his arm went around her. She remembered the firm pressure of it. Then she'd landed atop him, his body between hers and the road, but nothing between it and his. Nothing because he'd chosen it to be that way. Always he chose her over himself. Did he not know that without him she wouldn't exist anymore anyway? Did he not know that? And then it was all over. He was simply lying there and this heart she pressed her ear to now, it was motionless. That had opened up such a void, an unthinkable void, and she had fallen into it. He was alive. He'd come back. But still she clung by her fingernails to the edge of the chasm of his loss, not fully able to haul herself back up.

Even holding him as she was, even listening to his beating heart, the horror of the living memory of it brought fresh tears. She lay there a full hour or more, pressed into him, listening, listening, listening as she cried. Then she slept, arms around him, cheek to chest. Her pillow was much too far from his heart.

All day she slept and woke, cried, slept and woke. He lay as he'd fallen asleep, unmoving, quiet. When she was awake, she kissed his face, whispered to him all the confessions of her pain, her fear. She began to need him to move, to return her touch, to answer her whispers, but he did not. Hours passed and he remained in the deepest places of sleep where Hersholtz's powder had sent him. It wasn't until the light began to fade from the evening sky that he sighed a bit and licked his lips.

It took him a long time to rise up through all the heavy layers of induced sleep. The fingers of his right hand moved on the covers and he tried to remember where he was, what day it was. Then he knew that Eden was there. The ends of her hair were moving delicately across his upper chest. He wanted to say her name but the effort of it was still beyond him for a while. Then he felt her lips on his and he managed a slight pressure in return.

She pulled her head back. "Marshall? Darling?" But that was exactly what she'd said last night when he lay unmoving in the snow. Something sharp yanked its way up through her own chest and fresh tears burst from her face. "Damn!" she whispered, angry that she couldn't stop them.

"D...damn?" he repeated.

She laughed, hiccupped, then cried again.

His left hand came up, touching her wet cheek. She was crying. Why was she crying? "Eden?"

She put her hand over his, nodding her head, not able to unthicken her throat to reply right then.

"Tears?"

She nodded again.

"Why tears?"

She only cried harder, clasping her arms around him again.

So he folded his around her back then moved one hand up to stroke her hair. "Shhh!" he murmured. "It's all right."

But it hadn't been all right. It had been all wrong and the wrongness of it had riddled her with holes, leaving her brittle, very, very breakable. And as she held him and sobbed, he remembered the why and pulled her body up a bit so that her face was next to his.

"We'll deal with this, my darling," he said softly. "Together, you and I, we'll deal with this."

Then his mouth found hers with a kiss of utter tenderness. She kissed him back, her lips frantic on his, seeking, almost devouring the aliveness she found in them until he kissed her more intensely, matching her eager hunger. She felt the rise of his wanting her against her thigh and pressed her hands into his shoulders, desperate to have him inside her. She wanted him there. She wanted him never not to be there and she made love with a flaming fierceness until she knew the warm, living essence of his manhood was flowing into her and somehow, somewhere, something inside her let go of a little of the pain.

Chapter 56

Edith had watched Eden carefully all during the little dinner Martha had made for them. Only Marshall and Eden, Ryan, Connie and herself were at the table, smaller again now that Harold had removed the leaves. Elizabeth was keeping Luke at Stuart's all day, thinking it best that Marshall not have to deal with a child quite yet. Edith had known Eden from the day she was born, had probably spent more time with her than Cerise, her mother, ever had. Even after Miles had been killed, she'd not seen her niece in quite the state she was now observing. Marshall was all right, but Eden was not.

When the meal was over and Marshall seemed engaged in conversation with Ryan, Edith pushed back her chair and leaned toward Eden. "Come with me a minute," she directed.

Eden opened her mouth to protest that she didn't want to leave Marshall, but Edith repeated firmly, "Eden, come with me now."

Connie watched the interaction silently, glad her mother seemed to be taking some action.

Eden sighed heavily. "All right, but just for a moment." She told Marshall she was going up to Edith's room for something and would be right back. Once there, she sat on the side of one of the beds, twisting her fingers in her lap.

"What's so important?"

"You are, darling. You're what's important."

Eden pressed her lips together, trying to still the trembling in her chin she felt starting again. Edith sat beside her, sliding her right arm around Eden's shoulders. "Talk to me, darling. Tell me what's going on inside you."

"I...I...don't think I can."

"Try. You need to tell somebody what you're feeling. That's been me more often than not."

"I'm not sure any more, Aunt Edith."

"Not sure of what?"

"That I can do this. That I...that I...can live with the risk of it."

"The risk of losing him?"

She nodded. "I love him so much, Edith, and there's nothing I want more than to be with him, but I'm so scared right now." She stared down at her own hands. "I wish...."

"What?" Edith urged when Eden remained silent for a long moment.

"Oh, Edith! Sometimes I wish I'd never met him. I know I was a zombie before I did, but...but...I didn't know, I didn't understand what this would be like, what this could be like." Tears began running down her cheeks. "I just...hurt...so bad. I can't stand it. It hurts too much. Too much."

Edith was quiet, trying to grasp all that Eden was saying. She, too, had never seen anybody quite so overwhelmingly in love as Eden was with Marshall. Connie was right about that. "You want to go back to your apartment, darling? You want that life again?"

Eden buried her face in her hands. "No," she moaned, shaking her head. "Without him, I'm not sure I want any life."

Edith bit down on her lip, appalled at what Eden was indicating. "Darling," she said softly, starting to smooth Eden's hair. "Is there any real choice? Isn't marrying him better than just...."

"That's it, don't you see? If I marry him, I'll have to live with losing him. I could stop the whole thing and not have to live with that. I don't know if I can live with that."

"Can you just stop loving, Eden? Is that possible?"

"I can't do that either. That's what's so horrible about it. I can never not love him."

"I believe that," Edith said gently, "and since that's so, would you miss out on years of being with him, of bearing his children, of loving him every single day...would you miss out on that, darling, because you're afraid of possible loss?"

"I just want to feel safe, to feel like I can love and not have it all snatched away. I'm just so afraid." She slid her spread fingers up through her hair and leaned forward, rocking slightly. "When I saw him last night and he was gone, oh, Edith, I couldn't stand it. I just couldn't stand it. Just looking at him and...and...he'd been singing there at Stuart's a little while before, and he was so beautiful to me, you know. Just everything about him was so beautiful, so alive. How could he be gone? How? Not him, Edith, not HIM! And I knew everything... everything...had become this huge, empty pit that I'd have to live in forever."

She turned, taking Edith's hands in hers. "I know he'd been in trouble before. I know that. I'd been there for that, for the mud, for the forest, but I was doing something, you know, I was getting him out or tracking after him. But last night he was just there one second and the next he wasn't and there wasn't a thing I could DO! He was just gone. It was done, over. Everything was over. And...and I got lost in that and can't find my way back." She began crying again and leaned way over, burying her face in her Aunt's lap. "I'm so lost, Edith. He was gone and I...I lost myself."

"Oh, darling," Edith said, blinking back her own tears. "I know you've been through so much the last couple of months and I know it sounds trite to say it, but haven't they been wonderful, too? Haven't you been happy?"

"Umm hmm," she murmured mufflediy, her face still buried in Edith's skirt. "I've never been so happy in my life."

"That's the way of it, Eden. That's truly the way of it. It's the light that makes the shadows. You know that, darling, you know that's how life is set up. You can wander for years in foggy gray, and I think you did after Miles, but then there was Marshall, dear Marshall, like some grand lighthouse on a high bluff and you stumbled all unaware into the beam of him."

Eden lifted her head, nodding. "He's like that, he is."

"So, then, you weren't in that gray space any more, right?"

"Umm hmm."

"But lights, by their very nature, cause shadows. Shadows simply don't exist if there's not a light, and the brighter the light, the deeper the shadows. That's what happened to you last night. You tripped over a shadow and fell flat on your face in it, and it was there because he made it be, he made it just because of the way he shines. And that's it, darling. You have to choose between the evenness of a steadily gray life or walking in his beam of light with shadows possible. That's what all of us have to choose. To have the light, you have to risk the shadows, but isn't that better than nothing but gray? Isn't it? I don't think we're put here on this earth to walk in gray. We can, and many, many people do, but it's, well, it's a lesser way. Life isn't meant to be an exercise in safety. Life is a sketch, Eden, that we draw without an eraser, and we can take our pencil and make neat little lines but the picture is flat and lifeless unless we highlight it with light and take our fingertip and rub in some shadows. Light and shadows, that's what makes it real, that's what gives it value."

She brushed away the tears that remained on Eden's cheek. Eden looked at her aunt, really looked at her. "You know about shadows. Were there shadows when Uncle Dean...?"

"I don't think I loved him with the grand passion I see in you for your Marshall, but I loved Dean completely in my quiet, steady way. He was the only man I ever even thought about marrying. Such a good, kind man he was. You know he died with his head on my lap? I was sitting on the couch and he was resting, hadn't been feeling well, and I was stroking his hair. Do you remember how wavy and soft it was?" She gave a small little laugh. "No, I guess that wouldn't be something you'd ever think about. But it was. I always liked to touch it." She sighed, then continued. "The attack came so fast and he was gone before I could even reach for the phone. I sat there the longest time after I knew he was gone, just stroking his hair. So, yes, darling, I've walked through my own shadows.

Everybody does. If there's any light at all in their lives, they do. Would I go back and not have Dean, go back and have only gray so that I would avoid that day he died in my lap and his hair was still soft under my fingers?" She shook her head then put her hand on Eden's shoulder. "I live now in the lights of you and Connie. I could have lost both of you when the sleigh tipped. Would I rather not have you two, would I rather not have the risk of losing you? I wouldn't, Eden. I really wouldn't."

Eden sighed, rubbing her hand back and forth across her forehead. "Everything would be so gray without him, Edith." She smiled slightly to herself. "He doesn't even know what light is, not really, and yet he shines with it more than anyone I've ever known."

"Loving him is good, isn't it?"

"Oh, Edith, it's so wonderfully good."

"Isn't that what matters, darling? At the end of everything, isn't all that matters that we love, that we've been loved? No shadow is more important than that. No risk is more terrible than not having that."

Eden was chewing her lower lip, thinking hard. Edith added, "There's one more really important thing, darling. That's Marshall himself. He was the one who died last night. Have you stopped at all and thought that in that moment he, too, lost his whole future with you? What if he were so consumed with fear that he might die that he decided he couldn't marry you?"

Eden's eyes widened. "He wouldn't!"

"No, I don't think he would. But if he did, isn't that the same thing you were thinking about? Wouldn't that inflict as much pain on you as he would be in if you back out of his life now?"

"He wouldn't understand, Edith. He'd think I was like Beatrice, that I couldn't love him because of the blindness. I know he would! It would hurt him so badly."

"Think about that, darling. Think about him more than about what you're feeling. Didn't all this happen last night because he was thinking about you? Didn't the whole forest scene happen because of the same thing? Do you love him less, Eden, than he loves you? He risks his life out of his love for you. Can you risk his death out of love for him? Can you love him that much? Do you love him that much?"

"Oh, Edith, I feel like such a...."

"No, darling, you don't need to go there. There's only one place you need to go and that's to him, to him fully and openly and love him in spite of the risk, in spite of the shadows." She paused, her eyes gentle on her niece. "When I've found myself in some shadow in my life, I've always known that it was there, that it was only there, because a light had made it. If I stopped and looked at the light instead of the shadow, I seemed to understand things and they all fell into perspective. It's how I've lived my life, darling. And you know me, you know how I think. You know that I truly believe that the reason for life is so that we're better when we leave it than when we arrived."

Eden put her arms around her aunt. "I remember when I was little and you told Connie and me that if we tripped over a stumbling block, we should climb up on it and turn it into a stepping stone."

Edith laughed lightly. "I did say that, didn't I? And it's true. It's what you need to do now to get through this. Your wedding is less than a week. Don't waste these days in mourning over an almost-was. I always thought you'd be so happy if you ever loved again, if you ever were preparing for a wedding again. Connie and I are here with you. Can we enjoy this week, darling? Can it be a time of preparation with joy? You've got an absolutely marvelous man who loves you completely. Don't let any of this slide away, ok?"

Eden looked at her watch. "Ahhh!" she moaned. "I've been gone way longer than I told him."

"Some way longs are necessary so that entireties can happen."

Both women stood and Eden hugged her aunt again. "Do you know how dear you are to me?"

"I do," Edith smiled. "Now, if you're ready, go find him. Dare to love, Eden. Always."

Eden blew Edith a kiss and ran out the door.

She found him in the parlor, seated at the piano. Ryan was in the kitchen talking with his father and Connie. Coming up to the bench, she put her arms around his neck, laying her lips on his ear. "Marshall Sinclair, will you marry me?"

He laughed. "I do believe I shall." Then he turned on the bench, sliding his legs around the end, and took her in his arms. Something had changed with her. He wasn't sure just yet what it was, but there was a definite tone of happiness again in her voice. Tipping his chin up, he said, "Kiss me?"

She put her lips on his, saying as she did, "And I'll never ever stop. Ever."

"Is that a promise?"

"With all my heart, yes."

He touched her face with his fingertips. "You're all right?"

"Some way longs are necessary so that entireties can happen."

"Should I ask what that means?"

"Nope," she replied. "You don't need to ask. You just drink your orange juice and rest and let me love you."

"There was something in that, wasn't there?"

"You bet. Hersholtz was making sure you didn't go bungee jumping today."

"Is it ok if I skip more orange juice and just let you love me?"

She didn't answer. She just kissed him as thoroughly as is humanly possible.

Chapter 57

The two of them spent a while in the parlor after that and he played several old songs for her, ones his parents used to sing years ago. He knew them all, the music, the words, could hear a song once and then play it, and these particular ones he'd heard countless times, the notes sliding gracefully out from under his mother's fingers. She asked him to sing, too, and he did, pleased that she was herself again enough to be interested. He did *When You and I Were Young, Hear the Wind Blow, My Old Kentucky Home,* several Stephen Foster ones, his voice stronger than the day before.

She sat beside him, her head on his shoulder, letting the peace of being beside him slowly fill her empty places. Martha looked in the door, smiled, and went back to her kitchen. Edith took a book into the living room. Ryan had carried Connie up the stairs. Everybody quite purposely left the couple in the parlor alone.

Some time later they moved to the couch. "I like this couch," he said softly, his mouth quirking in a bit of a grin. There were a lot of memories connected with it.

"Was that just yesterday morning you asked me to marry you?"

"No," he replied. "I've loved you since before I knew you were you. No, that's not right, either. Somehow I've always known you were you, I just didn't know who was you or where you were, but I asked you to be mine long ago when we were just sparkles of thought in the mind of God. I know that's right. I feel the rightness of it."

"I think sometimes," she murmured, leaning close, "that I've come to the furthest reaches of loving you, that I know the all of it and I'm so filled with it the seams of my soul begin to stretch. But I never do. I get to the edges of what I know of loving you and I find it's not an edge at all." She sighed contentedly, rubbing her cheek lightly over his beard. "It just goes on and on and on, and I can't even begin to grasp the vastness of it. I...I've never known anything like this at all, Marshall. I've never known what it's like not to have a horizon where something ends." She kissed his chin. "There are days when the blue of the sea and the blue of the sky are so the same that the water fades into the air, merges with it with no visible line, and the ocean doesn't end and the sky doesn't begin. It's like that. It just goes and never stops, is never contained, never has boundaries."

He startled her slightly by whispering, "Sight," and turning his head away.

"What, darling? Oh, I'm sorry. I guess I use too many purely visual images."

He put his palm across his eyes and leaned his face forward.

"What? What is it?"

"I don't know what it is, Eden, what it was." He lifted his head, turning it toward her. "Something. Some sort of...something."

"When? What do you mean, sweetheart?"

"Last night. Something."

"Last night?"

"When the sleigh tipped. Something."

"When you hit the road? Is that what you mean?"

"Just after that...then."

"After? But...."

"I know, but that's what I mean."

She pressed her hand to her mouth. What was he talking about? After he hit the road, his heart stopped. How could there be something?

"I...," he began, faltering, searching for words.

"Something happened after...after...?"

He nodded. "I think so. It was all so confusing. I didn't know what was happening, what had happened. Everything was...different."

"Different how?"

"I can't describe it. There were...things."

"Things?"

"Yes, things. Around me, close to me. I knew they were there."

"That's good, isn't it, knowing they were there?"

"But I couldn't feel them, Eden. I couldn't hear them. But I knew they were there."

Her brow knit. She had no idea what he meant. "What sort of things?"

"Shapes. Some kind of...shapes." He shook his head. "I guess they were shapes. I don't know."

"Shapes? Like what? People?"

"I don't think so. It was so different. I knew they were there and I didn't touch them. They weren't making any noise, but they were there."

"Big?"

"I didn't seem to know what big was. They were just...there. I remember it being ok somehow. It was odd but it didn't really bother me." He shook his head again as though trying to clear it so he could grasp what he needed to communicate to her, to himself.

She could see plainly that it was bothering him. Whatever it was, if it hadn't bothered him then, it was bothering him now. "You were lying in the snow. Could it have just been the snow that was around you?"

"I don't think that was it. It was different...and I was moving through it."

"Moving?" He hadn't moved at all there in the snow. He was dead. He couldn't move. Her eyes suddenly widened. Could that be it? "Remember, darling, there in the mud when you couldn't breathe and you said for a moment you felt this sense of detachment, like you were just about to float away but didn't because I started beating your back?"

He clamped his tongue between his lips. "You think...?"

She nodded. "It's possible. Was there anything else, anything at all?"

"Punctures. There were lots of little punctures."

"In you? Was something poking at you?"

"Not like that, no. They were around me, above me. Little punctures."

Punctures? What could he mean by that? What would seem like punctures to him? "Close to you?"

"I don't know, Eden. I couldn't tell. They were just there, like this space I live in all the time had been pierced from somewhere outside. I have no idea what they were, what could do that." Again he shook his head. "They were just...there," he repeated.

"And you knew they were there?"

He nodded.

"But you didn't touch them?"

"I didn't touch them, no."

"Or hear them?"

"No."

"Marshall?"

"What?"

"Did you see them?"

His whole body jerked slightly. "That...that couldn't be what...seeing...is? Could it?"

"I don't know, darling. Something happened in that moment that your heart stopped. Maybe it was."

"But the punctures? I don't understand the punctures."

"You keep calling them that, Marshall. But what if, what if they were stars?"

His lips parted and his breathing grew rapid, shallow. "No. I don't...."

"Why not? Remember that study you told me about?"

"But, in the mud, I didn't...."

"You didn't die in the mud."

"But...."

"Think about it. The 'somethings'. What if they were the big evergreens that grow all along the lake road?"

"Like...that? An evergreen is like...that?"

"Well, maybe in the night it could seem like that, and then above them would be the stars. It was nearly midnight and the clouds were almost gone. I remember watching the stars as we drove along."

"But I didn't think stars were...."

"Like punctures? Weren't there old stories from ancient peoples who thought the stars were holes in the sky and the light shone through from the other side? Wasn't there something like that?"

He nodded, then buried his face in his hands. "I don't think I...."

She slid her arms around his back, realizing the truth of what Edith had said. Marshall was the one who'd died. He had his own issues to deal with. She'd better buck up and stop thinking about herself and think more about what he needed. She could see this was huge for him. He seemed absolutely shocked. If it were true and he'd seen for that small moment in time, it had been night and everything was shaded and shadowed, the colors barely there. The evergreens would seem foreign, especially if one were right in them. And stars, how did one understand what starlight was when one had no visual experience, had had no chance to develop the concepts that sighted people took so for granted? And it had all been very brief. She found herself not wanting him to think that was all there was to sight but, then, how would he handle even that little oblique brush with it? She didn't want him changed by it. Not that! He was so content in how it was he had to go through the world. That couldn't be taken away from him. It just couldn't!

"Marshall?"

His face was still in his hands and she could feel a slight trembling in his shoulders as he strained to come to terms with this experience. "Stars?" he was repeating. "Stars?" He shook his head. "It can't be. I was so...wrong." A shudder went completely through him. Had he been wrong about everything? Suddenly the world was an unfamiliar place. If that was what stars were like, if that was how people whose eyes weren't 'broken' knew they were there, then what was there he had been right about? Something like a small moan escaped his lips.

No, she thought, *no.* She didn't want the tables turned like this. Not like this! She didn't want him to be the one who was left suffering and in pain because of what happened last night. What had he said? He'd been so wrong? Yes, that was it. He hadn't known about the stars. How could he know what they were like?

She got up and crouched in front of him, taking his face between both her hands and saying his name strongly, firmly. When his attention seemed to have moved to her, she removed her hands from his face, picked both of his up and placed them on either side of her own face.

"Describe me."

"What?"

"Describe me. Right now. Describe me."

"Oh, Eden, I...."

"Now. Right now."

He sighed. "You're beautiful, all inside you're beautiful, and you know how to love and love and not let go. You won't stop. You see something you have to do and you manage to do it no matter how hard it is, like getting me out of that stream of mud or tracking all the way through that forest in the cold."

"More," she urged.

"Dogs like you. That's because of your loyal heart and the natural goodness of who you are." He seemed to be forgetting a little about what he'd been getting lost in, was concentrating on what she'd asked of him. "And you've been sad a lot. You have Edith and Connie, but part of you hurts still because people who should have been there for you weren't, and that's made you a little unsure about trusting life. You're smart, smarter than even you know, and you understand a lot about people and you know how to put it down in words."

"And?"

"You like it when there's just the two of us. You liked it when you and Connie had shared times growing up, when not a lot of other kids were around. And you adore Edith because she's the one who has been there for you. You've always wished she were your mother, and, to all intents and purposes, she is."

"And?"

"And you want to be happy. You want to love me. But it frightens you. You fight so hard to make it all right, but it still frightens you, especially when there's nothing to fight. You're really strong inside when you've got that something there to battle but if it's not there, then you've only got hurt left and...."

"You know me, don't you?"

He nodded. "It's important. It's who you are and I love who you are."

"Does red hair matter?"

"What?"

"Does red hair matter? You didn't mention that I have red hair or that I weigh, well, no matter what I weigh. You described who I am, what makes me me, not what color my hair is. I know you know it's auburn, but does it matter? Isn't what matters that I am consumed with love for you, waking, sleeping, and that all that I am, all that matters, is known to you, understood by you?"

"Where are you going with this, darling?"

"Are you wrong?"

"Wrong?"

"Yes, are you wrong about your concept of me?"

"I don't...."

"Has anything about your concept of me changed? Since last night, has it changed?"

He shook his head.

"Is everything important still the same?"

"You...are...everything important."

She smiled. God, how she loved him! "Do I love you less than last night?"

Now he smiled slightly. "I think maybe you love me more."

"Let me tell you something," she continued. "I do love you more. You do that to me. You. Who you are, who you've been, who you'll become. You. Everything about you, everything in you. I love that, I love all of that, everything that goes into making Marshall Marshall. You are so much more than anything I ever dreamed of and that you love me is a constant amazement and joy to me. And, darling, you know about stars. Not only do you know all the natural and scientific reasons they're there, but you understand the essence of them the same way you understand the essence of me. You understand the meaning of them and how the human heart responds to them in thoughts and words made into poetry and prose. I think how vast the number of people there are who don't care about the stars, who pay no attention to them, don't have the capacity to appreciate them. But you do. I've read things you've written about them, and you're right on. You know how to capture the heart of a star. That's what matters. Just like with me. I know you know me and when you describe me, you describe who I am, not that my hair is red. I could dye it purple tomorrow and all the things you said about me would still be true. You know me, you've captured the heart of me."

She lifted herself up enough to kiss him. "Just a bit ago Aunt Edith helped me understand about what matters. I'd let it start to slip through my fingers, and she showed me how to cup them back into a bowl and hold on, how to keep what's important where it belongs. I know this is a big deal for you, darling, but foundationally you're not wrong about things. You're really not. Your concept of things is so much more beautiful, so much more 'right' because you see to the heart of it all. Don't do what I was doing, darling. Don't lose anything, don't lose any part of yourself and let precious things slip away."

She laughed a wry little laugh. "Listen to me, sounding like Edith. I think she must've gotten to me even more than I realized. But all I know, darling, is that this is right. You are who you are, how you are, and I find the package of you entirely wonderful." Then she did laugh at the double meaning. "Well, that, too! But not only that. I love absolutely everything that's gone into making you Marshall, and your concept of the world is part of that, a wonderful, beautiful part of that. I adore your concepts. You're not wrong. You're not. Just be you. Just let me love you. You. That's who I want to love. Can we do that? Can we both not let the sleigh ride change us so that we've lost something? We already had everything that's important, everything that matters. Can't we hold onto it? Can't I take you upstairs and unwrap that package?"

She made him laugh. He hadn't expected to laugh, not right now, but she did it, and she was offering him love with both her hands. It was what he wanted. He knew he had more thinking to do about last night, but she'd made him put it in better perspective. There were concepts, and then there was death. Death rendered star concepts irrelevant, but he was here and she was here and he reached out literally and took the intangibility of her offering into his hands, merged it with his own, and offered it back to her. That was the way of it and he knew his concept of that was absolutely spot on.

"Did you say something about a package?"

Chapter 58

"They're not coming, are they?" Connie cast a look from Eden to Edith.

"No, they're not," Eden replied, "but you knew that already."

Edith made a little sound with her tongue. Cerise just didn't know how to come through for Eden when she should but, then, hadn't it always been that way?

Cerise was three years younger than Edith, had been born with Maureen O'Hara hair that she now kept dyed. The names of the two sisters said it all. Edith, solid, dependable, probably a bit old-fashioned in her values and outlooks. And Cerise. Where had they come up with that for a name anyway? And she'd always been about as easy to tie down, as available to latch onto as a bit of summer sky. Cerise cared about Cerise. She found it convenient to let Edith take care of Eden along with Connie. It left her freer to come and go as she pleased, and she pleased a lot. Edith didn't mind for her own sake. She'd have loved to have had five or six kids of her own, but Connie was her only child. It was for Eden's sake that she minded. A kid knew when its mother wasn't interested.

Then Cerise had gone and had a second child, Mason, four years younger than Eden. Edith had never figured that out. Mason had grown up independent, a bit wild, but had joined the Navy several years ago, surprising everybody. Now he was stationed in the Philippines. Eden had called him first, already almost certain he couldn't get leave to come for the wedding. He couldn't. She didn't blame him for that. Military life was like that. Vacations in Aruba were another matter, a matter of choice. But she had come to expect almost nothing when it came to what her mother would choose, not if it involved any inconvenience to her own plans. And her father? He walked, always, in Cerise's shadow, more interested in keeping the peace, keeping her happy, than in what might be going on with anyone else in the family, and that was what Eden had come to expect from him. He was a pleasant man, naturally quiet, and not a boat rocker, not even really an oar manner. He left that to Cerise. She determined where their little boat went, always had, always would.

Marshall was leaning against the doorframe of Edith's room, where Eden had called her parents. It seemed unimaginable to him that one's parents could be alive and not interested in coming to their own child's wedding. His parents would have made it up to the inn for New Year's Eve if they'd had to walk on their knees. How very strange, and sad, it was.

"It's snowy," Eden shrugged. "You know Mom and the snow."

Indeed Edith did. Even as a kid Cerise had never liked to play in the snow. It was wet and, worse, cold. Cerise loathed cold. Edith was amazed she'd actually lived in Pittsburgh as long as she had. Of course, she left it for long periods of time. She left it as often as she could. Eden had not even bothered to tell her mother about the accident with the sleigh. All she would have gotten in response was a lecture on the dangers of traveling in snow and a suggestion she consider marrying someone who didn't die. Cerise was blunt that way. Eden hadn't wanted to have to deal with what to say to her mother in reply to such things, not with Marshall standing right there.

She turned and looked at him, his left shoulder pressed against the frame, a rather displeased look on his face. "It'll be all right, darling," she said, getting up and walking to stand in front of him. "It's what I expected."

"Still...," he replied, standing straight.

"I've got Edith and Connie. They're the ones I really need anyway." She turned her head, smiling at her aunt and cousin, then back to Marshall. "And you. Always you."

He slid his arms around her. "I love you," he whispered. Edith's eyes filled with tears.

"Well, what's next?" Connie said. "When do you want to go into Bellefonte and look for a dress?"

"Maybe tomorrow, Con," Eden said softly. "I think I'd just like to stay here today." The truth was, that though she felt somewhat recovered from the trauma of Marshall's death, she knew she was not completely over it. The thought of leaving him even for a trip to Bellefonte for the dress just did not appeal to her. All she wanted was to be with him, as close as she could get.

"But if they don't have something you like, then...," Connie began, thinking of what a short time remained to come up with what was needed.

"I could come, too," Marshall volunteered, realizing why Eden wanted to remain at the inn.

"But the groom can't see the dress before...." Connie turned red and clapped her hand over her mouth. *Stupid, stupid, stupid!!*

But Marshall laughed. "We don't have that problem, now do we?" He kissed Eden's hair. "In fact, I have a particular request I'd like to make concerning that. Since I'll be standing there by the fireplace when you come into the parlor, darling, I won't be able to have the experience of that first sight the groom has of his bride. You'd walk in and I wouldn't know, wouldn't know at all, what you were wearing."

"I hadn't thought of that," Eden said. "What do we do?"

"I'd like to know the dress before we get to that part of things. I'd like to gaze at it, if I might, preferably with you in it."

"Gaze at...?" Connie had no idea what he meant.

Eden, though, knew he wanted to touch the dress, touch it all over so he knew the shape and form of it, the material, the fold and the drape, but all she could think was his hands exploring over the dress and she stood on tiptoe to whisper in his ear. "I might not make it into the parlor, you know. I might have to...."

He smiled widely and Connie, getting the idea of it, just shook her head fondly. "You two might have to get a room so he can, um, gaze at the dress."

"We have a room," Marshall grinned. "I could gaze at it there."

"You can gaze, darling, but the whole room thing is going to have to wait until after the ceremony or there won't be a ceremony."

Martha came up then behind Marshall. "Speaking of ceremonies, I've just talked with Reverend Powers. He does this sort of thing for folks around here, folks that don't have a regular church in the area but would like someone other than a magistrate to marry them. He says he'd be delighted to come to the inn. You'll like him. Really nice man."

"Oh, Martha, thank you!" Eden smiled. "I had no idea who we'd get on such short notice."

"Short notice is my specialty," Martha laughed. "And Joan asked if she could make your cake. She's mighty good at it. Just give her an idea of what you'd like, and she'll whip it up for you."

"Chocolate?" Marshall said hopefully.

"With raspberry jam between the layers?" Eden added.

"You like raspberry jam on cake?" he asked.

"Is that ok?" she responded, worriedly.

"Ok? It's what my mother always used to do. I didn't know if anybody else did that, too, or not."

Edith laughed, listening to them. "She grew up with my raspberry jam in cakes, Marshall."

Marshall smiled in the direction of Edith's voice. "Edith, you are absolutely the best."

"It needs white icing, though," Connie interjected. "Wedding cakes need white icing."

"Fine by me," Marshall said, "just so long as it's chocolate and raspberry underneath."

"I'll let her know," Martha nodded. "Did I hear someone mention Bellefonte? Are you going dress shopping today?"

"Tomorrow," Eden said softly. "I'd rather go tomorrow."

"That will be all right, darling." Edith laid her hand briefly on Eden's arm. "I'm sure we'll find what you want. You do what you need to today." Her eyes flashed toward Connie, warning her daughter not to push further on the matter.

Marshall kissed the top of Eden's head. "I'll wait for you back in our room. Come whenever you're finished here."

He actually wanted a quiet moment just to think. He and Wadsworth slipped quickly down the hall and into their room. Inside the door, he paused, then reached out and flipped the light switch on, off, then on again. What was it like, a room brightly lit? What was...lit? It had been there ever since Christmas night, that desire to understand. Usually he managed to sit on it effectively enough that it didn't haunt him, but not since the sleigh ride. Sitting on the side of the bed, he touched his lids with his fingertips, sighed, then laid back on the pillows.

Concentrating so hard on what he was thinking, he didn't hear Eden open the door and come in. She stood there silently a long moment, watching him. He was lying on the bed, his knees bent, his right hand cupped over both eyes, his left hand cupped over that.

She'd never seen him do something quite like that. As she watched, he probed a bit at his eyelids with his fingertips then let his left arm fall straight out from his body on the bed, while keeping his right over his eyes. She walked softly around the bed, leaned over, and slid her palm into his where it lay atop the covers.

He jerked slightly, startled that he'd been unaware of her coming, then moved his right hand from his face as his lips curved in a smile of greeting. Sitting on the bed, she bent enough to kiss the fingers of the hand she was holding. "You were thinking about your eyes?"

He nodded. "So much I thought I'd dealt with seems to have gotten stirred up."

"Tell me," she urged. "What sorts of things?"

"All my life I've tried to understand, tried to grasp as best I could what people meant when they said they were seeing something. Jeff used to talk and talk with me about it, about what it was like to see." He touched his lids again with his right hand. "I just can't quite imagine what it is these things are supposed to do, you know. How it is they gather the information they do without touching or hearing or smelling? It's like science fiction to me that there's this other way, this way that provides so much knowledge of what's out there. It's always been so utterly foreign to me, so not a part of how I live, how I make my way, how I do what I do. All I know is that almost everybody else has this, this whateveritis, that gets them through the world, that lets them drive cars, that lets them dance in crowded rooms, that lets them know when Uncle George has come into the room before he speaks."

He rubbed his hand back and forth across both eyes. "Helen Keller said, 'Death is no more than passing from one room into another. But there's a difference for me, you know. Because in that room I shall be able to see.'" His left hand was still in hers, but he moved to rest his right forearm across his eyes. "I always wondered what that meant to her, what the thought of being able to see meant to her, what sort of concept she'd come to about it, especially since she had to imagine what hearing was like, too."

His tongue came out a bit, wetting his lips. "I've tried ever since I can remember not to let it be hard, that knowing nearly everybody else had some way of knowing things I didn't have. And I was so comfortable moving around and living in the world as I know it, that it truly didn't matter all that much. I've always been curious about it, though, just what it is, what it might be like, but there's never been any real way for me to know. Then," he paused, blowing out a breath, "there was the sleigh ride and something... different...was there, there in my familiar, comfortable space."

He sat up, turning to sit cross-legged on the bed, facing her, holding out his right hand, too, so that both her hands were in both of his. "I can't even begin to describe what it was like in any way that makes sense. It was a bit as though I were hearing words, only I'd never heard anything before and I couldn't understand what was being said, only that I knew somehow they were words. I just couldn't attach any meaning to them, so the sound of them simply flowed over and around me but didn't get in me." Shaking his head, he continued. "That's not really even close, though. It was more than that. Something, some... things... were there and I knew they were there but I didn't know how I knew. I had no way of relating to how I knew. It's just so hard to explain, but if it was seeing, even some little part of seeing, I want to understand it. I couldn't tell what anything was. I mean, I thought I understood about pine trees, but if that's what was there in the space with me, then it wasn't like anything I've ever thought about pines."

"The circumstances were really different, darling," Eden said, wanting desperately to enter into what he was feeling, was trying to express. "If it was sight, then it was during a time when nothing would have been the same for you in any way. People, live people, don't just rise up through the pine boughs like that. If it had been me, I'm not sure even I would have understood what was going on. And for you...."

"I always thought sight was more than that," he said seriously. "It just didn't seem, whatever it was, quite good enough to be sight."

She smiled fondly at him. "From what you said, it sounded like you had a face full of pine branches. That's not much, especially in the middle of the night, for anybody to see. Now if you'd been in a brightly-lit hospital room, it might have been a different story. But not you. Nope. You have to go and die in forests at night."

He chuckled a bit. "I'd say I'd try to do better next time, but you'd probably...."

"I would," she interrupted. "I'd scream. I really would."

"I thought so."

"You have an abominable track record, I hope you know, Dr. Sinclair. It's something I've been wanting to talk to you about."

"In what way?"

"About being here at the inn. Don't get me wrong, I love the inn. I'm crazy about Martha and Harold and their family and all, but I'm really wondering if maybe we shouldn't go back to Pittsburgh before too much longer. I just don't think I can handle any more of the sorts of things that seem to happen to you in this quiet, peaceful spot."

"It is a bit ridiculous, isn't it?"

"More than a bit, darling. A lot more than a bit."

"Would you like to go home, really?"

"Home?"

"To Mount Lebanon. To our home."

"Our home," she repeated. "Your house?"

"No," he said firmly. "Not my house. Our home."

"Not to your house? You don't want to live in your family's house after we're married?"

He shook his head, laughing. "I do want to live there. With you. Our home."

"Oh!" she exclaimed, feeling obtuse. "Oh, yes! I'd love that! I want so much to see where you grew up and to live there." She blinked a bit. "I can't imagine how wonderful it would be to live there."

"With me."

"Oh, Lord, yes, with you." She leaned further forward so that her face was against his chest. "But no sleighs."

"No sleighs," he promised. "Not even a skateboard."

"You didn't?"

"No, I didn't," he smiled. "Just roller skates."

"Oh, Lordy," she moaned. "Do you have bubblewrap?"

"Kiss me," he said, "and forget the bubblewrap."

"Yes, Sir," she replied obediently as he lay back again, pulling her with him. And she did forget about it. Completely. Bubblewrap was not on her mind at all as his lips, warm and moist, pressed into hers.

Chapter 59

Parachute silk. That was it. She didn't know why it had never come to her before, but now as she lay still beneath him, the image, the feel of it was perfectly clear. When he took her up, lifting her till her nerves imploded and exploded all at once and then she lay as she was immediately after, it was like lying on grass somewhere as a huge white parachute slowly settled over her. It settled in folds of wispy silk, in gentle layers brushing against the walls of her being, inside and out, a silent floating down so delicately light, so completely perfect in its contrast to the exquisite piercingness of mere seconds before. Then she lay completely enfolded in its lingering silky touch, somehow a part of both the grass and the silk, her being spreading out, becoming wider again in the release from long minutes of intense ingathering.

His face was buried where her neck curved into the line of her shoulder and, listening to his breathing, she knew he, too, was settling, was with her under the soft drape of the white canopy. She felt utterly separated from anything else in the world but him. The togetherness with him was all there was and her hands curved up around his back as though to make the moment stretch its boundaries of time. He was no longer supporting himself on his arms and most of his weight was fully on her, yet not heavy in that way a woman's body has of shaping to hold her mate's without discomfort. She let her mind explore the fact of that, wondering, appreciating that it should be so. She liked the feel of his weight atop her, liked the sense of covering it gave her. The parachute silk had faded now, leaving only him. Only him. How totally sufficient that 'only' was.

She felt his lips move on her neck and then he rolled mostly off her, and as he melded himself to her right side, he slid his bent right leg atop hers. Sighing happily, she turned more toward him and his right hand slipped up her ribcage then over and down her arm where he laced his fingers into hers. He nuzzled his nose to her ear. "I really like it," he murmured.

"What?"

"Your outfit.'

"My wedding dress?"

"Oh, I'll like that, too, but I mean your current outfit."

"My birthday suit?"

"Mmm hmm, that. I really like that."

She laughed, turned a bit, and nipped at his nose. "No zippers, no buttons," she chuckled.

"One button," he corrected and before she could stop him, had moved and blown a big, loud raspberry in her navel.

She shrieked then clapped a hand over her mouth, looking toward the door. "Do you suppose they heard?"

"Heard what? That I love you?"

"Yeah, that."

"Probably," he replied helpfully.

Wadsworth had sat up at the sound of her shriek, his ears pricked sharply toward the bed. "He's staring at us," Eden announced.

"He never tells. It's ok."

"But he's watching."

Marshall chuckled. "Wadsworth, lie down!" he ordered with mock firmness.

Wadsworth promptly turned his back on them and settled down, his chin on his front paws. "Good boy," Eden breathed.

"Me?" Marshall asked playfully.

"You, too, but you're definitely not as obedient as he is."

Marshall affected a wounded expression. "Ask me anything and I'll do it."

"Ooo," she grinned, "that could be interesting. Let me think."

A series of rather risqué thoughts popped immediately into her head, but, leaning on her elbow looking down at him beside her, she was again consumed with her need for him always to be all right. She bit her lip and in a barely audible voice whispered, "Don't die."

His expression changed instantly and, reaching for her, he pulled her down and wrapped his arms around her. "I will someday, darling," he said tenderly, kissing his way around her face, "but what I can promise you is that I'll do everything I can to make sure that's on some vaguely distant day, far, far in the future. But I'm here now, right here, and now is what we've got." He kept kissing her as he spoke. "And life is made up of all our nows stacked one atop the other. It's up to us if each now is lived in happiness and love or in fear of possibilities. What I want for us, for you and me, Eden, is to make our stack a good one. I don't know how tall it will be but I do know I want it to, how was it Luke was talking about the Christmas tree...sparkle? That's it. I want it to sparkle."

"This one," Eden said, her fingertips lightly touching the shoulder of the dress the slim, older woman was holding on the hanger. "This is definitely it."

"Don't you want to try it on first?" Connie suggested.

"Oh, I'll try it on," Eden nodded, "but I already know it's the one."

The six of them, Martha and Edith, Connie and Ryan, Eden and Marshall, were all tucked around in the small open area of the narrow shop in Bellefonte. They'd driven out the morning of the next day in Martha's large station wagon on their dress-finding mission. Miss Amity, the proprietor of the Somewhere In Time vintage clothing shop, had suggested several dresses before bringing out this one from further back on a rack. Marshall sat on a small wooden chair immediately behind where Eden was standing and she maintained contact with him by keeping the calf of her right leg pressed slightly against his shin.

"What's it like?" he asked.

"It is ivory, Dr. Sinclair," Amity began, but Eden lifted her hand and the shopkeeper stopped.

"It's ivory, yes," Eden smiled, "but that's not what matters." She took Marshall's hand and moved it to the dress.

"Silk?" he asked, his fingers gathering up a fold.

"Yes, silk. Soft, flowing, drapey silk...like...like...a parachute." She blushed and Connie shook her head, wondering why.

"It's from the 1930's," Amity offered, "made in the style one might have seen in the movies of the day."

Eden took the dress behind a thick curtain and quickly slipped it on. "Oh, Eden!" Edith breathed as her niece stepped out so they could see. "It's lovely. You're lovely."

Eden smiled and came close to Marshall again, bending to whisper, "I know we can't do it properly here, but I want you to have some idea right away." She guided his hand to her hip where he let it slide over the curve of that then move to her sleeve. The feel of the fabric under his fingertips reminded him of Christmas morning in the parlor when he'd asked her to marry him.

"It's like your gown," he said softly. "It's wonderful."

"I'll model it just for you later, ok?"

"Good," he said, blowing out a little breath, adjusting his position on the seat.

The dress was fitted through the bodice, waist, and hips, but was cut to flare out around one's lower legs with the slightest movement. The neckline was deeply draped and though it had long sleeves with tight, wide cuffs, the very full sleeves themselves were slit completely down their length so that her arms showed slim and bare in their silky surround. The material was gathered at the top of each shoulder and each had a row of five very small, covered buttons sewn there. She liked the texture that gave the dress, something specific for his fingers to wander through. She'd thought of lace for that purpose, and possibly embroidery, but the silk of this slid over her like a second skin and she, too, remembered Christmas morning. It was thin, almost weightless, and she shivered right there in the store at the delightful thought of his hands on it.

"What about a veil?" Connie asked.

"No veil," Eden said firmly. "Maybe a flower." She turned to Marshall. "What sort of flower for my hair, darling?"

"A gardenia," he replied immediately.

"There you have it!" she smiled at Connie. "I'll be needing a gardenia."

Martha laughed lightly. "No problem with the decision-making process here, is there?"

"No daffodils?" Connie couldn't help but interject.

"Daffs have their uses," Eden grinned widely, "but I'm going for scent here."

"Then your bouquet should be gardenias, too, probably," Connie continued.

"Do I need a bouquet?"

"Yes, you need a bouquet." Connie was firm.

"You're bossy," Eden said affectionately.

"I'm the matron of honor. It's my job." Then Connie rolled her eyes. "I hate the word 'matron.'"

Ryan chuckled. "Well, you're not very matronly, Con. We could refer to you as the 'best woman.'"

"That might work. I'm definitely not a 'maid'.

Ryan's smile widened. "Definitely not."

Martha rolled her eyes. "Behave!" she hissed fondly at her son.

The gown was purchased and then Connie found a mid-calf dress from the 1940's she liked, made from a pale rust-colored jersey that would coordinate well with the rest of the bridal party.

"Do I get to feel it?" Ryan whispered.

"Sure," she replied, then handed him the dress on its hanger. "Here."

"That is not what I had in mind."

The dresses, in their long plastic bags, were laid carefully in the back of the station wagon then they headed for lunch at the mill. "I love this place," Eden said, glad to be back, reaching out to touch the thin branches tied to the square posts.

Edith was enchanted. "It's like something out of a fairy story," she commented, delighted. "You almost expect the amber lights to come loose and fly around the room."

"Like fireflies," Eden added.

"Yes, just like that."

Ryan, walking close behind Connie, blew lightly on her neck. "Or like that," he whispered.

"Behave!" she grinned, half-turning.

"It's too late. Never learned how."

"Well, I can't teach you."

"I know," he laughed, sliding his arm through hers and unabashedly doing a little two-step past a table, "and isn't that grand?"

She tipped her head back, joining in his laughter. Eden, holding Marshall's hand, said, "Looks like some other folks have found how to make their nows sparkle, too."

Edith, looking from one of her girls to the other, discovered she was feeling a definite sparkle herself. Then her eyes found Martha, who was studying her son with appraising eyes, her lips curving into a smile. Silently she reached out and, taking Martha's hand, gave it a slight squeeze.

Chapter 60

"Back there?"

"I could ask Ryan to take me. That might be better. I don't want to stir up unpleasant memories for you, darling."

"Unpleasant is hardly the word," Eden sighed.

"That's what I mean." He cocked his head, listening. "I hear Ryan in the kitchen." He started to rise from the piano bench.

"No," she said. "If you need to go back there, I want to be with you."

She'd come into the parlor after having been talking for some time upstairs with Connie, finding him sitting at the piano, his fingertips exploring lightly over the keys, not pressing hard enough to make sound. The day before had been thoroughly pleasant, finding her dress, enjoying a long lunch at the mill, pressing close to him during the drive back to the inn. But now he had a deeply lost-in-thought expression on his face and when she'd sat beside him on the bench and asked him about it, he almost reluctantly explained that he'd been thinking again about the pines the night of the sleigh accident.

"The skies are gray again," Eden commented, looking out the window, "but no new snow. The days are really short right now, aren't they?"

A slight smile curved his lips. "Winter," he said softly. "For me the days grow colder, but not shorter."

She touched his arm. "There is so much I need to learn to understand about what it's like for you."

His hand found her hair. "I wish there were some way I could understand, in return, what it's like for you. That's one reason I want to go back to the pines. I keep trying to come to grips with what happened that night but I don't seem to be getting anywhere with it."

About fifteen minutes later, bundled in their coats, Wadsworth in harness, they got out of Eden's car where Ryan had described to them the accident had happened. Eden had no memory of the surroundings. Her entire focus that night had been on his half-open eyes, the absence of a throbbing pulse in his neck. Then nothing. She didn't like being there again. But Marshall had such an intent expression on his face as he tipped his head into the wind that she figured if she just concentrated on him now, she'd manage to get through the next few moments. She saw the rock just beside the road, the one the sleigh runner had hit, and a shudder went through her as she recalled the sensation of the fall, of Marshall's arm going around her, holding on, keeping her safe.

"Do you remember falling?" she asked, her voice catching.

"Up till when my back hit the road. That's it. After that, I just seemed to be somewhere else. Here, yet not here. Where are the pines?"

"About ten steps straight in front of you. There are some young, shorter ones then a clump of larger ones right behind them. The biggest one sort of leans toward the road, hangs over the smaller ones."

He dropped the harness and walked forward, his hands extended. He was holding his breath, though he didn't realize it. His fingers found the outer branches of the small trees and he paused there, running his hands over the tips of the pine needles. It was a very familiar sensation, especially after his time in the forest so recently. He'd come in contact with countless pine trees on his long trek. Moving his right hand to his face, he inhaled the scent from the trees on his palm. This was how he knew pine trees. Touch. Scent. Lifting his chin again, he listened.

A chill December wind played through the tall pines, the sound it made creating for him the sense of the trees over his head, bringing into being their presence. If there had been no wind, only the small pines would exist for him. Without the wind, the reality of his world was edged by whatever could be touched by his body. But the sounds resulting from the wind's passage placed him inside a larger space.

The wind slowed, dying down for a moment, and the tall pines disappeared as completely as if they'd never existed. They were not really there, not for him. Then the wind picked up again and the pines returned. In the world of the blind, it was like that, things going and out of existence, often very rapidly. If a man in a park played his guitar, it was part of his world. When he stopped, his presence was gone. Everything in his world of sound came and then went. Nothing continued like it did for those with sight, who knew the man was in the park even when he wasn't playing. For him, there was no world where things simply are. If someone said there was a kite sailing up toward the clouds, it wasn't really there, not for him. It had always been like that. Except Christmas night. Then he had known the pines were there. The tall ones. The ones he couldn't reach.

How?

How did Eden know they were there? She was still standing beside the car yet she had told him about the tall pines behind the younger trees. She knew. She knew without touching them or smelling them. She knew without the wind. She simply...knew. Because she could see them. And what did that mean? Seeing them.

He stepped forward more so that he was surrounded by young pine branches. That, too, was familiar, but that night his sense of touch, of smell, did not seem to be available to him. He stood, unmoving, trying to remember, trying to grasp how he'd known that something was there with him. It was entirely elusive, though, like holding partially-set gelatin in his hands, and the sense of it kept leaking through his mental fingers so that in some frustration he clutched the clumps of needles closest to him. He needed to hold onto... something.

"How?" he muttered. "How?"

Being here wasn't helping. He was simply feeling more removed from the experience of that night. It had been very fleeting, the whole thing, and during it he'd had no idea of what was happening. He stepped quickly back out of the small pines, his heel catching on a root, and sat down hard on the narrow shoulder of the road. Both Eden and Wadsworth came hurrying up.

"I'm fine," he growled, but made no move to get up.

Now even the small pines were gone. Nothing had an abiding presence.

Eden, disturbed by the look on his face, squatted beside him, her hand on his shoulder. "What is it, darling?"

He tried to smile for her but couldn't quite manage it. "I'm afraid it jangled me. That night. It took my comfortable, familiar world and it knocked it sideways a bit." He put both hands on his temples. "It made understanding what it is that you do so easily, made understanding that more important. I just...can't...I...."

She sat beside him on the cold ground, putting her arms around him. "I want so much to help you, sweetheart. I just don't know what to do."

He rubbed his fingertips hard across his forehead. "I need to let go of this, Eden. I need for it to stop haunting me." A small laugh escaped his lips. "Jeffrey would have my hide for letting this throw me for a loop."

She wanted to say something important, something that mattered, but couldn't think of a thing.

He moved his hand in a wide motion, letting it come to rest on his chest. What was going on inside him was always more real than what was outside. "It's my world, Eden, it's how the world works for me. But I...I...."

"What?"

"I sometimes wonder how I have the gall to try and write a book about a seeing world. Why am I doing that? I must have it all entirely wrong." He shook his head. "I should write what I know." He shook his head again. "What do I think I'm doing?" He said it to himself, then turned to her once more. "It's nothing but hearsay, you know, when I describe what it's like for Morgan. Nothing but hearsay." He squeezed his eyes tightly shut.

She'd never seen him quite like this. "I...," she began, but he jerked suddenly.

"Let's go back now," he said, starting to rise, extending a hand to help her.

"You're sure?"

"I'm done here. No point in keeping you out in the cold."

She didn't like the set of his jaw, but she kept quiet as he curved his hand around Wadsworth's harness and they headed together to the car. He was silent on the short ride back to the inn, silent as they came through the main entrance. At the bottom of the staircase he finally spoke. "I'm going up to the room for a while." He didn't suggest she come with him and so she stood, eyes stinging somewhat, watching him and Wadsworth mount the steps. He was hurting and he'd pulled it all into himself.

"Oh, Marshall," she whispered as he turned the corner at the top and disappeared.

Chapter 61

He sat at the desk, his palm spread over the Braille printout of what he'd written so far of his novel set in the opening days of the Revolutionary War. The tip of his forefinger rested on Morgan Kent's name. Morgan Kent, a sighted man in a sighted world. What did he really know of that? Sure he knew the war backwards and forwards, and he'd spent many days in Williamsburg, getting to know the place where Morgan lived, getting to know it as a blind man got to know something, anything. Got to know the scents of it, its sounds, the feel of its pickets and hedges, but Morgan knew what it *looked* like.

Williamsburg was ephemeral for him. He knew that. The bell in the tower of Bruton Parrish Church did not exist unless it were ringing the hours. It was not there, then it rang and existed...briefly...was silent and gone again. But Morgan could stand there on the Duke of Gloucester Street and look up at the bell. Its presence for him was steady, solid. Not only could Marshall not look up at the bell, he couldn't grasp what looking up was, and right now that lack, that inability to grasp, was washing over him like the mud had in the bottom of the gully. It was choking off his air supply and his fingers closed spasmodically on the top page, crumpling it.

It wasn't that he needed to see. No, that wasn't it. That wasn't what was drowning him. He needed to understand what seeing...was. What did it mean to look up at the tower and see the bell? How did that work? How did one apprehend the knowledge of the presence of the bell when it was silent? His mind was brilliant, quick, retentive, but it could not wrap itself around what seeing was. For the first time in his life he felt encapsulated. He didn't like it.

Lifting his hand with the crumpled page in it, he closed his fingers more tightly, crushing the page into a wad which he pressed against the side of his face. He sat there like that a long time, breathing through his mouth, his eyes tightly shut. "Damn it to hell!" he moaned, then threw the wad across the room, startling the dog, who scrabbled to his feet.

He folded his forearms atop the stack of papers, laying his head on them. Morgan was slipping away from him. Or was he? Had he ever really been able to get inside Morgan's head? Wasn't a good author supposed to be able to look through the eyes of his character? Well, there was no chance of that, now was there? He sat straight and using both hands, pushed the manuscript off the side of the desk, intending it to land in the wastepaper can that was usually situated midway there. The can, though, was several inches further back than normal and more pages sifted down to the floor than made it into the container. He could tell from the sound that was what had happened and he laughed, an entirely mirthless laugh, and buried his face back in his arms.

What was the matter with him? He was getting married in a couple of days to a woman he adored and yet here he was like some internal combustion engine on overload. Married. Maybe that was it? After Beatrice, he'd presumed he'd simply live alone the rest of his life. He'd gotten quite good at it, in fact. Now here he was letting someone commit to joining her life in every way to his. She couldn't really know what that would be like for her, not really. He felt jarred right down to his core by his inability to grasp sight. It had simply never mattered all that much before, then his world had been punctured by what Eden said were probably stars, only they were unlike any concept he'd ever even wildly considered for stars and whatever they were was so utterly nebulous to him it amounted to little more than grasping at the fog. His mind came away that empty of comprehension, but the effort of it had dented his peace. That was it. He felt...dented.

She opened the door as soundlessly as she could, her eyes dropping to the wad of crumpled white paper on the floor just inside. He was at the desk, his forehead resting on its surface, his hands folded over the top of his head. Her breath caught in her throat. She tiptoed several steps closer, noticing the mound of pages on the floor. He was throwing his book away. Yes, that was what he was doing.

Wadsworth, aware as usual of Marshall's mood, did not rise to greet her but remained where he was lying, his eyes going from Eden to the man at the desk and back again. What Marshall was feeling had communicated itself to him and he lay there, confused, anxious.

She paused, unsure of what to do. If Marshall knew she was there, he gave no sign of it. Should she touch his shoulder? Speak? Indecision kept her where she was a long moment until he let out such a ragged sigh that nothing mattered but that she be beside him. Kneeling to the left of his chair, she started to slide her arms around his waist. He jumped slightly at her unexpected touch, then lifted his head, turning his body in the chair more toward her. She didn't say anything, nor did he. She just laid her face in his lap and he folded over her, resting his cheek on her back.

He had not been aware she'd entered the room, not until he felt her arms start around him. He'd thought he wanted to be alone, but with her there, with her head in his lap, all he desired was to be close to her. So he laid his own head on her back, joining her in a place where words were not necessary. For a long, long time they remained like that, something in him quietly filling through her presence. After a while she whispered, "I'm here, my darling."

He breathed in a long, still somewhat shaky breath. "I'm trying to be here." He meant that. He wasn't fully there, not yet, but he was trying. It was not so simple to let go of something as monumental as this whole thing had become to him. It had altered his perception of his relationship to the rest of the world and as much as it hurt, that meant her, too. She lived in that world of steady solidness from which he was ever set apart. His tension had gotten a fierce headache fairly well locked in place. "Head hurts."

She loosened her arms. "Come over to the bed."

"I can't, not right now."

"Not that," she chuckled. "Just come. You'll see."

She propped herself with pillows against the headboard as he lay on his back, head in her lap. A bit of smooth cream on her fingertips, she began a soft, circular motion on his temples. He sighed, moaning gratefully, as her fingers moved across his forehead, sliding around his brow bone, down under his eyes, back up to his temples. She kept at it a long time, occasionally pressing harder here and there.

"Feels so good," he murmured, starting to drift into sleep. "So good."

His lips parted as his breathing grew deep and regular. Still she kept up her massaging movements, only stopping when she was absolutely sure he was sound asleep. Looking down at him, it occurred to her that they were in the same positions as when she'd sat with him on the muddy path in the rain. She leaned forward as she had then, only this time not to shelter his face from the downpour, but to place a soft kiss on his lips.

"You are so stuck with me, Doctor Sinclair," she said, tracing a fingertip along his chin line. "No matter what insecurities you might have come up with, you are stuck, completely and utterly stuck." She smiled down at him. "You need to know that, mister, really you do."

Sitting back against the headboard again, she looked across the room toward the desk, a frown line creasing her forehead as she stared at the scattered pages of his book on the floor beside it. He was more upset than she'd realized. What had he been thinking, feeling, to do that? She looked back down at his face, calm and relaxed in sleep, utterly beautiful, utterly precious to her. Some minutes later, she got a cramp in her right calf and shifted her position slightly. He sighed in his sleep, turning his cheek more against her lap. She smiled fondly at him. How far they'd come since that day in the rain. Her fingertips moved, lingering on his cheeks as they had when the thick layer of mud had begun to dissolve, revealing his features for the first time. Even then she'd known, even then, that she was connected somehow to this man. His hands rested atop his chest and she studied the way his fingers were made, her lips curving as she recalled how intimately those fingers had come to know her body. His fingers. She looked at his left hand. Wedding ring! His wedding ring would go there. Only she'd forgotten about that. Oh, good Lord! She didn't have a wedding ring for him. Cheeks puffed out, she stared up at the ceiling. Martha. Martha would know what to do, where to get one in this part of Pennsylvania. She glanced at the door, wishing she could talk with her. No, that could wait. Her hands cupped around his cheeks. This was where she belonged. "Please don't feel that way, my darling," she whispered. "You are the bulwark of my life, my high tower. Does it sound silly," she asked conversationally even though he was asleep, "that you've become rather a rampart for me?" She smiled to herself as she got a mental image of a castle keep, with him as its defensive wall. "You're there now, you know, solid and strong between me and all the 'leftness' of my life. I stand on the walkway you've brought to me and I can look out at the future, at our future, mine and yours, and what's always been a little tentative in me is strengthened by your presence. I...," she paused because his lips had begun to curve.

"You are a very medievally-minded woman, Eden McLaughlin, but how I do love you."

Chapter 62

"Why?" she asked softly, her fingers playing gently in his hair as his head still lay in her lap.

"Why are you medievally-minded?"

"Not that," she smiled, her fingers now tracing down his brow and around to his cheekbone. "Why the book?"

He didn't answer, just lay there silently for a while. She waited, knowing she didn't need to repeat her question.

"I don't think I can...," he began, then stopped, pressing his lips together.

"You can't what?"

"I don't think I can write Morgan any more. I don't think I could ever write him."

"Because he's sighted?"

He nodded his head. She closed her own eyes a moment, not sure what to say. The sleigh accident had affected him profoundly, even more profoundly than she'd thought at first. This was too important, she knew, for her to spout something stupidly affirmative. He deserved better than that. So she sat there, thinking, massaging his temples again, pleased when the new tension in his brow began to relax again. She'd been there with him as he'd written every word since late October, offering her opinions, her advice, her insight. But... still.

"Something is lacking." She said it in a tone that was neither statement nor question, but somehow in between the two.

He nodded again and she moved her hands away, but he reached up, found them, and guided them back. "Head still hurts?" she asked.

"It's getting better. You make everything better."

"How can we make the book better?" She didn't try to say it was wonderful the way it was, even though she truly thought it was quite splendid. That it wasn't right in his opinion was what mattered, was what needed to be addressed.

Again he was silent a while, just letting her fingers do their circular motion on both temples. After several minutes, she leaned forward a bit, wondering if he had gone back to sleep, but she saw his tongue lick his lips just then and knew he was thinking.

"You're good, you know, with words," he said softly. "What if...?"

"If...?"

"What if you become a real writing partner and not just an advisor? What if," he paused again, "we change the whole thing around and write it together, really together?"

"In what way, darling?"

"We could keep the setting. I think I'd like to do that, but we could make it different, angle it differently."

"I'm not following you."

He took her right hand in his, moving it to his mouth where he began kissing her fingertips. "What if we make it more of a love story and one of them is blind?"

"You mean...?"

"You write the sighted one. Completely. You can do it."

"The Scribbling Sinclairs?" she chuckled.

"Or the Sinclair Scribes," he said, rolling onto his belly and wriggling back to nestle his face in her lap.

She leaned down, kissing the back of his head. "You intend to make Morgan blind?"

"It doesn't have to be him, you know," he said, his voice muffled in her slacks. "We could have Susannah be the blind one."

"Susannah?" Her eyes widened a bit. In what had been written already, Susannah, the daughter of a prominent Williamsburg attorney, was planning a trip to England over the vehement objections of her father. "But...but...then...you'd have to write her and that would leave me writing....."

"It would, indeed," he said, lifting his head a bit.

"Wouldn't that be odd?"

"Why?"

"Well...."

"Don't women write male characters all the time?"

"I suppose so."

"You know so, and the book would just list us both as authors, which is rather appealing as no one would even know who wrote what."

He pushed himself up on one elbow. "You can keep McLaughlin if you like."

She touched his nose lightly. "I don't like. I fully intend to be sincerely Sinclair."

He laughed, batting at her hand. "Sincerely Sinclair. I like that. 'Hello. I'm Marshall Sinclair and this is my wife, Sincerely.'"

"You are bad," she announced firmly, pushing his shoulder so he rolled over again on his back. "Bad bad bad. And you definitely deserve this." She grabbed his ear lobe between her teeth just enough so he couldn't easily pull it free.

He wrapped his arms around her neck. "Who knew you were so violent, Sincerely?"

She let go. "Full disclosure before the wedding." She moved then and took his lower lip between her lips, pressing tight.

He tried to laugh but couldn't manage it with what she was doing. "Brumftt."

Releasing her hold, she asked, "What?"

"I said, 'brutal.' You are a brutal, medieval woman." Then he did laugh.

"And you want me, don't you?" She nipped at the end of his nose.

His hands slid up to either side of her head, his expression suddenly serious. "I want you more than I've ever wanted anything." He held her face there a moment, directly over his, almost touching, then pulled her down, her mouth atop his own.

Some time later they lay cuddled together beneath the sheet, her head on his shoulder. "I want so much...," she sighed.

"To...?"

"I want to understand everything about you, to know as much as I can, as I possibly can, of what it's like for you. I want to get into the very 'innerness' of it, darling. I want to...to...follow sight beyond all seeing to some meeting place with you."

He tipped his head to kiss her hair. "That's what's been bothering me, Eden, what I've been yearning to do with you, to know what it's like for you, and I've been working at it so hard, just trying and trying to know something I can't know until I'd begun to lose sight...." He stopped and smiled. "So to speak. To lose sight of the fact that happiness has very little to do with outward circumstances." His hand moved down her body, lingering over the curve of hip. "I know I've erred in my concepts of light, of color, but I also know that this is you, my Eden, and most important of all," he touched her forehead, then her heart, "I know that this is you and I have not erred in that."

Chapter 63

Susannah paused, the late morning sunlight warm on her uplifted face as she stood alone on the bottom step of the back entrance to her father's house on Nicholson Street. Stepping onto the walkway, she smiled as the sole of her shoe settled on the second brick which had a slight tip to its right. She was as familiar, as comfortable as it is possible for anyone to be. That brick had greeted her foot nearly every day of her life since she'd learned to walk. Once, her father had thought to have the gardener relay it, but she had convinced him to let it be. It was one of her countless touchstones that guided her way, that let her know precisely where she was.

The backyard gardens of Williamsburg were all laid out in a very orderly fashion, brick pathways marching straight through neatly-trimmed low hedges of boxwood. They were framed in pickets, with picket gates counterweighted by small cannonballs so they closed easily and firmly. Her father had taken great pains with the ordering of his own garden so that his only child might have the greatest possible freedom to walk there. There had been much concern offered, much pity even, when Susannah had been born completely without sight eighteen years ago. That her mother had died three days later from childbed fever only added to the general feeling that life would be a nearly impossible thing for the baby. Her father, though, had been determined from the start that she be given every opportunity for happiness and fulfillment.

Myra, his housekeeper, had a six-year old daughter, Layla, who became Susannah's constant companion, watching over her, going with her as she toddled around the neatly-kept house and ventured into the back garden. Harmer Wellington was a busy man, his law practice thriving, and these days, with such Colonial discontent beginning to fill the very air, spent less time with his daughter than he would have preferred. But Layla, now at twenty-four, was Susannah's best friend and he knew that, in her company, she would always be all right.

This morning, though, Layla was inside, helping Myra with preparations for the dinner Harmer was having that evening. Both Washington and Jefferson would be there, as would several of the more vocal members of the town. But Susannah knew the garden, knew it perfectly, and had no need of being guided along its paths. Harmer had seen that specific markers were made a part of it so that she would be at ease there. Fifteen steps straight down the central brick path brought her to the garden seat just off the right-hand side. She didn't even really need to count her steps any more. Her sense of the distance, of the time it took to get there, was all that was required and now she walked there, settling the skirt of her lawn morning dress around her, the fingers of both hands curved over the smooth, front edge of the large wooden seat as she leaned forward, taking in the glorious scents of late May.

Her father had taken her on trips to Boston, to Philadelphia, New York and even down to Charleston, but Williamsburg was always and ever home and she knew their carriage had arrived back in her beloved town as soon as it passed the first hedges of boxwood. There were those who did not like the smell of box, but she had never understood the why of that. Yes, it had a strong, distinctive scent, but it was so entirely connected to her love of place that, for her, it was simply wonderful. As the days grew warmer with the ascending sun, so did the scent of box ascend. It was what made Williamsburg Williamsburg.

The windows of the house were open and the sounds of clinking dishes as the large dining room table was being set, the swish of a broom, a rug being beaten in the side yard, floated to her ears, familiar and dear. Myra called out an order to someone and Layla was singing as she moved about the kitchen.

Standing again, Susannah adjusted the ribbon of her hat and turned down the walkway to the left. Just a few steps brought her to where the foxglove border was and she stopped, her hand reaching out expectantly to touch a tall, strong spire of bloom. Her fingers moved slowly, lovingly down its length, curving around and sometimes into the series of individual trumpets that formed the spire. The foxgloves grew up through clumps of daisies mixed with poppies and her hands continued down, brushing over the hard button centers of the daisies, fluttering lightly on the more delicate petals of a poppy.

Just past the foxgloves was a statue of an angel her father had shipped from England some years ago. She could never pass it without letting her hands flow down the length of one extended wing and up the other. The right wing had a small chip missing, but she liked even that as it was such a familiar tactile thing for her hand. Only Layla in all the world knew that Susannah talked to the angel, had even named it Marietta, had told it her secrets, had, as a small child, asked it to take messages to her mother.

Beyond the angel, a very low hedge of box marked the outer edge of the herb garden that backed up to the picket fence. Harmer had arranged seats for her all through the garden and she sat again in the midst of the herbs. This was possibly her favorite spot in the yard. She leaned a bit, her fingers touching the nearby lemon balm. Deliberately she squeezed a leaf then lifted her hand to her face, the scent of lemon strong on her skin. Rosemary, thyme, dill, fennel, basil, chamomile grew in neat partitions close by. Off to her right were the chives, whose soft spiky tops were among her favorites. Lavender grew next to the pickets and just down from them was the taller tansy. Getting up, she went straight to where she knew the tansy was, breaking off some to bring back to the house. Myra had been complaining of ants in the pantry this week and could probably use more tansy.

"I like it, Marshall," Eden said. "You're making the Williamsburg as you know it, and I can tell I'm going to be fonder of this Susannah than I was of the one you had before. What next?"

"Yes," Marshall smiled, "what next?"

"Me?"

"It would seem so."

"Oh, gosh," she sighed, looking at the keyboard. She'd just entered what he'd dictated about Susannah. Morgan. Morgan wouldn't be so into the scents. He'd be visual. If he saw Susannah, it would be how she looked, how the place where she was looked.

Morgan walked out the back entrance of the Raleigh Tavern, following the straight path through the series of small yards, and turned left down Nicholson Street. He was warm and removed his hat to wipe his coat sleeve across his brow. He'd come to prefer walking down Nicholson toward the Palace Green rather than the busier Duke of Gloucester, which paralleled it one block over. Nearly all the businesses of the small town were clustered on Duke of

Gloucester and he liked to think as he walked, undistracted by the bustle of the more occupied street. It was amazing how much more rural Nicholson seemed despite its proximity to the main thoroughfare. There were even some open fields and sections of woods still present. He was not yet used to the Virginia tidewater heat, having spent his life in Kent, and when he saw a small dirt path leading off into the shade of a weeping willow, turned aside.

The path led him by a neat white house with second-story dormers. Well, that could be said, now couldn't it, for most of the houses in Williamsburg. He was thinking deeply of what George Wythe had just told him in the Raleigh, and wasn't paying attention to what lay beyond the picket fence to his right. Pickets were everywhere in Williamsburg and one soon stopped noticing them, really, only focusing on their presence when presented with a gate one must open to proceed. He had intended to go straight down Nicholson, cross the Palace Green, and continue his conversation with Mr. Wythe in the back office of his large brick home that faced the far side of the Green.

Wythe was a wise, experienced man who had even taught Jefferson and was possibly the main luminary of the town. Morgan did not agree, not yet, with all the man's opinions of matters of current import, but he found himself wanting to hear more and more of what he had to say. Wythe had still been speaking with several men in the tavern when Morgan left, so he knew he had time to dawdle a bit here in the shade.

Shrugging out of his light brown jacket, he folded it over his left arm, feeling much more comfortable in just his white shirt. His chestnut brown hair was clubbed neatly back, tied with a black ribbon, and the Virginia sun had already tanned his face more deeply than it had ever been. Straight brows over deep green eyes....

Marshall laughed. "It seems to be a green-eyed world we live in."

"Shhh!" she said. "I'm...creating."

"Eventually," he said, kissing the top of her head, "I do hope so."

...that were looking inward as Mr. Wythe's last words replayed in his head, failed to see the small stone protruding through the ground. He tripped and only by flailing his arms managed to keep to his feet. His coat had fallen, though, onto the path and he stooped to pick it up, frowning as he shook off the clinging dust. Sighing, he stood there, undecided if he should continue on the shady path or venture back out into the sun of Nicholson.

"At least he didn't fall into a gully," Marshall commented wryly.

"Not every story begins with mud," she replied.

"Ours does."

"Well, this one's got dust. It hasn't rained for two days at least."

"And how do you know that."

"I just do. So there. Now shush!"

Something white moved, catching his eye, and he turned, trying to discern what it was.

"It will, of course, be Susannah?" Marshall interrupted.

"Shush!"

"So brutal," he sighed, "so very, very brutal."

"You got it, Mister, and you ain't seen violence yet like you will if you don't let me think."

"Would that be a promise?"

Someone was standing on the other side of the pickets, a young woman who seemed absorbed in tracing the outline of a fig leaf. He stepped back more deeply into the shadows cast by several young maples so he could study her without being observed. Possibly it was the way the dappled sunlight glinted on her almost golden hair....

"Golden is good."

She ignored him.

...that caught his eye the most. She had taken off her hat as he had, and it hung by its ribbon from her left forearm, some sort of ferny green plants placed into its crown. She was in profile to him, her lips curved in a smile. Even though he'd been in Williamsburg for three months now, he knew immediately he'd never seen her before. He would have remembered. Fascinated, he watched the movement of her fingers around the lobed edges of the leaf. She seemed to be exploring it as though it were somehow important. A slight breeze blew out her skirt, showing the sprigs of violets on the soft, white lawn of the dress. A wide lavender ribbon was tied as a sash about her waist. How was it he had not seen her before?

His eyes moved for a moment to the house fronting the garden. Harmer Wellington's. He'd never been inside, but he'd met Mr. Wellington several times in the Raleigh. He and Wythe, both attorneys, were good friends. Was she Wellington's daughter? If he were to step out on the path again, were to continue on his way, would she notice him and could he then speak to her? As he was pondering the propriety of this, a slender black woman came out the back door of the house, calling, "Susannah! You got to come back inside now, Susannah. Mama needs to know which dress you want her to iron up for dinner tonight."

Susannah. He rolled the syllables of her name silently over his tongue, tasting them sweetly like sugared cream.

"I like that. That's good." He tried it himself, saying 'Susannah' long and slow. It came out beautifully, somehow sensuous.

"Can't do that with 'Eden', I'm afraid," she sighed, dropping her hands from the keys to her lap.

He lifted her hair, kissing the back of her neck. "There are many, many things I can do with Eden," he whispered into her ear.

"Would that be a promise?" she echoed his earlier words.

"It would."

Susannah released the fig leaf with some reluctance. Her father's dinner parties were entirely political anymore and she didn't particularly enjoy being in attendance. At least she was expected to excuse herself as soon as the meal was over while the men went into the parlor to talk for hours over drinks. Bending, she snapped off a few stalks of lavender, tucking them in her sash.

"I'll be right there, Layla," she called back, though still she lingered where she was.

He watched her, aware from her actions, that she did not want to leave. He, too, wished most fervently that she would stay but, eventually, she turned away from the white fence and he stepped forward to see her for as long as he could, smiling to himself as she passed the angel statue, trailing her fingers along its wings. When the back door closed behind her, he came up to the fence, staring over at the angel. "You pale," he said, addressing it, "in comparison."

The angel, guardian of secrets, did not reveal that he was the only other person who had ever spoken directly to her.

Eden hit the 'save' button, then printed it out in Braille for him. "I'm hungry," she announced as the printer completed its afterwhir. "Is that Martha's barley soup I smell?"

"What about promises?"

"I do much better in collecting on promises when my tummy's not growling."

"I can live with that," he chuckled.

She stood, looking at him, and wondered when she'd ever get past that little jolt in her belly whenever something brought to mind the fact that he almost didn't live. It lurked there in the shadows of her happiness, ready to stab its barb all too often. She knew it was because of Miles dying in the snow, because she felt so 'left' by that, so 'left', too, by her parents. That Marshall might leave, however unwillingly on his part, was woven into the matrix of her being. She knew it was possible. She knew that all too well and a shudder went through her just as he laid his hand on her arm.

His brow knit. "Are you all right?"

She turned, sliding her arms around his waist, pressing into him. "I love you," she murmured into his chest.

He rested his cheek atop her hair. "You are so infinitely precious to me," he whispered back.

She squeezed her arms tighter. If only she never had to let go.

Chapter 64

"You know a lot about gardens," Eden commented after she'd eaten nearly half a bowl of barley-beef soup.

"My mother," he replied, wiping his lips with a paper napkin. "She planted flowers everywhere in our yard. It's one of my favorite ways to remember her, coming up behind her as she knelt at the edge of the lawn, holding the root ball of some perennial. Thanks to her I've learned to identify quite a number of plants by smell or touch."

"What's your favorite?"

He thought a moment. "Probably McKenna columbines. They have a fantastic shape with those spurs out their backsides, you know. I remember the first time I really explored one. It seemed like some alien flower left by moonpeople to me."

"You were into rocket ships?"

"Entirely. Then I discovered dinosaurs."

"So Williamsburg must have been a treat for you," Martha added from near the stove, taking the conversation back to gardens. She'd heard them talking about the town as they'd entered the kitchen. "I haven't been there for at least thirty years."

"They keep improving it, Martha," he explained, "making it more and more authentic all the time. They've even redone the gardens, getting them back more true to Colonial times."

"I like that even though the war is about to start, the gardens are still an important part of the story," Eden mused.

"You can't really write about Williamsburg and not have gardens be a part of it," Marshall smiled. "Even many of the most famous patriots were gardeners."

"Who?" Martha asked.

"Take Jefferson himself. He wrote, 'No occupation is so delightful to me as the culture of the earth, and no culture comparable to that of the garden. Though I am an old man, I am but a young gardener.'"

"Have you ever planted anything yourself?" Eden was suddenly curious.

"When I was about six, my mother had me dig a fairly large hole in the far left corner of the back yard. I still remember how great the shovel felt in my hands and the heaviness of lifting it full of dirt. There was some sort of pleasure in making that mound of dirt. I knelt beside it and ran my hands over it, quite proud of myself. Dad brought up a small willow tree with its roots in burlap but I got the thing into the hole all by myself. They said that was important. Then I shoveled the dirt back and watered it. It's still there. Gotten quite huge now. Willows grow fast, you know. They wanted me to plant something that would last, something that I could put my hands on and feel the changes in. I can't even get my arms around it now." He smiled to himself. "But when I'm home and go out there where it is, I always remember that day."

A slow smile spread across Morgan's face as he approached the front walkway of the Wellington home. It had been quite simple. He had been sitting across Wythe's writing table from him, listening to the man recount in some detail the Colonial problems with taxes when Wythe had suddenly mentioned that if he wanted to hear passion on the subject, he should listen to Patrick Henry.

"He will, in fact, be at Harmer Wellington's dinner table tonight," Wythe commented.

Morgan, carefully maintaining a composed face, had replied, "I should very much like to meet Mr. Henry."

Wythe had smiled. "I'm quite sure there would be no problem with Wellington should you accompany me. I'll send Joshua over with word to expect one more for dinner."

And so it had come about. Now here he was, changed into a light linen coat the better to withstand the evening's heat, Mechlin lace foaming nicely at his throat and wrists. Patrick Henry was not on his mind. Would she, Susannah, would she be in attendance?

"Ah, Mister Kent," a warm, friendly voice boomed not far behind him. George Wythe was stepping out of a small carriage.

"Good evening, Sir," Morgan greeted, tipping his head. "You are certain this is no imposition on the Wellingtons?"

"None at all. Joshua brought back word that Harmer would be delighted to entertain the young Englishman so recently arrived. Just expect that you will be fairly inundated with talk from a more Virginian perspective." He smiled again, patting Morgan's arm. "Come, let us go inside together."

"Sneaky fellow, your Morgan," Marshall commented as she read aloud what she was writing.

"Hey, a man's gotta do what a man's gotta do."

"And you know this how?"

"Because it's the same for women. That's how. And just what is your feminine side up to at the moment?"

"My feminine side?"

"Well, we've gender-switched, have we not? So what do you know about female primping?"

"I doubt Susannah is much of a primper," he smiled. "Let me see...."

Susannah sat quietly on the padded bench as Layla finished tying the slender blue ribbon about her neck."There, Susannah, you're all done now."

Susannah's hand went to her throat where a single pearl was centered on the ribbon. She sighed. "More politics. Always more politics." Not that they were not important. She realized fully that they were. It was just the very constantness of them these days. No one seemed to talk of anything else and especially not the men her father was friends with. Dinner would be like that, earnest men earnestly talking politics, and now the word 'war' was being more openly bandied about.

She was glad she had no brothers to send off to battle, glad her father was too old. He was too old, wasn't he? Surely he'd not have to fight? Why couldn't things just stay the way they were?

Slowly she descended the staircase, knowing her father would be waiting at the bottom step, ready, as always to take her arm and lead her into dinner. The buzz of male voices came to her from the dining room. She would be the only woman present. The familiar distance was covered with sure steps, her hand resting lightly on her father's arm as male forms moved quietly out of their way. Her chair was pulled out and she settled into it with a slight swish of silken skirting. As soon as she was seated, a dozen more chairs were scraped out and then back in, her father taking his seat at the opposite end from her.

"I can hear the sound of that," Eden said.

"Where is Morgan?" Marshall asked.

Both because he was new to Virginia and new to Wellington's table, Morgan had been honored by being seated on the side of the long table just to Susannah's right.

"You would have him there," Marshall smiled.
"I would, indeed," she grinned, beginning to type again.

Morgan had been standing, his back to the fireplace, when Susannah had entered the room. He smiled an entirely inward, satisfied smile, hoping she would look his way as she passed, but she kept her lashes somewhat lowered, her head slightly tipped. She was, though, even lovelier if possible than when he'd first seen her in the garden. Her gown was a pale blue watered silk with a fichu made from extremely thin and delicate ivory lace. That both Washington and Jefferson sat on either side of his host did not attract his eye so much as the way the pearl at her throat rose and fell with the gentle motion of her breathing.

Too late he became aware someone was addressing him and looked embarrassedly down the table, finding it was Washington himself. "And so, Mr. Kent, I am given to understand you come to us from...Kent? An interesting bit of naming, if I might say so." Washington's blue eyes were kind, interested, in his square, grave face.

"I have always found it so myself," Morgan nodded back. "It has been the family name for at least five hundred years, so it's origin is lost in some distant fog, though it is probably not amiss to presume it was taken up by early settlers in the region."

"And what brings you, Mr. Kent, to Virginia at such a time as this?" The speaker sat to Jefferson's left, his voice completely unlike Washington's cultured tones. The man was almost gaunt in his rather shabby clothes, his face long, eyes piercing. He sounded backwoodsy in his brogue and his question was presented more as an inquisition than an inquiry.

"I have come on behalf of certain shipping interests of my father's, Mr. Henry," he replied, knowing this had to be who the man was.

"And will you be staying long?" Henry pursued.

"I am finding the business to be more complicated than expected, Sir," Morgan explained mildly, "and as yet have no knowledge of the length of my stay."

"Then you do intend to return to England? Before war breaks out?"

"You think it will actually come to that, Mr. Henry? The thought of this undeveloped land rebelling against the massive power of England is hard for me to comprehend."

"I think you will find...."

"Now, now, Patrick," Wellington said pleasantly, "let us enjoy our meal before we get into talk of war. Such matters are best discussed with a fine brandy in one's hand, are they not?"

Morgan looked gratefully at his host, a sturdy sort of man, broadened somewhat with age, silver hair in a neat queue. "Susannah," Harmer said, "that is Mr. Kent to your right, darling. Mr. Kent, my daughter, Susannah. Forgive me for my late introductions."

Marshall chuckled softly, then took his turn.

She had been listening to him talk, judging from the sound of his voice that he must be several years younger than the rest of the men in the room. Turning her head toward him at her father's introduction, she still kept her eyes cast slightly downward, though a small smile curved her lips. "Mr. Kent," she acknowledged.

"This calls for a more rapid back and forth," Eden observed, her fingers beginning to fly over the keys.

She did not lift her eyes to him. Was she so shy she could not do such a thing? Somehow he had not thought that of her. "My pleasure, Miss Wellington," he replied softly. If he hoped for more, he did not then receive it for she turned back to her plate, waiting quietly as she was served, then reached for her glass. Her hand went past it and the gray-haired serving man leaned just enough forward to whisper in her ear, "Myra put it more to the right, Miss Susannah."

"Thank you, Micah," she also whispered, her hand following his directions, fingers curving around the stem of a tall goblet.

Morgan paused in his own reach for his glass, observing her. How strange.

She wasn't sure why, but not finding the glass easily had flustered her. After she took a sip, she dropped her hands to her lap, completely unable to recall the arrangement Myra had told her that the food would be on her plate. She wasn't hungry anyway. Would anyone really notice should she not eat anything?

The other guests at the table had been there often, were well aware she could not see and so used to it that it had long since ceased for them to be a matter unusual in any way. Most of them had known her since her girlhood. Perhaps it was the presence, so close to her side, of the visitor from England that had her off balance? With some innate sense, she knew he was studying her.

It looked to him as though she might be somewhat ill and his brow knit in concern. "Are you all right, Miss Wellington?" he asked, keeping his voice low.

She sighed. Might as well get on with it. Lifting her chin, she turned her face fully toward him, no longer keeping her eyes shaded by lashes. She waited a moment, long enough for him to see that she was not looking back at him, and said somewhat resolutely, "I am fine, Mr. Kent, thank you, but I would appreciate it if you would be so kind as to inform me if my spring peas are at 10 o'clock or at 3."

He was entirely taken aback. Her eyes were a lovely, bright sky blue. He had known somehow they would be blue, but he felt nearly slapped across the face by the fact that there was no answering light of sight in them. His mouth dropped slightly open, his breath not coming for a long minute as he gazed at her. She was presenting herself to him quite openly. He had no doubt of that. What he doubted was his own perception so he shook his head as though to clear some obstruction from his brain, but her eyes remained the same and then she asked him something about...peas? Ten or three? What did she mean?

"I...I'm sorry," he stuttered. "Peas?"

"Yes," she said, "on my plate. I've quite forgotten where they might be."

"Plate?" he repeated blankly.

"Like a clock face. If you do not mind."

Realization came to him. "Three, Susa...Miss Wellington. They are most definitely at three o'clock."

His almost use of her given name had not passed unnoticed. Again she did not know the why of it, but his slip settled her back into her composure. "I thank you, Mr. Kent, for your kindness." Picking up her fork, she confidently moved it toward the peas, smiling just a bit as she did so because she knew that if she ever encountered this Mr. Kent again, she would, inevitably, think of spring peas.

She was blind. He'd had no idea. She'd moved so assuredly down the garden path then she'd come into the dining room on her father's arm. There had been nothing, not a thing, to let him know. He looked at her again, more freely since he knew she would not really know how intently he did so.

As she wrote that, Eden clearly remembered doing exactly the same thing with Marshall the evening of the apple pie. She stopped writing, looking fondly across the room at him where he sat in the rocker, stroking Wadsworth's fur. *If you were a pussycat, Waddy,* she thought, *you'd be purring loudly right now.*

"You're not writing?" he asked.

"I'm busy loving you."

He smiled, holding out both arms in her direction, and she left the computer, crossing the room to sit in his lap. Putting his arms around her, he helped her settle into him, her head on his shoulder, her legs curling up. She closed her eyes and they just rocked together for a while. She hadn't meant to at all, but she felt so warm and safe, so entirely sheltered there with him, that the gentle motion of the chair lulled her into sleep.

He rested his cheek atop her head as he liked to do, listening to the even rhythm of her breaths. "How I love you, Mrs. Sinclair," he whispered into her hair, then added, "Sincerely."

Chapter 65

She did not turn her head toward him again, feeling somewhat embarrassed she'd been so brazen about her peas with a complete stranger. Her smoked pheasant had been cut before being placed on her plate as meat always was when guests were invited for dinner and her father wanted to spare her the difficulty of knife and fork. The knife lay, unused, just to the right of her plate and she took the end of it in her fingers, rolling it back and forth an inch in both directions, her lips pressed together. She had not been hungry and the one bite of peas was not sitting well. Mr. Kent's eyes were on her. She felt them. What must he be thinking of her request about her plate? She drew in a long breath, hoping the peas would settle in her stomach. Breathing. That's what she needed to do. She needed to breathe, but not here. She needed to be in the garden. Her other hand, in her lap, folded and refolded a section of the tablecloth. Had dinner really only just begun?

Morgan's eyes were, indeed, on her. She had seemed all right for a moment but now had that almost ill expression again. He wanted to say something but felt suddenly completely inept. "You...you are not hungry, Miss Wellington?"

"No," she murmured, thirsty but not wanting to reach for her glass with him engaged in such close observation of her movement.

He had no idea how the thought came to him, but he was suddenly entirely aware that she wanted to reach for her glass but would not do it. She was uncomfortable. She wished to leave but would not do that, either. Before he could think twice about it, his own hand reached out, quite deliberately fumbling his goblet and knocking it over. Every eye at the table turned in his direction. Just a drop or two of white wine had spattered to the puffed sleeve of her dress, but his own linen coat had a large wet area.

"Miss Wellington," he said contritely, "I am so sorry. I fear I've gotten wine on your gown."

Micah came quickly up behind her as she began to push her chair back. "Susannah?" It was her father's voice.

"If you do not mind, Father, I think it best if I leave the table." Micah guided her out of the room.

Harmer gazed at Morgan, who stopped mopping with his napkin long enough to smile rather shyly back at him. Wellington had been observing Morgan's response to Susannah for some time, as he always did when anyone was meeting his daughter for the first time. He had seen her missed reach for her goblet earlier, seen her lift her chin and speak with Mr. Kent. Kent did not impress him as a clumsy man. Indeed, one of the things Harmer had noticed about him as he'd entered his house was the quiet grace with which he moved. The corner of Harmer's mouth twitched in a slight smile. "Perhaps your coat will not be ruined if you applied some water right away?" he suggested.

The coat was new, expensive, and this was the first time Morgan had worn it. It was, he thought, a small price to pay, however, to relieve Susannah of her discomfit. "That may be true," he agreed, however.

Micah had come back to the dining room after seeing Susannah to her quarters. "Micah," Harmer said, "would you please show Mr. Kent to kitchen where his jacket might receive proper attention?"

Morgan stood, leaving his napkin on his chair. There was something odd about Wellington's response. It was almost if the man wanted him out of the dining room. He tipped his head toward the seated men and said, "Excuse me while I attend to this small matter."

Harmer kept his eyes on Morgan. He did not know this young Mr. Kent. George Wythe, however, had spoken glowingly about the man's integrity of character and George was a master at sizing up men. He watched Kent move toward the door, remarking to himself again at the carriage of his body and the graciousness with which he took his leave as Washington said something quietly to him as he passed.

"What did Washington say?" Marshall asked.

"I don't know. I wasn't close enough to hear."

Marshall smiled. "And where were you?"

"I was already in the kitchen, getting the water ready."

"Very kind of you."
"I'm a very kind sort of woman."
"What kind of kind woman?"
"I thought you knew."
"I think I do, but it's always nice to experience it again."
"You want to experience me?"
"Almost constantly."
"I know just how you feel," she giggled.
"And how do I feel?"
"Great. You feel absolutely great, especially certain parts of you."
He began chuckling, too. "I think I'd better marry you very soon."
"I think you had."
"How about New Year's Eve? Are you free?"
"I'm afraid I'm not free, Dr. Sinclair. I am hopelessly enslaved by my devotion to you."
"Washington, Jefferson, and Wythe all freed their slaves."
"But I do not wish to be free."
"And what is it you do wish?"
"I wish to be Mrs. Dr. Sinclair."
"I think that can be arranged."
"Speaking of which, is there anything left we do need to arrange?"
"You could arrange to come over to the bed."
"What about Morgan?"
"I don't think I want Morgan in the bed."
She laughed aloud. "But Susannah went upstairs. I thought you were going to send her out to the garden so she could breathe."
"The chapter is not yet over."
She got up from the computer chair, crossing to the bed where he sat on its edge, coming right up to stand between his legs. "Morgan and Susannah can take care of themselves. Why don't you take care of me and I take care of you?"
He lay backwards on the bed, his feet still on the floor.

Morgan followed Micah out the rear door and down a brick path to the right. "Kitchen, Mr. Kent," Micah announced, holding the door wide.
Morgan stepped inside. It was quite hot in the small outbuilding and he was grateful to shrug off his jacket. Micah went up to Myra, who was drizzling honey over the evening's dessert. After he'd explained about the wine, Myra looked from Micah to the young man standing in the doorway. Mr. Wellington had never done anything like this before with a guest. She knew him well enough after all these years, though, to know that he also never did anything without some purpose.
"Susannah's gown, too?" she asked, actually of Micah.
But Morgan answered. "Just a drop or two. I'm sure the dress will be fine."

Myra narrowed her eyes. This must be the extra guest Joshua had said would be coming for dinner. She'd never seen the man before. He did cut a fine figure, though, even with his jacket wet and hanging from his hand like that.

Some time had passed and Eden was back at the keyboard. Marshall asked, "What does Morgan look like to you?"

"He looks like you, darling, exactly like you at twenty-four except that he's clean-shaven and his hair is longer."

"But you wrote that he cuts a fine figure."

"Do you not know what a fine figure you cut?"

"I have never actually thought about what sort of figure I cut."

"Well, you can believe me. It's fine indeed, especially with suede elbow patches. Or...."

"Or?"

"Nothing."

"Nothing?"

"Yeah, nothing is good. Very fine."

Myra took the jacket, examining the wine stain. "Linen don't clean all that well," she said, "but I'll try. You give me a little time here, all right?"

"I'd appreciate anything you can do," he smiled. "Might I wait out in the garden? I'm afraid I'm finding Virginia a bit warmer than I'm accustomed to."

"Is that a set-up?" Marshall asked, trying not to grin.

"If you want it to be."

Layla helped Susannah out of the tightly-laced blue gown. "Just something cool," Susannah said as Layla scanned through the selection of dresses. "I'm not going back into dinner."

When she was changed and Layla had gone downstairs to help bring in the desserts, Susannah sat by the open window of her bedroom, fanning herself. She let the thin ribbon at her waist slide again and again through her fingers. She knew her father's friends would have already forgotten her hasty departure, but what must Mr. Kent think? Not that it mattered. He was merely visiting Williamsburg and would be going back to England soon. She leaned her elbows on the windowsill. He did have a nice voice, though, deep, somehow extraordinary to listen to. Why had he almost used her given name?

A moth, in the gathering dusk, brushed past her cheek. The air had cooled in the last few minutes. Perhaps she would walk in the garden a bit while the men finished their dinner. The sound of their voices, rising up the staircase, would keep her from sleeping anyway. The garden would be quiet and she could sit on a bench and just breathe. Yes, she would do that.

Slipping down the back stairs, she paused, listening for a moment to Patrick Henry. She was not fond of the brusque manner in which he spoke. Closing the back door behind her, she walked silently out into the garden.

"Ooo," Eden cooed happily, "you sent her out."

"You knew I would."

"One had hopes."

Morgan had gone down the path leading by the angel statue, drawn there because it obviously meant something to Susannah. He paused directly in front of it, studying it. Her wings were spread wide and because he was the son of a shipping family, he considered what it must have taken to pack it for safe shipping. Reaching out, he touched one of the wings, noticing it had a chip missing.

"So," he said, "you are an angel with a slightly broken wing."

Susannah stopped at the intersection of the main path with the one that led past the foxgloves. Distinctly she heard a voice, a male voice. Someone was in the garden. She listened. It was the voice of Mr. Kent. Whatever was he doing out in the garden when dinner was not yet over? Who could he possibly be conversing with? She listened more, but only heard the one speaker. Then it dawned on her he was addressing her angel. Her lips parted in surprise and she took several soft steps down the side path, knowing from the feel of the air on her face that night had fallen, hoping he would not notice her presence. She was not, by nature, an eavesdropper, but no one had ever talked to her angel before except her and she found she needed desperately to know why this stranger to town would do such a thing. What could he possibly find to say?

"Did it break in shipping," Morgan continued, "or did you collide with a star on your way to Earth?" He smiled to himself. "I think I like the star better. Does your Susannah know you are chipped? Yes, she would. I expect she knows you completely."

The statue was about three and a half feet tall and stood atop a low block of square marble. Leaning a bit, he looked at her up-tipped face. "Your lips are carved well," he said, "though not so perfectly as hers." He traced a fingertip along the angel's lower lip. "I wished, you know, at dinner that I might be able to do that. You are lucky that you get to be in her company so freely, so openly, while I, well, it would be entirely unseemly for me to be alone with her." He paused, then sighed, "Yet."

Susannah had rested her palm on the twisty trunk of a small crape myrtle. Unconsciously, her fingers tightened as she listened.

Morgan could now only see the dimmest outline of the angel. "I don't know why I'm telling you all this. Perhaps it's because there isn't a soul on this side of the Atlantic that I would feel free to tell, and something about you says to me that you know how to keep a secret so I'm counting on you to keep mine. This is all very strange for me. Not just that I find myself in a garden at night speaking to a statue, pardon me, an angel, but that some part of me has, in a single surprising day, been put rather completely in the hands of another. I think it was the sunlight on her hair earlier today that began to crack some defense in me. She is, you know, far more angelic than you and as nice, I am sure, as you are, never once have your fingers traced the outline of a fig leaf and ended their movement in the inner boundaries of my soul."

Susannah had to put a hand over her mouth for fear her intake of breath would give away her presence. Fig leaf? Mr. Kent had seen her today with the leaf? He must have been on the path while she was in the herb garden. She'd had no idea anyone was that near.

"Does that happen a lot?" Eden asked.

"Probably a great deal more than I can ever know. Unless someone chooses to speak, to make some sound, to wear some distinct scent, it is most often entirely up to them whether I know they are there or not. And I have been told that when Wadsworth and I are together, with him in harness doing his job, then every eye turns and follows us as we pass."

She knew that was true. She'd seen that for herself in Bellefonte and in restaurants. "I don't think I'd like that."

"There is nothing I can do about it, Eden. It is the way of things."

He paused a moment, then asked, "Do you want Morgan to love her so quickly?"

"I do," she replied firmly. "The only reason I did not love you in the first minutes after I came upon you was that you were too coated with mud for me to discern who you were."

"And when did you do that?"

"In my lap, when the raindrops began to wash the dried layers away. It was the first spattering of rain on your face that began to open the way to the boundaries of my soul." Saying those words made her think of what she might say to him day after tomorrow when she made her vows to him. She was not certain she wanted to prepare something ahead of time. It would be best to stand there, her hands in his, and say what came to her heart in that moment. It would, she realized completely, have to be that way.

Chapter 66

She should leave, really she should. This was not right, this listening to someone else's private conversation, but it was about her, wasn't it, and he was talking to her angel. She'd found herself liking his voice there in the dining room, though he'd actually not said all that much. Now, here in the dark garden, he spoke at some length, spoke things she'd never heard anyone say before, especially not about her. People always tended to keep her packed in cotton wool, always watched both their manners and their speech in her presence, but this Mr. Kent ...what was his given name? She couldn't remember. This Mr. Kent was speaking so entirely openly, so vulnerably. How could she turn away from his words?

She took another step closer, a small twig from the crape myrtle snapping under her slipper. She stopped, transfixed, mortified.

Morgan, too, stopped what he was saying. "Is my coat ready?" he asked, presuming the older man had tracked him down.

There was no reply. "Is someone there?" he called, slightly louder.

Susannah pressed her lips together. How often she had asked those same three words. In the night, Mr. Kent was not far removed from the state in which she lived. She tried backing up a step or two, caught her heel, and a short, surprised, "Oh!" escaped her.

Before she could step again, he was there. She heard his long strides quickly covering the short distance on the brick walkway and then his presence arrived, hardly two feet in front of her.

"Susa...Miss Wellington!" he breathed, utterly shocked. "I...I...."

"I'm sorry, Mr. Kent. I did not know you were there when I came into the garden for a breath of air. I...I...did not mean to...to intrude on your privacy. I...."

"No," he hastened to say. "This is your garden. It is I who am the intruder. My coat...in the kitchen...my coat is being rinsed and I...I...came down the path because it was cooler. I did not think...I mean...I did not know...."

He was flustered, completely and utterly flustered, and the fact of it set her at ease. "The wine? My gown was barely dampened at all. Your coat...?"

"I fear my coat received the main portion of the goblet's contents."

"Thank you," she barely whispered.

"For spilling my wine?"

"Yes," she replied, her head tipped down and slightly turned away, "for spilling your wine."

So, she knew. How could she possibly know? The moon suddenly sailed from behind a bank of clouds. She was so close. He wished she would lift her head, lift it so he might see silvered light pooling on her brow, her cheeks.

She had no way of knowing the change of lighting there in the night, but without knowing, she slowly raised her chin, her face pulled upwards rather magnetically by the nearness of his presence. She heard a small gasp of sharply inhaled breath from him, but had no idea why.

"Sus...," he began, but said no more. He would betray himself, he knew, if he spoke. Her name was there in his mouth, hovering closely over his tongue, had been there since he'd said it earlier this day. It wanted to be pronounced, wanted to find its life in the space of air between their two faces, but the silence lay between them instead of her unspoken name. A breeze, making its way around the corner of the house, blew loose a long strand of her hair, then as quickly as it had come, was gone. The waving lock settled in a curve down her neck, over her collarbone. His eyes followed it as though it were some pathway leading.... No. He must stop himself, must not think such things in her presence while she stood there before him, radiating purity. He did not think it was her blindness alone that made this so. No, there was something innate in her that would have been this way no matter her circumstance. The fact of blindness only served, prism-like, to focus it, to make the colors of it clearly evident. He wondered then how it had come about, her blindness, and how long ago?

"I should go," she said.

"Yes." But neither moved.

The last thing he wanted was that she should go. It was, he knew, inappropriate beyond all words for him to be with her like this, not only alone, but alone at night, and yet the thought of her going was nearly unbearable. What could he do, what say, to prolong this moment however briefly?

"I have met your angel," he ventured.

How well she was aware of this, but she gave no indication that she was. "Marietta."

"Marietta?"

"Her name." She smiled. "I thought she must have a name."

"Marietta," he repeated softly.

In all her life she'd never heard the word spoken so. His voice touched some response in her and she trembled slightly. He had gifted her and was completely unaware.

"I should go," she said again, knowing the truth of it, but the words coming with slow reluctance.

"Yes," he, too, said again as in the very moment his mind searched for some small thing to prevent it. "You...you...grow figs here?" He bit his lip. Could he have said anything more inane? Good Lord, was he twelve again?

"Yes, we do," she replied, seeming not to notice his wild grasping for conversation. "Nearly every home in Williamsburg has at least one fig tree."

"You...you were born here?"

"I was. I have lived here all my life." She paused. "Is this your first visit to America, Mr. Kent?"

He wanted to say, My name is Morgan, Susannah. *He wanted to say,* This required formality is killing me, Susannah. *He said, "Yes, my first."*

"At dinner I heard you say you did not know how long your visit might last."

He wanted to say, I have no idea how I could ever leave. Not now. *"It will last as long as I need to be here."*

Why was it she hoped he needed to be here a long, long time?

Mike, looking in the mirror, straightened his rust-colored tie. One corner of his mouth quirked up in an extremely wry grin. "We who are about to die, salute you," he intoned. The week since Christmas had passed slowly, dripping like cold molasses down the calendar of his days. He'd gone about his work, had gotten a drunk sixteen-year old out of the mangled wreckage of a car, had stopped the bleeding when Simon Mackerel sliced a vein in his forearm, had transported a stroke victim to the hospital and released a toddler who'd gotten his head stuck in the rails of his grandfather's old bedstead. Such was the rhythm of his life. He lived it basically for the benefit of others. He frowned at his reflection, awash in that moment in the awareness he had no personal life, nothing he could call his own.

The phone rang and he sat on the small bed as he picked up the receiver. Ryan's voice was there, asking if he wanted him to pick him up for the wedding. "Nah," Mike said, "I'll get there under my own steam, I think. Thanks, though." He wanted to have his own vehicle there. That way he could leave when he wanted. Actually, he didn't want to go at all but, as usual, he wasn't doing what he wanted.

He turned his head, eyeing the half-empty whiskey bottle on the bedside table. He could really use another stiff one. Help him get through this blasted thing he had to get through. His large hand reached out, curling around the bottle's neck, beginning to lift it off the table.

"No!" he snapped, talking to himself. "Dammit, man, you've got to have more courage than what's floating around in there." He set the bottle back down, eyeing it drearily. It had been full last evening. It was how he'd gotten through the hours. "Stupid bastard," he growled, standing abruptly and grabbing his overcoat off a chair. "Stupid, stupid bastard!"

"It's Mike!" Luke called out, opening the door of the inn a few minutes later. "Hi, Mike."

"Hi, yourself," Mike said, a big smile plastered on his face as he shrugged out of his coat, hanging it on the rack near the door. "Good to see you, Squirt. How's it going?"

"Come see the decorations, Mike," Luke urged. "Come and see!"

"Right behind you. Like your suit, by the way."

"You do? It's really ok?"

"It's really ok," Mike pronounced gravely. Luke was wearing the old suit Ryan had as a boy. Martha found it in the attic, adjusted it here and there, and sent it off to the cleaners.

"It's chocolate and cream," Luke said, proudly indicating the tweed of his jacket.

His mother, passing by on her way to the kitchen, chimed in, "And you look good enough to eat!"

Luke laughed. He was happy today. He hadn't seen all that much of Marshall all week but today would be different. Today he was Marshall's best man. Today he got to have the wedding rings in his pocket. Marshall had said he was important enough to do that. He positively glowed.

While everyone was buzzing about downstairs, completing final preparations, Marshall and Eden were still upstairs in their room. "It's ok we're not going on a honeymoon right away?" he asked.

"I don't know what could be more honeymoon than what we've been living right here at the inn, darling," she replied. "Besides, we're going to the Lake District in April. That's sort of our official honeymoon, isn't it?"

He didn't answer. "Come closer," he said.

She was in her wedding gown, had recently come out of the bathroom after putting on her make-up, and he had not yet gotten to gaze at her. Eden knew what he wanted. It was for this moment she had picked out this particular dress with all its interesting tactile features. "I don't know...." she whispered, her voice trailing off.

"What is it, darling?"

"I don't know if I'll make it to the wedding if you, um, gaze really well at me right now." She was serious. The lightest touch from him was always her complete undoing.

He smiled. "If you don't make it, I won't be making it, either."

"That's what I'm afraid of," she gulped.

"I'll only gaze just a little, all right? But I truly do need to know before you come into the parlor."

"I know," she said softly, coming close to where he sat on the window seat in his rust-colored tweed with its suede elbow patches and one shoulder patch. "You look splendid, you know." She touched his cheek lightly.

"Just a little," he repeated. "But not after. After is different."

"Yes," she murmured. "After is different."

He reached out, placing a palm on either of her hips. She gasped sharply.

His head cocked, face intent, he slid them down the length of her legs, exploring briefly how the silk flared below her knees. His hands moved up to her waist, lightly touching the fit of the gown over her breasts, running along the deeply-draping neckline. She was trembling and couldn't stop. His hands paused and she thought she might die on the spot. "Just a little," she reminded, seriously considering abandoning the ceremony altogether.

He stood, his hands moving on, down her arms, his fingers tracing the edges of the long slits in the sleeves, then reaching in, finding her arms, moving back up to the covered buttons on her shoulders. He cupped her chin and ever so gently kissed her softly on her mouth. "Just a little," he whispered.

"I can't walk," she said. "I think I'm going to fall over."

He took her hand. "We'll go together."

"You promise?"

"Always," he breathed, moving toward the door.

Chapter 67

"You're not coming down the stairs?" Connie asked.

"I just came down the stairs," Eden replied.

"But doesn't the bride come down the stairs, when there are stairs, so she can be seen?"

"I've already been seen," Eden smiled, looking up at Marshall at her side, then back at her cousin.

"Not thoroughly," Marshall whispered in her ear and she giggled.

Martha bustled up, glowing more than the Christmas tree which still stood in a corner of the parlor. "Reverend Powers is here," she announced. "Come let me introduce you."

They followed her into the living room where the pastor was talking with Harold.

"Peter," Martha began, "this is our bride and groom, Eden McLaughlin and Dr. Marshall Sinclair."

The pastor turned, his eyes running appraisingly over the couple as he extended his hand. "Eden, Marshall, this is Reverend Peter Powers," Martha continued the introduction.

Eden saw a tall man, at least 6'5", in his early forties, with short, neatly-waved brown hair streaked with just a bit of gray. Peter shook Eden's hand and then smoothly took Marshall's. He noticed a slight smile twitching the corners of Eden's mouth. "It's the name, isn't it?"

She nodded without replying and he added, "Sounds like something out of a book or something, doesn't it?" Then he smiled broadly. "And I've even got brothers named Paul and John."

"Are all of you ministers?" Eden asked.

"John is, but Paul's a stand-up comic." He shrugged. "Sort of balances the two of us out somehow."

Marshall found himself liking the friendly, open tone of the man. "We truly appreciate your coming over like this on New Year's Eve, Reverend Powers."

"Peter," the minister corrected pleasantly, "and I love weddings. It's the happiest thing I do."

Martha left the three of them together to discuss some details about the ceremony, going back into her kitchen to check on the platters of hors d'oeuvres she and Elizabeth had made. Smiling to herself, she straightened the parsley stem of a calla lily. Those she made by using a biscuit cutter to form circles from the center of white bread slices. She rolled them flat, spread whipped white cream cheese on them, lay a piece of parsley stem out one side and a thin, pointed strip of carrot out the other, then pinched it shut at the parsley end. They made perfect, edible calla blossoms and really suited a wedding table.

The cake Joan had made stood grandly on the counter, its chocolate layers and raspberry jam hidden beneath white icing. She didn't know why, but Eden had requested that she make a single, large maple leaf as the topper. Since it was also New Year's Eve, and Eden had left her free to do whatever else she wanted, Joan had made streamers out of peach-colored icing, which trailed their way artfully down the three graduated layers of the cake. It was very pretty, even though to its maker it didn't look all that much like a wedding cake.

Elizabeth was pinning a gardenia on Luke's lapel. "Don't squirm!" she scolded gently. "I don't want to stab you."

"Mike's here," Luke replied, grinning up at the big man standing just behind him, his own gardenia already in place. "He'd save me."

Elizabeth's eyes flickered over to Mike's. She'd known him her entire life and though he'd never spoken of Eden to her, she knew.

Mike saw the awareness in her eyes and sighed imperceptibly. "It's all right," he whispered.

"Is it?" She finished pinning Luke's flower and straightened.

He shrugged just a bit. "As right as it can be anyway. Wasn't meant to be. Simple as that."

"But...walking her in...."

"I know. Can't let her down."

"Have you ever let anybody down, Mike?"

"You could ask my ex-wife that, Liz. I'm sure she'd have an answer for you."

The doorbell rang and Martha hurried past to answer it. Dr. Hersholtz stood there, smiling in the twinkling lights strung around the porch. "I brought Maria with me. Seemed easier to come in one car since we both just got off duty at the hospital," he explained.

Marshall turned at the sound of Hersholtz' voice. "I'm so glad you could come, Doctor," he greeted warmly. "I know New Year's Eve is probably a busy night at the hospital."

"Just as glad not to be on duty, let me tell you," Hersholtz replied earnestly. But he patted his coat. "Got my phone, though. Just hope I don't get called back."

"Maria?"

"Here, Marshall," the dark-haired nurse answered from the doctor's right side.

Marshall held out both hands, saying something to her in Greek, to which she replied in kind then she held out a small package, placing it in one of his hands. "And, yes, I am a Greek bearing gifts," she laughed softly. "So you'd best beware of me tonight."

Mike had come out to the entrance hall in time for this last interchange. He recognized Maria from the hospital, though she looked entirely different with her long hair loose and not dressed in her nurse's pants and loose-fitting top. "Hello, Maria," he greeted. "Mike. From the EMT guys."

"Yes," she smiled. "I've seen you often around the hospital. It's nice to finally meet you in a non-medical situation."

Hersholtz cocked one eyebrow dramatically and squeezed Marshall's forearm. "And you keep it that way, you hear me!"

Marshall laughed. "I'll most certainly try."

"Well, make it a resolution for the new year, young man. I'm tired of giving you the MFP award, you know."

"MFP?"

"Most Frequent Patient."

Marshall laughed again but Eden wasn't at all sure just how funny she found that.

Everyone greeted everyone, Marshall attempting to keep his hand on Eden's arm in the now-crowded room. Wadsworth sat on the wide bottom step of the staircase, keeping an eye on Marshall. After his paws had gotten stepped on twice, he'd reluctantly moved at Marshall's urging off to one side. Elizabeth had tried to tuck a gardenia under his collar, but he was having none of it and shook it immediately out.

There was to be nothing formal about this wedding. Eden and Marshall had made that plain from the beginning. There would be music, though not at all what one thought of as wedding music, but it was to be a gathering come together to share in the unrehearsed words that these two people wished to say to one another. Not even Connie or Edith knew what piece Eden had chosen as her entrance music. The walk was short with little need for something like Pachelbel's Canon in D that was so popular for that purpose nowadays. Martha, who would play it, found the selection interesting, perfect for Eden, and much to Eden's delight, Martha had even agreed to sing it, understanding that the words were as important, or more so, than the music itself.

While everyone else took their places in the parlor, Eden and Mike went together to the living room on the far side of the entrance hall. He kept having to remind himself to breathe. The ivory silk flowed with her as she moved, the most feminine motion he'd ever seen. Her auburn hair, somehow made more glorious in contrast with the ivory, was piled atop her head in loose curls while lots of tendrils waved down her neck. Among the curls gardenias were pinned as Marshall had requested and her bouquet, too, was mostly gardenias with some trailing ivy and a bit of stephanotis. The perfume from the flowers was strong yet elegant. Yes, that was how she looked to him. Elegant. And very, very desirable.

She turned, facing him. "Thank you, Mike," she said softly.

"For walking you in?"

"For everything. You've been the best friend I could possibly have."

Damn! There she went, using the blasted f-word. His nostrils flared and he had to literally bite his tongue to keep from replying that being her friend had nearly crushed his heart.

"And for Marshall, too," she continued. "You mean the world to both of us."

The muscle under his left eye twitched. Couldn't trust his own dammed body any more.

Wadsworth sat just to the left and slightly rear of where Marshall stood, his back to the fireplace. He kept his nose lightly pressed against the outside of Marshall's leg. Marshall was very aware of its presence there. It was only right. Wadsworth was serving in the capacity of Best Dog. Just beyond him stood young Luke, his right hand curled tightly over the two rings in his pocket. Marshall had given them to him moments before. Luke didn't know when in his whole six years of life he'd ever been trusted with something that important. He was sweating a bit from the gravity of his charge and from being so close to the fireplace. His thick lenses were fogging and as he looked up at Marshall, it seemed he saw him through a gathering mist. He knew he needed to wipe his glasses, but that would require his letting go of the rings and there was no way he would do that.

Peter Powers stood, composed and quiet, just to Marshall's right, curious himself as to how this particular ceremony would unfold. He really had little to do tonight other than to make some short opening remarks, say a prayer, and pronounce them husband and wife. He loved that last part. There was this moment out of all time where a man and a woman were not married, then he said the words and everything changed for them. One second they were not and the next they were. As many weddings as he'd performed, he always treasured that moment, always regarded it with the awe which it deserved. He smiled to himself and glanced over where Martha was seated at the piano. There was something entirely intimate about the way these people were gathered in this room. There was a warmth present, not just from the fireplace or the lights of the tree and the many candles placed about, but more from the good will of those present, from the fact that the old year was ending here with this ceremony, with this couple who had already been through so much, had come out the other side of it all and were going together into a new season.

Connie was not going to be walking in as matron of honor, but had already taken her place. Ryan, seated on the arm of the couch, studied the play of firelight on her peach-colored gown. She smiled at him, aware of his gaze. Edith, too, was aware.

At the first note of the music, Mike gathered everything he had within him, leaned down and kissed Eden's forehead. "You have my blessing," he said, his voice barely audible. And she did. He wanted the best for her. He had from the beginning. He just had to come to terms that it was not him. So he held his left arm out and she slid hers through it.

"Mike," she whispered, "you are the best."

Her gaze then turned raptly toward the entrance hall they would cross and then onward into the parlor. He followed her line of vision and made a huge, unseen effort, untying the ropes he'd stretched weeks ago from his heart towards hers. She needed to be free of them even though she didn't know they were there. Perhaps someday he would be someone else's best, but he was not hers.

He smiled down at her. "Ready?" he asked.

Chapter 68

The corners of Eden's lips twitched slightly in a little grin as she headed toward the living room. She doubted any other bride had ever come in on just this music and rather expected a bit of a reaction to it, but the music was not for anyone in the room but her and Marshall. The lyrics would be the beginning of what she wanted to say to the man who stood there waiting for her by the fireplace, and as soon as she saw him she forgot there were any others present.

Martha played a short introduction and then her clear soprano filled the room. "Ah, sweet mystery of life at last I've found thee." Connie's eyes opened wide and she stared at her cousin. Eden, though, was blissfully unaware of all the eyes upon her. The only eyes that mattered were the ones beholding her from deep in the soul of the man in rust-colored tweed. It was toward that she walked as Martha sang the words to the Victor Herbert song. "Ah, I know at last the secret of it all. All the longing, seeking, striving, waiting, yearning... the burning hopes, the joy and idle tears that fall."

Marshall knew the song. It had been one of his mother's favorites. Eden had no way of knowing that, though, had no way of knowing how often he'd stood as a boy beside the piano bench as his mother sang it to his father, how his father always took his mother's face in his hands when the last note faded away and kissed her. He'd never thought of it as a bridal entrance song, but knowing she was on her way, was coming toward him as the familiar words winged around him with all their memories of love, brought sudden tears that blinking could not quite stem. Then she was there. Mike had taken her right hand and placed it in Marshall's left, stepping back and away, and Marshall was enveloped in the beauty of love, old and dear, flowing on and into love that was new and nothing less than everything. His fingers laced through hers, lifting her hand to his lips as Martha sang, "And 'tis love and love alone the world is seeking. And 'tis love and love alone that can repay. 'Tis the answer, 'tis the end and all of living. For it is love alone that rules for aye."

Peter was wise enough to let the silence continue after the last note had faded. The moment was full without words from him. Marshall still held Eden's hand to his lips. It seemed everyone in the room was holding their breath. Then he whispered, "'Tis the end and all of living," and still clasping it, lowered it to his side, turning his face toward Peter.

Mike had watched Marshall's face when the music started, had seen the naked emotion spread over it then center into what he felt for Eden. Despite his own dreams, the deep stirrings in his own heart towards her, something in Mike felt suddenly humbled as he watched Marshall. Then Mike's eyes turned down towards Eden and the response that was there in her uplifted face, the utter completeness of her love and commitment, made him feel like an interloper onto a brightly-lit stage where he had not been cast in a role. He realized his attempt at rope cutting a moment before, though from a genuine heart, had been feeble at best. *No*, he said firmly to himself, *no. This is not yours. This never was.* And he knew it. No more self-deception. He knew it entirely and the knowing lifted something from him so that he was suddenly able to inhale a breath more deeply than he had for some time. He noticed Ryan was studying him and gave the barest of thumbs-up, to which Ryan lowered his lashes in a quiet acknowledgement between life-long friends.

Ryan had been worried all day about Mike, what with Eden so completely unaware of what she'd asked him to do for her. He had no doubts that Mike would make it through the ceremony. He'd grown up knowing that core of strength in Mike that stood despite the storms. Yes, Mike would make it through the ceremony, smiling and gracious. It was after that worried Ryan. After, when Mike would be alone again in his cabin. He saw Mike's gesture with his thumb, knew Mike meant it in a way to encourage Ryan not to worry. He'd seen the long breath, the shift in the way Mike was holding his shoulders, but had no idea what his friend was thinking in that moment, but he closed his lids briefly to let him know he'd seen. He'd try to stick as close to Mike as he could after the ceremony, but there would come that time when Mike went home. It was inevitable. His jaw tightened. What then?

Edith, her eyes, too, going from Marshall's to Eden's, dabbed at her face with a tissue she'd been smart and tucked up her sleeve. To love...again...to love...even more. *Yes, my darling, yes.*

Peter Powers gazed from face to face around the room. For the first time in his career in the ministry he was not so sure another word needed to be spoken, not in the whole ceremony. Everything needful was already lying quite bare, quite fully expressed. For a moment he was actually tempted to say *I now pronounce you husband and wife* and just be done with it. The thought of Jesus coming up to John the Baptist in the Jordan came to his mind. Jesus did not need to be baptized, not really. He had no sin to wash away and yet he came, saying to John's protests, "Suffer it to be so now, for thus it becometh us to fulfill all righteousness." And, in that spirit, Peter smiled a small, close-lipped smile then said, "There is already so much welcome in this room that it would be redundant of me to bid you welcome. Indeed, I find a certain redundancy in that I should speak at all, and, yet, welcome felt is only magnified by welcome spoken and so I do say *welcome.* I say it now in the original sense of the word...well come... for we have, each one of us by our own paths, well come to this moment where we are privileged to witness, to be a part of the union of this man and this woman. Marshall, Eden, though this is not a church, the ground where you stand is holy ground because God is here and there is no ground where He is not. You bring to this moment all you have been, all you are, all you hope to be, and you give it, give it freely one to the other. What needs to be said in this place needs to be said, not by me, but by you to the other. And so it is in the beauty of the simplicity of that that I ask you now to face one another, holding both hands, as Marshall makes pledge and promise to the woman who is becoming his wife."

Eden turned enough to hand her bouquet to Connie, then back to face Marshall, slipping both her slender hands into his much larger ones. His fingers were warm, holding hers firmly yet softly, his face was tipped down toward hers just as though he were looking into her soul, and she knew he was. Firelight and candlelight danced on his features, highlighting brow and curve of cheek, golden, amber, like his suede. His face was the most wonderful thing she'd ever seen in her life, his green eyes open, trusting her with their lack of vision. No, there was nothing about this man that lacked vision. Not one thing.

He was rubbing the pads of both thumbs across the backs of her hands, suddenly finding it hard to speak. He swallowed to ease the thickness in his throat and slid his left hand up past her wrist a bit, just enough to run his fingertips over the wide, tight cuff, to find the beginning of the long slit, enough to get in touch again with the reality of her dress. Then he returned his hand to hers.

"Eden," he said, his deep voice warmed by firelight and emotion into a rich honey-flow of sound, "Eden." He said it twice, then paused. "In times past, the use of a given name was not taken lightly but was something both earned by acquaintance and given as favor. I say your name., Eden, and I am humbled by the fact of my right to have it on my tongue." He smiled. "It is, I know, an old-fashioned concept and yet it has great value to me, for in this world where things so often are taken before they are given, part of my pledge to you as my wife is that I will ever honor you, will ever treasure all things, no matter how small, that you bring to me, will do my best always to recognize the value of the gift of you. It is nothing less than grace you offer me, the giving of favor with no qualifications to be met, no boundaries to speak of edges or ends. And it is how I promise to love you, with no edges and no endings. What I feel for you comes from a source that fills as I pour it out. It is, somehow, not only in me, this well that has no bottom, but I find myself immersed in it from without. I swim in it, breathe in it, my heart beats in it, and all I want is to take you into it with me, around me, in me."

He paused again, rubbing his thumbs more. "I had hoped, for years I had hoped, that somewhere my beautiful half existed, that half of me that was parted from me upon my coming into this world." He lifted his chin a moment toward the ceiling, then turned his face back down to her. "I find a destiny, a strange, unbelievable destiny in how your path finally crossed mine. We all dream, each of us, how love will come. Never once did I ever imagine it would come to me in a flow of icy mud when my last breath was only one gasp away." He shook his head a bit and smiled again. "But you got me up and out of so much more than mud. You got me up and out of a way of thinking, of living, that had grown all too settled into solitude. I thought I had passed some point where I would come to know the warmth of love freely given, but you rose upon my life like that sun I've never seen, scattering away all my lonely shades, and in your presence I know what sunlight is. There are a thousand thousand words I could say to you, I whose tools of trade are words, but three small ones say everything. I love you. I simply, completely love you and I give you my vow today that I will never stop, that I will be faithful to you, loving you and none other beyond the end of my days. Freely, as God has given me life, do I join my life today to your life."

He stopped, but his mind was still racing with all the possibilities he could have said to her. Was it enough? Had he said enough? The thousand thousand words were all bumping into each other for a single intense moment when he'd finished, but he drew in a long breath, lifted both her hands in his, kissed the back of one and then the other and whispered, "I love you," and the words unspoken were suddenly all said.

Eden was blinking hard. He had both her hands in his and she had nothing to wipe them away with, so several larger teardrops tracked down her cheeks. "I...I...didn't kn... know," she rather stammered, "I never even dreamed that my heart could hold as much love as it's doing at this moment, and it's you, my darling Marshall, it's you who has filled it so. I feel it expanded, still expanding, in my chest because it wants, it needs, it simply must reach out and wrap itself around you, through you. You come to me, bringing all that you are, and I am left in amazed wonder that you have. I am so completely yours that to promise faithfulness seems entirely unnecessary, and yet I do speak the words to you that I will love you always, love you and none other."

There was no one else in the room. There was just her and Marshall and endless space around them and in their coupled solitude she said to him what lay in her heart, genuine, even slightly awkward. "Some place, some time, I don't know exactly where or when, I think I'd lost myself these last few years. Then I almost literally stumbled across you and in finding you, I found me again. You've given me not only you, you've given me back to myself but in a new and different way. You've made me more than I ever was, and all that I am with you, because of you, all of it, every bit, wants nothing else but to cherish and adore you. This I promise you, Marshall Sinclair, that I choose freely to walk beside you into the future. I trust you with everything I am and I pledge to you that it is safe for you to trust me with everything you are. You make each moment of my life more beautiful and kind simply by your presence. You are my rock, my home, my safe harbor and you have made me believe again that anything is possible. I first loved you in the rain, and I promise to love you when the grass is fresh and filled with daisies and when it's dry and even the weeds have died. I will love you in snow and sunshine, in darkness and in light. You have attached wings to my heart and I ache with the longing, the necessity to soar into your being. Marshall, you are the chosen companion of my heart, and it is with gladness and unending joy that I join my life today to your life."

Peter spoke again. "Marshall, do you have Eden's ring?"

Luke's sweaty little hand was curled tightly, still, about the two rings in his pocket. He repeated Marshall's careful instructions to himself. *First the small ring, then the big. First the small, then the big.* They were waiting. Oh, no! Suddenly he wasn't sure which ring was small and which was big! He loosened his grip, feeling them frantically with his fingers. One of them settled way down in the deep corner of the pocket of the old suit. Which one did he still have in his hand? He couldn't tell! He couldn't...tell! It felt big to him, but then his own fingers were so small that any adult ring felt big. His forefinger scrabbled after the one nestled in the pocket corner. It was wedged! He closed his eyes tightly, concentrating desperately on getting it loose so he could tell if it was the big one or the small one. Marshall said he was important enough to do this, old enough to be given this special job. Marshall said....oh! He got it! Yes, yes! That one was bigger than the other. Now which one did he give first? He couldn't remember! Then he felt Marshall's right hand gently cup his cheek. It was patient, kind. He opened his eyes, blinking up at Marshall's face, forgetting that he couldn't look back at him.

"I...I...," he stuttered, then suddenly remembered. *First the small, then the big!* He slid the big one way down over his thumb and withdrew his hand from his pocket, holding out the smaller ring, almost gasping in relief. Then he realized Marshall couldn't see his hand and so, using his left hand, he turned Marshall's over and laid the ring with his right on

Marshall's palm, pressing it down just a bit to be sure he knew it was there. Marshall smiled at him just as though he could see him, then turned and handed the ring toward Peter.

Peter took the ring from Marshall's palm, and prayed, "I ask the blessing of our Lord Jesus Christ on this ring, on the one who gives it and the one who wears it." He got the ring back into Marshall's hand and Marshall turned to face Eden again, holding it between his thumb and the tips of his fingers. She couldn't get a clear look at it, but she lifted her left hand so that the very end of her ring finger contacted his fingers. He held the ring there, passing the end of his tongue quickly over his lower lip.

"More than once I've quoted to you *God planted a garden eastward in Eden*. Eden was God's gift to man, a place where all his needs were met, a place of extreme beauty, extraordinary peace and communion. In you, God has gifted me, my Eden, and in you all my needs are met, in you I have found the extremity of beauty and peace and communion." He began to slide the ring, bit by little bit, as he spoke, turning his fingers enough so that she could see its top. He'd asked that she leave her engagement ring in place for the ceremony. The wedding ring had an almost odd-looking curve worked into its top with a small lily made from intricately fitted little diamonds. When it reached the base of her finger, he gave it one more gentle push and the curve of the wedding band fit in a perfect snuggle around the star of her engagement ring. He kept his fingers on it as he continued. "In Eden, heaven and earth met and were one as the stars shine over the lilies of the field, the lilies of the garden." He raised his left hand, sliding its palm under her hand, then completely covered it with his right. "Together, the lily and the star have become the symbol of unity, where all that has always been and all that is to come are one with all that now is. I give this ring to you, my darling Eden, as a sign of completeness, as a symbol that a star, however large, however bright, however...conceived of...is but a light alone unless it shines upon a garden. And with this ring I do thee wed, taking you unto me as my wife and the beloved of my heart, acknowledging the oneness that is ours and pledging to do everything in my power to seal that for all eternity." He moved his top hand away and bent his head to kiss her rings.

Luke managed a smoothly successful transfer of the larger ring to Marshall, and when it, too, had been blessed and passed into Eden's hands, she stood silently a moment, looking at it on her palm. She'd known the fact of its goldenness would mean little to Marshall, so with Martha's expert help, she'd found a small jewelry shop just down the street from the hospital where a very elderly jeweler had listened carefully to her explanation, her reasons why she needed something tactile to give her groom. The jeweler had offered to engrave the ring in Braille, but somehow that was not what Eden wanted. He showed her, though, how small engraving of any sort on a ring would be very difficult, if not impossible, to discern clearly by fingertip alone. It was, indeed, he said, why the Braille dots were raised and not indented. She had asked if it were possible for him, then, to emboss something on a ring for her. He had stared at her, his eyebrows raised so much that his forehead was a roadmap of wrinkles. That was a much more time-consuming matter, much more labor-intensive and required a thicker gold ring to begin with. Did he have such a ring? He did, but it was two sizes larger than she needed and would have to be resized. It had all proven rather complicated, but she was persistent and within two days time he had actually produced what she wanted.

She lifted his left hand, beginning a slow slide of the ring down his finger. "Marshall," she said, then decided she wanted him to be able to touch the ring, so pushed it all the way on and guided his right hand where she wanted it to be, gently pressing his forefinger down atop the band. As he realized what was centrally embossed and smiled, she continued. "For every great change in our lives, there is some catalyst, some something that sets it all in motion. For us it was a single maple leaf cart-wheeling across a sidewalk and then coming to rest as though to be sure it were properly noticed. That simple leaf changed my path and, in so doing, changed everything, bringing me to you, bringing you into my life, leading us to where we stand today. So it occupies the central place on this ring I give you, my love, and is also symbolic of my pledge to you that I will never treat lightly or take for granted the unexpected pathways, the joys and blessings of life. For you are my joy and my blessing, the end and the beginning of all my paths, and the companion with whom I shall walk them."

His fingers moved past the embossed maple leaf, tracing the letters that encircled his ring. *ALWAYS* was spelled in gold, raised like the leaf. Each letter was very distinct, carefully, painstakingly done to make it easily discernible. "I thought of all the things I might want to put on your ring and many, many words came to mind, but in *always* I am promising you that always I shall love you and be faithful to you, always I shall be with you no matter how wonderful or how sad the time may be, always I shall give you my loyalty, my trust, my devotion." She ran her own fingertip around the word. "Always, Marshall. Always in all ways I take you as my wedded husband."

With Eden's left hand resting atop Marshall's, Peter then reached out, laying his right hand over theirs. "Lord, I ask Your seal and Your blessing on the covenant this couple has made before You and in the presence of family and friends. Grant them a special grace whereby each one will prefer the other's good. May they always be too brave to be unkind. May each one add their courage to the other. May they always forget what ought to be forgotten, and recall, unfailing, all that ought to be recalled. Lord, gift them with patience, gentleness, and tender hearts for each other. Grant that each one may not so much seek to be consoled by the other as to console, to be understood as to understand. May each sow joy in the other's sadness, light in the other's darkness, faith in the other's doubt. Let them not defer or neglect any kindness, any good thing they can do for one another. Give them the gift of finding joy everywhere and leaving it behind them in the hearts of others when they go. In Jesus' name. Amen."

He removed his hand, smiling widely at them. "And now, inasmuch as Marshall and Eden have made their pledge and promise each to the other and have declared the same by the giving and receiving of rings and the joining of hands, by the power invested in me by the state of Pennsylvania, I pronounce that they are husband and wife in the name of the Father, and of the Son, and of the Holy Spirit. Marshall, you may kiss your bride!"

And he did. Quite tenderly, though very thoroughly. The others in the room cheered and clapped and, completely spontaneously, Martha launched into Irving Berlin's *Always* on the piano. Marshall grinned at the sound of it and with his arms still around Eden, sang it to her.

I'll be loving you, always-
With a love that's true, always-
When the things you've planned need a helping hand,
I will understand, always-always.
Days may not be fair, always-
That's when I'll be there, always-
Not for just an hour, not for just a day,
Not for just a year, but always.

Then he buried his lips in her hair, whispering, "Always, my darling. Always."

Chapter 69

Mike stood, one foot on the low hearth, hands resting on the mantel, staring down at the fire. Closing his eyes, he let himself enjoy the scent of wood smoke, the crackle and pop of heating sap, the warmth of the flames on the front of his body. Behind him, the room was filled with voices, laughing convivial voices, sharing the joy of the evening's event. New Year's Eve. Not just a wedding, but New Year's Eve. He smiled slightly wryly to himself. Endings. Both of them, endings. For him anyway.

Marshall and Eden were planning on going back to Pittsburgh soon. Just as well. Some friendships were a bit wearing on the heart. The last two months, though, were a time he knew he'd never forget, especially that day on Coopers Ridge when he and Eden had been tracking Marshall hour after hour. It was exhausting, both emotionally and physically, that day, but she had been right there beside him the whole way. Letting go of her was not easy. The wedding had helped, actually. Witnessing what passed between Marshall and Eden as they made their vows...how could any man even think of interfering with that? Even continuing to think about Eden as he had been doing would be nothing less than obscene after that.

"You've been an EMT here a long time?"

A soft voice came from just to his left and he opened his eyes, turning his head. "Oh, hello, Maria. I didn't realize you were there." Taking his hands off the mantel, he faced her. "Yes, yes, I have," he replied, "ever since I came back home after the army."

"You were born here, then?"

He nodded, making an effort to center his attention on the nurse. "Lived here all my life. Well, except for that stint in the military. I love it here." He smiled at her. "You haven't been here all that long, have you?"

"Only since August. It's very different from where I was before."

"Where would that be?"

"Philadelphia. Big city hospital. Very busy. Very hectic. Very crowded. It's why I came here. I wanted to try something else, something smaller, more personal."

"And is it?"

"Smaller?"

"More personal?"

"Somewhat."

"Only somewhat?"

"It seems to be taking me a while to fit in, to get to know people." She gave a small laugh. "Not too many Greeks here in the forest."

"I heard you speaking Greek with Marshall that day in the hospital."

"Ah, you remember that?"

"Not too much Greek spoken in forest hospitals," he grinned. "I found it memorable."

"He was a very special patient." She looked across the room to where he was standing beside Eden, talking with Ryan and Connie. "A very special man."

"He is, indeed," Mike nodded.

"I was honored he asked me to come today," she added, "and it's nice to get out on New Year's Eve, too."

Mike looked at her, really looked at her, for the first time. Thick, shining black hair waved down to the top of her shoulders, framing an oval face with, he realized with a bit of a start, absolutely enormous brown eyes under finely winged brows. The firelight reflected in them, amber dancing in the brown so darkly brown it was almost black. She said something but he was studying the amber lights so intently he didn't catch her words.

"I'm sorry...?"

"I was just saying that it was good to be out of my apartment tonight. New Year's Eve and all."

"You live in town?"

"About three blocks from the hospital, yes. I generally walk to work, which is why my car wasn't at the hospital and Dr. Hersholtz kindly offered to drive me to the inn." She gazed around the room. "I've never been here before. It's really lovely, especially all decorated like it is tonight."

"Harold and Martha are wonderful folks," Mike smiled. "Their son Ryan's always been my best friend. I've spent probably more time in this house than in my own home over the years."

"You live near-by?"

"Got a log cabin I built just down the road. It's on the land where my parents' house used to be."

"Used to be?"

"Yeah. Burned down in the early 90's. Not a trace of it left anymore."

"I'm sorry," she said genuinely. "It had to be hard to lose that."

He shrugged just a bit. "Nice, though, to still be able to live on the land. Good hunting and fishing, too." He cocked an eyebrow. "You ever been fishing?"

She laughed again. "I'm afraid not. I did have an aquarium in my bedroom for a while. Does that count?"

"Would you like to give it a try? Come spring, you think you might like to try your hand at it?"

As she looked up at the face of the tall man with the silvering hair and light blue eyes, she thought just maybe she might. She smiled, full, well-shaped lips parting to reveal white teeth. "I wouldn't know what to do, I'm afraid."

"I know what to do," he said softly.

Luke came up to Marshall, tugging lightly at the hem of his jacket to let him know he was there. "Your eyes were working tonight, Marshy. I saw them."

"Working? What do you mean, Luke?"

"They made tears. They were working."

Marshall smiled. "They did, didn't they?

"They were happy tears? Like on Christmas Day?"

"Very happy, Luke. I'm as happy today as I've ever been in my life."

"Did I do ok, Marshy? I was worried I wasn't a good best man."

"You were a great best man, Luke. I couldn't have been more pleased." He squatted in front of the little boy, holding his arms out.

Luke hugged Marshall's neck. "Thank you for thinking I was special enough," he whispered.

"Oh, Luke," Marshall said fondly, "you are more special than you have any idea."

"Like you," Luke pronounced gravely.

"Like him," Eden confirmed.

Maria had gone into the kitchen to offer Martha her help in serving the hors d'oeuvres. As Connie was also there, Ryan walked up to where Mike still stood near the fireplace, running his thumb pad absently around the rim of a glass of beer. "You doing ok?" Ryan asked, briefly gripping Mike's arm.

"Fine," Mike nodded, draining the last of the beer. "Just fine."

Ryan studied him. "You mean it?"

"Yeah," Mike affirmed. "Bit surprised about that myself."

"The nurse have anything to do with that?"

"Maria?"

"Yep."

"I'm going to teach her how to fish this spring."

"That so?"

Mike grinned. "Give a nurse a fish and you've fed her for one meal. Teach a nurse to fish and you've fed her for a lifetime."

"You thinking about feeding this one?"

"Too early to tell. But...." He shrugged.

"But is good," Ryan chuckled.

Maria came back into the parlor with a tray of salmon creamed cheese stuffed into tiny, hollowed tomatoes. Mike was standing right where she'd left him so she headed toward him and held out the tray. "These look interesting," she said.

Mike popped one into his mouth. "Martha makes interesting combinations."

"Interesting combinations can be good things," Ryan smiled, looking from Mike to Maria. "Hello. I'm Ryan. Welcome to the inn."

She inclined her head slightly and returned his smile. "It's good to be here. My first time."

"And not your last, I hope."

Her eyes flickered very briefly to Mike then back to Ryan. "Are you home for long?"

"Just for the holidays, I'm afraid, then it's back to the salt mines in Cleveland."

"He's helping a friend set up a travel agency," Mike explained. "What are you planning for after that?" Mike continued.

Ryan's eyes were following Connie as she brought her mother a fresh drink. "Remains to be seen, Mike, but I'm thinking."

"Time to cut the cake," Martha announced. She and Joan had gotten the cake into the dining room where it sat, centered grandly on the lace tablecloth.

Marshall and Eden were directed to the best place for them to stand and Eden described the cake to him. "Guess I can't really gaze at the cake, eh?" he remarked.

"Not unless you want Joan to smack your hands," Eden laughed.

"Is the maple leaf standing up or lying down?" he asked.

"Kind of propped up at an angle. It's made from really stiff icing and is almost like a big cookie. I wish I had the actual one pressed. I'd frame it and hang it on the wall. Just had no idea at the time, you know. It was simply a leaf."

He slid his palm around her waist. "Life is like that. Most times we don't know the significance of things that cart wheel across our sidewalks. Only later. Only then do we understand how in their simplicity they've changed everything."

"I'm so glad," she whispered, leaning into him, "I'm so glad I found you."

"I'm glad you found me, too," he smiled. Then he felt Martha pressing the handle of a cake cutter into his right hand. Eden quickly laid her hand atop his. "We'll have to do this together," he said very low.

She guided his hand toward the cake, pressing down when it was in the right place to cut. After they'd made the initial cut, Joan took over and finished the slice, putting it on a white china plate and handing it to Eden. Eden broke off a small piece, leading his fingers to it. "Don't let me poke it in your eye," he chuckled.

She picked up her own little piece. "I'm right here," she said, guiding him just enough, then waiting quietly. His face went all intent as he concentrated on doing this right. He found her cheek with the tip of his little finger then moved his hand slightly left. Her mouth was open and he got the small bite quite neatly inside.

"Perfect," she affirmed, her mouth still full. "Your turn." She actually bumped his lip a little, getting icing on it. He smiled and started to lick it but she said, "No, let me," and stood on tiptoe to kiss it off.

"Much better," he agreed. Everyone was very quiet, watching, and it was easy for him to feel like he and she were the only ones in the room. His hand moved higher up her back and he kissed her again, a real kiss, not just an icing removal sort. "My wife," he whispered.

A cell phone rang. Hersholtz uttered a quiet "Damn!" and reached into his pocket. He went out into the front entryway a moment then returned hurriedly. "Sorry," he said, "but I've got to go back to the hospital. One of my patients is arresting." He looked at Maria. "I'm afraid if you want a ride, you'll have to come with me now."

"Certainly," she replied. "Let me get my coat."

"I could drive her home," Mike offered. "If you'd like to stay, that is."

"You wouldn't mind?"

"Not at all. That way you can have a bit more New Year's Eve."

"Yes, I'd like that. Thank you, Mike."

Ryan tried not to grin but was not fully successful in the effort.

"And you haven't gotten a piece of cake yet," Mike added, finding he really did want her to stay.

"No, I haven't, have I."

Joan had been cutting slices, much larger ones than were usually served at receptions, and he picked up one of the plates, handing it to her. "Can't go to a wedding and not have cake."

"I suppose you can't," she smiled.

"Too bad there's not room to dance," Ryan spoke up.

"What about the porch?" Connie suggested. "Would that work?"

Ryan's eyes lit up. "Great! Most of the porch furniture is stored away for the winter so that's the biggest open space we've got around here. Get your coat! I'll put batteries in the CD player and we've got us a ballroom. Come on, Mike. You and Maria come on out with us."

"Would...would you like to?" he asked.

She nodded, intrigued by the concept of a New Year's Eve dance on a frosty porch.

"Do you want to go, too?" Eden whispered to Marshall.

He shook his head no. The porch was still a space too small for him, especially with other couples that he would bump into, and he was feeling a little tired. It had been a long day and he still wasn't back up to his normal energy after the pneumonia. He had plans, too, for when the party was over and he and Eden could be alone. He wanted to save his strength for that. "Could we just sit by the fire for a while?"

"Sounds good to me, darling." She'd been aware for a little while that he was flagging a bit. He held his mouth differently when his energy level was down. "I'll take some hot tea with us. I think I'm ready for a cup."

When both of them were snuggled closely together on the couch, Wadsworth lying almost across their feet, and the two couples were getting the porch set up for the music, the rest of those present in the inn all set about putting away leftovers and cleaning up. They were going to spend the night at Stuart and Joan's so that the bride and groom could have the inn to themselves. Elizabeth and Dale had already taken Luke over there. Marshall rested the side of his head against Eden's, listening to the happy chatter from the kitchen, the clink of dishes, the shutting of cabinets. From the porch came the sound of Ryan's laugh as he struggled to sort out the CDs with frozen fingers. "Gloves," he groaned. "someone get me gloves!" A log crumbled into embers.

"This is so good," Marshall murmured, utterly at peace.

"Why don't you rest just a minute?" Eden suggested.

"You wouldn't mind?" he asked drowsily.

"I need you rested. How else will you ravish me tonight?"

"You want to be ravished?"

"Mmm hmm. Most definitely."

"I'd better rest, then," he half chuckled, half sighed. "Just for a moment, though."

In less than a minute his head grew heavy and sagged against hers. His left hand was in her lap and she smiled contentedly down at it, at the way his wedding band looked. He was her husband now. Her husband. She squeezed her eyes tight. *Please protect him. Oh, God, please, please keep him safe.*

Maria had on a deep blue coat with a light blue cashmere scarf tucked about her neck. Still she shivered slightly as they waited for Ryan to get the CD player going. Mike, beside her, felt the shiver and turned, lifting her scarf up more, settling it higher so it covered part of her ears. "That's better," he pronounced softly, his hand brushing her cheek as he moved it away. She was standing directly under the porch light and it cast long shadows of her lashes over her cheekbones. Why had he never noticed how lovely she was? "Play something slow, Ryan," he said, not taking his eyes off her.

"Well, all I've got here are Mom's CDs so I don't think there's any Crowded House."

Ryan put in a CD then laughed as *Red Sails in the Sunset* began to play. "That'll do," Mike said, taking a step closer to Maria, holding out a hand for her to take. Her fingers were soft, small in his, vaguely electric. He wasn't sure, not yet, if she'd be stiff against him in the newness of their acquaintance, but she, too, took a step forward and as his other hand slid around her back, he was suddenly completely aware of her yielded suppleness against him, a willingness to let him guide her into the music. The awareness shot through his entire nervous system, a mingling of surprise and delight.

Ryan just let the whole CD play, one old love song after another drifting through the crisp night air. With each one, Mike held Maria a little closer than he had with the song before. Harold poked his head out the door. "Countdown to midnight's on now."

Mike paused, looking down at Maria's uptipped face. "Happy New Year," she whispered and his hands moved as though by their own volition, framing her face. He kissed her, just lightly, his lips warming atop hers, feelings stirring deep in his gut.

"Happy New Year, Maria," he said, lifting his lips enough to speak, then kissing her again with growing firmness.

Marshall had awakened moments before, just sitting still, listening to *When I Grow Too Old Too Dream*. His hand had sought, had found, Eden's and when the final whoop of the countdown came from the kitchen, he pulled her to him, his mouth gentle yet eager on hers. A new year was beginning and it was his wedding night.

Chapter 70

She'd kicked off her ivory satin high heels near the dresser and was now sitting on the edge of their bed, watching Marshall as he stood a moment just inside the doorway, his hands on the frame, paused like something existing out of time. She didn't mind that he kept standing there. He was obviously thinking deeply and she loved the sight of him, the way he looked in his rust-colored tweed. Something in her was still trying to process that he was her husband. Dr. Marshall Sinclair...her husband.

Everyone had gone to Stuart's now, everyone but for Mike and Maria. Mike was driving Maria into town in his truck. He'd seemed more his old self later this evening, friendly, relaxed. She was glad. She'd seen him from time to time through the window that looked out on the porch. He was resting his cheek on Maria's dark hair as they danced.

Marshall took a couple of steps into the room, closing the door behind him. He knew where everything in this room was and as he passed the rocking chair, slipped off his jacket, hanging it over the wide oak back.. His cravat and vest joined it and he unbuttoned the top several buttons of his ivory shirt, then continued on to where Eden sat. She watched him intently, her eyes wide and very bright, her body already trembling at his approach.

Kneeling in front of her, he lifted both her hands in his, burying his cheek in her palms. "My wife." He said the words, his voice low, deep, with rather an echo of awe in his tone that moved her so profoundly that she wrapped her arms lightly about his head, pressing it against her breasts.

They passed a long moment, just so, neither moving or speaking. Then he leaned back enough for her to see his face. "There was a time when only your hands were mine to touch, there that day in the parlor, and times when I wanted you so terribly but the sling did not permit. And then, so very briefly, I could give all myself to you." He smiled wryly. "But forests and pneumonia interrupted that and it has only been in the last week that there has been full freedom to love you as I want, as I must." He kissed her palms, one then the other. "Now, tonight, we are in the opening hours of a new year, the opening hours of our marriage, and it is, in its way, such a new beginning, such...well, there is so much freshness to it that it is almost like the first time." He kissed her palms again. "And it is the first for me to love you as my wife. Please," he barely whispered, his fingertips on her neck, "let me...as though I've never gazed at you before."

A soft moan was the only answer she could manage.

His fingers moved up her neck, very, very slowly, then curved along her jawbone, exploring her face. Everywhere he touched, little charges of electricity ran along the pathways of her nervous system. He pulled her lower lip slightly down, feeling the moisture inside, then pressed her back on the bed, rising to lean over her, replacing his fingertips with his own lips. He kissed her a long, long time then with his mouth still on hers, his hands began to move again, down her neck, pausing at the rows of silk-covered buttons on her shoulders. She felt his lips smile just a little over hers, then his right hand found the long slit in her sleeve and he moved it inside and down the length of her arm. Everything he did was very, very slow.

He undid the small buttons and her bodice was loosened so that he could slide her gown down over her shoulders. He kissed his way along her collar bone, followed the curve of her shoulder and sent his lips like butterfly wings skimming down to her wrists. There were more buttons on the wide cuffs and he raised himself enough to undo them, smiling again when her arms were free and she lay bare to her waist.

She unbuttoned his shirt, her palms sweet and hot over his pectorals. His shirt fell to the floor and he lifted her feet, slipping his own out of his shoes, as she lay back full upon the bed, him half atop her. Her back tensed, arched, as he loved his way down her torso rib by rib. She lifted her bottom enough so that he could slide the gown down, down past her hips and was only vaguely aware that he took it on past her ankles and it joined his shirt then his slacks on the rug. A moment more and nothing, not the filmiest bit of lace, lay between his hands and her skin. The parachute settled over them, spreading its gentle sigh of self over his back, enveloping her in its silken folds of released tension.

He lay there, giving her a moment, giving him one but, his being enmeshed in the wonder she was his wife, he loved her again then folded his arms around her, pressing her cheek to his chest, and just held her. There was no parachute this time. He had taken her beyond where parachutes could fly. She had exploded and little pieces of her being settled down to earth, leaving trails akin to those huge willow-like fireworks that sift serenely through a July night. She was the sifting trails of light, and she was also the dark surface of the river that greeted them, reflected them, and then flowed on. And then there was peace and quiet and...him...his arms still holding her.

He lay quietly, his lips buried in her hair, aware of the gradual slowing of the pulse in her temple that rested just below his collar bone. Her skin, softly moist and warm against his, began to cool and he listened as her breathing calmed. The full length of her nestled securely against him, she drifted into sleep. Waking so recently from his nap, he was not tired, and so simply remained still, loving the feel of her in his arms, loving the stir of emotions she generated in his heart. His wife. He loved, too, how she responded to his lightest touch, how she trusted him to lift her up and not let her fall, how he could lift and lift her and that in his knowing of her she was satisfied. His hand moved down, cupping over the bare curve of her hip, and she stirred, burrowing even more closely against him. That he also loved and every masculine, protective feeling in him wrapped itself around her nearly as tangibly as his arms.

He did not know when he, too, drifted into sleep, nor even that he had. He only knew that he awakened sometime in the night to her touch on his thigh. He started to prop himself on his left elbow, but she pressed her hand against his chest so that he lay back, lay still. Her breath moved warmly up his ribs, his neck, over his eyes, then concentrated in his ear. "Allow me," she whispered, "to gaze at my husband."

In less than a minute she had gazed at him so well his hands were fisted into the sheets and his lips pressed tightly together. She touched her tongue to them, prying them slightly, and felt them open to her then close over her mouth. Her fingertips trailed over his inner thigh and he gasped, releasing her lips, so she moved her mouth down his body again, kissing the small chest tube scar on his side. Its presence brought clearly to her all that he had suffered, all the pain he'd endured. Now she had him, she had him here, safe in their marriage bed, and she was determined that all he would endure would be the touch of her hand, of her mouth, on his skin. She smiled to herself, her mind filling with all sorts of things for him to endure this night.

Chapter 71

It was 3 AM and Mike sat in his old rocker, pushing it gently with the toe of one shoe, staring absently into the fire he'd made. He and Maria had sat in the cab of his truck for at least two hours before he escorted her to the door of her apartment building. Not that they'd done more than a gentle bit of kissing. It was her openness, her genuineness that got to him. She was simply entirely real, entirely without pretense and they had talked and laughed and talked some more. He had felt like some swinger of trees who had let go of a branch without knowing if another lay at all within reach, only to find his fingers closing over slender bark, finding purchase so quickly that he was still inwardly startled by the fact of it. She had been there the whole time, well, the entire autumn, and he had never really even focused on her as a person. In the hospital she moved with this air of quiet competence, her own attention centered on the well-being of her patients. To him she had simply been part of the overall atmosphere of the hospital itself.

"Damn fool that you are, Mike Johnson," he said, smiling to himself as a sudden bright flame flared up.

His thoughts turned to Eden, to how he'd come running up the path through the downpour to find her sitting there, leaning forward to shelter Marshall. They were a unit, the two of them, even then, even before they realized they were. He'd seen it, seen it plain as day, yet still he'd dreamed. He shook his head. "Damn fool!" he repeated softly. She could have come back to the inn from the hospital that very first night. There was no reason for her not to, no reason but that the unrealized bonds with Marshall had already secured their position. She stayed because he was there. She could not leave him, not even then, not even knowing that she could not. She simply...stayed.

And that time by the icy river, when she started off alone in the direction she believed he'd gone. He'd never seen such utter determination, such force of will. He grinned at the memory of how she'd pushed Barry flat when he tried to stop her. Nothing would stop her...ever...from getting to Marshall. Yet he had taken her to the cafe and bought her dinner and dreamed. He closed his eyes and just rocked a moment, contemplating his own compounding of his foolishness. Perhaps it was merely a mark of how the solitude of his life had begun to wear on him. It had just seemed so unlikely that he would ever know anything more than that, and then there she was, sitting on that path, rain beating on her back as she offered herself as shelter. The sight of it had moved something profoundly inside him. It was all so completely different from anything his ex-wife would have done. Then when he found her sleeping on that uncomfortable little hospital seat and had carried her down the hall in his arms. That had done it, that warm softness of her lying against him.

He went over it all, every bit, shining the light of understanding on all the whys of his responses to her. He should have disliked Marshall intensely, but he couldn't. He liked the man, a lot, and that had made it all the worse. Eden had only friendship to offer him. Nothing more had obviously ever occurred to her, and why should it? He recalled the November days when he'd come regularly to the inn and the three of them had played with Wadsworth, had sat in Martha's kitchen and munched her cookies. He thought about it all and he let it sift through his fingers. It was all right. At last it was all right. It had become all right during the wedding ceremony, and it was only after it was all right that he had discovered Maria. He liked that. It meant something to him that had been the order of things. Sure, there were no guarantees with Maria, not yet, but he was encouraged enough that he smiled, picturing how her dark hair had looked under the porch light. He let his lids close, beginning to drift off right there in the rocker, and for the first time since the end of October, the eyes that filled his mind were brown and not green.

Harold was snoring, as usual, but that wasn't what was keeping Martha awake. She was used to that. It was the clicking of Wadsworth's nails on the hardwood floor of the bedroom at Stuart's house. All night the dog paced back and forth past the closed door, stopping now and then to snuffle at the small crack at its bottom or give a scratch or two in hope that someone would let him out. From time to time he took his nose and poked the old brass doorknob enough to make it rattle.

Martha snapped her fingers and Wadsworth padded over, putting his muzzle in her hand, staring at her with pleading eyes. "I'm sorry, boy," Martha whispered, "but even you have to let them have this one night all to themselves. I know it's hard, but they'll be over here by afternoon for New Year's dinner. Just be patient, ok. They'll be here. I promise."

Eden woke around seven. She wasn't sure why, because they could sleep as late as they liked, but she drifted inexorably up through layers of some dream and blinked open her eyes. She had left the bathroom light on all night, its door open, because she'd wanted to be able to see him. Now as she lay there, she was very glad of it because the winter dawn had not yet begun. He was on his back, arms at his sides, very deeply asleep. She propped herself up on her right elbow so she could watch him. The quilt was pulled up over most of his chest, but his arms were atop it, were still bare. She watched him for a long time, wanting to kiss his lightly-parted lips but refraining lest she wake him. As she gazed at him it seemed suddenly that his eyes were half-way open and the bathroom light on his face was that of the moon. That icy spear stabbed through her gut again. He was only sleeping, wasn't he? Wasn't he? She had to be sure. Leaning over him, she put her cheek near his mouth. The soft movement of his warm breath on her skin left her weak with relief and she lay back on her pillow, her teeth sunk into the back of her right hand to keep herself from whimpering aloud.

She hadn't got rid of it, that fear of unbearable loss. Miles' death had nearly done her in and here she'd gone and given her whole heart to a man who'd nearly died twice, had died once. She turned her head again, dropping her hand down, looking at his profile limned in the bathroom light. When he was deeply asleep he always rolled over onto his back, but it made him positively look laid out. Suddenly she couldn't bear it and slipped out of bed, going to the window and raising the blind. She stood there, naked and shivering as the moonlight poured through the glass, her hands fisted into the curtains for support.

Did he know, could he possibly know how all that had happened to him had affected her? And each day she loved him more than the day before so that the thought of the loss of him was an ever-increasing thing. Sometimes she thought she'd mastered it, maybe even forgotten about it, but something always seemed to bring it back, something as simple as the way he was sleeping. She turned to look at him again. He'd lain just like that in the ICU when he was unconscious from pneumonia and exhaustion. Why couldn't he sleep on his side?

She jerked herself back toward the window, pulling too hard on the curtains. The rod gave way, collapsing with its load of curtains, coming apart in the middle as it fell. One of the center ends scraped across her shoulder and with her hands tangled in the material, she lost her balance and fell hard on her hip, most of the curtains billowing down around her. She let out a small cry as she fell and then just sat there, large tears rolling down her cheeks, feeling as though in her fears, she had let him down.

Marshall's dreams were scent-filled, tactile things, accompanied by sounds, often by music. He was deep in one, the fragrance of her skin in his nostrils, the small sounds of delight she was making causing him to smile, his fingertips tingling as he slid them down her thigh. Then something, he had no idea what, jarred him awake and he sat up, his left hand instinctively going out to where Eden should be lying. The covers on her side of the bed had been thrown back.

"Eden?" he called, concern starting to grow. "Eden, darling?"

There was no answer so he sat straighter, listening. From near the window he could hear her breathing rather raggedly. "Eden?" he called again, scooting rapidly across the bed then hurrying toward the window. He literally bumped into her and sank quickly to his knees beside her. "What's happened?" he asked, his hands encountering the strange folds of cloth draped across her lap and one shoulder. "What's this?"

Still she did not answer and his fingers found her face, found the wetness of her tears. He sucked in a quick breath. "Darling, did I hurt you?" Why was she crying? Had he been clumsy in his need for her?

He slid his arms around her, starting to scoop both her and the material up, but she made a sharp little sound of pain. "You're hurt? Darling, are you hurt?"

"My sh...shoulder," she said. "Curtain rod."

Curtain rod? This mass of cloth was the...curtains? "Where?" he asked, trying to feel her face.

"No, my shoulder. Nothing big I think." She was sniffing now, trying to stop the tears.

His fingers went to her shoulder, finding a rough-edged scratch about three inches long. Lips pressed together, he did scoop her up then, heading with her toward the bed.

His foot caught in the curtains and he almost fell, but managed to right himself and set her atop the mattress.

"Wait there," he said firmly and made his way around the bed to the bathroom, coming back in a brief moment with a tube of something. "Tell me I haven't got the toothpaste."

She looked at the tube. "Neosporin," she read aloud.

Very gently he spread some over her scratch then, setting the tube aside, asked again, "What happened?"

She felt the tears well again and turned her head and shoulders away from him, her hands still clutching the curtains. He followed down her arms with his own hands, slowly, carefully, uncurled her fingers and pushed the curtains off the bed. Then he lay back, taking her with him, enfolding her in his arms, murmuring endearments into her hair. She needed time and he was good at giving people time. One thing resulting from blindness was a great deal of patience. If he had been somehow inept, she would tell him when she was ready.

She had no idea of what he was thinking might be the cause of her tears. She was just grateful that he was holding her, was not insisting that she talk. What she wanted was simply to lie there in his arms, her cheek against his chest, listening to the beating of his heart. The bullet in Miles' neck had torn through an artery and he had bled out rather rapidly. She thought about that a lot right after he died, how his heartbeats must've grown fainter and fainter there in the snow. Heartbeats had come to have a great significance to her. And...then...Marshall had had none. That was a week ago today. Only a week. So she pressed her ear more firmly into his flesh, hungry for the regular rhythm of its beating. If only she could encapsulate this moment, just live inside it and only it. It was unrealistic, impossible. She knew that. She just didn't know how to stop the wanting of it. He had talked with her before about it and what he'd said made sense and she'd thought it had helped, but watching him sleep, just watching him sleep, had sent it all flooding over her. Against her will, more tears escaped.

He felt the new wetness on his chest and his brow creased in concern. "Did...did I do this?" he whispered.

He had, not at all like he thought, but he had. She, ashamed of her weakness, just gripped onto him more tightly, unable to stop wetting his chest. He moved one hand up, curving it about the back of her head in some nameless gesture of communication. She liked it there.

Very slowly she calmed. The way he was holding her, the little things he kept saying softly, it was all too beautiful, but even as she sailed her ship into the harbor of it, she thought of how the beauty of this moment was utterly transient. It was like watching a sunset with colors so vivid it nearly hurt the soul just to look at it. But you could never hold onto a sunset. It was, inevitably, over. And night always came. Miles had died in the night. So had Marshall. But, oh God, just listen to those strong heartbeats under her ear. She began to count them, not realizing she was doing so aloud.

After a while, Marshall put his lips to her temple. "What?" he murmured.

"Oh!" she became aware she'd been audible. "Heartbeats," she said sheepishly.

"My heartbeats?"

"Mmm hmm," she nodded, keeping her ear where it was. "Heart's beating."

"This is good?"

"Very good," she sighed. "Keep it up."

He smiled. "I shall surely try."

A new tear trickled down. "Is that it? Eden? Is that it?"

She turned her head, burying her face completely against his chest. "A week ago today...is that it?"

She managed the barest nod.

"Oh, my darling," he sighed. "It's all right. I'm all right. That's over and done. We've only just begun, you and I."

She mumbled something against his chest. "What was that?" He hadn't been able to catch a word.

Moving her head enough to speak clearly, she repeated, "You sleep like the dead."

"I sleep...?"

"You do!" she said more definitely, lifting her head entirely off his chest. "You look like you're lying in a coffin instead of on a bed."

He was rather taken aback. "What....?"

She realized she was sounding ridiculous and heaved a big sigh. "It's not your fault. It just scares me."

"Is that what just happened?"

"Mmm hmm."

He kissed her eyes. "Is that better?"

"Some."

He moved his lips down her throat. "How about that?"

"Getting better," she allowed.

He paused. "Darling, I don't know what I can do about that other than sew a golf ball into the back of my pajamas."

"You aren't wearing pajamas."

"Oh, yeah," he chuckled. "Problem there, eh?"

"I rather like no pajamas."

"No pajamas, no golf balls," he reminded.

Chapter 72

"Mom," Ryan said, walking into Joan's enormous kitchen where Martha, Joan, Elizabeth, and Joan's daughters were already preparing New Year's dinner. "Would you invite Maria to eat with us?"

Martha turned toward her son, wiping her hands on her apron. "You wouldn't happen to have any ulterior motivation for that request, now would you?"

"Most definitely," he grinned, lifting her hand and kissing it despite its dusting of flour. "Mike's invited, is he not?"

"He's always invited. You know that."

"So, will you give Maria a call? I just happen to have her number." He handed her a small slip of paper.

"Matchmaker," she accused fondly.

He just cocked his head, continuing to grin. "You seen Con?"

"In the den, with her Mom. Give them a sec. Seemed like they were in some deep discussion."

"Ok," he replied amiably, scooping a fingerful of cookie dough from a bowl on the counter.

"Raw eggs," she admonished.

"Yeah, good, eh?"

"About Connie...."

"What about her?" he smiled, leaning against the counter, contentedly licking his finger.

"You know what I mean."

"I do," he agreed.

"So...what?"

"Somethin's up, Mom," he admitted, smiling broadly, lips together, shaking his head from side to side.

"They'll be going back to Pittsburgh tomorrow, won't they?"

He sighed. "Yeah, they will and I've gotta get myself up to Cleveland."

"Which leaves you, where?"

"Leaves her in Pittsburgh and me in Cleveland."

"And....?"

"And I intend to do something about that as soon as I can."

Her lips twitched into a smile. "I saw that," he added.

"It just makes me happy," she said softly. "Happy for you, happy for the possibilities with this new family I've gone and got so darn fond of."

"We do have possibilities," he nodded, meeting her gaze.

Connie and Edith sat side by side on a small couch, talking about their upcoming return to Pittsburgh. Edith had been asking pretty much the same things Martha had been asking Ryan. "What's great, Mom," Connie was saying, "is that we're both in the same business and Ryan has a lot of experience in opening new travel agencies. We're thinking, when he's got this one in Cleveland on its feet, we're thinking of, maybe, starting one together in Pittsburgh."

Even though she loved wisely and with open hands, Edith's heart plumped a bit with sudden gladness. Connie would be staying in Pittsburgh and so would Eden. Her New Year's cup was full. She blinked back quick tears.

"What, Mom? What is it?"

"I love you so much," Edith smiled. "That's all."

"Oh, Mom, do you have any idea how enough that is?"

Luke, not really aware of the intensity of Wadsworth's concentration on only one thing, opened the front door to see how his snowman was doing. He and Ryan and Connie had built it in the yard after breakfast and he wanted to be sure it wasn't melting or anything. Wadsworth bolted down the entrance hall and was out the door before Luke was even aware of the dog's presence. "*STOP!*" he shrieked as Waddy made straight for the back road that ran close to the lake.

Ryan heard Luke's cry and ran to the hall just in time to see Wadsworth disappear around the bend in the road. "Get him, Ryan!" Luke wailed. "Make him stop!"

Ryan shook his head. "Nothing's going to make that dog stop, Luke. He wants to get to Marshall."

"But he'll get lost! And Marshy needs him."

"He won't get lost, Luke. No need to worry about that. He knows right where he's going." He pulled out his cell phone, though, pausing to check his watch for the time first. *Should be ok...by now,* he thought, suppressing a grin, then dialed the inn's number.

Eden picked up the extension in the kitchen. She and Marshall had just finished a rather late breakfast. "Hello."

"Ryan here, Eden. Just wanted to give you a head's up that company's on its furry way."

"Wadsworth?"

Marshall's ears pricked up.

"Yeah, he escaped captivity and is headed down the lake road toward the inn. Will you give me a call when he gets there? Luke's worried."

"What's up with Wadsworth?" Marshall asked as she hung up the phone.

"Evidently he got loose from Stuart's house and is coming here. Alone. Will he be ok? Should I drive out and look for him?"

"He'll be ok," Marshall smiled. "He'll be just fine."

"Is it that homing device for guide dogs you have implanted in your wrist?"

He laughed. "Something like that."

She went to the door, looking toward the lake road. No sign of him. She pressed her lips together. Damn dog had wormed his way into her heart right along with his master. Well, he'd just better not go and fall off any cliffs between Stuart's and the inn. Damn dog!

Marshall came up behind her, putting his hands on her shoulders. "You worried?" he asked.

"He's part of you," she murmured. "Somehow he's part of you. He means a lot to me."

"He'll be fine."

She wheeled on him. "You always say that! Then you go off somewhere and a building falls on you."

"Aren't we talking about Wadsworth?"

"We're talking about a doggy extension of you, Marshall. A bear is probably eating him as we speak."

"You did think he was a bear once, if I recall."

"It's not funny," she griped, grabbing her coat off the hook and stepping out onto the porch where she could get a better view of the end of the lane.

He followed her, but with no coat. She looked at him then closed her eyes tightly. What was she to do? Bubble wrap was simply not an option. He put his arms around her and she whispered, "You drive me crazy, you know."

"Like this?" and he nibbled at her neck.

"No coat."

"Ah," he murmured, "but this is a much better way." And he continued his nibbling.

Her entire pelvis was coming alive in response. How could she concentrate on worrying about Waddy when he was doing that to her neck? "Stop that!"

"Really?" He nibbled up to her ear.

She was lost and she knew it, so turned to face him. "No, not really." He kissed her lips and she put a palm on either side of his face. Abruptly she pulled back. "Your cheeks are cold."

"It's January first."

"That's right, and you're on the porch with no coat."

"Whither thou goest...."

Without another word she took his hand and went back into the entrance hall. "Coffee, mister," she announced, leading him toward the kitchen.

"I'm fi...." he began to protest.

"Don't you dare say it!" she growled. "It's only been days since you had a tube jammed through your ribcage."

"Aren't we supposed to be worrying about Wadsworth and the bears?" He sat on a stool, accepting a steaming mug from her hand.

"You were letting me do all the worrying. There was a definite inequity of worrying going on."

"But he will be fine, Eden. He will."

"Did you know 'fine' is a four-letter word, my dear?"

He sipped his coffee, the corners of his mouth twitching, which made it rather more difficult. "Married life is proving to be very interesting, Mrs. Sinclair."

He said it with a smile but suddenly she was utterly stricken by the way she'd been behaving and turned, gripping the edge of the sink, tears welling again.

"Eden?" he said into her silence. When she still didn't answer, he set his mug on the counter, trailing his fingers along the Formica edge until he came to the sink. She was leaning forward over it, her hair hanging down. His hand moved up her back and he could feel the shaking of her soundless crying. "Oh, Eden! I didn't mean anything by that."

"It's not you," she said without turning. "It's me. I...I'm not doing this right."

"You're not doing what right, darling?"

"Being your wife. Loving you. I'm not doing any of it right."

He took her shoulders, turning her to face him. "You love me perfectly. Don't you know that?"

She shook her head and hiccupped. "No. I don't know that. You have no idea how wrong I do it."

"Because you worry? Do you mean because you worry about me?"

She nodded. "It's more than worry. I think I'm scared to death."

He thought of the sleigh accident Christmas Day, how he'd come back to himself only to find she'd completely collapsed, had retreated somewhere so far from conscious bearing of what had happened it had taken hours to revive her. He wanted to promise her he'd always be ok, had wanted to promise her that before, but you could never really promise such a thing. "I've put you through so much, my darling, way too much."

She hiccupped again, wiping at her face. "Only because you try to protect me."

"I couldn't let them take you, Eden, and I couldn't let you fall on the road. I just...."

"I know," she said, "I know, but maybe you have to let me fall. I can bear that better than losing you."

But he couldn't promise her that, either, so he just held her to him. "Can we be happy, darling? Right here in this minute we've got? Can we take that and just be happy in it?"

She sniffled. "Maybe...if the bears don't eat Waddy."

Just at that moment a series of sharp barks sounded at the front door. "He's here!" she gasped, breaking from his arms to sprint toward the door.

He was left standing in the middle of the kitchen, so began to walk rapidly after the sound of her footsteps, smiling as he heard her open the door and delightedly cry, "Waddy!" But he misjudged the location of the stool and walked right into it, knocking it over on its side, and falling with it onto his knees. He was still on all fours when Wadsworth burst into the kitchen and practically hurled himself atop Marshall, whom he considered to be in prime 'play' positioning.

Eden made it back to the kitchen just in time to see Waddy topple Marshall over onto his side. Her eyes took in the fallen stool and she shouted, "No, Waddy!"

But Marshall rolled onto his back and Wadsworth straddled him, furiously licking his face. "It's ok, Eden," he managed to get out, though his tongue got licked in the process. "He's just glad to see me."

She watched them a moment. Marshall had his hands buried in the thick fur of the dog's neck and Wadsworth's tail was beating a tattoo on the fallen stool. Marshall laughed, turning his head away from the licking a bit, but Waddy just went for his ear and he laughed again then wrapped his arms around the big dog, pulling him down onto his chest. And she saw the boy that was still in the man and she loved them all, the man, the boy, the dog. They were hers, hers to love, all of them. She squatted beside them and Wadsworth craned his neck out, swiping his tongue wetly down her cheek. "Happy New Year's, Waddy," she said. "Welcome home."

Marshall let go of Wadsworth with his right hand, reaching it out to her. "No bears," he said softly.

She took his hand, warm and vibrant with life, in both of hers. "No," she whispered, "no bears. Not today."

Chapter 73

About three in the afternoon Eden and Marshall, with Wadsworth along, drove over to Stuart's house. Neither of them mentioned anything about the sleigh they'd ridden in a week ago to do the same trip. Connie and Ryan were the first to greet them as they arrived at the door. Connie threw her arms around her cousin in a welcoming hug, but Eden flinched just a bit.

"What's the matter?" Connie asked, moving her arms away from Eden's shoulders.

"Curtain rod," Eden replied. Connie raised her eyebrows.

Ryan noticed a slight limp to Marshall's walk as he crossed the wide porch. "You hurt your leg, Marsh?"

"Kitchen stool."

Ryan looked at Connie then back at the newly-weds. "And just what sort of wedding night did you two...have?" Then he chuckled. "Sounds a bit rough."

Connie poked Ryan in the ribs. "Don't ask that, for Pete's sake."

Ryan chuckled again. "Why not? May be some useful information there."

Martha came bustling up. "Happy New Year's," she said warmly. "What's all this about kitchen stools and curtain rods?"

"We're not supposed to ask, Mom," Ryan added, rolling his eyes at Connie, "but I think they broke your inn last night."

"Oh, Ryan!" Connie poked him again.

"This morning, actually," Marshall said, quite calmly, and it was Eden's turn to roll her eyes. "Stool's fine and we rehung the curtains before we left," he added.

"Rehung...?" Martha's mouth dropped open a bit.

Ryan had to clap a hand over his mouth to keep from laughing out loud. Connie glared at him and he gasped out, "I'm not even gonna ask which room the curtains fell down in."

Connie grabbed his arm and dragged him out of the entrance hall, mumbling something about "uncivilized" as she went.

"Are you both all right?" Martha asked.

"Just a couple of bruised knees and a scraped shoulder," Marshall replied. Ryan was still close enough to hear and totally unable to stifle a big, snorting laugh.

The three still by the door turned as Mike's truck pulled up. He went around and opened the passenger door, handing Maria out.

"Mike's truck?" Marshall asked, recognizing the sound of the engine.

"He's brought Maria," Martha added, pleased. Ryan had called Mike after Maria had accepted the invitation to dinner, letting him know so he could offer her a ride if he wanted. Obviously he had wanted.

Ryan escaped Connie and still with a smile on his face came back when he heard Mike's arrival. The smile broadened when he saw Mike take Maria's hand as she stepped down from the high cab of the truck. Martha leaned close to her tall, slim son. "Pleased with yourself, are you?"

"This is a good thing, Mom. You know that."

She did, indeed. She'd known Mike for too many years not to have been aware of the expression on his face when he looked at Eden. She also knew how entirely Eden's focus was on Marshall. Mike would be hurt, was hurt. It had been inevitable. Then Connie and Ryan had immediately clicked. She couldn't be sorry about that. She just couldn't, but her heart ached for Mike's aloneness. Then last night at the wedding, well, after the wedding, it seemed someone might just have stepped into his circle of light. So she went forward to greet Maria with genuine warmth.

"I'm so glad you could join us today, Maria. You, too, Mike." She looked from him back to Maria. "Mike's been a part of this family ever since he was a boy." She didn't add *except for when he was married and his wife wasn't particularly fond of coming over here or to the inn.*

Maria smiled in return. She was an only child, raised by quiet, bookish parents, and wasn't used to such an enormous group of happily interacting family members. Mike knew this about her now and gave a gentle squeeze with his hand that still held hers.

Marshall, too, picked up the slight, soft hesitation in her voice and said something to her in Greek that made her stifle a small chuckle. The combination of that with the gentle pressure of Mike's large fingers served to get her past the noisy greetings on the porch. She was, she found, entirely glad she had come. Her eyes flickered briefly up to Mike's strong profile beside her.

Ryan, ever observant, saw the glance, closed his own eyes a moment and blew out a long breath.

"You ok?" Connie asked.

"I've been very ok for a week now," he grinned, opening his eyes and looking down at her. He touched her cheek with the back of his knuckles.

Her eyes misted over. "I don't know how I'm going to be able to leave tomorrow." Her chin began to tremble. "You'll. Hurry, won't you?"

"Cleveland holds very little attraction for me anymore," he said softly. "I'll be in Pittsburgh before the end of January. I promise."

The dinner at the big table was different in many ways from the one a week ago. There were no covert glances from Mike in Eden's direction. He'd settled quite comfortably into letting her sail off into the happiness she shared with Marshall. He would always be terribly fond of her, he knew, but it was an easy fondness now, uncomplicated by dreams. Ryan and Connie were no longer just getting to know one another. Marshall was a week further along in his recovery and was feeling much less tired than he had Christmas Day. Luke, though, still sat at Marshall's side and Wadsworth was mostly tucked under his chair. Wadsworth's job, his desire, was to be close to Marshall but the evenness of that had been disrupted so often in the last two months that it was hard for him to lay back and just trust any more that Marshall would always be near. So he rested his muzzle atop the toe of Marshall's left shoe and remained on the alert, not distracted from his vigilance even by the nearly overwhelming scents of food wafting down from the laden table. And there would be no sleigh ride to take them back to the inn.

Martha looked around the table, her gaze settling on first one and then another of those gathered around it. Tomorrow so many of them would be leaving. She watched Luke's eager little face turned up to listen to what Marshall was saying to him. Elizabeth and Dale were taking him home tomorrow. She worried about him, about the near inevitability of what the doctors said was coming for him. Marshall seemed to make it all seem better somehow, not so frightening. She was glad Luke had this time with him, wished, though, it could be more. Her eyes passed on to where Ryan was whispering something in Connie's ear. He was happier than she'd seen him in years. He'd said there were possibilities there. Watching the two of them, Martha didn't think possibilities was quite good enough a word. And if...? She let her mother's heart, her grandmother's heart linger on what that might mean. Connie would be family, real family, then, and if Connie were family, then Eden and Marshall would also be family. They might return for more gatherings like this, and Marshall might still be there for Luke. She wanted this table gathered like this again. She wanted it more than anything.

Mike laughed quietly and Martha looked at him. His attention was centered entirely on the lovely, quiet nurse beside him, and Maria would not be going far away, only into the town where the hospital was, the hospital Mike worked out of. *Thank You, God*, Martha whispered. *Thank You for all of it.*

After dinner, they gathered in the living room and Martha sat at the piano, playing a lot of the old standards. Marshall knew the words to them all and the others joined in when they, too, remembered lyrics. Martha loved it when Marshall sang as she played. She'd miss that. When she played *Wonderful, Wonderful Copenhagen* and his deep baritone filled the room, Ryan took Connie's hand and swept her out into the wide hallway, curving her around to the grand, full tones of the piece. Several of them sang *Scarlet Ribbons* and *Three Coins in the Fountain* together. It was all very old-fashioned, very warm, very together. Martha smiled as she played, as she sang, thinking this was as near to heaven as it could get on this earth for her. Her fingers moved into *Till the Clouds Roll By* and on through *On the Street Where You Live.*

"Come," Marshall urged, "let's all sing one more, all of us together." As they started to get to their feet and join him, he added, "This was the theme song of my family when I was a kid. We sang it more times than I can count. And you," he slid his right arm around Eden's waist, his left over Luke's shoulders, "are my family now."

So he led them into a happy, laughing rendition of Harry Woods' 1927 *Side By Side.*

"Oh, we ain't got a barrel of money...maybe we're ragged and funny...but we'll travel along, singin' a song...side by side. Don't know what's comin' tomorrow...maybe it's trouble and sorrow...but we'll travel the road, sharin' our load...side by side. Through all kinds of weather... what if the sky should fall...just as long as we're together...it doesn't matter, doesn't matter at all. When they've all had their quarrels and parted...we'll be the same as we started...just trav'lin' along...singin' a song...side by side."

And it seemed to him, there in that warm, loving room, that Jeffrey and his mother and father were singing, too. He smiled and laughed and blinked tears at the same time. He tipped his face toward the ceiling, mouthing silently, "I love you," then put his lips to Eden's ear and whispered, "I love you, Mrs. Sinclair."

Chapter 74

Edith rode back to the inn with Harold and Martha. She wanted to get her things, Connie's as well, packed up and ready for their departure in the morning. Ryan had taken Connie out for a while in his car, saying vaguely they'd be at the inn later. Marshall and Eden remained a bit longer after dinner, reluctant to say good-bye to Luke. Elizabeth and Dale were staying on at Stuart's, planning to get an early start from there.

Luke had come to where Marshall was seated on the couch and without preamble, climbed up onto his lap. "Marshy," he said, "it's Luke."

Marshall tried not to grin. "I sort of thought it might be you."

"Is it really all right?" Luke's voice seemed very small.

"Is what all right, Luke?"

"The darkness that you live in. Is that really all right?"

"Luke, it's not darkness for me." He'd tried to explain this before. Eden sat nearby, listening intently, and Elizabeth came and perched on the far arm of the couch. "It's hard to put it into words. For me, since I am never in the light that makes it true that I am also never in the dark."

"But is it...scary?"

"No, Luke, it's not scary. It's what I know. I have no need to be afraid of it because it's just how things are for me."

"But...," Luke's voice became almost inaudible, "I don't know it like you do. Won't that make it different for me?" Even though he was still so young, he'd obviously thought a lot about this.

"It would be somewhat different, yes," Marshall agreed. "I never had to get used to changes but, Luke, you've seen the clouds and the mountains and the far end of the field. You know what that's like and I can only try to imagine such things so some things are easier for me and some things are easier for you."

"Marshy, I'm worried about being alone in the darkness." His mother pressed her hand to her mouth.

Marshall wrapped his arms gently about the boy. "Close your eyes a minute, Luke." Luke did. "Am I still here?" Marshall asked and Luke whispered, "Yes, Marshy. You're there."

"Let me tell you something my mother told me when I was about your age that made me feel a whole lot better." He paused a moment, clearly hearing his mother's voice. "O Lord, You have searched me and known me; You know when I sit and when I rise, You know my thoughts from afar, my going out and my lying down and are familiar with all of my ways. Before a word is on my tongue, You know it completely, O Lord. You hem me in--behind and before--and have laid Your hand upon me. Where can I go from Your Spirit? Where can I run from Your presence? If I go up to the heavens, You are there; if I make my bed in the depths, You are there. If I take the wings of the morning and dwell in the uttermost parts of the sea, even there Your hand will guide me, Your right hand will hold me fast. If I say 'Surely the darkness will hide me and the light become night around me,' even the darkness will not be dark to You and the night will shine like the day for the darkness and the light are both alike to You."

He rested his chin lightly atop Luke's head. "That's part of Psalm 139, Luke. My mother used to read that to me a lot, and do you know what she told me it meant?"

"What, Marshy, what does it mean?"

"Even though there is a difference between light and darkness, God is greater than that difference. They don't exist for me, Luke, either light or darkness because of my blindness. God is bigger than all of it, larger than the world of light, undefeated by the darkest dark, and He's above it all, making them one by joining them together with His presence. He's the God of everything, Luke, absolutely everything and it doesn't matter where I live, whether it's dark or light because He is there, knows me, and I'm not alone, I'm never alone."

"Your Mom knew about all that?"

"She did, Luke. And she helped me understand it. So, just like I'm with you when your eyes are closed, just like I know you and I have my hands on you even in the dark, there's never a place you can go where He's not already there and never a place you can be where He can't put His hand on you."

Luke opened his eyes, looking seriously up at Marshall's face. "When you were left in the forest by the bad guys, was He there? Did you always know He was there?"

It was a profound question from one so young. He'd been trying to take the transcendent concept of Psalm 139 and put it into words a boy could understand. He'd always thought he understood it himself and, more often than not, he did walk in the knowledge of it, but he recalled all too well moments there on Coopers Ridge when he'd felt utterly, utterly alone, desperately lost in his aloneness. How could he explain that to Luke?

"There are great truths, Luke, things that simply are true whether we are resting in them or not. When I broke that branch and started down the long hill, I asked Him to guide me, to get me down, and I knew He was doing that but, yes, there are those times when we are just too sick and too tired and feeling so very lost that we can forget what we know and start to think it's all just up to us. It's what makes us human, and even though I'm all grown up, I still sometimes lost my sense of Him. It didn't mean He wasn't there or that He didn't know just where I was. It just meant I was too messed up to remember that. I wish I could say I didn't do that, but I did. The important thing is that no matter what I was feeling, He was still there. He never left, He never stopped knowing where I was. I just stopped knowing that He knew. It was me, not Him, and, in the end, I did get down the hill."

"If you didn't," Luke was very quiet, "would He still have been there?"

Marshall kissed the top of Luke's head. "Yes, Luke, He would have been there, even then."

"Does...does He get mad at us when we forget to know?"

"No, Luke, He doesn't get mad. He just stays with us and waits for us to remember."

Luke leaned into Marshall's chest. "I don't want you to go to Pittsburgh."

Marshall squeezed his eyes tightly shut a moment. "I know, Luke, I know, but we'll be together again. I promise. Nothing's going to keep me away from the inn."

"But I might not be able to see you, Marshy, by next Christmas." He closed his eyes.

"Then we'll still be together," Marshall breathed, "just like this."

Elizabeth let the tears roll freely down her cheeks as she watched the blind man holding her going-blind son, the two of them completely together. Eden, reaching back to put her hand on Elizabeth's arm, found herself thinking that just maybe Victor Hugo had a point. Maybe there was such a thing as that 'cavern of deep harmony.' Watching Marshall, it was easy to believe there was.

Back at the inn later that evening, Eden sat in Marshall's lap in the rocker in their room. It was what she wanted, just to have him hold her quietly and rock. Her eyes were closed and she let herself be entirely absorbed by the feel of his arms around her, the motion of the rocker. His cheek rested on the side of her head, his breath soft and warm on her hair. It was the ending of the first day of the new year and she was doing what he'd asked; she was resting in the happiness of the moment and it was enough.

They were staying on at the inn for a few more days. Marshall's house in Mount Lebanon hadn't been lived in for several months and he'd arranged for Sylvie, his mother's long-time housekeeper, to come in and get it ready for them. When he'd stay there from time to time rather than at the university, he'd sleep in his old bedroom, but he wanted something different from that to bring Eden home to so he'd asked Sylvie to arrange a complete refurbishing of the master bedroom suite that had been his parents'. He'd told her basically what he wanted done, that Eden herself would be adding to it what she liked after they got settled.

Home. He was going home and bringing a wife with him. The big stone house had seemed so empty for so long. It was why he stayed there so infrequently anymore. But now it would be a home again. He sat there with her cuddled in his lap, thinking of her there, there in that place that had been the center of his life from its very beginning. He'd stopped by briefly before coming to the inn early last autumn, he and Wadsworth walking through the rooms. There'd been a hollowness to it, as though all the sounds of all his memories echoed off the walls. Locking the door behind him, he'd had no idea when he'd return. His arms tightened slightly around her and his lips began to roam through her hair.

Chapter 75

It was quiet in the inn the next day. The family had scattered early, heading to their respective homes. After breakfast, Marshall and Eden went back up to their room.

"It will be a good time to write," Eden said as they went up the stairs side by side, closely followed by Wadsworth.

"I think I can manage to write," Marshall grinned, "for a while."

Eden settled at the computer. "Has anyone noticed our young couple is alone in the garden?" she asked.

"Not yet. Everybody's busy right now."
"Ok," Eden smiled. "Let me see...."

The sounds of the tree peepers grew louder in the night around Susannah and Morgan as they stood on the brick walkway. As was typical with Williamsburg houses, the front door aligned with the back, a wide hallway joining the two. Both doors stood open, permitting the evening breeze to cool the adjoining rooms, and the voices of the male guests, now congregating in the back parlor for cigars, brandy, and further intense discussion, floated out into the garden.
"Will they miss your presence," Susannah asked, "now that dinner is over?"
"Unlikely," he smiled down at her. "It was your father's own suggestion that I take my stained coat out to the kitchen."
"He suggested that?" How strange. Why had he simply not asked Micah to take the coat?
Again his mind raced, seeking for words. Everything that came to his mind was nothing he could say aloud. "I...," he began, but paused, unsure.

"Hmmm?" Eden said. "I think my own mind is racing to find words for Morgan to say."
"That's because it's the 1770's and he wants to do this...." He leaned over, nibbling her ear, kissed his way across her cheek until his lips found hers, surrounded hers, then a long moment later, "...but all he can do is stand there and call her Miss Wellington."

"...Miss Wellington," he breathed.

Marshall chuckled, "Took me literally, did you?"
"I take you any way I can get you, Dr. Sinclair."

Susannah held her breath. The night air was heady with the scent of herbs, of jasmine, and through the scent floated the sound of her name in his deep voice. Her hand lifted, her fingers spread delicately as though she might encounter her name there in the night and it would alight on her fingertip and she would feel the brush of its wings.
"What?" he asked, fascinated by the motion of her hand.
"Nothing," she whispered, "or possibly much." His presence made her feel confused, almost as though the bricks beneath her slippers had shifted position and she was no longer sure which way the path led. She swayed slightly, disoriented, and his hand came quickly, gripping her elbow.

"Ah, ha!" Eden said with a bit of a smirk. "You are going to let him touch her."
"So....?"

He felt the deep lace sewn there on her gown crush under his fingers, felt the slimness of her arm and was careful to support her but not bruise. "Sus...you...."
"I think I might need to sit for just a moment," she whispered, her feeling of disorientation only increasing as his hand clasped her arm.

Keeping his hand there, he guided her a short distance to one of the garden benches, seeing that she was seated and then squatting in front of her near her knees. "Should I get someone?" he asked, concerned.

"No. I am all right. Truly." His hand was gone from her arm, but she was entirely aware of his presence right there, low in front of her. "I do not know why I...," but she did. Somehow it was him. How could that be? That he was there in her familiar garden had made all her well-known pathways unstable and she was not even sure which bench she was seated upon nor which way led back to the house.

He watched her face there in the moonlight, saw a series of emotions pass over her features. "Susannah." It was said barely audibly, said in an overflow of tenderness that leaked out of his heart. He did not mean for her to hear it. He said it to himself, for himself.

But her ears were keen with much need of careful listening. What was it about his voice, about how he'd said Marietta and now her own name that made them sound so different? "Mr. Kent?"

He leaned forward. She'd said his name very softly.

"Mr. Kent?" she repeated and he leaned more, overbalancing himself and coming down hard on one knee, his right palm ending on the edge of the bench, dangerously close to her leg. He pulled himself away so quickly that he fell back onto his rear on the walkway. For several seconds he was utterly appalled, then it all began to seem quite ridiculous to him and he covered his eyes loosely with his hand and began to chuckle.

Susannah had no idea what to make of what was happening. She'd felt the slight brush of his hand down her leg, then his little gasp as he pulled back, heard the sound of his impact on the bricks. Nothing remotely like this had ever happened in the garden before. She needed to know what was going on, so she now leaned forward, stretching out her hand to find his face right there before her. He seemed to have a hand over his eyes and was shaking his head slowly as he laughed. "Mr. Kent?" she tried for the third time, her fingers lightly remaining on the knuckles of his hand.

His laughter ceased at her touch, but he left his hand there because she was allowing her fingers to stay. "I am," he whispered.

"You are...?"

"Mr. Kent, Morgan Kent," he smiled, peering at her through a gap in his hand.

Morgan. Ah, yes. How could that have slipped her mind? It was, perhaps, the things she'd heard him say to her angel that emboldened her, though she did drop her hand back onto her lap. "Morgan Kent. I think I am glad you came to dinner."

"I wished to meet Patrick Henry," he said, "...and other people."

"You must not let Mr. Henry bother you," she responded, remembering his sharp questioning. "He is an intelligent man, but passionate about his beliefs to the point of bluntness."

"I was not bothered," he replied truthfully. His attention, indeed, had been centered on dinner guests seated much more closely to him. "And your father is a gracious host."

"Though that he would send you to the kitchen still puzzles me," she commented, then was quiet as the sound of Mr. Henry's voice, raised loudly in defense of some point he was making, came from the house. "They will be at that for some hours yet." She let out a long breath then suddenly remembered he must be sitting on the walkway. "You have not injured yourself?"

He got his feet under himself and rose, dusting off his knee breeches. The evening had proven rather rough on his new suit. "I, too, am all right," he said, "just a new layer of Williamsburg dust." Williamsburg, he'd discovered very soon after his arrival, seemed often coated in a fine layer of dust that rose from the unpaved streets, settling on everything from the horse-blocks to flower petals. He was still patting at his pants when she stood.

"It must be very late," she murmured. "I should...." But she turned her head to her left and then to her right. Truly she had no sense of where she was.

"Is something the matter?"

"I...I don't know which way I should go." Then she bit her lip, hating that he should find her so helpless in her own garden. It was not an opinion she wanted him to have of her. She had simply never gotten so turned around out here before and felt embarrassed by it.

He had witnessed her sure steps earlier that day, so sure that he had not had any idea that she was blind. He did not understand that his presence was her handicap. She was extending her arm out to the right, hoping to encounter some marker that would set her aright. His slid his left palm under her searching hand. "May I?"

She paused. In this world she inhabited, the touch of a hand often came out of nowhere, was not there and then suddenly was. She was used to it, though it still often disturbed her, made her feel vulnerable, bringing to her attention yet again that though others had some way of knowing where she was, she could not know that of them until they chose to let her know. But his hand was warm under hers and she did not start at his touch. She wanted to say to him that this being directionless in her own yard was entirely unusual, that she was not some helpless girlchild who could not find her way, that she was perfectly competent in getting where she wanted to go, but the warmth of his touch was spreading along her arm and at the moment she barely knew up from down. What was the matter with her?

He stepped around beside her and she moved her free hand to her throat where her pulse was beating way too rapidly. "I believe this may be the way," he said softly.

"It...it is better if you simply let me rest my hand on your arm," she explained. "For me that is better."

"Of course," he replied, holding out his left elbow and moving her hand there. "I fear I am new at this."

"It is not the same for me. It is all I know."

"All?" he repeated, stopping again and looking down at her. "Always? You have never...?"

"I have never. No."

"But...."

"Ah, waste no pity on me, Mr. Kent. My life is beautiful and gentle. I am a lucky woman, very blessed."

Again his eyes roamed her moonlit features. Her chin was tipped and she was entirely sincere in her words. With his right hand he lifted hers from his left arm, lifted it to his lips for the merest brush of a kiss, then replaced it on his sleeve. "I, too, am glad I came for dinner."

"Mr. Kent," Micah had turned the walkway corner and appeared suddenly, "Myra say she finished all she can do for your jacket. Say to come'n fetch you from the garden." His eyes had widened considerably when he saw that Mr. Kent was standing there in the dark with Susannah's hand on his arm.

"Well, at least they seem to have made some progress," Eden sighed.

"Progress was a very slow process then," Marshall smiled.

"Speaking of progress, I was rereading what you'd written already about Morgan and the beginning of the Revolution. Don't you think we can keep an awful lot of that? We'd just need to work in more of the Susannah parts, but all that led into the war is fine the way it is."

"I was rather thinking that myself," Marshall agreed. "But speaking of progress of another sort...." He slid his hand down her throat.

"You do realize," she said, "that you are acting like a newly-wed and the progress of your hand will drastically curtail any Morgan might hope to make.

Chapter 76

"What about the old *'publish or perish'* thing for college professors?" Eden asked, buttoning her long coat just inside the front door. The family had scattered early, heading to their respective homes.

"You mean because we got so little written today?" Marshall was sliding on his gloves.

"Right. We didn't even get them out of the garden."

"You're in a hurry to do that?"

"Not really. I kinda like them out there. When they come in, it won't be the same, but I thought maybe you had some sort of deadline you needed to meet."

"I've already met my deadline. This is extra."

"You've met...what did you write? It was published?"

"It was. A thematic guide to American poetry."

"An anthology?"

"Not an anthology, more of a topical exploration."

They, along with a loose Wadsworth, were now going down the front steps, planning to walk out to the dock.

"What's that? What sort of topics?""

"Oh, things like life and death, suffering and joy, memory, time and change. I begin each chapter with a favorite quote of mine and then discuss the concepts that unify certain poems."

They reached the end of the dock, having passed where he'd collapsed after making his way out of the forest. "Suffering and joy," she whispered. "The inn has taught me more about both of those."

" I'm so sorry, darling."

"Sorry? About what?"

"That your suffering in this place has been centered around me."

Taking both his hands, she turned to face him. "So has my joy, Marshall, so has my joy."

"You're truly happy?"

"I don't think it's possible to be any more truly happy than I am now."

He leaned his face close to hers, his breath warm on her cold cheeks. She never took such things for granted, not anymore. She touched each moment that he was present to her, explored every nook, every crevice of its seconds then slid it deep inside her memory where it would be safe. "I love your breath," she murmured. He smiled and pressed his mouth to hers.

They stood there a long while, arms about each other's waists, listening to the now-familiar sounds of the winter lake. "Will you be sorry to go?" she asked.

"Only in that this is where I found you. If I were leaving you, then yes, I would be sorrier than I can imagine, but since we're going home together, no. I want very much to know the reality of your presence in that house." He was silent a moment, remembering how full of sound and life the house had been for so many years. The last time he'd stood there in the big living room, there had been only quiet. He thought about that from time to time, the starkness of the contrast. It was there he'd composed much of his chapter on loss.

"Can we go home soon?" she asked.

"Just a couple more days, darling."

"Then can we keep Morgan and Susannah in the garden a while longer?"

"Even after Micah has come?"

"I'd like for them to stay."

"All right. Let's give them more time."

"Mr. Kent will be along presently, Micah," Susannah said, startling both Morgan and Micah.

"But Miss Susannah, Myra'll flay me alive if I leave you out here with...."

"Then don't tell her."

"Miss Susannah!" Micah's eyes widened even more. "You never...."

"That's right, Micah. But I am right now. So you just go back to the kitchen and tell your sister that you found Mr. Kent and informed him his jacket was ready and he said he'd be there shortly. Right now he's examining the...the herb garden."

Morgan had his lips pressed together, trying to suppress a wide grin. He kept silent, letting her work it out.

Micah turned grudgingly, muttering something about how the devil had done caught the child, but he went, nonetheless, casting a few distrustful looks over his shoulder once or twice.

"I don't think he likes me," Morgan offered.

"He doesn't know you."

Morgan thought about that for a moment. Was she saying that she felt she knew him well enough to remain alone with him in the garden? "What if your father comes looking for you?"

"He saw me go upstairs during dinner. He won't come looking. Besides, Mr. Henry would be terribly insulted if father left the room during one of his speeches."

She continually surprised him. Just minutes earlier she'd seemed confused and a bit lost. Now she was standing there having arranged to spend more time in the garden, in the garden ...with him.

"Have you ever considered a career in espionage?" he asked rather boldly.

She laughed, a lovely soft sound that made him ache with the pleasure of her nearness. "I fear I have been quite forward," she continued. "What must you think of me?"

He had too many answers for that, so many they stumbled over one another and only a small, "That you are lovely, indeed," made it into sound.

"You see, Mr. Kent...."

"Morgan," he interrupted. "Please? If it's at all all right, please?"

"You see, Morgan, if I were not blind, I would never consider doing this, doing what I've just done, but I cannot see your face, cannot know in the ways that everyone about me seems to know, the manner of man you are by your outward appearance." She laid her hand on his arm. He jumped slightly, surprised again. "All I have is what I know from touch, from the sound of your voice, the scent of the pomade in your hair."

She stopped, somewhat appalled at herself. Usually she sat quietly, waiting for such information as she could gather to come to her. Now she found herself reaching out, almost taking it. It was entirely new, rather heady, but Micah had come and Morgan was about to follow him to the kitchen. She was not ready that this moment with him should end. If Myra knew.... She hoped, though, that Micah would not tell. Even if he did, even if she had to face Myra's scolding, it would be worth it. She'd arranged this moment. For the first time, ever, she'd arranged a moment. Did he find her exceedingly forward? Was there time these days for all the required reticence? War was coming. The distant voices of her father's dinner guests confirmed that. Perhaps Morgan would have to sail for England before such things became impossible? Perhaps he would never be alone in her garden again? No, she was not ready that this moment should end.

"Susannah," he said, this time to her, for her. He was still somewhat in a state of shock, so unexpected was what she had done, but the name, her name, had to be spoken. What was he to do now? They were standing just around the corner from the central path that led directly to the open back doorway. That he was here with her was such an entire breach of acceptable behavior on his part that...damn it! Did he care?

"Come," he urged, "sit with me on the bench in the herb garden." Then, at least, what she'd told Micah about examining the herbs would be true. This time he knew to extend his bent arm, to let her rest her hand atop it, as they walked back down the brick walk. He was very aware of her skirts moving against his leg and had to control his breath, making it regular and even with great effort.

She sat well to one side, leaving room for him, pressing her skirts to herself. When he settled beside her, she let go of them and they billowed out again, nearly covering his right leg. He gasped as though her hand had touched his thigh. Hearing the sound he made, she turned her face toward him in the moonlight. "Have I done something amiss?"

"You could not. Ever." He whispered the words, finding it hard to believe he was actually sitting here with her.

"I would not ask Myra that," she smiled, "nor even Micah."

"You have asked me," he replied, "and you could not." Words were so hard to come by. His lips were dry, his tongue thick in his mouth. He was dreaming. He'd gone back to his room

in the boarding house and he was dreaming. None of this was real. Nothing like this could be real. That must be it.

"Tell me, Morgan," she said, "about your home in Kent. Where were you born?" She knew nothing like that about him yet she knew already everything.

"Reculver," he replied, "a small and very old town on the eastern coast. There is a church there that the sea will take some day."

"Have you family?"

"A sister, older, married and the mother of four. And my father, of course."

"You have always lived there?"

"Not always, no. My father has many business ventures because of his shipping company. He has always liked to check on things in person, so I grew up going wherever he happened to be."

"And schooling?"

"A tutor who traveled with us. Father wished for me to learn all the modern European languages. When I was older, I went to Harrow." He shrugged. "I am expected some day to take over the shipping company."

"And is this what you wish to do?"

It had never been entirely what he wished to do, more what he was expected to do. Right now he had no reply. All his wishes seemed centered on the slim form so near beside him.

"Morgan?"

"Pardon?" he whispered.

"Is this what you wish to do?"

"No one has ever really asked me, Susannah, what it is I wish to do. I find myself bumbling for some answer."

"I understand," she said softly, her hand finding his forearm again. "Though I have known only kindness and love, I am expected to agree with all that anyone considers best for me. I am cared for like a pot of heliotrope, watered, tended, and have nothing asked of me but to sit there, look pretty, and smell nice."

His smile widened and, without thinking, he laid his hand atop hers. "I think I am beginning to understand that there is ever so much more to you than a pot of heliotrope."

She had not flinched when his hand came unexpectedly atop hers. It was large and warm and felt wonderful there. "My father built this garden for me." She tipped her head. "He wanted to make a place for me to be free in, not just inside the house. Here, yes, it is for me the heart of the world, of my world. Still because of my eyes, because there is simply nothing to be done about them, I am more often than not a flowerpot. I have so often wished...."

"What, Susannah, what have you wished?"

"That there were some way for me to read. All by myself, to read what I want to read."

"No Braille?" Eden asked.

"Not yet."

"I hadn't really thought of that. No wonder she feels like a flowerpot."

"And no Wadsworths, either."

"Everything I know from books," Susannah continued, "has been read to me. Not everybody reads aloud all that well, you know. It can be hard to get the feeling of something when it's being read by a flat voice, or a stumbling one." It occurred to her then that he probably read aloud quite wonderfully.

He was thinking about how many lines of type his own eyes had scanned, how it might feel if he could not do that, had never been able to do that. Into his silence she said, "But you must know, Morgan, that I require no pity."

"Susannah, I do not wish to pity you. I want only to understand."

"I am not sure it can be done."

"It can be...tried."

"Why would you do that?"

"It matters. You have taken my breath away this day , Miss Susannah Wellington, and understanding you suddenly matters a great deal."

"You do not mind?"

"Mind?"

"That I cannot see you?"

"I think, perhaps, you have seen me, indeed."

She turned toward him more and he removed his hand from atop hers. "May I?" she asked, lifting her hand toward his face. "It is, of course, not the same at all, but it gives me some little idea."

He didn't know, at first, what she meant, but her hand sought out his cheek and her fingertips moved up and around his face. He closed his eyes, letting her hand go where she willed, scarcely breathing because of the intimacy of it all. No one had ever touched his face like that and he nearly trembled under her seeking fingers. They did not speak. There was only the rustle of the mulberry leaves, the always-present night peepers, the distant murmur of male voices, a carriage passing down Nicholson Street. He floated in the moment, scarcely feeling as though he were touching the bench.

Again she had surprised herself, asking a man she'd only just met if she could touch his face. She'd actually felt very few faces, her father's, Layla, Myra, her Aunt Clara, who lived in Richmond. It was not something one did casually, but here she was, running a fingertip down his fine, strong nose, discovering that he had straight brows and a cleft in his chin. It was a very different face than her father's. She'd been thinking for some minutes that she wanted to touch it, wanted to know more of what he was like. He was tall. At 5'2" herself she knew that from standing next to him. Her father was only 5' 6". She liked the sense of height she got from being near him.

He did jerk slightly when her fingertips found his lips. Her touch there was nearly more than he could bear, was more than he could bear in absolute stillness. His entire body was awake, almost vibrating. She had no idea what her touch was doing to him. His lips parted under her fingers, his breaths coming in short little puffs.

She pulled her hand away. "Are you all right?"

"No," he whispered, opening his eyes, "I am not."

"What...?"

"Susannah. Have you any idea how much I want to kiss you?" There, he'd said it. As unconscionable of him as it was to have said it, he had. Now she would want to leave. He'd ruined it. It wasn't done. It simply was not done like that.

She pulled back a little, licking her lips. Parker Harrelson had kissed her once, lightly, briefly on her cheek. Parker's father owned one of the big plantations up the Neck from Williamsburg, but kept a house in town as well. Parker was twenty-three, rather spoiled, but had paid a great deal of attention to her in the last couple of years. She had never once even thought of touching his face, however. Layla said it was evident from the way Parker looked at Susannah, that he'd probably be asking her to marry him one of these days. The prospect had never been all that exciting to her. Though her father and Parker's were friends, Harmer was not terribly pleased about the match, either. He didn't trust Parker. The man was too fond of himself. He'd expressed that opinion to his daughter more than once.

Morgan waited a moment, then gathered his muscles to stand. "I...." He started to apologize, but she put her hand back on his arm.

"Morgan Kent," she said, "I think I might like that."

"You...?" Morgan sucked in a long breath. This was not real, but she leaned toward him somewhat and lifted her chin. Nearly dazed at first, he moved his right hand up, touching her hair, then ever so gently sliding it behind her head, guiding her face to his. His lips found hers, just grazing lightly across them, then moving back, cupping over her upper lip a moment, then down to her lower. He wanted desperately to surround her mouth with his, to plunge inside it, but he had just enough reason left in his brain to control himself. He pressed both his lips to hers, only slightly touching the tip of his tongue to hers, almost moaning with his wanting of her.

It was the most purely male encounter she'd ever had and something deep in her belly seemed to flip right over. It was the most natural thing in the world for her to return the pressure of his lips. As she did, his kiss became even more ardent until he suddenly pulled completely away.

"I can't...I must...," he stammered, wiping a hand roughly across his face. He stood, walked about five paces away, came back and sat quickly again. Wordlessly, he gripped her shoulders, pulled her to him, and kissed her absolutely thoroughly.

Her mind swam, fell off whatever platform it usually sat serenely upon, spinning on some unknown ground that had suddenly come into existence inside her soul. Her belly flipped again and something strange and new flowed up and down the nerve paths of her lower torso. She...wanted. She had not known what wanting was, but her body, her being, wanted his.

He felt it, felt her yielding in his arms, felt his control entirely slipping away. "No," he gasped, hating the word even as he said it. He straightened his arms, hands still on her shoulders, holding her away from himself. "You...I....it's not...I...."

She managed a little smile, though she was panting slightly through parted lips. Nothing, she knew it, nothing would ever be quite the same again. His hands dropped and he started to stand. "I should go," he whispered hoarsely. "I...."

She was reaching a hand out toward him and he took it, letting her pull it to her face where she buried her cheek in his palm. She showed no indications of letting it go, so he stood quietly, watching the moonlight on her bowed head, his mind racing. Finally he squatted in front of her, his hand still pressed to her cheek. "I love you," he said, his voice catching. "I love you already, Susannah Wellington, and I don't know what to do about it."

"Stay," she whispered, turning her cheek so that she could kiss his palm. "Don't go back to England."

Chapter 77

'Stay,' she had said and suddenly everything back in England, his father, his older sister, the shipping company, all of it, seemed worlds away, was, in fact, worlds away. He ran his fingertip down her cheek in the moonlight. He had come to the New World and found her. Everything was new here; he was new here. In the night, with the breeze tossing the tree canopies, he was aware of the vastness of the land beyond where he sat. It went on endlessly, so far as anyone knew, mysterious, mostly unexplored...new. He felt himself becoming one with it in its sudden likeness to himself, to all that he was feeling. What would he do if he should stay? How would he earn a living? And war was coming. This new land would be taking up arms against the old. If he stayed, he would inevitably find himself a part of that. His father would never understand, never forgive. He would be cut off from all he'd known, all that was familiar to him. Yet Susannah had laid her hand atop his now and by the simple act of that, had branded his soul. He knew this woman. All his life he'd known her. He just had not found her yet, not until this day.

"Morgan?"

"Forgive me. My thoughts are like wild birds blown in the wind." He tipped his head down, the imagery of that clear in his mind. "I'm casting my nets, seeing what I can gather."

"Thoughts of England?"

"Yes, of England...of many things."

She turned her head away and up. "I had no right to ask such a thing of you."

With his fingertips he gently turned her face back toward his. "You have more rights than you can imagine, my Susannah."

She was not sure why or how he could say such a thing. She only knew that in this night, in this garden, she was no longer the same person she had been a few hours ago. He sat beside her, one of his hands still lying beneath hers, and his presence radiated across the small space between them more vividly than any presence she had ever known. She simply 'felt' him as though every cell of her body were in contact with his.

"I know that feeling," Eden smiled, turning from the computer to touch Marshall's face.

"It's how my body responds to yours," he said softly, "even when we are not touching." He kissed her hair. "There are times when your soul passes through mine and my soul bends with the movement of it like a willow in the breeze."

Eden blinked back sudden tears. "I think," she whispered, "that I know the fullness of what it is to love you and then you come and pour more of yourself into me and I understand that my concept of fullness is so inadequate."

He smiled. "It's what life is about, you know, awareness, becoming steadily more aware."

A sudden sound of carriages, of horses being mounted, of men's voices saying their farewells beyond the front pickets, interrupted the moment.

"Oh, my!" Susannah cried softly. "Is it that late? Father will...."

"Come," Morgan said, standing, holding her hand. "I'll walk with you near to the turning of the path. When you have gone inside, I shall wait a few moments, then go to the kitchen for my coat."

Together, they went quickly down the brick walk. Morgan peered around a large boxwood toward the back of the house and when he was satisfied no one was there, turned back to Susannah. "It seems all right. I think no one will see you should you go up the back stairs."

She took one step to go, then stopped. Despite the awkwardness that would ensue should they be discovered, she found it simply terribly hard to walk away from him.

When she'd taken her hand from his, he'd felt a nearly physical pain. Then she stopped and he took her in his arms, pressing her close against him, his lips warm, almost desperate, on hers. He had not kissed her like this, standing, the length of her against the length of him, and he was completely staggered by it. Only because he must, did he finally release her.

"Go...quickly," he whispered hoarsely, his lips brushing one last time over hers. Then, his hand gripping a branch for support, he watched her slip down the central walk and to the side where a small door led to the back stairway. She paused once on the single outside step, turning back toward the garden, then opened the door and was gone.

He stood quietly, his hand still tight around a twisty branch. He did not yet trust his legs alone to support him. Trying to keep some awareness of how many minutes were passing eluded him. His mind was not at the moment capable of such prosaic thoughts so he simply stood there, leaning slightly forward, breathing through his mouth. After a while he lifted his head, looking at the moon through the branches of the tree. It did seem to have sailed somewhat further on its course through the night, so he released his grip, suddenly aware that his palm and fingers were stinging from the tightness of his hold on the bark. Rubbing his hands together to ease that, he went to the turning and made his way to the kitchen.

A single candle guttered on a long table, casting feeble shadows around the room. Myra had gone, but his jacket hung on the back of a wooden chair. He lifted it off, but did not put it on. The night was still too warm, the jacket damp. He went outside, standing there a while, contemplating the back door of the house. It was closed now for the night. He had not taken his leave of his host. What must Mr. Wellington think of his manners? Well, nothing to be done about it now. He would have to think of some explanation for his continued absence from the dinner. Noting that a portion of the walkway led to a side gate, he moved in that direction. When he was about halfway to the gate, a male voice said quietly, "Good night, Mr. Kent."

His forward motion halted as suddenly as though he'd been shot and his head snapped to the side. The moon had disappeared beyond a cloud, leaving the garden quite dark, and all he could make out was the end of a lit pipe.

"Sir?" he said hesitatingly.

"It's me, Wellington," came the voice. "I often sit here in the late evening, having a quiet smoke, enjoying the air."

"I did not see you, Sir."

"I know," the voice replied with just a hint of a chuckle.

Morgan turned to face the still unseen form, able to locate Wellington only by the presence of his pipe. "I wanted to...." he began.

"I trust Myra improved the condition of your coat?"

Morgan lifted the arm his coat hung across. He'd not actually taken the time in the dim room to examine it and now he could not see it at all. "Quite fine," he said nevertheless. "Please extend my gratitude to her."

The glowing end of the pipe tipped briefly down as Harmer nodded. "And the garden. I trust you found it an adequate place to wait?"

"I...yes...um...yes, Sir. It is a most excellent garden."

"Did you enjoy the smell of the herbs?"

"Herbs. Yes. Great smell. Very fine. Yes."

"You missed some excellent conversation, I fear."

"Yes. I know. I'm sorry about that, Sir. In future I shall try to be more careful with my wineglass."

"George Wythe asked that I bid you good night for him."

"Oh? Yes. He is a fine man, Mr. Wythe is. I've gotten very fond of him."

"And he of you, so it seems."

"Really? Well, I've been honored to spend time in his company. He is very wise on matters of...of...current import."

"And how do you feel, Mr. Kent, if I might ask, on matters of current import?"

"Um. Well, Sir, I find my feelings to be in rather much of a flux right now. Much that is new to me is rapidly becoming very, um, important."

"It sounds, Mr. Kent, as though you have a great deal of thinking to do."

"Yes," he agreed simply.

"Well, then, best be getting on home so you may do so." Harmer was smiling broadly at the young man, though Morgan could not see.

"Yes, Sir. You're probably right, Sir. Well, good night, Sir. I thank you with all my heart for allowing me to come for dinner. I am...most grateful and obliged."

"Good night, Mr. Kent. Watch that high brick just before the gate."

"Good night, Sir. Thank you again." Morgan hurried through the darkness toward the gate, tripping over the brick.

Harmer stood, walked out on the path as the moon sailed free, watching Morgan fumbling with the gate latch. "Parker Harrelson," he murmured to himself, "you may just have met your match."

Eden had been writing both Harmer and Morgan and sat back with a satisfied grin. "So," Marshall said, as she read aloud what she'd written, "you intend for there to be a rivalry?"

"Someone needs to be a Patriot and someone a Tory, you know. I find it interesting that the native-born Virginian will fight for England and the newly-arrived Englishman will fight for Virginia."

All along Marshall had had Morgan becoming a Patriot, eventually under Lafayette's command. Now that he was rewriting the book with Eden taking an active role, he had let her rather take the lead on where the romantic side of the story might go. His thematic guide was done, and he'd decided the novel and its coming changes would be a good bonding time for him and Eden, a chance to work together to a mutual end, to feel out how one another approached story-building. It was new to him, this give-and-take in writing, a release of his usual full control over the actions of his characters, but with Eden he found he enjoyed it.

"And what unit will Parker fight with, do you think?" he asked.

"Simcoe. That seems most logical as most of his Rangers were Virginians anyway."

"Well, then, I guess we'd better bring young Mr. Harrelson more into the storyline, eh?"

"Tomorrow," Eden replied. "Right now I'm a bride in desperate need of attention."

"Hmmmm?" he said, thoughtfully tapping his chin. "I just might have some attention to spare."

"You better, mister," she laughed, rising and backing him toward the bed.

CHAPTER 78

Morgan paused just outside the picket gate, leaning back on it. He felt like a complete idiot. Susannah's father had taken him totally by surprise there in the dark. How long had he been there? He wiped a palm over his face, feeling sweaty. Then he'd gone and tripped over the brick right after Wellington had warned him about it. Damn!

Entirely distracted, he cut down Botetourt Street, heading for Duke of Gloucester. A cold tankard of ale. Yes, that was what he needed! The Raleigh would still be open. Half-way down Botetourt, though, he stepped into the midst of a very large road apple. It's scent, instantly released fully into the humid, night air, rose up around him, making him gag. He saw a small wooden bench not far away, and made for it. As he sat there, not ten feet from Duke of Gloucester street, holding his shoe gingerly with one hand while scraping at its bottom furiously with a small stick he'd found, a tall form paused on the corner of the intersection.

"Would that be you, young Kent?"

Morgan held the stick still, peering at the source of the male voice. The outline of the form was familiar to him and could belong to none other than George Washington. "I...," he began, but stopped, aware of the unpleasant nature of his current engagement.

Washington began to walk toward him. "Oh, God," Morgan moaned to himself. He'd just made a fool of himself in front of Wellington, and now here came Washington.

"You are all right?" Washington asked, concerned at Morgan's cut-off reply.

"I am fine, sir," Morgan said, standing on one leg, keeping his sock-clad foot a bit in the air. "Just a small inconvenience, I fear."

Washington cocked an eyebrow, smelling the inconvenience clearly. "Ah, I see." He smiled and sat on the bench. "Do continue, Mr. Kent."

"But...but...sir?"

"The digestive by-products of the equine world and I are well-acquainted. As a farmer, I have found it inevitable."

Morgan, more familiar with what was said about this man than with the man himself, hesitated.

Washington patted the bench beside him. "Sit, Mr. Kent, if you wish to remove it before it crusts."

Morgan couldn't help himself. He let out a small, delighted laugh. Washington looked up at him, a slight grin curving his lips. "You find me amusing?"

Morgan sat. "I find you...real...sir. I was not sure that was actually the case."

Now Washington laughed, more of a deep, rumbling chuckle. "Just don't tell anybody about that. We shall keep it between ourselves, you and I, that bit of information."

Morgan began to scrape carefully at his shoe again, very aware of how each movement of his stick through the horse dung stirred its scent afresh. Washington tipped to his right, scanning the ground, then leaned down. "Here," he said, handing a larger stick to Morgan, "this may prove a more useful tool."

Taking the stick, Morgan paused in his cleaning task. "You were born here, were you not? Right here in Virginia?"

"I was, indeed. It is my great honor to call myself a Virginian."

"I'm trying to understand what that's like, sir, what it means to the heart and the mind to be a Virginian."

"You have decided to become one, Mr. Kent?"

"I'm not sure, not sure of anything right now, sir. I didn't think...I never planned...."

"Mr. Kent, let me ask you something."

"Sir?"

"Do you know how it is we make God laugh?"

"Sir?"

"We tell Him our plans." He patted Morgan's knee.

"Oh!" Morgan was rapidly losing his power of coherent thought. First Susannah in the garden, then Mr. Wellington by the house, now George Washington and God and the horse manure here in the quiet night. None of them said, did, things that Morgan expected they would. His jacket, which had been lying across his right thigh, chose that moment to slip to the ground.

Washington reached it before Morgan even began to move. "This, I presume, is the jacket upon which the wine was deliberately spilt?"

"The...deliberately?"

"It was a gentlemanly thing you did. Miss Wellington was most discommoded at the dinner table."

"I...I didn't think anyone...knew...that. About my jacket, I mean."

"You sat at table, young Mr. Kent, with some of the most observant men in the colonies." Washington smiled, handing the jacket to Morgan.

Morgan had set his shoe down, resting his sock foot atop the other. "I'm sorry I did not get to be a part of the after-dinner conversation."

"There will be other times, I am sure. Some evenings there are more important things to tend to than conversation."

Good Lord! Did everyone know he'd been in the garden?

"This interest in Virginia, is it serious?" Washington continued.

"It seems to be becoming steadily more so, sir."

"Well, stay close to George Wythe. Any questions you have, he will have the answers to."

"You feel certain that war is coming?"

"I see little way these days that it may be avoided. It is not a thing I would choose, being all too familiar with the means and effects of war, but if it comes, it will be fought with more heart and courage than England may expect to face."

"You've been a part of the British army yourself, though. I don't understand how...."

"Virginia," he said softly. "That is what it comes down to, son, Virginia. The past will not matter if war comes, only that Virginia be safe."

"But Braddock," Morgan continued, stubborn in his lack of understanding. "Back in England, we know the stories, how brave you were there with Braddock when the French and Indians ambushed."

Washington chuckled again. "Stories, eh? The truth of the matter is that I had been so sick with influenza during the march toward the Forks of the Ohio that I had to ride in one of the wagons. During the Battle of Monongahela, I could barely sit my horse." He leaned back a little, lacing his fingers, remembering."Two horses were killed under me, though. Came down hard and it was even harder for me to get back up. Later, I counted four balls that had gone through my uniform." He sighed. "But that is simply the way it is for a soldier. He fights even when he cannot stand." His gaze locked on Morgan. "If you stay in Virginia, you may discover this for yourself."

"I know," Morgan whispered.

"It is something that must be considered. All of us face many hard choices in these times." He stood, straightening his jacket. "I must be on my way."

"Thank you, sir," Morgan said, standing as well, balancing carefully. "I am glad you, you... stopped by."

Washington chuckled again, nodding down at Morgan's boot. "Good luck with that. It is a common hazard one faces afoot in the Williamsburg dark."

Morgan stood, watching Washington's figure until it disappeared around the corner. Then he sat heavily, his mind filled with what they'd talked about. Yes, hard choices, many hard choices, but Susannah's face came, dancing before the eyes of his memory. Some choices just might come more easily than others.

"I both am eager to go and reluctant to leave," Eden sighed, snapping her largest suitcase shut. She sat down on the bed beside it, looking around the room that had become so familiar, so full of memories. Marshall was coming through the bathroom door, a small kit of supplies in his hand. Marshall. All of it, every single bit of it, centered around, on, and in him.

"Would you like to stay longer? We can."

"No, I'm ready to walk in the door of your house."

"Our house," he corrected with a smile.

"Our house. I need to make memories there, too."

Setting the kit down atop the dresser, he moved toward her, his hand running along the suitcase until he found her. Squatting in front of her, he took both her hands in his. "This means the world to me, Eden, that you should be coming to live there. I'm not sure I can really convey all it means to me. The house, it was always, has always been such a part of me. My roots are there, going down under the foundation stones of it in a way that they can never be pulled." He kissed her hands, his face very serious, then continued. "When I'd be away from it and know I was coming back, my thoughts would fly, like birds, ahead of me, but I lost that. For two years now the birds have not wished to fly. I'd still think of it often. It just came inevitably to mind. It's so connected with the how and the why of me, but my nostalgia for it became more of a despair that the life of it was gone."

He licked his lips. "When I was little, I used to imagine I could hear the heartbeat of the house. It was very real to me, but the heartbeat stopped and the silence it left in the house was a heavy, dulled thing. Now you come to it and I know, I simply know, that I shall hear its heartbeat again. It will be home, Eden, a thing it's not been for way too long."

Eden tended to think in terms of what Marshall brought to her life, the change, the veritable lifting he'd caused, not what she might bring to him. Leaning forward, she kissed the top of his bowed head. "How do I love thee? Let me count the ways," she murmured. "I can hardly wait."

She opened the bedroom door, a couple of bags in her hands, to find Mike standing there, poised to knock.

"Mike!" she greeted, smiling. "I'm so glad you came."

"Hadda come say good-bye, you know," he replied. "Thought I could give a hand, too, with the bags." He looked into the room, spotting Marshall. "Hey, there. Got a bag I can help wrestle down the stairs?"

"Hello, Mike," Marshall said, holding out his hand. "I'm pleased we don't have to leave without my having a chance to tell you again how grateful I am for all you've done, for all you've been."

Mike came into the room, shook Marshall's hand, then stooped to ruffle Wadsworth's fur. "All three of you have been really special to me."

"Where's Maria?" Eden asked.

"She's on duty right now. Asked me to say her good-byes for her."

"And how's that going?"

"Goin' just fine, Eden. Just fine."

"I'm glad, Mike," Eden smiled. "Really glad."

Mike went over to the dresser. "I 'spect you're plannin' on takin' this dollhouse thingamajig?"

"Definitely," Eden laughed. "In fact, I'd appreciate it if you'd carry it out to the car for me."

"You got it!" Mike said, picking it up as well as curling his fingers through a big suitcase handle.

Martha and Harold were waiting by the front door. "I'm going to miss you all," Martha said, holding out her arms to hug Eden. She was blinking hard, trying to hold back tears. "Never had guests before who became part of the family." She gripped Marshall's arm. "Who's going to appreciate my cookies now?"

"I'll still be around, Martha!" Mike called back over his shoulder as he crossed the porch. "You ain't gettin' rid of me."

"We'll be back, Martha," Marshall said. "This place means a lot to us. You mean a lot to us. I hope you know that."

"I do," Martha sniffed, her chin quivering. "I've just gotten so used to you all being here. It's going to seem empty without you."

When the final good-byes were said, the car all loaded, Wadsworth sitting in the back seat beside the dollhouse, Eden backed slowly out of her parking place. Martha, Harold, and Mike were all beside the house, waving. She described it for Marshall and he waved back.

"What a monumental difference a choice of inn makes," he commented as they headed for the road.

"Don't it just!" Eden said firmly. "Don't it just!"

Marshall laughed, moving his hand to her right leg. "I love you, Mrs. Sinclair."

Chapter 79

"That was interesting," Marshall commented as Eden drove them southwest away from the inn.

"What was interesting?"

"That section you wrote with Washington and the horse manure. I never really thought of them in the same sentence before."

"You never wrote a book with me before," she laughed. She had written that entire encounter on Botetourt Street by herself.

"Are we there yet?"

"Are you going to say that a lot?"

He chuckled. "For some reason I just had to ask that."

"Pest!" she chortled.

"Are we there yet?"

Her shoulders shook with repressed laughter. "And here I thought you were a dignified professor."

"I am dignified," he replied, sitting up even more straight and squaring his shoulders. "Are we there yet?"

"Did you do that to your parents?"

"Constantly." He shrugged. "When you can't see where you are, it becomes a more valid question."

"I know," she said softly, briefly lying her hand atop his where it rested on her leg. "What are the birds doing?"

"The birds?"

"Your birds. Are they flying ahead of you to Mount Lebanon?"

"Oh, them. They've already been back there for some time now."

"What kind of birds are they?"

"Homing pigeons," he grinned.

"And what do these pigeons do when they get there?"

"They roost. Somewhere high. And preen their feathers while they roll their beady little eyes waiting for me to come."

"Ooo," she mock-shuddered. "They won't keep me awake at night, will they?"

"Oh, no. That I plan on doing myself."

They paused for coffee in Altoona, then headed west on 22. "Let's have lunch in Murrysville," she suggested. "I'd rather not have to think about finding food when we get to Mount Lebanon."

"Sounds good to me," he agreed.

She pulled into the parking lot of a restaurant called 'Dick's Diner'. "Looks kinda like an Eat 'n Park," she explained as she cut the engine, "only the sign says it's family-owned, not a chain." As they waited a moment to be seated, she eyed the pies behind the counter. "We'll have to have a piece of pie. I've never seen such giant, thick meringues in my life."

"They have lemon meringue?" he asked.

She peered more closely. "Looks like."

"Good. My favorite."

"I didn't know that."

"What's your favorite?"

"Strawberry-rhubarb."

"Well, I didn't know that so we have some intense pie-finding-out to do, it would seem." He grinned at her, his hand locating the back of her neck, his fingers caressing it.

"Marshall," she whispered, "the people at that first table are staring at us."

"Staring people have never bothered me. Not once."

She stepped lightly on his foot. "I have plenty of plans to bother you."

"Are you making promises again?"

"You bet'cha."

"Dogs aren't allowed," a plump waitress said, coming up and stopping in front of them.

"Guide dog," Eden replied, indicating the harness.

"Hmmm? He's big. Let me see if I can find a table out of the way."

"Behind a large plant in front of the entrance to the rest rooms will be fine," Eden said.

Marshall snorted, his shoulders shaking. "You're bad," he said softly, his lips nearly in her hair.

"You ain't seen nothin' yet, big boy. Just you get me home and I'll show you bad."

He lost it then, a full-out laugh escaping. Putting a hand over his mouth, he shook his head. Then, suddenly serious, touched her hair. "You make me laugh." He blew out a long breath. "I haven't laughed much for a while." His hand traced down her hair, finding her lips so he knew exactly where they were. He kissed her, right there in the entryway of Dick's Diner. "Thank you," he murmured.

Eden, after his kiss, saw past his shoulder into the main area of the restaurant. Every eye was on them. The corner of her mouth twitched. She didn't mind. It was true, she didn't. Marshall was smiling, Wadsworth was pressed against the fronts of their legs, and they were almost home. She was filled with an overflow of both gratitude and happiness. "We just got married," she announced loudly, smiling widely. Everyone in the room clapped, a few of them calling out congratulations or whistling, and Marshall, never once having been bothered by stares, kissed Eden again.

"This is it?" Eden asked, pulling into the drive that ran along the left-hand side of a large stone house.

"If it's 333 Mayhaven, it is," Marshall replied. "Until I get out of the car, I have no real way of knowing."

"It's big."

"Try to imagine it in spring. There's a huge difference to the feel of the yard."

In January, patches of snow lay here and there, mostly close to the several large oaks that graced the lawn. She could see that there was a rhododendron in front of a bay window, but most of the shrubs and plantings had lost their leaves and she couldn't identify them. Marshall had always described it as a big house, but she'd never quite imagined it was this big. Her mind flashed to her one-bedroom apartment about twenty minutes away.

She sat silently in the car a moment, just staring at the front of the house. It looked big enough to be two or three fairly large houses all put together. Because of the different levels of the tiled roofline and the way sections of the house stuck out further than other parts, that joining together of more than one house seemed even more real. It was made of stones in many shades, going from light beige to darker brown. All the windows she could see on the front of the house had leaded, diamond-paned glass. Yes, this was definitely Mount Lebanon, the best part of Mount Lebanon. Her mind flashed back to the first time she'd seen the address, there on Wadsworth's muddy dog tag as Marshall lay trapped in the gully. Now she was here and this was hers.

The house was solid, anchored somehow to the land, durable as well as beautiful. You could tell from the size of the oaks it had been there for a while, that it was comfortable with itself. She, though, suddenly felt uncomfortable with it, felt invisible armor come from deep in her being and deploy about her person.

"It's all right, darling," Marshall whispered, extremely sensitive to such things. "Just imagine me on a tricycle heading straight for an oak tree. It will seem less formidable then."

"You rode a trike?"

"Was supposed to stay in the driveway with Jeff watching, but I always seemed to veer off across the lawn toward the trees."

She attempted a smile. "It...is...your house, isn't it?"

"It's where I grew up, yes, but it's waiting for a woman named Eden to put her mark on it."

"I could run into a tree. That would probably leave a mark." She took his hand. "Oh, Marshall, I feel rather overwhelmed. I'm not sure...."

"What, darling?"

"That I, that I belong in a place like this."

"Do I belong here?"

"What? You?" She looked at him. "You belong perfectly."

He nuzzled her cheek with his nose then kissed her. "And do you belong with me?"

"Don't think I don't see where you're going with that," she breathed, his lips still hovering just above hers.

"I'm going inside, that's where I'm going, and Mrs. Sinclair belongs there with Mr. Sinclair."

Wadsworth, aware of where he was, was pacing back and forth in the rear seat, his tail thumping hard now and then on the doll house. "I'd better let him out," Marshall said, "before he home-wrecks the doll house."

He opened his door then stopped. "How far down the driveway did you park?"

"You're directly opposite the oak that grows closest to the house."

"Thanks!" he said over his shoulder, already turning, letting Wadsworth out. Wadsworth ran across the front yard, sniffing here and there, then loped back to Marshall. "Let's get Eden," Marshall said, bending over the dog. Together the two of them walked around the back of the car. "Leave the bags for now. I'd like you to see the house first unencumbered."

Wadsworth, wearing neither harness nor leash, danced beside them as Marshall and Eden walked hand in hand toward the front door. Marshall had wanted her to enter there and not through the closer side entrance. He unlocked it, opening the thick wooden door and propping open the storm door with his leg. "Mrs. Sinclair," he smiled, holding out his arms.

She came into them, expecting a kiss, but he scooped her up, grinning, "There's only one proper way for a bride to cross her threshold." He did kiss her then. As he stepped through the doorway with her in his arms, he was kissing her.

The storm door smacked shut behind them and he walked five steps forward and turned through a large archway, still holding her, letting his body be all the shield she'd need. "Living room," he announced.

She made no move for him to set her down. His arms around her were almost feathered things as she lay in the nest of his presence. "Describe what you see," he said into her hair, "so that I can feel the room through your eyes, through what you notice about it."

"Well, the thing that strikes me first is the fireplace. You could roast a boar in there!"

He laughed. "Look through it. You see the dining room?"

"Yep. Dining room's there." The massive fieldstone fireplace opened doubly so that both rooms shared the same chimney.

"What else?" he asked.

"Portrait over the mantel. Who's that? He looks rather like you."

"My great grandfather, Francis Hardin Sinclair."

"Go closer. I want to see him better."

Marshall carried her almost up to the fireplace. Quietly she studied the face in the old oil painting. The resemblance to Marshall was actually quite striking, the shape of the head, the cleft in the chin, the bridge of the nose, but it was the eyes that had grabbed her and wouldn't let go. The brows were straight, like Marshall's, the upper lids with that same slant down over the eyes, but these eyes looked back at her, intense, intelligent, vibrant. It was, for a moment, as though Marshall himself were looking at her and something caught in her gut then splashed up, stinging her eyes.

Marshall felt her tense in his arms. "What is it, darling?"

"N...nothing," she stammered, turning her face into his shoulder.

"It's not nothing. Please, darling. I need to know."

"He was looking at me."

"Who?"

"Your great grandfather. He was looking at me with your eyes."

"Ah." Marshall understood. He ordered Wadsworth to the kitchen where he knew Sylvie would have water and food waiting for him, and without a word, carried Eden through the living room and down a back hall to the master suite. He moved with utter assurance, equal to that of any sighted person. He knew this house perfectly.

In the bedroom he lay her gently on the new king-sized bed he'd had Sylvie order. His parents' bed had occupied this space. He wanted it all new for Eden and for himself, though. Getting up on the bed, kneeling beside her, his hands moved toward her. She blinked back her tears. Marshall was going to look at her.

Chapter 80

Eden came back to herself slowly, lying there on the big bed trying to decide if she'd fallen asleep. Her eyes roamed the walls of the room, more than half- expecting to see scattered particles of her being dribbling down the wallpaper towards the wainscoting. She had exploded. Under his hands, after a long, long time, she had simply exploded. Not completely clear as to whether it had been Marshall's intention, the result had been that now as she gazed around at what was their bedroom, she knew she had already become irretrievably connected with the fiber of this house. He had done it. He had taken her hesitancy and blown it asunder, had blasted it apart, sending the cellular structure of her soul into the house itself.

She became aware his hand still rested on her thigh and turned her head to look at him. He lay on his back, completely unclothed, and sound asleep, his lips curved into the slightest of smiles. Letting her eyes roam freely down the length of him, her own lips curved broadly. He was the most beautiful man she had ever seen. He was, though, beautiful to her not just in this body that lay beside hers, but in himself. He was beautiful, everything that made him, visible, invisible, all of it.

The late afternoon light, muted by the heavy weight of January, braved its way through a giant bay window that overlooked a very private back yard. The glow highlit for a moment something very russet draped over a slipper chair not far from the window. Carefully, she rose from the bed and walked across the deep pile of the emerald green carpet, stopping to finger the material. It looked like a woman's robe. She knew Marshall had had all his parents' things taken out of the master suite. It must be for her. Picking it up, she let the heavy satin of it flow like melted chocolate over her skin as she put it on.

"Thank you, darling," she breathed, looking back at her sleeping husband.

There was still enough light, though it seemed to be fading rapidly, and she tucked herself up atop the wide window seat, pressing her nose to the glass as she tried to get some idea of what the area behind the house looked like. A series of low terraces, made of flagstones, fell gently away from the house down a slope to an area of what she thought might be hemlock trees. Between the terraces and the trees lay an expanse of lawn where she could easily imagine Marshall playing as a boy. There were perennial borders, not much to look at in the depths of winter, as well as lots of shrubs and other trees. She wondered where his willow was. You couldn't see it from here.

Knowing he'd like to be with her as she saw the house for the first time, she decided to limit herself to areas she had already been with him. That pretty much left only the hallway and the living room, so she padded softly in the direction of the fireplace. Wadsworth heard her and came out of the kitchen just as she stopped to examine the portrait over the mantel again.

"Hullo, boy," she murmured, scratching behind his ears before she turned her full attention to Francis Hardin Sinclair. The eyes were Marshall's still, but now even that had changed. Now she knew that whenever she passed through this room and the painted eyes were looking at her, now she knew that she would always remember Marshall's scooping her up in his arms and taking her to the bedroom, their bedroom, to gaze at her. There were no tears that needed blinking back.

She jumped, startled, at a touch on her left shoulder.

"I see you found the new robe," Marshall whispered into her hair, his hand sliding over the satin covering her arm.

"How did you know where I was?"

"I followed your scent," he smiled. "You leave a soft trail of roses in the air."

"You were asleep. I came out to look at...."

"At great grandfather, eh? He'd have loved you, you know. All the Sinclair men would have loved you."

She knew he had to be thinking, then, of Jeffrey and his father, both of whose lives had been such an integral part of this house. "Would you show me your room, darling, your old room?"

It wasn't until then she turned to face him and saw he was still naked. "Sylvie's not here, is she?" she asked quickly.

"Not today. I wanted us to have the house all to ourselves when you first arrived."

"Whew!" she sighed dramatically. "You're not leaving much to the imagination right now, I hope you know."

"Is that not good?"

"Oh, it's good, it's very, very good. In fact, it's so good that if you don't put a robe on, I shall ravish you right here in front of the fireplace, mister."

He grinned. "Later, when the fire is lit."

"Then put something on because the flesh is weak and so is the spirit right now and your virtue is in grave, grave danger."

He chuckled. "My virtue has never been in danger in this house before."

"Not once?"

"Not once."

"You never....?"

"Not here, no."

"So that...in the bedroom...that was...?"

"Yes," he replied, kissing her ear. "And now I'm not sure we really have to wait for the fire."

"It looks like there's a fire laid, and I see long matches."

His lips had moved from her ear down to her throat. "I don't need matches."

She gasped as his tongue found her flesh. "I don't...don't...'spect that you do."

"Wa...Wadsworth?" she croaked. "What about Wadsworth?"

"Kitchen!" he ordered.

"Poor Waddy."

"He'll live. I, however, am in serious danger of spontaneous combustion."

"We...we can't have...that."

He tipped her back onto the thick, sculptured area rug that lay in front of the hearth. She found herself looking over his shoulder straight into the eyes of Francis Hardin Sinclair. "Great grandpa is watching," she sighed.

"He'll just have to get used to it, now won't he?" Then his lips moved lower and she forgot about everything but what he was doing. He was such a 'giver' during their love-making. She'd come to know that he preferred to gaze at her first, moving his hands and lips over her in slow, lingering motions so that he felt every inch of her body come to life under his touch, felt like she was satisfied that she was 'seen', that he was satisfied that he was aware completely of her in that moment. It was only after that that the real give and take of lovemaking came into play. But he had done that there in the bedroom, knowing that she especially needed to feel seen by him this afternoon. So now she pressed enough on his shoulder for him to understand she wanted him to roll over onto his back. Her robe lay across the nearby coffee table, its sash come loose and coiled just out from her hand. Her fingers found it and, using its satin end very like the daffodil, she took him where she wanted, there in his first time in front of the fireplace, not once thinking of Francis Hardin Sinclair.

"Is it auburn?" he asked later. "I wanted it to be auburn, to match your hair." He was letting the satin sash slide over and over through his fingers.

"It's definitely auburn." How clearly she remembered back to what seemed a lifetime ago when he was explaining about colors to her, how he got some sense of them.

He took the sash and wrapped it loosely three times around her lower arm then three around his own. "In Celtic weddings they often used ribbons as a sign of bonding, of the man and the woman joining together. 'And so the binding is made,'" he quoted almost in a whisper.

"I am," she replied, her voice husky with emotion as she buried her face in his chest, "completely and utterly bound to you."

They lay like that a long time, just breathing together in the silence as the last bit of daylight muted then faded into darkness. Finally she opened her eyes, disoriented in the blackened room. "I can't see a thing."

She heard his chuckle. "Neither can I."

She'd lifted her head, but now let it lie back against him again. So, was this what the house was like for him? No, not really. For him it was a familiar place, with familiar things in a familiar absence of light.

"Listen," he whispered.

She became aware that the only sound she'd been hearing was his heartbeat under her ear and that had been enough, had been a sound the parameters of which defined her own livingness, but now, because he asked, she turned her head, waiting for the house to speak to her as it spoke to him. From the corner to the right of the fireplace came a steady, rather solid-sounding, tick-tick-tocking. She vaguely remembered a tall grandfather clock standing somewhere there. It was a large tick, suitable for the pendulum of a large clock. If she listened very carefully, she could make out that muffled creak of old wood settling like old bones for a winter night. The furnace kicked in and hummed mechanically for a while. The house seemed to respond to the fresh inflow of warmed air by settling in slightly different patterns. There was a little scritch-scratch of sound against a front windowpane.

"The pink dogwood," Marshall explained when she asked. "It insists on growing a little too close to the house."

"I expect you hear memories, too."

"Lots of memories. Birthdays, Christmases, little boys, young men. But we are making new memories, you and I, Eden, and they will become a part of the house."

She thought about feeling splattered on the bedroom walls not long ago. "Yes," she agreed, "I can already feel that happening."

From the kitchen came the click of dog claws on the floor and a tentative whuffing noise. "I bet Waddy needs out," she said, starting to rise. "He's part of the sound of the house, too."

"I'll get him, darling. Why don't you see if you can get the fire going? I'll be right back."

He helped her to her feet. "Wait just a second." Passing easily around the coffee table, he switched on a lamp near the couch for her, then he was off for the kitchen.

The fireplace screen on this side was one of those metal curtain ones with chains you pull to open. She struck one of the long matches and found that the fire had been expertly laid with lots of kindling so that it caught immediately. Pulling the chains again, she settled back on the rug, not putting on her robe since he didn't have his with him. She'd heard the kitchen door open and close then the clink of some glasses. Before long Marshall returned with a bottle of wine tucked under his right arm, two goblets in one hand and a platter of cheeses, olives, small crisp breads, and a dip in the other. He could carry things in both hands because he knew the house so well.

"Sylvie thought of everything," he grinned, setting the platter on the coffee table.

The fire was crackling and spluttering as it caught. "Ah, pine," he said, pleased. "Pine is not necessarily the best firewood, but it's probably the noisiest. They always used it a lot for my sake. Nice 'n sappy."

After the fire had gotten going, she'd turned off the lamp so that the only light in the room came from the flames. As he settled beside her on the rug, she was glad for just the fire, enjoying the play of light over his body. He held out his right arm and she nestled into the curve of it.

"Home," he sighed, "I'm really home."

Chapter 81

Marshall woke in the wee hours, having no idea what time it was until several minutes later the clock chimed three. He was aware of Wadsworth snuggled against his back while Eden was spooned into his front. His family. The years in this house flowed and the currents had brought him to this present moment. How different it was from before, but how very alive it had suddenly become again after those long months when it had all seemed to settle into some stagnant pool.

Late in the evening Eden had fallen asleep in his arms there in front of the fireplace. He'd let Wadsworth back inside earlier and when no further sounds came from the living room, the dog had made his way out of the kitchen and settled with a sigh against Marshall's back. Marshall had pulled a soft afghan over them, even Wadsworth, and lay a long while listening to the breathing of the two living beings he loved most in the world. He was literally cocooned there between them, a feeling of utter contentment enveloping him.

His left arm was over Eden's shoulder as she lay on her right side and his hand rested just above her breast. Very, very lightly he let his fingers cup around it with just enough pressure to feel its soft give. It was so completely female there under his strong fingers that he began to respond to it and quickly moved his hand away. Time enough for that later. She was sleeping deeply now and he wanted her to rest. Besides, Wadsworth had lifted his head at Marshall's small movement and given him a long, lazy lick on his left shoulder blade.

Now as he lay there, he heard the sharp spatterings of sleet against the living room windows. January. So far from the time of daffodils. He smiled again, thinking of how that particular flower had taken on a whole new meaning for him. The sleet continued for a long time. He'd call Sylvie first thing and tell her not to try coming over. Mayhaven was a cobbled road and even slipperier when iced than pavement was. Eden and he could spend the day exploring the house together. For some reason they hadn't managed to get very far with that yesterday evening. Maybe they might even write a bit more of Morgan and Susannah. Finally he drifted off again, his left hand resting fairly safely on her hip.

Eden woke just after dawn, managing to turn in Marshall's arms without waking him. This left her face to face with him, mere inches between their noses. His breath was soft and warm against her skin and she opened her mouth so it could flow inside her. She lay like that for long minutes, inhaling as he exhaled, feeling absolutely at one with this man. She wanted to touch his face, to trace her fingertip down the line of his nose, across the curve of his lips, but she settled for bringing her open mouth closer so that the merest fraction separated it from his parted lips and his breath flowed more directly into her.

Wadsworth shifted position and, just slightly roused from sleep, Marshall licked his lips. His tongue encountered something soft almost against his and though he was far from awake, he instinctively tipped his chin and pressed his mouth to hers. Wadsworth's head came up enough that his eyes met Eden's. She focused intently on them and with her right hand made a gesture toward the kitchen. He sighed, she could swear it was a sigh, and moved out of the room as she silently promised him she'd let him out in a bit, but, darn it, she was still on her honeymoon.

She loved that his lips were on hers in his sleep. Carefully she let her tongue enter his mouth, running it along the ridge of his upper teeth before she searched out his tongue. An instant stirring against her thigh let her know he was waking up and she began to kiss him more thoroughly. He woke suddenly, a deep, primal sound rising up his throat, and she took the sound into herself as well. Her hands were on his back, pressing him urgently against her as though she could push the cells of his being into her own cells. For one fleeting moment she visualized that, something the opposite of a cell dividing, making two new cells. No, this was a separate cell coming home again, pressing through the walls, its nucleus merging back again with another. It was an act not of creation, but of re-creation and she wanted it with a surging desperation. That such a thing was not possible, not here on earth anyway, urged her on that there might be as much of him inside her as could be. It had started with his breath and then his guttural waking sound, followed by his tongue and then the warmth against her leg was within her, too, and still she pressed her hands as hard as she could against his back, wanting endless more of him.

When their lovemaking was done, he thought of saying something about never having been awakened in quite so splendid a way before, but he was sensitive to her mood and, instead, lay still inside her, his arms wrapped about her as she buried her face in his neck. He was quiet a long time, then whispered into her hair, "I'm not going anywhere, my darling." He splayed his left hand fully across her back and his right behind her head. "My wife," he whispered, his lips against her temple. As a sudden gust blew a hard rush of sleet against the tall windows, he pressed her closer and added, "My wife, in our home." Then he let out a long, satisfied breath, the warmth of which flowed down her cheek, over her collarbone, and curved around her breast. She nestled into him. He was the home she'd come to live in, him, and not a stone building. The building only mattered because it was some sort of tangible extension of him.

After a while his tummy growled loudly and he said hopefully, "You getting hungry, darling?"

All they'd had since lunch yesterday at the diner had been the little tray of snacks Sylvie had left in the refrigerator for them. The kitchen. Eden hadn't really seen the kitchen yet. She wondered just what all she might find in there. Marshall got to his feet, extending a hand back down to her. She shrugged into her new robe then looked at him standing there as unadorned as he'd come into the world. "Come," she said, taking his hand. "We'd better go find your robe or I'll never be able to keep my mind on food."

In the bedroom, she watched as he deftly unhooked his robe from a hanger on the back of the door. It was dark green in a thick, soft flannel and as he belted it around his waist, she had to admit she liked it better when he was au natural but it was light out now and he couldn't just parade around in front of the windows. The thought sent her to the bay window that overlooked the back yard. The sky was a leaden gray, heavy with cold precipitation that wavered back and forth from sleet to frozen rain.

"Glad it didn't do this yesterday," she commented, "the weather, I mean."

"Sylvie," he said. "I've got to call Sylvie." He used the bedroom phone and then together they went to the kitchen.

"Wow!" she said, flipping on a few wall switches that illuminated every nook and cranny of the place. Her eyes, though, sought one particular thing. "There it is," she announced happily.

"There what is?"

"The peanut butter cookie table." How long ago now it seemed that he'd told her about pressing out the peanut butter balls with the bottom of a glass. "Do you...?"

"If the stuff's in the pantry, sure," he replied, knowing instantly what she meant, "but maybe not for, um, breakfast."

"Lunch, then," she persisted. "Peanut butter cookies for lunch."

He laughed. "Diet's all shot to hell. I can see that already!"

"You can see that?" she repeated softly.

"Yes, I can see that," he nodded, "just like I can see you."

"You gaze at cookies?" She suddenly needed to be flip again.

"Hey! A good cookie is a marvelous thing to touch, um, behold."

The kitchen was a warm, homey place despite being maybe ten or more times the size of the one in her apartment. The countless cabinets were polished cherry wood and all the countertops were a light beige granite, even the top of the sizable central island with its extra sink. "Your Mom liked Tuscany?" she ventured, looking around at the decorations.

"One of her favorite places," he replied. "I guess that's pretty evident in here, eh? You can change it however you like, though."

"I like it fine," she smiled. "You can take me there sometime when the sunflowers are in bloom and we'll just add more stuff to it."

"Ah," he said, "that's what we'll have to do, follow the flowers around the world, like some people follow the big surfing waves. Daffodils in the Lake Country, lavender in Provence, sunflowers in Tuscany."

"And poppies," she added. "I understand Italy has a lot of those."

"And poppies," he agreed. "Definitely poppies. What about waffles?"

"You know where the waffles bloom?"

"Yep," he grinned, "right over here." He trailed his hand along the edge of a long counter, then reached out. "That is if it's still where it used to be." His fingers found a round waffle iron. "None of those new-fangled square waffles for the Sinclair boys," he said before he realized he'd done it.

Eden knew instantly that a memory of Jeff had just walked into the room. "Round's good!" she hastened to say. "Fit on the plate better that way anyway, I always say." She looked around. "You know where the bowls might be?"

He knew the kitchen quite well and before they started on the waffle batter, he took her on a tour of all the cabinets and drawers. There was a huge pantry, too, a breakfast area with its own oval table set neatly in front of another bay window overlooking the back of the house, an entrance to a laundry room and beyond that a door to the garage. A door to the right of the breakfast area led directly to the back yard. Marshall let Wadsworth out. "Bet he doesn't stay long, not with all this ice." In less than two minutes the big dog had announced he was ready to come back in.

One side of the kitchen island had a row of four tall swivel chairs along it and they sat companionably side by side as she poured ingredients into a large glass bowl and he stirred the batter. When four waffles had been made, three for him and one for her, they had a leisurely breakfast with orange juice, tea, sliced peaches, and the waffles, her first real meal in her new home. She looked the length of the kitchen with its beamed ceiling hung with copper pots and many kinds of oddly-shaped baskets. What a lovely room, like something straight out of a magazine. *You gonna fit in here, kid?* she asked herself silently. But one look at Marshall hungrily stuffing a large bite of syrup-dripping waffle into his mouth was all it took to give her the answer to that.

Despite there being a dishwasher, she hand-washed the few dishes and he dried and put them away. She liked watching his confident movements in this large kitchen. As for

Marshall, he felt so complete, all the way down to his toes, to be in this house again, to be happily in this house again. The large, glazed tiles under his bare feet were familiar territory. He remembered stories his mother would tell about how he'd zoom around this very floor in his wheeled walker that the doctor had said would be too dangerous for a blind baby. Jeff had thought otherwise, though, and the walker the older brother had used was brought out of the attic for the use of the younger. He'd loved the thing, propelling himself with his chubby little legs as fast as he could go. There were still dents in the lower regions of the island counter where he'd crashed over and over into it. Jeff was always nearby, would dash up and usually manage to catch him before he flipped head-first onto the tiled floor. Marshall had never been all that cautious about exploring his unseen world and when he was given this wonderful wheeled contraption while still very young, it had been like wings for him.

Marshall paused at one of the corners of the island, following down its edge with his right hand until he came to a fairly deep dent in the cherry wood. Eden saw the motion and asked him about it, how it got there.

"Me," he grinned. "I got it there. Thirteen months old at the time." And so he told her about the walker.

Eden touched the dent herself. Marshall. The whole history of Marshall was literally engraved on this house. There was no way she could not love it. "Started young, did you," she cracked, though, "with the whole gully syndrome?"

"Very young," he admitted, "though I promise I won't bang into kitchen counters anymore."

"You better not, mister!" she said, her voice starting out flippant but then breaking. She slid her arms around him. "You just damn well better not."

He heard the change in her voice. "Could I distract you with the offer of a shower?"

"I don't know that's distracting enough."

"Um, a joint shower?"

"You can make it really distracting?"

"So distracting you won't even notice the water or the soap."

"What if I want to notice the soap?"

"All right. I'll be sure you notice the soap."

Chapter 82

Marshall felt so content, wandering through the big house with Eden as she was seeing it for the first time. He was walking with her through the one place that had always been the physical center of his world, and her entering into it beside him was more important to him than even he had realized it would be. He wanted her to see everything, be aware of what it meant to him, so a constant stream of anecdotes flowed from him as they walked from room to room.

Eden's favorite so far was the room that had been Marshall's father's study. It was paneled floor to high ceiling in a rich wood that seemed to glow from within. There was a stone fireplace here, too, a beamed ceiling, and a tall diamond-paned series of windows looked out toward the front of the house. A deep burgundy rug lay over a polished hardwood floor. There were paintings on the walls of old English manor houses, the largest of those centered behind an enormous roll-top desk.

Marshall stopped beside the desk, letting his fingers play over a carving on the wood.

Watching him, it really hit Eden how, though he knew this room intimately, he only knew it piece by little piece. He'd never gotten the over-all sense of it like she had merely upon walking into it for the first time. Had anyone even ever told him about the beams in the ceiling or did the sighted people merely take them for granted? She'd ask about that some other time.

On the other side of the room from the roll-top was another desk, very long and not so deep, with quite a breath-taking array of technical equipment on it from end to end and two matching swivel chairs in front. Marshall led her there, past the central set-up of furniture covered in soft café-au-lait leather, saying, "This is where we'll write Morgan and Susannah." He smiled at Eden. "It's probably got more bells and whistles for me than I'll need now that you're writing, too."

"I like this room," she said, turning her head to take it all in again. "It's a good room for writing in." She looked back at the old roll-top. "Your father, Jonathan, did he write, too?"

"Ledgers, account books, things like that," Marshall explained. "He was a financier. I guess that's the best description of what he did. Very good at it, too, which is why this house is as it is."

"I remember at the inn," she continued, "your telling me how so much of the wood in the house was carved because he wanted you to have plenty of things to touch."

"Yes, after I was born, he had a lot of the wood completely redone just for me. Sometimes it was...," a thought struck him and he broke off in mid-sentence. "Come with me." He took her hand again. "This is a bit over-the-top, perhaps, but I want you to see something."

He led her up the main staircase, a marvelous structure with spiraled railings under the wide banister and the most amazing newel post she'd ever seen. They went up to the second floor, didn't stop but turned to go up another flight of somewhat less grand steps, where he paused, his hand on a door knob. "The attic," he said. "I'm going to show you the Christmas present he gave me the year I was eight."

"I love old attics," she replied. "So you keep the Christmas presents of your youth up here, then?"

"Only this one."

"Why this one?"

"You'll see," he answered with a wide grin and opened the door.

He ushered her into a large room with sloped ceilings, remembering to flip the light switch for her, something else Jeff had drilled into him. As she looked around, she didn't see anything particularly striking beyond the usual array of attic items: several pieces of old furniture, cardboard boxes, a steamer trunk, shelves with smaller boxes on them, a bicycle, and in a corner, a battered blue tricycle. That last item did catch her eye. Marshall's tricycle that he'd run into the tree while riding.

"What...?" she asked.

"Oh, not in this room. There are three rooms up here. The next two are my present."

"Your present takes up two rooms?"

"My present IS two rooms."

"Now I'm really curious," she admitted. What in the world had Jonathan come up with that would need two rooms?

Marshall opened another door, flipped another switch. "Make sure we turn these off," he said over his shoulder. "I tend to forget that end of it."

He stepped aside, then, letting her enter the room, which was about a quarter of the size of the larger room they'd just left. There was only one thing in it and that occupied most of the wall directly across from her.

"A...a...wardrobe?" She walked toward it. It was about the most glorious wardrobe she'd ever seen, though, completely covered with intricate carvings that seemed to tell a story. Bending close, she studied those on the left door panel a moment, then straightened and turned her head toward Marshall. "Oh, my goodness! THAT wardrobe!"

Marshall chuckled. "Yes, that wardrobe. You see, when I was a little boy I was entirely enthralled with Narnia. My father must've read the whole series of books to me more times than I can count. I just never got tired of them, and that Christmas when I was eight, he decided he wanted to make it as real as possible for me, so he commissioned this wardrobe. Since I couldn't see the pictures in the books, he had them carved on it. Here...," He found her hand and unerringly guided it down to the bottom section of the right-hand door. "That's Susan and Lucy riding on Aslan." He closed his eyes. "I wanted to do that so badly, ride Aslan like that, you know."

"This is just amazing, darling," she said, straightening again. "What a wonderful present."

"This is just the beginning," he grinned, opening both doors to reveal a rack of fur coats.

"No!" she laughed. "Not fur coats, too!"

"This one belonged to my grandmother," he said, running his hand down a long sleeve. "I don't know where he found the others but, come."

"Come?"

"What good is a wardrobe if you can't go inside it?"

Indeed, the thing was so big that even fully-grown Marshall could stand easily in it, which she noted as he stepped inside and held his hand back out for hers. She stood there a moment, something in her finding it totally unbelievable that she was about to take his hand and actually step inside a wardrobe full of fur coats. She'd read the books herself and seen the movies, too, but what she was looking at right now was still unbelievable. "Ok," she finally said and, inhaling a deep breath, took his hand.

Immediately she was enveloped in fur and let herself settle into the sensation of being Lucy. "Are you Peter or Edmund?" she whispered to Marshall, whose front was pressed delightfully close to hers.

"Peter, of course," he chuckled.

"Well," she replied, "I must tell you that with you all pressed up close to me like you are, I'm not feeling all that sisterly toward you at the moment."

He laughed again. "I don't think I've ever had a better time inside this wardrobe." Then he cleared his throat loudly. "So we'd best be on our way."

She turned back to open the doors but he stopped her arm. "Not that way."

"He...didn't...?" she almost gasped.

"Oh, but he did."

She looped her fingers through his belt and followed him toward the back of the wardrobe. There was a second row of fur coats then a third. The side of the wardrobe hadn't looked anywhere near that deep! "How....?"

"Shh!"

When pine branches began to touch her face instead of fur, some childish instinct in her almost began to feel nervous and her fingers tightened their grip on his belt. The last of the coats left behind, they stepped out into a thick clump of evergreen trees of all sizes. "What the...?"

"Artificial Christmas trees," Marshall explained. "This is the third room. It's big like that first part of the attic and my father had the walls of the wardrobe extend out into this one to make room for rows of coats and give you the feeling like you were going somewhere. Then out here he put a couple dozen different-sized Christmas trees."

She was standing ankle-deep in artificial snow. "He gave you...Narnia? He actually gave you Narnia?"

There was sort of a path through the trees and he took her around a curve of that.

"There."

A lamp post. A real lamp post stood in the 'snow'. Not far from that was an almost life-sized stuffed male lion. "Where could he get...?"

"Right down in Canonsburg. You know Sarris, that chocolate factory? They have a display room filled with stuffed animals, many of them large as life. That's where he got it."

She walked around the lion, touching it here and there in wonder. "Did you sit on it?"

"There were days I almost lived on him," he replied softly, his voice full of memories as he buried his fingers in the mane. "Sometimes I could even feel the wind in my face. He took my favorite story and made it real for me." He tipped his chin suddenly, blinking back tears, the sound of his father's deep voice coming to him as clearly as the touch of the fur beneath his hand. This was the first time since his parents had died that he'd been up to the attic.

Eden walked around the lion, took his arm, and together they went to the lamp post where she indicated she'd like to sit in the snow. For the next hour the two of them leaned against the post, their fingers interlaced, as Marshall told her stories about these two rooms, sometimes Jeff with him, other times alone. He pointed out the wall rack with its rubber swords, told her which shield was Peter's and therefore the one he'd used. "Sword fighting is hard when you can't see what the other guy is doing with his weapon. That's why they're a really soft rubber. Maybe I can't see," he paused, "but I still liked the feel of it in my hand."

She closed her eyes, leaning her head against his shoulder. Somehow she found it quite easy to imagine him with sword and shield.

Chapter 83

Marshall led Eden back down to the second floor where his boyhood bedroom was located. He paused, his hand on the doorknob. If the house itself were the center of his universe, this room had always been for him the heart of the house. "It's a bit of a mish mash," he explained, smiling, before opening the door. "I liked to keep the things I was familiar with when I was smaller and just add new things as time passed. Has a bit of everything, I think."

He opened the door and they entered together. The room was large, located directly above the living room, with double diamond-paned windows that overlooked the front yard. Eden had been eager for some time to see this inner sanctum of his. A double bed with a carved oak headboard occupied a corner away from the windows. Directly in front of the windows sat a desk with an amazingly large worktop. An array of stereo equipment was arranged just to the left of the desk and Eden noted that the room had been wired for surround sound. The system could play CDs, tapes, or records and nearby shelves were stacked with those, each sporting a label in Braille. Two tall bookcases were filled with Braille books. These were the things belonging to the more adult Marshall, but what caught Eden's eye the most were the things left over from his boyhood. From the ceiling hung the solar system, each planet on its own wire.

Marshall took a few steps forward and without hesitation reached up and curved a palm under the Earth. "Jeff rigged this when I was about nine so I could understand the relationships between the sizes of the planets." He tapped it with a finger, sending it into a bit of a spin.

Eden wandered over to a long table against the right-hand wall where several big models were set up. There was a beige castle, comprised of large chunky pieces that could be easily rearranged. It was filled with knights, horses, a few ladies, even a phoenix perched atop a tower. To its left was a western stockaded fort, complete with cavalrymen and Indians. Marshall followed the sound of her steps, touching briefly a knight on a rearing horse.

"It helped, you know, being able to run my hands over three-dimensional things. Then all I had to do was enlarge them in my mind to understand the size of a real castle." He dropped his hand to his side.

"Buildings, structures of any sort, are hard for a blind person to grasp. I can walk up and lay my hand on a wall and know if it's brick or stone or wood, but when it goes up out of my reach, it's not really there for me. And trees...." His fingers found the canopy of a perfectly-formed oak tree about ten inches tall. "This very tree was the one that gave me the understanding I needed." He closed his eyes a moment, remembering. "That's why it's still here."

She gazed at him, aware that she loved him more, not at all sure just how that could be, but knowing it was true. Each moment she loved him more than the moment just passed. "May I hold it?"

He picked it up, placing it in her hands. She closed her own eyes, running her fingers over it, its complicated layers of foliage, its branches and trunk, trying to get inside what it was like for him, never having seen a tree in its entirety. "I'm glad you've kept it," she said. "It should be kept always."

He took her down the hall to Jeff's room, where the walls were filled with sports posters, maps, aerial views of the Grand Canyon and Ayers Rock. Shelves contained model motorcycles, sports trophies, books on military history. "Mom wanted to keep it just as he left it," Marshall said.

At the other end of the second floor, the hallway opened into a large parlor-like area filled with comfortable, padded furniture in shades of dusty rose and beige. There was a TV, more shelves of books, and a square table with four chairs. In front of a window stood possibly the largest globe Eden had ever seen, a good three feet in diameter. Fascinated, she walked toward it, finding that all the features had been raised so that Marshall could discern the outlines of the continents, could feel the mountain ranges and even the larger rivers.

He heard the familiar squeak it made as she turned the globe. "Ah, 'Marshall's World,'" he chuckled. "That's what Jeff always called it." A quick stab of longing for his brother made its way through his chest. Eden could see the sudden moisture of it in his eyes, bkut this was what she had wanted, to see him here in the pottery where his vessel had been fashioned. She took his hand, pressing his knuckles to her lips.

"Thank you," she murmured.

"For what?"

"For bringing me here, for making me a part now of all this."

"All this is alive again for me, you know, because you are here." He took her in his arms and they stood together for several minutes, not speaking.

After lunch, they settled themselves side by side at the computer downstairs. "It feels like it's been ages since we've written Morgan and Susannah," she sighed as the computer booted up.

After his encounter with George Washington, Morgan tugged his shoe back on and walked to the corner of the Duke of Gloucester Street. He looked to his left where he could see the lights from the Raleigh Tavern sending out their glow into the night, pondering if he really wanted to go there or not. Quite a number of horses were still hitched in front of it and small groups of men stood about on the walkway, their voices engaged in serious discussion. No, he wanted to be alone, so he continued across the main street and down another short block, turning left on Francis Street. He'd rented a room on the second floor of a gracious white house not far from the turning to the Capitol building. Opening the picket gate, he walked up to the front of the house and sat on the stoop, his elbows on his knees, his chin in his hands. His jacket lay on the step beside him as he closed his eyes, listening to the night, imagining again what it must be like for Susannah.

A single rider passed, tipping his hat when he noticed Morgan, who had kept his eyes closed and so did not respond. Williamsburg. It seemed its own world now to him, an entire microcosm totally separated from anything he had known before, anywhere he had been before. There were men here he admired, men worthy of admiration. In his days in the maritime trading business, he'd not come across such a concentration of men of principled mind, men who made him examine his own thoughts, his own motivations for being. It was affecting him more each day that passed, and today, today had been remarkable in every way. Here in the late evening of that day, he found he had more to think about than he seemed quite able to manage. The main stream of his thoughts, though, were not of Washington or Wythe or

Henry but rose on strong wings like geese into the winds of the flyway that would take them home. The image of that fit for never before had he felt such a sense of migratory pull, as though there were some place he simply must arrive or die.

Eden had been writing and she stopped, turning to him. "It's like that, you know, for me. I must arrive not at you, but somehow in you, in order now to live."

"It says it well, darling, the 'migratory pull'. I like that. I understand that." He touched her cheek. "And it is that way, as well, for me."

He began to dictate and she typed his words.

Susannah lay on her bed, unable to sleep. Something in her was deeply amazed. In her garden, at the center of her world...he. Morgan, there in her garden. How? Her mind struggled, trying to wrap itself about the thought that such a thing had happened, had happened without her looking for it, had just simply...happened. Her fingers found her lips, lingering there, remembering his. She had only met him, and yet his lips had known hers. Such things did not occur, but this had. This was real. Morgan...in her garden. No one knew. Only she, only he. She smiled, pleased at that, at how it was a personal thing between them. Was one allowed, really, to have such a personal thing with someone only just met? She didn't care. Morgan had been in her garden and life was not the same as it had been when last she lay in this bed.

She became aware of the pulse in her neck and moved her fingers there, feeling the rapid beat of it. She would not sleep, could not sleep. That she knew. Moving her legs over the side of the bed, she reached into the ewer there, wetting her hands, running them over her cheeks, down her neck. Her breasts ached, as though yearning for his touch. They had never ached before. Not ever.

"Ok, how do you know about aching breasts, mister?" Eden asked.

Marshall chuckled. "I'll never tell."

She swiveled her chair to face his. "Oh, yes, you will!"

He shook his head firmly side to side, his lips together, curving in a smile.

"Fess up!" she insisted.

So he took his hand and with fingers light as butterfly wings, moved it in a slow curve around her left breast. The breast began to ache, yearning toward him. "Like that," he whispered as she gasped.

She blew out a few long breaths. "Ok, but that's still me with the aching breast. How do you know they ache?"

"Because doing that makes parts of me ache," he replied, "and I just transpose that onto a female form."

She slid her hand up his thigh then inward. "Here?" And was pleased that he, too, gasped in response.

"There," he nodded, his voice cracking on the single syllable.

"You realize it's going to take us a long, long time to write this book?" She began to pull her hand away, but he put his over it, moving it back.

"Book? Was there a book?"

She grinned. "I'm in no hurry."
"I am," he sighed.
"To finish the book," she chuckled.
"Oh, that. That's not what I meant."
"I know."

Chapter 84

"I'm hungry," Eden announced.
"For what?" Marshall asked, grinning as he finished rebuttoning his shirt.
"For something I've dreamed of ever since I first heard of this house."
"I thought we'd done that. Several times."
"Oh, yes, and it was very good, too!" she laughed, reaching over to tickle his chest. "But I have something else in mind."
"Yes?"
"Something almost equally tactile."
"You have my attention."
"But more fattening."
"I'm not fattening in the least," he smiled.
"True. I find you very slimming."
"It's the exercise involved."
"Yes, lots. But this, this is fattening."
"What is?"
"What I'm hungry for."
"Um, could you be possibly a bit specific? Roast pig? A brick of Velveeta?"
"Peanut butter cookies." She pressed her nose into his cheek.
"Ah!" he said, understanding. "At the big kitchen table, with a wet cloth and a fork?"
"You got it!"
"Now? You want to make cookies now?"
"Can we?"
"I don't see why not," he said, turning his head to kiss her nose.
Together, Wadsworth at their heels, they went into the kitchen. "Where would the peanut butter be kept?" Eden asked as Marshall settled into a chair at the table.
"Second cabinet to the right of the microwave."
Soon she had a large glass bowl out and was happily adding ingredients as Marshall stirred. "You're such a marvelous stirrer," she purred, kissing his ear, "and so manly as you do it."
He'd gotten flour on his cheek and she thought he looked entirely adorable.

When the dough was ready, she spread long sheets of waxed paper atop the table and assembled everything they would need to make the cookies the way he described they had always done it. Taking a spoonful of the dough, he rolled it into a neat little ball and set it in front of her.

"Now the glass," he said, and she picked up the juice glass with the small square of wet cloth fastened to its bottom with a rubber band and squished the ball.

"You did this, right?" she asked.

"That was my main job," he smiled, dipping a fork in a small bowl of flour and pressing it twice across the flattened dough.

They developed sort of an assembly line process and she was fascinated watching his fingers find the dough and deftly press the tines across it first one way and then at right angles. If it weren't for the fact that he wasn't looking down at what he was doing, you'd never have suspected he was doing it all by touch alone. Eden had heated both ovens and soon the smell of dozens of peanut butter cookies filled the large room.

"So familiar...," he murmured, lifting his chin to let his being float in the scent.

Wadsworth thought it smelled wonderful, too, and sat near the table, doggie drool dripping slowly off the tip of his tongue.

She came up behind Marshall, sliding her arms around his neck and he raised both hands, cupping them about her forearms. "This is just what I wanted," she whispered.

"You are just what I wanted," he said, leaning his left cheek over onto her arm.

"It's just that this, all this, is such a part of you and there's nothing I want more than to belong to everything that has anything to do with you." She kissed his hair. "You do know you mean absolutely, totally everything to me, don't you?"

He nodded, keeping his cheek on her arm, letting his eyes close, utterly content.

She made a pot of hot tea and they took their cups and a big plate of warm cookies into the living room, cuddling by the fireplace. Breaking off a piece of cookie, she touched it to his lips.

"Open," she said and when he let his lips part, she placed it as gently as a communion wafer on his tongue. His presence in her life did that, took all the ordinary moments and somehow made them holy.

He closed his mouth, keeping the bit of cookie on his tongue, letting the flavor of it fill him. "Here, Marshall darling," his mother's voice said. "This is the first cookie of the batch." "Hey, Marshy!" Jeffrey laughed. "You got cookie crumbs on your chin!" "I love you," Eden said, unable to resist touching his lips with her fingertips.

His throat constricted with emotion and for a moment he was unable to swallow the cookie. Feeling his lips tighten, she asked quickly, "Are you all right?"

He nodded, managed to get the piece down, and when she moved her hand, he said, "There's just so much, you know, so much that's a part of such a simple thing."

"I know," she replied. And she did.

They spent a long time there, close together, drinking the tea, eating cookies. Wadsworth made a little whuffing sound from time to time and Marshall would break off some of his cookie and feed it to him. "You get your teeth brushed today, I hope you know," he laughed, rubbing behind a pointy ear.

Later they put on heavy coats and boots and went out through the kitchen into the back yard, holding onto each other as it was fairly slippery with ice. She wanted to see his willow tree. Carefully they made their way to the far back corner where it grew, had grown since he'd planted it as a boy. The icy snow was somewhat littered in its vicinity with the thin whips that willows lose in the harshness of winter.

"We're here," she said when they'd reached the outer bounds of the branches that draped nearly to the ground.

He slipped off his gloves, probing with both hands, his fingers contacting slender willow branches completely coated in ice. He smiled, running his hands up and down a long length of them. "Hello, old friend," he murmured.

He led her under the willow, its ice clattering as they moved through layers of drooping branches toward the fat trunk of the tree. He stopped, standing perfectly still, as though listening to some arboreal voice only he could hear. Eden tipped her head up, enthralled. She'd never stood inside a willow in the winter. It seemed to her, in its icy encasement, as though she were in the secret place under a frozen waterfall. It was magical, visual, for her in its glassy and graceful beauty. For him? It must be a different experience for him and she took one of his hands in hers and closed her eyes. The wind blew a thin willow wand against her cheek, a streamer of pure coldness, smooth and wet as her skin melted an outer layer of ice. With her eyes closed she could better hear the music of the tree its branches made, as like wind chimes they brushed against one another. The gracefulness was no longer visual, but something she was lightly enclosed within, a sense of a gracefulness that touched the heart with its invisibility. And this was Marshall, too, she knew. The willow's roots were his roots, connecting him to this place.

She breathed slowly, adrift in the shared moment and time didn't really pass. Time was lost but with no sense of loss. Standing in the middle of perfection was like that, and she knew that without him, without what he brought to her life, she would be still living in poverty of soul. *I love you.* The words welled within her and yet did not seek verbal expression. Sound, any sound, other than the music of the tree and the beating of her heart, would dispel this moment. So she simply breathed the words voicelessly, letting them fill her lungs over and over, as she held his hand under the willow.

Chapter 85

The following morning a bit of January thaw seemed to be taking hold and a great deal of the ice had melted. Sylvie arrived, eager to see Marshall again and meet his bride. She entered through the side door into the laundry room, bustling happily into the kitchen where Marshall and Eden sat at the breakfast table, just finishing eggs scrambled with cheese and sun-dried tomatoes.

"Marshall!" she sighed, content at the sight of him where he belonged. She'd never liked it that he'd spent so much time at the university in that tiny room he had there.

"Sylvie," he smiled in return, standing for one of her hugs.

Sylvie was in her late fifties, rather well-rounded, with a beaming face that reflected her Polish descent. Gray streaked through her short, tightly-curled brown hair. He held his arms out for her greeting, knowing exactly what she liked to do. Her plump arms went around his middle and she squeezed hard as he tried to avoid letting a little 'oomph' escape his lips.

Eden, watching, grinned. Sylvie was part of this house, too, and she obviously adored Marshall. Eden rose, waiting, as Sylvie patted Marshall's cheeks, studying his face.

"You look good," she finally pronounced, "though still a bit thin." She knew about what he'd been through with the gully and the convicts, though not the sleigh accident.

Satisfied, she turned toward Eden and smiled beneficently. "You saved him," were the first words out of her mouth.

"I think he's saved me every bit as much as I saved him," she smiled, her eyes going to Marshall.

Sylvie saw the look, saw all the love it contained, and again she was satisfied. "You are a good wife for him. I see that." She nodded her head several times. "Yes, a good wife."

"The best, Sylvie," Marshall affirmed.

"The roads are all right this morning?" Eden asked.

"The roads? Pah! I never mind the roads. It's him." She looked, brow knitted, at Marshall. "He is the one who should be more careful where he walks."

"I am careful," Marshall smiled.

"You think I do not know of the gully, then? Or of the forest?"

"I called and told you about the gully," Marshall reminded her, "and the forest was all over the newspapers."

"Does she know about the sleigh turning over?" Eden asked.

"Shhh!" Marshall made a little face.

"Sleigh? There was a sleigh? Did you get hit by a sleigh?" She narrowed her eyes at him.

"No, Sylvie, I didn't get hit by a sleigh, just tossed out of one but, as you see, I'm fine."

"He's always 'fine,'" Eden sighed, "even when...."

"Shhh!" Marshall said again.

Sylvie pushed him, making him sit back down. "Tell me," she ordered. "What is it you do not wish me to know, my Marshall?"

"It was night," he sighed, "of Christmas Day. We were returning to the inn. Sleigh hit a rock and flipped us out on the road. That's all."

"And you were not hurt?" She looked from his face to Eden's.

"I wasn't," Eden said quickly. "He...he cushioned my fall."

"With what?"

"Um, with himself."

"And you were not hurt?" She rested her hand on his shoulder. He tipped his face down, not wanting to replay this in front of Eden, but Sylvie was a pit bull when she wanted to know about something. He wasn't sure what to say that wouldn't trigger something in Eden.

"You hesitate?" Sylvie noted. "Why?"

"He died," Eden said softly.

"What?" She put her hand under his chin, lifting his face up, his reluctance clearly writ. "What does Eden mean you died?"

"Just briefly," he whispered. "Very briefly."

"Tell!"

"There were four of us in the sleigh. Ryan, the other man, hit my chest really hard. Started my heart again. I'm fine. I'm really fine."

"Marshall," Sylvie said, touching her head, "if you could see, you would know how much gray I have now in my hair. Most of it is because of you."

"Mom used to say the same thing," he grinned, trying to lighten the mood.

"She would have been entirely white with what has happened to you since you were last in this house," Sylvie said firmly.

"But I'm home again now, and I've brought my bride with me, and we need to figure out where to have some sort of reception dinner for the folks here in the city who didn't come to the inn."

"Are you thinking a restaurant or here?" Eden asked.

"You could have it here. I could cook," Sylvie offered.

"I know you could," Marshall replied, patting her arm, "but that's a lot of extra work. I was actually thinking of a restaurant or some sort of small banquet hall."

"What about Monterey Bay on Mount Washington? I've always loved the view from up there."

Then she realized what she'd said. He'd never seen the glorious panorama of the city at night all spread out below, across the confluence of the rivers. He'd never seen any view. "They've got great food," she hurried to add.

"You'd like that?"

She'd only eaten there once, in fact, as it was quite expensive. "No, it doesn't have to be there. It would cost a fortune."

"That's not an issue," he smiled. "Remind me to talk to you later about that. Let me ask you again. Would you like that?"

"I don't think it matters, really, where we have it. You pick a place, any place."

"All right," he said, his lips smiling.

"Here, let me take these." Sylvie began clearing away the breakfast dishes.

Marshall stood, following her to the sink. "I want to tell you again what a great job you did with the master bedroom. I appreciate it all so much. It's perfect."

After they were dressed, Eden spoke up. "Do you think since the roads are ok today that we could go by my apartment? There are some things there I'd like to bring here soon and I need to decide what to keep and what to get rid of with the rest."

"I'd very much like to see where you lived."

She smiled at him, noting once again how he always used words like 'see' and 'look'. "It's not much." Not much, for sure, compared to this.

"It's where you lived, Eden. It matters."

Coated and gloved, they went out to Eden's car, which had been moved into the garage.

Wadsworth jumped into the back seat and Eden headed north out of Mount Lebanon toward Crafton. "To think you were so close," Marshall mused as she drove. His hand moved to her right leg. "How could I not have known?"

Eden pulled up in the parking lot of a yellow brick, three-story apartment building, sitting a moment, staring at it out the windshield. It had been all right. Nothing more than that. It was where she slept, where she hung her clothes. There was no feeling of home about it, none, and her eggs didn't seem to be sitting well on her stomach this morning, adding to a certain sense of malaise she had.

"What?" he asked when she didn't move.

"Just looking at it, thinking." She described it to him, even the long rust stain down the bricks where an old gutter had developed a large hole. Thank goodness her lease was due to be renewed the first of February. She could leave it free and clear as she'd already paid the rent through January.

Wadsworth was in harness on his left and she took his right hand as they walked toward the door. Her apartment was on the second floor, on the back of the blocky, flat-roofed building. She felt like an alien as she went up the stairs and down a long hallway. Had she really lived here? It wasn't just a lifetime ago, it was somehow more than that. As she unlocked the door, she turned her head, looking at Marshall waiting beside her.

Him, that's what made her an alien here. Maybe she'd lifted him out of the gully, but he'd lifted her out of her whole life, set her down in a place wholly new, wholly different.

He'd set her down with him and that was where she belonged. With him. But here he was standing in her past and it just seemed terribly odd to her.

He reached out, touching her cheek. "It's all right," he whispered.

"How did you know?" she breathed. "How do you always know?"

"You've merged with me. I can't not know."

"I love you, Marshall Sinclair."

"I know."

She opened the door, aware he wouldn't know the arrangement of the rooms, the furnishings, glad he had Wadsworth in harness. She gave him a quick tour. There was only the small living room, one bedroom, a little kitchen with room for a table at one end. When he was seated on her bed, she rummaged through her closet and her dresser, packing into a suitcase some items she'd been wishing she had. The furnishings had come with the apartment, so there was nothing large she'd have to deal with. She and Connie could pack some cardboard boxes with her few decorative items, the books, CDs, things like that. Other than that, there would just be the rest of her clothes, make-up, a bit of jewelry. It wouldn't be complicated at all leaving here.

She sat down next to him, taking his hand, needing the contact, sighing as she looked around the room, her stomach still rather 'off'.

"You weren't happy here?" he asked.

"I was a widow here," she replied, her voice low, "a widow who went to work and came here to sleep, maybe read, watch a DVD."

"What about work? Do you want to start back soon?"

"I don't know. I'm not sure. I just...."

"What?"

"I just want to be with you, and you're not teaching right now. I don't want to go off and leave you during the day."

"You don't have to, you know."

"What do you mean?"

He lifted her hand, kissing her knuckles. "Remember I told you my father was a financier and that he was good at it?"

"Umm hmm," she nodded.

"Well, he was, shall we say, very, very good at it."

"How good?"

"Extremely good, almost unbelievably good."

"What are you saying?"

"I'm saying basically that neither of us has to work unless we want to. If you'd like, we can just write, become full-time authors. Maybe travel, let you see the Li River Valley, that sort of thing. Then you can write about it."

She blinked, trying to comprehend what he was saying. "You mean...?"

"I do mean, yes."

"Really?"

"Really." He began to smile broadly.

"Oh, my goodness!" She stood quickly, then felt dizzy, really, really dizzy. "Ohh!" she gasped.

"What's wrong?" He stood, too.

"I think I'm going to...." And she started to crumple.

"Eden!" He managed to grab her before she hit the floor and, his face a mask of worry, lay her on the bed, leaning over her, his hands moving over her face. "Eden?"

He thought he knew where the bathroom was and hurried there, almost tripping over the suitcase she'd left sitting in the middle of the room. He found a wash cloth, wet it, and came back to the bed, kneeling beside it, gently wiping her face. "Eden," he murmured, "come on, Eden. Wake up."

She moaned and turned her head to the side. "Wh...what?"

"You fainted, darling. Are you ill?"

The thing that had been playing around in the back of her mind the last few days, suddenly surfaced. "I think," she licked her lips, "I think, Marshall, that I'm pregnant."

Chapter 86

Marshall paused, wet rag still poised in mid-air, his lips parting. He looked absolutely stunned.

"Is...is that ok?" she asked, then she noticed his jaw was working. "Is it too soon? Is that it?" Tears welled in his eyes, lots of them, overflowed, big, silent tears that began to drip down his cheeks. Leaning more forward, he still said nothing, only laid his head on her chest where she could feel the wetness through her blouse.

"Marshall?"

He was still silent for what seemed a terribly long moment. Wadsworth, concerned, made a few low whuffing sounds, poking at his leg with his nose. Finally, without any attempt to dry his cheeks, he straightened, gathering her into his arms. He tried to speak, made a little croaking sound, and just pressed her carefully to himself. She waited, almost holding her breath. His chin was atop her head and she couldn't see his face.

He cleared his throat, trying again. "We...we...I don't...." He cleared it again, blowing out a long breath. "We don't know, we really don't know how empty our cup is until it suddenly fills to the brim and splashes over in its fullness. I...for so long...I thought...I just expected...I never...."

He changed her position so she could see his face. "Family. That was everything to me for most of my life. Everything. What mattered, all that really mattered, you know. Then it was gone, all of it...gone. And then...," he squeezed his eyes tightly closed, "there was you. You. In the most isolated, desperate aloneness of my life...you. And...and...now this. You're making me a whole new family and I...."

She cupped his face in her hands. "I love you," she whispered, kissing him softly.

"Oh, Eden!" He began kissing all over her face.

"So," she managed to gasp, "it's ok then?"

"How much?"

"How much is it ok?"

"How much pregnant?"

"Rather completely, I'd say."

"How...?"

"I had a bit of help in that department," she chuckled, "as you may recall."

"How long?"

"Not long. I think I'm just sorta beginning."

"September? Early September?"

"Probably. I'll need to see a doctor before long to get a real due date."

His hand came up to his mouth, and he tipped his head down, closing his eyes. "You all right?" she asked.

He nodded, not lifting his head. "What's going on?" she tried.

"Heart's expanding."

"Like the Grinch?"

"Something like that," he smiled, now raising his head, "only I've never stolen a Christmas tree."

"Good thing. Our little Cindy Lou Sinclair might not like that."

He laughed at that. "Cindy Lou, eh?"

"Well, that was the kid in the story, you know, Cindy Lou Who."

"Might be a boy."

"Ok. Horatio Grumsdorfer Sinclair."

"Gads!" He shook his head. "Good thing we have about eight and a half months to arm wrestle over this."

"Good thing," she agreed. "Can we have lunch now? I'm hungry."

He took both her hands in his. "You're really all right now? You scared me when you fainted."

"Turn about's fair play," she smiled. "Yes, I'm fine." Then she chuckled because that's what he always said. "I really am and junior wants to eat."

He stood, taking Wadsworth's harness in his left hand, reaching for hers with his right.

"Suitcase," she said.

" I don't want you carrying that and I want to hold onto you on the stairs. I can't have you fainting again and falling down the steps."

He got it out the door to the hallway. Bob, who had an apartment on the same floor, was just coming out his door. He was a gym teacher at the local high school. "Bob!" she called out, pleased at the timing. "Could you do me a favor?"

"Hey there, Eden. Good to see you back." He came down the hall toward them, noting the harness and the guide dog.

"Bob, this is my husband, Marshall. Marshall, Bob."

"Husband, eh? Well, glad to meet you, Marshall."

"I'm going to be living in his house now," Eden explained. "Would you mind getting this suitcase down the steps for me? I'd really appreciate it."

"Sure. No problem." He carried it all the way out to her car, in fact.

She drove to the Olive Garden in Greentree. "He wants pasta."

"Who wants pasta?"

"Horatio wants pasta."

He shook his head, his lips curving into a smile. "All right, then, pasta."

"Can't disappoint the little guy."

"With a name like that, he's bound to encounter at least a little disappointment."

"Not from me. He wants pasta. I give him pasta."

The travel agency where Connie worked was just a bit down Greentree Road from the restaurant, so after Horatio had his fill of pasta, they stopped by there.

"Eden!" Connie looked up from her computer. "Marshall! How great you guys stopped in."

"I've got good news," Eden beamed.

"I can always use some of that, Cuz. Lay it on me."

"You're going to be an aunt."

Connie's eyes widened. "Really? Wow!"

Connie was Eden's first cousin, but no sisters had ever been closer, so in her mind, 'aunt' was the proper word. "Probably September," Eden added. "Haven't been to the doctor yet."

"You heard from Ryan?" Marshall asked.

"Constantly." Her eyes flickered to her computer screen. "He's working to get that Cleveland office in shape. Says he'll be here as soon as he can."

"I really like him, Connie," Eden smiled, "and it doesn't hurt that he's Martha and Harold's son, either."

"How're the new digs?" Connie asked.

"I want you to come over when you get a chance. You've got to see it for yourself." She wrote down the address on a piece of paper, handing it to her cousin. "Bring Edith. We'll have dinner or something."

"She'll like that. I'll like that. Where you two off to now?"

"Back home," Marshall said. He wanted to be alone with her...soon.

Sylvie had gone by the time they arrived and Marshall led her into their bedroom, having gotten Wadsworth settled by the living room fireplace with a large rawhide chew. He closed the door. "Where are you?"

"Sitting on the bed."

"Good choice." He walked toward her, exuding something almost startlingly male. Not that he didn't always, but there seemed to her eyes something slightly different, almost more. Had fatherhood done that to him? She didn't know, but she was ready to find out. She lay back as he crossed the room.

"You're feeling all right, right now?"

"I think I may even be a bit better than all right."

He smiled, kneeling beside the bed. "I need to gaze at your tummy."

"It looks just the same right now."

"I know, but it's not. It's utterly changed."

She raised her arms over her head while he unbuttoned her blouse and pulled its hem out of the waistband of her slacks. Then he pulled her slacks halfway down over her hips so her torso lay bare. She bit her lip, looking at the intensity on his face. He laid both of his palms across her flat belly, closing his eyes, just leaving them there a long while, then moving them, replacing them with his left cheek.

"I love you," he murmured.

"Me?"

"Both of you." Without opening his eyes, he said almost dreamily, "Did you ever think that this is the only time that two souls occupy the same space at the same time?" He sighed. "Mother and child." His voice held a quiet note of awe.

"I need you," she whispered.

He lifted his head and, sliding his hand inside her slacks, pushed them all the way down, setting them on the floor, then kissed his way up her legs, lingering over her belly as his hands reached behind her, unfastening her bra. She loved looking down at his face when he was loving her, and right now she thought of Michelangelo running his expert hands over some piece of marble he was about to carve. "Cararra," she mumbled.

"What?" He paused briefly.

"Quarry. Italy."

"Michelangelo's?"

"Umm hmm. I was feeling like a block of marble. Remember how he said the sculpture was already in the marble and he just had to find it, remove the pieces that didn't belong, and the sculpture would appear?"

"Are you my block?"

She nodded, "Mmmm."

He smiled. "You're not very square, you know, and other than your clothing, I don't think there's anything that needs removing, but," his tongue slid down her throat, "I'll see what I can do."

Chapter 87

"Coming from the South Hills, you know we could've just driven up the back side of Mount Washington," she commented, getting out of the car in the parking lot at the edge of the Ohio River.

"No inclines on the back side."

"True, but there are roads."

"Special night," he grinned, letting Wadsworth out of the back seat. "Calls for special transport."

"You like the incline, I take it?"

He nodded, "Yup."

"Yup?"

"I'm allowed to yup from time to time." He grinned again.

"Maybe in old Tucson or Dodge, but this happens to be Pittsboig, dear lit professor mine."

"Yup." And he took hold of Wadsworth's harness. "Wait there. Let me come around the car to where you are."

He'd been zealous in his protectiveness for the last week ever since she'd fainted there in her old apartment. She'd been dizzy two or three times, but hadn't keeled over again. She smiled, thinking that for a blind man he sure kept an eagle eye on her.

They had to go up a steep flight of steps, turn a corner, and follow the covered walkway to the lower station of the Duquesne Incline. "So, you come here often, mister?" she asked as he stood in line to purchase their tickets.

"Jeffrey and I used to like to ride this together. He'd describe everything you could see from the cable car. Just seemed like a good way for us to get up to Monterey Bay this evening." Perhaps, too, it was his way of taking his brother along with them. There was so much of his new life he wished he could share with Jeff.

There were only three other people in the old car, January not being a major time for sight-seeing in the 'Burgh. There were two cars, an up and a down, that passed each other halfway along the tracks. Both of them were original, dating from the May 20, 1877 opening of this incline. They took their seats on one of the wooden benches that ran around the interior edges of the car and rose up the steep tracks at a stately six miles an hour.

It had been some years since Eden had ridden in one and she peered out the window at the city, its lights already on in the early darkness of the winter evening. "Tell me what this is like for you?" she asked him, her voice low.

"It's a working museum, you know, and it takes me right back over the years to when the tired workers would ride this home. I'm aware of the sensation of rising and the cars have a particular scent of old wood and polish. I know the city's out there and we're going high, so that we're above it, with the rivers below. I imagine the lights are on now?"

"Yes, the lights are on." She knew he had no real understanding of what that meant and a lingering pang of wishing he did shot through her and she squeezed his hand more tightly.

"Are they like the punctures?"

He hadn't really spoken for a while about what he'd seen that brief moment his heart had stopped there on the snowy road by the sleigh. "Sort of like that, only bigger, and more of them, and more colors. Lower down it's all kind of a golden glow." She studied his face. "You still think about that?"

"Sometimes. It's hard not to, you know." He was quiet a moment. "I just wish I could understand what it is that you do with your eyes. I want to know that because it's your world. It'll be the baby's world, too and I...."

"You are my world, Marshall."

He smiled and leaned to kiss her lightly.

When they arrived at the top, they were still early for the reception, so walked along Grandview Avenue for a while. It was a Saturday night and the area they were in was lined with restaurants, all on the north side of the street so they'd have views of the city. Monterey Bay, though, was across the street and able to be so because it was atop the second highest building on Mount Washington. Only the Trimont Tower was higher. She looked at the black shape of that and frowned, trying not to think of the architect who lived there, glad she'd never ridden the Duquesne Incline with the man.

After half an hour, they turned back toward the Monterey Bay. Marshall had invited a number of his colleagues from the university, some neighbors from Mount Lebanon, two or three writers he knew, a few friends he'd grown up with, and Sylvie. Ryan had been able to make it down from Cleveland, and was bringing Connie and Edith. Eden had asked Marti from the newspaper, several of her former co-workers, some friends.

"I miss Martha and Harold," she whispered as they went in the main entrance and into the glass elevator that would take them to the top of the building, "and Luke, and Mike and Maria." She sighed. "I think I came to feel closer to them than most of the people who're coming tonight." Her parents, of course, would not be in attendance.

A large section of the restaurant had been reserved for their guests. She walked with him through the big round pillars painted like palm trees, toward their tables. Connie was already there with her mother and Ryan, who stood, beaming at them. Ryan couldn't look at Marshall without remembering his desperate blow to the man's chest, so it always made him feel better to see Marshall looking happy, and alive. "I understand congratulations are in order," he greeted.

Edith positively glowed. She felt like a grandmother-in-waiting. Eden, for all intents and purposes, was as much her daughter as Connie. She looked from Eden to Marshall and back again. Yes, they were happy, complete. Her eyes traveled then to Ryan, who'd taken hold of Connie's hand. Her girls, her two girls, both loved by wonderful men.

"What are you smiling at, Mom?" Connie asked.

"My cheeks are happy," she replied.

Gradually the rest of their guests trickled in and there was much hand shaking, hugging, well-wishing, introducing. Marshall and Eden sat at a table with Edith, Connie, Ryan, and Sylvie, Wadsworth tucked part way under Marshall's chair. The restaurant was a popular one and quite crowded, with diners and waiters moving about. It was famous for its fish, which were flown in daily from as far away as Hawaii.

"How long are you here?" Eden asked Ryan.

"Have to be back in Cleveland for Monday morning," he replied, "but I'll have most of the day tomorrow with Connie."

"He's found a place for our travel agency," Connie smiled, "out in Robinson where all the new shops and houses are going in."

"Good spot," Marshall nodded.

"I understand you two are going to England in early April. That still on?"

"Very on," Eden smiled. "Marshall hasn't had his Christmas present yet, you know."

Marshall whispered something in her ear about how he'd unwrapped her and she giggled.

"Isn't that your birthday, Marshall?" Edith asked.

"Yes. April 7th."

"You taking the furry one, I presume?" Connie continued.

"Don't leave home without 'im," Marshall grinned.

"I can help with the paperwork and stuff for him to go overseas if you like."

"I'd appreciate that. Thanks, Connie."

The dinner went well. At one point, Eden guided Marshall around all their tables so they could speak again with their guests. Sylvie offered to drive Edith home so Ryan and Connie could go off together. They went out the front entrance in a group and Eden watched tall, slim Ryan head off down Grandview, his arm around Connie's shoulders then she and Marshall crossed to the upper station of the incline and descended to the lower parking lot. She leaned her head on his shoulder, finding she got tired more easily these days. She'd taken a home pregnancy test that had confirmed what she thought, and had an appointment with her doctor early next week.

Marshall felt her head grow heavier on his shoulder and knew she'd fallen asleep. He wished he could drive her home. How that was done totally escaped him, how people knew where other cars were, when to turn, when to stop. Scattered punctures had not revealed things like that to him. The sighted world was still a mystery. He sighed and woke her gently.

"We're down," he said.

"Down what?" she mumbled.

"Down the hill. Have to get off the car, darling."

He half-supported her along the covered walkway and down the steps, then opened her car door for her. She got in, folded her arms on the steering wheel, and rested her head on them. "So tired," she sighed.

Marshall let Wadsworth in the back seat, then got in beside Eden, pulling her over against himself. "There's no hurry. Rest a while longer."

Obediently, she immediately went back to sleep while he held her, listening to the night sounds along the river. An hour later a train rumbled noisily along the near-by tracks and she woke with a start. "Where...?"

"Parking lot."

"Did I sleep?"

"For a while, yes. Are you rested enough to drive?" Damn, but he wanted to do that for her!

She yawned widely. "Umm hmm." Then she turned, studying his profile in the parking lot lights. His jaw seemed set a bit tightly.

"Sorry I made you wait," she murmured.

"I didn't mind."

"Is something wrong?"

"I wanted to drive you home. It didn't used to matter I couldn't."

"I know, darling, I know. But just like you didn't mind waiting, I don't mind driving. Really I don't."

He turned his face toward the side window, his lips pressed together. It mattered to him. For the first time in his life it really, really mattered. "You're tired, pregnant," he mumbled. "I should be able...."

"Turn around," she said, tugging on his coat sleeve, "please."

Reluctantly he did and she slid closer to him, putting her arms around him. "Don't," she whispered, her mouth close beside his face. "Please don't. You are so utterly complete to me, so entirely whole. Don't waste time with this. Please." She began to kiss his cheeks, his temple. "Please?"

He turned his head, taking her mouth with his. Just then there was a loud tap on her side window. A policeman shined his flashlight into the car. "Move along, folks," he said. "Get a room."

He walked away and both of them laughed. "Shall we get a room?" she asked.

"I know just the one," he replied, his dour mood completely broken.

Marshall's tension had communicated itself to Wadsworth, and at the sound of the laughter from the front seat, he let out a loud bark, joining in. Eden started the car, heading home, her two guys in the car with her. She wondered if there were a third? Well, it was a bit early yet to know that.

Chapter 88

Marshall's lawyer came to the house for a meeting and while he was occupied with that,

Connie and Eden drove together to Eden's old apartment to gather up the remainder of the things Eden wanted to take. "Don't lift anything too heavy!" Marshall called after his wife as she left the house.

"Protective, isn't he?" Connie remarked.

"I fainted the last time I was at the apartment," Eden shrugged.

" Because of the pregnancy?"

"Seems like it. I've been dizzy a lot since. Haven't always let Marshall know."

"Is that something you should keep from him?"

"He worries."

"And you've never worried about him?"

"I'm an expert. That's how I know what it's like, what little good it does."

"Is that why he wanted to be sure I came along with you today?"

"Probably. He doesn't like me to be alone."

"Maybe you shouldn't be alone? You think of that?"

Charles Gromley, an older man who'd been Marshall's father's attorney ever since Marshall could remember, walked into the den, opening a leather briefcase he'd set on the desk. "Everything, eh?"

"Absolutely," Marshall nodded. "I want everything I own also in my wife's name."

"Do you have any idea, Marshall, just what it is you own?"

"Some. Probably not entirely."

"Would you like me to explain?"

"Might as well. I've never really needed to know before."

So for the next hour the two men sat in the then while Charles went through Marshall's holdings, his investments, his accounts. "The will, too," Marshall spoke up. "I need you to draft a new will. Didn't have anybody to leave all this stuff to before."

Charles studied the younger man. "I heard you almost died last fall."

"You heard right," Marshall affirmed. "Did die once. Really got me in touch with how lax I've been with my paperwork. I want these drawn up immediately, Charles."

Charles chuckled. "You sounded like your Dad just then."

Connie and Eden carried the rest of her clothes on their hangers, draping them over the back seat of Connie's car. She didn't take any kitchenware. Her new kitchen had more equipment than she'd ever seen. Besides, she liked using things she knew Marshall's mother had cooked for him with. There were two small boxes of books, one of make-up and jewelry, one with CDs and DVDs, a sack with her shoes. Her DVD player, stereo, and TV she was giving to Connie, who would pick them up another time when she had male help.

Charles had just left when the women got home. They only took the boxes as far as the garage, unsure just where to put them. The clothes they hung in the large closet that was Eden's in the master bedroom.

"Gotta go now," Connie said. "Mom's going to meet me for lunch."

"Give her a kiss for me," Eden smiled, "and thank you! I don't think I could've managed this without you."

"Marshall was right, eh?" They were in the bedroom and could hear him in the bathroom. "Hi, Marsh! Bye, Marsh!" Connie called as she left.

"Bye, Connie!" he answered. "Be right out, darling," he added for Eden.

She felt really drained and stared at the bed. Maybe she could sneak a quick nap before they had lunch? Her nose was a bit drippy from being out in the cold, so she walked around to the far side of the bed where a box of tissues sat on the end table. She pulled one out, but dropped it on the carpet.

"Drat!" She bent quickly over to pick it up. Everything went black and she just continued forward, ending face-down in a little crumpled heap between the end table and the corner of the bedroom. As she'd fallen, her right arm had gotten hooked through the lamp cord, and the lamp went down with her, hitting the wall and breaking the china base. Her arm was cut, not badly, but blood trickled from the middle of her lower arm down to her wrist.

"Did you drop something, darling?" Marshall came out of the bathroom, still drying his hands.

"Eden?"

She didn't answer. "Are you here, darling?" He moved around the room, coming within a foot of her head. Hmmm? There was no sense of her present in the bedroom. Perhaps she'd gone to the kitchen. It was lunchtime and Horatio was often hungry.

He walked into the kitchen, calling, "Eden?" He could hear Wadsworth near the back door, busily working on his rawhide chew. Other than that, there wasn't a sound from inside the house.

He went into the den, the living room, the dining room, calling her name. Stopping at the base of the staircase, he wondered if she might have gone up there. Quickly he went up to the second level, calling out as he went up and down the hall, poking his head into each room. Back downstairs, he returned to their bedroom. "Darling?"

She wouldn't have gone outside, would she? He went back to the kitchen, called out into the rear yard, did the same with the laundry room and the garage. Her car was there. She hadn't driven anywhere and her purse was on the kitchen counter. He stopped in the hallway to the bedroom suite, listening intently. He'd heard some sort of sound while he was still in the bathroom. What could it have been? It had sounded close, like it was in the bedroom. His hands trailed over the dressers. Everything seemed to be in place atop them. He even opened the two closet doors, anxiety growing exponentially in his chest. She had to be somewhere, yet the house had this sense of emptiness about it, the like of which he hadn't felt since that last time he was here before going to the inn.

"No," he said to himself, "it can't be empty like that. She's here. She's got to be here."

He went to the bed, running his hands over it, then touched the things on the bedside table closest to him. No, everything was all right. Walking around the bed, he felt along the window seat, then headed toward the other table. His foot came down on something unfamiliar and he checked his step before his weight went on it. Kneeling, he felt forward. It was her left arm.

"Eden?" He leaned over her, trying to find her face. It was down and turned away from him, her hair spilling over the bit of cheek that was not in the carpet. Brushing the hair back, he touched her closed lids, then found the pulse in her neck. His hand slid down her right arm, encountering wet stickiness. She was bleeding! He scrabbled to his feet, intending to call 911, but she made a soft moaning sound and he dropped back to his knees.

"Eden? Darling?" His heart was pounding.

"Mar...Marshall?"

"I'm here, oh, darling, I'm here."

"T...tissue," she mumbled. "Dropped tissue." She tried to turn.

"Don't move," he urged.

"Not broken," she managed. He scooped her up then, laying her on the bed.

"You're sure?"

"Am," she sighed. "Just...," she blew out a long breath, "just blacked out."

"You fainted?"

"Think so. Dropped tissue. That's...."

Speaking was a bit of an effort. Bending over to pick up the tissue was the last thing she remembered. Her eyes moved slowly to the side, toward the end table. "Lamp's gone."

"Must be what broke. Your arm's cut, darling." He went to the bathroom, returning with a wet cloth, pressing it over where he felt the stickiness. She'd lifted the arm while he was gone, noting that the cut didn't seem that big.

"Don't worry," she whispered. "It's just little." He couldn't tell that for himself, though, and he didn't want to probe at her fresh wound with his fingers. He'd touched half the house in looking for her.

He leaned over her, wrapping her in his arms. "I couldn't find you," he moaned. "I couldn't...." A shudder went completely through him. What if she'd been seriously injured, had been bleeding badly the whole time he vainly went from room to room? For the first time he completely tuned in to him alone in the house with a crawling baby. "Oh, God, oh, God, oh, my God," he groaned.

"You did find me, Marshall, you did."

"In the last place I looked, the very last place," he croaked.

"Did you check in Narnia?" He shook his head. "Then it wasn't the last place, was it?"

She was feeling better and wanted to sit up but his arms were tightly around her. She squirmed and he got the idea, loosening enough to let her prop against the head board, but not really letting go of her. His face was visible to her now, though, and she read an absolute desolation there. He kept whispering over and over, "I couldn't find you...."

She closed her eyes, trying to imagine what it would be like to be in utter darkness and trying to locate something, some one. "It's all right," she tried to soothe. "I'm all right. You did find me. You did."

He was biting his lower lip so hard she was afraid his teeth were going to sink through the flesh of it, so she kissed his mouth softly again and again until he stopped. "Right here in the bedroom. You were here, right here. I didn't know." This was worse than not being able to drive her home the other night, much worse. Never had he felt so incomplete, so lacking. The bile of it rose stingingly up his throat and he stumbled for the bathroom, throwing up over and over.

Wetting a bath towel, he wiped his face roughly, let it drop to the floor, and clung with both hands to the side of the sink. He knew there was a mirror there, knew what the function of a mirror was, though, as with so many things, it was something he couldn't really grasp. He was supposed to be able to stand where he was, look straight ahead, and see himself, whatever seeing was. He was supposed to know what his face looked like without touching his face. He was supposed to be able to look in a room and know where his wife was. His grip on the sides of the sink tightened and a sound like some low, primal growl began in his gut and shoved its way up through him, out of his mouth, and he banged his forehead into the useless mirror, sending jagged crack lines all through it.

"Marshall!" Eden called, but he didn't come.

She got off the bed, walking to the bathroom, appalled at seeing him there, holding onto the sink while blood dripped from his forehead into the oval, granite bowl. A little cry escaped her and she clutched his right arm. He'd broken the mirror. That was what she'd heard, and he'd obviously broken it with his face. "Oh, my darling!"

The bathroom smelled of his vomit, which though it was in the toilet bowl, was unflushed. Quickly she flushed it, grabbed another, smaller towel to wet, took his hand and led him to the bed. Her own cut had pretty much stopped bleeding, but he'd split his skin right at his hairline and blood dripped down over both his closed lids. She didn't need to ask why he'd done it. His repeated 'I couldn't find you's' were evidence enough. She also remembered back to the days right after the sleigh accident when she had been so afraid he would be lost in that brief, inconclusive experience he'd had that might or might not be sight. He couldn't change, couldn't lose that marvelous assurance of who he was, of how he made his way in the world. Now she feared the same thing again.

As he lay down, he folded his arms over his face and she had to pry them away. He'd gotten blood on them, too, by doing that. "Do you love me?" she breathed.

He gritted, "I love you so much, but it's not enough."

"Why isn't it enough?"

"I thought it would be. I wanted you, wanted a family so much, I thought it would be enough." He twisted his head from side to side miserably. "But it's not enough. I'm not enough."

He was slipping away into some trough of despair and she had to prevent his plunge. She lay down, mostly atop him. holding his face with her hands. She'd been in that trough herself there a few days before their wedding when the thought of the loss of him almost led her to run away, not to risk the pain of his death ever again. She had eyes that weren't 'broken' as Luke called them. She didn't even need glasses yet she couldn't keep him from harm. She'd been right beside him when the sleigh started to flip and he'd still died, right beneath her body he'd died when she was in full contact with him. The impossibility of always protecting had been a lesson she wasn't sure she'd yet fully learned. She still worried about him. How compounded that must be, keeping the beloved from harm, when it must be done totally without light, without the information that came to one by seeing?

"You shielded me," she said softly near his ear, "in the sleigh accident. You protected me entirely. You kept the convicts from taking me into the forest. Then, alone and sick, you found your way out, found your way home."

His chin quivered and his eyes stayed tightly squeezed shut. "In...in the forest, I was the one...the one lost. I was...was trying to find...me, get me out."

"Yes, but for me. You did that for me."

He nodded. "But you weren't lost. I wasn't trying to find you. Not like now. I tried and tried and tried," a tear welled despite his tightened lids, "and I couldn't...do...it. I couldn't find you. I need...," he gasped in a sharp breath, "I need to...to be able to...find you. I...."

He tried to twist his head away, but she held on. "I'm not going to let you go, Marshall Sinclair. Do you hear me? I am NOT going to let you go!"

"Why?" he groaned, his whole face almost crumpling.

"Don't you know you are the best, the most wonderful, the most unimaginably glorious thing that's ever happened to me? EVER! Don't you know how much you mean to me, how I can't possibly live without you, can't even begin to think of living without you? You almost died three times at the inn, my darling. This was just a little faint. Don't do this to yourself. Don't do this to me. Please, darling!"

"The baby." His chin was still trembling. "I can't keep our baby safe. I don't know...I...."

"We'll work out ways. Lots of blind people have raised kids. We'll find out stuff, figure it out. It'll be ok. We can do it. You can do it. I know you can. I do!"

He heaved an enormous sigh. The memory of searching the house, of not finding, was still so fresh. She still lay atop him and his arms slid around her back. She rested her face against his, his blood getting on her cheeks and nose. Gradually she felt his tension begin to leave somewhat. He seemed exhausted and she was still tired from packing up things in her apartment. They slept as they were, her heart right above his.

Sylvie came in the house an hour later, intending to straighten up after lunch and maybe polish some of the silver in the dining room breakfront. Eden's car and purse were there, so she knew they must be home. Besides, Wadsworth was in the kitchen, meaning Marshall had to be about somewhere. She went down the hall just to check and see if their bedroom door were closed. It was open and she paused outside, half-turning away. They were asleep. She smiled and decided to close the door, make sure any noise of her cleaning didn't disturb them. Her hand on the knob, she cast a quick, fond look at them, then froze. Eden lay atop Marshall and both their faces were turned toward the door, both covered with blood. Her piercing shriek reverberated through the house, awakening them. They sat up, blinking sleepily toward the doorway.

More sharp shrieks preceded her as she ran to the bed. She could barely breathe as she clutched at them here and there. Murderers had been in the house, had stabbed them.

"Where?" she shouted, wanting to know where the knives had found their mark.

"Wh...what?" Marshall stammered, not fully awake. He felt frantic hands moving over his chest. "Eden?"

"Blood!" Sylvie moaned. "Blood everywhere! Oh, my God, blood everywhere!"

"Sylvie?" he tried.

"My darling Marshall. You're alive! Where have you been stabbed? Where?"

His hand went to his face, feeling the caked, dried blood. "Mirror," he said in feeble explanation. "No knives."

"Mirror? They attacked you with mirrors?" Sylvie was on the verge of keeling over herself.

"No, no, Sylvie. It's all right."

"And you?" She began feeling Eden.

"Lamp," Eden stated uninformatively, then suddenly remembered when they'd arrived at Stuart's house for New Year's Day dinner, wounded by curtain rods and kitchen stools, and how Ryan had reacted to that with laughter. She definitely felt discombobulated at the moment and began to giggle.

"It's her arm," Marshall explained. "The lamp broke and cut her arm."

"But her face! Blood all over!"

"My blood," he said quietly, and touched his hairline.

Finally deciding that brigands had not almost killed them, Sylvie caught her breath and leaned to check his forehead and then Eden's arm. "Stitches," she pronounced. "Get coats. I'm driving you both to St. Clair Hospital."

"But Sylvie...," he protested.

"Now!" she stated even more firmly. She got them up and hustled them out to the kitchen, glaring at Wadsworth, who was just swallowing his last bit of rawhide chew. "So," she growled, "if it had been murderers, would you have left the chew and saved your people?"

Wadsworth gave her a sloppy doggy grin and came over to sniff at the scent of blood on said people. "He would have, Sylvie," Marshall said, remembering the dog's unflagging tracking of him through the forest, how he'd brought Eden to the gully. "I told him he was off duty and gave him the chew." He paused to rub Wadsworth's neck, then grabbed the harness near the door.

"He's coming, too?" Sylvie frowned.

"Always," Marshall replied.

In the car, with their faces more on his level as the three of them sat in the back seat, Wadsworth was much more intent on exploring the presence of blood. Marshall buckled on his harness during the five minute drive to St. Clair. Sylvie pulled into the emergency entrance and two attendants hurried out.

"Looks a heckuva lot worse than it is," Eden said quickly before they could bring gurneys. "We can walk."

A male nurse tried to put them in separate exam rooms but Marshall was having none of it. Sylvie sat in the near-by waiting room, holding Wadsworth's harness. "Poor boy has spent way too much time in hospital waiting rooms of late," Eden sighed as she and Marshall were led down a corridor.

"This is highly irregular," the nurse said, pulling back a blue curtain but Marshall had a grip on Eden's hand and nothing was going to make him let go. He held onto it the entire time a young female nurse washed their faces and arms to determine just who was bleeding where. Eden's cut was handled with three small butterfly bandages and Marshall was basically glued.

"No stitches," Marshall announced as they came back out to the waiting room.

Sylvie's eyes narrowed. "In and out this time, is it? Not like your usual."

"Good thing Hersholtz isn't here," Marshall said wryly, remembering his doctor's yoyo string remark.

"Let's go home," Eden sighed. "Horatio's hungry."

Chapter 89

While Marshall and Eden ate lunch, Sylvie went to their bedroom to take care of some of the damage. The glass from the lamp was cleaned up, the bedding changed, the blood-stained items being treated and then put in cold water to wash, and the bathroom sink and floor cleaned. She called for a new mirror to be installed.

Afterwards she shooed the two of them to the bedroom so they could have some privacy and talk more. On her trips through the kitchen while they ate, they'd seemed too silent to her. She hadn't even been able to coax Marshall into a real smile with a cookie.

He sat on the side of the bed, his shoulders slumped. Eden came up in front of him, straddling his legs, resting her wrists on his shoulders. "I love you," she said softly.

"I know," he replied in a whisper. "I love you, too."

"We need to talk about this," she added.

"I have a lot of thinking to do," he said, not lifting his head.

"You're hurting." He nodded. "I can't let you hurt alone."

"I need to think," he repeated, turning his head to one side.

"Baby's coming. Thinking's not going to change that."

"I know. It's not just that. It's...."

"What?"

"Everything. Me."

"And me? Am I in that?"

"Most of everything is you," he replied, finally turning his face toward hers.

"Do you wish we'd never...."

"No. Not for a minute. You are all that's good in my life."

She slipped the tips of the fingers of her right hand under his chin. "So what's there to think about?"

"I need to...I have to...I...."

"You really want some quiet time right now?"

He nodded. "If...if you...."

"For you, anything." She got off his lap, kissed him gently, and walked toward the door. "I'll be back after while." She remained standing in the doorway long enough to see him lie back on the bed, his feet still on the floor, and fold his arms over his face. Sighing, she closed the door so that he could hear her close it, then went back to the kitchen.

"He asleep?" Sylvie asked, putting the last of the lunch dishes in the dish washer.

"No. Suffering."

Sylvie's left eyebrow shot up but she didn't say anything about it. Instead, she asked, "Want to whip up something special?"

"What did you have in mind?"

"Maybe a lemon meringue pie from scratch?"

Eden remembered what he'd said about that kind of pie when they'd stopped at Dick's Diner in Murrysville on the way back from the inn. It would give her something to do other than staring out a window and worrying. "Sure," she half-smiled.

Marshall lay like that a long time, his thoughts a tangle of half-followed trails with no endings. He knew from all the places he'd walked while searching for Eden that he must've come within a matter of inches from her right toward the beginning. What if it had been an artery that the lamp glass had cut? He simply did not know what to do with the fact that she could have bled to death right there in their bedroom while he was only inches away.

It all came back to the whole damn sight thing. Most people in the world would have found her instantly, using this special something they all had. He went over every second of that odd rise of his there on Christmas Day when his heart wasn't beating. Was there something there, anything that he could latch on to, that would have helped him find her when finding was an utter necessity? But what Eden had said were probably snowy pine boughs hadn't even seemed like that to him. They were a mishmash of unrecognizable forms and he had no way of discerning what they even were. His mind didn't work that way, didn't connect form with vision. There was simply no connection. And the punctures. That was almost worse, absolutely totally confusing to him. How did the sighted take that and use it to gather all the information they did?

He remembered sitting on the blanket with Eden that fall day when she'd described the distant trees, the presence of the groundhog, the slope of the hill, the stumps and rocks.

She did all that from where she sat, without touching any of them. She knew. Dammit, she

KNEW! How...how did she know? How did that work?

He thought of Horatio or little Cindy Lou Sinclair crawling toward the top of the staircase or picking up a piece of glass. He wouldn't know. Never before had the need to know mattered so much. As a boy he'd gone blithely about, quite secure in his world with all its enclosing parameters of little import. He went where he wanted to go, did what he wanted to do, or so it had seemed. Jeffrey made it seem that way. So did his parents. And he had believed it had been enough. It had been enough. Until now. He was almost overwhelmed with the sudden fall from grace he was experiencing. Even alone on Coopers Ridge, he hadn't felt like this, and he'd managed to get down, to get himself out, get to a place where he could be found. Just like he'd always done. As hard as it was, he had done it...and it had been enough.

Not now.

Eden could have bled to death, and he would not have been enough. The baby...the stairs...whatever. He wouldn't be enough. Reaching for a pillow, he grabbed it and put it over his face, refolding his arms over that. Nothing helped. He couldn't shut out the fact of his lack. It was screaming loudly in his ears, pounding in his veins, and his head hurt with it. He tossed the pillow aside and lay still, hoping the inner cacophony would calm.

The loss of something important lay over him heavily, so heavily that his ribs almost ached with the weight of it. It was new and he wasn't used to it, didn't know what to do with it. Balling both hands into fists, he pressed them over his eyes. It was the same old thing of not being sure it was so much that he needed to see as that he was desperate to understand what seeing was. How could he not know something as important as that, as common?

He thought back to that rainy day on the inn porch when he'd described to Eden all the different sounds the rain made, how they revealed the world to him, gave it presence and dimension it didn't have without it. How feeble that now seemed. With a single turn of her head, she would know all that and so much, much more. He felt circumscribed and there was nothing to be done about it. This was the way life was for him, always had been, always would be but, before, it had been enough.

He'd never really had to be responsible for anybody but himself, and a narrowed world for himself had always worked fine. He went, he did, he functioned damn well, but a wife was in his world now, a child was coming, and that changed everything. A convulsive sob rose up from his chest and he clamped both hands over his mouth, rolling sideways, burying his face in the bedspread.

He was like that when Eden quietly opened the door. Tears instantly stung her eyes. He was hurting even more than she'd thought. She couldn't turn away and go back to the kitchen now, not now, so she went to him, sat on the bed beside him and lay her hand on his head.

He hadn't wanted her to find him like this. "I'm...I'm sorry," he murmured, moving his hands away from his lips.

"For what? For loving me, for wanting to take care of me?"

He stayed on his side, but his arms went around her waist. "I wanted...wanted to...."

"Marshall, I want you to hear me. Everything I need, absolutely everything, and more than I ever thought or imagined, all of it, you give me that. I had lost myself and you even gave that back to me. You found me and returned me, made me whole again, made me more whole than I'd ever been in my life. You, you did that. You do that. You not only gave me you, you gave me back me, and now you've given me someone who's a part of both you and me. I'm so happy about that. It'll be all right, really it will. We'll work together and we'll make it all right. I need you to believe me on that."

He sighed, the longest, most ragged sigh she'd ever heard. She began to comb the fingers of her right hand through his hair. "Just let me love you, darling. Just let that be enough."

"You've always been enough," he whispered. "I'm just not...."

She put a finger over his lips. "You are, you so very much are."

"I want...."

"Shhh!" she murmured, leaning back so she was beside him, running the backs of her fingers along his cheek. "You are what I want. Just the way you are." She touched his cheek some more. "And that happens to be absolutely perfect in every way, you hear me, in every way. I adore the man you are and no man has ever, ever, done more for a woman than you've done for me. I mean that with all my heart and I mean it because it's the truth."

"But...."

"No, no but's. Not a single one. Not ever. You fill me up so that I overflow, lift me to places where joy dances naked in the wind."

"Naked in the wind?" he repeated.

"Umm humm."

"We should try that sometime."

She smiled. He was coming back. "In the daffodils preferably."

"Definitely daffodils," he agreed, nuzzling his face in her hair.

"Definitely Daffodils. Is he related to Sincerely Sinclair?" she asked with a small chuckle.

"Lovers," he whispered. "Most scandalous."

"Well, then," she said, unbuttoning his shirt, "why don't we...?" But his mouth had found hers and she couldn't finish whatever it was she'd been going to say.

Chapter 90

"You look nervous," Eden said, smiling at Marshall. He'd moved the single chair in the small room next to the examination table where she sat, her legs dangling.

"I've never been to an obstetrician before."

"Get used to it, big boy," she chuckled. "I like you here with me."

The door opened and an attractive, brown-haired woman in her late forties came in. "Hello, Dr. Pratner," Eden greeted. "This is my husband, Marshall Sinclair."

Sophie Pratner had been Eden's gynecologist since before her marriage to Miles and she smiled as she greeted Marshall, who had risen and extended his hand in her direction. Ah, he was blind, she noted, taking the proffered hand firmly in hers. She sat on a little rolling stool and they chatted briefly, with her going over some basic pregnancy preliminaries.

"She's fainted...twice," Marshall said, his voice low, rather grim.

"Not unusual for early pregnancy," Dr. Pratner said. "She'll be getting her sea legs before you know it." She turned to Eden. "I'd like to do some blood work, get a urine sample. When you're further along, we'll do a sonogram. It's too early for that right now."

She left and a nurse came in, taking Eden's blood, then showing her to a restroom for the sample. She was also weighed then taken back to the room where Marshall waited. When Dr. Pratner returned, she did a pelvic exam. "Yep," she smiled, "baby's on its way all right." She caught Eden's quick look at her husband, noting it was mingled with joy and concern.

"Is that good news?" Pratner asked.

"Very good," Marshall replied, but his smile was just slightly tremulous.

"Ok, guys, what's up?"

"He's concerned about being blind and having a baby in the house."

"I lost her a few days ago," Marshall sighed heavily. "She'd fainted in the corner of our bedroom and it took me a long time to find her. I...," he pressed his lips together, "I want a family more than anything, Dr. Pratner, I truly do. I'm just concerned."

"Ah, I see," Pratner said, studying his face.

"That's the problem," Marshall added wryly. "I don't. What if the baby is crawling and I...."

"What if, Marshall, you take the 'what if's' as they come? A person can 'what if' themselves into a chasm and get buried alive by them."

Both Marshall and Eden snorted loudly. "That was funny?" Pratner asked.

"It's how we met," Eden supplied. "He'd fallen into a chasm and was drowning in liquid mud."

"I've heard of interesting first dates, but that one takes the cake," Pratner said, shaking her head. "Well, look at it this way, um, take it this way...you know from experience what that's like then, yes? So don't do that again. There's a lot of help and advice out there for just this situation and if you take it one step at a time, you can deal with one aspect of it at a time. That way it doesn't become a mudslide."

"I understand that," Marshall said softly, "and it's what I want to do. It's just...."

"You don't feel quite adequate? Is that it?"

Marshall nodded, lacing his hands tightly in his lap.

"Dr. Pratner, I can't begin to tell you how more than adequate my husband is. He's saved my life twice now, both times at great personal cost." Eden reached out, curving a hand over his shoulder, pressing her fingers firmly into it. He unlaced his hands and put one of his atop hers.

Dr. Pratner smiled again. "It seems to me the two of you have a good foundation going between you to build a life on, to build a family on. Let it come. Enjoy it. Wring every drop of joy you can out of every single moment."

The corner of Marshall's mouth began to twitch. "Did you ever think of coaching for the NFL?"

Pratner laughed. "Too sweaty! Now then, back to the pregnancy. From what I can tell so far, you should be due around mid-September. Looks like you got pregnant somewhere near New Year's."

"We got married New Year's Eve," Eden volunteered.

"Ah ha!" Sophie Pratner chuckled. "That may explain it, then."

"She's all right, though, doctor, even with the fainting?"

"She's quite healthy," Pratner affirmed. "She'll do just fine."

"What about him?" Eden asked. "I'm not so sure he'll do just fine." She was flooded with a clear image of Marshall gripping the bathroom sink, blood streaming down his face. That couldn't happen again.

"There's a lot of modern technology out there these days," Pratner went on. "Explore around, see what you can find, what works for you."

"What do you think she meant?" Eden asked as she drove them home.

"I imagine she meant I could bug you."

"What?"

"Some sort of small electronic device that could send a sound signal if...if you...."

"If I fainted again?"

"Would...would...."

"For your peace of mind, my darling, anything, absolutely anything."

"I'll make some calls this afternoon," he said, letting out a long breath of relief.

Thank goodness, she thought. Something. Anything.

And, so, by the next afternoon Eden was wearing a rather attractively-wrought silver bracelet that had a bit of complicated electronics tucked away beneath a pearl setting. If Marshall were trying to find her and she, for some reason, were non-responsive, he could press a button on a little device in his pocket which would activate a loud buzz that would lead him to her. He sat beside her on the couch, his fingers exploring the bracelet.

"You don't mind? It's not too...."

"I don't mind at all. It's really quite lovely." And it would certainly help to keep the bathroom mirror intact, not to mention his head. She touched his cheek. "Have I told you lately how much I love you, Dr. Sinclair?"

"Yes. But you can always, um, show me." He grinned. "I like that, you know."

"So I've noticed."

February passed rather quickly. They decided that, come spring, they'd add a new room onto the back of the house just off their bedroom. That way the nursery would be right there, and not upstairs. Marshall was very pleased about that. They were also rather enjoying not knowing if it were Horatio or Cindy Lou, not that they were actually going to use either of those names, so decided in case they continued with the not wanting to know, to do the nursery in creamy yellow, spring green, and white. Marshall and Eden talked at some length about the meaning and connections with those colors and he felt he had somewhat of a concept of them, especially liking the connotation of the light green with the first sprouting leaves of spring, tender, delicate, like a baby. It was going to be a big nursery, with room for two rocking chairs and a play area so when the child was a toddler there would be a place for it to play close by that didn't involve stairs.

"You see?" Eden said. "No mudslides. We're taking the 'what if's' one at a time." She looked at her husband, who was stirring the waffle batter. "You are more peaceful about it, aren't you?"

He held the large wooden spoon up high, letting the batter drip back into the bowl. "Peace, like a river..." he sang with a bit of a chuckle.

"A river of waffle batter? Just, um, how peaceful is that?"

"It's a peace that will shortly solidify and not only that, will taste good."

"Mmmmm, peace that tastes good. Nice concept."

"Is the waffle iron hot?"

"Yep."

"Give it a try then." He put the spoon back in the bowl and pushed it toward her. When he heard her move the bowl and then the sizzle as she poured batter into the waffle iron, he added, "Yes."

"Yes?"

"Yes, I'm more peaceful."

Leaving the waffle to its cooking for a moment, she came around the kitchen island and kissed his lips lightly. "Your peace is my peace," she whispered, then kissed him again. It was true. Her worry about his well-being had been greatly subsumed by her worry over his worry about her well-being. Which, actually, come to think of it, *was* worrying over his well-being, was it not? Ah, it sounded too complicated when you tried to put it into words like that, but there had been no more incidents, no fainting, and with his knowing he could find her, with the decisions they were making about the baby, a steady, quiet peace had begun to radiate from him again.

Ryan had finished helping his friend set up the travel agency in Cleveland and was now in Pittsburgh. A new mall had opened out toward the airport, not an enclosed or even a strip mall, but one designed to look more like a street with shops on both sides. He and Connie had rented there and were busily engaged in getting their very own travel agency running. It was a dream come true for the both of them, being able to design it the way they liked.

"So it's just a little over a month, right," Ryan asked, "that you two head for England?"

"April 5th, yes," Eden affirmed. "Flying into Manchester then making our way to the Lake Country."

"I presume Waddy here's traveled overseas before?" At Marshall's nod, Ryan continued, "So he's micro chipped already?" Marshall nodded again. "Has he been into the UK?"

"Germany and Switzerland," Marshall supplied, "oh, and Spain, but not the UK."

"We were checking the State Department guide for access policies for service animals into the UK for you," Connie said. "He'll need a blood test and proof he's been treated for ticks and tapeworm and is free of rabies, but I imagine you have most of his documentation."

"Right," Marshall smiled, knowing she meant Wadsworth's certificate of training from the guide dog school. His documentation would be sent by fax ahead of their flight to the Animal Reception Center at Manchester and when they arrived, a sticker would be attached to the dog. At least Wadsworth wouldn't have to spend time in quarantine.

"It seems like a lifetime since Christmas," Eden sighed, "and now England is finally getting close." She touched Marshall's arm. "And your birthday."

"And my birthday," he repeated, "in England, with you."

"Waffle batter," she whispered.

He smiled. "Yes, waffle batter."

Ryan cocked an eyebrow dramatically.

"Peace becoming solid," Eden said. "Don't ask. I doubt I could explain."

Chapter 91:

Throughout February Marshall and Eden had picked carefully through his original manuscript, choosing sections both large and small that could easily be kept. Even Morgan's conversations with George Wythe, Washington, Henry and others at the Raleigh could be kept the way they were. What they had to do was weave a net of Morgan and Susannah and lay it gently over that framework, fitting it in.

February was an unstable month, swinging wildly between ice and thaw, potholing the roads, and lending itself to much time spent by the large living room fireplace or in the big study, fashioning their net of words. Eden experienced some morning sickness, but nothing too terrible, and Marshall was unfailingly attentive.

"Who's at the door?" Susannah asked as Layla came back into the parlor.

"Young Harrelson," Layla replied, her tone clearly indicating her displeasure.

Susannah sighed. "I suppose you'll need to show him in."

"I am in," Parker said, brushing past Layla, hardly breaking stride as he pressed his hat into her hands. He stopped a few feet out from where Susannah, dressed in pale rose, was seated.

Layla's fingers curled over a section of the brown tricorn, crushing it slightly as she watched Harrelson's back. "I'll be lettin' your father know he's here," she said pointedly, a bit too much emphasis on the word 'he'.

Parker's head turned toward her. "No hurry," he said.

His ice-blue eyes glinted in the morning light streaming through the parlor's white lace curtains, his pale blond hair neatly queued. Man ain't got no lashes, *Layla thought. Parker's short blond ones hardly showed at all.* Looks like a pig. *Well, his nose wasn't short and pudgy, though, was it? It was very narrow and quite long and he tended to lift his chin and look down the length of it.*

He'd turned his attention back to Susannah, who looked to Layla's protective eyes like a white hen being sized up by a fox. Pressing her lips together, she left the room, hung the hat on a rack near the door, then hurried to find Mr. Wellington. "Sure don't want that man alone with her," she muttered under her breath.

"Good morning, Parker," Susannah said, not extending her hand.

Parker looked briefly at the sunlight in the window then back at Susannah, a vision of loveliness to his eager eyes. It was, indeed, why he wanted her. She was undoubtedly the most beautiful woman in Williamsburg and would be a perfect ornament for his arm. That she was blind was, indeed, detrimental, but women needed leading around anyway and where he wanted to lead this one was to his bed. With war so near, he wanted to lock in his right to that fairly soon.

"Miss Susannah," he responded, taking a couple of steps closer, "my father is having a ball at Graylands Saturday next and I was...."

"Good day, Mr. Harrelson," Harmer Wellington said firmly, appearing through the side door to the parlor. "What is this about a ball?"

Parker inclined his head toward Harmer. "I was just telling Miss Wellington about the ball my father is having at our plantation up the Neck. I...he...wished me to extend his invitation to you and your daughter if that is...."

"You think a ball is appropriate, Parker, what with war doubtlessly on the horizon?"

"I think it may be more than appropriate, Sir. It may be necessary."

"And how might that be?" Harmer cocked an eyebrow.

"Soon there will be no time, no opportunity for such endeavors and one must enjoy them while one may."

"Interesting way of looking at it," Harmer said, not smiling.

Parker shifted uncomfortably, aware Mr. Wellington was sizing him up. Mr. Wellington always seemed to do that, especially now that Parker was a man grown.

"Percival feels the same, does he?" Harmer continued.

"My father, yes, he does." Actually the whole thing had been entirely Parker's idea and his father had taken a great deal of convincing, but Parker wanted to get Susannah there and propose to her that night.

Harmer was not unaware of Parker's intentions regarding Susannah. The man practically salivated when he looked at her. At the thought, Harmer's upper lip curled slightly in disgust. As a boy, Parker had been self-centered and thoughtless, traits that only seemed to have been magnified in his manhood. As long as he was alive, Harmer thought, his beloved child would never end up in the clutches of such as he. He cleared his throat. "I understand, Parker, that you bear a great sense of loyalty to the English king."

"To our king, yes, yes, I do." He eyed Harmer, aware the man entertained the likes of Patrick Henry at his dinner table, dinners to which he himself was never invited.

"Well, then, there is an Englishman rather newly arrived in Virginia and, perhaps, being so fond of things of an English nature, you might consider expanding your invitation list to include him?"

Harmer never asked anything of him. Here was a chance to do something that might impress his future father-in-law. "Certainly, Sir. What is his name?"

"Morgan Kent. His father owns a large shipping company." That was all the information he'd give Parker. He'd not mention Morgan's age, nor his grace, nor his own recent hopes regarding him.

"Where might I find him?" Parker asked.

"Oh, I shall be glad to extend the invitation on your behalf, Parker. Don't trouble yourself about it."

Parker dipped his head, looked quickly at Susannah, then back at Harmer. "So, Sir, I take it that this means you and Sus....your daughter will be in attendance?"

"We shall," Harmer smiled, walked further into the parlor, and added, "Here, allow me to escort you to the door."

"That Harmer," Marshall chuckled, "he's quite the schemer."

Eden had been writing Harmer and curved her lips in a smile. "Sometimes a father's gotta do what a father's gotta do." She looked up at Marshall, who was standing behind her chair as she typed. "So what does Susannah think of all this?"

When her father had mentioned Morgan, Susannah's lips had parted rather dramatically, but Parker was looking at Harmer at the time and didn't see her response. What her father had said was so entirely unexpected she had no idea what to think. She had not said a word during the whole interchange between the two men and when she heard the front door close and her father's footsteps come back into the room, she said quickly, "Father? You...you...?"

"I happen to be quite fond of our young Mr. Kent," he replied, carefully observing the emotions that passed over his daughter's face.

"You...you are? I didn't...."

"Indeed so. I've spoken with him several times in the Raleigh since he attended our dinner here. He is developing a fine appreciation, I find, of matters of a colonial nature."

Her father had not mentioned that he had seen Morgan again. She found that, though she had not encountered him again, he was never far from her thoughts. Did he think still of her? Was she untoward in hoping that he did, that he must?

"It is all right with you, Susannah, if I invite him to attend the ball?"

"All right? Um, yes, Father. It is all right."

Harmer smiled. Morgan's simple act of deliberately spilling his wine so that Susannah might have reason to escape an uncomfortable situation had quite won him over. No one, especially no young man, had ever been that thoughtful, that discerning of her needs. He knew they had spent time in the garden that night, indeed, he'd gone out of his way to make that possible. Such was his measure of Mr. Kent. Ever since, he'd found his daughter smiling to herself in a way he'd never seen her do before. He worried about her. He was aging, would not be there to watch out for her well-being forever. The thought of Parker swooping her off to his bed was beyond repulsive to him. He'd seen her face when he'd entered the parlor, her cheeks stiff, her mouth set, and because he'd been facing her when he'd mentioned Morgan's coming to the ball, he'd seen her reaction to that as well.

"Well, my darling," he said, coming to give her a kiss on her cheek, "I must be off. I have a meeting with Wythe this morning."

She reached out her hand, touching his face as he bent. "I love you, Papa," she whispered.

"I know." He tapped the end of her nose lightly with a fingertip.

He walked briskly down Nicholson Street then headed across the Palace Green toward Wythe's brick home on the far side. He was half way across when he saw Morgan coming out Wythe's front door and walking toward the Green. He stopped where he was, waiting.

Morgan saw Mr. Wellington and raised his hand in greeting, hurrying his steps toward him. "Good morning, Sir," he greeted. "I see you are on your way where I have just departed."

"Indeed I am," Harmer smiled, "and most propitious it is to encounter you."

Morgan raised his eyebrows, curious as to what Wellington might mean.

"There is to be a ball Saturday next at Graylands, Mr. Kent. That is the plantation on the James about six miles up the Neck. My daughter and I will be attending and Parker Harrelson, son of the host, has most kindly extended the invitation to include you."

"Me?"

"Yes, Mr. Kent, you. Is that something you might possibly consider?"

Susannah! Susannah would be there! His eyes almost ached with his need for the sight of her. Harmer's lip twitched as he read that clearly exposed on the young man's face. "Why, yes, yes, Sir! I would be most delighted to attend! Certainly! Yes!"

"Good. Susannah and I will be going by carriage, of course, but we would be pleased to have you accompany us on the way by horseback if that is amenable to you, since you don't know the way."

Morgan's lips had parted in much the same way Susannah's had. "I should be most, um, most grateful, Sir. Yes."

That very afternoon Morgan ordered a new suit made for himself, not that his Susannah would see him in it, but he wished to look his best for the occasion, nonetheless. The endless days had passed, their hours creaking almost agonizingly slowly by as though turned by some ancient waterwheel that shuddered and groaned with the effort of the weight of their minutes. Now he stood before the old mirror in his room in the Francis Street boarding house, studying himself as best he could with a great deal of the silvered backing missing from the aged glass. His coat and knee breeches were a deep, rich claret, with fine white lace foaming over the claret and silver damask tunic-vest. His chestnut brown hair was only lightly powdered, held in its queue by a strip of claret velvet. His new shoes were black with silver buckles. He stood there, cocking his head, white lace falling across his clasped hands. "You'll do," he said to himself, unused to this new need to appear at his best, picked up his black cloak lined with matching claret, and strode to the stables to get his bay gelding.

Tying the bay to the post outside Wellington's white house, he mounted the two steps to the front entrance. Before lifting his hand to knock, he closed his eyes a moment, breathing slowly in and out in an effort to calm his racing pulse. Susannah. He was about to see Susannah again. He was still standing like that when Micah opened the door.

"You all right, sir?" Micah asked. He'd seen Morgan coming up the front walk but the man had not knocked.

Morgan's eyes flew wide. "Oh, um, yes, Micah. I'm fine. Would you please let...."

"Come on in, Mr. Kent," Harmer said heartily. He'd been crossing the entrance hall as Micah had opened the door. "Let me see if my daughter is ready." He took Morgan's hand briefly then went up the main stairs to Susannah's room.

"Mr. Kent has just now arrived, Susannah," he said, and she turned on the vanity bench where Layla was placing a last pin in her hair. He heard her suck a breath in as she turned and he smiled.

"I'm ready, Papa," she said as Layla stepped back, her grin of approval going from ear to ear. Susannah had no idea of how fine she looked.

Harmer crossed to her as she stood, offering his arm. "Let us go down then, shall we?"

Morgan paced back and forth across the wide entry hall, unable to remain still, but when Susannah appeared at the top of the steps, he stopped, absolutely rooted to the spot. She was wearing what looked like iced-pink silk, draped over a wide hoop that swayed when she paused at the top. The fullness of the skirt only emphasized her tiny waist. Her bodice was embroidered with small, slightly darker pink rosettes with a hint of green leaves, and two stiffly-ruffled rows of white lace framed the upper curves of her breasts. The sleeves were tight to the elbows where more lace draped in scalloped curves. Her golden hair was done up in a complicated series of curls, worked with pink and white ribbons, while two long pipe curls hung down one side of her neck, around which she wore a thin silver chain with a single large pink pearl.

He was staggered. Harmer, seeing how struck through to the core the young man was, smiled slightly. Together he and Susannah descended the wide staircase. As they came closer to him, Morgan was not at all sure he would live through the moment. His heart seemed to be ricocheting wildly off his ribcage. When they reached the bottom, he tried to speak, but his voice had deserted him. Desperately, he cleared his throat.

"Mr. Kent, if you don't mind," he took Susannah's hand off his own arm, transferring it to Morgan's, "would you wait with my daughter while I get our cloaks?"

Micah had already gotten them, but Harmer made a hand gesture to shoo him back. Neither Susannah nor Morgan had been at all aware of Micah.

Susannah, as she'd descended the stairs, had begun to sense Morgan's presence there in the entryway, knew he was watching her. She didn't think ever in her life she'd been so excited by any other moment. Morgan. He was there. Every cell in her being began to vibrate, a fact not missed by her father as her hand on his arm began to tremble.

She heard Morgan clear his throat then was astounded by her father moving her hand to his arm. Her astonishment immediately gave way, though, to her awareness of her hand being on his arm. Again. Not since that night in the garden, but now again. Her lips curved and she said, "Mr. Kent," then under her breath added, "Morgan."

Morgan had to clear his throat yet again. He was still blinking in his own surprise at what Mr. Wellington had done. His voice low, cracking with emotion, he managed to whisper, "I've missed you so."

Her smile widened. "And I you." A crease of worry formed on her brow. "Is...is father...?"

"He's not returned yet. I...I...." He lifted a hand, briefly touching her cheek. "Ah, Susannah, I cannot begin...."

"I know," she said softly. "I, too."

"I need to kiss you." His whispering voice broke in a moan.

A loud 'Ahem' sounded from the next room and Harmer slowly reappeared, two cloaks over his arm. He handed one to Morgan. "Help her with this while I get my own on, Morgan."

Both Susannah and Morgan noticed her father's use of his first name.

Holding her dark pink satin cloak in both hands, Morgan stepped around behind her, placing it over her shoulders. Harmer seemed busy with getting his own cloak straight, so Morgan let his hands linger, then slide slowly down the curve of her shoulders. He'd stopped breathing while he did so.

"Thank, thank you, Mor...Mr. Kent," Susannah murmured, trembling again at his touch.

"Looks like we are ready," Harmer announced, placing Susannah's hand on his own arm and heading toward the door, which Micah was holding open for them.

Morgan walked immediately behind them, his eyes following the sway of Susannah's hoop as she went down the two front steps. Joel, Harmer's coachman and Layla's brother, had pulled the carriage around to the front and Harmer handed his daughter carefully up inside. It was a small one, with only room for two passengers, and a top that could be pulled down in back. As the evening was quite comfortable, it had been folded back and when mounted on Gideon, his bay, and riding beside it, Morgan had a clear view of Susannah's profile. He was in no hurry to arrive at Graylands. Just riding there so close to her had him entirely content.

"So, Morgan," Harmer said as they left the edge of the town, heading up the Richmond Road in gathering twilight, "how far have you been up the Neck since you've been here?"

"Not so far as Graylands, Mr. Wellington," he replied. "My business keeps me mostly in Williamsburg with occasional trips over to Portsmouth. I hope in future to make it up to Richmond, though."

"My sister Clara lives in Richmond," Harmer continued. "I expect she'll be coming down to Williamsburg when...if...," he looked sideways at Susannah, his voice trailing away.

"If what, Papa?"

Harmer sighed. "If I have to go to Philadelphia, my darling."

"Oh, Papa! I thought you would be able to stay here!"

"It is looking more and more like I shall be needing to go," he said, but added, forcing brightness into his voice, "but your Aunt Clara is a most capable woman." He didn't want to send Susannah to Richmond, not while Williamsburg was still safe. She was much more comfortable in her own home, her own garden, and he wanted that for her.

He patted her hands. "Let's not think about that now. Tonight is for music."

"I have a question," Eden asked. "Myra, Micah, Joel and Layla, are they slaves?"

"We haven't dealt with that, have we."

"No, and we must. I don't want them to be slaves."

"They certainly don't have to be," he said. "Let us have the Wellington family living in Williamsburg for, oh, three generations, and Myra's family with them for that long as well. Even if they started out as slaves way back then, they haven't been for many, many years. I think they've become more like part of the family over time and especially now with Susannah being motherless and blind, Harmer really depends on them."

"So where do they live?"

"It's a big house," Marshall smiled, "and there are two rooms downstairs. Myra and Layla share one and Micah and Joel the other."

They traveled in silence for a while, Susannah very aware of the presence of Morgan and his horse just to her left. Harmer was, too, and wished that she could see him, his cloak spread over the bay's flanks, the way he sat his saddle.

When they reached Graylands, a steady stream of carriages and horses was arriving, voices were lifted in greeting, torches lighting the front of the plantation crackled in the night air. Morgan dismounted and as Harmer seemed to wait, he handed Susannah down from the carriage, watching with utmost care that her slippered feet found the small steps.

Harmer, getting out of the carriage, spotted Wythe arriving. "George!" he called. "A moment!" He turned to Morgan, asking him to escort Susannah inside while he had a word with his friend. "I wasn't sure you'd actually come to Harrelson's," he chuckled, moving away from Morgan and Susannah.

"One tries to remain civilized as long as possible, Harmer," Wythe smiled. "I heard Patrick Henry was not invited, however."

Morgan was trying to decide just how much longer he should continue to be surprised by what Harmer Wellington did. He watched the two older men a moment then, with Susannah on his arm, walked between the line of torches toward the huge double front doors of Graylands. Like silk and satin butterflies, the gaily bedecked men and women of the lower Neck moved along before and behind them, Loyalist and Patriot, resplendent and still together in the exquisite early June night.

Parker stood on the wide colonnaded porch that ran the width of the front of the house, his eyes scanning the arrivals, looking for the Wellingtons. When he finally located Susannah, his lips pressed into a thin white line. That was not her father on whose arm she rested her hand. He'd never seen the man before. He went down the top three of the six wide, white steps that led to the porch, waiting for them to come. "Miss Wellington," he said rather loudly, announcing his presence to her. "Where is your father?"

"Good evening, Parker. I believe he is speaking with Mr. Wythe."

"Who might this be?"

"This is Mr. Kent, Morgan Kent. He did not know the way and so accompanied us."

"Ah, Mr. Kent," Parker said, his eyes scanning down the man's impeccable attire. "From England."

Morgan smiled. "Yes, from England." He dipped his head politely.

"Well, glad you could come. I'll take Miss Wellington from here." With a deft movement he placed himself between them and managed to move her arm on to his. "Please, Mr. Kent, do go inside. There is refreshment," he smiled with his mouth but not his eyes, "and the best of the young ladies of Virginia."

"But...," Susannah started to protest as Parker led her firmly and rather rapidly up onto the porch and toward the door.

Harmer came up behind the once-again astonished Morgan. "Man's a first-class ass," he rumbled close to Morgan's ear, only serving to further Morgan's astonishment. "Watch yourself around him. He wants her."

Harmer passed him and went inside. Morgan stood where he'd stopped on the steps, staring at the open doorway, trying to make sense of what had just happened. Wythe paused at his left side. "Coming in, Morgan?"

"What? Oh, yes, Mr. Wythe. I am." He walked along at Wythe's side, finding himself inside the grandest house he'd been in since he'd come to the Colonies. Its ballroom was larger by far than that in the Governor's Palace back in town. Hundreds of candles, their light multiplied by huge mirrors on the walls, lit the room. In one corner a small orchestra played, the notes sent forth by violin and cello soaring over the large, colorful crowd. Finding himself a place to one side, he looked for Susannah. Ah, there! Parker had led her to a seat at the front of the room and was handing her a cup of punch. Her expression he could tell, even though she was rather distant from him, was not very happy. He studied young Harrelson. She'd called him Parker. They must have known each other for a while, had possibly grown up together. He frowned, then was startled by Harmer's hand on his shoulder.

"I didn't know," he began but was cut off by Harmer.

"Not much to know, Morgan. Parker wants her because she's the prettiest thing in the Colonies. Doesn't care a fig about who she is, what she likes, what she needs. He just wants her."

"I take it, Sir, that fact does not please you?"

"It pleases me not at all. Not at all."

"Is that why...?"

Harmer looked up at the taller Morgan, his face a mask of innocence. "Why...?"

"My coat, the garden?"

Harmer smiled, then looked back across the room at his daughter, his expression changing to one of fatherly concern. "I want only the best for her. That man is not the best." His gaze turned back up to Morgan. "She doesn't dance, you know. Too much moving around in circles on her own. She's afraid she'll bump into people, be some sort of spectacle." He sighed, looking again at Susannah. "Keep that in mind tonight. She doesn't, but she wants to." His eyes settled on Parker, dressed in midnight blue. "But Parker, he likes to dance. He'll be out on the floor with the ladies soon. You'll see." With that, he moved away into the crowd.

Morgan kept to the edge of the ballroom, but moved further along, more toward the end where Susannah sat. Parker had taken a seat to her right, his eyes on the dancers, the fingers of one hand tapping on his leg in time to the music. Morgan had no idea of how he expected this evening to go, but it had not involved watching his Susannah sit forlornly beside another man. Yet, this was that man's home and he was his guest, so he waited, keeping his eyes on them.

Parker knew he'd have to wait till later, till most of the dancing was done, before he could possibly lure Susanna out to the porch and ask her to be his wife. He glanced sideways at her. She was unutterably lovely, yes, she was, and her scent of roses went straight to his groin, making him shift in his seat. "I don't suppose you'd try a dance with me," he tried as the music stopped for a moment.

"You know how I feel about that, Parker," she said, her voice low. She wasn't quite sure why she even came to occasions like this. She did enjoy the music, though, and the sounds of the others dancing, the sense of excitement in the air.

A rather attractive young brunette stood alone not far away and Parker watched her hips swaying as the music began again. "Would you mind terribly if I...?"

"Go right ahead, Parker," she encouraged. "I don't mind at all." She truly didn't. What was it to her if he danced with another woman?

Parker frowned, wishing it did matter to her. He could see it didn't, though, so he stood and approached the brunette and soon they had turned with the music and disappeared into the massed dancers.

Morgan smiled, came around the corner of the ballroom, and slid into Parker's vacated chair. "Susannah," he said, lightly touching her arm.

"Morgan! I didn't know where you'd gone."

"I've been here. I was wondering if you, would you, come outside with me? Now."

"But Papa will...."

Morgan caught sight of Harmer only twenty feet away and Harmer dipped his head and winked at him. "Your father won't mind. I have that on good authority." He stood. "Please?"

More than anything she wanted to be in a garden with him again. "Oh, yes!"

Making sure to stay out of Parker's sight, he led her carefully through the crowd to a side door he'd noticed that opened onto a patio, paved with brick, with a garden area just beyond. A tall, neatly-clipped boxwood grew at the edge of the patio and he went behind it, instantly pulling her into his arms, his mouth, warm, finding hers with a kiss that lasted nigh unto breathlessness for them both. He was aware of her breasts pressed against his chest and he felt himself responding to it, felt himself filling with such an aching need of her that he trembled under the strength of its onslaught. He knew he should step away, but he couldn't, so he stood there and ached and held her pressed against the length of himself, his heart pounding, and kissed her again and again.

Marshall cleared his throat as Eden finished reading aloud what she'd just written. "I'm not sure I can stand much more like that and not grab you up and run to our bed. Just hearing you read that makes me ache."

"It does? Oh, good!" She began typing again.

"You are a cruel woman," he sighed. "I hope you know that."

"Oh, I do, I do!" she chuckled, "but I fully intend to do something about that ache in just a minute."

"A short minute?"

"Maybe fifty-six seconds," she replied, her fingers still flying over the keyboard.

He sighed dramatically and she let out a full-blown laugh. "I love you, Sinclair."

"Prove it."

"Fifty-six seconds. Come on, jump in with Susannah."

"All I want to do is jump in with you."

Susannah could barely stand. The rush of feelings through her had turned her legs to jelly and it was only his arms about her that kept her upright. "Oh, Morgan," she gasped when his lips moved to her neck. "I...I...." There were no words. Her mouth found his forehead and she kissed her way across it.

"I'm getting really uncomfortable here," Marshall said, his voice rather hoarse.

"Hang in there. We're almost done."

Without conscious thought, his hands had begun to fumble with the laces at the back of her dress. Suddenly he became aware of what he was doing and dropped his arms to his side. "Oh, Susannah...I...I...." He had nearly lost control of himself and he turned away, his face pressed into the tall boxwood. When her hand slid down the length of his back, he moaned audibly, knowing they must go back inside or else he would....

"Uhhhh!" Marshall echoed Morgan's moan.

"Now, now," Eden said. "He's resisting."

"This is just the second time he's been with her. I'm your husband. I don't have to resist."

The orchestra began a new piece, the music wafting out onto the patio. Perhaps? "Susannah," he said, turning to face her, "give me your hand."

Her brain felt entirely fogged by what was going on in her body. "What?"

"Your hand," he repeated, reaching to take it though she hadn't lifted it. "Come." He led her back on to the bricks. Yes. He wanted to remain with her but knew he had to stop kissing her. "Listen," he said, and she cocked her head, aware again of the music.

It was a minuet and ordinarily he would have had to let go of her hand, only returning his to hers from time to time, but he adjusted the steps, keeping hers always in his.

Susannah knew the basic steps of the dance. Her father had led her through them more than once in their wide entryway, but it was never something she would engage in in public, not with all the other dancers moving so closely nearby. She hesitated.

"It's all right," Morgan whispered. "It is but you and I and the music and I will not let go of you nor let you stumble."

For some minutes he guided her in smooth turns and movements and a smile began to curve her lips more and more. She was at a ball and she was dancing, and not only dancing, but dancing with him. A small, lilting laugh of joy came from her just as the piece ended and Morgan bowed, pressing his lips to the back of her hand, then just stood there, filling his eyes, his senses with the pleasure of her presence.

Parker, finished with the brunette, had been looking for his intended. He circled the ballroom twice, not able to locate her, then noticed the door to the patio was open. Perhaps she'd gone out for a breath of air? He knew she tended to spend an inordinate amount of time in her gardens. Irritated that he must look for her when she should have been in her seat awaiting his return, he walked out onto the bricks, stopping, aghast, when he saw she was, my God, dancing with that Englishman. He watched them a while, his muscles tensing and when he heard her happy little laugh, he ground his teeth. So, that's the way it was, was it? Then the music stopped and the usurper had the gall actually to kiss her hand! Something in him exploded and his hand found a buggy whip that had been left lying on a small metal table just outside the door. He curled the fingers of his right hand around its handle, his mouth squared in fury.

Morgan took a few steps back from Susannah because he wanted to see the full length of her. His back was to the house and her face was bathed in the glow of the lights through the huge windows. "Susannah Wellington," he said, emotion wetting his eyes, "I love you."

Something white hot wrapped itself around his neck, sinking into his flesh, and he was yanked backwards off his feet, his head smacking hard against the bricks. The world tilted and he fell off into whirling blackness.

Chapter 92

"I'm ready now," Eden said brightly, turning in her swivel chair to face Marshall.

"I'm not," he sighed.

"What happened?"

"You killed him."

"Did not!"

"I thought you intended to wait for battle to smite the poor fellow."

"I did, but opportunity presented itself."

"Bloodthirsty woman."

She grinned. "Are you saying you're not aching any more then?"

"My head aches in sympathy with Morgan."

"Oh, well, then. We can write some more."

"It's a plot. It's all a dastardly plot."

Harmer had noticed Parker heading toward the patio door and followed. He'd seen Morgan and Susannah's earlier movement through it and was concerned as to what young Harrelson might do. He stepped out on the patio just in time to hear Morgan say he loved Susannah then the black whip uncoiled in Parker's hands and Morgan went flying backwards.

"PARKER!" he bellowed, running out and past him.

His shout attracted the attention of those inside near the doorway and soon more than a dozen people had streamed out onto the patio. Susannah stood where she was, utterly confused. "Papa?" she said, with no idea what had happened or where Morgan was. She'd heard the crack of a whip. She'd ridden in enough carriages to know the sound well. That had been followed by a loud thud whose source she couldn't determine.

Harmer had knelt beside Morgan, who lay sprawled on his back, a bright red line around his neck oozing blood down onto his white lace. "Someone get Graves out here," he said, not looking up. Graves was Williamsburg's leading doctor and Harmer had seen him inside not long ago. A young man turned and sprinted back inside the house.

"Morgan?" Harmer said, touching his cheek but getting no response.

Susannah stepped forward, her hands wide, searching, finding her father's bent back. "Papa? What's happened? Where's Morgan?"

"He's right here, Susannah," Harmer replied, guiding her hands down to Morgan's chest.

Her breath hissed sharply in. "He's hurt? Why? How is he hurt?"

"You want to tell her, Parker?" Harmer growled.

Parker stood quietly, still gripping the whip. "He had no right."

"No right to what, Parker, dance with my daughter?"

"I was going to ask her tonight."

"Ask me what?" Susannah almost shouted, her hands moving over Morgan's chest.

"To be my wife, that's what. He had no right."

"Your wife? I would never be your wife, Parker!"

Her searching fingers found Morgan's face. His eyes were closed, his lips parted. "What happened to him, Papa? Did I hear a whip?"

"His neck," Harmer said grimly. "Parker yanked him backwards. I fear he's hit his head."

Dr. Graves pushed his way through the gathered crowd, kneeling across Morgan from Susannah. He slipped a hand beneath Morgan's head and came away with blood on his fingers. "Man's likely cracked his skull," he said, looking at Harmer then to Susannah, who seemed to be getting more and more distraught by the moment.

The crowd didn't exist for her, Parker no longer existed, her father and Dr. Graves barely did. "Oh, Morgan," she moaned, needing to keep her fingers in contact with his face.

"Best get him inside," Graves said. "Let me see him better in the light."

Several men lifted Morgan, carrying him in and laying him on a sofa in the parlor off the ballroom. Parker had come along. "Put a towel down!" he snapped. "He'll get blood on the upholstery."

Percival looked at his son. "Give me that!" he said sharply, snatching the whip out of Parker's hand. "What were you thinking? A guest at our own party?"

"He had no right," Parker repeated dully, frowning as Susannah crouched beside the sofa, murmuring softly to Morgan.

A servant brought Dr. Graves a wet towel and a large piece of white linen. Graves turned Morgan's head, using the towel to clean away the clotted blood from his hair. "Doesn't look like he needs stitching," he pronounced, "wound's not all that big. More'n likely he's pretty well concussed, though." He tore a long strip from the linen and wrapped it around Morgan's head. "Not much I can do for him, I'm afraid. Just need to see when he wakes up, if he wakes up. Might be best just to put him to bed here. See what happens."

Susannah felt like she might faint and was vaguely aware her father had his hand gripped around her upper arm. "Not here!" she hissed through her teeth. "I won't have him left here at Parker's." She turned her face toward her father's. "I won't!"

"You want us to...," Harmer began.

"I do," she nodded vigorously.

"Our carriage is too small, Susannah."

"I came in my larger one, Harmer," George Wythe spoke up. "Take it and I'll ride back to town in yours."

Several minutes later they had Morgan lying slightly awkwardly across one seat inside Wythe's larger carriage, angled a bit as he was too tall and his legs curved to one side toward the floor. Harmer had put a pillow under his head and was seated facing Morgan. He'd tried to get Susannah to sit beside him, but she'd settled herself on the carriage floor so she could be close to Morgan, who had not yet stirred. Her pink silk skirts billowed up around her and she punched them down, shifting, trying to get them under control. Someone had handed Harmer a small lantern with a fat candle in it and the light from that flickered and danced around the carriage's interior. Harmer looked at Morgan's face, his concern mounting the longer it took for the young man to come to himself.

"Will he be all right, Papa?" Susanna had a hand resting on Morgan's chest so she could feel the rise and fall of his breathing.

"Of course he will, my darling. Of course he will."

"I'll stop by in the morning, Harmer," Dr. Graves said through the window, "see how he's coming along."

The ball had been rather effectively terminated and small clumps of people began to get in their carriages or riders mount their horses. A few hung around outside, talking in low voices.

Susannah jostled against her father's legs as the carriage began to move. "I was so happy," she whispered, "so happy tonight."

"You danced, my darling?"

She nodded, not answering, exploring Morgan's face with her left hand as she tried to steady him with her right. "I didn't know it was possible...."

"What, Susannah?"

Tears trickled down her cheeks. "To love so deeply so quickly. I didn't know that was possible."

He loves you, then?"

"I don't know how or why, but, yes, he does, Papa."

"He'll be all right. You'll see. He'll be all right." He had to be. This all had come about much more rapidly than Harmer had ever had any idea it might and now it was evident how much his child had invested herself in this young man. He stared at Morgan. Come on! *he willed silently. Wake up!*

But they did the six-mile trip back to Williamsburg without him stirring. Wythe had followed closely behind in Harmer's small carriage, Morgan's horse tied to its rear, and when the two pulled up in front of the Wellington house, Joel ran inside to get Micah, then the two of them, along with Wythe's driver, got Morgan into the house and up the stairs.

Myra came into the room, clucking when she saw Morgan, not quite sure why the man whose coat she'd cleaned had been brought into this house, but as soon as she caught sight of Susannah's face, she began to understand. "All you get yourselves out of here," she said, shooing the men out of the room. "Layla," she called, "bring me the ol' nightshirt Mister Wellington left on the nightstand." She turned to Susannah. "You, too, honeychild. Not fittin' you be in here with me gettin' some man out of his clothes."

"Do you think I can see anything, Myra?" Susannah said firmly, settling in a chair not far from the bed. "I'm not leaving him."

"Ain't fittin', Susannah. You know that."

"I don't care about that right now, Myra. You just do what you have to do and I'll be right here in this chair." She folded her arms across her chest defiantly, blinking hard in an attempt to keep her tears back.

Layla came in with the nightshirt, a basin of water and several cloths. Myra muttered under her breath, but began unbuttoning his vest, glancing every few seconds over her shoulder at Susannah with a frown. "Never heard tell of no lady in no room while no man bein' all undressed."

"Look at his neck, Mama," Layla said softly, pushing down the lace at the top of his shirt.

"Lordy!" Myra exclaimed. "How'd that happen to him?"

"Parker's whip," Susannah said through her teeth.

"Parker? He done this to this young fellah?"

She nodded, half-rising from her chair. "How bad is it?"

"Cut pretty deep, Susannah," Layla said. "Most like leave a scar, I 'spect."

"Here, girl. Lift him so's I can get that coat off him."

When they had his coat, vest, and shirt off, Myra tipped his chin up and gently wiped his neck with the water, applied some of her own homemade ointment, and wrapped a thin strip of clean linen around his throat a couple of times. She absolutely would not take off his breeches, though, until she and Layla had Harmer's night shirt on him and pulled down as far as it would go. It was, of course, much too short as Morgan was quite a bit taller, but it covered what it needed to. Still scandalized by Susannah's presence in the room during such an activity, she placed her bulk between the young woman and the man lying on the bed before she began to slide his breeches off. Layla had taken the white shirt out to the kitchen to soak in cool water to see if the blood would wash out. "Man's always gettin' somethin' on his clothes," she murmured to herself as she pressed it down so the water completely covered it.

When she got back upstairs, Morgan was safely tucked under a sheet and a light blanket, his arms resting atop them at his sides. Susannah's chair was closer to the bed now and she was reaching to find his hand. "Susannah," Layla said softly, "don't you want to get yourself out of them fancy clothes? Be more comf'table, I think."

"I'm all right, Layla." She didn't want to leave him long enough to do something like that.

"I can bring your shift in here for you."

"Susannah ain't gonna undress with that man in the room!" Myra exclaimed, horrified at the mere thought.

"He's unconscious, Mama," Layla pointed out and she left to get the shift.

It took some coaxing, but Layla got Susannah to let her unlace her. The ice-pink silk slid to the floor in a puddle, several large smears of dirt marring its formerly pristine beauty. Myra picked it up, looking at it and emitting a heavy sigh. Even Susannah had to admit movement was much easier when the hoop had dropped around her feet. The layers of petticoats came off, the whalebone corset, and with each layer Myra looked suspiciously at Morgan as though she were ready to clout him with a vase if he dared wake up during the process. He remained satisfactorily inert, though, and she made a little sound of relief when Susannah was clothed in her long night shift. Still, it wasn't right for her to be thusly attired and in a room with a man. Myra's sensibilities were entirely shaken.

Free from her encumberments, Susannah sat again, leaning toward the bed, finding Morgan's left hand and holding it between both of her own. Myra gathered up the discarded clothing, carrying it out of the room, mumbling, "He'll sure nuff have to marry that girl now." Just outside the door, she stopped and looked back inside. "He sure nuff will."

"What, Myra?" Harmer had just arrived back at the upper hallway.

"That man, Mister Wellington. Ain't fittin' she in her shift and in there with him. He's gonna have to marry up with her after this."

Harmer smiled. "I think she just might be in favor of that, Myra."

Her eyes narrowed and she shook her head, continuing along the hallway, her arms full of bundled clothing.

"How is he?" he asked, stepping into the room.

"Oh, Papa, he won't wake up," Susannah sighed. "I don't know how to help him."

"There's not much can be done except wait," he said, coming around behind her chair and putting his hands on her shoulders. How strange, he thought, looking past his daughter's head to where Morgan's hand lay limply between hers. It had only been days since he'd first laid eyes on the man and now here he was, dressed in his own nightshirt, his own daughter desperately clinging to his hand. He looked very young lying there, very vulnerable with the bandages around his head and neck. 'Please, Morgan,' he whispered under his breath, 'be all right.'

Both Layla and Myra were gone and Harmer crouched beside his daughter's chair. "I suppose it would be useless to ask you to get some rest?"

"Ummm," she said absently.

Sighing, he stood. "I'll come back in a little while. Do you want me to ask Layla to wait with you?"

She shook her head 'no'.

He watched her a while from the doorway, then closed it with a sigh.

Alone with Morgan, she moved to sit on the side of his bed, her fingers tracing the edges of both his bandages. His last words to her had been 'I love you.' They couldn't be his very last words. "I love you, too, Morgan Kent," she whispered fiercely. "You hear me? I love you, too!"

She leaned close, touching his lips with hers. His were warm, soft, but slack and unresponsive and she yearned for their returning pressure. Still she kept hers there against his a while, her tears falling on his face. Would her tears bring him back to her? But they didn't and, suddenly terribly tired, she lay down atop the covers, her neck over his arm, which she pulled up and around herself, holding it there.

Harmer checked in on them an hour later and just stood a while, quietly watching the two young people on the bed. He shouldn't permit her to lie beside him like that. It was unthinkably improper but, then, Susannah's life was different from most and he himself had played a role in getting her to this point. He wasn't sorry about that. If life had taken its ordinary path, she would have probably ended up the mistress of Graylands, and with a philandering husband who took her to his bed when he wasn't with some other woman. He'd spent years trying to make sure her life wasn't 'small'. He loved her more than anything in this world and that's what he wanted to continue in her experience, that she be loved more than anything. He'd seen that in Morgan's eyes. Please God they'd open again and he'd see that once more. He wasn't at all sure he could bear watching Susannah have her heart broken.

Taking a small quilt off a chest, he placed it gently over his daughter then went downstairs to find Myra. He intended to tell her not to go up to the room where Morgan lay, not tonight.

She would surely make Susannah get up and he wanted her to have the comfort of these moments so near him, no matter how improper that might be.

Chapter 93

His head hurt. Oh, God, how his head hurt! He was rising up through thick layers of clinging blackness and the further he rose, the more his head hurt. Was there no way he could simply let go, simply slide back down into the nothingness where there was no pain? He tried, desperately he tried, but his rise continued inexorably, accompanied now by a low moan coming up his throat. He felt nauseated and clamped his teeth, fighting the bile back down. Where he was, what had happened, were not thoughts he felt well enough to bother with. Surviving the next second. That was enough.

He lay there, his eyes still closed, breathing slowly, absolutely swallowed by the pain in his head. His right hand fisted in the covers but his left seemed somehow positioned where he couldn't do that. Effort could not be spared to think of the why of that, either. He gritted his teeth, fighting down more bile, more ragged moans that kept trying to force their way through the bile and find expression on his lips. Minutes did not so much pass by as stab their way, one by one, along some tortuous route of time.

It took him quite a while to venture to open his eyes and when he finally managed a half-lift of his weighted lids he seemed to have no ability to focus and there were two wavering forms in the dim light where one bedpost rose darkly in the room. He closed his eyes again, willing himself to fall into some abyss of blackness, but it wouldn't come. Then he became aware his back and shoulders hurt, too, and tried to shift himself a little without moving his head. Something seemed to be pinning his left side, though, preventing that and he opened his eyes a slit, turning his head just slightly to the left. That small motion, though, sent fresh waves of pain ripping into his head and the taste of bile came into his mouth. He faded then into blessed nothingness, brief as it was, and came to himself moments later, his head still turned to his left.

Again he opened his eyes a slit, that need to shift to relieve his back and shoulders very present. Why couldn't he? Something was there on his left arm. He licked his dry lips, his mouth bitter, and tried to discern what it was. A single candle, burned down to a mere inch in remaining height, sat on a stand beside the bed. Yes, he was in bed. He'd decided that much, though it had taken great effort to get that far with his thinking. He blinked several times, trying to see well enough to understand what held down his arm. Briefly he made the mistake of looking directly at the candle's flame and the light from it pierced his brain as though someone had driven a stake through each eye. He had to close his eyes and take a while to recover. Lying there like that, he wasn't sure he wished to open his eyes again, but the need to know what was on his arm prevailed after an unknown length of time and he barely cracked them.

Hair, blonde hair. That was his first impression. He wasn't entirely sure, however, it was hair as it waved and moved in his distorted vision. It was taking much too much energy to discover what was beside him and he didn't dare turn his head more to facilitate the process. He let his eyes close again, but his body had tensed with the pain, only serving to magnify it. A long, broken moan escaped his lips. Breathe, he told himself, just breathe. He inhaled through his nose, held it a moment, then let it slowly out through his mouth. Again and then again. It finally came to him that he was aware of the sound of soft breathing even when he was holding his own breath. His eyes slivered open. A curve of something white was there, mere inches from his face, its top edge limned with candlelight that wavered in his sight.

What? He blinked again, forcing his gaze downward without moving his head. It was, no, that wasn't possible. Despite the cost, he did tip his head more, sinking his teeth into his lower lip. It was, yes, a cheek, Susannah's cheek. His breath came out of him as though he'd been struck a blow to his chest. Every muscle tensed in utter shock and once again he fell into the abyss. Slowly he drifted back upwards, impelled by some need to know that had followed him in his plunge.

His eyes opened and her face was there, right beside him, her face. He felt bleary with confusion, with a loss of sense of place, of time, of event. This was truly impossible that she should be there. There was no way. Something was wrong with him, very wrong, though he had no idea what. She could not be there, she simply could not. His eyes closed as he dealt with the unreality of it. Why was his mind doing this to him? Had he somehow fallen ill? Where? Where had he been last?

Even if she were not really there he needed to see her phantasm, so he looked again. Her face was somehow vague, distorted by his inability to focus clearly, but it was her face. If only this were real. If only she were really there. He sighed in his longing for that to be so. It took a while longer for it to dawn on him that she was why he couldn't move his arm. A phantasm wouldn't be tangible, wouldn't have weight to pin him so.

Morgan's arm seemed to be both under and curved around her. He tried to think of the why of that but could come up with nothing. His left hand had not fallen away because she had both of hers over it, holding it to her chest. If he were imagining this, he thought he was doing a very good job of it. He wanted to see her more clearly, forgot himself, and shook his head a bit, which sent him into such a spasm of pain that he pulled his knees up, a sharp gasp of agony escaping his lips.

Susannah woke abruptly at the sound, her half-sitting motion releasing his arm, which he instinctively lifted, pressing both hands to his face. "Morgan! Oh, Morgan, you're awake!"

His teeth were clamped on his lip and he couldn't answer, gasping as wave after wave of shark teeth slashed their way back and forth through the inside of his head.

She heard the sounds he was making and her hands sought his face, finding his clamped hands. "Oh, Morgan," she moaned, desperate to do something that would help.

After long minutes, he stretched his legs out again, let his hands fall to his sides, and just lay there, each breath accompanied by a small little sound of hurt. As though from inside some minute speck of space somewhere deep inside himself where his consciousness had gone, he felt her fingers begin to move over his face. He was separated from that, though, his body a mere dull encasement for that tiny speck, and it was like a great distance separated him from what she was doing. She whispered his name over and over and for him her voice came from some hazy mountaintop, filtered through vast layers of clouds.

"Please, Morgan," she begged, "please be all right!"

He couldn't move, couldn't speak, could only lie there and wait. If he survived this... then... but not yet.

Susannah remembered that Layla had brought a fresh basin of cool water and a cloth before she'd left. It should be on the night stand. Perhaps that might help? She twisted around, her hands exploring toward where the little table was. Her fingers found the candle flame first, and she jerked back with a small exclamation. Soon, though, she'd located the basin and had wet the cloth. Feeling with her left hand, she touched his face, then with the cloth in her right began with the lightest touch she could manage to wipe his face.

It felt good, what she was doing. Wetting the cloth again, she folded it, laying it over his brow, which felt even better. He let out a long, sighing breath and filled his body with himself again. Her hand was still on his cheek and he lifted his, covering it. "I wish you were really here," he managed to mumble, his eyes closed.

She leaned forward, brushing her lips across his, having gotten way beyond any sense of reticence with him. Her lips still light and warm atop his, she whispered, "I love you, Morgan Kent. With all my heart I adore you."

His eyes came half-way open. Her face was right there and she lifted it enough so that he could see all of it. Her features still moved for him, not remaining in place where they should, but it was the face that occupied his heart and he sighed, "Susannah."

"I'm here," she said.

"Wh...where?"

"In my house. We, Papa and I, brought you home from Graylands."

"Graylands?"

"The ball. Remember we were at the ball?"

"Wh...what?"

"Parker." He saw a frown crease her brow.

"He...he...?"

"He came up behind you with a whip. Your neck. He pulled you backwards."

"I...I danced...didn't I? With you? Outside?"

"Yes, that's what we were doing when he came."

"I didn't...."

"He was behind you. You wouldn't have known."

"Neck?" He moved his hand down, discovering the bandage, aware for the first time of a line of stinging that curved completely around it.

She lifted his hand away, kissing it several times. "You...you're...here?"

"I am here, yes."

"Real? You...you're...real?"

He saw her smile and something in him strengthened in response to the fact of her reality. But how? How was she here with him? Why was she allowed to be here with him? "You can't...."

But she pressed a finger to his lips."But I am and I shall continue to be." She removed the cloth, wetting it again, replacing it.

"Head hurts," he mumbled.

"You fell backwards onto the bricks Papa said."

"Your father...he...knows you're...."

"Yes, Morgan, he knows."

"But...."

"It's all right. I promise you, it's all right."

"I can't...," but his lids were too heavy and a pathway had opened again for him to sink into darkness. Briefly, he lifted them a slit, looked at her with a mixture of amazement and longing, but turned and let himself fall.

Under her hands, she felt the change in him, the relaxation of his tense muscles. He had come back to her, though, and her world had ceased its wobble.

Chapter 94

Sometime in the wee hours Harmer came back into the bedroom, finding Susannah seated on the side of the bed, holding both his hands in hers. "Still the same?" he asked, discouraged.

"No, Papa. He woke up and we talked. He's in very much pain, though, I fear."

Harmer came up beside the bed, holding the candle he carried closer. Morgan looked as he had the last he'd seen him. "You're sure it wasn't a...."

"No, Papa, it wasn't a dream. I explained to him what happened but he has a hard time staying awake."

Morgan moaned and opened his eyes. "Mr....Mr. Well...Wellington." He blinked slowly several times.

"Good to see you back, my boy. You had the lot of us mightily worried."

"I...you...." He closed his eyes. "Two...two of you."

"Double vision, is that what you mean, son?"

"Mmmmm."

"I'll talk to Graves about that come morning. You rest as best you can, and you, Susannah, I must insist...."

"I'm fine, Papa. I slept a while."

"Not enough."

"Enough for now." She lifted one of Morgan's hands to her cheek. Turning her face to her father, the hand still held in place, she said, "He came back."

Morgan, his eyes closed, smiled slightly. "Love you," he mumbled then he faded again.

"What are we going to do with him, Susannah?" Harmer asked.

"He can't go back alone to that room on Francis Street. No one will watch over him there."

Harmer studied his daughter. Yes, without sight, she was, indeed, watching over him. "We shall discuss that in the morning," he said, not knowing what else to say at the moment. "Let us see what Dr. Graves says about his condition."

Susannah dozed from time to time the rest of the long night, but mostly sat, holding his hands or touching his face. When Harmer came back in the morning, he watched her more for a time. His daughter was utterly changed from the young woman who knew nothing of loving or being loved by someone her age. Morgan had come into her world and everything was different, she was different. She seemed more a woman now than a girl. The expressions he saw on her face had nothing to do with girlish things. Still, it would not work for him to allow a young man to remain in his house with his daughter. Perhaps he could hire someone to care for Morgan at the boarding house?

Myra was standing in the doorway. "Doc Graves come, Sir."

"Thank you, Myra. Please show him on up."

"Mmmmm."

Morgan was rousing again. Good, Harmer thought. It would be best if he were awake when Graves were here. Doctor could probably tell more about how he was doing that way.

"Good morning, Harmer," Graves said, entering the room. "How is the young man?" Susannah had moved to the chair and Dr. Graves leaned over the bed, lifting one of Morgan's eyelids.

"Ahhh!" Morgan moaned. "Hurts."

"The light hurts?"

Morgan nodded then nearly lost consciousness again, his face contorting with pain. Graves exchanged a look with Harmer. "Can you open your eyes?" he asked Morgan.

Harmer pulled the velvet overcurtains, blocking out most of the morning sunlight. Morgan lifted his lids halfway. Graves held up a forefinger. "How many?"

"T...two," Morgan gasped then closed his eyes.

Graves drew in a long breath. "Man's got a really severe concussion," he said, straightening. "Could take him some weeks to get past this, maybe more."

"Weeks?" Harmer hadn't expected that.

"Needs rest, lots and lots of rest. Not much moving around. These things can be slow, Harmer." He set about unwrapping the bandage Myra had put around Morgan's throat. "I see Myra did her usual excellent job. Her ointment works better than mine." He made a fresh bandage for it. "Just keep it clean and it should heal fine."

When Graves had gone, Harmer pulled a chair around close to where his daughter sat. "I shall hire someone trustworthy, Susannah, to stay at the boarding house with Morgan."

"No."

"No? What do you mean 'no,' Susannah? I can think of no other way to deal with this. Morgan may have a long convalescence and needs someone there for him."

"Yes, he does."

"Who do you have in mind?"

"Me."

Somehow he'd thought she'd say that. He sighed. "That is not possible, my darling. You know the two of you together cannot be allowed. I have made an exception this last night because of its emergency nature, but you cannot continue in this manner. Surely you must know that."

"I do know that."

"Then what are you saying?"

"I want him to remain here, in our house."

"Have I not just said that is not possible?"

"You have."

"Why then...?"

"I wish to make it possible."

"He...he's right, Sus...Susannah," came Morgan's weak voice from the bed. "I can't...can't stay here."

"Why can't you stay here? I want to hear you say why you can't."

"Be...because your rep...reputation...be ruined. Can't."

"Do you think I care about that?"

"I c...care."

Harmer smiled in spite of himself. Morgan was a good man. "Thank you, Morgan," he said. "Maybe you can talk some sense into her."

"I...I should go...now."

"Can you even lift your head off that pillow?" Susannah asked, knowing well the answer.

He tried to raise himself up, pushing with his elbows, gasped and fell back, almost passing out. Susannah waited a while for him to recover, she needed him conscious for what she intended to say.

"What are you waiting for now?" Harmer asked.

"You shall see soon enough," she smiled.

"Need help," Morgan managed. "Get...downstairs. Need help." He looked blearily at Harmer.

"I can get Micah and Joel," Harmer offered.

"That won't be necessary," Susannah said firmly.

"Susannah! Enough of this! Morgan is right. You don't even have a brother in this house we could say he's visiting. There's just me and you and you are a young unmarried woman."

"What if I weren't?"

"What could you possibly mean by that?"

Susannah moved again, sitting on the side of the bed, taking Morgan's hand. "Morgan Kent," she said, holding her voice steady with some effort, "will you marry me?"

"What!" Harmer burst out.

"Wh...what?" Morgan gasped, feeling quite dizzy.

"I said," she straightened her shoulders, kissed his hand, "will you marry me?"

"Susannah! You've seen him twice! I know I've...."

"Yes, you have, Papa. The bottom line is, do you trust me to know my own heart?"

"Do I...?" He stared at his only child. She was a level-headed girl, no, woman, and had never been given to flights of fancy, fits of temperament, or self-indulgence. Her blindness had brought an early seriousness and maturity, but she was not really very experienced with men. Then he gazed at Morgan, remembering the light in his eyes as he looked at Susannah, his kindnesses, his thoughtfulness, how she had laughed so happily when he'd gotten her to dance. "I trust you, my darling one," he said softly. "It's just that I...."

"Morgan, do you love me?"

His head was pounding because his heart was racing so. "With...with all my heart, Susannah, but...."

"What possible 'but's' can there be?"

"How...how can you be sure...of me...how you feel?"

"I've never been so sure of anything in my life, Morgan Kent."

"Is...is...this just so I won't...go?"

"That may be the catalyst of the moment," she admitted, "but it's what I want. You are what I want and I want you here, with me, forever, not just while you're getting well, you hear me, but forever."

"You're really serious, Susannah?" Harmer questioned, hundreds of thoughts racing madly through his head.

"Never more so, Papa."

"Morgan?" Harmer asked, coming now to stand close to the other side of the bed, looking down at him. "How do you feel about this?"

"I...I...want to get on my knees...ask her proper."

"You do want to marry her, then?"

"I never...never...dreamed she would...want me...like that."

Susannah kissed his hand again. "Is that a yes, my darling?"

"N...no. I won't...can't have you ask me. Not right." He screwed his eyes tightly shut, gathering himself. "They...they say that sometimes no matter what the attitude of the body, the... the soul is on its knees. I ca...can't get on mine right now," he paused for several deep breaths, "want to but can't. So, Sus...Susannah, can you take this from me as though I were? My...my soul is on its knees. Can...can that be enough?"

Silently she leaned forward, kissing his lips very softly.

He covered his face with his hands for a moment and when he let them fall away, Harmer saw there were tears in his eyes and held his own breath, waiting. "Mr. Well...Wellington, I'd like...like to ask you, Sir, for the honor of your daughter's hand in marriage."

Harmer's eyes began to sting. He looked from his sightless daughter to the struggling young man on the bed, who was trying so hard to do everything right for Susannah's sake. They fit. Good Lord in heaven the two of them did just fit. "Yes, Morgan," he said, "you have my blessing."

Tears began to stream down Susannah's face, tears she ignored because all her concentration was on Morgan. Morgan forced his eyes fully open and reached for her left hand, which lay in her lap as she sat on the bed. One by one he slowly, tenderly kissed each of her fingertips then laid her palm over his heart and pressed his atop it. "Susannah Wellington," he said, his voice stronger than before, "will you grace my life by consenting to be my bride?"

A ragged sob tore out of her, then she straightened again. "Yes," she replied, "yes with all the love in my heart behind it."

"I'll call the Rector," Harmer said.

"Today."

"Yes, Susannah, today. Is that all right, Morgan?"

Morgan had never once considered he'd get married flat on his back or, worse, spend his wedding night unable to lift his head from a pillow, but, well, this was Susannah. "Today," he echoed, barely remembering not to nod his head. A sudden thought hit him. "No ring."

"I would be both pleased and honored, Morgan, if you would consent to give my daughter the ring I gave her mother twenty years ago."

"Tr...truly, Sir?"

"Oh, Papa!" Susannah cried. "I'd love that! Mama's ring, yes!"

"Guess that settles that," Morgan managed, feeling himself starting to drift as the constant pain tired him quickly.

"You rest now, Son," Harmer said, a deeper fondness in his voice. "I'll make arrangements."

And so it was that wearing Harmer Wellington's night shirt and unable to lift his head, Morgan Kent, quite newly arrived in America, married Miss Susannah in a bedroom with George Washington, Thomas Jefferson, George Wythe, Myra, Layla, Micah, Joel, and Harmer himself standing around. The Rector of Bruton Parish Church officiated, the bride wore lavender and lace and the groom made his vows, gave his bride her mother's ring, and managed to kiss her before he drifted away.

In the parlor, the guests were served cakes and tea, but did not stay long. Going back up afterwards where Morgan lay in a deep sleep, Harmer slid his arm around his daughter's waist. She leaned her head against his shoulder, sighed with a great happiness, and said, "So, it's all right for him to stay now, Papa?"

"Yes, Mrs. Kent, it is perfectly all right."

Chapter 95

Sometime in the night, he had no idea just when, Morgan awoke, taking a long moment to orient himself as to his whereabouts and circumstances. While he'd slept, Harmer had a small cot moved in next to the bed, between it and the window, and Susannah was sleeping on it, her arm up onto the higher bed, holding his left hand. Morgan ran his thumb pad lightly back and forth over her fingers. His wife. Good Lord above, Susannah Wellington was now Susannah Kent. It was more than he could get his mind around. And with her father's blessing, too.

He thought back to their time in the gardens behind this very house, how he'd wanted to say her first name but had no right. Now, beyond all belief, she was his wife. "Wife," he said the word aloud, a slight smile on his lips. Fine lot of a husband he was right now, though. They'd obviously thought him too injured for her even to sleep in the same bed with him. But she was here, next to him, and he had her hand in his. Now he whispered the word, "Susannah," with the new-found pleasure in his total right to say it.

It had only been so very recently he'd even arrived in Virginia. He thought about his days here before he'd seen her by the fig tree. Even then, even at that very moment as he watched her hands trace the lobes of the large leaf, he'd known he'd never be the same. Then it hit him fully. He'd committed himself to being a Virginian. His father! A sudden pain raced through his head, back to front, as he tensed. His father would never understand, would disown him, but Susannah's hand lay within his and that had become the foundational meaning of his life.

He knew, too, that even apart from her, he'd been steadily going down the path of Colonialism. Being here, right here in Williamsburg, with access to the Apollo Room in the Raleigh Tavern, that room that to him seemed the beating heart of the New World, filled with the men who made it so, all of that had been getting inside him, taking up residence. That he had gotten married now was like pressing the seal into the soft wax that made the document official. He'd become a Virginian, both by heart and by marriage. It was his choice, what he wanted, no matter the cost.

There was so much to think about, so very much, but he drifted back into a deep sleep, still holding his wife's hand.

It took him the better part of two weeks to stop seeing double, to be able to lift his head and not feel like he was going to pass out. Micah and he had developed a friendship as the older man was the one who tended to him when he couldn't get out of bed to use the chamber pot. Micah grew very fond of the young man, who was unfailingly kind to him. This was aided by the mere fact, too, of how clear it was to everyone that he made their Susannah happy. All of them had watched her grow from babyhood and felt very protective of her. Morgan had come, suddenly and unexpectedly, and made her happier than any of them had ever seen.

Myra fussed over him, making him soups, soft breads, little sugary pastries. Harmer had sent Joel to the Francis Street boarding house to pack his things and bring them to what was now Morgan's new home. That he was so incapacitated and in such pain when he first became a part of the household, that this had been done to him by someone they all disliked, resulted in the protectiveness they felt for Susannah being extending to wrap around him as well. Motherless, having spent his life with a business-like, sharp-minded father always on the go, being cosseted was a wonder to him.

The first time he'd tried to stand, he was so instantly dizzy that he'd collapsed, scaring everyone half to death as it was by the barest margin that Micah had been able to prevent his head from striking the dresser as he fell. Dr. Graves came by from time to time and once told Harmer that he'd actually been surprised Morgan had not died or ended in a coma as the concussion was so severe.

It wasn't till the fourth week of their marriage that Susannah felt he was well enough for her to sleep in the same bed with him. They, of course, had cuddled and kissed before, but it still hurt him to move his head very much and she wanted him to be able to sleep with whatever comfort he could manage. Often at night, though, he would wake, aware of her on the low cot beside his bed, and he railed inwardly at himself for not being able to make her truly his wife. Once he'd pushed himself up on his elbow, wanting to look at her face in the moonlight, but the price he'd paid in pain had made him hesitate to repeat that endeavor. He found that if he lay perfectly still, the pain would subside to a low throb, but he also knew that such enforced inactivity was taking its toll on his bodily strength and he wanted so desperately to be strong for her.

Now she lay beside him and the covers had been thrown back as it was early July and quite warm despite a light breeze stirring the lace at the open window. He was aware of Susannah's almost total inexperience with men but also remembered clearly how she'd responded to him both in the gardens here and at Graylands. He was on his left side, having slowly and carefully moved to arrange himself to face her, and his fingers trailed down the exquisite curve of her cheek.

She was smiling at him, her long hair loose about her shoulders, and wearing a pale blue night shift with a white satin tie that held the scooped, gathered neckline together in the front. It occurred to him that for her sake, it was probably wise that he introduce her a little at a time to married love. His own body had already responded to her mere presence beside him and the increased sexual tension had raised his usual head throb to a higher level, a fact he was trying to ignore, though not always successfully. He was breathing carefully, hoping to get past that, but the more he looked at her, the further down her neck his fingers went, the more aroused he became with a resulting constant increase in his head pain. Still, he didn't stop. His body felt at war with itself, the needs of one part aggravating the hurt in another, but he pressed his lips tightly together, determined to know at least the outer edges of what it meant to be husband to her.

Susannah sighed and lifted her chin as his fingers moved down her neck. She'd spent so many days now in deep concern for him that being his wife had taken second place to being his nurse. She knew he didn't want that. She didn't want that, either, but fate had thrust this upon them and it would pass. All she had to do was wait, care for him, and he would be himself again. Now she lay quietly, except that wherever his fingers touched, her flesh became warm and trembled. She had no idea what it meant to be a wife, but she trusted this man implicitly, and she, too, remembered how her body responded to his, how even that first night in the garden she had become aware of want.

His hand traced her left collarbone, hesitated, then found the satin tie, undoing it. A large fold of her shift slid down, revealing her right breast, his hand paused, hovering a long while. She didn't move, waiting, very aware of what her clothing had done. Morgan was breathing faster, through his parted lips, and left his hand several inches above her, closing his eyes briefly, willing his head to cooperate. Slowly his lids opened and even more slowly he allowed his hand to lower, his palm curving over her breast.

She sucked in a long, open-mouthed gasp of air. Nothing had ever felt like that before and as his hand moved gently around her breast, under, over, then found its way under her shift to her left, areas further down her body flooded with an aching need, way beyond what she'd experienced from being kissed and she pressed herself against him.

He leaned forward, kissing his way around her breasts, delighted by her response, but was only able to maintain that position for a moment or two before he had to lie back. "I'm...I'm sorry," he mumbled.

Now she had pushed herself up on her arms, leaning over him. "Don't you dare, my darling. You are mine and I am yours and when it is time, everything will...."

"But I want you so, Susannah. I want you now."

"I know." She ran the backs of her fingers across his brow, trying to erase the furrow she felt there. "Shh! Let it go. It will come."

He made a sharp, cut-off laughing sound, that she, whom he was trying gently to introduce to love, had to comfort him. He was twenty-three and desperately tired of being an invalid. His hand came up behind her head, pulled it down, and he proceeded to kiss her as thoroughly as he ever had until he gasped, clutched both sides of his head with his hands, making little "uhhn uhhn" sounds deep in his throat.

Susannah fumbled for the basin, wetting a cloth, trying to push his hands aside so she could wipe his face. "Listen to me, Morgan. Nothing is more important than getting you through this, getting you well again. Nothing! Please, darling, please don't make yourself suffer over it. Please don't!"

"I just...I just...."

"I know, I know. But relax now, please. Let your head rest."

"I think I've come to loathe my head," he sighed, then took a deep breath.

"It's my husband's head," she smiled, "and I'm quite fond of it. So stop."

"I love you," he murmured.

"I love you, my darling." She folded the cloth, leaving it on his forehead, and lay beside him again, pulling his arm up and over her in that way she liked.

"Is it still all right?"

"What?"

"That you married me?"

"Oh, Morgan! It's so much more than all right. It's wonderful."

"Even with all this?"

"Even with all this, yes. Now rest."

She could hear him trying to even his breathing out and after a while knew he'd fallen asleep.

Two weeks more and he was up and around, slowly and carefully, but he even made it out to the garden. He was very weak and had to lean on Micah still, but just being outside was a marvel to him. Harmer had a padded lounge chair set for him not far out from the rear door and he'd stretch out there, loving the dappled sunlight on his face as the breeze stirred the trees. The mid-summer perennials were blooming now and the air smelled glorious. Susannah would sit beside him and they talked and talked, finding out all the details of each other's lives, sharing the secrets of their hearts.

By the end of July Morgan had been able to make love to his wife and what had long been a thorn in his side turned into a bubble of happiness. The only thing still hanging over him was his father's response to the long letter he'd sent early in July. It, of course, took weeks for correspondence to get from Virginia to England and then back again and he wasn't even sure if his father actually were in England in the first place, his shipping interests often taking him abroad, which would only lengthen the time for a reply.

By early August it was becoming evident that Harmer would be going to Philadelphia at the end of the month with Washington and Jefferson. That his daughter was married and there was a man in the house was a great comfort to him, but still he sent for his older sister, Clara, in Richmond. Clara's husband had been killed in a fall from his horse after only two weeks of marriage. She had never remarried and had continued all these years to live in the large house in Richmond that had been their home.

Clara arrived the third week of August in a flurry of luggage. "With the world the way it is," she announced, "one never knows how long one might be required to stay." Clara smelled of lavender sachet and had an ample bosom upon which to comfort anyone who needed it. She adored her only niece. Smoothing her gloves, she sized up the young man leaning against the front door frame. So this was Morgan Kent, the man who had married her Susannah. Harmer had written her in some detail about the events surrounding that and she had been most curious to see him for herself, wanting to know if her own opinion would match that of her brother's.

Morgan was dressed in light fawn breeches with a darker tan jacket. Her immediate impression was that he was quite handsome but much too thin. He'd obviously lost weight during his ordeal. At her approach, he smiled, pushed himself off from the doorway and came down the two steps to greet her. "Aunt Clara," he said in a deep voice she instantly found enjoyable to listen to, "it is my honor and great pleasure to meet you at last."

He looked slightly older than twenty-three to her probing eyes. Great pain over many weeks would do that to one. When he smiled there were a few lines that crinkled at the corners of his eyes, two around the edges of his mouth. Nothing that took away, mind, from his attractiveness and might well even add to it with that air of maturity they lent. "Dear Morgan," she smiled, holding out her hand, over which he bowed, lifting it and placing a light kiss. "You are much improved, then?"

"Much," he said, looking back as Susannah appeared in the doorway, delayed by Layla's not being able to find the sash to her dress. With some ease she came down the steps, where Morgan took her hand.

"Aunt Clara?"

"Here, darling child," Clara said, enveloping Susannah in an enormous hug.

Watching, Morgan smiled. He knew how reluctant Susannah had been to have her father travel to Philadelphia soon, but Aunt Clara's arrival seemed to smooth that somewhat. Morgan could understand why Harmer wanted her there in his absence. Morgan was still not back to where he'd been before, and Clara fairly radiated competence. She'd come and watched over Susannah several times in her growing up when Harmer had to be away and couldn't take his daughter along. Her evident love for Susannah also gratified him. He wanted for her that she be loved as much as possible.

"So," Clara continued, still holding onto her niece, "you have now a husband who loves you."

"And whom I love," Susannah added. "I am very happy, Aunt Clara."

"So I see." She did, indeed. Susannah glowed with that satisfied happiness that comes from a good marriage.

And so Aunt Clara settled in the back bedroom she always used when visiting and outdid even Myra in clucking over Morgan, making sure he ate an amount she considered satisfactory, that he wasn't on his feet too long. He reminded her somewhat of her own young long-lost husband and her heart instantly went out to him, her protectiveness surrounding him. Between Susannah, Clara, Myra, and Layla, Morgan was nearly inundated with feminine care. He found he rather liked it and got a certain amount of pleasure in seeing how happy it made them to fuss over him. He still tired easily, still had days when his head pounded, but he was overall really much better and improving steadily...and his wife was truly his wife in every way. That pleased him the most.

Chapter 96

"Well," Eden sighed, "we've got them up to August."

"We only started in May, you know," Marshall pointed out.

"And it's a lengthy war. Good thing you've already done so much of that." She looked at him a long moment. "I was surprised she asked Morgan to marry her."

"I was surprised when Parker almost killed him," he grinned.

"It gave you the perfect set-up, though, didn't it?"

"Indeed. I think it will work much better now when he finally goes off to war that he is her husband. Changes the level of it."

"Husbands in danger. I can relate to that," she said softly.

"We weren't married yet."

"I've been married to you since before I was born."

It was early September, eleven days after Harmer had left for Philadelphia that a thick packet arrived for Morgan. Micah carried it in to the parlor where Morgan was sitting on the couch, listening to Susannah play the harpsichord.

"Ah, I'm glad she plays," Marshall commented.

"You play. Actually, I wish you played more. I love it when you do."

"This evening, then, after dinner."

"Good."

They'd been so occupied of late with plans for the nursery and writing the novel that it had been more than two weeks since he'd played his piano. With the trip to England growing so near, they'd wanted to get as much done on the book as possible, and only a month after they would return home, there was a meeting in Campeche, Mexico they had to attend. Well, Marshall had to attend it, but she was definitely going along. It seemed his father's business interests were somewhat more involved than he'd realized. That he practically owned a large factory in the Yucatan seemed strange to both of them.

"For you, Sir," Micah said, presenting the packet to Morgan.

Morgan took it, turning it over in his hands. At first he'd thought it might be from his father, but the return address was from a London solicitor whose name he only vaguely recalled having heard before.

"What is it, darling?" Susannah asked, dropping her hands to her lap.

"I'm not sure." He undid the thin leather tie that bound the packet shut, letting the outer paper sift down to the rug by his feet. Brow furrowed, he unfolded the top paper, a letter of some sort, and began to read. Clara, knitting in a chair across the room, set her needles down, watching Morgan. His face paled and he turned to one side, placing a hand over his eyes.

"Morgan?" Clara said, concerned. She'd come to know he was waiting for a letter from his father. If this was it, then the man had not taken his son's news well.

From the way Clara had said his name, Susannah instantly knew something was amiss. She left the harpsichord and sure-footedly crossed the room to the couch, sitting beside him. With her hand, she found the packet on his lap, raised her hand more and discovered the position he was in. "Darling? Is it news from your father?"

He sighed and turned back, his lips pressed into a tight line, his eyes dropping again to the letter he held. "Not from him, no. About him."

"What...?"

"He's dead. This is from his solicitor. Seems his heart failed in mid-July. My letter arrived after he was gone." He looked at Susannah. "He never knew about us, about my decision."

"Oh, darling!" She touched his cheek. "I'm so sorry."

He set aside the letter, unfolding more papers, glancing at them one after the other. It was his father's estate. His older sister was well provided for and the bulk of it had been transferred into Morgan's name. With war coming, Morgan wasn't quite sure what that would mean. He had no intention of going back to England to run a shipping business. Since he'd been feeling better, he'd been handling certain matters for it here in Virginia but war would mean the cessation of trade. Perhaps if he hurried, if there were yet time, he could have a certain amount of that shifted so it would be available to him here in the Colonies. He would have to ask George Wythe for advice.

Already Patrick Henry was referring to himself as an 'American' and openly discussing the formation of five or six thousand men into Virginia companies. Morgan knew a non-importation bill had been introduced in the Burgesses in an attempt to send a clear message to Britain. It seemed every day brought them closer to the brink of war, and now the Continental Congress was in session in Philadelphia. He needed to think, but one of his headaches was getting a firm grip since he'd tensed so while reading the news about his father.

"I'm fine," he said, kissing Susannah's cheek and rising to his feet.

Eden looked at Marshall. "He's like you, my love. He's always just 'fine.'"

"No train tracks through the middle of Colonial Williamsburg for him to get his legs cut off," Marshall shrugged with a grin.

"And a good thing that is, too, mister. I have a hard enough time keeping you off the tracks."

"I'm fine," he said, tipping his chin up.

"I need to speak with Mr. Wythe," he explained. "There's a ship leaving for England on the morning tide and it seems I need to make certain arrangements."

"You're not...you wouldn't...." Susannah gasped.

"Oh, sweetheart, not me! No. I need to send letters as soon as possible to deal with my father's shipping company. I'm afraid a great portion of it will simply be lost to me but I would like to see what I can salvage before war comes. I'm hoping Mr. Wythe can draw up some legal documents for me in response to these." He kissed her again. "I'll return as soon as I can, darling." He strode quickly toward the door, the papers in his hand, forgetting his hat.

When he'd gone, Clara said, "He didn't look right to me, Susannah. I think he had one of his headaches."

"Micah," Susannah called, "will you please follow Morgan. He's going to Mr. Wythe's and I just want to make sure he's all right."

Micah went to the door, smoothly taking Morgan's hat off the rack as he passed. He was a quiet man, but he noticed everything. Once past the front pickets, he saw Morgan striding along Nicholson toward the Palace Green.

It was hot, a brilliant sun beating down on his bare head as he hurried along, his mind racing with the fact of his father's death and with all that needed attending to as quickly as he could. He had last seen his father in the spring, just before he sailed for Virginia. It had never occurred to him he'd never see him again. Even though Edward Kent was not a warm man by nature, Morgan had spent most of his life in his company and the thought that he was gone forever pierced through him in ways even he had not realized it would.

He crossed the Green, unaware of the Palace to his right, of the lawn beneath his shoes, of Mr. Peterson who bid him good day. On the far side of the Green, he stumbled, braced himself against a stout maple, and simply stopped there, leaning his forehead against the bark, his head pounding. He was tense and he'd walked too fast and he needed to sit down.

Across the street was a bench that backed up to Wythe's front wall. He made for it almost blindly, sitting heavily, the papers sliding from his hand to the brick walk. Leaning forward, he held his head, rocking just slightly. Then Micah was there, gathering up the papers, setting them on the bench beside Morgan. He waited until Morgan straightened and dropped his hands to his lap. "Forgot your hat," he said quietly, proffering the object.

"What? Oh, Micah. I...I'm...."

Micah set the tricorn atop the papers. "I'll just be lettin' Mister Wythe know you're here," he said, turning to mount the four steps to the small porch and pull the bell at the black front doors.

Wythe himself, who had been passing through his entrance hall, opened the door. "Micah, what brings you here today?"

Micah stepped back, half-turning, nodding toward where Morgan sat on the bench. "Mister Kent, he got things he needs to speak with you about, Sir, but he ain't doin' so well this minute."

"Help him inside, Micah." Wythe turned to call down the hall. "Jerusha, I'll be needing a glass of cool water in my office."

"Mister Kent, Sir, the door's open now. You come with Micah an' let's go on in."

"Thank you, Micah." With a sigh, Morgan stood, and Micah took hold of his arm, picking up the hat and papers with his free hand.

Wythe's office was at the rear of his house, at the end of the wide hallway on the left. It was in here that he had taught Jefferson much of what made him the man he'd become. Micah got Morgan settled in a chair, then said, "I'll just be waitin' for you out front," then he was gone.

Jerusha, Wythe's housekeeper, came in with a large glass of water on a small tray, cool and fresh from the pump house. Morgan took it gratefully, his hand shaking a bit as he drank it. "Didn't realize it was so hot today," he said, smiling weakly.

Wythe had been through every step of this ordeal with Morgan and was well aware of the toll it had taken on the young man. He completely doubted if he himself would even have survived it. Never one to beat around the bush, he asked straight off, "Has something happened, Morgan?"

Morgan lowered the glass, adding his left hand to hold it as well as though it were suddenly heavy, his eyes fastened on the remaining water. "My father is dead," he said, his voice low.

"I am sorry to hear of that, Morgan. You have my most sincere condolences."

Morgan lifted his eyes to the older man's face, "Thank you, Sir." He set the glass down on the round table with its dark green cloth and fumbled to pick up the slim stack of papers, handing them toward Wythe. "I...I'd like your advice, Sir, on what to do about these, given the present circumstances."

Wythe took the papers, looking through them, then smiled at Morgan. "I think I can help you with this, my dear young man." And for the next hour and a half the two men worked intensively preparing documents to be sent out on the morning tide. Wythe even arranged for one of his men to deliver them to Capitol Landing.

"I can't tell you how grateful I am, Sir," Morgan said, standing to leave. His face was pinched with pain from the effort of the concentration required to handle all the many legal details and his headache had settled completely down the back of his neck as well as in his head.

Looking at him, Wythe said, "Let me arrange for my carriage to take you home, Morgan."

"It is only a matter of three blocks, Sir," Morgan protested.

"Nonetheless, I beg you to indulge me in this."

And so it was, with Micah riding up front with Wythe's driver, Morgan was delivered safely into the arms of Susannah...and Clara...and Myra...and Layla. Before he knew what happened, he was tucked up into bed, the curtains were drawn, he'd been fed soup, and his wife was sitting on the edge of his bed, folding a cool, damp cloth.

"You push yourself, my darling," she said.

"It had to be done. There is so little time left."

"I am sorry about your father."

"My news would not have pleased him. I know that."

"But you were not disowned. He died feeling as he always did for you. Perhaps that was for the best."

"I didn't like the thought that he could despise me."

"You are his son, his only son. I doubt that he would have despised you."

Morgan, though, was not so sure about that. Edward Kent's life was entirely English. He would never have understood, never countenanced his son choosing Virginia. He thought about his earlier conversation with Washington about what it meant to be a Virginian, what it might cost one to make that choice. Sighing, he closed his eyes. He was very tired. Making a little murmuring sound, he began to drift into sleep. "Home," he said, his voice barely audible, "Virginia."

Susannah smiled, unutterably glad that he had come to feel that way. Virginia had always been, would always be, home for her, but Morgan had come into her life and now he was, for her, the heart of that home, the very soul of it. He was sleeping now, and she leaned forward, resting her cheek on his chest so that she might hear home's heartbeat.

Chapter 97

Eden stood part way into the living room, watching Marshall. He was seated in a wing-back chair, Wadsworth's chin resting on one of his knees, the big dog's eyes turned up, raptly staring at his master's face. Music was playing, the surround sound filling the room with it. She recognized it as Strauss but couldn't quite put a name to it. Marshall was moving his hand in that way he had of almost literally touching the notes, of his motion being somehow inside the music, and he had a wide smile on his face, his head tipped back, eyes closed.

She loved him so much she wasn't sure she could contain it. Not wanting to interrupt him, she remained silent, trying to keep even her breathing quiet.

He sensed her presence nonetheless and, still smiling, held out his hand to her so she would continue on to him. She came and sat on the arm of the chair, sliding her right arm behind his neck. "Strauss?" She said it softly, hopefully unobtrusively.

"Johann, yes."

"You like this piece. I can tell."

"I like it very much. Listen to the section that's just about to start."

She closed her eyes, the music alive, pulsing, swinging, her body swaying inevitably to its call. "It's happy," she said. "There's no other word for it. It makes me happy to listen to it. What is it?"

"*Roses From the South*. Even the title is happy I've always thought."

"That particular part, it's almost extraordinary in its exuberance, its joy."

"Merry-go-round," he smiled.

"What?"

"At Kennywood, the big, old merry-go-round."

"Yes, I've ridden it many times."

"Can one ride a merry-go-round and not smile?" he asked.

She thought about that a moment. All her merry-go-round memories were, indeed, happy ones.

"As fine as the word 'carousel' is, I've always preferred the more descriptive 'merry-go-round,'" he said. "I used to go to Kennywood with my family and my favorite ride was the big merry-go-round. Do you recall the tiger?"

"I do, yes. Was that your favorite mount?"

He nodded. "Most of them, of course, are horses, but the first time my hands found the tiger, I knew I wanted it to be him I rode. I didn't always get the tiger. Sometimes someone else already had him, but whenever I could I did."

"You, riding tigers, yes, I can definitely relate to that." She was picturing the carousel, all its lights, its panoply of colors, the very visualness of it. "What was it like for you, darling, when you were on the merry-go-round?"

"Motion, the smooth up and down, the sense of around and around, the air blowing past my face, my hair moving with it, and music, music like that part of Roses. It would just rise up my core as I rode, filling me with the joy of its notes, and burst out my face in a wide smile. I can't hear Roses without imagining the feel of the merry-go-round."

"The whole piece is very, well, sort of 'swingy', you might say. Makes you want to move to it, to whirl around some glowing, marbled ballroom."

He ran his hand lightly down her arm. "I imagine that must be marvelous, but not a thing I can do." He made a small, indeterminate sound. "But the merry-go-round, that was possible. It's still there, you know. Maybe this summer we can give it a go? It's gentle enough, I expect, even for a lady great with child." His hand continued on to her slightly curving belly. "There are even a couple of very sedate compartments, like seats on a carriage, depending on just how, um, great you are."

"I want to see you ride the tiger," she chuckled.

"I haven't, not for many years now."

"Well, we shall just have to remedy that, now won't we?"

"I'd like that."

"What's your absolute favorite Strauss?" she continued, leaning to kiss the top of his head.

"Probably the *Emperor Waltz*. There are parts to that that just go right through my soul."

"Anything especially?"

"I like the whole thing, but toward the end the music slows and there's a section where a few notes become so piercingly bittersweet that...."

"That what?" He'd left the sentence unfinished and she wanted to know.

"It's like...like...love. The notes there actually ache with it, with longing, with...with... possibilities of separation. I think of stories when I hear them. The ball when sudden word passed and all the uniformed officers left their ladies to go fight at Waterloo. Like that, aching yet filled with the depth of the beauty of the mere existence of love."

"Is your Susannah going to know that?"

"Eventually, yes," he said quietly.

"I know it," she barely whispered.

"Love, to be full, to be mature, has, inevitably, to confront it. Often, I think the aching is a way we come to understand the depth of love."

She thought about what he was saying, that toward the end of Roses lay the utter joy of the merry-go-round and toward the end of Emperor lay the ache of Waterloo, and she knew that the two were actually one and could not really be separated without there being some great lack of fullness.

In mid-October, the Fairhaven, one of Edward Kent's smaller vessels, docked at Capitol Landing, bringing with it one Anderson Charles, sent by the solicitor in London who was handling the Kent estate. Anderson, a short, rather stout man in his early 30's, hired a small carriage to take him into Williamsburg, letting him out at the white house on Nicholson Street where Micah showed him into the parlor.

"Morgan Kent?" Anderson said, looking across the room at the young man who'd stood, laying aside a book.

"At your service," Morgan replied.

"Sir, I am Anderson Charles, representative of Martin Howard, your late father's solicitor."

Morgan's eyes widened in surprise. "You have come this far?"

"Your father, Sir, he left most specific and detailed instructions on the matter at hand, requesting in, um, certain eventualities that these," he lifted a leather valise he'd been holding at his side, "be hand delivered into your care should you not have returned to England. When Mister Howard received the recent communications from you and Mister Wythe regarding your father's estate, he dispatched me to bring them." He took a few steps forward, setting the valise near Morgan's feet.

"Please, Mr. Charles, do be seated while I have a look at these. Brandy?"

Anderson nodded, much fatigued by his trip, and sat back, watching, as Morgan took the valise to a small table and opened it. Inside was a copy of his father's will, documents stating he was now the sole owner of Kent Shipping, more papers detailing locations of properties, investments, lands, buildings, etc. When he came to a listing of finances, he cocked an eyebrow, looking over the paper at Anderson.

"You have been to Philadelphia before coming here?"

"Yes, Sir, I have. Mister Howard has arranged," he eyed Morgan, "since your original missive stated your clear intention to remain in the Colonies, for your father's bank accounts to be transferred to Philadelphia." A slight look of disapproval crossed Anderson's bland features.

Morgan noted, and the corner of his mouth twitched in a quickly-repressed smile. "I take it you are returning to London shortly, Mr. Charles?"

"As soon as possible, yes. I wouldn't want to be trapped over...."

"Of course not. That would be most unfortunate." He stood and came around from behind the table. "Please accept my most sincere gratitude for bringing me this and for what you have done on my behalf. I should like to write Mister Howard a letter for you to take with you. I shall have it delivered this evening to...." He looked at Anderson inquiringly.

"The King's Arms, Sir."

"Of course," Morgan smiled, walking the man to the door.

Susannah came in the back door, her small wicker basket filled with late fall gatherings from the rear garden. "Was someone here, darling? I thought I heard a carriage stop out front."

Morgan crossed to her, kissing her forehead. "It seems I am not to be quite the church mouse I'd thought." He was pleased. For some months now he'd been living almost entirely under the largesse of Harmer Wellington. It was still a fact, an undeniable fact, however, that war was shortly inevitable and shipping would be disrupted. At least the bank accounts were now in the Colonies. If the coming revolution succeeded, and he was as yet not at all sure that would be possible so unlikely did that outcome seem, but if it did, perhaps, just perhaps enough could be salvaged that would enable him to make a living. Surely the war would not last too long. The odds were so stacked in favor of England. What would become of the company, of him, should England win? If he fought on the side of Virginia against his king, he would be considered a traitor. All of them would, Washington, Jefferson, Henry, all subject to hanging. If he fought. Yes, that was the question. What would he do when the time came? He could never take up arms against Virginia, not now, but men his age would be expected to do something. His arms tightened around Susannah. He knew what he would do. He did. He had to help preserve all that mattered to her because now it all mattered to him. He couldn't sit by and let it be swept away. He would go. When the time came he would go. He just had no idea right now how that might come about, where he would go. His cheek atop her head, a sigh escaped him.

"What are you thinking?" she asked.

"I'm thinking how much I love you, how very much you mean to me."

Morgan was right. By November trade was almost at a standstill. The winter passed, everyone rather on edge as though waiting for some giant shoe to drop from Mount Olympus. Harmer came and went, came and went on various trips. As Morgan's health had fully returned some while ago, Clara decided to accompany Harmer to Richmond in March of 1775 where he went to attend the second Virginia Convention. It was there that Patrick Henry gave his soon-to-be famous 'Give me liberty or give me death' speech. He had a way about him, you had to give the man that much, of stirring the hearts of his listeners. His passionate belief in the cause of liberty was contagious and Virginia's governor, John Murray, Lord Dunmore, seemed constantly to add fuel to the patriotic fires in the hearts of men.

Late on the night of April 20th, Morgan was awakened by the sound of drums. He lay there trying to determine the why of them. Again the drums sounded and his heart beat faster as he recognized it as the call of the Independent Companies to arms. He sat up, then walked to the window, opening it to the cool spring air, leaning out a bit to discern its direction. It wasn't far and seemed to him to be coming from the Duke of Gloucester Street, possibly the Powder Magazine. That must be it.

Quickly he began to dress. "What are you doing, Morgan?" Susannah asked.

He'd dropped his boot and sat on the chest at the foot of the bed, grabbing for it, yanking it on. "Something's going on at the Powder Magazine. I mean to see what it is."

She heard the distinct sound of him buckling on his sword, something he'd never done before except for some friendly practice with Thomas Sutter once in a while. That he was doing so at night and in a hurry sent a chill of foreboding through her. He came to the side of the bed, gripped her shoulders and kissed her briefly but firmly, then said, "I'll send Layla in to stay with you until I come back."

He half-walked, half-sprinted down Botetourt Street, turning right on Gloucester, the drums swelling and fading, swelling again as he hurried along. A few horses galloped past him and there were shouts, loud voices here and there in the night. He almost stumbled into Sutter as he neared the court house.

"Tom!" he cried, "Do you know what's happened?"

"It's gone, Morgan. The powder's gone."

"What?"

What they didn't know was that secret orders had come from the British ministry to the royal governors to move the military stores so that the colonists couldn't have access to them. Word had not had time yet to reach Williamsburg but the very day before, in Massachusetts, attempts by Governor Gage had resulted in the conflict at Lexington. In Virginia, Governor Dunmore had waited until after midnight then had marines from the armed schooner Magdalen remove the powder to the vessel. They had been discovered, but the powder was already gone. The drums, then, had raised the Companies. A crowd of citizens had gathered in the streets and seemed now to be moving toward the Palace Green. Morgan and Thomas went along with them.

"He won't let our spokesman in," growled a man Morgan recognized as the proprietor of a carpenter's shop.

"Did you hear?" asked another man. "He's armed his servants."

People were muttering, shaking their fists at the Palace, and Morgan began to wonder if they would actually attack the brick building and drag Dunmore bodily out onto the Green. It was only Peyton Randolph's arrival, riding up onto the Green with his new authority of being the President of the Congress at Philadelphia, that stopped them. The crowd began to disperse when he promised them he would make a formal demand for the return of the powder. They dispersed, but they were still muttering, still angry.

"This doesn't look good," Thomas said, shaking his head.

No, Morgan thought, it didn't look good, not at all. What would Dunmore do next?

He didn't return the powder, making up some excuse about needing it in case there were a slave uprising in a neighboring county. Patrick Henry was having none of it and assembled a corps of volunteers at New Castle, marching toward Williamsburg. When he got to within sixteen miles of the town, he was met by some of Virginia's delegation on their way to Philadelphia. They informed him that Dunmore was frightened by what Henry was up to and when Henry demanded the value of the powder, which was 330 pounds, he got it, sent it immediately to the treasury in Williamsburg and his volunteers disbanded on May 4th and went home. Henry himself, being a delegate to Congress, left for Philadelphia a week later.

Dunmore, greatly irritated, threatened to burn Williamsburg. He didn't do so, but he issued a proclamation against Patrick Henry and some of his 'deluded followers' which forbade everyone from countenancing them at all. His Palace he surrounded with cannon, turning it into a garrison and fortifying it.

"This is most injudicious," Morgan sighed, standing at the end of Nicholson and looking toward the Palace. "He is doing everything possible to isolate himself and make the Virginians, make us," he amended, "feel separated from him and what he represents."

Thomas, a tall, raw-boned, and dark blond young man Morgan's age, was studying law at William and Mary. He nodded his head. "Look there, Morgan. Going through the Palace gate. Isn't that...."

"Parker Harrelson," Morgan finished for him. "Yes, I understand he practically lives at the Palace now that Dunmore is gathering his adherents about him."

Nine days after the first shot had been fired at Lexington, an exhausted express rider brought the news of it to Williamsburg, then rode on toward the Carolinas. Morgan and Thomas had been at the Raleigh when the rider practically fell in the front doorway, muddy, worn, quite haggard, yet with an excitement in his voice as he told about the small bridge where the first official shots of the war had rung through the springtime air.

"It's coming, Morgan," Thomas said.

"It has come, Tom. It's here." He was thinking of the Scots, who carried a fiery cross to call the men to grab their swords and gather for battle. As he watched the rider gulp down a tankard of ale, he could almost see such a cross superimposed over the man. The news he carried would ignite every single one of the colonies.

Letters from Dunmore to ministers had been found, publicly read, their meanness causing the governor to be even more despised. The first week of June several barrels of powder were discovered under the floor of the magazine, evidence that Dunmore had plans to blow it up. On the 7th, a rumor circulated rapidly through town that the Magdalen was coming up the river with a hundred royal marines. Instantly the men of Williamsburg flew to arms. The rumor proved false, but Dunmore was shaken by the readiness of the people to seize arms whenever alarmed, and his fear of personal violence increased to the degree he took his family and left Williamsburg, going to Yorktown, then aboard the Fowey, a British man-of-war, becoming the first royal representative to, as the townspeople put it, 'abdicate government'.

"Dunmore refused?" Morgan stood just inside the high brick wall surrounding the capitol building. He'd been waiting for Harmer to come out, intending to walk home with his father-in-law.

"We pledged our honor to the safety of his person," Harmer shrugged, "but he was adamant about not leaving the ship."

"What else did he say?"

"He demanded that we present ourselves aboard his ship. Then he says he'll sign the bills the Burgesses passed."

"You're not going? Surely you'll not?"

"There is, pardon my language, no way in hell that that will happen."

"What do you think will be the consequences of this?"

"We've adjourned until October."

"But won't that...." Morgan was surprised.

"Not really. A committee of the delegates has been appointed as a permanent convention."

Harmer turned, looking back at the capitol building. "They've been entrusted with unlimited powers of government. Their intention, Morgan, is to raise an armed force of large enough size to defend the colony. This, you realize, along with Dunmore's flight, will effectively terminate royal power in Virginia."

Morgan wiped his hand across his mouth. What would England's response be to that?

By late July Susannah was pregnant. As happy as the prospect of fatherhood made Morgan, he was concerned that he might have to leave Williamsburg and join the fight before the baby was due in March of 1776. One had no idea from day to day what course events would take and the effect they might have on daily life. The thought of not being there when his child was born weighed heavily on him...and to leave Susannah while she was pregnant? No, he mustn't do that. Perhaps the gods would grind their mills more slowly? It was a hope he had.

He was thinking of that in September as he lay beside her in bed. It was still warm, the window was open, and a maple leaf floated through. He watched it do a little flip in the air, then settle atop Susannah's stomach. He simply stared at it a while in the pale light, meditating on how it lay right above where the baby was growing. Susannah was asleep and his eyes moved from the leaf up to her face, which was tipped toward him. There were times when he could hardly grasp all that had come to pass in his life, the fact that this utterly adorable creature was his wife and lay beside him, carrying his child.

Unable to resist, he picked up the leaf, holding it close to his face, studying its structure and veining. How strange that it should come in the window as it had and settle just there. "Is there some meaning, some portent in your coming?" he whispered as though addressing the leaf itself.

"Portent?" Marshall chuckled. "Are you making reference to our 'wheeling mapled portent' that led you to walk in the woods rather than down to the lake that fateful day?"

"Just maybe," Eden replied. "It was a very significant leaf, you know."

"One I shall never forget," he added, "as it saved my life."

"It was a good maple leaf, indeed."

"Is this one?" he asked.

"Not so much, I think. I wanted him to be lying beside her in early autumn while she's pregnant and the leaf just, well, happened."

"So, what is he thinking now as he holds it?"

Morgan twirled the leaf, rolling its long stem between his thumb and forefinger. Could it possibly mean anything? Perhaps the very looming quality of a great war beginning led his thoughts down such odd pathways. He didn't know. He just lay there, twirling it, trying to find some sense of his own place in the inexorable march of events. Finally, with a sigh, he laid the leaf back atop Susannah. "It's your leaf, little one," he said softly to his unborn child. "It came for you, not for me."

Gazing at it for a while longer it suddenly came to him that a leaf only floated away from its tree because it had become detached from its source, was no longer able to receive nourishment from its tree, was no longer alive and growing. A shudder went through him and he snatched up the leaf, crumbling it in his fist. "No," he said, "no you don't!"

He'd said that more loudly than he'd intended and Susannah woke up. "What? Did you say something, darling?"

"Nothing important," he replied, leaning to place his lips softly atop hers, the crumbled leaf still in his tightly clenched hand.

"Mmmmm," she murmured against his lips. "Feels good."

"How good?" he asked, reaching over her to let the bits of leaf sift to the floor.

"Very, very good."

He found he had a deep need to get past that thought the leaf had generated and so reached under the cover, curving his hand over her not really mounded yet belly. Then he pushed the cover down, pulled up her night shift and covered both her and his child with countless small kisses.

Chapter 98

Susannah sat alone in the parlor, holding a stack of letters from Morgan. At the bottom of each he'd turned the page over and poked pinholes through in the shape of a heart. She ran a fingertip over one of them, smiling at his way of sending her an 'I love you'. There were no letters just to her as husbands off in war wrote to their wives, none because she could not read them. Every letter that came had to be read by her father or Aunt Clara and by the very nature of that, tended not to carry with it the feelings she knew lay in his heart.

Sighing, she touched another page, finding the heart there. Which letter was it? She had no way of knowing if it were one written shortly after he'd gone north in August of 1776 to join Washington or one written in a frigid January from their horrid winter encampment at Morristown, New Jersey. He was often very descriptive of his surroundings, though she knew he must leave out most of the details of hardship and suffering.

"What is it really like for you, my darling husband?" she whispered aloud into the quiet room. She thought of Morristown and then Valley Forge the following winter. He'd gotten the long, thick muffler she'd knitted for him, the two pair of socks Clara had made, but she knew he had to have been so cold, so very cold. He would mention the cold in passing then go on to describe in great detail the strength and courage of Washington and how it inspired him to carry on.

His first Christmas away he'd been with Washington as he crossed the Delaware and attacked Trenton. She hadn't, of course, known that Christmas Day what he was doing. All she knew was that he was far away, was cold, was in constant danger of sickness, injury, death. She'd sat in a rocker that evening near a fireplace, listening to the crackle of the burning logs, feeling their warmth on her face, feeling the hole in her heart that his absence left. Then Myra had brought in little George for her to nurse. Thank heavens Morgan had still been home on March 4th when his son had been born. He'd named him George after both Wythe and Washington. George Harmer Kent was in his tenth month that Christmas and his father had missed so much of his life.

He'd made it through the battle of Brandywine in September of 1777 unscathed but had gotten a slight flesh wound in his left arm at Germantown in early October. "Nothing to worry about," he'd written but she'd worried anyway. He'd exulted over the news of the Patriot victory at Saratoga but she'd been glad he wasn't there. He was a captain now and had been assigned to Lafayette's section of the army. He wrote even more about the young Marquis than he had about General Washington, glowing reports of his character, his intelligence, his care for his men. For her, the best thing about Morgan's being with Lafayette was that the Marquis was now in Virginia, which meant Morgan was also in Virginia.

Her fingers traced again a heart. It was June 22, 1881 and she'd seen him exactly twice since August of 1776. Twice. George had turned five in March and had no idea who his father was. Cornwallis had moved his army up into Virginia from the Carolinas recently and Lafayette was shadowing him as he moved south down the Neck, ever closer to Williamsburg. What, she wondered, would it be like if the British actually occupied the town?

Morgan was wondering the exact same thing as he carefully pricked another heart for his wife at the bottom of a new letter home. Home. He closed his eyes, letting his own fingers run over the outline. How he yearned for his home, for Susannah, for little George who was not so little any more, for the others there who had become his family, Harmer, Clara, Micah, Layla, Myra, Joel. Missing had become an almost continual pain tucked into his heart. So many years. How could it have possibly been so long? He hadn't seen George since he was three. If... when...the war ever ended, he'd have to start all over with his son and the fact of that galled him terribly. Yet he was doing what he had to do, what he must do, and the thought that still everything could so easily be lost, that all the years could have been spent in vain, loomed ever-present. Unless the French fleet came, and came to the right place at the right time, there seemed no real hope for anything but defeat.

For some time now Lafayette's army had been moving as Cornwallis' moved, not really engaging, just keeping close, keeping a constant awareness of their presence. That Cornwallis was now so close to Williamsburg was never far from Morgan's mind. He would occupy the town. That much was inevitable. Then what?

He ran a hand around inside his collar. It was hot, excessively hot, this June in Virginia and he took off his dark blue Continental jacket, hanging it over the back of his camp chair. It seemed in this man's army one was either freezing or broiling or sopping wet. Rolling up the sleeves of his white shirt, he fanned himself with the piece of paper he'd been writing on. Two years since he'd seen Susannah. My God, two years. Now he was so close he could mount Gideon and be there in a day or two. Only the British army was between him and home. Only that. But the nearness of it to his home weighed heavily on him.

Yet once again he looked at the letter in his hand. How he wished he could write private things to his wife that only she would read. It would, possibly, have made the long separations more bearable. But always he had to keep in mind as he wrote that Harmer would be the one reading the letter aloud, him or Aunt Clara. He did write endearments, yes, but not of the kind his soul yearned to write. Placing a kiss on the heart, he folded the letter then sealed it, turning to slide it into the pocket of his jacket. With the two armies in their current positions, he wasn't at all sure a letter would even get through.

Leaning back in his small chair, he contemplated the immediate past. On May 24th Lafayette had written Washington, saying that he was "not strong enough even to get beaten." The Marquis' general plan had been to keep himself between Cornwallis' much larger force and a line of communication to the north. Washington still expected that the main British attack would fall on New York City and he and his army remained in the north. Wayne, though, had marched south to join Lafayette, whose army was comprised mainly of militia. In early June Banastre Tarleton, who'd gained the nickname in the Carolinas as 'the Butcher', had been sent by Cornwallis in an attempt to capture Jefferson at Monticello. Tarleton had 189 dragoons and 70 mounted infantry with him, but Jefferson had been warned and escaped. Cornwallis' other dragoon legion was under the command of Lt. Col. John Graves Simcoe and was made mostly of colonists loyal to the Crown, mounted on the best of the blooded horses of Virginia. Harmer had written Morgan that Parker Harrelson had joined them, the Queen's Rangers, as they were called, and they, too, were in Virginia, attacking here and there.

What bothered Morgan the most was that in the third week of April, Simcoe's Rangers had been in Williamsburg, had forced the Virginia militia under James Innes to retreat from the town. Surely Parker would have left Susannah alone? Morgan hadn't had a letter from Harmer since before then so didn't know if there had been any encounter or not.

There had been. Layla had opened the door to find Parker standing there, resplendent in his green dragoon uniform. Her lip had curled slightly at the sight and Parker had simply brushed past her and entered the parlor unannounced. Harmer had been over at William and Mary on business and Susannah was alone, seated at the harpsichord. He stood there a moment in the middle of the room, just looking at her. She was still the most beautiful woman in Williamsburg and it had been a thorn in his side that she had chosen Morgan over him. Since he'd gone off to war, he'd only had women in taverns or among the camp followers, women who were nothing like the lovely flower she was.

"They're going to lose, you know," he said.

She knew the voice, though she'd not heard it for a long while. "Parker. What are you doing here?"

"I wanted to see you."

"It's not your place to see me, Parker. I'm married, a mother."

"I heard you'd had his whelp. Have you seen him recently?"

"That is none of your business."

He smiled. "You haven't, have you? You probably don't even know if he's still alive."

"I know...no, I shall not speak of him, not to you."

"It's been a long war, Susannah. You're probably lonely."

"Not for the likes of you, Parker. I...just go, please."

He came closer, standing beside the small bench on which she sat. "I want you to know, Susannah, that when this is all over, when their army has lost and he's been hung for treason or left dead on some battlefield, then I will come for you. I still want you even though you weren't wise enough back then to know what was best for you."

She tipped her head. "You will go now. You have no idea what you're talking about."

"You think not, do you?" He clutched her shoulders, pulling her to her feet, kissing her hard, invading her mouth with his tongue, bruising her lips. "That," he said, "is what you've been missing, my dear, and when your Mr. Kent is in his grave, that is what you'll have. I promise you."

He turned on his heel with a sharp jingle of spurs, went to the entrance archway of the parlor and paused. "Remember that, Susannah. That's why I've come today, to promise you that. Believe me, I'll make it happen. I will. You know I will."

When the front door had closed, she'd hurried to her room, dipping her hands in the ewer near her bed, washing across her mouth over and over. She was still doing so when her door opened and little George came in. "Mama?"

"Oh, sweetheart, I'm all right, everything's all right." She gathered him up in her arms, sitting with him on the edge of her bed. She'd never seen him, but she knew how much he looked like his father. Everyone remarked on it, on his green eyes, his brown wavy hair, and she'd felt his straight brows, the cleft in his little chin, the general shape of his face. He was her

tangible piece of the love between her and Morgan, something of him she could hold. Parker's words about Morgan's death had been a knife in her heart and she pressed George close, kissing and kissing the top of his head.

Now, here in the last week of June, she knew Simcoe's men were back. As her fingers rested on the heart, she thought of Parker's unwelcome visit in April, her other hand going to her mouth, wiping across her lips. So lost in thought was she that she hadn't heard the door open, was unaware she wasn't alone until a male voice said, "You wish another kiss?"

"What? Parker?"

He came and knelt on one knee beside the rocker, knocking Morgan's letters off her lap onto the floor. "It will be over soon. I feel it. Then you will be free, Susannah, to be mine."

"Are you mad, Parker? Do you truly think that even were I widowed I would ever...ever... be with you?"

"I shall be part of a great, conquering army, my dear, and you, yes, you, will be my personal conquest. This ridiculous notion of a country separate from England will die, he...will die, and you will need caring for. My father is dead, you know, and Graylands is mine. I shall take you there and you will be mine, too, and be glad of it."

"I would die first." Her words came as a broken whisper.

He laughed. "You think that now, but in time you'll come to your senses. A woman like you needs a strong, capable man to watch over her."

"Like me? You mean blind?"

"Blind, yes, and lovely. You are lovely, you know, my Susannah."

"I am not your Susannah. I...Morgan...."

"I shall kill the man myself if need be." He wished he knew where Morgan was so that could be facilitated. He'd heard he'd joined Washington so he was probably still somewhere in the north. He indulged, though, in a pleasurable mental image of choking the life out of him and leaving him on the Wellington doorstep. Yes, wouldn't that be a fine thing?

"Cornwallis, you know, will march into Williamsburg this week." When she started, he smiled. "You didn't realize he was that close, did you? Yes, this week. I know this for a fact. He is but a couple day's march away. The French have not come and Lafayette is but a boy and no match for Cornwallis. You'll see." He laughed again. "Well, maybe you won't 'see', but you'll hear it all, I'm sure, as the most splendid army in the world takes over the town. We will be here and there's nothing your Morgan can do about it." He rose up a bit, taking her shoulders again, preparing to kiss her.

Susannah could feel his face getting close to hers, feel his breath, and the memory of his revolting kiss flooded through her. She spat in his face, startling him. He pulled back his arm, almost slapping her, but controlled himself at the last second. Instead, he stood, the fingers of his left hand bruising her upper right arm he gripped her so firmly. His eyes narrowed, he stared down at her, wanting both to hit her and kiss her. He released his grip. "With the British army occupying Williamsburg, know that I will be back. Count on it!" Then he was gone again and Susannah pressed her hands to her face, trying to hold back her tears.

"He's not very nice," Marshall remarked in obvious understatement.

"If he had a long black moustache, I 'spect he'd be twirling it," Eden smiled, "but we need a set-up for Spencer's Ordinary."

"Poor Morgan," Marshall sighed.

"Yes, poor Morgan," Eden agreed.

"I know what I'm going to do about it," he added.

"Do you now? Are you telling?"

"Not yet," he smiled, "but wait and see."

It was how their way of writing together had developed, each one having to respond to the actions the other wrote. The book was, in fact, more their feeling their way into each other, reflecting their own story, what they knew personally of love and of pain, in what happened to their characters. It was an exercise in togetherness and sometimes it was even a game.

CHAPTER 99

Parker intended to come back to see Susannah again the following day, the sight of her having aroused his need to see her more, but Simcoe's Queen's Rangers were sent out on the 23rd of June on a raid to destroy boats and supplies, farms and mills on the Chickahominy River just west of Williamsburg. On the 25th, Cornwallis marched into town, Tarleton raising the British flag over the old capitol building and the remaining Loyalists in town coming out to celebrate. Simcoe's raid was an easy couple of day's work with little fuss involved. The night of the 25th, however, word of the raid was received in Lafayette's camp. The Marquis had been hoping for an opportunity for a small engagement without having to face the full strength of the British army and immediately sent out Colonel Richard Butler, a veteran Continental officer, to intercept them.

Lafayette had very little cavalry but as so many of Simcoe's men were mounted, he sent horsemen under Major McPherson to join with Butler's corps of troops and riflemen. A certain Captain Morgan Kent was among the horsemen, smiling because each hoof beat took him closer to Williamsburg.

Simcoe, alerted to Butler's pursuit, looked for a local loyalist to participate in a ruse to lure his enemy into a trap. Unable to find such a man, Simcoe planted false information in the mind of a local rebel, sure that he would pass it on to Lafayette. Most of the night of the 25/26 was spent, therefore, by the Patriots heading to attack a campsite just vacated by Simcoe's men. Butler, frustrated upon discovery of the ruse, sent ahead an advance party of fifty horsemen with fifty infantrymen riding double behind them.

Morgan was tired, having ridden all night and now had the unaccustomed presence of another man riding double behind him. He was sweating, too, as even the nights this June did not cool much. The man behind him had a musket and was to be set down when the enemy was contacted. Morgan himself had a pistol and his saber as most mounted Continental units weren't often able to find enough rifles for more than a handful of men in each troop.

Parker. He was with Simcoe, Morgan knew. The Queen's Rangers, he also knew, were an elite corps that had fought in every major campaign since the operations in Pennsylvania in 1777. Accompanying the Rangers this day were two rifle units, one a Hesse-Kassel jager unit, and a mounted unit of New York volunteers. Simcoe would not let anyone serve with him unless they'd merited the right so as not to 'contaminate' his regiment with anything less than excellence. Also with him was a unit of North Carolina Loyalists who were performing the non-combat duties of herding the cattle Simcoe had rounded up and guarding the provision wagons he was taking to Cornwallis.

The woods were thick and often swampy and the infantry with Simcoe had encamped just south of the Williamsburg road for breakfast. The fields and orchards here were surrounded by rail fences and both the Williamsburg road and the Jamestown Road that crossed it were also lined with them. Simcoe's cavalry had thrown down some of them to provide access to the meadows and the nearby stream for their horses and to give themselves greater freedom of movement to support the infantry and the cattle and wagons. Spencer's Ordinary was a small tavern with a house and barn at Lee's farm nearby.

Major McPherson, in his eagerness to engage the enemy, attacked Simcoe's videttes to the west of the road, a premature act that gave both Simcoe's cavalry and infantry time to assemble. McPherson had also not waited for Butler to bring up the main body of around five hundred troops.

"There!" cried one of McPherson's men.

A Simcoe vidette was riding around a hill and McPherson ordered his horsemen after him, not realizing they were deliberately being led away from the Rangers, who were now mounting. One of Simcoe's men led a charge toward them and McPherson was knocked from his horse, severely injured. Morgan, now riding alone, reined in close to the fallen major, prepared to offer assistance but a hussar had him in his sights and the slam of a ball through his left shoulder sent him flying backwards off Gideon. He crashed down hard on his back, lying there sick and dizzy from the shock as the battle continued around him. Simcoe's Captain Ewald led a bayonet charge that passed right over him, though one of the hussars fell close to Morgan, shot through the head, his bayonet landing across Morgan's legs.

Morgan pressed his right hand to his shoulder, feeling the blood seeping through his fingers. Oh, God, he thought, so close, a mere six miles from Williamsburg. Clamping his teeth, he tried to fight off the pain, tried to concentrate for a moment on the image of Susannah's face. Insects buzzed about him in the meadow and the sun beat steadily down on his face. He licked his lips, suddenly terribly thirsty.

Simcoe, concerned that Lafayette might be closer than he thought, withdrew from the field but when he reached a defile on the Williamsburg Road decided there was no sign of pursuit and turned back. Butler, too, realized he was all too close to Cornwallis' main force and pulled back. Simcoe, reinforced now by more units of the British army led by Cornwallis himself, returned to the battlefield to look for casualties and prisoners.

Flies began crawling on Morgan's sweaty face, on the blood stain on the front of his jacket. He tipped his head back, seeing that he was lying near one of the rail fences, and pushing with his feet, squirming through the grass, he got himself up next to it. Grabbing the lowest rail, he hooked his right arm over it, dragging himself to a seated position. McPherson was moaning in agony where he lay and Morgan looked at him blearily. The hussar's brains coated a small section of the tall grass.

Gideon stood in the field just a yard or two from the fence. If he could get to his feet, if he could stand, maybe he could make it to his horse, maybe. He turned his body so he was on his knees facing the fence. His left arm was useless so he used his right again, hooking it now over the second rail, to try to stand. The world tilted and he squeezed his eyes tightly closed, waiting for it to stop turning.

"Mr. Kent, I do believe."

Parker, returned with Simcoe to the field, had spied Morgan, his eyes attracted by the man's attempts to pull himself upright at the fence. Hardly able to believe his good fortune, he walked, pistol in one hand, saber in the other, across the meadow, stopping about three yards back.

Morgan turned his head, blinking, trying to focus. "Wh...who?"

Parker inclined his head in a smiling, mini-bow. "Parker Harrelson, at your service. I had no idea you were back in Virginia," he paused to peer at Morgan's uniform, "Captain." He took several steps closer. "Did you know I've seen your wife twice of late? Did she tell you that?"

"My...my...Susannah?"

"Yes, Susannah, a most arousing kisser. Only she will shortly not be your Susannah but mine. I intend to make the poor widow my wife, mistress of Graylands. Do you like the sound of that, Captain Kent?"

"Wife...no...I...." He tried to straighten more but Parker, not wishing him to stand, shot him through his right thigh and he began to fall, clutching desperately at the rail, on his knees, leaning into the fence.

Almost absently, Parker let his pistol fall into the grass as he began walking closer. "She was always too good for you. Surely you must have known that, miserable little merchant that you are, yet still you married her, married the one woman I'd chosen to be my wife. Do you hear me, Kent? MY wife!"

With a grim smile of utter satisfaction, he slashed his saber across the kneeling man's back, watching as almost in slow motion Morgan's arm slipped loose from the rail and he toppled silently sideways and lay still.

"Harrelson! What in hell are you doing?" It was Simcoe himself, sitting on his horse several yards away. "This battle is over. We're here for our wounded and to take prisoners, not continue fighting with injured men." He'd seen Parker slash the helpless man and frowned deeply. "Your actions bring no honor to the Rangers, sir, none at all, and you will report to me back in Williamsburg." Simcoe wheeled his horse away.

Parker was too elated to feel much concern over Simcoe's displeasure. He knelt beside Morgan, grabbing his hair and lifting his head. The man was dead. He smiled again and let Morgan's head drop back to the ground. Standing, he looked around, then walked to Gideon and took his dangling reins, leading him up to the fence. Two young British infantrymen were passing nearby and he got them to heft Morgan up, laying him facedown across the saddle. He didn't want to lift him himself because he'd end up with blood on his uniform. Mounting his own horse, he took Gideon's reins and headed toward Williamsburg, whistling a tune as he rode. He paused once for a long drink from his canteen and stared with satisfaction at the size of the bloodstains on the back of Morgan's blue coat. Such a nice present he had for Susannah. His pleasant meditation of leaving her dead husband on her doorstep had never been far from his mind. Now it would be reality. Sometimes life was just so good!

He rode into Williamsburg, crossed the Palace Green, and headed happily down Nicholson Street toward the Wellington house. He'd gotten as far as the pathway that led down the side of their yard when two of Simcoe's lieutenants rode up from Botetourt Street.

"Captain Harrelson!" one of them called. "Lieutenant-Colonel Simcoe wishes you to accompany us to his quarters immediately."

Parker looked at Morgan and sighed. Ah, well, the man wasn't going anywhere, now was he? Just a brief reprimand and he could return and complete his little mission. "You can go on the doorstep a bit later, Captain Kent." He flipped Gideon's reins over a picket in the fence near the fig tree and followed the two junior officers toward the Duke of Gloucester Street.

Gideon knew where he was, knew his stable was just there in the far back corner of the yard. He was hungry, thirsty, and tired. Tossing his head, the loose loop came over the top of the picket and he went down alongside the fence, turning to his right. Not far along the back fence was a larger gate, one Morgan had taught him to open with his nose by pressing on the latch. Now he opened it and walked into the yard, smelling hay and oats, scenting water. He stopped suddenly and turned when a loud sound from the street startled him and Morgan slipped feet-first off the saddle, crumpling in a heap on the grass.

The jolt of that jarred a bit of sensibility into Morgan, who had been lapsing in and out of consciousness for the last several minutes, and he blinked his eyes open, trying to focus, trying to determine where he was. Everything was blurry but he vaguely made out a white shape. What was it? He squeezed his eyes shut then opened them wide. Marietta? No, how could it be Susannah's angel? Still...it looked like Marietta. How? The last he remembered was a searing pain in his back, sometimes the sound of whistling and a word or two from Parker. He wriggled forward, every inch a mile of pain and weakness. He had no strength, none at all, but he had to get to the angel even though he didn't know why he did. All he could do was pull himself with his right arm and push a bit with his left leg. Nothing else seemed to work. His right hand came down on something. Brick? Yes, the upturned brick edging of the back of the garden. He gripped it, dragging himself into the flowerbed, closer to the statue. The bed was long and narrow and he managed to clutch at the angel's base, raising his head just enough to see that, yes, it was Marietta. He looked up at her profile, smiled slightly, then collapsed onto his side, rolling over onto his back, crushing the foxgloves.

Joel came out of the stables, heading for the kitchen, thinking of the stew Myra was making for lunch. He almost tripped when he saw the saddled horse standing in the middle of the yard grazing. "Gideon?" Good Lord above, it was Gideon! Quickly he strode to the horse. Why hadn't Morgan...? Then he saw the blood on the saddle and sucked in a deep breath. Instantly his eyes began to search the yard. Where? There by the statue. He ran through the flowers, kneeling beside the fallen man, seeing the blood from bullet wounds in his shoulder and leg. Then he was up again, sprinting for the house.

The back door was open to let in the air and he ran straight through it into the parlor. Susannah and Clara were seated on the sofa, both knitting, and Harmer was standing by the front window, watching British troops in the street, a frown on his face.

"Mister Wellington!" Joel gasped, waving his arm toward the back of the house. "Come quick! Morgan in the flowers."

Harmer turned, staring at the excited man. "What are you talking about, Joel? Calm down and tell me what you mean."

"Shot, sir. Morgan...in the flowers...shot!"

"In the...? Morgan? Morgan's here?"

"By the angel...in the flowers."

"Good Lord!"

Joel was running out the back again with Harmer not far behind. Susannah's knitting had slid to the floor and she was on her feet, going as fast as she could in their wake. Clara was calling, "Susannah, no!" but nothing would stop her from going, not if Morgan were there.

"Oh, my God!" Harmer moaned, sinking to a crouch beside Morgan, seeing the two bullet wounds. "Morgan?" He touched the young man's cheek then Susannah was there, too, practically falling herself into the flowers as she groped to find her husband.

"Is...is it him, Daddy?"

"It's Morgan, darling, yes. He's been shot." He looked up at Joel, who was shifting from foot to foot in anxiety. "How did he get here?"

"I don' know but Gideon come home an'...an'"

Clara arrived, having routed out Micah and Myra to come with her. Layla she'd sent upstairs to watch over George.

"Micah, good," Harmer nodded. "We've got to get him into the house. Help me."

Micah slid an arm under Morgan's shoulder to begin lifting him but pulled it back when he felt sticky wetness. "Wait," he said, turning Morgan just enough to reveal the long saber wound.

Harmer closed his eyes, opening them when Susannah cried, "What? What is it?"

"He's hurt more than I thought," Harmer said, his voice cracking. "Come now, let's get him up."

Morgan opened his eyes a bare slit. "Not...not inside. No."

"Morgan, thank God!" Susannah gasped.

"Why, son?" Harmer asked. "What do you mean?"

"Parker...he...he's coming back."

"Parker? He did this?"

Morgan nodded slightly. "Heard say...coming back...doorstep."

"Doorstep?"

"Me...doorstep...leave...you find. Thinks I'm...thinks I'm dead."

"He plans to leave you on our doorstep?" Harmer's mouth dropped open in ghastly amazement.

"Doorstep...yes. Not find me...look. Not inside. Not...." His eyes closed.

Harmer licked his lips, looking from Micah to Joel to Myra. "We'll have to hide him then."

"That Parker devil's gonna look for him. You know that," Myra said, her practical mind racing. "We got to make him keep thinkin' our Morgan here's dead. He's lost a lotta blood an' we have to do somethin' 'bout that but we still got to make the devilman think what he thinks." Myra, in action, was like a drill sergeant and when she knew what was the best thing to do, it got done. "My kitchen," she announced firmly. "Bring him to my kitchen an' we'll take care of him."

Carefully, the three men lifted Morgan and carried him into the backyard kitchen house, where Myra spread a cloth quickly over the large preparation table. "Joel," she said, "you get yourself out to the back fence and dig up somethin' that'll pass as a grave so we can tell the devil we done buried our man, then you take them broken flowers an' pile 'em on it so's there a reason they got broke. An' take care o' that horse, too."

She looked at Susannah, who was pale and shaking. "Susannah, this ain't no place for you, child."

"I'm not leaving him, Myra, so don't bother asking." She wiped a hand across her face. "I'm not."

There was no time to argue with her. No one knew when Parker might return and before they could hide Morgan, his bleeding must be stopped. She asked Clara if she'd go watch George and send Layla to her as she needed her help. Morgan was lying on his back and Myra got Harmer and Micah to sit him up enough to remove his coat and shirt while she took a small knife and cut open his tight-fitting white pants above his leg wound. The front shoulder wound seemed to have stopped bleeding, but blood was still steadily seeping from his thigh. She sighed and slid the blade of a larger knife into the cooking fire.

Harmer cocked a brow at her but she shrugged and said, "No other way, not with the time we got, not with that bleedin'."

Morgan was making little, low moaning sounds and Susannah, leaning near his head, kept brushing his hair back from his face, whispering into his ear. "You're home, my darling, you're home. We've got you and everything will be all right. You'll see, my love, it will be all right."

But Harmer and Myra exchanged a look across the table that said neither of them were at all sure about that. Morgan's skin was almost white because of blood loss and he was obviously in shock. Now there would be more pain. Layla came in, her mouth setting in a grim line when she saw Morgan. Myra handed her a bottle of whiskey, and she poured some over the front thigh wound and on his shoulder.

"You best stand back, Susannah," Layla said as Myra approached the table with the glowing knife. Micah held down Morgan's shoulders and Layla his legs as Myra pressed the end of the blade above the leg wound. Morgan's head came up off the table, his back arched, and a cry began to escape his lips. Tears in his eyes, Harmer clamped a hand firmly over his son-in-law's mouth so that no one passing by might hear his scream. Susannah was shaking, tears streaming down her face, then everything was silent as Morgan lay limp and quiet on the table.

Harmer and Micah then turned him over. They'd noticed earlier that both balls had passed all the way through him and so there needed to be no digging to remove them. More whiskey was quickly poured. The exit wounds of both balls seemed to be bleeding the most. As Parker had shot his leg from the back, it was the front of his thigh that needed cauterization, but the hussar had hit him from the front and Myra pressed the reheated blade to the back of his shoulder. He'd done a long slide into darkness with what she did to his thigh and now lay unmoving as she tended to his shoulder. His face was turned to his left and Susannah kept touching his cheek.

The long slash across the middle of his back from side to side was also still bleeding and Myra debated quickly cauterizing that, too, but it was so long and she knew that so much tissue around it would be damaged if she did that. "Layla," she almost hissed, "fetch me my sewin' basket." While Layla was gone, Myra applied a second, careful dose of the whiskey along the nearly straight wound.

"She's very competent, your Myra," Marshall commented.

"Indeed she is," Eden agreed. "If she'd lived in our modern times, the woman could've been the CEO of a corporation."

Her lips pursed intently, Myra chose a curved darning needle and some thick black thread then set about stitching the wound as quickly as she could. That Morgan still lay perfectly unmoving was a great help to the process. There was no time for proper poultices and bandaging, not yet. She felt in her bones that Parker would be back any moment and she wanted to have just Micah and Layla with her to finish what she intended to do.

"Sir," she said, looking at Harmer, "I know what's got to be done now an' if you'd kindly take Susannah inside the house an' maybe get her to lie on the sofa like she's laid all low with grief when that devilman comes, that'd be a big help."

"You plan to hide him out here, Myra?" Harmer asked.

Myra nodded. "'Behind them barrels an' sacks. Devilman search the house for sure but maybe not here so well."

"What if he wakes and makes noise or moves?"

"I'll take care o' that, too. Don't you worry none. I know what to do."

Harmer smiled slightly. He believed she did. "Thank you, Myra," he said sincerely. "I am more grateful to you than I can say."

Susannah didn't want to leave but Harmer talked her into it simply because it would be safer for Morgan if she did. Once inside the house, she did lie on the couch and it wasn't hard at all to look like she was distraught because she was. She felt clammy and her pulse was pounding in her neck.

In the kitchen Micah was asking, "How're you gonna keep 'im from movin' or makin' noise he wakes while that Parker man lookin' for 'im?"

"Like this," Myra said and with Layla's help and a fresh sheet from the clothes line, began to swaddle him like a newborn, wrapping the cloth around him and tucking it in on itself tightly, which was both good for his injuries and kept his arms pinned to his sides and his legs together.

Micah pulled the barrels out further from the back wall of the kitchen and Layla tossed some more laundry from the clothes lines on the floor there to pad it a bit before they laid Morgan down. The bloody sheet from the table, Morgan's coat and shirt, Myra grabbed up and stuffed into a barrel, then put its lid on again and set some onions atop it.

Morgan on the floor, moaned again. She'd hoped he'd stay unconscious longer and, sighing, tied a large knot in a big cloth table napkin and gagged him. "I'm sorry 'bout this, my sweet Morgan, but we can't have that devil hearin' you, so this is for your own good."

Micah pushed the barrels back close against Morgan and Myra and Layla piled several layers of empty burlap sacks over him. As a last touch, Myra picked up a big basket that was filled with freshly-picked herbs and set it on the sacks over his legs. Micah set a few full sacks of flour and potatoes on the barrels, making the barrier higher as Layla wiped off the big table and arranged several pots and bowls on it.

Parker was in a foul mood, having been dressed down by Simcoe at some length, but he cheered somewhat as he rode along Nicholson, getting closer to Wellington's house. It was worth it, the stern reprimand, worth it because of the result his actions on the battlefield would now have. He could almost taste the pleasure of dumping Kent on the doorstep. Maybe Susannah might even trip over his body? Wouldn't that be a sight! He turned into the little path where he'd left the dead man, glowering when he saw the horse was no longer there. Standing in his stirrups, he looked across the garden, and when he noticed someone moving near the stables called out, "You there! Come over here!"

Joel took a deep breath and crossed the yard to the herb garden by the fence. "Sir?" he said, doffing his hat.

"I left a horse here not more than an hour ago. What happened to it?"

"Oh, that be Gideon, Mister Kent's horse, Sir. He come home with Mister Kent dead on his back. Mister Wellington, asked me to bury him there," he pointed to the far fence line in the rear of the yard, "so's Miss Susannah she not have to have his body lyin' about."

"Buried him? You buried Kent already?" His brows rose incredulously.

"Yes, Sir. That's what Mister Wellington want me to do. I can show you if you want."

"I do want! Parker snapped.

"Back gate, Sir," Joel pointed and Parker spurred his horse to ride down the fence line then turn right while Joel sprinted to the gate, opening it for him. Parker dismounted just outside and strode through, glaring at the groomsman. Joel led him past some large lilac bushes to where there was an obviously freshly-dug grave. It was only a foot deep, but it was the surface size of a grave and Joel had mounded the dirt up rather effectively then sprinkled the broken foxgloves over it.

Parker stood looking down at it, feeling robbed. Finally he said, "She knows he's dead, then?"

"Sir? Mister Morgan? Yes, Sir, Miss Susannah knows."

"Good," he said, then turned, looking toward the back of the house then down at the grave again. Something didn't seem quite right. Without another word to Joel, he began walking quickly through the yard toward the open back door. Susannah heard his spurs as he came down the back entry and a shiver of fear went through her lest he discover Morgan.

Parker paused in the archway to the parlor. Susannah lay on the couch, her eyes closed. Harmer stood nearby, drinking a glass of water, his hand shaking, both because he wanted the effect of that for Parker's sake and because it really was shaking on its own somewhat. So much was at stake in this moment.

"Parker," Harmer said, "you've heard?"

"I've heard Kent was killed. Is that true?"

Harmer looked devastated. "I'm afraid so." He glanced at his daughter. "My poor Susannah is quite prostrate with grief."

Parker walked to the couch, looking down at her, seeing tears still wet on her face. Her grief seemed real enough. He touched her arm but she only moaned and turned on her side, her face against the back of the couch.

Good girl, *Harmer thought. He hadn't wanted her to have to endure speaking with Parker.*

Parker straightened. "You won't mind, then, if I have a look around."

"There's no need for that, Parker, but, of course, I don't mind. Since you came in the back, I trust you've seen his grave."

Susannah moaned again and her shoulders shook. It wasn't feigned. She knew all too well Morgan could still die.

"Very well," Parker said stiffly and went quickly up the stairs, looking in each bedroom, under every bed, even inside a large wardrobe. In George's room he gazed at the child a moment. The brat looked like his father. He couldn't possibly have him at Graylands. Downstairs, he checked under the dining room table, in the pantry, lifted the lid of a big chest in the hall. Morgan was not in the house. Still not completely satisfied, he stalked out the back entrance, going around the brick path to the cookhouse.

Myra was stirring a big pot of stew, to which she'd added a lot of onions and herbs, its scent filling the room, covering that of blood and evaporating whiskey. Layla was at the table, mixing bread dough in a large bowl. They both watched silently as he moved around the room, tipped a barrel, frowned, then left. He walked across the yard back to the grave, stared at it briefly, then bent and picked up a long stem of lavender-colored foxglove. He twirled it between his thumb and forefinger, then slid the fingers of his left hand down the stem, shredding off the trumpet-shaped blooms. A bee inside one of the trumpets stung his thumb. With a low curse, he sucked on the sting, his brow deeply knitted. Tossing the bare stem back onto the dirt, he turned on his heel, went to his horse and mounted.

Chapter 100

Morgan came awake, desperately hot, fighting for breath. He'd lost all touch with where he was, what had happened. The only thing he knew was that he had to get out of wherever he was and he had to get out now. He struggled, only to discover to his horror he couldn't move, couldn't even wiggle a fingertip. Opening his eyes, he could see only the vaguest, filtered light and something fine and powdery sifted down into his eyes, forcing him to close them again. He was soaked in his own sweat, overwhelmingly hot, and the containment he was in added immeasurably to that. Air. He needed more air, required great gulping gasps of it but something large was in his mouth, holding his tongue down and he couldn't suck in enough. He needed to swallow, too, but he couldn't do that, either, couldn't make the slightest sound. His mind reeled with lack of understanding, with not enough air, and sheer terror, cold and stark, shot through him, accompanied by nearly unbearable pain. He'd been buried alive. Somehow he'd been buried alive and his mind screamed, long, utterly soundless screams as his throat worked with the fruitless effort to swallow. It was too much and his consciousness crashed, splintering on the rocks of it, swallowing him into darkness.

Joel rushed back into the house. "He's gone! Devilman done rode down the street."

"Thank God!" Harmer sighed. "Now let's get Morgan inside."

Again Susannah followed the two men out the back door, still feeling weak from the stress of having Parker in the house. Myra looked up from her stewpot at their entrance into the cookhouse.

"Where is he?" Harmer asked, noting with satisfaction there was no trace of Morgan anywhere in the room. "He is here, isn't he?"

"Behind the barrels. Devilman come an' he didn't find him." She smiled at the recollection of Parker's frustration as Micah and Joel began removing the filled sacks from the tops of the barrels. "Hurry up now," Myra urged. "We got to get his wounds tended better."

Susannah was holding onto the doorframe, feeling the need of support as she listened to the sounds of the sacks being tossed aside, the scrape as barrels were moved. Layla and Myra began pulling off the empty sacks and when Harmer could see Morgan he gasped. "Good Lord! What have you done to him?"

"Had to keep him quiet. Was the only way with so little time."

Harmer knew she was right. He himself had clamped a hand over Morgan's mouth as Myra cauterized the thigh wound, but the sight of him with the gag in his mouth and so completely bound up almost made him sick to his stomach. "Well, let's get him up out of there and quick about it."

He worked at untying the gag while Myra and Layla undid the big sheet binding him. Myra had used a knot gag as it was more effective in preventing sound. It held his mouth open but pressed down on his tongue and Harmer worked gently in getting it out of his mouth. Damn, but that had to be uncomfortable. Morgan lay entirely limp, though, and Harmer was glad he'd been unconscious the whole time and hadn't had to deal with the gag or the bindings. That would have been too terrible.

They gathered him up, loosened sheet and all, and managed somewhat awkwardly to get him in the house and up the stairs. George heard a bumping in the hallway and opened his door, peering out. Harmer saw him but for a moment was too occupied with getting Morgan into a bedroom to do anything about it. When Morgan lay on the towels Layla had quickly spread, Harmer went back down the hall and squatted in front of the wide-eyed little boy.

"We have a guest, George, but he's been hurt really, really badly and we need to take care of him. He'll be all right, so don't you worry." He didn't want to come out and say it was George's father in case the child might mention it to someone he shouldn't.

He stood, looking over George's head at his sister. "Clara, I don't think this is the place for George right now. You must have seen Parker when he came upstairs and heaven only knows if the man might come back or not and what would happen then. I'd like George out of here for a few days at least. Will you pack him a bag and take him down the street to Sally

Woolworth's? Lawrence is his best playmate and they're always trying to spend more time together. Ask Sally if it's all right for George to spend a while there. Tell her Susannah is, no, tell her I'm indisposed and it would be a great favor if she'd let him stay."

"Certainly, Harmer." Clara looked down the hall. "How...how is he?"

"Not well, not well at all, I'm afraid." He whispered it quietly so George wouldn't hear.

"Do you really think Parker might come back?"

"He well may. There's no way of telling. I'm hoping the way Susannah looked and the fact of the fresh grave will be enough to dissuade him from returning. Lafayette has to be close now or Morgan wouldn't be here. Hopefully the British army won't remain in Williamsburg for long."

Before going back to the room where Morgan lay, Harmer went down the stairs, opened a high drawer in a cabinet and pulled out a pistol. Carefully loading it, he took it with him back up the stairs, laying it on a small round table near the bedroom window.

Eden looked at Marshall. "You didn't mention the pistol."

"I didn't, did I?" he smiled.

"What have you got planned, wily husband o' mine?"

"You'll see."

"I love you anyway," she laughed.

"I know."

"You don't usually write what Harmer does," she added.

"It needed to be done."

"Are you going to have him shoot Parker?"

"You'll see."

"You are a brute, I hope you know, keeping your loving wifeypoo in the dark and her preggers 'n all."

His lips twitched but he didn't reply.

"You are not going to 'fess up, are you?"

"Write, and let's see how this goes."

"Damn the torpedoes," she chuckled, turning back to the keyboard.

Myra bustled into the room as Harmer turned from the table, looking back at the bed.

"Is it ok if I'm writing him again?" Eden asked.

"Quite fine. I only needed him to do that one thing."

"Well, sir, meeting your needs is one of my highest priorities."

"And you do it so well," he grinned.

Myra had a large basket of bandaging and a jar of something with a spoon in it. "What's that?" Harmer asked. "It looks like honey."

"It is, warm honey. Layla, child, you come help me with this." There was a big chest at the foot of the bed for holding blankets and she set the basket and the honey jar down on it. Layla folded some gauze-like material into thick pads, setting them on a towel, and Myra spread spoonfuls of honey on them, warmed so it would absorb more quickly into the cloth.

Susannah was seated in a chair close to the bed, holding Morgan's hand. At Myra's suggestion, Harmer and Micah removed his tall black boots, unbuckled his pants and carefully pulled them off over his leg wound. Layla washed around the thigh wound, wiping away the dried blood, cleaning it well, then Myra laid a honey-soaked pad over it, binding it in place with a long strip of thin cloth as she explained that there was nothing better than honey for taking care of possible infection in a wound. They had two beehives in the backyard and an ample supply of it. The same was done with his shoulder wound, then he was turned and the two bullet wounds there taken care of. The long saber slash took more care because of its length but finally he was well-bandaged. Myra wanted him propped with pillows slightly on his right side so that he wasn't lying flat on his back because of the wounds there. Layla washed his face and arms and they covered him up to his waist with a light-weight sheet. Harmer, at Susannah's request, had kept up a description of what was being done to Morgan and when the others left the room, she took his hand again, kissing his palm.

Here he was, terribly injured once more, and by Parker again. She'd never actually felt hatred for anyone, but him she could hate with every fiber of her being, and hanging over it all was the possibility the man might return. If he found Morgan still alive.... No, she wouldn't go there.

For hours, all afternoon, he lay there not stirring while she held his hand and talked to him, telling him all about George, about how much she'd missed him, telling him he was home now, in his own bed, and she was there with him. The room seemed stifling hot to her and she fanned him, wiped his face with cool water, not heeding her own sweat trickling between her breasts. He was home, Morgan was home, and his hand was sandwiched between both of hers. He was alive and she would will him to remain so. He couldn't die now, not when she'd just got him back after so long. He'd live, he would, and the war would be over for him. She wouldn't have to hear the door close behind him as he left to go back to the army.

"Never again," she whispered, "never, ever again."

Just at dusk he stirred, his head turning a bit, and he licked his lips. She'd had her hand on his cheek then and felt his movement. "Morgan? Morgan, darling, it's me. Come back to me, sweetheart. I'm here, I'm here with you."

His features tightened as he became aware of pain and he let out a long, sighing moan. "You're hurting, aren't you?"

She hurried to the door, calling down the stairs for Myra. "He's waking up," she explained, "and he's in a lot of pain. Can you help him? Please, can you help him?"

The British had taken every bit of medical supplies in town, needing them for their men. There wasn't even a drop of laudanum to be had anywhere. Myra went back to the kitchen, boiled water and mixed two teaspoons of finely powdered white willow bark in it, letting it steep. When it was ready, she poured it into a mug and took it upstairs.

Morgan was almost fully conscious, enough so that Myra could lift his head and help him drink the willow tea.

"That's how Bayer discovered aspirin, you know," Eden said, "from the salicin in white willow bark."

"Myra knows her stuff. Honey and willow bark. She's doing right by him."

"He needs to live," Eden smiled.

"I'm glad to hear it."

"It takes longer to work, but it's supposed to last longer, the willow bark. It's an anti-inflammatory as well as a pain-reliever."

"Doesn't really help much with fever, though," he said.

"I'm not going to let him have a fever. The honey'll work."

"You are merciful, wife."

"I have my moments."

"That's twice already I've thought you might kill off our hero."

"Close, but no cigar."

"Antiquated phrases as well, eh?"

"I like antiquated things. You yourself will be turning thirty-seven very soon and I'll like you even then."

"You are taking me to the daffodils for that, are you not?"

"Yes, I plan to do all sorts of tortuous daffodillian things to you on your birthday."

"Oh, good," he laughed.

Morgan got down most of the tea and about half an hour later, went to sleep. Myra sighed contentedly, pleased that it was sleep and not unconsciousness.

"He be all right, Susannah. You'll see. He'll be just fine."

Just before midnight when everyone was asleep, a dark form slipped behind the boxwood under the parlor window. It was so beastly hot all the windows had been left open and it was easy for the tall man to make his way silently over the sill and into the room.

Chapter 101

Marshall touched Eden's cheek so she'd look up at him. "Would you mind, darling, if I write the next part?"

"This is because of your set-up, right?"

"It is."

"Go for it. I'm curious as to what you've got in mind."

Parker stood there in the darkened parlor, waiting for his eyes to adjust.

"That's right, isn't it? Don't sighted people do that?"

"Perfectly right. You're doing fine."

He'd just come from the back yard where he'd been to the supposed grave again. This time he'd stuck his saber into the mound of soil and when it had gone down only a bit over a foot, it struck solid, hard dirt. So, they'd lied to him, all of them. Susannah hadn't been widowed, not yet.

Now, inside the house, he made his way carefully toward the staircase. He'd taken off his spurs before coming in the window and wasn't wearing his saber any longer. Quietly, he went up the steps and down the hall past three closed bedroom doors. The one at the end had been left open so the air would move through better for Morgan's sake. Parker stopped in the doorway, staring at the bed, fairly well revealed in the moonlight. A large padded chair with a stool had been pulled up on the far side of it and Susannah was asleep there, her hand lying just beside Morgan's on the sheet. He closed the door behind himself, turning the lock.

Coming close to the bed, he looked down at the sleeping man. He was shirtless and Parker could see the thin line of an old scar around his neck. Parker smiled, remembering the whip, glad it had left a mark on Morgan. He let his hand, fingers spread wide, hover just a couple of inches over the sleeping man's face, savoring his utter vulnerability. So, *he thought,* you need a bit more help in dying, do you? *Putting his knee on the bed atop Morgan's undamaged right arm at the wrist, he let his long, strong fingers slide around the man's neck, another of his fantasies finding fulfillment.*

Morgan woke at the sharp pressure on his wrist, groggy, blinking his eyes. Before he had his eyes fully open, he was being choked and couldn't make a sound. He arched his back, kicking a bit with his feet, but he was so weak from blood loss he had almost no strength to fight back and the one arm he could use at all was firmly pinioned. His pulse began to pound in his ears as the grip on his throat tightened and his head was filled with a loud roaring.

Parker was finding it so easy that it wasn't all that much fun. He wished Morgan could offer him a little more fight but the man's eyes were already beginning to roll back in his head. Perhaps he should simply break Morgan's neck and be done with it? No, the slow process of choking was better and he smiled as he pressed his fingers harder, tighter.

Susannah, deep in emotionally-exhausted sleep, woke with a start at the movement on the bed. "Morgan?" He wasn't making a sound. She reached out for him, encountering Parker's arm and jerked back, startled.

"You stay out of this, Susannah."

It was Parker's voice. What was he doing in here? She shook her head, trying to clear the sleep from her brain, then reached out again, following his arm down to his hands on Morgan's throat. "NO!" she screamed, clawing at his fingers.

"Stay back, Susannah," he said, his voice low, deadly.

She screamed again, this time a shrill, wordless shriek of desperation. Parker released his right hand, backhanding her hard and she flew backwards, falling over the stool, lying stunned on the floor as he renewed his grip on Morgan's neck.

"Susannah!" It was Harmer, pounding on the locked door. "What's going on? Let me in! Let me IN!" When there was no response, he turned, intending to go downstairs and get his pistol to shoot the lock off. He stopped after just two steps. Damn! The pistol was in the room.

Morgan had passed out and Parker smiled with satisfaction. Almost there. Just a moment more and he'd be dead, be really dead this time.

"Parker, stop!"

Ah, so his wife-to-be had roused. "Soon," he said, smiling, continuing to choke Morgan, not looking at her.

"Parker, stop now."

Something in her voice made him look over at her, his grip on Morgan only loosening slightly. She was standing there, leaning against the table, shaking from head to foot, holding a pistol pointed toward him. The trembling, blind woman was almost laughable and, indeed, a small chuckle escaped him. "Put that down, you goose, before you shoot your foot off." He tightened his grip again. Time to end this.

Susannah raised the pistol just a little, judging by Parker's voice where he must be. Holding her breath, she fired it, heard a sharp gasp and a thick thud.

The sound of the shot made Harmer slam his shoulder against the door in frantic desperation. The lock gave and he practically fell into the room. Grabbing the edge of the bureau to keep on his feet, he stood there, his breath heaving, trying to make out what was going on. A dark form lay diagonally across Morgan on the bed. Susannah was backlit by the moonlight coming in the window and he couldn't see her face. He went unsteadily to the bed, finding the form to be Parker's. Pulling on him to get him off Morgan, he let him slide onto the floor.

"Susannah?" He began to walk around the bed. It wasn't until he was right beside his daughter that he saw his pistol still held out in her trembling hands.

"Daddy? I...I...." She fainted and he caught her, lowering her to the carpet.

Myra and Layla, roused from sleep in their first-floor room, burst through the doorway, each with a lighted candle. Harmer, in his nightshirt, stood, shaking his head, looking from Susannah to Morgan to Parker.

"Good Lord Amighty!" Myra cried, staring at the carnage. As Layla lit the lantern on the bureau and a better light filled the room, she, too, looked at the three unmoving forms. Susannah was Myra's first concern, had been since the day she was born and her mother died.

"She...she's fainted...I think," Harmer croaked. "She...she...shot Parker."

"She...? Land o' Goshen, how'd she do a thing like that?" She knelt beside Susannah. "Child, you wake up now, you hear me?"

Almost obediently Susannah moved and began to try to sit up. "Mor...Morgan? Parker was choking him." She pushed Myra's hands away. "Help Morgan," she insisted.

Layla stepped over Parker, holding the lantern closer to Morgan. His throat was marred by deep finger imprints. Leaning close, she waited to feel his breath on her cheek. It was there, thank the good Lord, but very shallow. She wet a towel in the ewer and wiped his face and neck and he began to cough and gasp.

Harmer had turned Parker over. A bright red stain had spread over the center of his chest. Susannah had killed him. He looked across the bed at his daughter, who'd been helped by Myra into the chair and was leaning toward Morgan, her fingers finding his head. Good Lord, she'd actually killed the man all by herself.

"He's all right?" he asked Layla.

"He's comin' 'round," she replied, still pressing the cold cloth to his throat. "Look like he was almost gone, though," she added, glancing at Susannah. "You saved him sure, Susannah," she said, shaking her head in wonder.

"Devilman, he's dead?" Myra asked.

"Completely dead," Harmer affirmed. "My God! What are we going to DO with him?"

"You sit yourself right there, child," Myra ordered Susannah, "an' don't you move." She walked toward the door. "You all take care of Morgan. I'll be right back."

Harmer went around and crouched in front of Susannah. "Are you all right, my darling?"

"Daddy...I...I...."

"I know. You did fine. You did the right thing. He would have killed Morgan, almost did. I'm very proud of you."

Tears dripped down her cheeks. "I...I...wasn't sure where...where to shoot. Oh, Daddy! What if I'd hit Morgan?"

"You didn't. I couldn't have shot more true myself. Don't think about that now. Just think how you kept your husband alive."

"But, Daddy, I...I...killed him. I...."

"Can you think of a man needed killin' more'n that one?" Layla asked.

"She's right, darling, she's so right. Now Morgan will be safe in the house, you'll be safe."

Myra came back with both Micah and Joel. Pointing to Parker on the floor, she said, "We need us a grave, a real grave this time."

"Where you want that, Mama?" Joel asked.

"'Behind the stable where you put the muck-out should do just fine."

Joel smiled. "I like that."

"Do that now while it's still dark. Come mornin', flatten that empty one and put turf on it. We don' need that one no more."

The two men carried Parker down the stairs, dumping him unceremoniously behind the stable while they set to shoveling. When the hole was deep enough, they dropped him in. Joel grinned, "Wait, Micah. Somethin' I want to do first."

He went to the manure pile, got a big shovelful and tossed it in atop the dead man. Micah liked the idea and joined him and between the two of them they made a nice layer of it over the body before filling the rest in with dirt. They didn't mound it up, but kept the top flat, then moved the compost heap atop it, a mixture of rotting vegetation, hay, manure, and worms.

"Now that's what I call fittin'!" Micah beamed.

Since the moonlight was sufficient and they were so wide awake, they went on and tended to the pretend grave near the lilacs, flattening it, and moving some turf from just outside the back pickets to the top. "I'll water that come mornin'," Micah said, "an' nobody'll ever know there was ever no grave there."

Joel clamped his hand on his uncle's shoulder. "We got ourselves two graves nobody never know about."

Back in the bedroom, Morgan was slowly coming around. His throat hurt and he couldn't speak but the cool water Layla was using felt good and he looked at her gratefully. She pulled off the sheet covering him as it had a large bloodstain on it. His chest, too, needed washing again because of Parker's blood and she tended to that. There was only a little on the carpet beside the bed and she poured a glass of water on it to let it soak while she went to get a scrub brush and some soap.

Myra brought both Susannah and Morgan cups of cold apple juice to drink. Morgan had a hard time swallowing and took his time as she held the cup to his lips, taking tiny sips.

Harmer could see the questions in Morgan's eyes and gave a brief account of the door being locked and Parker inside trying to strangle him. Morgan turned his eyes toward Susannah and Harmer said, "Yes, she saved you. Looks like she shot him right through the heart."

Morgan lifted his right hand, trying to reach across himself to where she was on his left, but couldn't. "Susannah," Harmer said, "come around over here. He's wanting you."

When she sat there on the edge of his bed, he took her hand, moving it to his lips and gently kissing it. "I love you," she whispered and he moved her hand to his face so she could feel him nodding yes.

Layla gathered up the sheet and took it down to soak with the other two in a big tub of cold water. Morgan's blue coat and his shirt, she'd burned as they were too damaged for further use. Soon, she smiled, other than the healing Morgan, there would be no trace that any of this had happened today.

"Ooo," Eden said admiringly, "you do know how to be brutal, don't you? I quite like the inventive use of the manure, I must say."

"He had it coming, don't you think?"

"No more black moustache twirling for him. So, do they live happily ever after?"

"Yep," he grinned, "bluebirds singing on the windowsill 'n all."

"Well, Cornwallis did move his army out of Williamsburg on July 4th, so he was only there from June 25th till then. After that they wouldn't have to conceal Morgan's presence anymore."

"Then Yorktown in October. I don't think we'll send Morgan there, though."

"So," Eden smiled, "the war's over for him, just as Susannah said."

"Now he can get to know his son." He knelt beside her computer chair, placing both palms on her gently mounding middle. "Just like I get to know our little Horatio in there."

"Only you're not allowed to ride off and join Washington when the kid's a mere, what, five or so months old."

"I promise, no riding off to join Washington."

"I'll hold you to that, mister."

Chapter 102

"Do you think this jacket is too warm?" Eden asked, holding out the particular article in question for Marshall to touch.

"Probably good to have it along," he nodded. "It can still be cool this early in April. Maybe the lighter one as well, just in case."

"It seems like ages since we first planned to go on this trip," Eden added.

"Christmas morning," he smiled. "Yes, my birthday has seemed a long time in coming."

"Wednesday," she said. "Now it's only just until Wednesday."

It was very early Monday morning, April 5th, and their flight would leave in four hours. A lot of careful thought and planning always went into his trips, especially overseas ones, as there were paperwork and arrangements to be made for Wadsworth's accompanying Marshall. Luckily Manchester was one of the UK airports with an Animal Reception Centre, which made everything a lot easier. His passport documentation had already been sent there by fax, regulation for service animals. In addition there was documentation he was free from rabies, had been treated for ticks and tapeworm, been microchipped, had a blood test, a certificate from the Seeing Eye School about his training, and the car safety harness required since Eden had arranged for a rental car to drive them up into the Lake District.

It was late evening as Eden looked with a brief glance to her left at the spreading pink sunset. She was driving north on the M6 and rather nervous about it.

"You're very quiet, darling," Marshall said.

"I'm concentrating on driving on the wrong side of the highway," she sighed heavily. "I want us to live to get to the daffodils, you know."

Marshall touched the Braille dial of his watch. "Almost six. Must be pretty dark by now."

"Sun's setting. Just about gone. Lots of pink still, though."

"Pink," Marshall repeated. "Baby laughter. That's what Jeff said, that pink was baby laughter." He rested his right palm on her leg. "I'll be meeting pink fairly soon."

"Do boy babies laugh in pink?" Eden asked.

"I think all baby laughter is pink," he grinned. "You turned," he commented then. "Where are we now?"

"Off the M6, heading diagonally northwest into the Lake District. Not much further to go, thank goodness."

It was with some relief that she pulled up in the small parking area of the B&B they were staying at near Windermere. She'd specifically wanted something close by the long, finger-like lake and just a short drive from Grasmere, where Wordsworth's Dove Cottage was. After she'd parked, she simply sat there a moment, her fingers still curled tightly around the steering wheel.

"Darling?" He wondered why she wasn't moving.

"Fingers are stuck," she sighed. Indeed, she'd been gripping the wheel very tightly the whole way.

He reached out his right hand, sliding up the curve of the wheel till he came to her hand, then cupped it over hers. A gentle heat radiated from his flesh into hers. With his left hand he unbuckled his seat belt and leaned close to her, uncovering her fingers so he could kiss them.

She smiled, watching his profile in the dim light. "I love you!" she murmured.

His lips twitched and he just silently raised himself more so he could kiss her further hand. With his head so closely in front of her, she leaned and kissed his cheek. "Happy Birthday eve eve," she whispered in his ear.

The B&B was named Sheepsrest. It was too dark now to see if there were actually any resting sheep in the large pasture that ran from the front of the place down toward the lake, but she'd liked the name and that had been one of the deciding factors in her choice.

After they'd registered and Mr. and Mrs. Finchley-Harrow, the owners, had greeted Wadsworth and made a bit of a fuss over him, they were shown through the living area, a white-washed space with dark wood hand-hewed ceiling beams. It was a simple place, nothing modern, nothing fancy, and just what she wanted for them. The furniture was padded in rose fabric that matched the curtains and she noted a doorway leading into what looked like a garden beyond. As they moved, she described for her husband what she was seeing, rested his hand on a supporting beam just behind the couch so he'd be aware of its presence. In the months since late October she'd gotten used to his not seeing where they were, well, mostly used to it. Whenever they came to a new place like this that he'd not been before, though, there was still that bit of a pang that ran through her, that wishing he could see it for himself, could experience it in the way she did.

Marshall ran his hand around the sharp corners of the post then along the back of the couch. "I'll remember this is here," he said quietly.

"Dog isn't in to chasing sheep at all, now is he?" Mr. Finchley-Harrow asked, pausing at the bottom of a flight of narrow stairs that would lead them to the guest rooms on the second floor. Wadsworth was the first guide dog that had ever stayed there.

Marshall smiled slightly. "No worries there. The only thing he herds is me. That's his entire focus, what he's trained for."

"It's just the animal is so big," Mr. Finchley-Harrow added. "Could bring down a sheep if he had a mind to, no problem for him at all."

So Eden told him the story of the two blueberry muffins on the dock and how Wadsworth had simply let them roll past right in front of him. "That's how well-trained he is. He still constantly amazes me."

They had eaten in Manchester and Eden was really tired from the travel and the tenseness of driving in England. She lay on the bed, letting her head rest on the pillows. Marshall sat on the edge of it, his hand exploring the round knob at one end of the footboard. "Brass?"

"Yep. We got four knobs like that. Big old trunk at the foot of the bed, so watch for that. Row of windows on the wall to my right, small wooden chair beneath them. Wardrobe to right of windows, couple of end tables, lamps, dresser across from the chest. Floor's wide, dark planking, small white throw rug beside the bed on your side. Very simple arrangement of furniture."

"Good. Won't take much to get used to it then." He heard her tired sigh and slipped her shoes off, setting them carefully just under the edge of the bed where he sat so he wouldn't trip on them later. Turning back he rubbed her feet a while then moved a bit more up the bed and very, very gently rubbed his palms over the lower part of her abdomen where the pregnancy had begun to swell.

"Mmmmm. Feels good. Could you do my back?" She rolled over and he massaged her back and shoulders, aware after a while she'd fallen asleep.

He'd taken off Wadsworth's harness, setting it atop the trunk, then made his way around the foot of the bed, locating the wooden chair. There were, he found, three windows above it, the middle one open. He turned the chair so it faced the window and sat down, just listening. There was the click of Wadsworth's nails on the bare floor then a happy dog sigh as he settled atop the throw rug. Eden was breathing softly on the bed behind him. The three of them, together within the same four walls, all healthy, all safe. The way life should be.

He turned his attention to the outside. The lake wasn't far. He could smell its water. There was a barn somewhere nearby, too, a barn with hay, a barn with a door that creaked when someone opened it. A light scent of manure came to him, not enough to be unpleasant really, just there to announce the presence of farm animals. Someone walked on a pea gravel path. He could tell from the sound of it that the gravel was small, round underfoot. The person coughed once, then moved away.

Going back to the bed, he rested a hand on Eden's shoulder. Still asleep, still dressed in her travel clothes. She was lying on her front and his fingers found the buttons at the waistband of her skirt, deftly unbuttoning them. Somehow he managed to slide her skirt off without waking her but knew that further efforts would inevitably fail. Getting out his own pajamas, he was soon lying beside her, though she was taking up pretty much most of the center of the bed.

In the morning when Eden awoke, she instantly looked for him and smiled fondly when she saw his rear half off the bed and, even asleep, his hand curled around one of the poles of the headboard, hanging on. Getting up, she padded around the bed and tried to scoot him a little, but her touch woke him.

"*Two Years Before the Mast*," she said.

"What?"

"The way you're gripping that pole it looks like you've spent the night on a tossing ship holding onto the mast for dear life."

Awake now, he grinned. "Perhaps you should do a body check to make sure all my limbs are intact?"

"I can see them. You're not covered, you know. They're all there."

"I'm not covered because you were sleeping atop them all."

"You tryin' to make me feel guilty, Mister?"

"A limb check would more than make up for lack of covering."

"OoOOoo, you're a tough cookie, you are!"

"Biscuit. We're in England now."

"Then you're a tough biscuit," she amended.

"Doesn't sound the same somehow," he observed.

Very lightly, she bit his rear that hung over the bed. "Ahh!" he cried, rolling forward into the center. "You bit my buns, woman!"

"Biscuits. I couldn't push you. Biting seems to have worked."

On his back now, he held out both arms. "It's my birthday eve now. Be nice."

"How nice?" She got up on the bed.

"Very, very nice."
So she was.

After breakfast they walked out the front of the B&B and Eden described how the plantings there sloped down to a level area of lawn beyond which sat a gray fieldstone wall with a sheep pasture on the other side.

"Are they resting?" he asked.

"They seem quite engrossed in munching the grass, though I do believe I see one at rest."

"Good. Then the name is not deceiving. A sheep resting at Sheepsrest. Is there a gate?"

"Yes, just off a bit to the right."

"How far to the lake?"

"I'm not good at distances. Um, maybe a ten minute walk."

"Would that be ten minutes of walking fast or ten minutes of ambling?"

"In my condition, I'm a definite ambler."

"You want to?"

"Amble?"

"Umm hmm, then we can come back and drive up to Grasmere and see Dove Cottage if you like."

Wadsworth was in harness because Marshall was in an unfamiliar place both in and out of the house, but Marshall pulled back on the handle so Wadsworth would go more slowly across the pasture for Eden's sake. He held her left hand in his right as they made their way, Eden keeping watch for sheep poop as she wasn't sure just how much of an obstacle Waddy might consider such a thing, or not.

The morning sun was on their backs as they were on the eastern side of the lake, heading toward it. "What do you know about Windermere?" she asked, knowing he would, inevitably, be a font of information.

"It's eleven miles long," he explained as they walked, "but only a half mile wide, gouged by a retreating glacier as all the lakes here were. This one is the largest natural lake in England."

When they got to the wall at the far end of the pasture, they paused, leaning against it. "I can see an island some distance off to my left," Eden said.

"That would be Belle Isle, by far the largest of the eighteen islands in the lake. It's privately owned. Forty acres."

"How neat to live on your own island," she chuckled.

"You want to do that some day?" he asked seriously.

"Probably not. I just want to live wherever you live. Doesn't matter to me just so long as you're there and I'm there."

He slid his arm around her back and side by side they lifted their faces into the wind.

Grasmere was at the top edge of Rydal Water, a much smaller lake just north of Windermere. Eden, a bit more comfortable with the driving today, found a place to park not far from the white-washed cottage.

"Looks like there are already a number of sight-seers," she commented.

"It's a popular place. Almost everybody who comes to the Lake District knows about Wordsworth and they want to see his home at least once."

She described the two-story whitewashed cottage to him. "It's got a gray roof and two chimneys. There are a number of vines climbing up the white walls. We have to go through a gate in a stone wall again to get inside."

They stopped inside an upstairs window, Eden looking back at the town. "Everything here seems to be built out of the same gray stone as the front wall. There's kind of a jumble of buildings, all with chimneys, and I see a taller wall, taller than people's heads, with a garden inside. Looks like the garden's just stuffed with large plantings."

"Gray," he repeated, thinking about what to her was an obvious color.

"A soft gray," she continued, "like the fog, only solid. I like, however, that Dove Cottage itself is white as it makes it stand out somehow."

"White is one of the harder colors to grasp," he said.

"Think of a page with no Braille on it," she tried. "A page you can run your fingers over and nothing is there yet. It's all just waiting to be made into something."

His hand came out, finding her hair. "I think I like auburn better." He kissed her then, not caring there were four other people in the room. "And we're very busily already making our lives into something," he murmured into the auburn.

Chapter 103

"You know," Marshall commented, "I have no idea what he looked like."

"Wordsworth?"

"There must be a portrait around here of him somewhere. Will you describe him to me, darling?"

She found one downstairs and studied it silently a while, Marshall's hand on her arm. "He looks like a poet," she began.

"I'm a poet," he chuckled. "Does he look like me?"

"Not in the least, but he looks like what you think of when you think of a poet."

"I don't look like a poet?" One of his brows arched up.

"He looks pale, delicate. You look like you just returned from smiting the Mongols."

"I have never smitten...ever!" The eyebrow went higher.

"Yes, yes, you have. You smote my heart the day I met you. It's never been the same since. I was completely...smited."

"I don't think smited is a word."

"Well, it should be. Anyway, in this portrait he has a high forehead, thin brownish hair, long sideburns. You both do have a cleft in your chins, though yours is, um, more finely formed. He has nice lips."

"Better than mine?"

"No lips are better than yours. He doesn't have the cute little cupid's bow your lips make."

"Cupid's bow? I'm not sure that sounds all that, um, manly, especially for a Mongol smiter."

"Trust me. They're plenty manly. His are softer, fuller, is all."

"What else? What's his nose like?"

"Fairly long, thin, with a slight, very slight arch high on the bridge. He looks tired, worn sort of. His right hand is to his forehead. Nice long fingers, something delicate about them, too."

"Obviously not a smiter, then."

"Obviously not. He's looking down though not really at anything. More like he's thinking, his mind turned inward."

"Probably thinking of daffodils, no doubt."

"Inevitably. Say, I've seen some scattered here 'n there as we've driven today. When do you want to, um, do daffodils, officially?"

"Tomorrow. We could spend the whole day tomorrow daffodilling."

They walked through the town, around a curve, to St. Oswald's where Wordsworth was buried.

"It's a lovely setting," Eden said. "Just a simple gray church with a fat, square tower, points on each top corner, a small window high on each side of the tower, clocks below the windows, but there are shrubs and trees all around so it looks like it was plopped into a garden, and beyond it is a high hill with a rocky top."

Inside, the church was cool, two rows of pews separated by a wide, dark gray slate aisle, its thick stone walls whitewashed, its peaked ceiling magnificently beamed. Eden watched Marshall run his hand down the edge of one of the stone arches then along the back of a pew. "It's nice in here," he smiled. "I like the feel of it."

She wanted him to see it. How could he appreciate the ceiling beams if he couldn't see them?

"You're quiet," he said softly. "Are you all right?"

"I want you to see it," she murmured.

"It's all right. Really it is."

"It's not always all right with me. I wish it were, but it isn't."

"I know, and it's all right that it's not all right, if that makes sense."

She led him down the aisle to a glass case near the altar. "His prayer book. It's here inside the case."

He rested a palm flat on the top of the case, then moved it to cup her cheek. "I love you," he whispered, "without limit."

Wordsworth was buried toward the back of the churchyard, his marker very simple and serving both him and his wife, Mary, who had lived nine years after his death. Appropriately, there were a few daffodils in bloom. Their children, Dora, William, Thomas, and Catherine were close by. They also found Hartley Coleridge, Samuel Taylor Coleridge's oldest son. Behind the small upright marker for Wordsworth was a flat one with deep carving. Marshall squatted beside it, letting his fingers trace the words, his eyes closed, a small smile on his face.

"What are you thinking, darling?" Eden asked, standing just to his right side.

"I'll tell you in the daffodils tomorrow."

"I'm glad you know daffodils," she said, more to herself than to him.

He tipped his head up toward her, his eyes open again. "I have known a daffodil in the uttermost carnal sense of the word 'knowing,'" he grinned. "Thanks to you," he added.

"I wish," she sighed, "you could know that again in the midst of a whole field of them. Alas, there would be the voyeuristic eyes of mutton-on-the-hoof watching."

"Mutton-on-the-hoof? How romantic."

"Darn beasties never give one any privacy in the midst of daffodil fields," she grumped dramatically.

"Nor, one suspects, would the countless spring hikers."

It's a shame," she said, "a real shame, it is."

"The thought is quite intriguing, I must say," Marshall observed, getting to his feet.

They drove back down to the town of Ambleside, at the northernmost tip of Windermere, had lunch in a nice little pub, then began to follow one of the easier-to-manage paths that led through the countryside. In a steep meadow they paused, sitting on the grass, the lake's end spread below them.

"There are a lot of small boats, mostly sailboats it looks like, but none of them seem to be sailing right now. They remind me of gulls at rest, just bobbing on the water, which, by the by, is very, very blue, bluer than the sky is today. On the far side, the grass comes right down to the lake's edge and there are tons of trees everywhere right from the lake up to the hills rising beyond."

He lay back on the grass, folding his arms under his head, letting the sunlight bathe his face, the light breeze blow over it. "Smells wonderful. Something just so clean about it."

Wadsworth lay close beside him, his chin resting on Marshall's thigh. "I have a sense of being up," he added, "of space below me, of distance." Lips curving with contentment he began to quote, "Oh, I have slipped the surly bonds of earth and danced the skies on laughter-silvered wings; sunward I've climbed, and joined the tumbling mirth of sun-split clouds...."

"What's that from, darling?"

"It's the beginning of a poem called *High Flight*, written by John Magee, a nineteen year old airman who was killed in World War II. It came to mind while I'm lying here."

"Have you slipped the surly bonds of earth, my love?"

His hand found hers, lifted it to his lips. "Only because of you."

They walked some more then turned back to Ambleside where Eden had parked the rental car. In a small shop there, she found a painting of daffodils that she loved and bought it to hang in their house in Mount Lebanon as a remembrance of the day.

That evening, after dinner in the town of Windermere, they drove south along the lake, finding a place they could park near the shore and settling down atop a large rock as the sun set.

"This is about the most peaceful thing I've ever seen," she remarked quietly.

"Tell me."

"There's a tree, its branches still bare and looking black with the light now behind them. It curves out gracefully over the lake from our left, four swooping branches over the water itself. But it's the glow, an absolutely creamy yellow glow that's spread over the blue of the waters and the lower parts of the sky. It's warm, alive, the glow, like...like...what you feel in your heart when you're with the one you love. Like that."

She took his hand, placing it on her chest. "It's this, what's in here, what you've made be in here. The color's like that. It's so full a color you wonder how you can contain it, how your ribs don't crack with it, why the lake and the sky don't explode with it and spatter it on your face."

He knew about that inner glow, loved that he did, but the slightest frown briefly crossed his face as, definitely unbidden, unwelcome, the tiny punctures in the blackness came into his memory. They had been nothing like what she was describing, nothing at all. Someday, as Helen Keller had said, he would walk into that other room and he would see. With what he hoped was not a visible effort, he contained the memory of the punctures, settling into what must be, finding his contentment in the glory of the inner glow that pressed against the inside of his ribs.

"Happy birthday!" Eden smiled, kissing him awake Wednesday morning. "It's the day of the daffodils!"

"Much better than the *Day of the Jackal*."

"Or the *Day of the Triffids*."

"Or the *Day of the Living Dead*."

She laughed, adding, "Or *The Night of the Day of the Dawn of the Son of the Bride of the Return of the Revenge of the Terror of the Attack of the Evil, Mutant, Alien, Flesh-eating, Hellbound, Zombified Living Dead Part 2: In Shocking 2-D*."

"You made that up," he accused.

"Did not. It's the longest-titled film in the English language, though it's often called NOTDOT for short. Was made by James Riffel in '91 by redubbing the '68 *Night of the Living Dead* with comedic dialog. So there!"

"Wow! I'm impressed! You have started off my thirty-seventh year by definitely impressing me."

"Though I have never seen it," she admitted.

"Thank goodness!" he laughed.

After breakfast they drove north again. "You'd think, really you would, that Worddy could have at least been satisfied to write his poem about the daffodils along the shore of Grasmere or Windermere or even Rydal Water but, no, he had to go all the way up to Ullswater to find daffodils inspiring enough to write about."

Marshall was distracted by her use of 'Worddy'. "That, I take it, is to differentiate him from Waddy, the dog?"

"You must admit that Wordsworth and Wadsworth are all too similar, all too similar."

"But Wordsworth was a last name and Wadsworth a middle."

"Yes, but Waddy has only Wadsworth and no first or last." The dog in question hung his head over the back of the front seat, happily drooling on her shoulder.

"Well, it was Worddy's sister Dorothy who saw the daffodils anyway and she liked them so much he wrote the poem about them. And Ullswater's not all that far. After all, the Lake District is only about thirty-five miles north to south and thirty-five miles east to west. How far can you have to travel in that?"

"Man should've gone to Texas. Then he'd know what distance is."

Marshall just shook his head, chuckling.

Eden drove until she found the Gowbarrow area by Ullswater. That's where the original, poemed daffodils had been seen. Sure enough there they were, daffodils near the lake. Pulling over she said, "Well, how about that!" and quoted the beginning of the famous poem:

I wandered lonely as a cloud
That floats on high o'er vales and hills,
When all at once I saw a crowd,
A host of golden daffodils;
Beside the lake, beneath the trees,
Fluttering and dancing in the breeze

"I am," she added, "definitely not lonely as a cloud."

"Are there many?" he asked.

"Well, I'm not sure it's an actual, um, host. Maybe a crowd. I do see some fields further ahead and off more away from the lake, though, that are definitely hosted. We can go there next."

They got out and walked to the edge of Ullswater. "These are 'beside the lake, beneath the trees'. Here. Bend here and put your hand out."

He let his fingers glide over four or five of the flowerheads. "The edge of the lake?"

"About six steps to your right."

"About?"

"Well, six of my steps. Four and a half of yours."

He took three steps then felt carefully with his foot. One more and just a bit and the toe of his shoe tipped over the edge.

"Stop now!"

Marshall crouched again, his left hand on a daffodil, the fingers of his right trailing into the water, a smile spreading over his face. She watched him intently. This was his experience of Wordsworth's daffodils being 'beside the lake.' That glow from last night's sunset threatened to break her ribs as she looked at him, loving everything about him. Lifting his hand from the water, he found the large tree just to his right. "Beneath the trees...," he whispered to himself, something in him satisfied. He was here, here in the spot where the daffodils, the most famous daffodils in all the world, had grown on April 15, 1802.

Sitting back against the tree, his fingers explored the daffodil growing closest to him. A single daffodil. Then they flowed over two, three, a dozen. His head tipped down, he blinked several times, filled with some inexpressible feeling that had slid quietly in. Then he held out his hand and Eden came, sitting beside him for a long while as they said nothing, just listened to the lapping of the lake against the shore.

He drew in a great breath, holding it, then letting it slowly out. "The sense of it is just so present, so now," he said softly.

"Of William and Dorothy being here?"

"Umm hmm. It's something I think about so often. I was thinking about it yesterday but it's even stronger here."

"What you were going to tell me in the daffodils?"

He nodded, leaning his head back against the tree. "Maybe, I don't know, maybe it's because I live in a world that has no edges. Maybe because of that."

"What do you mean, darling?"

"There's this...this...endlessness to where I live. Edges don't exist unless I've encountered them with my hand, unless my toes have stuck out over them. Otherwise, they're not there. Maybe... maybe it's that way with...with time, too. I don't know. I just think about it a lot."

"In what way?" She wanted to understand what he was trying to say.

"There's this poem. It keeps going around and around in my head. About that."

"A poem? Who wrote it?"

"I did. Only it's never been written down. I just think it."

"About time?"

"About the edgelessness of time. The edgelessness of...of...now."

"Now?"

"Did you ever think that every moment that has ever been, ever, was just as present, just as real, just as 'now' for the people living it as this moment you and I are in? What if...if...there are no edges to 'now'? What if instead of making some long line, they all just overlap? I know it probably doesn't make any sense, but sometimes I'm just so aware of them, of all of them. I've wondered if it's my concept, my experience of the world, this place I live in, that moves with me as I move, that has no edges, maybe it's that that makes me think about it. Like here, now, that first daffodil moment overlaps with this one, that somehow it's not simply gone, that somehow, I can't begin to understand how, that their 'now' is still real like our 'now' is real. Sometimes I just feel merged with it. Yes, I think that's the word I'm looking for, merged. That in my experience of my particular 'now', all the other 'nows' are still there and...and...I'm aware of them, of their value, of their intrinsic worth." He closed his eyes.

"I don't think I'm explaining this all that well. I'm not sure it's something that can really be explained. It's more a feeling I have, an awareness of things not lost. I wonder if it's at all like that for God. He's got no edges, isn't trapped in time. Wouldn't He be aware of every pain ever felt, every joy, every loss and gain? Perhaps all of it, every bit of it, exists in Him and it's all still important, all still matters? I see Him as the Lord of Nows, of all nows, free of boundaries and any constraints of time."

"You have a poem about it, about all the 'nows'?"

He nodded again. "It's been in my head for years. It comes back to me in moments like this and won't let go until my mind runs through all its lines."

"Would you say it for me?"

"You would be the only person who's ever heard it. I've kept it in the secret places of my heart, but you, you are there now where it is. I call it *All Things Always* and tried to write it as a sighted person would." He paused, caressing a daffodil's edges. "It just dawned on me I've never said it aloud."

She touched his cheek. "I love you so very much, Marshall Sinclair."

"It's a little odd. Maybe," he murmured, then cleared his throat.

"In the soft encircling of the night
Where velvet blackness serves for lids
That have no need of closing,
And sense of time and even place
Hang loosely in the quiet space
Where I lie, thoughts reaching out like hands,
To grasp the unity of things...
My place in the continual flow
Of life and thought and feeling,
And I am full aware of the edgelessness of me...
How this night is all nights ever known,
And my thoughts are kin to everything that's been.
That this very 'nowness' of my now
Is just a spreading blur across the face of time,
A blending part of every now not lost as
I touch my tear-dropped cheek and my fingers know
The feel of tears a thousand years gone by
And more.
In my unenclose-ed night I feel the breath of wind
On tear-wet face when locusts ate the wheat,
When husband did not return from war,
When news, given, brought sorrow to an aged heart.
I lift my hands into remembered sunlight,
Feeling warmth of newly-coming spring
When winter went into reluctant thaw,
Revealing tenderness of grass to clothe the land
So the sheep did not lay themselves to die;
And heat unbearable in the desert sand
When way was lost in Sinai in the noon,
Lips cracking under blue just far too blue.
I lie, rocked in the swelling deep of ocean waves,
A speck upon the vastness of all seas;
I hear the snap of canvas in the wind,
The sound of whales singing in the dawn.
I know the brush of hair upon my cheek,

The touch of someone loved beyond compare;
I ache with muscles trembling from the day
Of planting rice beside my mud-squished toes,
Hear the welcome home of my dog's bark
With ears that also heard the trumpets blow
The charge against the castle's guarded walls
And felt the sudden swish of parted air
When arrow sped along the contour of my brow.
I know the sticky feel of brightened blood,
Scented silver as it flows and will not stop,
And that awareness of the coming night
With its hope the moon will rise in time,
Revealing paths now hidden through the trees
So the joy of finding lostnesses will well anew.
I breathe, chest rising, falling now again,
And know the breaths of millions in my lungs,
Each moment real, each breath of lifted chest,
As meaningful, as real as mine.
Sometimes, lying on my bed, it is all there,
All of it...all that once has ever been,
All that will ever be...
A panoply, a quilted work, woven into a single piece
Spread over and around me as I lie.
The reality, the 'presentness' of moments come
But not yet...gone,
Not gone because I know and feel them
In the air, all around me, all the times,
All the loves, all the living moments
Of each life that ever was or will be lived,
All the senses of their expectations,
All the long and weary waits,
All the fallings in and out of love,
The babies born, the young men dead in war,
The sight of land when months were spent at sea,
The sight of her come home, at last, again.
The squint when sunlight was too bright,
The laying of a loved one in the grave
And going home alone to sit and mourn.
All of it is there, each single moment of each single life,
Existing, real, in the air around me as I lie
Awake in the lilac-scented night
And see the fullness of the glowing moon
Seen by every single one who's ever looked,

And we see it, smiling, they and I.
I hear that certain metallic scrape of sword,
The sizzle of bacon in the iron pan,
And know the sudden lurch of gut
When foot has slipped upon some mountain height;
The taste of chocolate on my hungry lip,
The gentleness of sleeping after pain,
The thatch-leak that drips upon the hearth
Just in the place the cat prefers to lie,
The tilt of chin when pride has suffered blows,
The fear when riders come, approaching in the dark.
All the sights, all the sounds, all the feelings, always,
Never lost, not unremarked, not worthless
In the sum of things
For every tired flex of hand upon some well-worn hoe,
Every fear of loss, each glad-greeted hug,
Each wipe of sweat from every sunshined brow,
All times that baby cries have creased the night,
Each ring of every single chiming bell,
Flows about me in the ever-living now,
So I can feel all feelings ever felt,
And hear the singing notes of songs not writ,
Can see the ship arriving at the shore,
And know the racing rumble of a thousand hoofs
And none of it is past, none still yet to come,
But all in all is always, ever,
In some mystery never-told,
Where now is always, ever, now,
Where all the breathing, living moments
Wrap themselves about me
And are mine."

He finished and sat, rubbing his right thumb pad over his left palm. She moved even closer to him, tracing his lips with a fingertip.

"Marshall, you take me places I've never gone before, where I've never thought there were places to go, and you show me, always you show me, the wonder that is you. I can't begin to tell you what you've done with this moment, how you've lifted it, infused it with so much more than I was aware it held. You do that for me, Marshall. You do that constantly and I'm filled with gratitude that you are you and that there was a particular now in which you came to love me. I look at the daffodil beside my leg and I see it in double exposure with the now of the cartwheeling maple leaf that led me to you. I see all our nows, maybe not so clearly as you see all those myriad nows in your poem, but it's a beginning for me to see them all almost as one thing, that first raindrop on your muddy cheek, the wondrous ones like that...that first moment I knew your heart was not beating, all of them. They all make up the story of us, are the building blocks of how I love you, why I love you. I just need some time to think about it more, to let a fuller understanding of it come to me, but this I know already. My love for you, all the moments, all the nows of that, are alive, are on-going, will always be so. I have no doubt of that, none at all. I look at you, touch you, and they're all there, every one of them, real, alive, present. I...I...well, I'm kind of blithering on, aren't I?", present. I...I...well, I'm kind of blithering on, aren't I?"

He turned more toward her and without a word slid both arms around her. A sudden breeze came in off the lake, blowing her hair, making the daffodils dance, and sitting there among them, he kissed her in their 'now' and almost...almost...heard Dorothy comment to her brother, "William, will you just look at THAT!", not meaning daffodils at all.

They sat there for some minutes longer, then walked back to the car where Eden reached in and picked up a small backpack that Marshall presumed contained a picnic. Once across the road they continued to a larger area of daffodils growing thickly up a slope toward some distant woodlands.

"Too thick," Eden said.

"Too thick? Is it possible for daffodils to be too thick?"

"I don't want us to crush them."

"Why would we crush them? Well, so many of them anyway?" He thought of the one most thoroughly-crushed daffodil back in their room at the Morning Glory Inn Christmas day.

"You'll see," she grinned.

"You mean when we sit to have lunch?" She didn't answer. "Is that what you mean?"

"No." She continued onward, pleased when she got closer to the woods and the daffodils became more scattered. Suddenly she stopped, putting an arm on his shoulder. "A deer. It's grazing just beyond the daffodils."

"We could be quiet. Maybe it won't run away."

"I don't intend to be quiet."

"You don't?" His lips parted. "You don't have in mind, not here, not where someone could...?"

"Well, I do have that in mind, but I'll wait till we get back to Windermere. This is something else."

"You know I have no idea what you mean."

"Yes, and I'm quite pleased about that."

"Aren't we going to eat, then? Isn't that what you have in the backpack? You should've let me carry that in the first place."

"It ain't heavy, it's my backpack. To paraphrase a song."

"What do you have in it that's such a secret?"

"You'll find out just as soon as I locate the perfect spot, kinda flat, not many daffodils."

"No crocodiles?"

"Yep, none of them either."

"What's this about, Eden?"

"It's about your birthday. It's about the night we got married and there was a certain activity on the porch of the inn that we weren't a part of."

He thought back to New Year's. Ryan had taken Martha's CD player out on the porch. "You mean...?"

"The cat is out of the proverbial bag, or," and she unbuckled the strap on the backpack, "more correctly, the CD player is out of the pack."

"You brought a CD player...to England?"

"Battery-powered. Not too many plugs in the woods." She liked the place where they now stood. "Here. Here is the place."

"What?"

She set the player on a stump, pressed *play* and *Va Pensiero* wafted up through the branches. "Our song," she said simply. She walked up close, facing him, taking his hand.

"Dancing? You want to dance...here?"

"No people, nothing to bump into. Just you and me. Yes, I want to dance with my husband on his birthday."

He bit his lip for a moment. "I'm not...."

"Yes, yes, you are. Remember how you and your Mom danced in the gym all those years ago? Now it's my turn. Just listen, move into it like you do with your hand, only use your whole body."

He felt a little awkward at first, was very aware of counting his steps...ONE two three, ONE two three...but then his natural affinity with music took over, his inborn grace rose up, and he smiled, leading her in a sweeping waltz. "Oh, Eden," he exclaimed, throwing back his head, "this is wonderful!"

She'd made a whole CD of just *Va Pensiero* playing over and over so they danced and danced and then they danced some more. She looked up at his face, a look of amazement still on his features. "Happy birthday," she said again. "Happy, happy birthday, my darling husband."

CPSIA information can be obtained
at www.ICGtesting.com
Printed in the USA
BVOW03s1236061017
496650BV00010B/2/P

9 781545 613146